IOLA LEROY
by Frances E. W. Harper

Perhaps the best-selling [...] 19th century, *Iola Leroy* [...] dignity of slavery, a [...] mother, and the heroine's rejection of a wealthy white suitor. This 1892 novel has many of the hallmarks of sentimental 19th-century literature—with one innovative literary difference. Light-skinned Iola proudly identifies herself as an African-American and dedicates herself to the welfare of black people instead of selfishly "passing" as white.

THE MARROW OF TRADITION
by Charles W. Chesnutt

Based on the infamous Wilmington Massacre of 1898, this realistic, hard-hitting novel confronts the origins and effects of white supremacist politics that dominated the turn-of-the-century South. Chesnutt's 1901 novel describes how race hatred estranges two families tied by blood and mutual economic interests, as violence erupts in a small southern city where blacks must choose between resistance and reconciliation.

THE SPORT OF THE GODS
by Paul Laurence Dunbar

This brilliant work from the man Booker T. Washington described as the "Poet Laureate of the Negro Race" gives a grim, ironic look at urban black life. Portraying a southern black family that migrates to New York's Harlem, Dunbar provides no facile solutions in a ground-breaking picture of the urban ghetto. First published in 1902, this is a truly seminal novel in American literature, marking the transition from the antebellum period to the Harlem Renaissance.

WILLIAM L. ANDREWS is Joyce & Elizabeth Hall Professor of American Literature at the University of Kansas. He is the author of *To Tell a Free Story: The First Century of Afro-American Autobiography, 1760–1865* and editor of two other Mentor anthologies, *Three Classic African-American Novels* and *Collected Short Stories of Charles W. Chesnutt*.

AFRICAN AMERICAN STUDIES

(0451)

THE AFRICAN-AMERICAN NOVEL IN THE AGE OF REACTION

THREE CLASSICS

Edited and with an Introduction by

William L. Andrews

A MENTOR BOOK

MENTOR
Published by the Penguin Group
Penguin Books USA Inc., 375 Hudson Street,
New York, New York 10014, U.S.A.
Penguin Books Ltd, 27 Wrights Lane,
London W8 5TZ, England
Penguin Books Australia Ltd, Ringwood,
Victoria, Australia
Penguin Books Canada Ltd, 10 Alcorn Avenue,
Toronto, Ontario, Canada M4V 3B2
Penguin Books (N.Z.) Ltd, 182–190 Wairau Road,
Auckland 10, New Zealand

Penguin Books Ltd, Registered Offices:
Harmondsworth, Middlesex, England

First published by Mentor,
an imprint of New American Library,
a division of Penguin Books USA Inc.

First Printing, July, 1992
10 9 8 7 6 5 4 3 2 1

 REGISTERED TRADEMARK—MARCA REGISTRADA

Library of Congress Cataloging Card Number: 91-68367

CONTENTS

INTRODUCTION

THE AFRICAN-AMERICAN NOVEL came into existence in the 1850s in response to a single dominant sociopolitical issue—slavery and its attendant evils, racism and discrimination based on color. After the Civil War cleansed the American social fabric of slavery, most pioneers of African-American fiction shelved their previous literary ambitions, replacing them with speaking and writing activities that they felt would more directly address the social concerns of the post-slavery era. Frederick Douglass, author of *The Heroic Slave* (1853), the first work of African-American fiction, devoted his energies in the years after 1865 to journalism, lecturing, and stump speaking for the Republican party. William Wells Brown, whose *Clotel, or the President's Daughter* (1853) gained international attention in the antislavery movement, revised his novel three times in the next fourteen years. But after *Clotelle, or the Colored Heroine* (1867), which left his heroine operating a school for Mississippi freedpeople after the war, Brown abandoned fiction for history writing and temperance lecturing. Nothing is known of Harriet E. Wilson, author of *Our Nig* (1859), the first novel by a black American woman, after 1860. Martin R. Delany, whose black nationalist novel, *Blake, or the Huts of America*, appeared in 1859 in serialized form, went on to write of his travels in Africa and to author a treatise on ethnology. But no one from the first generation of black American novelists seems to have made a concerted effort to pursue a career as a fiction writer or even to undertake a second novel. In several respects, therefore, one might say that the cause of antislavery became an end in itself for the early African-American novel.

During the twenty-five years following the collapse of

slavery, only a handful of African-American novels were published. Little is known about the contents or the authors of most of these obscure books. Undoubtedly the black American press, especially after 1870, lent its auspices to more than a few black short story writers as well as to an occasional serialized novel. But the only African-American novelist of the 1870s and 1880s about whom much is known is James H. W. Howard, whose best-known work, *Bond and Free; A True Tale of Slave Times* (1886), seems more intent on reiterating earlier attacks on slavery than identifying the social ills of its own day. Meanwhile increasingly ominous developments on the political front, particularly in the South, beckoned black writers back to the novel of purpose as a means of addressing reactionary trends in race relations that came to a head during the last decade of the nineteenth century.

By bringing Reconstruction to an end in the South in 1877, the Republican party in the North and its partners in big business and finance served notice of their willingness to bargain away black civil rights in the South in exchange for a white-controlled political system receptive to northern investment. Many white supremacists found federal encouragement in the 1883 U.S. Supreme Court ruling that declared the most far-reaching civil rights legislation passed during Reconstruction to be unconstitutional. During the late 1880s the first laws mandating segregation in railroad transportation swept through the South. The 1890s saw first Mississippi, then South Carolina, and eventually every southern state systematically altering its constitution to deny blacks the right to vote. When the Supreme Court ruled in 1896 in favor of the South's "separate but equal" racial doctrine, the federal government put its stamp of approval on state laws requiring cradle-to-grave segregation of the races. An age of reaction, which threatened to reverse all the political and economic advances black America had earned since Emancipation, settled over the United States. Realizing that they could no longer expect support from the federal government in their struggle for dignity and opportunity in the South, many blacks concluded that their best hope lay in cultivating their own resources for the uplifting of the race. Among these resources was the literary imagination, which writers like Frances Ellen Watkins Harper believed could be used both to inspire blacks to high ideals and to educate whites about the capacities and achievements of African-Americans.

In *Iola Leroy* (1892), the culminating work of Harper's remarkable literary career, a major character issues a call for the kind of African-American writing to which Harper devoted herself throughout her adult life: "out of the race must come its own defenders. With them [i.e., black Americans] the pen must be mightier than the sword. It is the weapon of civilization, and they must use it in their own defense." Born in Baltimore, Maryland, in 1825 to free parents who died when she was a child, Frances learned from her uncle and guardian, the abolitionist Rev. William Watkins, lessons in selflessness and social activism that she would always live by. After receiving a basic education from her uncle, Frances worked as a domestic, a seamstress, a sewing instructor, and a schoolteacher until 1853, when she decided to commit herself full-time to the antislavery effort. Moving to Philadelphia, she lived at a station on the underground railroad and began contributing poetry to abolitionist periodicals. In 1854 she was appointed traveling lecturer for the Maine Anti-Slavery Society and published *Poems on Miscellaneous Subjects*, which went through at least twenty editions in the next seventeen years. In 1859 the *Weekly Anglo-African* published her short story, "The Two Offers," which is considered the first contribution to this genre by an African-American.

Marriage in 1860 to Fenton Harper, a Cincinnati farmer, limited Frances Harper's work on behalf of antislavery and women's rights. But when her husband died in 1864, she returned to lecturing and writing. The cessation of the Civil War allowed her to travel widely in the South, where she urged the newly emancipated black people to seek a just reconciliation with their white neighbors and work toward the moral and social betterment of all. Her southern experience contributed much to one of her most innovative books of poetry, *Sketches of Southern Life* (1872), which offers an informal history of Reconstruction as seen through the eyes of the shrewd and resilient former slave, Aunt Chloe Fleet. Besides her highly visible participation in the American Women's Suffrage Association, Harper also assumed leadership of the African-American division of the Women's Christian Temperance Union in 1883. She continued to publish occasional poetry, essays, speeches, and serialized fiction until her death in 1911. But *Iola Leroy, or Shadows Uplifted*, which was published in 1892 in both Boston and Philadelphia and which went through five printings in its first year, constitutes the most enduring work of Harper's later years as a writer. No other African-American novel of the nineteenth century, with the possible exception of the four editions of Brown's *Clotel*, enjoyed as wide a readership as *Iola Leroy*.

That Harper knew and was influenced by William Wells Brown's novel has been noted by a number of critics. Like Clotel, Iola Leroy is a beautiful, fair-skinned, high-minded woman of hardly distinguishable African descent. Both Clotel and Iola suffer the indignities of slavery; both commit themselves to finding family members from whom slavery has separated them; and, in the case of the 1867 version of *Clotelle*, both devote themselves to the education of freedpeople after the Civil War. These fairly obvious similarities suggest the grounding of *Iola Leroy* in the antislavery literary tradition of the 1850s and 1860s. Yet *Iola Leroy* does not simply rehearse the outrages of slavery. The novel begins at a moment late in the Civil War when a group of North Carolina slaves realize they have the opportunity to escape bondage and join the approaching Union army. Some of the slaves make plans immediately to seize their freedom, while others resolve to remain at home, some because of obligations to family members, and in one instance because of a sense of loyalty to a master. Notable here is Harper's emphasis on the diversity of the slaves' sense of purpose and responsibility. Immediate personal freedom is all-in-all to some, but just as understandable and respectable are those who set aside their individual desires and choose instead to honor previous commitments to others. This tension between personal fulfillment and identification with the welfare of the group—be it the black family, the black community, or humanity in general—is debated repeatedly in *Iola Leroy* and is resolved by every major character in the same way, that is, by placing the best interests of others before self-satisfaction.

This theme of altruistic self-sacrifice is just one way in which *Iola Leroy* displays its ties to the nineteenth-century tradition of women's fiction. The title character of the novel confronts challenges to her moral and social ideals reminiscent of those that the heroines of popular white women's fiction had to contend with. These challenges are epitomized in Iola's decision, not once but twice in the novel, to reject the marriage proposal of a sincere white suitor, Dr. Gresham. Again, however, Harper's adoption of the conventions of a well-established type of fiction bears her distinctive stamp. For when Iola Leroy ponders the ultimate decision a woman must make in nineteenth-century fiction, that is, whether and whom to marry, Iola does so as an *African-American* woman. Every choice she makes as a typical women's fiction heroine—how to recover her long-lost mother, how to support herself, whom to reject and accept in marriage—she considers in light of the fact that she has chosen to identify herself as a black person. To Harper such an identification amounts to an almost holy calling of service to the least advantaged of black Americans. If Iola Leroy seems at times so wise and noble and self-sacrificial as to be a virtually bloodless ideal, one should remember that until Harper's novel no African-American female character had been treated as worthy of such idealization in the nineteenth-century women's fiction tradition. Basing her heroine's moral superiority on her dedication to the welfare of black people rather than on her superficial affinities with whites was Harper's way of arguing that even the most talented and privileged of black women had to conceive of their traditional responsibilities to family as embracing the entire black community. Thus even when Iola decides to marry, it is with the understanding that she and her African-American husband will return to the South to "labor for those who had passed from the old oligarchy of slavery into the new commonwealth of freedom."

Set in the turbulent years of the Civil War and early Reconstruction, *Iola Leroy* deplores southern mob violence, including public lynchings and other atrocities, and condemns efforts in the South to deprive the freedpeople of the right to vote. In keeping with the antislavery movement's belief that society would reform only when the hearts of its individual members were redeemed, Harper appealed to the conscience of her readers as the ultimate wellspring of social change. As she affirmed in one of her speeches on the solution of America's racial problem, "it is the inner life that develops the outer." Thus, when asked to name the "one remedy by which our nation can recover from the evil entailed upon her by slavery," Iola Leroy unequivocally replies, "a fuller comprehension of the claims of the Gospel of Jesus Christ, and their application to our national life." Having become at the end of the novel southern missionaries for Harper's African-American social gospel, Iola, whose "life is full of blessedness," and her husband, Dr. Latimer, "a leader in every reform movement for the benefit of the community," look to the future with optimism and faith.

At the end of Charles W. Chesnutt's *The Marrow of Tradition* (1901), the leading male character, who is, like Harper's Dr. Latimer, a light-skinned black physician laboring in the South for the welfare of his people, has much less reason to contemplate his region's future hopefully. The town of Wellington, North Carolina, where Chesnutt's novel is set, has just undergone a terrible race riot, plotted and directed by a cadre of white supremacists intent on overturning the town's biracial, democratically elected government. Few who read *The Marrow of Tradition* when it first appeared would have overlooked the similarity of the novel's climactic events to the infamous Wilmington Massacre of November 1898, when violent means were used to impose white supremacy on a North Carolina town that Chesnutt had often visited during his youth. Although born in Cleveland, Ohio, in 1858, Charles Waddell Chesnutt grew up in Fayetteville, North Carolina, scarcely one hundred miles up the Cape Fear River from Wilmington. In "down-east North Carolina," Chesnutt received his formal education at a school founded by the Freedmen's Bureau. He also got a good deal of informal instruction in the folklore of the black South while working in his father's grocery store. From 1872 to 1883, Chesnutt devoted himself to public school-teaching, rising from a teacher's assistant to principal of the State Colored Normal School in Fayetteville. Chafing against the restrictions of segregation and believing that he could make a better living, as well as do his part to combat racial discrimination in America, with his pen, the aspiring black author moved back to Cleveland in 1884. While establishing a prosperous legal stenography business that enabled him to offer his family a comfortable middle-class existence, Chesnutt devoted his spare hours to writing fiction.

His first literary success came in August 1887, when the *Atlantic Monthly* published "The Goophered Grapevine," an unusual dialect story that featured Chesnutt's knowledge of southern black "hoodoo" practices as well as his subtle, ironic wit. For the next decade Chesnutt worked at the craft of short-story writing. He was eventually rewarded in 1899 with the publication of two collections of his stories, *The Conjure Woman*, composed of a series of tales of slave life patterned after "The Goophered Grapevine," and *The Wife of His Youth and Other Stories of the Color Line*, a volume concerned primarily with the problems faced by people like Chesnutt, that is, light-skinned, middle-class African-Americans who lived in the urban North. Houghton Mifflin, Chesnutt's prestigious Boston publisher, was sufficiently pleased by the sales of his short story collections and by the positive reviews written by such eminent literary figures as William Dean Howells that it wasted little time in bringing out Chesnutt's first novel, *The House Behind the Cedars*, in 1900. This book about a beautiful young woman who attempts to pass for white helped introduce Chesnutt as a social problem novelist. He hoped his second and more hard-hitting novel of purpose, *The Marrow of Tradition*, would cement his grasp on a large readership and have the kind of impact on public opinion that *Uncle Tom's Cabin* had had fifty years earlier. Unfortunately, although *The Marrow of Tradition* was widely reviewed as timely and provocative, it did not sell well enough to satisfy its author. Chesnutt would publish one more novel about racial conditions in the South, *The Colonel's Dream* (1905), but after the disappointing reception of *The Marrow of Tradition*, he treated fiction writing as an avocation rather than a full-time career. Through the early decades of the twentieth century, black America held his turn-of-the-century fiction in high esteem because of its literary craftsmanship, realistic treatment of the American color line, and commitment to racial justice. Today Chesnutt is generally recognized as the first African-American novelist to engage a substantial national audience with a seriously conceived and artistically sophisticated social message.

The Marrow of Tradition confronts head-on the origins and effects of white supremacist politics, which by the turn of the century had taken control of most of the South. In contemporary popular novels by post-Reconstruction southern apologists like Thomas Nelson Page and Thomas Dixon, the traditions of the Old South—especially the glorification of white "blood," the necessity of black subjugation, and the wisdom of an aristocratic monopoly on power—were receiving a literary face-lift. Page's *Red Rock* (1898) and Dixon's widely-read *The Leopard's Spots* (1902) portrayed white supremacist violence as the justifiable means to a beneficial end, that of a New South where blacks and whites would coexist in an orderly, peaceful, and wholly segregated way. One of Chesnutt's major purposes in writing *The Marrow of Tradition* was to tear away the New South's mask of progress and reconciliation to reveal the corrupt marrow of its guiding principles and ideology.

The Marrow of Tradition's main thread of action knits together the lives of two families: the Carterets, who represent the postwar southern aristocracy, and the Millers, a mixed-race couple who embody their creator's idea of the progressive New Negro. Philip Carteret's obsession with white supremacy leads him to mastermind the race riot that destroys Dr. Miller's hospital in the process of overthrowing Wellington's government. Carteret's wife, Olivia, also poisoned by racism and envy, has long disavowed her relationship to her half-sister, Janet Miller, wife of the black doctor and the product of a secret marriage between a white aristocrat and his former slave. In spite of each Carteret's best efforts to keep separate from the Millers and to maintain their supposed superiority over them, fate repeatedly implicates each family in the fortunes of the other. At the end of the novel Philip Carteret is forced to acknowledge his dependence on Dr. Miller for the medical skill that can save Carteret's mortally ill son. Olivia Carteret is also forced to acknowledge Janet Miller as her legitimate half-sister and rightful co-heir to their father's estate. Chesnutt thus manages the outcome of *The Marrow of Tradition* so as to remind his readers that artificial caste and class divisions cannot permanently sever the ties that bind humanity together in mutual social need and moral obligation.

Just as *Iola Leroy* represents a notable African-American contribution to antislavery and women's fiction traditions, so *The Marrow of Tradition* displays clear affiliations with the late nineteenth-century school of American realism. Unlike the idealized mulattas and mulattos of Harper's imagination, William and Janet Miller are conceived with distinct strengths and weaknesses. Their personal desires and self-interest sometimes vie with their perception of what Harper would have regarded as their higher mission. The Millers' internal struggles, which would seem out of place in *Iola Leroy*, reveal Chesnutt's commitment to represent honestly the ambivalences that he felt characterized the situation of many mixed-race people. William Miller's foil in the novel, Josh Green, a working-class black man willing to die to defend his people, might be regarded as more heroic than the circumspect mixed-race physician who refuses to sacrifice himself to the cause of violent resistance to Carteret's henchmen. Yet in the almost Darwinian world of *The Marrow of Tradition*, it is Miller, not Green, who survives the bloody massacre and is then able to take a difficult step toward healing the wounds exacerbated by the new white racism. Consistent with the perspective of such realist writers as William Dean Howells and Edith Wharton, Chesnutt remained convinced that, despite the heavy weight of tradition oppressing the ascendant forces of change in the South, individual moral initiative could still make a positive difference. The closing line of the *The Marrow of Tradition*—"there's time enough, but none to spare"—testifies to Chesnutt's determination to be realistic about the precariousness of the southern situation without sounding so pessimistic about its solution that his readers would decide the region's racial problems were hopeless.

The final bleak lines of Paul Laurence Dunbar's *The Sport of the Gods* (1902)—"they knew they were powerless against some Will infinitely stronger than their own"—stands in stark contrast to both the assured optimism of *Iola Leroy*'s conclusion and the urgent call for action implicit in the ending of *The Marrow of Tradition*. Yet if there was one black writer at the turn of the century whom most American readers would not have considered despairing, especially about black people's lot in life, it would have been Paul Laurence Dunbar. Dubbed the "Poet Laureate of the Negro race" by Booker T. Washington, Dunbar was best known for his lively verse in black dialect, which earned the praise of sophisticated critics and popular readers alike. But he also produced a sizable body of short stories and novels, of which *The Sport of the Gods* has received considerable attention as a major novel of protest and the first extensive portrayal in fiction of life in twentieth-century Harlem.

Dunbar was born in 1872 in Dayton, Ohio, to former Kentucky plantation slaves, whose stories of their pre-emancipation experiences stocked the future writer with much valuable literary material. His parents were divorced when he was four years old. He grew up under the care of his watchful and encouraging mother, Matilda Glass Dunbar. Dunbar was an excellent and respected student at Dayton high school; though the only black in the school he was elected president of his class and delivered the class's graduation poem in June 1891. Refused subsequent employment in Dayton newspaper and legal offices because of his color, Dunbar found a job as an elevator operator. Between calls he wrote poems and articles for various midwestern newspapers while studying his favorite poets: Tennyson, Shakespeare, Keats, Poe, Longfellow, and the Midwest's most famous regionalist, James Whitcomb Riley. In 1893 Dunbar saw into print *Oak and Ivy*, the first of more than a half-dozen volumes of poetry that he published in his short literary career. As the demand for his poetry grew and his literary friendships broadened, he began a correspondence with the black woman poet Alice Ruth Moore, whom he married in 1898. By that time Dunbar had become an internationally acclaimed black writer by virtue of the praise for and sales of his next two collections of poems, *Majors and Minors* (1896) and *Lyrics of Lowly Life* (1897).

During a triumphal reading tour in Great Britain in 1897 Dunbar went to work on his first novel, *The Uncalled* (1898), which, though a competently-told (and somewhat autobiographical) story of a young man who refuses to enter the ministry, was coolly reviewed because of its lack of African-American local color. Simultaneous with his first novel, Dunbar also brought out his first collection of short stories, *Folks from Dixie*, which dealt with black people from both the slavery era and the post-Reconstruction period. Many of the stories in this and three subsequent volumes of Dunbar's short fiction celebrate the simple pleasures of "down home" living for black Americans, who find fulfillment in their own communities apart from and seemingly unmindful of the world of whites. Only a comparative few of Dunbar's stories offer candid assessments of social problems occasioned by race. Typically the difficulties that blacks face in his stories arise from their own self-deceptions and misplaced priorities, not from deeper causes, such as white racism, that would require a profounder analysis of social and economic forces. Occasionally, however, Dunbar put aside the mask of sentiment, piety, and easy moralizing that he generally wore for the readers of his fiction, revealing his doubts about the faith in self-help maintained by a Frances Harper or the hope for social reform that a Charles Chesnutt clung to. *The Sport of the Gods* represents Dunbar's most thoroughgoing critique of myths that he, as well as Harper and Chesnutt, had subscribed to in much of their fiction, particularly the myth of the southern black community as self-sustaining and ultimately triumphant over injustice through a combination of faith in God and commitment to social struggle. As a foray into a grim, urban realism anticipating the work of Richard Wright, *The Sport of the Gods* might have signaled a turning point in the artistic evolution of Paul Laurence Dunbar. Unfortunately, the author's worsening health and harried finances allowed him little time or energy to explore this literary vein before his death in 1906.

Just as *Iola Leroy* and *The Marrow of Tradition* are grounded in crucial historical developments and social issues of the post-Reconstruction years and the white supremacist 1890s, respectively, so *The Sport of the Gods* addresses a major question affecting black America at the turn of the century—the advantages and disadvantages of black migration from the rural South to the urban North. As early as 1879 African-Americans had begun to leave the South in search of better opportunities on the plains of the Midwest. But not until the turn of the century did significantly large numbers of black southerners set their sights on northeastern big cities, launching what has come to be known as the "great migrations" of the first decades of the twentieth century. For Dunbar *The Sport of the Gods* serves as a kind of case study of migration, and he leaves little room in his chronicle of frustration and demoralization for anything but a negative judgment of the fate of black families who try to resettle in a city like New York. Explaining the causes of the tragedy of the Hamilton family in Harlem, Dunbar does not cite such familiar aspects of de facto racism in the North as joblessness or poor housing or restricted educational opportunity for blacks. Instead the author illustrates the lack of real community in northern cities, the empty hedonism, the collapse of "home life," and the indifference to the "old traditions" and "old teachings" that had long sustained black Americans, particularly in the South. Dunbar suggests that this lack of a moral and cultural foundation for a viable black community in the northern city almost guarantees that a well-meaning mother like Fannie Hamilton will fail to protect her children from exploitation by the hustlers and hangers-on who make up "the fast life" in Harlem. Revealing the futility of individual human will against destructive social forces unleashed in the city, *The Sport of the Gods* takes a leaf from novels of urban naturalism such as Stephen Crane's *Maggie: A Girl of the Streets* (1893) and Theodore Dreiser's *Sister Carrie* (1900).

After reading *The Sport of the Gods*, however, one comes away with the feeling that Dunbar found little consolation in the themes of human futility and fatalism that arise from his portrayal of black migration. Unwilling or unable to assume the posture of nonjudgmental detachment favored by the naturalist, Dunbar betrays a lingering allegiance to the moral idealism and activism of Harper and Chesnutt, even as he portrays their standards as quaintly alien to the code of the Harlemites who serve as the agents of the Hamilton family's dissolution. This desire for an alternative to mere cynicism helps explain the strongly satirical tone that the novelist takes toward many of his characters, including whites and blacks in the South and the North, conservative and "liberal" alike. Yet *The Sport of the Gods* lacks the moral consistency of great satire; even its attitude toward the city itself fluctuates between outrage and admiration, disgust and gusto. In other words *The Sport of the Gods*, much more than *Iola Leroy* or *The Marrow of Tradition*, is caught up in, and is indeed the expression of, a vision of irreconcilable contradictions in African-American life. At the end of the story Dunbar gives Berry and Fannie Hamilton a final respite from some of the more oppressive of these contradictions, but even this apparent sop to the weary reader cannot disguise the structural irony of the novel. After all, what does it mean that at the start of the story a hypocritical white self-protectiveness banishes the Hamiltons from their home, while at the end an equally contemptible white self-aggrandizement restores them to it? Is one supposed to feel relieved or dispirited, happy or sad, by this double reversal of the Hamiltons' fortunes at the hands of white "gods" who become themselves the sport of the author's irony?

The more one perceives the refusal of *The Sport of the Gods* to resolve itself as tragedy or comedy, as social study or satire, the more one wonders if Dunbar was trying to propose what we might call a "blues perspective" in which to interpret the fate of the Hamiltons. If the blues response to black experience highlights the ability to "laugh to keep from crying" over a perpetual condition of struggle, then the narrator's attitude toward the central figures in *The Sport of the Gods* may very well be associated with the blues. Moreover, the novel itself brings forth a model of blues commentary in the highly self-conscious self-contradictoriness of Sadness, the provocative con man-confidant of the doomed Joe Hamilton. In his wry humor, his disarmingly boastful confessions, his realistic estimate of himself and his world, and his ability to hold in the balance a tragic view of himself as victim and a comic self-estimate of his own failings, Sadness looks well beyond the worldview of most nineteenth-century black American heroes to anticipate the modern consciousness of a Jim Trueblood in Ralph Ellison's *Invisible Man* (1952) or a Shug Avery in Alice Walker's *The Color Purple* (1982).

The fate of the black family in *Iola Leroy, The Marrow*

of Tradition, and *The Sport of the Gods* serves as an index to the differences among Harper, Chesnutt, and Dunbar with regard to their novels' social vision and aesthetic credo. Harper's is a novel of unabashed family reunion. Its firmly resolved plot may be read as a metaphor of her belief that the African-American struggle could be brought to a just and meaningful conclusion and that art could and should serve as a light of inspiration toward that end. Chesnutt's tempered and chastened realism compelled him to balance one family's loss with another family's potential restoration at the conclusion of *The Marrow of Tradition*. By revealing the tragedy suffered by a black family because of white malice and indifference, Chesnutt hoped to drive home the necessity of his readers' taking the reins of his open-ended plot so as to bring the nation's story to resolution in a just social union. Dunbar's emphasis on the dissolution of a black family and its irretrievable loss testifies ostensibly to his inability to envision a community for blacks in northern cities or an alternative to their traditional roles as dependents on whites in the rural South. Yet the fact that Dunbar, of all turn-of-the-century African-American writers, determined to sing his urban blues without offering a shadow of a solution beyond the singing itself is perhaps more significant to the future of African-American literature than the work of Harper or Chesnutt. For in the unresolved, and seemingly unresolvable, problems that Dunbar posed in *The Sport of the Gods* we find the incipient call for a new fiction to confront new phenomena—the northern urban ghetto and the consciousness it instilled in black people—in ways that would take African-American fiction beyond the moral categories and accepted literary modes of the nineteenth century and place it in the forefront of the modern American novel.

—*William L. Andrews*

Iola Leroy
or
Shadows Uplifted

by

Frances E. W. Harper

TO MY DAUGHTER
MARY E. HARPER,
THIS BOOK IS LOVINGLY DEDICATED.

Introduction

I CONFESS when I first learned that Mrs. Harper was about to write "a story" on some features of the Anglo-African race, growing out of what was once popularly known as the "peculiar institution," I had my doubts about the matter. Indeed it was far from being easy for me to think that she was as fortunate as she might have been in selecting a subject which would afford her the best opportunity for bringing out a work of merit and lasting worth to the race—such a work as some of her personal friends have long desired to see from her graphic pen. However, after hearing a good portion of the manuscript read, and a general statement with regard to the object in view, I admit frankly that my partial indifference was soon swept away; at least I was willing to wait for further developments.

Being very desirous that one of the race, so long distinguished in the cause of freedom for her intellectual worth as Mrs. Harper has had the honor of being, should not at this late date in life make a blunder which might detract from her own good name, I naturally proposed to await developments before deciding too quickly in favor of giving encouragement to her contemplated effort.

However, I was perfectly aware of the fact that she had much material in her possession for a most interesting book on the subject of the condition of the colored people in the South. I know of no other woman, white or colored, anywhere, who has come so intimately in contact with the colored people in the South as Mrs. Harper. Since emancipation she has labored in every Southern State in the Union, save two, Arkansas and Texas; in the colleges, schools, churches, and the cabins not excepted, she has found a vast field and open doors to teach and speak on the themes of education, temperance, and good home building, industry, morality, and the like, and never lacked for evidences of hearty appreciation and gratitude.

Everywhere help was needed, and her heart being deeply absorbed in the cause she willingly allowed her sympathies to impel her to perform most heroic services.

With her it was no uncommon occurrence, in visiting cities or towns, to speak at two, three, and four meetings a day; sometimes to promiscuous audiences composed of everybody who would care to come.

But the kind of meetings she took greatest interest in were meetings called exclusively for women. In this attitude she could pour out her sympathies to them as she could not do before a mixed audience; and indeed she felt their needs were far more pressing than any other class.

And now I am prepared to most fully indorse her story. I doubt whether she could, if she had tried ever so much, have hit upon a subject so well adapted to reach a large number of her friends and the public with both entertaining and instructive matter as successfully as she has done in this volume.

The grand and ennobling sentiments which have characterized all her utterances in laboring for the elevation of the oppressed will not be found missing in this book.

The previous books from her pen, which have been so very widely circulated and admired, North and South—"Forest Leaves," "Miscellaneous Poems," "Moses, a Story of the Nile," "Poems," and "Sketches of Southern Life" (five in number)—these, I predict, will be by far eclipsed by this last effort, which will, in all probability, be the crowning effort of her long and valuable services in the cause of humanity.

While, as indicated, Mrs. Harper has done a large amount of work in the South, she has at the same time done much active service in the temperance cause in the North, as thousands of this class can testify.

Before the war she was engaged as a speaker by anti-slavery associations; since then, by appointment of the Women's Christian Temperance Union, she has held the office of "Superintendent of Colored Work" for years.

She has also held the office of one of the Directors of the Women's Congress of the United States.

Under the auspices of these influential, earnest, and intelligent associations, she has been seen often on their platforms with the leading lady orators of the nation.

Hence, being widely known not only amongst her own race but likewise by the reformers, laboring for the salvation of the intemperate and others equally unfortunate, there is little room to doubt that the book will be in great demand and will meet with warm congratulations from a goodly number outside of the author's social connections.

Doubtless the thousands of colored Sunday-schools in the South, in casting about for an interesting, moral story-book, full of practical lessons, will not be content to be without "IOLA LEROY, OR SHADOWS UPLIFTED."

William Still

CHAPTER I

Mystery of Market Speech and Prayer-Meeting

"GOOD MORNIN', BOB; how's butter dis mornin'?"

"Fresh; just as fresh, as fresh can be."

"Oh, glory!" said the questioner, whom we shall call Thomas Anderson, although he was known among his acquaintances as Marster Anderson's Tom.

His informant regarding the condition of the market was Robert Johnson, who had been separated from his mother in his childhood and reared by his mistress as a favorite slave. She had fondled him as a pet animal, and even taught him to read. Notwithstanding their relation as mistress and slave, they had strong personal likings for each other.

Tom Anderson was the servant of a wealthy planter, who lived in the city of C——, North Carolina. This planter was quite advanced in life, but in his earlier days he had spent much of his time in talking politics in his State and National capitals in winter, and in visiting pleasure resorts and watering places in summer. His plantations were left to the care of overseers who, in their turn, employed negro drivers to aid them in the work of cultivation and discipline. But as the infirmities of age were pressing upon him he had withdrawn from active life, and given the management of his affairs into the hands of his sons. As Robert Johnson and Thomas Anderson passed homeward from the market, having bought provisions for their respective homes, they seemed to be very light-hearted and careless, chatting and joking with each other; but every now and then, after looking furtively around, one would drop into the ears of the other some news of the battle then raging between the North and South which, like two great millstones, were grinding

7

slavery to powder. As they passed along, they were met by another servant, who said in hurried tones, but with a glad accent in his voice:—

"Did you see de fish in de market dis mornin'? Oh, but dey war splendid, jis' as fresh, as fresh kin be."

"That's the ticket," said Robert, as a broad smile overspread his face. "I'll see you later."

"Good mornin', boys," said another servant on his way to market. "How's eggs dis mornin'?"

"Fust rate, fust rate," said Tom Anderson. "Bob's got it down fine."

"I thought so; mighty long faces at de pos'-office dis mornin'; but I'd better move 'long," and with a bright smile lighting up his face he passed on with a quickened tread.

There seemed to be an unusual interest manifested by these men in the state of the produce market, and a unanimous report of its good condition. Surely there was nothing in the primeness of the butter or the freshness of the eggs to change careless looking faces into such expressions of gratification, or to light dull eyes with such gladness. What did it mean?

During the dark days of the Rebellion, when the bondman was turning his eyes to the American flag, and learning to hail it as an ensign of deliverance, some of the shrewder slaves, coming in contact with their masters and overhearing their conversations, invented a phraseology to convey in the most unsuspected manner news to each other from the battle-field. Fragile women and helpless children were left on the plantations while their natural protectors were at the front, and yet these bondmen refrained from violence. Freedom was coming in the wake of the Union army, and while numbers deserted to join their forces, others remained at home, slept in their cabins by night and attended to their work by day; but under this apparently careless exterior there was an undercurrent of thought which escaped the cognizance of their masters. In conveying tidings of the war, if they wished to announce a victory of the Union army, they said the butter was fresh, or that the fish and eggs were in good condition. If defeat befell them, then the butter and other produce were rancid or stale.

Entering his home, Robert set his basket down. In one

arm he held a bundle of papers which he had obtained from the train to sell to the boarders, who were all anxious to hear from the seat of battle. He slipped one copy out and, looking cautiously around, said to Linda, the cook, in a low voice:—

"Splendid news in the papers. Secesh routed. Yankees whipped 'em out of their boots. Papers full of it. I tell you the eggs and the butter's mighty fresh this morning."

"Oh, sho, chile," said Linda, "I can't read de newspapers, but ole Missus' face is newspaper nuff for me. I looks at her ebery mornin' wen she comes inter dis kitchen. Ef her face is long an' she walks kine o' droopy den I thinks things is gwine wrong for dem. But ef she comes out yere looking mighty pleased, an' larffin all ober her face, an' steppin' so frisky, den I knows de Secesh is gittin' de bes' ob de Yankees. Robby, honey, does you really b'lieve for good and righty dat dem Yankees is got horns?"

"Of course not."

"Well, I yered so."

"Well, you heard a mighty big whopper."

"Anyhow, Bobby, things goes mighty contrary in dis house. Ole Miss is in de parlor prayin' for de Secesh to gain de day, and we's prayin' in de cabins and kitchens for de Yankees to get de bes' ob it. But wasn't Miss Nancy glad wen dem Yankees run'd away at Bull's Run. It was nuffin but Bull's Run an' run away Yankees. How she did larff and skip 'bout de house. An' den me thinks to myself you'd better not holler till you gits out ob de woods. I specs 'fore dem Yankees gits froo you'll be larffin tother side ob your mouf. While you was gone to market ole Miss com'd out yere, her face looking as long as my arm, tellin' us all 'bout de war and saying dem Yankees whipped our folks all to pieces. And she was 'fraid dey'd all be down yere soon. I thought they couldn't come too soon for we. But I didn't tell her so."

"No, I don't expect you did."

"No, I didn't; ef you buys me for a fool you loses your money shore. She said when dey com'd down yere she wanted all de men to hide, for dey'd kill all de men, but dey wouldn't tech de women."

"It's no such thing. She's put it all wrong. Why them Yankees are our best friends."

"Dat's jis' what I thinks. Ole Miss was jis' tryin to skeer a body. An' when she war done she jis' set down and sniffled an' cried, an' I war so glad I didn't know what to do. But I had to hole in. An' I made out I war orful sorry. An' Jinny said, 'O Miss Nancy, I hope dey won't come yere.' An' she said, 'I'se jis' 'fraid dey will come down yere and gobble up eberything dey can lay dere hands on.' An' she jis' looked as ef her heart war mos' broke, an' den she went inter de house. An' when she war gone, we jis' broke loose. Jake turned somersets, and said he warnt 'fraid ob dem Yankees; he know'd which side his brad was buttered on. Dat Jake is a cuter. When he goes down ter git de letters he cuts up all kines ob shines and capers. An' to look at him skylarking dere while de folks is waitin' for dere letters, an' talkin' 'bout de war, yer wouldn't think dat boy had a thimbleful of sense. But Jake's listenin' all de time wid his eyes and his mouf wide open, an' ketchin' eberything he kin, an' a heap ob news he gits dat way. As to Jinny, she jis' capered and danced all ober de flore. An' I jis' had to put my han' ober her mouf to keep old Miss from yereing her. Oh, but we did hab a good time. Boy, yer oughter been yere."

"And, Aunt Linda, what did you do?"

"Oh, honey, I war jis' ready to crack my sides larffin, jis' to see what a long face Jinny puts on wen ole Miss is talkin', an' den to see dat face wen missus' back is turned, why it's good as a circus. It's nuff to make a horse larff."

"Why, Aunt Linda, you never saw a circus?"

"No, but I'se hearn tell ob dem, and I thinks dey mus' be mighty funny. An' I know it's orful funny to see how straight Jinny's face looks wen she's almos' ready to bust, while ole Miss is frettin' and fumin' 'bout dem Yankees an' de war. But, somehow, Robby, I ralely b'lieves dat we cullud folks is mixed up in dis fight. I seed it all in a vision. An' soon as dey fired on dat fort, Uncle Dan'el says to me: 'Linda, we's gwine to git our freedom.' An' I says: 'Wat makes you think so?' An' he says: 'Dey've fired on Fort Sumter, an' de Norf is boun' to whip.' "

"I hope so," said Robert. "I think that we have a heap of friends up there."

"Well, I'm jis' gwine to keep on prayin' an' b'lievin'."

Just then the bell rang, and Robert, answering, found Mrs. Johnson suffering from a severe headache, which he thought was occasioned by her worrying over the late defeat of the Confederates. She sent him on an errand, which he executed with his usual dispatch, and returned to some work which he had to do in the kitchen. Robert was quite a favorite with Aunt Linda, and they often had confidential chats together.

"Bobby," she said, when he returned, "I thinks we ort ter hab a prayer-meetin' putty soon."

"I am in for that. Where will you have it?"

"Lem me see. Las' Sunday we had it in Gibson's woods; Sunday 'fore las', in de old cypress swamp; an' nex' Sunday we'el hab one in McCullough's woods. Las' Sunday we had a good time. I war jis' chock full an' runnin' ober. Aunt Milly's daughter's bin monin all summer, an' she's jis' come throo. We had a powerful time. Eberythin' on dat groun' was jis' alive. I tell yer, dere was a shout in de camp."

"Well, you had better look out, and not shout too much, and pray and sing too loud, because, 'fore you know, the patrollers will be on your track and break up your meetin' in a mighty big hurry, before you can say 'Jack Robinson.'"

"Oh, we looks out for dat. We's got a nice big pot, dat got cracked las' winter, but it will hole a lot o' water, an' we puts it whar we can tell it eberything. We has our own good times. An' I want you to come Sunday night an' tell all 'bout the good eggs, fish, and butter. Mark my words, Bobby, we's all gwine to git free. I seed it all in a vision, as plain as de nose on yer face."

"Well, I hope your vision will come out all right, and that the eggs will keep and the butter be fresh till we have our next meetin'."

"Now, Bob, you sen' word to Uncle Dan'el, Tom Anderson, an' de rest ob dem, to come to McCullough's woods nex' Sunday night. I want to hab a sin-killin' an' debil-dribin' time. But, boy, you'd better git out er yere. Ole Miss'll be down on yer like a scratch cat."

Although the slaves were denied unrestricted travel, and the holding of meetings without the surveillance of a white man, yet they contrived to meet by stealth and hold gatherings where they could mingle their prayers and tears, and lay plans for escaping to the Union army. Outwitting the vigilance of the patrollers and home guards, they established these meetings miles apart, extending into several States.

Sometimes their hope of deliverance was cruelly blighted by hearing of some adventurous soul who, having escaped to the Union army, had been pursued and returned again to bondage. Yet hope survived all these disasters which gathered around the fate of their unfortunate brethren, who were remanded to slavery through the undiscerning folly of those who were strengthening the hands which were dealing their deadliest blows at the heart of the Nation. But slavery had cast such a glamour over the Nation, and so warped the consciences of men, that they failed to read aright the legible transcript of Divine retribution which was written upon the shuddering earth, where the blood of God's poor children had been as water freely spilled.

CHAPTER II

Contraband of War

A FEW EVENINGS after this conversation between Robert and Linda, a prayer-meeting was held. Under the cover of night a few dusky figures met by stealth in McCullough's woods.

"Howdy," said Robert, approaching Uncle Daniel, the leader of the prayer-meeting, who had preceded him but a few minutes.

"Thanks and praise; I'se all right. How is you, chile?"

"Oh, I'm all right," said Robert, smiling, and grasping Uncle Daniel's hand.

"What's de news?" exclaimed several, as they turned their faces eagerly towards Robert.

"I hear," said Robert, "that they are done sending the runaways back to their masters."

"Is dat so?" said a half dozen earnest voices. "How did you yere it?"

"I read it in the papers. And Tom told me he heard them talking about it last night, at his house. How did you hear it, Tom? Come, tell us all about it."

Tom Anderson hesitated a moment, and then said:—

"Now, boys, I'll tell you all 'bout it. But you's got to be mighty mum 'bout it. It won't do to let de cat outer de bag."

"Dat's so! But tell us wat you yered. We ain't gwine to say nuffin to nobody."

"Well," said Tom, "las' night ole Marster had company. Two big ginerals, and dey was hoppin' mad. One ob dem looked like a turkey gobbler, his face war so red. An' he sed one ob dem Yankee ginerals, I thinks dey called him Beas' Butler, sed dat de slaves dat runned away war some big name—I don't know what he called it. But it meant dat all ob we who com'd to de Yankees should be free."

13

"Contraband of war," said Robert, who enjoyed the distinction of being a good reader, and was pretty well posted about the war. Mrs. Johnson had taught him to read on the same principle she would have taught a pet animal amusing tricks. She had never imagined the time would come when he would use the machinery she had put in his hands to help overthrow the institution to which she was so ardently attached.

"What does it mean? Is it somethin' good for us?"

"I think," said Robert, a little vain of his superior knowledge, "it is the best kind of good. It means if two armies are fighting and the horses of one run away, the other has a right to take them. And it is just the same if a slave runs away from the Secesh to the Union lines. He is called a contraband, just the same as if he were an ox or a horse. They wouldn't send the horses back, and they won't send us back."

"Is dat so?" said Uncle Daniel, a dear old father, with a look of saintly patience on his face. "Well, chillen, what do you mean to do?"

"Go, jis' as soon as we kin git to de army," said Tom Anderson.

"What else did the generals say? And how did you come to hear them, Tom?" asked Robert Johnson.

"Well, yer see, Marster's too ole and feeble to go to de war, but his heart's in it. An' it makes him feel good all ober when dem big ginerals comes an' tells him all 'bout it. Well, I war laying out on der porch fas' asleep an' snorin' drefful hard. Oh, I war so soun' asleep dat wen Marster wanted some ice-water he had to shake me drefful hard to wake me up. An' all de time I war wide 'wake as he war."

"What did they say?" asked Robert, who was always on the lookout for news from the battle-field.

"One ob dem said, dem Yankees war talkin' of puttin' guns in our han's and settin' us all free. An' de oder said, 'Oh, sho! ef dey puts guns in dere hands dey'll soon be in our'n; and ef dey sets em free dey wouldn't know how to take keer ob demselves.' "

"Only let 'em try it," chorused a half dozen voices, "an' dey'll soon see who'll git de bes' ob de guns; an' as to taking keer ob ourselves, I specs we kin take keer ob ourselves as well as take keer ob dem."

"Yes," said Tom, "who plants de cotton and raises all de crops?"

> " 'They eat the meat and give us the bones,
>   Eat the cherries and give us the stones,'

"And I'm getting tired of the whole business," said Robert.

"But, Bob," said Uncle Daniel, "you've got a good owner. You don't hab to run away from bad times and wuss a comin'."

"It isn't so good, but it might be better. I ain't got nothing 'gainst my ole Miss, except she sold my mother from me. And a boy ain't nothin' without his mother. I forgive her, but I never forget her, and never expect to. But if she were the best woman on earth I would rather have my freedom than belong to her. Well, boys, here's a chance for us just as soon as the Union army gets in sight. What will you do?"

"I'se a goin," said Tom Anderson, "jis' as soon as dem Linkum soldiers gits in sight."

"An' I'se a gwine wid you, Tom," said another. "I specs my ole Marster'll feel right smart lonesome when I'se gone, but I don't keer 'bout stayin' for company's sake."

"My ole Marster's room's a heap better'n his company," said Tom Anderson, "an' I'se a goner too. Dis yer freedom's too good to be lef' behind, wen you's got a chance to git it. I won't stop to bid ole Marse good bye."

"What do you think," said Robert, turning to Uncle Daniel; "won't you go with us?"

"No, chillen, I don't blame you for gwine; but I'se gwine to stay. Slavery's done got all de marrow out ob dese poor ole bones. Ef freedom comes it won't do me much good; we ole ones will die out, but it will set you youngsters all up."

"But, Uncle Daniel, you're not too old to want your freedom?"

"I knows dat. I lubs de bery name of freedom. I'se been praying and hoping for it dese many years. An' ef I warn't boun', I would go wid you ter-morrer. I won't put a straw in your way. You boys go, and my prayers will go wid you. I can't go, it's no use. I'se gwine to stay on de ole place till Marse Robert comes back, or is brought back."

"But, Uncle Daniel," said Robert, "what's the use of praying for a thing if, when it comes, you won't take it? As much as you have been praying and talking about freedom, I thought that when the chance came you would have been one of the first to take it. Now, do tell us why you won't go with us. Ain't you willing?"

"Why, Robbie, my whole heart is wid you. But when Marse Robert went to de war, he called me into his room and said to me, 'Uncle Dan'el, I'se gwine to de war, an' I want you to look arter my wife an' chillen, an' see dat eberything goes right on de place.' An' I promised him I'd do it, an' I mus' be as good as my word. 'Cept de overseer, dere isn't a white man on de plantation, an' I hear he has to report ter-morrer or be treated as a de-serter. An' der's nobody here to look arter Miss Mary an' de chillen, but myself, an' to see dat eberything goes right. I promised Marse Robert I would do it, an' I mus' be as good as my word."

"Well, what should you keer?" said Tom Anderson. "Who looked arter you when you war sole from your farder and mudder, an' neber seed dem any more, and wouldn't know dem to-day ef you met dem in your dish?"

"Well, dats neither yere nor dere. Marse Robert couldn't help what his father did. He war an orful mean man. But he's dead now, and gone to see 'bout it. But his wife war de nicest, sweetest lady dat eber I did see. She war no more like him dan chalk's like cheese. She used to visit de cabins, an' listen to de pore women when de overseer used to cruelize dem so bad, an drive dem to work late and early. An' she used to sen' dem nice things when they war sick, and hab der cabins white-washed an' lookin' like new pins, an' look arter dere chillen. Sometimes she'd try to git ole Marse to take dere part when de oberseer got too mean. But she might as well a sung hymns to a dead horse. All her putty talk war like porin water on a goose's back. He'd jis' bluff her off, an' tell her she didn't run dat plantation, and not for her to bring him any nigger news. I never thought ole Marster war good to her. I often ketched her crying,

an' she'd say she had de headache, but I thought it war
de heartache. 'Fore ole Marster died, she got so thin an'
peaked I war 'fraid she war gwine to die; but she seed
him out. He war killed by a tree fallin' on him, an' ef
eber de debil got his own he got him. I seed him in a
vision arter he war gone. He war hangin' up in a pit,
sayin' 'Oh! oh!' wid no close on. He war allers blusterin',
cussin', and swearin' at somebody. Marse Robert ain't a
bit like him. He takes right arter his mother. Bad as ole
Marster war, I think she jis' lob'd de groun' he walked
on. Well, women's mighty curious kind of folks anyhow.
I sometimes thinks de wuss you treats dem de better dey
likes you."

"Well," said Tom, a little impatiently, "what's yer
gwine to do? Is yer gwine wid us, ef yer gits a chance?"

"Now, jes' you hole on till I gits a chance to tell yer
why I'se gwine to stay."

"Well, Uncle Daniel, let's hear it," said Robert.

"I was jes' gwine to tell yer when Tom put me out.
Ole Marster died when Marse Robert war two years ole,
and his pore mother when he was four. When he died,
Miss Anna used to keep me 'bout her jes' like I war her
shadder. I used to nuss Marse Robert jes' de same as ef
I were his own fadder. I used to fix his milk, rock him
to sleep, ride him on my back, an' nothin' pleased him
better'n fer Uncle Dan'el to ride him piggy-back."

"Well, Uncle Daniel," said Robert, "what has that got
to do with your going with us and getting your freedom?"

"Now, jes' wait a bit, and don't frustrate my mine. I
seed day arter day Miss Anna war gettin' weaker and
thinner, an' she looked so sweet and talked so putty, I
thinks to myself, 'you ain't long for dis worl'.' And she
said to me one day, 'Uncle Dan'el, when I'se gone, I
want you to be good to your Marster Robert.' An' she
looked so pale and weak I war almost ready to cry. I
couldn't help it. She hed allers bin mighty good to me.
An' I beliebs in praisin' de bridge dat carries me ober.
She said, 'Uncle Dan'el, I wish you war free. Ef I had
my way you shouldn't serve any one when I'm gone; but
Mr. Thurston had eberything in his power when he made
his will. I war tied hand and foot, and I couldn't help it.'
In a little while she war gone—jis' faded away like a

flower. I belieb ef dere's a saint in glory, Miss Anna's dere."

"Oh, I don't take much stock in white folks' religion," said Robert, laughing carelessly.

"The way," said Tom Anderson, "dat some of dese folks cut their cards yere, I think dey'll be as sceece in hebben as hen's teeth. I think wen some of dem preachers brings de Bible 'round an' tells us 'bout mindin our marsters and not stealin' dere tings, dat dey preach to please de white folks, an' dey frows coleness ober de meetin'."

"An' I," said Aunt Linda, "neber did belieb in dem Bible preachers. I yered one ob dem sayin' wen he war dyin', it war all dark wid him. An' de way he treated his house-girl, pore thing, I don't wonder dat it war dark wid him."

"O, I guess," said Robert, "that the Bible is all right, but some of these church folks don't get the right hang of it."

"May be dat's so," said Aunt Linda. "But I allers wanted to learn how to read. I once had a book, and tried to make out what war in it, but ebery time my mistus caught me wid a book in my hand, she used to whip my fingers. An' I couldn't see ef it war good for white folks, why it warn't good for cullud folks."

"Well," said Tom Anderson, "I belieb in de good ole-time religion. But arter dese white folks is done fussin' and beatin' de cullud folks, I don't want 'em to come talking religion to me. We used to hab on our place a real Guinea man, an' once he made ole Marse mad, an' he had him whipped. Old Marse war trying to break him in, but dat fellow war spunk to de backbone, an' when he 'gin talkin' to him 'bout savin' his soul an' gittin' to hebbin, he tole him ef he went to hebbin an' foun' he war dare, he wouldn't go in. He wouldn't stay wid any such rascal as he war."

"What became of him?" asked Robert.

"Oh, he died. But he had some quare notions 'bout religion. He thought dat when he died he would go back to his ole country. He allers kep' his ole Guinea name."

"What was it?"

"Potobombra. Do you know what he wanted Marster to do 'fore he died?" continued Anderson.

"No."

"He wanted him to gib him his free papers."

"Did he do it?"

"Ob course he did. As de poor fellow war dying an' he couldn't sell him in de oder world, he jis' wrote him de papers to yumor him. He didn't want to go back to Africa a slave. He thought if he did, his people would look down on him, an' he wanted to go back a free man. He war orful weak when Marster brought him de free papers. He jis' ris up in de bed, clutched dem in his han's, smiled, an' gasped out, 'I'se free at las'; an' fell back on de pillar, an' he war gone. Oh, but he war spunky. De oberseers, arter dey foun' out who he war, gin'rally gabe him a wide birth. I specs his father war some ole Guinea king."

"Well, chillen," said Uncle Daniel, "we's kept up dis meeting long enough. We'd better go home, and not all go one way, cause de patrollers might git us all inter trouble, an' we must try to slip home by hook or crook."

"An' when we meet again, Uncle Daniel can finish his story, an' be ready to go with us," said Robert.

"I wish," said Tom Anderson, "he would go wid us, de wuss kind."

CHAPTER III

Uncle Daniel's Story

THE UNION had snapped asunder because it lacked the cohesion of justice, and the Nation was destined to pass through the crucible of disaster and defeat, till she was ready to clasp hands with the negro and march abreast with him to freedom and victory.

The Union army was encamping a few miles from C——, in North Carolina. Robert, being well posted on the condition of affairs, had stealthily contrived to call a meeting in Uncle Daniel's cabin. Uncle Daniel's wife had gone to bed as a sick sister, and they held a prayer-meeting by her bedside. It was a little risky, but as Mr. Thurston did not encourage the visits of the patrollers, and heartily detested having them prying into his cabins, there was not much danger of molestation.

"Well, Uncle Daniel, we want to hear your story, and see if you have made up your mind to go with us," said Robert, after he had been seated a few minutes in Uncle Daniel's cabin.

"No, chillen, I've no objection to finishin' my story, but I ain't made up my mind to leave the place till Marse Robert gits back."

"You were telling us about Marse Robert's mother. How did you get along after she died?"

"Arter she war gone, ole Marster's folks come to look arter things. But eberything war lef' to Marse Robert, an' he wouldn't do widout me. Dat chile war allers at my heels. I couldn't stir widout him, an' when he missed me, he'd fret an' cry so I had ter stay wid him; an' wen he went to school, I had ter carry him in de mornin' and bring him home in de ebenin'. An' I learned him to hunt squirrels, an' rabbits, an' ketch fish, an' set traps for birds. I beliebs he lob'd me better dan any ob his kin'. An' he showed me how to read."

20

"Well," said Tom, "ef he lob'd you so much, why didn't he set you free?"

"Marse Robert tole me, ef he died fust he war gwine ter leave me free—dat I should neber sarve any one else."

"Oh, sho!" said Tom. "Promises, like pie crusts, is made to be broken. I don't trust none ob dem. I'se been yere dese fifteen years, an' I'se neber foun' any troof in dem. An' I'se gwine wid dem North men soon's I gits a chance. An' ef you knowed what's good fer you, you'd go, too."

"No, Tom; I can't go. When Marster Robert went to de front, he called me to him an' said: 'Uncle Daniel,' an' he was drefful pale when he said it, 'I are gwine to de war, an' I want yer to take keer of my wife an' chillen, jis' like yer used to take keer of me wen yer called me your little boy.' Well, dat jis' got to me, an' I couldn't help cryin', to save my life."

"I specs," said Tom, "your tear bags must lie mighty close to your eyes. I wouldn't cry ef dem Yankees would make ebery one ob dem go to de front, an' stay dere foreber. Dey'd only be gittin' back what dey's been a doin' to us."

"Marster Robert war nebber bad to me. An' I beliebs in stannin' by dem dat stans by you. Arter Miss Anna died, I had great 'sponsibilities on my shoulders; but I war orful lonesome, an' thought I'd like to git a wife. But dere warn't a gal on de plantation, an' nowhere's roun', dat filled de bill. So I jis' waited, an' 'tended to Marse Robert till he war ole 'nough to go to college. Wen he went, he allers 'membered me in de letters he used to write his grandma. When he war gone, I war lonesomer dan eber. But, one day, I jis' seed de gal dat took de rag off de bush. Gundover had jis' brought her from de up-country. She war putty as a picture!" he exclaimed, looking fondly at his wife, who still bore traces of great beauty. "She had putty hair, putty eyes, putty mouth. She war putty all over; an' she know'd how to put on style."

"O, Daniel," said Aunt Katie, half chidingly, "how you do talk."

"Why, it's true. I 'member when you war de puttiest gal in dese diggins; when nobody could top your cotton."

"I don't," said Aunt Katie.

"Well, I do. Now, let me go on wid my story. De fust time I seed her, I sez to myself, 'Dat's de gal for me, an' I means to hab her ef I kin git her.' So I scraped 'quaintance wid her, and axed her ef she would hab me ef our marsters would let us. I warn't 'fraid 'bout Marse Robert, but I warn't quite shore 'bout Gundover. So when Marse Robert com'd home, I axed him, an' he larf'd an' said, 'All right,' an' dat he would speak to ole Gundover 'bout it.' He didn't relish it bery much, but he didn't like to 'fuse Marse Robert. He wouldn't sell her, for she tended his dairy, an' war mighty handy 'bout de house. He said, I mought marry her an' come to see her wheneber Marse Robert would gib me a pass. I wanted him to sell her, but he wouldn't hear to it, so I had to put up wid what I could git. Marse Robert war mighty good to me, but ole Gundover's wife war de meanest woman dat I eber did see. She used to go out on de plantation an' boss things like a man. Arter I war married, I had a baby. It war de dearest, cutest little thing you eber did see; but, pore thing, it got sick and died. It died 'bout three o'clock; and in de mornin', Katie, habbin her cows to milk, lef' her dead baby in de cabin. When she com'd back from milkin' her thirty cows, an' went to look for her pore little baby, some one had been to her cabin an' took'd de pore chile away an' put it in de groun'. Pore Katie, she didn't eben hab a chance to kiss her baby 'fore it war buried. Ole Gundover's wife has been dead thirty years, an' she didn't die a day too soon. An' my little baby has gone to glory, an' is wingin' wid the angels an' a lookin' out for us. One ob de las' things ole Gundover's wife did 'fore she died war to order a woman whipped 'cause she com'd to de field a little late when her husband war sick, an' she had stopped to tend him. Dat mornin' she war taken sick wid de fever, an' in a few days she war gone out like de snuff ob a candle. She lef' several sons, an' I specs she would almos' turn ober in her grave ef she know'd she had ten culled granchillen somewhar down in de lower kentry."

"Isn't it funny," said Robert, "how these white folks look down on colored people, an' then mix up with them?"

"Marster war away when Miss 'Liza treated my Katie

so mean, an' when I tole him 'bout it, he war tearin' mad, an' went ober an' saw ole Gundover, an' foun' out he war hard up for money, an' he bought Katie and brought her home to lib wid me, and we's been a libin in clover eber sence. Marster Robert has been mighty good to me. He stood by me in my troubles, an' now his trouble's come, I'm a gwine to stan' by him. I used to think Gundover's wife war jealous ob my Katie. She war so much puttier. Gundover's wife couldn't tech my Katie wid a ten foot pole."

"But, Aunt Katie, you have had your trials," said Robert, now that Daniel had finished his story; "don't you feel bitter towards these people who are fighting to keep you in slavery?"

Aunt Katie turned her face towards the speaker. It was a thoughtful, intelligent face, saintly and calm. A face which expressed the idea of a soul which had been fearfully tempest tossed, but had passed through suffering into peace. Very touching was the look of resignation and hope which overspread her features as she replied, with the simple child-like faith which she had learned in the darkest hour, "The Lord says, we must forgive." And with her that thought, as coming from the lips of Divine Love, was enough to settle the whole question of forgiveness of injuries and love to enemies.

"Well," said Thomas Anderson, turning to Uncle Daniel, "we can't count on yer to go wid us?"

"Boys," said Uncle Daniel, and there was grief in his voice, "I'se mighty glad you hab a chance for your freedom; but, ez I tole yer, I promised Marse Robert I would stay, an' I mus' be as good as my word. Don't you youngsters stay for an ole stager like me. I'm ole an' mos' worn out. Freedom wouldn't do much for me, but I want you all to be as free as the birds; so, you chillen, take your freedom when you kin get it."

"But, Uncle Dan'el, you won't say nothin' 'bout our going, will you?" said the youngest of the company.

Uncle Daniel slowly arose. There was a mournful flash in his eye, a tremor of emotion in his voice, as he said, "Look yere, boys, de boy dat axed dat question war a new comer on dis plantation, but some ob you's bin here all ob your lives; did you eber know ob Uncle Dan'el gittin' any ob you inter trouble?"

"No, no," exclaimed a chorus of voices, "but many's de time you've held off de blows wen de oberseer got too mean, an' cruelized us too much, wen Marse Robert war away. An' wen he got back, you made him settle de oberseer's hash."

"Well, boys," said Uncle Daniel, with an air of mournful dignity, "I'se de same Uncle Dan'el I eber war. Ef any ob you wants to go, I habben't a word to say agin it. I specs dem Yankees be all right, but I knows Marse Robert, an' I don't know dem, an' I ain't a gwine ter throw away dirty water 'til I gits clean."

"Well, Uncle Ben," said Robert, addressing a stalwart man whose towering form and darkly flashing eye told that slavery had failed to put the crouch in his shoulders or general abjectness into his demeanor, "you will go with us, for sure, won't you?"

"Yes," spoke up Tom Anderson, " 'cause de trader's done took your wife, an' got her for his'n now."

As Ben Tunnel looked at the speaker, a spasm of agony and anger darkened his face and distorted his features, as if the blood of some strong race were stirring with sudden vigor through his veins. He clutched his hands together, as if he were struggling with an invisible foe, and for a moment he remained silent. Then suddenly raising his head, he exclaimed, "Boys, there's not one of you loves freedom more than I do, but—"

"But what?" said Tom. "Do you think white folks is your bes' friends?"

"I'll think so when I lose my senses."

"Well, now, I don't belieb you're 'fraid, not de way I yeard you talkin' to de oberseer wen he war threatnin' to hit your mudder. He saw you meant business, an' he let her alone. But, what's to hinder you from gwine wid us?"

"My mother," he replied, in a low, firm voice. "That is the only thing that keeps me from going. If it had not been for her, I would have gone long ago. She's all I've got, an' I'm all she's got."

It was touching to see the sorrow on the strong face, to detect the pathos and indignation in his voice, as he said, "I used to love Mirandy as I love my life. I thought the sun rose and set in her. I never saw a handsomer woman than she was. But she fooled me all over the face and eyes, and took up with that hell-hound of a trader, Lukens; an' he gave her a chance to live easy, to wear fine clothes, an' be waited on like a lady. I thought at first I would go crazy, but my poor mammy did all she could to comfort me. She would tell me there were as good fish in the sea as were ever caught out of it. Many a time I've laid my poor head on her lap, when it seemed as if my brain was on fire and my heart was almost ready to burst. But in course of time I got over the worst of it; an' Mirandy is the first an' last woman that ever fooled me. But that dear old mammy of mine, I mean to stick by her as long as there is a piece of her. I can't go over to the army an' leave her behind, for if I did, an' anything should happen, I would never forgive myself."

"But couldn't you take her with you," said Robert, "the soldiers said we could bring our women."

"It isn't that. The Union army is several miles from here, an' my poor mammy is so skeery that, if I were trying to get her away and any of them Secesh would overtake us, an' begin to question us, she would get skeered almost to death, an' break down an' begin to cry, an' then the fat would be in the fire. So, while I love freedom more than a child loves its mother's milk, I've made up my mind to stay on the plantation. I wish, from the bottom of my heart, I could go. But I can't take her along with me, an' I don't want to be free and leave her behind in slavery. I was only five years old when my master and, as I believe, father, sold us both here to this lower country, an' we've been here ever since. It's no use talking, I won't leave her to be run over by everybody."

A few evenings after this interview, the Union soldiers entered the town of C——, and established their headquarters near the home of Thomas Anderson.

Out of the little company, almost every one deserted to the Union army, leaving Uncle Daniel faithful to his trust, and Ben Tunnel hushing his heart's deep aspirations for freedom in a passionate devotion to his timid and affectionate mother.

CHAPTER IV

Arrival of the Union Army

A FEW EVENINGS before the stampede of Robert and his friends to the army, and as he sat alone in his room reading the latest news from the paper he had secreted, he heard a cautious tread and a low tap at his window. He opened the door quietly and whispered:—

"Anything new, Tom?"

"Yes."

"What is it? Come in."

"Well, I'se done bin seen dem Yankees, an' dere ain't a bit of troof in dem stories I'se bin yerin 'bout 'em."

"Where did you see 'em?"

"Down in de woods whar Marster tole us to hide. Yesterday ole Marse sent for me to come in de settin'-room. An' what do you think? Instead ob makin' me stan' wid my hat in my han' while he went froo a whole rigamarole, he axed me to sit down, an' he tole me he 'spected de Yankees would want us to go inter de army, an' dey would put us in front whar we'd all git killed; an' I tole him I didn't want to go, I didn't want to git all momached up. An' den he said we'd better go down in de woods an' hide. Massa Tom and Frank said we'd better go as quick as eber we could. Dey said dem Yankees would put us in dere wagons and make us haul like we war mules. Marse Tom ain't libin' at de great house jis' now. He's keepin' bachelar's hall."

"Didn't he go to the battle?"

"No; he foun' a pore white man who war hard up for money, an' he got him to go."

"But, Tom, you didn't believe these stories about the Yankees. Tom and Frank can lie as fast as horses can trot. They wanted to scare you, and keep you from going to the Union army."

"I knows dat now, but I didn't 'spect so den."

"Well, when did you see the soldiers? Where are they? And what did they say to you?"

"Dey's right down in Gundover's woods. An' de Gineral's got his headquarters almos' next door to our house."

"That near? Oh, you don't say so!"

"Yes, I do. An', oh, golly, ain't I so glad! I jis' stole yere to told you all 'bout it. Yesterday mornin' I war splittin' some wood to git my breakfas', an' I met one ob dem Yankee sogers. Well, I war so skeered, my heart flew right up in my mouf, but I made my manners to him and said, 'Good mornin', Massa.' He said, 'Good mornin'; but don't call me "massa." ' Dat war de fust white man I eber seed dat didn't want ter be called 'massa,' eben ef he war as pore as Job's turkey. Den I begin to feel right sheepish, an' he axed me ef my marster war at home, an' ef he war a Reb. I tole him he hadn't gone to de war, but he war Secesh all froo, inside and outside. He war too ole to go to de war, but dat he war all de time gruntin' an' groanin', an' I 'spected he'd grunt hisself to death."

"What did he say?"

"He said he specs he'll grunt worser dan dat fore dey get froo wid him. Den he axed me ef I would hab some breakfas,' an' I said, 'No, t'ank you, sir.' An' I war jis' as hungry as a dorg, but I war 'feared to eat. I war 'feared he war gwine to pizen me."

"Poison you! don't you know the Yankees are our best friends?"

"Well, ef dat's so, I'se mighty glad, cause de woods is full ob dem."

"Now, Tom, I thought you had cut your eye-teeth long enough not to let them Anderson boys fool you. Tom, you must not think because a white man says a thing, it must be so, and that a colored man's word is no account 'longside of his. Tom, if ever we get our freedom, we've got to learn to trust each other and stick together if we would be a people. Somebody else can read the papers as well as Marse Tom and Frank. My ole Miss knows I can read the papers, an' she never tries to scare me with big whoppers 'bout the Yankees. She knows she can't catch ole birds with chaff, so she is just as sweet as a peach to her Bobby. But as soon as I get a chance I will play her a trick the devil never did."

"What's that?"

"I'll leave her. I ain't forgot how she sold my mother from me. Many a night I have cried myself to sleep, thinking about her, and when I get free I mean to hunt her up."

"Well, I ain't tole you all. De gemman said he war 'cruiting for de army; dat Massa Linkum hab set us all free, an' dat he wanted some more sogers to put down dem Secesh; dat we should all hab our freedom, our wages, an' some kind ob money. I couldn't call it like he did."

"Bounty money," said Robert.

"Yes, dat's jis' what he called it, bounty money. An' I said dat I war in for dat, teeth and toe-nails."

Robert Johnson's heart gave a great bound. Was that so? Had that army, with freedom emblazoned on its banners, come at last to offer them deliverance if they would accept it? Was it a bright, beautiful dream, or a blessed reality soon to be grasped by his willing hands? His heart grew buoyant with hope; the lightness of his heart gave elasticity to his step and sent the blood rejoicingly through his veins. Freedom was almost in his grasp, and the future was growing rose-tinted and rainbow-hued. All the ties which bound him to his home were as ropes of sand, now that freedom had come so near.

When the army was afar off, he had appeared to be light-hearted and content with his lot. If asked if he desired his freedom, he would have answered, very naively, that he was eating his white bread and believed in letting well enough alone; he had no intention of jumping from the frying-pan into the fire. But in the depths of his soul the love of freedom was an all-absorbing passion; only danger had taught him caution. He had heard of terrible vengeance being heaped upon the heads of some who had sought their freedom and failed in the attempt. Robert knew that he might abandon hope if he incurred the wrath of men whose overthrow was only a question of time. It would have been madness and folly for him to have attempted an insurrection against slavery, with the words of McClellan ringing in his ears: "If you rise I shall put you down with an iron hand," and with the home guards ready to quench his aspirations for freedom with bayonets and blood. What could a set of unarmed and undisciplined men do against the fearful odds which beset their path?

Robert waited eagerly and hopefully his chance to join the Union army; and was ready and willing to do anything required of him by which he could earn his freedom and prove his manhood. He conducted his plans with the greatest secrecy. A few faithful and trusted friends stood ready to desert with him when the Union army came within hailing distance. When it came, there was a stampede to its ranks of men ready to serve in any capacity, to labor in the tents, fight on the fields, or act as scouts. It was a strange sight to see these black men rallying around the Stars and Stripes, when white men were trampling them under foot and riddling them with bullets.

CHAPTER V

The Release of Iola Leroy

"WELL, BOYS," said Robert to his trusted friends, as they gathered together at a meeting in Gundover's woods, almost under the shadow of the Union army, "how many of you are ready to join the army and fight for your freedom."

"All ob us."

"The soldiers," continued Robert, "are camped right at the edge of the town. The General has his headquarters in the heart of the town, and one of the officers told me yesterday that the President had set us all free, and that as many as wanted to join the army could come along to the camp. So I thought, boys, that I would come and tell you. Now, you can take your bag and baggage, and get out of here as soon as you choose."

"We'll be ready by daylight," said Tom. "It won't take me long to pack up," looking down at his seedy clothes, with a laugh. "I specs ole Marse'll be real lonesome when I'm gone. An' won't he be hoppin' mad when he finds I'm a goner? I specs he'll hate it like pizen."

"O, well," said Robert, "the best of friends must part. Don't let it grieve you."

"I'se gwine to take my wife an' chillen," said one of the company.

"I'se got nobody but myself," said Tom; "but dere's a mighty putty young gal dere at Marse Tom's. I wish I could git her away. Dey tells me dey's been sellin' her all ober de kentry; but dat she's a reg'lar spitfire; dey can't lead nor dribe her."

"Do you think she would go with us?" said Robert.

"I think she's jis' dying to go. Dey say dey can't do nuffin wid her. Marse Tom's got his match dis time, and I'se glad ob it. I jis' glories in her spunk."

"How did she come there?"

"Oh, Marse bought her ob de trader to keep house for him. But ef you seed dem putty white han's ob hern you'd never tink she kept her own house, let 'lone anybody else's."

"Do you think you can get her away?"

"I don't know; 'cause Marse Tom keeps her mighty close. My! but she's putty. Beautiful long hair comes way down her back; putty blue eyes, an' jis' ez white ez anybody's in dis place. I'd jis' wish you could see her yoresef. I heerd Marse Tom talkin' 'bout her las' night to his brudder; tellin' him she war mighty airish, but he meant to break her in."

An angry curse rose to the lips of Robert, but he repressed it and muttered to himself, "Graceless scamp, he ought to have his neck stretched." Then turning to Tom, said:—

"Get her, if you possibly can, but you must be mighty mum about it."

"Trus' me for dat," said Tom.

Tom was very anxious to get word to the beautiful but intractable girl who was held in durance vile by her reckless and selfish master, who had tried in vain to drag her down to his own low level of sin and shame. But all Tom's efforts were in vain. Finally he applied to the Commander of the post, who immediately gave orders for her release. The next day Tom had the satisfaction of knowing that Iola Leroy had been taken as a trembling dove from the gory vulture's nest and given a place of security. She was taken immediately to the General's headquarters. The General was much impressed by her modest demeanor, and surprised to see the refinement and beauty she possessed. Could it be possible that this young and beautiful girl had been a chattel, with no power to protect herself from the highest insults that lawless brutality could inflict upon innocent and defenseless womanhood? Could he ever again glory in his American citizenship, when any white man, no matter how coarse, cruel, or brutal, could buy or sell her for the basest purposes? Was it not true that the cause of a hapless people had become entangled with the lightnings of heaven, and dragged down retribution upon the land?

The field hospital was needing gentle, womanly ministrations, and Iola Leroy, released from the hands of her

tormentors, was given a place as nurse; a position to
which she adapted herself with a deep sense of relief.
Tom was doubly gratified at the success of his endeavors,
which had resulted in the rescue of the beautiful young
girl and the discomfiture of his young master who, in the
words of Tom, "was mad enough to bite his head off"
(a rather difficult physical feat).

Iola, freed from her master's clutches, applied herself
readily to her appointed tasks. The beautiful, girlish face
was full of tender earnestness. The fresh, young voice
was strangely sympathetic, as if some great sorrow had
bound her heart in loving compassion to every sufferer
who needed her gentle ministrations.

Tom Anderson was a man of herculean strength and
remarkable courage. But, on account of physical defects,
instead of enlisting as a soldier, he was forced to remain
a servant, although he felt as if every nerve in his right
arm was tingling to strike a blow for freedom. He was
well versed in the lay of the country, having often driven
his master's cotton to market when he was a field hand.
After he became a coachman, he had become acquainted
with the different roads and localities of the country. Besides, he had often accompanied his young masters on
their hunting and fishing expeditions. Although he could
not fight in the army, he proved an invaluable helper.
When tents were to be pitched, none were more ready
to help than he. When burdens were to be borne, none
were more willing to bend beneath them than Thomas
Anderson. When the battle-field was to be searched for
the wounded and dying, no hand was more tender in its
ministrations of kindness than his. As a general factotum
in the army, he was ever ready and willing to serve anywhere and at any time, and to gather information from
every possible source which could be of any service to
the Union army. As a Pagan might worship a distant star
and wish to call it his own, so he loved Iola. And he
never thought he could do too much for the soldiers who
had rescued her and were bringing deliverance to his
race.

"What do you think of Miss Iola?" Robert asked him
one day, as they were talking together.

"I jis' think dat she's splendid. Las' week I had to take
some of our pore boys to de hospital, an' she war dere,

lookin' sweet an' putty ez an angel, a nussin' dem pore boys, an' ez good to one ez de oder. It looks to me ez ef dey ralely lob'd her shadder. She sits by 'em so patient, an' writes 'em sech nice letters to der frens, an' yit she looks so heart-broke an' pitiful, it jis' gits to me, an' makes me mos' ready to cry. I'm so glad dat Marse Tom had to gib her up. He war too mean to eat good victuals."

"He ought," said Robert, "to be made to live on herrings' heads and cold potatoes. It makes my blood boil just to think that he was going to have that lovely looking young girl whipped for his devilment. He ought to be ashamed to hold up his head among respectable people."

"I tell you, Bob, de debil will neber git his own till he gits him. When I seed how he war treating her I neber rested till I got her away. He buyed her, he said, for his housekeeper; as many gals as dere war on de plantation, why didn't he git one ob dem to keep house, an' not dat nice lookin' young lady? Her han's look ez ef she neber did a day's work in her life. One day when he com'd down to breakfas',' he chucked her under de chin, an' tried to put his arm roun' her waist. But she jis' frew it off like a chunk ob fire. She looked like a snake had bit her. Her eyes fairly spit fire. Her face got red ez blood, an' den she turned so pale I thought she war gwine to faint, but she didn't, an' I yered her say, 'I'll die fust.' I war mad 'nough to stan' on my head. I could hab tore'd him all to pieces wen he said he'd hab her whipped."

"Did he do it?"

"I don't know. But he's mean 'nough to do enythin'. Why, dey say she war sole seben times in six weeks, 'cause she's so putty, but dat she war game to de las'.'"

"Well, Tom," said Robert, "getting that girl away was one of the best things you ever did in your life."

"I think so, too. Not dat I specs enytin' ob it. I don't spose she would think ob an ugly chap like me; but it does me good to know dat Marse Tom ain't got her."

CHAPTER VI

Robert Johnson's Promotion and Religion

ROBERT JOHNSON, being able to meet the army requirements, was enlisted as a substitute to help fill out the quota of a Northern regiment. With his intelligence, courage, and prompt obedience, he rose from the ranks and became lieutenant of a colored company. He was daring, without being rash; prompt, but not thoughtless; firm, without being harsh. Kind and devoted to the company he drilled, he soon won the respect of his superior officers and the love of his comrades.

"Johnson," said a young officer, Captain Sybil, of Maine, who had become attached to Robert, "what is the use of your saying you're a colored man, when you are as white as I am, and as brave a man as there is among us. Why not quit this company, and take your place in the army just the same as a white man? I know your chances for promotion would be better."

"Captain, you may doubt my word, but to-day I would rather be a lieutenant in my company than a captain in yours."

"I don't understand you."

"Well, Captain, when a man's been colored all his life it comes a little hard for him to get white all at once. Were I to try it, I would feel like a cat in a strange garret. Captain, I think my place is where I am most needed. You do not need me in your ranks, and my company does. They are excellent fighters, but they need a leader. To silence a battery, to capture a flag, to take a fortification, they will rush into the jaws of death."

"Yes, I have often wondered at their bravery."

"Captain, these battles put them on their mettle. They have been so long taught that they are nothing and no-

34

body, that they seem glad to prove they are something and somebody."

"But, Johnson, you do not look like them, you do not talk like them. It is a burning shame to have held such a man as you in slavery."

"I don't think it was any worse to have held me in slavery than the blackest man in the South."

"You are right, Johnson. The color of a man's skin has nothing to do with the possession of his rights."

"Now, there is Tom Anderson," said Robert, "he is just as black as black can be. He has been bought and sold like a beast, and yet there is not a braver man in all the company. I know him well. He is a noble-hearted fellow. True as steel. I love him like a brother. And I believe Tom would risk his life for me any day. He don't know anything about his father or mother. He was sold from them before he could remember. He can read a little. He used to take lessons from a white gardener in Virginia. He would go between the hours of 9 P.M. and 4 A.M. He got a book of his own, tore it up, greased the pages, and hid them in his hat. Then if his master had ever knocked his hat off he would have thought them greasy papers, and not that Tom was carrying his library on his head. I had another friend who lived near us. When he was nineteen years old he did not know how many letters there were in the A B C's. One night, when his work was done, his boss came into his cabin and saw him with a book in his hand. He threatened to give him five hundred lashes if he caught him again with a book, and said he hadn't work enough to do. He was getting out logs, and his task was ten logs a day. His employer threatened to increase it to twelve. He said it just harassed him; it set him on fire. He thought there must be something good in that book if the white man didn't want him to learn. One day he had an errand in the kitchen, and he heard one of the colored girls going over the A B C's. Here was the key to the forbidden knowledge. She had heard the white children saying them, and picked them up by heart, but did not know them by sight. He was not content with that, but sold his cap for a book and wore a cloth on his head instead. He got the sounds of the letters by heart, then cut off the bark of a tree, carved the letters on the smooth inside, and learned them. He wanted to learn how to write. He had charge of a warehouse where he had a chance to see the size and form of letters. He made the beach of the river his copybook, and thus he learned to write. Tom never got very far with his learning, but I used to get the papers and tell him all I knew about the war."

"How did you get the papers?"

"I used to have very good privileges for a slave. All of our owners were not alike. Some of them were quite clever, and others were worse than git out. I used to get the morning papers to sell to the boarders and others and when I got them I would contrive to hide a paper, and let some of the fellow-servants know how things were going on. And our owners thought we cared nothing about what was going on."

"How was that? I thought you were not allowed to hold meetings unless a white man were present."

"That was so. But we contrived to hold secret meetings in spite of their caution. We knew whom we could trust. My ole Miss wasn't mean like some of them. She never wanted the patrollers around prowling in our cabins, and poking their noses into our business. Her husband was an awful drunkard. He ran through every cent he could lay his hands on, and she was forced to do something to keep the wolf from the door, so she set up a boarding-house. But she didn't take in Tom, Dick, and Harry. Nobody but the big bugs stopped with her. She taught me to read and write, and to cast up accounts. It was so handy for her to have some one who could figure up her accounts, and read or write a note, if she were from home and wanted the like done. She once told her cousin how I could write and figure up. And what do you think her cousin said?"

" 'Pleased,' I suppose, 'to hear it.' "

"Not a bit of it. She said, if I belonged to her, she would cut off my thumbs; her husband said, 'Oh, then he couldn't pick cotton.' As to my poor thumbs, it did not seem to be taken into account what it would cost me to lose them. My ole Miss used to have a lot of books. She would let me read any one of them except a novel. She wanted to take care of my soul, but she wasn't taking care of her own."

"Wasn't she religious?"

"She went for it. I suppose she was as good as most

of them. She said her prayers and went to church, but I don't know that that made her any better. I never did take much stock in white folks' religion."

"Why, Robert, I'm afraid you are something of an infidel."

"No, Captain, I believe in the real, genuine religion. I ain't got much myself, but I respect them that have. We had on our place a dear, old saint, named Aunt Kizzy. She was a happy soul. She had seen hard times, but was what I call a living epistle. I've heard her tell how her only child had been sold from her, when the man who bought herself did not want to buy her child. Poor little fellow! he was only two years old. I asked her one day how she felt when her child was taken away. 'I felt,' she said, 'as if I was going to my grave. But I knew if I couldn't get justice here, I could get it in another world.' "

"That was faith," said Captain Sybil, as if speaking to himself, "a patient waiting for death to redress the wrongs of life."

"Many a time," continued Robert, "have I heard her humming to herself in the kitchen and saying, 'I has my trials, ups and downs, but it won't allers be so. I specs one day to wing and wing wid de angels, Hallelujah! Den I specs to hear a voice sayin', "Poor ole Kizzy, she's done de bes' she kin. Go down, Gabriel, an' tote her in." Den I specs to put on my golden slippers, my long white robe, an' my starry crown, an' walk dem golden streets, Hallelujah!' I've known that dear, old soul to travel going on two miles, after her work was done, to have some one read to her. Her favorite chapter began with, 'Let not your heart be troubled, ye believe in God, believe also in Me.' "

"I have been deeply impressed," said Captain Sybil, "with the child-like faith of some of these people. I do not mean to say that they are consistent Christians, but I do think that this faith has in a measure underlain the life of the race. It has been a golden thread woven amid the sombre tissues of their lives. A ray of light shimmering amid the gloom of their condition. And what would they have been without it?"

"I don't know. But I know what she was with it. And I believe if there are any saints in glory, Aunt Kizzy is one of them."

"She is dead, then?"

"Yes, went all right, singing and rejoicing until the last, 'Troubles over, troubles over, and den my troubles will be over. We'll walk de golden streets all 'roun' in de New Jerusalem.' Now, Captain, that's the kind of religion that I want. Not that kind which could ride to church on Sundays, and talk so solemn with the minister about heaven and good things, then come home and light down on the servants like a thousand of bricks. I have no use for it. I don't believe in it. I never did and I never will. If any man wants to save my soul he ain't got to beat my body. That ain't the kind of religion I'm looking for. I ain't got a bit of use for it. Now, Captain, ain't I right?"

"Well, yes, Robert, I think you are more than half right. You ought to know my dear, old mother who lives in Maine. We have had colored company at our house, and I never saw her show the least difference between her colored and white guests. She is a Quaker preacher, and don't believe in war, but when the rest of the young men went to the front, I wanted to go also. So I thought it all over, and there seemed to be no way out of slavery except through the war. I had been taught to hate war and detest slavery. Now the time had come when I could not help the war, but I could strike a blow for freedom. So I told my mother I was going to the front, that I expected to be killed, but I went to free the slave. It went hard with her. But I thought that I ought to come, and I believe my mother's prayers are following me."

"Captain," said Robert, rising, "I am glad that I have heard your story. I think that some of these Northern soldiers do two things—hate slavery and hate niggers."

"I am afraid that is so with some of them. They would rather be whipped by Rebels than conquer with negroes. Oh, I heard a soldier," said Captain Sybil, "say, when the colored men were being enlisted, that he would break his sword and resign. But he didn't do either. After Colonel Shaw led his charge at Fort Wagner, and died in the conflict, he got bravely over his prejudices. The conduct of the colored troops there and elsewhere has done much to turn public opinion in their favor. I suppose any white soldier would rather have his black substitute receive the bullets than himself."

CHAPTER VII

Tom Anderson's Death

"WHERE IS TOM?" asked Captain Sybil; "I have not seen him for several hours."

"He's gone down the sound with some of the soldiers," replied Robert. "They wanted Tom to row them."

"I am afraid those boys will get into trouble, and the Rebs will pick them off," responded Sybil.

"O, I hope not," answered Robert.

"I hope not, too; but those boys are too venturesome."

"Tom knows the lay of the land better than any of us," said Robert. "He is the most wide-awake and gamiest man I know. I reckon when the war is over Tom will be a preacher. Did you ever hear him pray?"

"No; is he good at that?"

"First-rate," continued Robert. "It would do you good to hear him. He don't allow any cursing and swearing when he's around. And what he says is law and gospel with the boys. But he's *so* good-natured; and they *can't* get mad at him."

"Yes, Robert, there is not a man in our regiment I would sooner trust than Tom. Last night, when he brought in that wounded scout, he couldn't have been more tender if he had been a woman. How gratefully the poor fellow looked in Tom's face as he laid him down so carefully and staunched the blood which had been spurting out of him. Tom seemed to know it was an artery which had been cut, and he did just the right thing to stop the bleeding. He knew there wasn't a moment to be lost. He wasn't going to wait for the doctor. I have often heard that colored people are ungrateful, but I don't think Tom's worst enemy would say that about him."

"Captain," said Robert, with a tone of bitterness in his voice, "what had we to be grateful for? For ages of poverty, ignorance, and slavery? I think if anybody should be grateful, it is the people who have enslaved us and lived off our labor for generations. Captain, I used to know a poor old woman who couldn't bear to hear any one play on the piano."

"Is that so? Why, I always heard that colored people were a musical race."

"So we are; but that poor woman's daughter was sold, and her mistress took the money to buy a piano. Her mother could never bear to hear a sound from it."

"Poor woman!" exclaimed Captain Sybil, sympathetically; "I suppose it seemed as if the wail of her daughter was blending with the tones of the instrument. I think, Robert, there is a great deal more in the colored people than we give them credit for. Did you know Captain Sellers?"

"The officer who escaped from prison and got back to our lines?" asked Robert.

"Yes. Well, he had quite an experience in trying to escape. He came to an aged couple, who hid him in their cabin and shared their humble food with him. They gave him some corn-bread, bacon, and coffee which he thought was made of scorched bran. But he said that he never ate a meal that he relished more than the one he took with them. Just before he went they knelt down and prayed with him. It seemed as if his very hair stood on his head, their prayer was so solemn. As he was going away the man took some shingles and nailed them on his shoes to throw the bloodhounds off his track. I don't think he will ever cease to feel kindly towards colored people. I do wonder what has become of the boys? What can keep them so long?"

Just as Captain Sybil and Robert were wondering at the delay of Tom and the soldiers they heard the measured tread of men who were slowly bearing a burden. They were carrying Tom Anderson to the hospital, fearfully wounded, and nigh to death. His face was distorted, and the blood was streaming from his wounds. His respiration was faint, his pulse hurried, as if life were trembling on its frailest cords.

Robert and Captain Sybil hastened at once towards the wounded man. On Robert's face was a look of intense anguish, as he bent pityingly over his friend.

"O, this is dreadful! How did it happen?" cried Robert.

Captain Sybil, pressing anxiously forward, repeated Robert's question.

"Captain," said one of the young soldiers, advancing and saluting his superior officer, "we were all in the boat when it struck against a mud bank, and there was not strength enough among us to shove her back into the water. Just then the Rebels opened fire upon us. For a while we lay down in the boat, but still they kept firing. Tom took in the whole situation, and said: 'Some one must die to get us out of this. I mought's well be him as any. You are soldiers and can fight. If they kill me, it is nuthin'.' So Tom leaped out to shove the boat into the water. Just then the Rebel bullets began to rain around him. He received seven or eight of them, and I'm afraid there is no hope for him."

"O, Tom, I wish you hadn't gone. O, Tom! Tom!" cried Robert, in tones of agony.

A gleam of grateful recognition passed over the drawn features of Tom, as the wail of his friend fell on his ear. He attempted to speak, but the words died upon his lips, and he became unconscious.

"Well," said Captain Sybil, "put him in one of the best wards. Give him into Miss Leroy's care. If good nursing can win him back to life, he shall not want for any care or pains that she can bestow. Send immediately for Dr. Gresham."

Robert followed his friend into the hospital, tenderly and carefully helped to lay him down, and remained awhile, gazing in silent grief upon the sufferer. Then he turned to go, leaving him in the hands of Iola, but hoping against hope that his wounds would not be fatal.

With tender devotion Iola watched her faithful friend. He recognized her when restored to consciousness, and her presence was as balm to his wounds. He smiled faintly, took her hand in his, stroked it tenderly, looked wistfully into her face, and said, "Miss Iola, I ain't long fer dis! I'se 'most home!"

"Oh, no," said Iola, "I hope that you will soon get over this trouble, and live many long and happy days."

"No, Miss Iola, it's all ober wid me. I'se gwine to glory; gwine to glory; gwine to ring dem charmin' bells.

Tell all de boys to meet me in heben; dat dey mus' 'list in de hebenly war."

"O, Mr. Tom," said Iola, tenderly, "do not talk of leaving me. You are the best friend I have had since I was torn from my mother. I should be so lonely without you."

"Dere's a frien' dat sticks closer dan a brudder. He will be wid yer in de sixt' trial, an' in de sebbent' he'll not fo'sake yer."

"Yes," answered Iola, "I know that. He is all our dependence. But I can't help grieving when I see you suffering so. But, dear friend, be quiet, and try to go to sleep."

"I'll do enythin' fer yer, Miss Iola."

Tom closed his eyes and lay quiet. Tenderly and anxiously Iola watched over him as the hours waned away. The doctor came, shook his head gravely, and, turning to Iola, said, "There is no hope, but do what you can to alleviate his sufferings."

As Iola gazed upon the kind but homely features of Tom, she saw his eyes open and an unexpressed desire upon his face.

Tenderly and sadly bending over him, with tears in her dark, luminous eyes, she said, "Is there anything I can do for you?"

"Yes," said Tom, with laboring breath; "let me hole yore han', an' sing 'Ober Jordan inter glory' an' 'We'll anchor bye and bye.' "

Iola laid her hand gently in the rough palm of the dying man, and, with a tremulous voice, sang the parting hymns.

Tenderly she wiped the death damps from his dusky brow, and imprinted upon it a farewell kiss. Gratitude and affection lit up the dying eye, which seemed to be gazing into the eternities. Just then Robert entered the room, and, seating himself quietly by Tom's bedside, read the death signs in his face.

"Good-bye, Robert," said Tom, "meet me in de kingdom." Suddenly a look of recognition and rapture lit up his face, and he murmured, "Angels, bright angels, all's well, all's well!"

Slowly his hand released its pressure, a peaceful calm overspread his countenance, and without a sigh or murmur Thomas Anderson, Iola's faithful and devoted friend, passed away, leaving the world so much poorer for her than it was before. Just then Dr. Gresham, the hospital physician, came to the bedside, felt for the pulse which would never throb again, and sat down in silence by the cot.

"What do you think, Doctor," said Iola, "has he fainted?"

"No," said the doctor, "poor fellow! he is dead."

Iola bowed her head in silent sorrow, and then relieved the anguish of her heart by a flood of tears. Robert rose, and sorrowfully left the room.

Iola, with tearful eyes and aching heart, clasped the cold hands over the still breast, closed the waxen lid over the eye which had once beamed with kindness or flashed with courage, and then went back, after the burial, to her daily round of duties, feeling the sad missing of something from her life.

CHAPTER VIII

The Mystified Doctor

"COLONEL," said Dr. Gresham to Col. Robinson, the commander of the post, "I am perfectly mystified by Miss Leroy."

"What is the matter with her?" asked Col. Robinson. "Is she not faithful to her duties and obedient to your directions?"

"Faithful is not the word to express her tireless energy and devotion to her work," responded Dr. Gresham. "She must have been a born nurse to put such enthusiasm into her work."

"Why, Doctor, what is the matter with you? You talk like a lover."

A faint flush rose to the cheek of Dr. Gresham as he smiled, and said, "Oh! come now, Colonel, can't a man praise a woman without being in love with her?"

"Of course he can," said Col. Robinson; "but I know where such admiration is apt to lead. I've been there myself. But, Doctor, had you not better defer your love-making till you're out of the woods?"

"I assure you, Colonel, I am not thinking of love or courtship. That is the business of the drawing-room, and not of the camp. But she did mystify me last night."

"How so?" asked Col. Robinson.

"When Tom was dying," responded the doctor, "I saw that beautiful and refined young lady bend over and kiss him. When she found that he was dead, she just cried as if her heart was breaking. Well, that was a new thing to me. I can eat with colored people, walk, talk, and fight with them, but kissing them is something I don't hanker after."

"And you saw Miss Leroy do it?"

"Yes; and that puzzles me. She is one of the most refined and lady-like women I ever saw. I hear she is a refugee, but she does not look like the other refugees who have come to our camp. Her accent is slightly Southern, but her manner is Northern. She is self-respecting without being supercilious; quiet, without being dull. Her voice is low and sweet, yet at times there are tones of such passionate tenderness in it that you would think some great sorrow has darkened and overshadowed her life. Without being the least gloomy, her face at times is pervaded by an air of inexpressible sadness. I sometimes watch her when she is not aware that I am looking at her, and it seems as if a whole volume was depicted on her countenance. When she smiles, there is a longing in her eyes which is never satisfied. I cannot understand how a Southern lady, whose education and manners stamp her as a woman of fine culture and good breeding, could consent to occupy the position she so faithfully holds. It is a mystery I cannot solve. Can you?"

"I think I can," answered Col. Robinson.

"Will you tell me?" queried the doctor.

"Yes, on one condition."

"What is it?"

"Everlasting silence."

"I promise," said the doctor. "The secret between us shall be as deep as the sea."

"She has not requested secrecy, but at present, for her sake, I do not wish the secret revealed. Miss Leroy was a slave."

"Oh, no," said Dr. Gresham, starting to his feet, "it can't be so! A woman as white as she a slave?"

"Yes, it is so," continued the colonel. "In these States the child follows the condition of its mother. This beautiful and accomplished girl was held by one of the worst Rebels in town. Tom told me of it and I issued orders for her release."

"Well, well! Is that so?" said Dr. Gresham, thoughtfully stroking his beard. "Wonders will never cease. Why, I was just beginning to think seriously of her."

"What's to hinder your continuing to think?" asked Col. Robinson.

"What you tell me changes the whole complexion of affairs," replied the doctor.

"If that be so I am glad I told you before you got head over heels in love."

"Yes," said Dr. Gresham, absently.

Dr. Gresham was a member of a wealthy and aristocratic family, proud of its lineage, which it could trace through generations of good blood to its ancestral isle. He had become deeply interested in Iola before he had heard her story, but after it had been revealed to him he tried to banish her from his mind; but his constant observation of her only increased his interest and admiration. The deep pathos of her story, the tenderness of her ministrations, bestowed alike on black and white, and the sad loneliness of her condition, awakened within him a desire to defend and protect her all through her future life. The fierce clashing of war had not taken all the romance out of his nature. In Iola he saw realized his ideal of the woman whom he was willing to marry. A woman, tender, strong, and courageous, and rescued only by the strong arm of his Government from a fate worse than death. She was young in years, but old in sorrow; one whom a sad destiny had changed from a light-hearted girl to a heroic woman. As he observed her, he detected an undertone of sorrow in her most cheerful words, and observed a quick flushing and sudden paling of her cheek, as if she were living over scenes that were thrilling her soul with indignation or chilling her heart with horror. As nurse and physician, Iola and Dr. Gresham were constantly thrown together. His friends sent him magazines and books, which he gladly shared with her. The hospital was a sad place. Mangled forms, stricken down in the flush of their prime and energy; pale young corpses, sacrificed on the altar of slavery, constantly drained on her sympathies. Dr. Gresham was glad to have some reading matter which might divert her mind from the memories of her mournful past, and also furnish them both with interesting themes of conversation in their moments of relaxation from the harrowing scenes through which they were constantly passing. Without any effort or consciousness on her part, his friendship ripened into love. To him her presence was a pleasure, her absence a privation; and her loneliness drew deeply upon his sympathy. He would have merited his own self-contempt if, by word or deed, he had done anything to take advantage of her situation. All the manhood and chivalry of his nature rose in her behalf, and, after carefully revolving the matter, he resolved to win her for his bride, bury her secret in his Northern home, and hide from his aristocratic relations all knowledge of her mournful past. One day he said to Iola:—

"This hospital life is telling on you. Your strength is failing, and although you possess a wonderful amount of physical endurance, you must not forget that saints have bodies and dwell in tabernacles of clay, just the same as we common mortals."

"Compliments aside," she said, smiling; "what are you driving at, Doctor?"

"I mean," he replied, "that you are running down, and if you do not quit and take some rest you will be our patient instead of our nurse. You'd better take a furlough, go North, and return after the first frost."

"Doctor, if that is your only remedy," replied Iola, "I am afraid that I am destined to die at my post. I have no special friends in the North, and no home but this in the South. I am homeless and alone."

There was something so sad, almost despairing in her tones, in the drooping of her head, and the quivering of her lip, that they stirred Dr. Gresham's heart with sudden pity, and, drawing nearer to her, he said, "Miss Leroy, you need not be all alone. Let me claim the privilege of making your life bright and happy. Iola, I have loved you ever since I have seen your devotion to our poor, sick boys. How faithfully you, a young and gracious girl, have stood at your post and performed your duties. And now I ask, will you not permit me to clasp hands with you for life? I do not ask for a hasty reply. Give yourself time to think over what I have proposed."

CHAPTER IX

Eugene Leroy and Alfred Lorraine

NEARLY TWENTY YEARS before the war, two young men, of French and Spanish descent, sat conversing on a large verandah which surrounded an ancient home on the Mississippi River. It was French in its style of architecture, large and rambling, with no hint of modern improvements.

The owner of the house was the only heir of a Creole planter. He had come into possession of an inheritance consisting of vast baronial estates, bank stock, and a large number of slaves. Eugene Leroy, being deprived of his parents, was left, at an early age, to the care of a distant relative, who had sent him to school and college, and who occasionally invited him to spend his vacations at his home. But Eugene generally declined his invitations, as he preferred spending his vacations at the watering places in the North, with their fashionable and not always innocent gayeties. Young, vivacious, impulsive, and undisciplined, without the restraining influence of a mother's love or the guidance of a father's hand, Leroy found himself, when his college days were over, in the dangerous position of a young man with vast possessions, abundant leisure, unsettled principles, and uncontrolled desires. He had no other object than to extract from life its most seductive draughts of ease and pleasure. His companion, who sat opposite him on the verandah, quietly smoking a cigar, was a remote cousin, a few years older than himself, the warmth of whose Southern temperament had been modified by an infusion of Northern blood.

Eugene was careless, liberal, and impatient of details, while his companion and cousin, Alfred Lorraine, was selfish, eager, keen, and alert; also hard, cold, methodical, and ever ready to grasp the main chance. Yet, not withstanding the difference between them, they had formed a warm friendship for each other.

"Alfred," said Eugene, "I am going to be married."

Lorraine opened his eyes with sudden wonder, and exclaimed: "Well, that's the latest thing out! Who is the fortunate lady who has bound you with her silken fetters? Is it one of those beautiful Creole girls who were visiting Augustine's plantation last winter? I watched you during our visit there and thought that you could not be proof against their attractions. Which is your choice? It would puzzle me to judge between the two. They had splendid eyes, dark, luminous, and languishing; lovely complexions and magnificent hair. Both were delightful in their manners, refined and cultured, with an air of vivacity mingled with their repose of manner which was perfectly charming. As the law only allows us one, which is your choice? Miss Annette has more force than her sister, and if I could afford the luxury of a wife she would be my choice."

"Ah, Alf," said Eugene, "I see that you are a practical business man. In marrying you want a wife to assist you as an efficient plantation mistress. One who would tolerate no waste in the kitchen and no disorder in the parlor."

"Exactly so," responded Lorraine; "I am too poor to marry a mere parlor ornament. You can afford to do it; I cannot."

"Nonsense, if I were as poor as a church mouse I would marry the woman I love."

"Very fine sentiments," said Lorraine, "and were I as rich as you I would indulge in them also. You know, when my father died I had great expectations. We had always lived in good style, and I never thought for a moment he was not a rich man, but when his estate was settled I found it was greatly involved, and I was forced to face an uncertain future, with scarcely a dollar to call my own. Land, negroes, cattle, and horses all went under the hammer. The only thing I retained was the education I received at the North; that was my father's best investment, and all my stock in trade. With that only as an outfit, it would be madness for me to think of marrying one of those lovely girls. They remind me of beautiful canary birds, charming and pretty, but not fitted for the wear and tear of plantation life. Well, which is your choice?"

"Neither," replied Eugene.

"Then, is it that magnificent looking widow from New Orleans, whom we met before you had that terrible spell of sickness and to whom you appeared so devoted?"

"Not at all. I have not heard from her since that summer. She was fascinating and handsome, but fearfully high strung."

"Were you afraid of her?"

"No; but I valued my happiness too much to trust it in her hands."

"Sour grapes!" said Lorraine.

"No! but I think that slavery and the lack of outside interests are beginning to tell on the lives of our women. They lean too much on their slaves, have too much irresponsible power in their hands, are narrowed and compressed by the routine of plantation life and the lack of intellectual stimulus."

"Yes, Eugene, when I see what other women are doing in the fields of literature and art, I cannot help thinking an amount of brain power has been held in check among us. Yet I cannot abide those Northern women, with their suffrage views and abolition cant. They just shock me."

"But your mother was a Northern woman," said Eugene.

"Yes; but she got bravely over her Northern ideas. As I remember her, she was just as much a Southerner as if she had been to the manor born. She came here as a school-teacher, but soon after she came she married my father. He was easy and indulgent with his servants, and held them with a very loose rein. But my mother was firm and energetic. She made the niggers move around. No shirking nor dawdling with her. When my father died, she took matters in hand, but she only outlived him a few months. If she had lived I believe that she would have retrieved our fortune. I know that she had more executive ability than my father. He was very squeamish about selling his servants, but she would have put every one of them in her pocket before permitting them to eat her out of house and home. But whom *are* you going to marry?"

"A young lady who graduates from a Northern seminary next week," responded Eugene.

"I think you are very selfish," said Lorraine. "You might have invited a fellow to go with you to be your best man."

"The wedding is to be strictly private. The lady whom I am to marry has negro blood in her veins."

"The devil she has!" exclaimed Lorraine, starting to his feet, and looking incredulously on the face of Leroy. "Are you in earnest? Surely you must be jesting."

"I am certainly in earnest," answered Eugene Leroy. "I mean every word I say."

"Oh, it can't be possible! Are you mad?" exclaimed Lorraine.

"Never was saner in my life."

"What under heaven could have possessed you to do such a foolish thing? Where did she come from."

"Right here, on this plantation. But I have educated and manumitted her, and I intend marrying her."

"Why, Eugene, it is impossible that you can have an idea of marrying one of your slaves. Why, man, she is your property, to have and to hold to all intents and purposes. Are you not satisfied with the power and possession the law gives you?"

"No. Although the law makes her helpless in my hands, to me her defenselessness is her best defense."

"Eugene, we have known each other all of our lives, and, although I have always regarded you as eccentric, I never saw you so completely off your balance before. The idea of you, with your proud family name, your vast wealth in land and negroes, intending to marry one of them, is a mystery I cannot solve. Do explain to me why you are going to take this extremely strange and foolish step."

"You never saw Marie?"

"No; and I don't want to."

"She is very beautiful. In the North no one would suspect that she has one drop of negro blood in her veins, but here, where I am known, to marry her is to lose caste. I could live with her, and not incur much if any social opprobrium. Society would wink at the transgression, even if after she had become the mother of my children I should cast her off and send her and them to the auction block."

"Men," replied Lorraine, "would merely shrug their shoulders; women would say you had been sowing your wild oats. Your money, like charity, would cover a multitude of faults."

"But if I make her my lawful wife and recognize her children as my legitimate heirs, I subject myself to social ostracism and a senseless persecution. We Americans boast of freedom, and yet here is a woman whom I love as I never loved any other human being, but both law and public opinion debar me from following the inclination of my heart. She is beautiful, faithful, and pure, and yet all that society will tolerate is what I would scorn to do."

"But has not society the right to guard the purity of its blood by the rigid exclusion of an alien race?"

"Excluding it! How?" asked Eugene.

"By debarring it from social intercourse."

"Perhaps it has," continued Eugene, "but should not society have a greater ban for those who, by consorting with an alien race, rob their offspring of a right to their names and to an inheritance in their property, and who fix their social status among an enslaved and outcast race? Don't eye me so curiously; I am not losing my senses."

"I think you have done that already," said Lorraine. "Don't you know that if she is as fair as a lily, beautiful as a houri, and chaste as ice, that still she is a negro?"

"Oh, come now; she isn't much of a negro."

"It doesn't matter, however. One drop of negro blood in her veins curses all the rest."

"I know it," said Eugene, sadly, "but I have weighed the consequences, and am prepared to take them."

"Well, Eugene, your course is *so* singular! I do wish that you would tell me why you take this unprecedented step?"

Eugene laid aside his cigar, looked thoughtfully at Lorraine, and said, "Well, Alfred, as we are kinsmen and life-long friends, I will not resent your asking my reason for doing that which seems to you the climax of absurdity, and if you will have the patience to listen I will tell you."

"Proceed, I am all attention."

"My father died," said Eugene, "as you know, when I was too young to know his loss or feel his care and, being an only child, I was petted and spoiled. I grew up to be wayward, self-indulgent, proud, and imperious. I went from home and made many friends both at college and in foreign lands. I was well supplied with money and, never having been forced to earn it, was ignorant of its value and careless of its use. My lavish expenditures and liberal benefactions attracted to me a number of parasites, and men older than myself led me into the paths of vice, and taught me how to gather the flowers of sin which blossom around the borders of hell. In a word, I left my home unwarned and unarmed against the seductions of vice. I returned an initiated devotee to debasing pleasures. Years of my life were passed in foreign lands; years in which my soul slumbered and seemed pervaded with a moral paralysis; years, the memory of which fills my soul with sorrow and shame. I went to the capitals of the old world to see life, but in seeing life I became acquainted with death, the death of true manliness and self-respect. You look astonished; but I tell you, Alf, there is many a poor clod-hopper, on whom are the dust and grime of unremitting toil, who feels more self-respect and true manliness than many of us with our family prestige, social position, and proud ancestral halls. After I had lived abroad for years, I returned a broken-down young man, prematurely old, my constitution a perfect wreck. A life of folly and dissipation was telling fearfully upon me. My friends shrank from me in dismay. I was sick nigh unto death, and had it not been for Marie's care I am certain that I should have died. She followed me down to the borders of the grave, and won me back to life and health. I was slow in recovering and, during the time, I had ample space for reflection, and the past unrolled itself before me. I resolved, over the wreck and ruin of my past life, to build a better and brighter future. Marie had a voice of remarkable sweetness, although it lacked culture. Often when I was nervous and restless I would have her sing some of those weird and plaintive melodies which she had learned from the plantation negroes. Sometimes I encouraged her to talk and I was surprised at the native vigor of her intellect. By degrees

I became acquainted with her history. She was all alone in the world. She had no recollection of her father, but remembered being torn from her mother while clinging to her dress. The trader who bought her mother did not wish to buy her. She remembered having a brother, with whom she used to play, but she had been separated from him also, and since then had lost all trace of them. After she was sold from her mother she became the property of an excellent old lady, who seems to have been very careful to imbue her mind with good principles; a woman who loved purity, not only for her own daughters, but also for the defenseless girls in her home. I believe it was the lady's intention to have freed Marie at her death, but she died suddenly, and, the estate being involved, she was sold with it and fell into the hands of my agent. I became deeply interested in her when I heard her story, and began to pity her."

"And I suppose love sprang from pity."

"I not only pitied her, but I learned to respect her. I had met with beautiful women in the halls of wealth and fashion, both at home and abroad, but there was something in her different from all my experience of womanhood."

"I should think so," said Lorraine, with a sneer; "but I should like to know what it was."

"It was something such as I have seen in old cathedrals, lighting up the beauty of a saintly face. A light which the poet tells was never seen on land or sea. I thought of this beautiful and defenseless girl adrift in the power of a reckless man, who, with all the advantages of wealth and education, had trailed his manhood in the dust, and she, with simple, childlike faith in the Unseen, seemed to be so good and pure that she commanded my respect and won my heart. In her presence every base and unholy passion died, subdued by the supremacy of her virtue."

"Why, Eugene, what was come over you? Talking of the virtue of these quadroon girls! You have lived so long in the North and abroad, that you seem to have lost the cue of our Southern life. Don't you know that these beautiful girls have been the curse of our homes? You have no idea of the hearts which are wrung by their presence."

"But, Alfred, suppose it is so. Are they to blame for it? What can any woman do when she is placed in the hands of an irresponsible master; when she knows that resistance is vain? Yes, Alfred, I agree with you, these women are the bane of our Southern civilization; but they are the victims and we are the criminals."

"I think from the airs that some of them put on when they get a chance, that they are very willing victims."

"So much the worse for our institution. If it is cruel to debase a hapless victim, it is an increase of cruelty to make her contented with her degradation. Let me tell you, Alf, you cannot wrong or degrade a woman without wronging or degrading yourself."

"What is the matter with you, Eugene? Are you thinking of taking priest's orders?"

"No, Alf," said Eugene, rising and rapidly pacing the floor, "you may defend the system as much as you please, but you cannot deny that the circumstances it creates, and the temptations it affords, are sapping our strength and undermining our character."

"That may be true," said Lorraine, somewhat irritably, "but you had better be careful how you air your Northern notions in public."

"Why so?"

"Because public opinion is too sensitive to tolerate any such discussions."

"And is not that a proof that we are at fault with respect to our institutions?"

"I don't know. I only know we are living in the midst of a magazine of powder, and it is not safe to enter it with a lighted candle."

"Let me proceed with my story," continued Eugene. "During the long months in which I was convalescing, I was left almost entirely to the companionship of Marie. In my library I found a Bible, which I began to read from curiosity, but my curiosity deepened into interest when I saw the rapt expression on Marie's face. I saw in it a loving response to sentiments to which I was a stranger. In the meantime my conscience was awakened, and I scorned to take advantage of her defenselessness. I felt that I owed my life to her faithful care, and I resolved to take her North, manumit, educate, and marry her. I sent her to a Northern academy, but as soon as some of the pupils found that she was colored, objections were raised, and the principal was compelled to dismiss her. During my search for a school I heard of one where three girls of mixed blood were pursuing their studies, every one of whom would have been ignominiously dismissed had their connection with the negro race been known. But I determined to run no risks. I found a school where her connection with the negro race would be no bar to her advancement. She graduates next week, and I intend to marry her before I return home. She was faithful when others were faithless, stood by me when others deserted me to die in loneliness and neglect, and now I am about to reward her care with all the love and devotion it is in my power to bestow. That is why I am about to marry my faithful and devoted nurse, who snatched me from the jaws of death. Now that I have told you my story, what say you?"

"Madness and folly inconceivable!" exclaimed Lorraine.

"What to you is madness and folly is perfect sanity with me. After all, Alf, is there not an amount of unreason in our prejudices?"

"That may be true; but I wasn't reasoned into it, and I do not expect to be reasoned out of it."

"Will you accompany me North?"

"No; except to put you in an insane asylum. You are the greatest crank out," said Lorraine, thoroughly disgusted.

"No, thank you; I'm all right. I expect to start North to-morrow. You had better come and go."

"I would rather follow you to your grave," replied Lorraine, hotly, while an expression of ineffable scorn passed over his cold, proud face.

CHAPTER X

Shadows in the Home

ON THE NEXT morning after this conversation Leroy left for the North, to attend the commencement and witness the graduation of his ward. Arriving in Ohio, he immediately repaired to the academy and inquired for the principal. He was shown into the reception-room, and in a few moments the principal entered.

"Good morning," said Leroy, rising and advancing towards him; "how is my ward this morning?"

"She is well, and has been expecting you. I am glad you came in time for the commencement. She stands among the foremost in her class."

"I am glad to hear it. Will you send her this?" said Leroy, handing the principal a card. The principal took the card and immediately left the room.

Very soon Leroy heard a light step, and looking up he saw a radiantly beautiful woman approaching him.

"Good morning, Marie," he said, greeting her cordially, and gazing upon her with unfeigned admiration. "You are looking very handsome this morning."

"Do you think so?" she asked, smiling and blushing. "I am glad you are not disappointed; that you do not feel your money has been spent in vain."

"Oh, no, what I have spent on your education has been the best investment I ever made."

"I hope," said Marie, "you may always find it so. But Mas—"

"Hush!" said Leroy, laying his hand playfully on her lips; "you are free. I don't want the dialect of slavery to linger on your lips. You must not call me that name again."

"Why not?"

"Because I have a nearer and dearer one by which I wish to be called."

57

Leroy drew her nearer, and whispered in her ear a single word. She started, trembled with emotion, grew pale, and blushed painfully. An awkward silence ensued, when Leroy, pressing her hand, exclaimed: "This is the hand that plucked me from the grave, and I am going to retain it as mine; mine to guard with my care until death us do part."

Leroy looked earnestly into her eyes, which fell beneath his ardent gaze. With admirable self-control, while a great joy was thrilling her heart, she bowed her beautiful head and softly repeated, "Until death us do part."

Leroy knew Southern society too well to expect it to condone his offense against its social customs, or give the least recognition to his wife, however cultured, refined, and charming she might be, if it were known that she had the least infusion of negro blood in her veins. But he was brave enough to face the consequences of his alliance, and marry the woman who was the choice of his heart, and on whom his affections were centred.

After Leroy had left the room, Marie sat awhile thinking of the wonderful change that had come over her. Instead of being a lonely slave girl, with the fatal dower of beauty, liable to be bought and sold, exchanged, and bartered, she was to be the wife of a wealthy planter; a man in whose honor she could confide, and on whose love she could lean.

Very interesting and pleasant were the commencement exercises in which Marie bore an important part. To enlist sympathy for her enslaved race, and appear to advantage before Leroy, had aroused all of her energies. The stimulus of hope, the manly love which was environing her life, brightened her eye and lit up the wonderful beauty of her countenance. During her stay in the North she had constantly been brought in contact with antislavery people. She was not aware that there was so much kindness among the white people of the country until she had tested it in the North. From the anti-slavery people in private life she had learned some of the noblest lessons of freedom and justice, and had become imbued with their sentiments. Her theme was "American Civilization, its Lights and Shadows."

Graphically she portrayed the lights, faithfully she showed the shadows of our American civilization. Earnestly and feelingly she spoke of the blind Sampson in our land, who might yet shake the pillars of our great Commonwealth. Leroy listened attentively. At times a shadow of annoyance would overspread his face, but it was soon lost in the admiration her earnestness and zeal inspired. Like Esther pleading for the lives of her people in the Oriental courts of a despotic king, she stood before the audience, pleading for those whose lips were sealed, but whose condition appealed to the mercy and justice of the Nation. Strong men wiped the moisture from their eyes, and women's hearts throbbed in unison with the strong, brave words that were uttered in behalf of freedom for all and chains for none. Generous applause was freely bestowed, and beautiful bouquets were showered upon her. When it was known that she was to be the wife of her guardian, warm congratulations were given, and earnest hopes expressed for the welfare of the lonely girl, who, nearly all her life, had been deprived of a parent's love and care. On the eve of starting South Leroy procured a license, and united his destiny with the young lady whose devotion in the darkest hour had won his love and gratitude.

In a few days Marie returned as mistress to the plantation from which she had gone as a slave. But as unholy alliances were common in those days between masters and slaves, no one took especial notice that Marie shared Leroy's life as mistress of his home, and that the family silver and jewelry were in her possession. But Leroy, happy in his choice, attended to the interests of his plantation, and found companionship in his books and in the society of his wife. A few male companions visited him occasionally, admired the magnificent beauty of his wife, shook their heads, and spoke of him as being very eccentric, but thought his marriage the great mistake of his life. But none of his female friends ever entered his doors, when it became known that Marie held the position of mistress of his mansion, and presided at his table. But she, sheltered in the warm clasp of loving arms, found her life like a joyous dream.

Into that quiet and beautiful home three children were born, unconscious of the doom suspended over their heads.

"Oh, how glad I am," Marie would often say, "that

these children are free. I could never understand how a cultured white man could have his own children enslaved. I can understand how savages, fighting with each other, could doom their vanquished foes to slavery, but it has always been a puzzle to me how a civilized man could drag his own children, bone of his bone, flesh of his flesh, down to the position of social outcasts, abject slaves, and political pariahs."

"But, Marie," said Eugene, "all men do not treat their illegitimate children in the manner you describe. The last time I was in New Orleans I met Henri Augustine at the depot, with two beautiful young girls. At first I thought that they were his own children, they resembled him so closely. But afterwards I noticed that they addressed him as 'Mister.' Before we parted he told me that his wife had taken such a dislike to their mother that she could not bear to see them on the place. At last, weary of her dissatisfaction, he had promised to bring them to New Orleans and sell them. Instead, he was going to Ohio to give them their freedom, and make provision for their future."

"What a wrong!" said Marie.

"Who was wronged?" said Leroy, in astonishment.

"Every one in the whole transaction," answered Marie. "Your friend wronged himself by sinning against his own soul. He wronged his wife by arousing her hatred and jealousy through his unfaithfulness. He wronged those children by giving them the *status* of slaves and outcasts. He wronged their mother by imposing upon her the burdens and cares of maternity without the rights and privileges of a wife. He made her crown of motherhood a circlet of shame. Under other circumstances she might have been an honored wife and happy mother. And I do think such men wrong their own legitimate children by transmitting to them a weakened moral fibre."

"Oh, Marie, you have such an uncomfortable way of putting things. You make me feel that we have done those things which we ought not to have done, and have left undone those things which we ought to have done."

"If it annoys you," said Marie, "I will stop talking."

"Oh, no, go on," said Leroy, carelessly; and then he continued more thoughtfully, "I know a number of men who have sent such children North, and manumitted, educated, and left them valuable legacies. We are all liable to err, and, having done wrong, all we can do is to make reparation."

"My dear husband, this is a wrong where reparation is impossible. Neither wealth nor education can repair the wrong of a dishonored birth. There are a number of slaves in this section who are servants to their own brothers and sisters; whose fathers have robbed them not simply of liberty but of the right of being well born. Do you think these things will last forever?"

"I suppose not. There are some prophets of evil who tell us that the Union is going to dissolve. But I know it would puzzle their brains to tell where the crack will begin. I reckon we'll continue to jog along as usual. 'Cotton fights, and cotton conquers for American slavery.' "

Even while Leroy dreamed of safety the earthquake was cradling its fire; the ground was growing hollow beneath his tread; but his ear was too dull to catch the sound; his vision too blurred to read the signs of the times.

"Marie," said Leroy, taking up the thread of the discourse, "slavery is a sword that cuts both ways. If it wrongs the negro, it also curses the white man. But we are in it, and what can we do?"

"Get out of it as quickly as possible."

"That is easier said than done. I would willingly free every slave on my plantation if I could do so without expatriating them. Some of them have wives and children on other plantations, and to free them is to separate them from their kith and kin. To let them remain here as a free people is out of the question. My hands are tied by law and custom."

"Who tied them?" asked Marie.

"A public opinion, whose meshes I cannot break. If the negro is the thrall of his master, we are just as much the thralls of public opinion."

"Why do you not battle against public opinion, if you think it is wrong?"

"Because I have neither the courage of a martyr, nor the faith of a saint; and so I drift along, trying to make the condition of our slaves as comfortable as I possibly can. I believe there are slaves on this plantation whom the most flattering offers of freedom would not entice away."

"I do not think," said Marie, "that some of you planters understand your own slaves. Lying is said to be the vice of slaves. The more intelligent of them have so learned to veil their feelings that you do not see the undercurrent of discontent beneath their apparent good humor and jollity. The more discontented they are, the more I respect them. To me a contented slave is an abject creature. I hope that I shall see the day when there will not be a slave in the land. I hate the whole thing from the bottom of my heart."

"Marie, your Northern education has unfitted you for Southern life. You are free, yourself, and so are our children. Why not let well enough alone?"

"Because I love liberty, not only for myself but for every human being. Think how dear these children are to me; and then for the thought to be forever haunting me, that if you were dead they could be turned out of doors and divided among your relatives. I sometimes lie awake at night thinking of how there might be a screw loose somewhere, and, after all, the children and I might be reduced to slavery."

"Marie, what in the world is the matter with you? Have you had a presentiment of my death, or, as Uncle Jack says, 'hab you seed it in a vision?' "

"No, but I have had such sad forebodings that they almost set me wild. One night I dreamt that you were dead; that the lawyers entered the house, seized our property, and remanded us to slavery. I never can be satisfied in the South with such a possibility hanging over my head."

"Marie, dear, you are growing nervous. Your imagination is too active. You are left too much alone on this plantation. I hope that for your own and the children's sake I will be enabled to arrange our affairs so as to find a home for you where you will not be doomed to the social isolation and ostracism that surround you here."

"I don't mind the isolation for myself, but the children. You have enjoined silence on me with respect to their connection with the negro race, but I do not think we can conceal it from them very long. It will not be long before Iola will notice the offishness of girls of her own age, and the scornful glances which, even now, I think, are leveled at her. Yesterday Harry came crying to me, and told me that one of the neighbor's boys had called him 'nigger.' "

A shadow flitted over Leroy's face, as he answered, somewhat soberly, "Oh, Marie, do not meet trouble half-way. I have manumitted you, and the children will follow your condition. I have made you all legatees of my will. Except my cousin, Alfred Lorraine, I have only distant relatives, whom I scarcely know and who hardly know me."

"Your cousin Lorraine? Are you sure our interests would be safe in his hands?"

"I think so; I don't think Alfred would do anything dishonorable."

"He might not with his equals. But how many men would be bound by a sense of honor where the rights of a colored woman are in question? Your cousin was bitterly opposed to our marriage, and I would not trust any important interests in his hands. I do hope that in providing for our future you will make assurance doubly sure."

"I certainly will, and all that human foresight can do shall be done for you and our children."

"Oh," said Marie, pressing to her heart a beautiful child of six summers, "I think it would almost make me turn over in my grave to know that every grace and charm which this child possesses would only be so much added to her value as an article of merchandise."

As Marie released the child from her arms she looked wonderingly into her mother's face and clung closely to her, as if to find refuge from some unseen evil. Leroy noticed this, and sighed unconsciously, as an expression of pain flitted over his face.

"Now, Marie," he continued, "stop tormenting yourself with useless fears. Although, with all her faults, I still love the South, I will make arrangements either to live North or go to France. There life will be brighter for us all. Now Marie, seat yourself at the piano and sing:—

'Sing me the songs that to me were so dear,
Long, long ago.
Sing me the songs I delighted to hear,
Long, long ago.' "

As Marie sang the anxiety faded from her face, a sense of security stole over her, and she sat among her loved ones a happy wife and mother. What if no one recognized her on that lonely plantation! Her world was, nevertheless, there. The love and devotion of her husband brightened every avenue of her life, while her children filled her home with music, mirth, and sunshine.

Marie had undertaken their education, but she could not give them the culture which comes from the attrition of thought, and from contact with the ideas of others. Since her school-days she had read extensively and thought much, and in solitude her thoughts had ripened. But for her children there were no companions except the young slaves of the plantation, and she dreaded the effect of such intercourse upon their lives and characters.

Leroy had always been especially careful to conceal from his children the knowledge of their connection with the negro race. To Marie this silence was oppressive.

One day she said to him, "I see no other way of finishing the education of these children than by sending them to some Northern school."

"I have come," said Leroy, "to the same conclusion. We had better take Iola and Harry North and make arrangements for them to spend several years in being educated. Riches take wings to themselves and fly away, but a good education is an investment on which the law can place no attachment. As there is a possibility of their origin being discovered, I will find a teacher to whom I can confide our story, and upon whom I can enjoin secrecy. I want them well fitted for any emergency in life. When I discover for what they have the most aptitude I will give them especial training in that direction."

A troubled look passed over the face of Marie, as she hesitatingly said: "I am so afraid that you will regret our marriage when you fully realize the complications it brings."

"No, no," said Leroy, tenderly, "it is not that I regret our marriage, or feel the least disdain for our children on account of the blood in their veins; but I do not wish them to grow up under the contracting influence of this race prejudice. I do not wish them to feel that they have been born under a proscription from which no valor can redeem them, nor that any social advancement or individual development can wipe off the ban which clings to them. No, Marie, let them go North, learn all they can, aspire all they may. The painful knowledge will come all too soon. Do not forestall it. I want them simply to grow up as other children; not being patronized by friends nor disdained by foes."

"My dear husband, you may be perfectly right, but are you not preparing our children for a fearful awakening? Are you not acting on the plan, 'After me the deluge'?"

"Not at all, Marie. I want our children to grow up without having their self-respect crushed in the bud. You know that the North is not free from racial prejudice."

"I know it," said Marie, sadly, "and I think one of the great mistakes of our civilization is that which makes color, and not character, a social test."

"I think so, too," said Leroy. "The strongest men and women of a down-trodden race may bare their bosoms to an adverse fate and develop courage in the midst of opposition, but we have no right to subject our children to such crucial tests before their characters are formed. For years, when I lived abroad, I had an opportunity to see and hear of men of African descent who had distinguished themselves and obtained a recognition in European circles, which they never could have gained in this country. I now recall the name of Ira Aldridge, a colored man from New York City, who was covered with princely honors as a successful tragedian. Alexander Dumas was not forced to conceal his origin to succeed as a novelist. When I was in St. Petersburg I was shown the works of Alexander Sergevitch, a Russian poet, who was spoken of as the Byron of Russian literature, and reckoned one of the finest poets that Russia has produced in this century. He was also a prominent figure in fashionable society, and yet he was of African lineage. One of his paternal ancestors was a negro who had been ennobled by Peter the Great. I can't help contrasting the recognition which these men had received with the treatment which has been given to Frederick Douglass and other intelligent colored men in this country. With me the wonder is not that they have achieved so little, but that they have accomplished so much. No, Marie, we will have our children educated without being subjected to the depressing influences of caste feeling. Perhaps by the time their education is finished I will be ready to wind up my affairs and take them abroad, where merit and ability will give them entrance into the best circles of art, literature, and science."

After this conversation Leroy and his wife went North, and succeeded in finding a good school for their children. In a private interview he confided to the principal the story of the cross in their blood, and, finding him apparently free from racial prejudice, he gladly left the children in his care. Gracie, the youngest child, remained at home, and her mother spared no pains to fit her for the seminary against the time her sister should have finished her education.

CHAPTER XI

The Plague and the Law

YEARS PASSED, bringing no special change to the life of Leroy and his wife. Shut out from the busy world, its social cares and anxieties, Marie's life flowed peacefully on. Although removed by the protecting care of Leroy from the condition of servitude, she still retained a deep sympathy for the enslaved, and was ever ready to devise plans to ameliorate their condition.

Leroy, although in the midst of slavery, did not believe in the rightfulness of the institution. He was in favor of gradual emancipation, which would prepare both master and slave for a moral adaptation to the new conditions of freedom. While he was willing to have the old rivets taken out of slavery, politicians and planters were devising plans to put in new screws. He was desirous of having it ended in the States; they were clamorous to have it established in the Territories.

But so strong was the force of habit, combined with the feebleness of his moral resistance and the nature of his environment, that instead of being an athlete, armed for a glorious strife, he had learned to drift where he should have steered, to float with the current instead of nobly breasting the tide. He conducted his plantation with as much lenity as it was possible to infuse into a system darkened with the shadow of a million crimes.

Leroy had always been especially careful not to allow his children to spend their vacations at home. He and Marie generally spent that time with them at some summer resort.

"I would like," said Marie, one day, "to have our children spend their vacations at home. Those summer resorts are pleasant, yet, after all, there is no place like home. But," and her voice became tremulous, "our children would now notice their social isolation and inquire the cause." A faint sigh arose to the lips of Leroy, as she added: "Man is a social being; I've known it to my sorrow."

There was a tone of sadness in Leroy's voice, as he replied: "Yes, Marie, let them stay North. We seem to be entering on a period fraught with great danger. I cannot help thinking and fearing that we are on the eve of a civil war."

"A civil war!" exclaimed Marie, with an air of astonishment. "A civil war about what?"

"Why, Marie, the thing looks to me so wild and foolish I hardly know how to explain. But some of our leading men have come to the conclusion that North and South had better separate, and instead of having one to have two independent governments. The spirit of secession is rampant in the land. I do not know what the result will be, and I fear it will bode no good to the country. Between the fire-eating Southerners and the meddling Abolitionists we are about to be plunged into a great deal of trouble. I fear there are breakers ahead. The South is dissatisfied with the state of public opinion in the North. We are realizing that we are two peoples in the midst of one nation. William H. Seward has proclaimed that the conflict between freedom and slavery is irrepressible, and that the country cannot remain half free and half slave."

"How will *you* go?" asked Marie.

"My heart is with the Union. I don't believe in secession. There has been no cause sufficient to justify a rupture. The North has met us time and again in the spirit of concession and compromise. When we wanted the continuance of the African slave trade the North conceded that we should have twenty years of slave-trading for the benefit of our plantations. When we wanted more territory she conceded to our desires and gave us land enough to carve out four States, and there yet remains enough for four more. When we wanted power to recapture our slaves when they fled North for refuge, Daniel Webster told Northerners to conquer their prejudices, and they gave us the whole Northern States as a hunting ground for our slaves. The Presidential chair has been filled the greater number of years by Southerners, and the majority of offices has been shared by our men. We wanted representation in Congress on a basis which would include our slaves, and the North, whose suffrage represents only men, gave us a three-fifths representation for our slaves, whom we count as property. I think the step will be suicidal. There are extremists in both sections, but I hope, between them both, wise counsels and measures will prevail."

Just then Alfred Lorraine was ushered into the room. Occasionally he visited Leroy, but he always came alone. His wife was the only daughter of an enterprising slave-trader, who had left her a large amount of property. Her social training was deficient, her education limited, but she was too proud of being a pure white woman to enter the home of Leroy, with Marie as its presiding genius. Lorraine tolerated Marie's presence as a necessary evil, while to her he always seemed like a presentiment of trouble. With his coming a shadow fell upon her home, hushing its music and darkening its sunshine. A sense of dread oppressed her. There came into her soul an intuitive feeling that somehow his coming was fraught with danger. When not peering around she would often catch his eyes bent on her with a baleful expression.

Leroy and his cousin immediately fell into a discussion on the condition of the country. Lorraine was a rank Secessionist, ready to adopt the most extreme measures of the leaders of the movement, even to the reopening of the slave trade. Leroy thought a dissolution of the Union would involve a fearful expenditure of blood and treasure for which, before the eyes of the world, there could be no justification. The debate lasted late into the night, leaving both Lorraine and Leroy just as set in their opinions as they were before they began. Marie listened attentively awhile, then excused herself and withdrew.

After Lorraine had gone Marie said: "There is something about your cousin that fills me with nameless dread. I always feel when he enters the room as if some one were walking over my grave. I do wish he would stay at home."

"I wish so, too, since he disturbs you. But, Marie, you are growing nervous. How cold your hands are. Don't you feel well?"

"Oh, yes; I am only a little faint. I wish he would never come. But, as he does, I must make the best of it."

"Yes, Marie, treat him well for my sake. He is the only relative I have who ever darkens our doors."

"I have no faith in his friendship for either myself or my children. I feel that while he makes himself agreeable to you he hates me from the bottom of his heart, and would do anything to get me out of the way. Oh, I am *so* glad I am your lawful wife, and that you married me before you brought me back to this State! I believe that if you were gone he wouldn't have the least scruple against trying to prove our marriage invalid and remanding us to slavery."

Leroy looked anxiously and soberly at his wife, and said: "Marie, I do not think so. Your life is too lonely here. Write your orders to New Orleans, get what you need for the journey, and let us spend the summer somewhere in the North."

Just then Marie's attention was drawn to some household matters, and it was a short time before she returned.

"Tom," continued Leroy, "has just brought the mail, and here is a letter from Iola."

Marie noticed that he looked quite sober as he read, and that an expression of vexation was lingering on his lips.

"What is the matter?" asked Marie.

"Nothing much; only a tempest in a teapot. The presence of a colored girl in Mr. Galen's school has caused a breeze of excitement. You know Mr. Galen is quite an Abolitionist, and, being true to his principles, he could not consistently refuse when a colored woman applied for her daughter's admission. Of course, when he took her he was compelled to treat her as any other pupil. In so doing he has given moral offense to the mother of two Southern boys. She has threatened to take them away if the colored girl remains."

"What will he do about it?" asked Marie, thoughtfully.

"Oh, it is a bitter pill, but I think he will have to swallow it. He is between two fires. He cannot dismiss her from the school and be true to his Abolition principles; yet if he retains her he will lose his Southern customers, and I know he cannot afford to do that."

"What does Iola say?"

"He has found another boarding place for her, but she

is to remain in the school. He had to throw that sop to the whale."

"Does she take sides against the girl?"

"No, I don't think she does. She says she feels sorry for her, and that she would hate to be colored. 'It is so hard to be looked down on for what one can't help.' "

"Poor child! I wish we could leave the country. I never would consent to her marrying any one without first revealing to him her connection with the negro race. This is a subject on which I am not willing to run any risks."

"My dear Marie, when you shall have read Iola's letter you will see it is more than a figment of my imagination that has made me so loth to have our children know the paralyzing power of caste."

Leroy, always liberal with his wife and children, spared neither pains nor expense to have them prepared for their summer outing. Iola was to graduate in a few days. Harry was attending a school in the State of Maine, and his father had written to him, apprising him of his intention to come North that season. In a few days Leroy and his wife started North, but before they reached Vicksburg they were met by the intelligence that the yellow fever was spreading in the Delta, and that pestilence was breathing its bane upon the morning air and distilling its poison upon the midnight dews.

"Let us return home," said Marie.

"It is useless," answered Leroy. "It is nearly two days since we left home. The fever is spreading south of us with fearful rapidity. To return home is to walk into the jaws of death. It was my intention to have stopped at Vicksburg, but now I will go on as soon as I can make the connections."

Early next morning Leroy and his wife started again on their journey. The cars were filled with terror-stricken people who were fleeing from death, when death was everywhere. They fled from the city only to meet the dreadful apparition in the country. As they journeyed on Leroy grew restless and feverish. He tried to brace himself against the infection which was creeping slowly but insidiously into his life, dulling his brain, fevering his blood, and prostrating his strength. But vain were all his efforts. He had no armor strong enough to repel the invasion of death. They stopped at a small town on the way and obtained the best medical skill and most careful nursing, but neither skill nor art availed. On the third day death claimed Leroy as a victim, and Marie wept in hopeless agony over the grave of her devoted husband, whose sad lot it was to die from home and be buried among strangers.

But before he died he placed his will in Marie's hands, saying: "I have left you well provided for. Kiss the children for me and bid them good-bye."

He tried to say a parting word to Gracie, but his voice failed, and he fainted into the stillness of death. A mortal paleness overspread his countenance, on which had already gathered the shadows that never deceive. In speechless agony Marie held his hand until it released its pressure in death, and then she stood alone beside her dead, with all the bright sunshine of her life fading into the shadows of the grave. Heart-broken and full of fearful forebodings, Marie left her cherished dead in the quiet village of H—— and returned to her death-darkened home.

It was a lovely day in June, birds were singing their sweetest songs, flowers were breathing their fragrance on the air, when Mam Liza, sitting at her cabin-door, talking with some of the house servants, saw a carriage approaching, and wondered who was coming.

"I wonder," she said, excitedly, "whose comin' to de house when de folks is done gone."

But her surprise was soon changed to painful amazement, when she saw Marie, robed in black, alighting from the carriage, and holding Gracie by the hand. She caught sight of the drooping head and grief-stricken face, and rushed to her, exclaiming:—

"Whar's Marse Eugene?"

"Dead," said Marie, falling into Mammy Liza's arms, sobbing out, "dead! *he died* of yellow fever."

A wild burst of sorrow came from the lips of the servants, who had drawn near.

"Where is he?" said Mam Liza, speaking like one suddenly bewildered.

"He is buried in H——. I could not bring him home," said Marie.

"My pore baby," said Mam Liza, with broken sobs. "I'se dreful sorry. My heart's most broke into two."

Then, controlling herself, she dismissed the servants who stood around, weeping, and led Marie to her room.

"Come, honey, lie down an' lem'me git yer a cup ob tea."

"Oh, no; I don't want anything," said Marie, wringing her hands in bitter agony.

"Oh, honey," said Mam Liza, "yer musn't gib up. Yer knows whar to put yer trus'. Yer can't lean on de arm of flesh in dis tryin' time." Kneeling by the side of her mistress she breathed out a prayer full of tenderness, hope, and trust.

Marie grew calmer. It seemed as if that earnest, trustful prayer had breathed into her soul a feeling of resignation.

Gracie stood wonderingly by, vainly trying to comprehend the great sorrow which was overwhelming the life of her mother.

After the first great burst of sorrow was over, Marie sat down to her desk and wrote a letter to Iola, informing her of her father's death. By the time she had finished it she grew dizzy and faint, and fell into a swoon. Mammy Liza tenderly laid her on the bed, and helped restore her to consciousness.

Lorraine, having heard of his cousin's death, came immediately to see Marie. She was too ill to have an interview with him, but he picked up the letter she had written and obtained Iola's address.

Lorraine made a careful investigation of the case, to ascertain whether Marie's marriage was valid. To his delight he found there was a flaw in the marriage and an informality in the manumission. He then determined to invalidate Marie's claim, and divide the inheritance among Leroy's white relations. In a short time strangers, distant relatives of her husband, became frequent visitors at the plantation, and made themselves offensively familiar. At length the dreadful storm burst.

Alfred Lorraine entered suit for his cousin's estate, and for the remanding of his wife and children to slavery. In a short time he came armed with legal authority, and said to Marie:—

"I have come to take possession of these premises."

"By what authority?" she gasped, turning deathly pale.

He hesitated a moment, as if his words were arrested by a sense of shame.

"By what authority?" she again demanded.

"By the authority of the law," answered Lorraine, "which has decided that Leroy's legal heirs are his white blood relations, and that your marriage is null and void."

"But," exclaimed Marie, "I have our marriage certificate. I was Leroy's lawful wife."

"Your marriage certificate is not worth the paper it is written on."

"Oh, you must be jesting, cruelly jesting. It can't be so."

"Yes; it is so. Judge Starkins has decided that your manumission is unlawful; your marriage a bad precedent, and inimical to the welfare of society; and that you and your children are remanded to slavery."

Marie stood as one petrified. She seemed a statue of fear and despair. She tried to speak, reached out her hand as if she were groping in the dark, turned pale as death as if all the blood in her veins had receded to her heart, and, with one heart-rending cry of bitter agony, she fell senseless to the floor. Her servants, to whom she had been so kind in her days of prosperity, bent pityingly over her, chafed her cold hands, and did what they could to restore her to consciousness. For a while she was stricken with brain fever, and her life seemed trembling on its frailest cord.

Gracie was like one perfectly dazed. When not watching by her mother's bedside she wandered aimlessly about the house, growing thinner day by day. A slow fever was consuming her life. Faithfully and carefully Mammy Liza watched over her, and did all she could to bring smiles to her lips and light to her fading eyes, but all in vain. Her only interest in life was to sit where she could watch her mother as she tossed to and fro in delirium, and to wonder what had brought the change in her once happy home. Finally she, too, was stricken with brain fever, which intervened as a mercy between her and the great sorrow that was overshadowing her young life. Tears would fill the servants' eyes as they saw the dear child drifting from them like a lovely vision, too bright for earth's dull cares and weary, wasting pain.

CHAPTER XII

School-Girl Notions

DURING IOLA'S STAY in the North she found a strong tide of opposition against slavery. Arguments against the institution had entered the Church and made legislative halls the arenas of fierce debate. The subject had become part of the social converse of the fireside, and had enlisted the best brain and heart of the country. Anti-slavery discussions were pervading the strongest literature and claiming a place on the most popular platforms.

Iola, being a Southern girl and a slave-holder's daughter, always defended slavery when it was under discussion.

"Slavery can't be wrong," she would say, "for my father is a slave-holder, and my mother is as good to our servants as she can be. My father often tells her that she spoils them, and lets them run over her. I never saw my father strike one of them. I love my mammy as much as I do my own mother, and I believe she loves us just as if we were her own children. When we are sick I am sure that she could not do anything more for us than she does."

"But, Iola," responded one of her school friends, "after all, they are not free. Would you be satisfied to have the most beautiful home, the costliest jewels, or the most elegant wardrobe if you were a slave?"

"Oh, the cases are not parallel. Our slaves do not want their freedom. They would not take it if we gave it to them."

"That is not the case with them all. My father has seen men who have encountered almost incredible hardships to get their freedom. Iola, did you ever attend an anti-slavery meeting?"

"No; I don't think these Abolitionists have any right to meddle in our affairs. I believe they are prejudiced against us, and want to get our property. I read about them in the papers when I was at home. I don't want to hear my part of the country run down. My father says the slaves would be very well contented if no one put wrong notions in their heads."

"I don't know," was the response of her friend, "but I do not think that that slave mother who took her four children, crossed the Ohio River on the ice, killed one of the children and attempted the lives of the other two, was a contented slave. And that other one; who, running away and finding herself pursued, threw herself over the Long Bridge into the Potomac, was evidently not satisfied. I do not think the numbers who are coming North on the Underground Railroad can be very contented. It is not natural for people to run away from happiness, and if they are so happy and contented, why did Congress pass the Fugitive Slave Bill?"

"Well, I don't think," answered Iola, "any of our slaves would run away. I know mamma don't like slavery very much. I have often heard her say that she hoped the time would come when there would not be a slave in the land. My father does not think as she does. He thinks slavery is not wrong if you treat them well and don't sell them from their families. I intend, after I have graduated, to persuade pa to buy a house in New Orleans, and spend the winter there. You know this will be my first season out, and I hope that you will come and spend the winter with me. We will have such gay times, and you will so fall in love with our sunny South that you will never want to come back to shiver amid the snows and cold of the North. I think one winter in the South would cure you of your Abolitionism."

"Have you seen her yet?"

This question was asked by Louis Bastine, an attorney who had come North in the interests of Lorraine. The scene was the New England village where Mr. Galen's academy was located, and which Iola was attending. This question was addressed to Camille Lecroix, Bastine's intimate friend, who had lately come North. He was the son of a planter who lived near Leroy's plantation, and was familiar with Iola's family history. Since his arrival North, Bastine had met him and communicated to him his intentions.

"Yes; just caught a glimpse of her this morning as she was going down the street," was Camille's reply.

"She is a most beautiful creature," said Louis Bastine. "She has the proud poise of Leroy, the most splendid eyes I ever saw in a woman's head, lovely complexion, and a glorious wealth of hair. She would bring $2000 any day in a New Orleans market."

"I always feel sorry," said Camille, "when I see one of those Creole girls brought to the auction block. I have known fathers who were deeply devoted to their daughters, but who through some reverse of fortune were forced to part with them, and I always think the blow has been equally terrible on both sides. I had a friend who had two beautiful daughters whom he had educated in the North. They were cultured, and really belles in society. They were entirely ignorant of their lineage, but when their father died it was discovered that their mother had been a slave. It was a fearful blow. They would have faced poverty, but the knowledge of their tainted blood was more than they could bear."

"What became of them?"

"They both died, poor girls. I believe they were as much killed by the blow as if they had been shot. To tell you the truth, Bastine, I feel sorry for this girl. I don't believe she has the least idea of her negro blood."

"No, Leroy has been careful to conceal it from her," replied Bastine.

"Is that so?" queried Camille. "Then he has made a great mistake."

"I can't help that," said Bastine; "business is business."

"How can you get her away?" asked Camille. "You will have to be very cautious, because if these pesky Abolitionists get an inkling of what you're doing they will balk your game double quick. And when you come to look at it, isn't it a shame to attempt to reduce that girl to slavery? She is just as white as we are, as good as any girl in the land, and better educated than thousands of white girls. A girl with her apparent refinement and magnificent beauty, were it not for the cross in her blood, I would be proud to introduce to our set. She would be the sensation of the season. I believe to-day it would be easier for me to go to the slums and take a young girl from there, and have her introduced as my wife, than to have society condone the offense if I married that lovely girl. There is not a social circle in the South that would not take it as a gross insult to have her introduced into it."

"Well," said Bastine, "my plan is settled. Leroy has never allowed her to spend her vacations at home. I understand she is now very anxious to get home, and, as Lorraine's attorney, I have come on his account to take her home."

"How will you do it?"

"I shall tell her her father is dangerously ill, and desires her to come as quickly as possible."

"And what then?"

"Have her inventoried with the rest of the property."

"Don't she know that her father is dead?"

"I think not," said Bastine. "She is not in mourning, but appeared very light-hearted this morning, laughing and talking with two other girls. I was struck with her great beauty, and asked a gentleman who she was. He said, 'Miss Leroy, of Mississippi.' I think Lorraine has managed the affair so as to keep her in perfect ignorance of her father's death. I don't like the job, but I never let sentiment interfere with my work."

Poor Iola! When she said slavery was not a bad thing, little did she think that she was destined to drink to its bitter dregs the cup she was so ready to press to the lips of others.

"How do you think she will take to her situation?" asked Camille.

"O, I guess," said Bastine, "she will sulk and take it pretty hard at first; but if she is managed right she will soon get over it. Give her plenty of jewelry, fine clothes, and an easy time."

"All this business must be conducted with the utmost secrecy and speed. Her mother could not have written to her, for she has been suffering with brain fever and nervous prostration since Leroy's death. Lorraine knows her market value too well, and is too shrewd to let so much property pass out of his hands without making an effort to retain it."

"Has she any brothers or sisters?"

"Yes, a brother," replied Bastine; "but he is at another school, and I have no orders from Lorraine in reference to him. If I can get the girl I am willing to let well enough alone. I dread the interview with the principal more than anything else. I am afraid he will hem and haw, and have his doubts. Perhaps, when he sees my letters and hears my story, I can pull the wool over his eyes."

"But, Louis, this is a pitiful piece of business. I should hate to be engaged in it."

A deep flush of shame overspread for a moment the face of Lorraine's attorney, as he replied: "I don't like the job, but I have undertaken it, and must go through with it."

"I see no '*must*' about it. Were I in your place I would wash my hands of the whole business."

"I can't afford it," was Bastine's hard, business-like reply. On the next morning after this conversation between these two young men, Louis Bastine presented himself to the principal of the academy, with the request that Iola be permitted to leave immediately to attend the sick-bed of her father, who was dangerously ill. The principal hesitated, but while he was deliberating, a telegram, purporting to come from Iola's mother, summoned Iola to her father's bedside without delay. The principal, set at rest in regard to the truthfulness of the dispatch, not only permitted but expedited her departure.

Iola and Bastine took the earliest train, and traveled without pausing until they reached a large hotel in a Southern city. There they were obliged to wait a few hours until they could resume their journey, the train having failed to make connection. Iola sat in a large, lonely parlor, waiting for the servant to show her to a private room. She had never known a great sorrow. Never before had the shadows of death mingled with the sunshine of her life.

Anxious, travel-worn, and heavy-hearted, she sat in an easy chair, with nothing to divert her from the grief and anxiety which rendered every delay a source of painful anxiety.

"Oh, I hope that he will be alive and growing better!" was the thought which kept constantly revolving in her mind, until she fell asleep. In her dreams she was at home, encircled in the warm clasp of her father's arms, feeling her mother's kisses lingering on her lips, and hearing the joyous greetings of the servants and Mammy Liza's glad welcome as she folded her to her heart. From this dream of bliss she was awakened by a burning kiss pressed on her lips, and a strong arm encircling her. Gazing around and taking in the whole situation, she sprang from her seat, her eyes flashing with rage and scorn, her face flushed to the roots of her hair, her voice shaken with excitement, and every nerve trembling with angry emotion.

"How dare you do such a thing! Don't you know if my father were here he would crush you to the earth?"

"Not so fast, my lovely tigress," said Bastine, "your father knew what he was doing when he placed you in my charge."

"My father made a great mistake, if he thought he had put me in charge of a gentleman."

"I am your guardian for the present," replied Bastine. "I am to see you safe home, and then my commission ends."

"I wish it were ended now," she exclaimed, trembling with anger and mortification. Her voice was choked by emotion, and broken by smothered sobs. Louis Bastine thought to himself, "she is a real spitfire, but beautiful even in her wrath."

During the rest of her journey Iola preserved a most freezing reserve towards Bastine. At length the journey was ended. Pale and anxious she rode up the avenue which led to her home.

A strange silence pervaded the place. The servants moved sadly from place to place, and spoke in subdued tones. The windows were heavily draped with crape, and a funeral air pervaded the house.

Mammy Liza met her at the door, and, with streaming eyes and convulsive sobs, folded her to her heart, as Iola exclaimed, in tones of hopeless anguish:—

"Oh, papa's dead!"

"Oh, my pore baby!" said mammy, "ain't you hearn tell 'bout it? Yore par's dead, an' your mar's bin drefful sick. She's better now."

Mam Liza stepped lightly into Mrs. Leroy's room, and gently apprised her of Iola's arrival. In a darkened room lay the stricken mother, almost distracted by her late bereavement.

"Oh, Iola," she exclaimed, as her daughter entered, "is this you? I am so sorry you came."

Then, burying her head in Iola's bosom, she wept convulsively. "Much as I love you," she continued, between her sobs, "and much as I longed to see you, I am sorry you came."

"Why, mother," replied Iola, astonished, "I received your telegram last Wednesday, and I took the earliest train I could get."

"My dear child, I never sent you a telegram. It was a trick to bring you down South and reduce you to slavery."

Iola eyed her mother curiously. What did she mean? Had grief dethroned her reason? Yet her eye was clear, her manner perfectly rational.

Marie saw the astounded look on Iola's face, and nerving herself to the task, said: "Iola, I must tell you what your father always enjoined me to be silent about. I did not think it was the wisest thing, but I yielded to his desires. I have negro blood in my veins. I was your father's slave before I married him. His relatives have set aside his will. The courts have declared our marriage null and void and my manumission illegal, and we are all to be remanded to slavery."

An expression of horror and anguish swept over Iola's face, and, turning deathly pale, she exclaimed, "Oh, mother, it can't be so! you must be dreaming!"

"No, my child; it is a terrible reality."

Almost wild with agony, Iola paced the floor, as the fearful truth broke in crushing anguish upon her mind. Then bursting into a paroxysm of tears succeeded by peals of hysterical laughter, said:—

"I used to say that slavery is right. I didn't know what I was talking about." Then growing calmer, she said, "Mother, who is at the bottom of this downright robbery?"

"Alfred Lorraine; I have always dreaded that man, and what I feared has come to pass. Your father had faith in him; I never had."

"But, mother, could we not contest his claim. You have your marriage certificate and papa's will."

"Yes, my dear child, but Judge Starkins has decided

that we have no standing in the court, and no testimony according to law."

"Oh, mother, what can I do?"

"Nothing, my child, unless you can escape to the North."

"And leave you?"

"Yes."

"Mother, I will never desert you in your hour of trial. But can nothing be done? Had father no friends who would assist us?"

"None that I know of. I do not think he had an acquaintance who approved of our marriage. The neighboring planters have stood so aloof from me that I do not know where to turn for either help or sympathy. I believe it was Lorraine who sent the telegram. I wrote to you as soon as I could after your father's death, but fainted just as I finished directing the letter. I do not think he knows where your brother is, and, if possible, he must not know. If you can by any means, *do* send a letter to Harry and warn him not to attempt to come home. I don't know how you will succeed, for Lorraine has us all under surveillance. But it is according to law."

"What law, mother?"

"The law of the strong against the weak."

"Oh, mother, it seems like a dreadful dream, a fearful nightmare! But I cannot shake it off. Where is Gracie?"

"The dear child has been running down ever since her papa's death. She clung to me night and day while I had the brain fever, and could not be persuaded to leave me. She hardly ate anything for more than a week. She has been dangerously ill for several days, and the doctor says she cannot live. The fever has exhausted all her rallying power, and yet, dear as she is to me, I would rather consign her to the deepest grave than see her forced to be a slave."

"So would I. I wish I could die myself."

"Oh, Iola, do not talk so. Strive to be a Christian, to have faith in the darkest hour. Were it not for my hope of heaven I couldn't stand all this trouble."

"Mother, are these people Christians who made these laws which are robbing us of our inheritance and reducing us to slavery? If this is Christianity I hate and despise it. Would the most cruel heathen do worse?"

"My dear child, I have not learned my Christianity from them. I have learned it at the foot of the cross, and from this book," she said, placing a New Testament in Iola's hands. "Some of the most beautiful lessons of faith and trust I have ever learned were from among our lowly people in their humble cabins."

"Mamma!" called a faint voice from the adjoining room. Marie immediately arose and went to the bedside of her sick child, where Mammy Liza was holding her faithful vigils. The child had just awakened from a fitful sleep.

"I thought," she said, "that I heard Iola's voice. Has she come?"

"Yes, darling; do you want to see her?"

"Oh, yes," she said, as a bright smile broke over her dying features.

Iola passed quickly into the room. Gracie reached out her thin, bloodless hand, clasped Iola's palm in hers, and said: "I am so glad you have come. Dear Iola, stand by mother. You and Harry are all she has. It is not hard to die. You and mother and Harry must meet me in heaven."

Swiftly the tidings went through the house that Gracie was dying. The servants gathered around her with tearful eyes, as she bade them all good-bye. When she had finished, and Mammy had lowered the pillow, an unwonted radiance lit up her eye, and an expression of ineffable gladness overspread her face, as she murmured: "It is beautiful, so beautiful!" Fainter and fainter grew her voice, until, without a struggle or sigh, she passed away beyond the power of oppression and prejudice.

CHAPTER XIII

A Rejected Suitor

VERY UNEXPECTED WAS Dr. Gresham's proposal to Iola. She had heartily enjoyed his society and highly valued his friendship, but he had never been associated in her mind with either love or marriage. As he held her hand in his a tell-tale flush rose to her cheek, a look of grateful surprise beamed from her eye, but it was almost immediately succeeded by an air of inexpressible sadness, a drooping of her eyelids, and an increasing pallor of her cheek. She withdrew her hand from his, shook her head sadly, and said:—

"No, Doctor; that can never be. I am very grateful to you for your kindness. I value your friendship, but neither gratitude nor friendship is love, and I have nothing more than those to give."

"Not at present," said Dr. Gresham; "but may I not hope your friendship will ripen into love?"

"Doctor, I could not promise. I do not think that I should. There are barriers between us that I cannot pass. Were you to know them I think you would say the same."

Just then the ambulance brought in a wounded scout, and Iola found relief from the wounds of her own heart in attending to his.

Dr. Gresham knew the barrier that lay between them. It was one which his love had surmounted. But he was too noble and generous to take advantage of her loneliness to press his suit. He had lived in a part of the country where he had scarcely ever seen a colored person, and around the race their misfortunes had thrown a halo of romance. To him the negro was a picturesque being, over whose woes he had wept when a child, and whose wrongs he was ready to redress when a man. But when he saw the lovely girl who had been rescued by the commander of the post from the clutches of slavery, all the manhood and chivalry in his nature arose in her behalf, and he was ready to lay on the altar of her heart his first grand and overmastering love. Not discouraged by her refusal, but determined to overcome her objections, Dr. Gresham resolved that he would abide his time.

Iola was not indifferent to Dr. Gresham. She admired his manliness and respected his character. He was tall and handsome, a fine specimen of the best brain and heart of New England. He had been nurtured under grand and ennobling influences. His father was a devoted Abolitionist. His mother was kindhearted, but somewhat exclusive and aristocratic. She would have looked upon his marriage with Iola as a mistake and feared that such an alliance would hurt the prospects of her daughters.

During Iola's stay in the North, she had learned enough of the racial feeling to influence her decision in reference to Dr. Gresham's offer. Iola, like other girls, had had her beautiful day-dreams before she was rudely awakened by the fate which had dragged her into the depths of slavery. In the chambers of her imagery were pictures of noble deeds; of high, heroic men, knightly, tender, true, and brave. In Dr. Gresham she saw the ideal of her soul exemplified. But in her lonely condition, with all its background of terrible sorrow and deep abasement, she had never for a moment thought of giving or receiving love from one of that race who had been so lately associated in her mind with horror, aversion, and disgust. His kindness to her had been a new experience. His companionship was an unexpected pleasure. She had learned to enjoy his presence and to miss him when absent, and when she began to question her heart she found that unconsciously it was entwining around him.

"Yes," she said to herself, "I do like him; but I can never marry him. To the man I marry my heart must be as open as the flowers to the sun. I could not accept his hand and hide from him the secret of my birth; and I could not consent to choose the happiest lot on earth without first finding my poor heart-stricken and desolate mother. Perhaps some day I may have the courage to tell him my sad story, and then make my heart the sepulchre in which to bury all the love which might have gladdened and brightened my whole life."

During the sad and weary months which ensued while the war dragged its slow length along, Dr. Gresham and Iola often met by the bedsides of the wounded and dying, and sometimes he would drop a few words at which her heart would beat quicker and her cheek flush more vividly. But he was so kind, tender, and respectful, that Iola had no idea he knew her race affiliations. She knew from unmistakable signs that Dr. Gresham had learned to love her, and that he had power to call forth the warmest affection of her soul; but she fought with her own heart and repressed its rising love. She felt that it was best for his sake that they should not marry. When she saw the evidences of his increasing love she regretted that she had not informed him at the first of the barrier that lay between them; it might have saved him unnecessary suffering. Thinking thus, Iola resolved, at whatever cost of pain it might be to herself, to explain to Dr. Gresham what she meant by the insurmountable barrier. Iola, after a continuous strain upon her nervous system for months, began to suffer from general debility and nervous depression. Dr. Gresham saw the increasing pallor on Iola's cheek and the loss of buoyancy in her step. One morning, as she turned from the bed of a young soldier for whom she had just written a letter to his mother, there was such a look of pity and sorrow on her face that Dr. Gresham's whole heart went out in sympathy for her, and he resolved to break the silence he had imposed upon himself.

"Iola," he said, and there was a depth of passionate tenderness in his voice, a volume of unexpressed affection in his face, "you are wronging yourself. You are sinking beneath burdens too heavy for you to bear. It seems to me that besides the constant drain upon your sympathies there is some great sorrow preying upon your life; some burden that ought to be shared." He gazed upon her so ardently that each cord of her heart seemed to vibrate, and unbidden tears sprang to her lustrous eyes, as she said, sadly:—

"Doctor, you are right."

"Iola, my heart is longing to lift those burdens from your life. Love, like faith, laughs at impossibilities. I can conceive of no barrier too high for my love to surmount. Consent to be mine, as nothing else on earth is mine."

"Doctor, you know not what you ask," replied Iola. "Instead of coming into this hospital a self-sacrificing woman, laying her every gift and advantage upon the altar of her country, I came as a rescued slave, glad to find a refuge from a fate more cruel than death; a fate from which I was rescued by the intervention of my dear dead friend, Thomas Anderson. I was born on a lonely plantation on the Mississippi River, where the white population was very sparse. We had no neighbors who ever visited us; no young white girls with whom I ever played in my childhood; but, never having enjoyed such companionship, I was unconscious of any sense of privation. Our parents spared no pains to make the lives of their children (we were three) as bright and pleasant as they could. Our home was so happy. We had a large number of servants, who were devoted to us. I never had the faintest suspicion that there was any wrongfulness in slavery, and I never dreamed of the dreadful fate which broke in a storm of fearful anguish over our devoted heads. Papa used to take us to New Orleans to see the Mardi Gras, and while there we visited the theatres and other places of amusement and interest. At home we had books, papers, and magazines to beguile our time. Perfectly ignorant of my racial connection, I was sent to a Northern academy, and soon made many friends among my fellow-students. Companionship with girls of my own age was a new experience, which I thoroughly enjoyed. I spent several years in New England, and was busily preparing for my commencement exercises when my father was snatched away—died of yellow fever on his way North to witness my graduation. Through a stratagem, I was brought hurriedly from the North, and found that my father was dead; that his nearest kinsman had taken possession of our property; that my mother's marriage had been declared illegal, because of an imperceptible infusion of negro blood in her veins; and that she and her children had been remanded to slavery. I was torn from my mother, sold as a slave, and subjected to cruel indignities, from which I was rescued and a place given to me in this hospital. Doctor, I did not choose my lot in life, but I have no other alternative than to accept it. The intense horror and agony I felt when I was first told the story are over. Thoughts and purposes have come to me in the shadow I should never have learned in the sunshine. I am constantly rousing myself up to suffer and be strong. I intend, when this conflict is over, to cast my lot with the freed people as a helper, teacher, and friend. I have passed through a fiery ordeal, but this ministry of suffering will not be in vain. I feel that my mind has matured beyond my years. I am a wonder to myself. It seems as if years had been compressed into a few short months. In telling you this, do you not, can you not, see that there is an insurmountable barrier between us?"

"No, I do not," replied Dr. Gresham. "I love you for your own sake. And with this the disadvantages of birth have nothing to do."

"You say so now, and I believe that you are perfectly sincere. To-day your friendship springs from compassion, but, when that subsides, might you not look on me as an inferior?"

"Iola, you do not understand me. You think too meanly of me. You must not judge me by the worst of my race. Surely our country has produced a higher type of manhood than the men by whom you were tried and tempted."

"Tried, but not tempted," said Iola, as a deep flush overspread her face; "I was never tempted. I was sold from State to State as an article of merchandise. I had outrages heaped on me which might well crimson the cheek of honest womanhood with shame, but I never fell into the clutches of an owner for whom I did not feel the utmost loathing and intensest horror. I have heard men talk glibly of the degradation of the negro, but there is a vast difference between abasement of condition and degradation of character. I was abased, but the men who trampled on me were the degraded ones."

"But, Iola, you must not blame all for what a few have done."

"A few have done? Did not the whole nation consent to our abasement?" asked Iola, bitterly.

"No, Miss Iola, we did not all consent to it. Slavery drew a line of cleavage in this country. Although we were under one government we were farther apart in our sentiments than if we had been divided by lofty mountains and separated by wide seas. And had not Northern sentiment been brought to bear against the institution, slavery would have been intact until to-day."

"But, Doctor, the negro is under a social ban both North and South. Our enemies have the ear of the world, and they can depict us just as they please."

"That is true; but the negro has no other alternative than to make friends of his calamities. Other men have plead his cause, but out of the race must come its own defenders. With them the pen must be mightier than the sword. It is the weapon of civilization, and they must use it in their own defense. We cannot tell what is in them until they express themselves."

"Yes, and I think there is a large amount of latent and undeveloped ability in the race, which they will learn to use for their own benefit. This my hospital experience has taught me."

"But," said Dr. Gresham, "they must learn to struggle, labor, and achieve. By facts, not theories, they will be judged in the future. The Anglo-Saxon race is proud, domineering, aggressive, and impatient of a rival, and, as I think, has more capacity for dragging down a weaker race than uplifting it. They have been a conquering and achieving people, marvelous in their triumphs of mind over matter. They have manifested the traits of character which are developed by success and victory."

"And yet," said Iola, earnestly, "I believe the time will come when the civilization of the negro will assume a better phase than you Anglo-Saxons possess. You will prove unworthy of your high vantage ground if you only use your superior ability to victimize feebler races and minister to a selfish greed of gold and a love of domination."

"But, Iola," said Dr. Gresham, a little impatiently, "what has all this to do with our marriage? Your complexion is as fair as mine. What is to hinder you from sharing my Northern home, from having my mother to be your mother?" The tones of his voice grew tender, as he raised his eyes to Iola's face and anxiously awaited her reply.

"Dr. Gresham," said Iola, sadly, "should the story of my life be revealed to your family, would they be willing to ignore all the traditions of my blood, forget all the terrible humiliations through which I have passed? I have too much self-respect to enter your home under a veil of concealment. I have lived in New England. I love the sunshine of her homes and the freedom of her institutions. But New England is not free from racial prejudice, and I would never enter a family where I would be an unwelcome member."

"Iola, dear, you have nothing to fear in that direction."

"Doctor," she said, and a faint flush rose to her cheek, "suppose we should marry, and little children in after years should nestle in our arms, and one of them show unmistakable signs of color, would you be satisfied?"

She looked steadfastly into his eyes, which fell beneath her truth-seeking gaze. His face flushed as if the question had suddenly perplexed him. Iola saw the irresolution on his face, and framed her answer accordingly.

"Ah, I see," she said, "that you are puzzled. You had not taken into account what might result from such a marriage. I will relieve you from all embarrassment by simply saying I cannot be your wife. When the war is over I intend to search the country for my mother. Doctor, were you to give me a palace-like home, with velvet carpets to hush my tread, and magnificence to surround my way, I should miss her voice amid all other tones, her presence amid every scene. Oh, you do not know how hungry my heart is for my mother! Were I to marry you I would carry an aching heart into your home and dim its brightness. I have resolved never to marry until I have found my mother. The hope of finding her has colored all my life since I regained my freedom. It has helped sustain me in the hour of fearful trial. When I see her I want to have the proud consciousness that I bring her back a heart just as loving, faithful, and devoted as the last hour we parted."

"And is this your final answer?"

"It is. I have pledged my life to that resolve, and I believe time and patience will reward me."

There was a deep shadow of sorrow and disappointment on the face of Dr. Gresham as he rose to leave. For a moment he held her hand as it lay limp in his own. If she wavered in her determination it was only for a moment. No quivering of her lip or paling of her cheek betrayed any struggle of her heart. Her resolve was made, and his words were powerless to swerve her from the purpose of her soul.

After Dr. Gresham had gone Iola went to her room and sat buried in thought. It seemed as if the fate of Tantalus was hers, without his crimes. Here she was lonely and heart-stricken, and unto her was presented the offer of love, home, happiness, and social position; the heart and hand of a man too noble and generous to refuse her companionship for life on account of the blood in her veins. Why should she refuse these desirable boons? But, mingling with these beautiful visions of manly love and protecting care she saw the anguish of her heart-stricken mother and the pale, sweet face of her dying sister, as with her latest breath she had said, "Iola, stand by mamma!"

"No, no," she said to herself; "I was right to refuse Dr. Gresham. How dare I dream of happiness when my poor mamma's heart may be slowly breaking? I should be ashamed to live and ashamed to die were I to choose a happy lot for myself and leave poor mamma to struggle alone. I will never be satisfied till I get tidings of her. And when I have found her I will do all I can to cheer and brighten the remnant of her life."

CHAPTER XIV

Harry Leroy

IT WAS SEVERAL weeks after Iola had written to her brother that her letter reached him. The trusty servant to whom she delivered it watched his opportunity to mail it. At last he succeeded in slipping it into Lorraine's mail and dropping them all into the post-office together. Harry was studying at a boys' academy in Maine. His father had given that State the preference because, while on a visit there, he had been favorably impressed with the kindness and hospitality of the people. He had sent his son a large sum of money, and given him permission to spend awhile with some school-chums till he was ready to bring the family North, where they could all spend the summer together. Harry had returned from his visit, and was looking for letters and remittances from home, when a letter, all crumpled, was handed him by the principal of the academy. He recognized his sister's handwriting and eagerly opened the letter. As he read, he turned very pale; then a deep flush overspread his face and an angry light flashed from his eyes. As he read on, his face became still paler; he gasped for breath and fell into a swoon. Appalled at the sudden change which had swept over him like a deadly sirocco, the principal rushed to the fallen boy, picked up the missive that lay beside him, and immediately rang for help and dispatched for the doctor. The doctor came at once and was greatly puzzled. Less than an hour before, he had seen him with a crowd of merry, laughter-loving boys, apparently as light-hearted and joyous as any of them; now he lay with features drawn and pinched, his face deadly pale, as if some terrible suffering had sent all the blood in his veins to stagnate around his heart. Harry opened his eyes, shuddered, and relapsed into silence. The doctor, all at sea in regard to the cause of the sudden attack, did all that he could to restore him to consciousness and quiet the perturbation of his spirit. He succeeded, but found he was strangely silent. A terrible shock had sent a tremor through every nerve, and the doctor watched with painful apprehension its effect upon his reason. Giving him an opiate and enjoining that he should be kept perfectly quiet, the doctor left the room, sought the principal, and said:—

"Mr. Bascom, here is a case that baffles my skill. I saw that boy pass by my window not more than half an hour ago, full of animation, and now he lies hovering between life and death. I have great apprehension for his reason. Can you throw any light on the subject?"

Mr. Bascom hesitated.

"I am not asking you as a matter of idle curiosity, but as a physician. I must have all the light I can get in making my diagnosis of the case."

The principal arose, went to his desk, took out the letter which he had picked up from the floor, and laid it in the physician's hand. As the doctor read, a look of indignant horror swept over his face. Then he said: "Can it be possible! I never suspected such a thing. It must be a cruel, senseless hoax."

"Doctor," said Mr. Bascom, "I have been a life-long Abolitionist and have often read of the cruelties and crimes of American slavery, but never before did I realize the low moral tone of the social life under which such shameless cruelties could be practiced on a defenseless widow and her orphaned children. Let me read the letter again. Just look at it, all tear-blotted and written with a trembling hand:—

'DEAR BROTHER:—I have dreadful news for you and I hardly know how to tell it. Papa and Gracie are both dead. He died of yellow fever. Mamma is almost distracted. Papa's cousin has taken possession of our property, and instead of heirs we are chattels. Mamma has explained the whole situation to me. She was papa's slave before she married. He loved her, manumitted, educated, and married her. When he died Mr. Lorraine entered suit for his property and Judge Starkins has decided in his favor. The decree of the court has made their marriage invalid, robbed us of our inheritance, and remanded us all to slavery. Mamma is too wretched to attempt to write herself, but told me to entreat you not to attempt to come home. You can do us no good, and that mean, cruel Lorraine may do you much harm. Don't attempt, I beseech you, to come home. Show this letter to Mr. Bascom and let him advise you what to do. But don't, for our sake, attempt to come home.

'Your heart-broken sister,

'IOLA LEROY.' "

"This," said the doctor, "is a very awkward affair. The boy is too ill to be removed. It is doubtful if the nerves which have trembled with such fearful excitement will ever recover their normal condition. It is simply a work of mercy to watch over him with the tenderest care."

Fortunately for Harry he had fallen into good hands, and the most tender care and nursing were bestowed upon him. For a while Harry was strangely silent, never referring to the terrible misfortune which had so suddenly overshadowed his life. It seemed as if the past were suddenly blotted out of his memory. But he was young and of an excellent constitution, and in a few months he was slowly recovering.

"Doctor," said he one day, as the physician sat at his bedside, "I seem to have had a dreadful dream, and to have dreamt that my father was dead, and my mother and sister were in terrible trouble, but I could not help them. Doctor, was it a dream, or was it a reality? It could not have been a dream, for when I fell asleep the grass was green and the birds were singing, but now the winds are howling and the frost is on the ground. Doctor, tell me how it is? How long have I been here?"

Sitting by his bedside, and taking his emaciated hand in his, the doctor said, in a kind, fatherly tone: "My dear boy, you have been very ill, and everything depends on your keeping quiet, very quiet."

As soon as he was strong enough the principal gave him his letter to read.

"But, Mr. Bascom," Harry said, "I do not understand this. It says my mother and father were legally married. How could her marriage be set aside and her children robbed of their inheritance? This is not a heathen country. I hardly think barbarians would have done any worse; yet this is called a Christian country."

"Christian in name," answered the principal. "When your father left you in my care, knowing that I was an Abolitionist, he confided his secret to me. He said that life was full of vicissitudes, and he wished you to have a good education. He wanted you and your sister to be prepared for any emergency. He did not wish you to know that you had negro blood in your veins. He knew that the spirit of caste pervaded the nation, North and South, and he was very anxious to have his children freed from its depressing influences. He did not intend to stay South after you had finished your education."

"But," said Harry, "I cannot understand. If my mother was lawfully married, how could they deprive her of her marital rights?"

"When Lorraine," continued Mr. Bascom, "knew your father was dead, all he had to do was to find a flaw in her manumission, and, of course, the marriage became illegal. She could not then inherit property nor maintain her freedom; and her children followed her condition."

Harry listened attentively. Things which had puzzled him once now became perfectly clear. He sighed heavily, and, turning to the principal, said: "I see things in a new light. Now I remember that none of the planters' wives ever visited my mother; and we never went to church except when my father took us to the Cathedral in New Orleans. My father was a Catholic, but I don't think mamma is."

"Now, Harry," said the principal, "life is before you. If you wish to stay North, I will interest friends in your behalf, and try to get you a situation. Going South is out of the question. It is probable that by this time your mother and sister are removed from their home. You are powerless to fight against the law that enslaved them. Should you fall into the clutches of Lorraine, he might give you a great deal of trouble. You would be pressed into the Confederate service to help them throw up barricades, dig trenches, and add to the strength of those who enslaved your mother and sister."

"Never! never!" cried Harry. "I would rather die than do it! I should despise myself forever if I did."

"Numbers of our young men," said Mr. Bascom, "have gone to the war which is now raging between

North and South. You have been sick for several months, and much has taken place of which you are unaware. Would you like to enlist?"

"I certainly would; not so much for the sake of fighting for the Government, as with the hope of finding my mother and sister, and avenging their wrongs. I should like to meet Lorraine on the battle-field."

"What kind of a regiment would you prefer, white or colored?"

Harry winced when the question was asked. He felt the reality of his situation as he had not done before. It was as if two paths had suddenly opened before him, and he was forced to choose between them. On one side were strength, courage, enterprise, power of achievement, and memories of a wonderful past. On the other side were weakness, ignorance, poverty, and the proud world's social scorn. He knew nothing of colored people except as slaves, and his whole soul shrank from equalizing himself with them. He was fair enough to pass unchallenged among the fairest in the land, and yet a Christless prejudice had decreed that he should be a social pariah. He sat, thoughtful and undecided, as if a great struggle were going on in his mind. Finally the principal said, "I do not think that you should be assigned to a colored regiment because of the blood in your veins, but you will have, in such a regiment, better facilities for finding your mother and sister."

"You are right, Mr. Bascom. To find my mother and sister I call no task too heavy, no sacrifice too great."

Since Harry had come North he had learned to feel profound pity for the slave. But there is a difference between looking on a man as an object of pity and protecting him as such, and being identified with him and forced to share his lot. To take his place with them on the arena of life was the test of his life, but love was stronger than pride.

His father was dead. His mother and sister were enslaved by a mockery of justice. It was more than a matter of choice where he should stand on the racial question. He felt that he must stand where he could strike the most effective blow for their freedom. With that thought strong in his mind, and as soon as he recovered, he went westward to find a colored regiment. He told the recruiting officer that he wished to be assigned to a colored regiment.

"Why do you wish that," said the officer, looking at Harry with an air of astonishment.

"Because I am a colored man."

The officer looked puzzled. It was a new experience. He had seen colored men with fair complexions anxious to lose their identity with the colored race and pose as white men, but here was a man in the flush of his early manhood, to whom could come dreams of promotion from a simple private to a successful general, deliberately turning his back upon every gilded hope and dazzling opportunity, to cast his lot with the despised and hated negro.

"I do not understand you," said the officer. "Surely you are a white man, and, as such, I will enlist you in a white regiment."

"No," said Harry, firmly, "I am a colored man, and unless I can be assigned to a colored regiment I am not willing to enter the army."

"Well," said the officer, "you are the d—d'st fool I ever saw—a man as white as you are turning his back upon his chances of promotion! But you can take your choice."

So Harry was permitted to enter the army. By his promptness and valor he soon won the hearts of his superior officers, and was made drill sergeant. Having nearly all of his life been used to colored people, and being taught by his mother to be kind and respectful to them, he was soon able to gain their esteem. He continued in the regiment until Grant began the task of opening the Mississippi. After weeks of fruitless effort, Grant marched his army down the west side of the river, while the gunboats undertook the perilous task of running the batteries. Men were found for the hour. The volunteers offered themselves in such numbers that lots were cast to determine who should have the opportunity to enlist in an enterprise so fraught with danger. Harry was one on whom the lot fell.

Grant crossed the river below, coiled his forces around Vicksburg like a boa-constrictor, and held it in his grasp. After forty-seven days of endurance the city surrendered to him. Port Hudson, after the surrender of Vicksburg, gave up the unequal contest, and the Mississippi was open to the Gulf.

CHAPTER XV

Robert and His Company

"GOOD MORNING, GENTLEMEN," said Robert Johnson, as he approached Colonel Robinson, the commander of the post, who was standing at the door of his tent, talking with Captain Sybil.

"Good morning," responded Colonel Robinson, "I am glad you have come. I was just about to send for you. How is your company getting on?"

"First rate, sir," replied Robert.

"In good health?"

"Excellent. They are all in good health and spirits. Our boys are used to hardship and exposure, and the hope of getting their freedom puts new snap into them."

"I am glad of it," said Colonel Robinson. "They make good fighters and very useful allies. Last night we received very valuable intelligence from some fugitives who had escaped through the Rebel lines. I do not think many of the Northern people realize the service they have been to us in bringing information and helping our boys when escaping from Rebel prisons. I never knew a full-blooded negro to betray us. A month ago, when we were encamped near the Rebel lines, a colored woman managed admirably to keep us posted as to the intended movements of the enemy. She was engaged in laundry work, and by means of hanging her sheets in different ways gave us the right signals."

"I hope," said Captain Sybil, "that the time will come when some faithful historian will chronicle all the deeds of daring and service these people have performed during this struggle, and give them due credit therefor."

"Our great mistake," said Colonel Robinson, "was our long delay in granting them their freedom, and even what we have done is only partial. The border States still retain their slaves. We ought to have made a clean sweep of the whole affair. Slavery is a serpent which we nourished in its weakness, and now it is stinging us in its strength."

"I think so, too," said Captain Sybil. "But in making his proclamation of freedom, perhaps Mr. Lincoln went as far as he thought public opinion would let him."

"It is remarkable," said Colonel Robinson, "how these Secesh hold out. It surprises me to see how poor white men, who, like the negroes, are victims of slavery, rally around the Stripes and Bars. These men, I believe, have been looked down on by the aristocratic slave-holders, and despised by the well-fed and comfortable slaves, yet they follow their leaders into the very jaws of death; face hunger, cold, disease, and danger; and all for what? What, under heaven, are they fighting for? Now, the negro, ignorant as he is, has learned to regard our flag as a banner of freedom, and to look forward to his deliverance as a consequence of the overthrow of the Rebellion."

"I think," said Captain Sybil, "that these ignorant white men have been awfully deceived. They have had presented to their imaginations utterly false ideas of the results of Secession, and have been taught that its success would bring them advantages which they had never enjoyed in the Union."

"And I think," said Colonel Robinson, "that the women and ministers have largely fed and fanned the fires of this Rebellion, and have helped to create a public opinion which has swept numbers of benighted men into the conflict. Well might one of their own men say, 'This is a rich man's war and a poor man's fight.' They were led into it through their ignorance, and held in it by their fears."

"I think," said Captain Sybil, "that if the public school had been common through the South this war would never have occurred. Now things have reached such a pass that able-bodied men must report at headquarters, or be treated as deserters. Their leaders are desperate men, of whom it has been said: 'They have robbed the cradle and the grave.' "

"They are fighting against fearful odds," said Colonel Robinson, "and their defeat is only a question of time."

"As soon," said Robert, "as they fired on Fort Sumter, Uncle Daniel, a dear old father who had been praying and hoping for freedom, said to me: 'Dey's fired on Fort Sumter, an' mark my words, Bob, de Norf's boun' ter whip.' "

"Had we freed the slaves at the outset," said Captain Sybil, "we wouldn't have given the Rebels so much opportunity to strengthen themselves by means of slave labor in raising their crops, throwing up their entrenchments, and building their fortifications. Slavery was a deadly cancer eating into the life of the nation; but, somehow, it had cast such a glamour over us that we have acted somewhat as if our national safety were better preserved by sparing the cancer than by cutting it out."

"Political and racial questions have sadly complicated this matter," said Colonel Robinson. "The North is not wholly made up of anti-slavery people. At the beginning of this war we were not permeated with justice, and so were not ripe for victory. The battle of Bull Run inaugurated the war by a failure. Instead of glory we gathered shame, and defeat in place of victory."

"We have been slow," said Captain Sybil, "to see our danger and to do our duty. Our delay has cost us thousands of lives and millions of dollars. Yet it may be it is all for the best. Our national wound was too deep to be lightly healed. When the President issued his Emancipation Proclamation my heart overflowed with joy, and I said: 'This is the first bright rift in the war cloud.' "

"And did you really think that they would accept the terms of freedom and lay down their arms?" asked Robert.

"I hardly thought they would," continued Captain Sybil. "I did not think that their leaders would permit it. I believe the rank and file of their army are largely composed of a mass of ignorance, led, manipulated, and moulded by educated and ambitious wickedness. In attempting to overthrow the Union, a despotism and reign of terror were created which encompassed them as fetters of iron, and they will not accept the conditions until they have reached the last extremity. I hardly think they are yet willing to confess that such extremity has been reached."

"Captain," said Robert, as they left Colonel Robinson's tent, "I have lived all my life where I have had a chance to hear the 'Secesh' talk, and when they left their papers around I used to read everything I could lay my hands on. It seemed to me that the big white men not only ruled over the poor whites and made laws for them, but over the whole nation."

"That was so," replied Captain Sybil. "The North was strong but forbearing. It was busy in trade and commerce, and permitted them to make the Northern States hunting-grounds for their slaves. When we sent back Simms and Burns from beneath the shadow of Bunker Hill Monument and Faneuil Hall, they mistook us; looked upon us as a lot of money-grabbers, who would be willing to purchase peace at any price. I do not believe when they fired on the 'Star of the West' that they had the least apprehension of the fearful results which were to follow their madness and folly."

"Well, Captain," asked Robert, "if the free North would submit to be called on to help them catch their slaves, what could be expected of us, who all our lives had known no other condition than that of slavery? How much braver would you have been, if your first recollections had been those of seeing your mother maltreated, your father cruelly beaten, or your fellow-servants brutally murdered? I wonder why they never enslaved the Indians!"

"You are mistaken, Robert, if you think the Indians were never enslaved. I have read that the Spaniards who visited the coasts of America kidnapped thousands of Indians, whom they sent to Europe and the West Indies as slaves. Columbus himself, we are informed, captured five hundred natives, and sent them to Spain. The Indian had the lesser power of endurance, and Las Cassas suggested the enslavement of the negro, because he seemed to possess greater breadth of physical organization and stronger power of endurance. Slavery was an old world's crime which, I have heard, the Indians never practiced among themselves. Perhaps it would have been harder to reduce them to slavery and hold them in bondage when they had a vast continent before them, where they could hide in the fastnesses of its mountains or the seclusion of its forests, than it was for white men to visit the coasts of Africa and, with their superior knowledge, obtain cargoes of slaves, bring them across the ocean, hem them in on the plantations, and surround them with a pall of dense ignorance."

"I remember," said Robert, "in reading a history I once came across at our house, that when the Africans first came to this country they did not all speak one language. Some had only met as mutual enemies. They were not all one color, their complexions ranging from tawny yellow to deep black."

"Yes," said Captain Sybil, "and in dealing with the negro we wanted his labor; in dealing with the Indian we wanted his lands. For one we had weapons of war; for the other we had real and invisible chains, the coercion of force, and the terror of the unseen world."

"That's exactly so, Captain! When I was a boy I used to hear the old folks tell what would happen to bad people in another world; about the devil pouring hot lead down people's throats and stirring them up with a pitchfork; and I used to get so scared that I would be afraid to go to bed at night. I don't suppose the Indians ever heard of such things, or, if they had, I never heard of them being willing to give away all their lands on earth, and quietly wait for a home in heaven."

"But, surely, Robert, you do not think religion has degraded the negro?"

"Oh, I wouldn't say that. But a man is in a tight fix when he takes his part, like Nat Turner or Denmark Veasy, and is made to fear that he will be hanged in this world and be burned in the next. And, since I come to think of it, we colored folks used to get mightily mixed up about our religion. Mr. Gundover had on his plantation a real smart man. He was religious, but he would steal."

"Oh, Robert," queried Sybil, "how could he be religious and steal?"

"He didn't think," retorted Robert, "it was any harm to steal from his master. I guess he thought it was right to get from his master all he could. He would have thought it wrong to steal from his fellow-servants. He thought that downright mean, but I wouldn't have insured the lives of Gundover's pigs and chickens, if Uncle Jack got them in a tight place. One day there was a minister stopping with Mr. Gundover. As a matter of course, in speaking of his servants, he gave Jack's sins an airing. He would much rather confess Jack's sins than his own. Now Gundover wanted to do two things, save his pigs and poultry, and save Jack's soul. He told the minister that Jack was a liar and a thief, and gave the minister a chance to talk with Uncle Jack about the state of his soul. Uncle Jack listened very quietly, and when taxed with stealing his master's wheat he was ready with an answer. 'Now Massa Parker,' said Jack, 'lem'me tell yer jis' how it war 'bout dat wheat. Wen ole Jack com'd down yere, dis place war all growed up in woods. He go ter work, clared up de groun' an' plowed, an' planted, an' riz a crap, an' den wen it war all done, he hadn't a dollar to buy his ole woman a gown; an' he jis' took a bag ob wheat.' "

"What did Mr. Parker say?" asked Sybil.

"I don't know, though I reckon he didn't think it was a bad steal after all, but I don't suppose he told Jack so. When he came to the next point, about Jack's lying, I suppose he thought he had a clear case; but Jack was equal to the occasion."

"How did he clear up that charge?" interrogated Captain Sybil.

"Finely. I think if he had been educated he would have made a first-rate lawyer. He said, 'Marse Parker, dere's old Joe. His wife don't lib on dis' plantation. Old Joe go ober ter see her, but he stayed too long, an' didn't git back in time fer his work. Massa's oberseer kotched him an' cut him all up. When de oberseer went inter de house, pore old Joe war all tired an' beat up, an' so he lay down by de fence corner and go ter sleep. Bimeby Massa oberseer com'd an' axed, "all bin a workin' libely?" I say "Yes, Massa." ' Then said Mr. Parker, 'You were lying, Joe had been sleeping, not working.' 'I know's dat, but ef I tole on Joe, Massa oberseer cut him all up again, and Massa Jesus says, "Blessed am de Peacemaker." ' "

"I heard," continued Robert, "that Mr. Parker said to Gundover, 'You seem to me like a man standing in a stream where the blood of Jesus can reach you, but you are standing between it and your slaves. How will you answer that in the Day of Judgment?' "

"What did Gundover say?" asked Captain Sybil.

"He turned pale, and said, 'For God's sake don't speak of the Day of Judgment in connection with slavery.' "

Just then a messenger brought a communication to Captain Sybil. He read it attentively, and, turning to Robert, said, "Here are orders for an engagement at Five Forks to-morrow. Oh, this wasting of life and scattering of treasure might have been saved had we only been wiser. But the time is passing. Look after your company, and see that everything is in readiness as soon as possible."

Carefully Robert superintended the arrangements for the coming battle of a strife which for years had thrown its crimson shadows over the land. The Rebels fought with a valor worthy of a better cause. The disaster of Bull Run had been retrieved. Sherman had made his famous march to the sea. Fighting Joe Hooker had scaled the stronghold of the storm king and won a victory in the palace chamber of the clouds; the Union soldiers had captured Columbia, replanted the Stars and Stripes in Charleston, and changed that old sepulchre of slavery into the cradle of a new-born freedom. Farragut had been as triumphant on water as the other generals had been victorious on land, and New Orleans had been wrenched from the hands of the Confederacy. The Rebel leaders were obstinate. Misguided hordes had followed them to defeat and death. Grant was firm and determined to fight it out if it took all summer. The closing battles were fought with desperate courage and firm resistance, but at last the South was forced to succumb. On the ninth day of April 1865, General Lee surrendered to General Grant. The lost cause went down in blood and tears, and on the brows of a ransomed people God poured the chrism of a new era, and they stood a race newly anointed with freedom.

CHAPTER XVI

After the Battle

VERY SAD AND heart-rending were the scenes with which
Iola came in constant contact. Well may Christian men
and women labor and pray for the time when nations
shall learn war no more; when, instead of bloody conflicts, there shall be peaceful arbitration. The battle in
which Robert fought, after his last conversation with
Captain Sybil, was one of the decisive struggles of the
closing conflict. The mills of doom and fate had ground
out a fearful grist of agony and death,

> "And lives of men and souls of States
>   Were thrown like chaff beyond the gates."

Numbers were taken prisoners. Pale, young corpses
strewed the earth; manhood was stricken down in the
flush of its energy and prime. The ambulances brought
in the wounded and dying. Captain Sybil laid down his
life on the altar of freedom. His prediction was fulfilled.
Robert was brought into the hospital, wounded, but not
dangerously. Iola remembered him as being the friend of
Tom Anderson, and her heart was drawn instinctively
towards him. For a while he was delirious, but her presence had a soothing effect upon him. He sometimes
imagined that she was his mother, and he would tell her
how he had missed her; and then at times he would call
her sister. Iola, tender and compassionate, humored his
fancies, and would sing to him in low, sweet tones some
of the hymns she had learned in her old home in Mississippi. One day she sang a few verses of the hymn beginning with the words—

> "Drooping souls no longer grieve,
>   Heaven is propitious;

> If on Christ you do believe,
> You will find Him precious."

"That," said he, looking earnestly into Iola's face, "was my mother's hymn. I have not heard it for years. Where did you learn it?"

Iola gazed inquiringly upon the face of her patient, and saw, by his clear gaze and the expression of his face, that his reason had returned.

"In my home, in Mississippi, from my own dear mother," was Iola's reply.

"Do you know where she learned it?" asked Robert.

"When she was a little girl she heard her mother sing it. Years after, a Methodist preacher came to our house, sang this hymn, and left the book behind him. My father was a Catholic, but my mother never went to any church. I did not understand it then, but I do now. We used to sing together, and read the Bible when we were alone."

"Do you remember where she came from, and who was her mother?" asked Robert, anxiously.

"My dear friend, you must be quiet. The fever has left you, but I will not answer for the consequences if you get excited."

Robert lay quiet and thoughtful for a while and, seeing he was wakeful, Iola said, "Have you any friends to whom you would like to send a letter?"

A pathetic expression flitted over his face, as he sadly replied, "I haven't, to my knowledge, a single relation in the world. When I was about ten years old my mother and sister were sold from me. It is more than twenty years since I have heard from them. But that hymn which you were singing reminded me so much of my mother! She used to sing it when I was a child. Please sing it again."

Iola's voice rose soft and clear by his bedside, till he fell into a quiet slumber. She remembered that her mother had spoken of her brother before they had parted, and her interest and curiosity were awakened by Robert's story. While he slept, she closely scrutinized Robert's features, and detected a striking resemblance between him and her mother.

"Oh, I *do* wonder if he can be my mother's brother, from whom she has been separated so many years!"

Anxious as she was to ascertain if there was any relationship between Robert and her mother, she forebore to question him on the subject which lay so near her heart. But one day, when he was so far recovered as to be able to walk around, he met Iola on the hospital grounds, and said to her:—

"Miss Iola, you remind me so much of my mother and sister that I cannot help wondering if you are the daughter of my long-lost sister."

"Do you think," asked Iola, "if you saw the likeness of your sister you would recognize her?"

"I am afraid not. But there is one thing I can remember about her: she used to have a mole on her cheek, which mother used to tell her was her beauty spot."

"Look at this," said Iola, handing him a locket which contained her mother's picture.

Robert grasped the locket eagerly, scanned the features attentively, then, handing it back, said: "I have only a faint remembrance of my sister's features; but I never could recognize in that beautiful woman the dear little sister with whom I used to play. Oh, the cruelty of slavery! How it wrenched and tore us apart! Where is *your* mother now?"

"Oh, I cannot tell," answered Iola. "I left her in Mississippi. My father was a wealthy Creole planter, who fell in love with my mother. She was his slave, but he educated her in the North, freed, and married her. My father was very careful to have the fact of our negro blood concealed from us. I had not the slightest suspicion of it. When he was dead the secret was revealed. His white relations set aside my father's will, had his marriage declared invalid, and my mother and her children were remanded to slavery." Iola shuddered as she pronounced the horrid word, and grew deadly pale; but, regaining her self-possession, continued: "Now, that freedom has come, I intend to search for my mother until I find her."

"I do not wonder," said Robert, "that we had this war. The nation had sinned enough to suffer."

"Yes," said Iola, "if national sins bring down national judgments, then the nation is only reaping what it sowed."

"What are your plans for the future, or have you any?" asked Robert.

"I intend offering myself as a teacher in one of the schools which are being opened in different parts of the country," replied Iola. "As soon as I am able I will begin my search for my dear mother. I will advertise for her in the papers, hunt for her in the churches, and use all the means in my power to get some tidings of her and my brother Harry. What a cruel thing it was to separate us!"

CHAPTER XVII

Flames in the School-Room

"GOOD MORNING," said Dr. Gresham, approaching Robert and Iola. "How are you both? You have mended rapidly," turning to Robert, "but then it was only a flesh wound. Your general health being good, and your blood in excellent condition, it was not hard for you to rally."

"Where have you been, Doctor? I have a faint recollection of having seen you on the morning I was brought in from the field, but not since."

"I have been on a furlough. I was running down through exhaustion and overwork, and I was compelled to go home for a few weeks' rest. But now, as they are about to close the hospital, I shall be permanently relieved. I am glad that this cruel strife is over. It seemed as if I had lived through ages during these last few years. In the early part of the war I lost my arm by a stray shot, and my armless sleeve is one of the mementos of battle I shall carry with me through life. Miss Leroy," he continued, turning respectfully to Iola, "would you permit me to ask you, as I would have some one ask my sister under the same circumstances, if you have matured any plans for the future, or if I can be of the least service to you? If so, I would be pleased to render you any service in my power."

"My purpose," replied Iola, "is to hunt for my mother, and to find her if she is alive. I am willing to go anywhere and do anything to find her. But I will need a standpoint from whence I can send out lines of inquiry. It must take time, in the disordered state of affairs, even to get a clue by which I may discover her whereabouts."

"How would you like to teach?" asked the Doctor. "Schools are being opened all around us. Numbers of excellent and superior women are coming from the North to engage as teachers of the freed people. Would you be willing to take a school among these people? I think it will be uphill work. I believe it will take generations to get over the duncery of slavery. Some of these poor fellows who came into our camp did not know their right hands from their left, nor their ages, nor even the days of the month. It took me some time, in a number of cases, to understand their language. It saddened my heart to see such ignorance. One day I asked one a question, and he answered, "I no shum'."

"What did he mean?" asked Iola.

"That he did not see it," replied the doctor. "Of course, this does not apply to all of them. Some of them are wide-awake and sharp as steel traps. I think some of that class may be used in helping others."

"I should be very glad to have an opportunity to teach," said Iola. "I used to be a great favorite among the colored children on my father's plantation."

In a few days after this conversation the hospital was closed. The sick and convalescent were removed, and Iola obtained a position as a teacher. Very soon Iola realized that while she was heartily appreciated by the freedmen, she was an object of suspicion and dislike to their former owners. The North had conquered by the supremacy of the sword, and the South had bowed to the inevitable. But here was a new army that had come with an invasion of ideas, that had come to supplant ignorance with knowledge, and it was natural that its members should be unwelcome to those who had made it a crime to teach their slaves to read the name of the ever blessed Christ. But Iola had found her work, and the freedmen their friend.

When Iola opened her school she took pains to get acquainted with the parents of the children, and she gained their confidence and co-operation. Her face was a passport to their hearts. Ignorant of books, human faces were the scrolls from which they had been reading for ages. They had been the sunshine and shadow of their lives.

Iola had found a school-room in the basement of a colored church, where the doors were willingly opened to her. Her pupils came from miles around, ready and anxious to get some "book larnin'." Some of the old folks were eager to learn, and it was touching to see the eyes which had grown dim under the shadows of slavery, donning spectacles and trying to make out the words. As Iola had nearly all of her life been accustomed to colored children she had no physical repulsions to overcome, no prejudices to conquer in dealing with parents and children. In their simple childish fashion they would bring her fruits and flowers, and gladden her lonely heart with little tokens of affection.

One day a gentleman came to the school and wished to address the children. Iola suspended the regular order of the school, and the gentleman essayed to talk to them on the achievements of the white race, such as building steamboats and carrying on business. Finally, he asked how they did it?

"They've got money," chorused the children.

"But how did they get it?"

"They took it from us," chimed the youngsters. Iola smiled, and the gentleman was nonplussed; but he could not deny that one of the powers of knowledge is the power of the strong to oppress the weak.

The school was soon overcrowded with applicants, and Iola was forced to refuse numbers, because their quarters were too cramped. The school was beginning to lift up the home, for Iola was not satisfied to teach her children only the rudiments of knowledge. She had tried to lay the foundation of good character. But the elements of evil burst upon her loved and cherished work. One night the heavens were lighted with lurid flames, and Iola beheld the school, the pride and joy of her pupils and their parents, a smouldering ruin. Iola gazed with sorrowful dismay on what seemed the cruel work of an incendiary's torch. While she sat, mournfully contemplating the work of destruction, her children formed a procession, and, passing by the wreck of their school, sang:—

> "Oh, do not be discouraged,
> For Jesus is your friend."

As they sang, the tears sprang to Iola's eyes, and she said to herself, "I am not despondent of the future of my people; there is too much elasticity in their spirits, too much hope in their hearts, to be crushed out by unreasoning malice."

CHAPTER XVIII

Searching for Lost Ones

To BIND ANEW the ties which slavery had broken and gather together the remnants of his scattered family became the earnest purpose of Robert's life. Iola, hopeful that in Robert she had found her mother's brother, was glad to know she was not alone in *her* search. Having sent out lines of inquiry in different directions, she was led to hope, from some of the replies she had received, that her mother was living somewhere in Georgia.

Hearing that a Methodist conference was to convene in that State, and being acquainted with the bishop of that district, she made arrangements to accompany him thither. She hoped to gather some tidings of her mother through the ministers gathered from different parts of that State.

From her brother she had heard nothing since her father's death. On his way to the conference, the bishop had an engagement to dedicate a church, near the city of C——, in North Carolina. Iola was quite willing to stop there a few days, hoping to hear something of Robert Johnson's mother. Soon after she had seated herself in the cars she was approached by a gentleman, who reached out his hand to her, and greeted her with great cordiality. Iola looked up, and recognized him immediately as one of her last patients at the hospital. It was none other than Robert Johnson.

"I am so glad to meet you," he said. "I am on my way to C—— in search of my mother. I want to see the person who sold her last, and, if possible, get some clew to the direction in which she went."

"And I," said Iola, "am in search of *my* mother. I am convinced that when we find those for whom we are searching they will prove to be very nearly related. Mamma said, before we were parted, that her brother

112

had a red spot on his temple. If I could see that spot I should rest assured that my mother is your sister."

"Then," said Robert, "I can give you that assurance," and smilingly he lifted his hair from his temple, on which was a large, red spot.

"I am satisfied," exclaimed Iola, fixing her eyes, beaming with hope and confidence, on Robert. "Oh, I am so glad that I can, without the least hesitation, accept your services to join with me in the further search. What are your plans?"

"To stop for a while in C——," said Robert, "and gather all the information possible from those who sold and bought my mother. I intend to leave no stone unturned in searching for her."

"Oh, I *do* hope that you will succeed. I expect to stop over there a few days, and I shall be *so* glad if, before I leave, I hear your search has been crowned with success, or, at least, that you have been put on the right track. Although I was born and raised in the midst of slavery, I had not the least idea of its barbarous selfishness till I was forced to pass through it. But we lived so much alone I had no opportunity to study it, except on our own plantation. My father and mother were very kind to their slaves. But it was slavery, all the same, and I hate it, root and branch."

Just then the conductor called out the station.

"We stop here," said Robert. "I am going to see Mrs. Johnson, and hunt up some of my old acquaintances. Where do you stop?"

"I don't know," replied Iola. "I expect that friends will be here to meet us. Bishop B——, permit me to introduce you to Mr. Robert Johnson, whom I have every reason to believe is my mother's brother. Like myself, he is engaged in hunting up his lost relatives."

"And I," said Robert, "am very much pleased to know that we are not without favorable clues."

"Bishop," said Iola, "Mr. Johnson wishes to know where I am to stop. He is going on an exploring expedition, and wishes to let me know the result."

"We stop at Mrs. Allston's, 313 New Street," said the bishop. "If I can be of any use to you, I am at your service."

"Thank you," said Robert, lifting his hat, as he left them to pursue his inquiries about his long-lost mother.

Quickly he trod the old familiar streets which led to his former home. He found Mrs. Johnson, but she had aged very fast since the war. She was no longer the lithe, active woman, with her proud manner and resolute bearing. Her eye had lost its brightness, her step its elasticity, and her whole appearance indicated that she was slowly sinking beneath a weight of sorrow which was heavier far than her weight of years. When she heard that Robert had called to see her she was going to receive him in the hall, as she would have done any of her former slaves, but her mind immediately changed when she saw him. He was not the light-hearted, careless, mischief-loving Robby of former days, but a handsome man, with heavy moustache, dark, earnest eyes, and proud military bearing. He smiled, and reached out his hand to her. She hardly knew how to address him. To her colored people were either boys and girls, or "aunties and uncles." She had never in her life addressed a colored person as "Mr. or Mrs." To do so now was to violate the social customs of the place. It would be like learning a new language in her old age. Robert immediately set her at ease by addressing her under the old familiar name of "Miss Nancy." This immediately relieved her of all embarrassment. She invited him into the sitting-room, and gave him a warm welcome.

"Well, Robby," she said, "I once thought that you would have been the last one to leave me. You know I never ill-treated you, and I gave you everything you needed. People said that I was spoiling you. I thought you were as happy as the days were long. When I heard of other people's servants leaving them I used to say to myself, 'I can trust my Bobby; he will stick to me to the last.' But I fooled myself that time. Soon as the Yankee soldiers got in sight you left me without saying a word. That morning I came down into the kitchen and asked Linda, 'Where's Robert? Why hasn't he set the table?' She said 'she hadn't seen you since the night before.' I thought maybe you were sick, and I went to see, but you were not in your room. I couldn't believe at first that you were gone. Wasn't I always good to you?"

"Oh, Miss Nancy," replied Robert; "you were good, but freedom was better."

"Yes," she said, musingly, "I suppose I would have done the same. But, Robby, it did go hard with me at first. However, I soon found out that my neighbors had been going through the same thing. But it's all over now. Let by-gones be by-gones. What are you doing now, and where are you living?"

"I am living in the city of P——. I have opened a hardware store there. But just now I am in search of my mother and sister."

"I hope that you may find them."

"How long," asked Robert, "do you think it has been since they left here?"

"Let me see; it must have been nearly thirty years. You got my letter?"

"Yes, ma'am; thank you."

"There have been great changes since you left here," Mrs. Johnson said. "Gundover died, and a number of colored men have banded together, bought his plantation, and divided it among themselves. And I hear they have a very nice settlement out there. I hope, since the Government has set them free, that they will succeed."

After Robert's interview with Mrs. Johnson he thought he would visit the settlement and hunt up his old friends. He easily found the place. It was on a clearing in Gundover's woods, where Robert and Uncle Daniel had held their last prayer-meeting. Now the gloomy silence of those woods was broken by the hum of industry, the murmur of cheerful voices, and the merry laughter of happy children. Where they had trodden with fear and misgiving, freedmen walked with light and bounding hearts. The school-house had taken the place of the slave-pen and auction-block.

"How is yer, ole boy?" asked one laborer of another.

"Everything is lobly," replied the other. The blue sky arching overhead and the beauty of the scenery justified the expression.

Gundover had died soon after the surrender. Frank Anderson had grown reckless and drank himself to death. His brother Tom had been killed in battle. Their mother, who was Gundover's daughter, had died insane. Their father had also passed away. The defeat of the

Confederates, the loss of his sons, and the emancipation of his slaves, were blows from which he never recovered. As Robert passed leisurely along, delighted with the evidences of thrift and industry which constantly met his eye, he stopped to admire a garden filled with beautiful flowers, clambering vines, and rustic adornments.

On the porch sat an elderly woman, darning stockings, the very embodiment of content and good humor. Robert looked inquiringly at her. On seeing him, she almost immediately exclaimed, "Shore as I'se born, dat's Robert! Look yere, honey, whar did yer come from? I'll gib my head fer a choppin' block ef dat ain't Miss Nancy's Bob. Ain't yer our Bobby? Shore yer is."

"Of course I am," responded Robert. "It isn't anybody else. How did you know me?"

"How did I know yer? By dem mischeebous eyes, ob course. I'd a knowed yer if I had seed yer in Europe."

"In Europe, Aunt Linda? Where's that?"

"I don't know. I specs it's some big city, somewhar. But yer looks jis' splendid. Yer looks good 'nuff ter kiss."

"Oh, Aunt Linda, don't say that. You make me blush."

"Oh you go 'long wid yer. I specs yer's got a nice little wife up dar whar yer comes from, dat kisses yer ebery day, an' Sunday, too."

"Is that the way your old man does you?"

"Oh, no, not a bit. He isn't one ob de kissin' kine. But sit down," she said, handing Robert a chair. "Won't yer hab a glass ob milk? Boy, I'se a libin' in clover. Neber 'spected ter see sich good times in all my born days."

"Well, Aunt Linda," said Robert, seating himself near her, and drinking the glass of milk which she had handed him, "how goes the battle? How have you been getting on since freedom?"

"Oh, fust rate, fust rate! Wen freedom com'd I jist lit out ob Miss Johnson's kitchen soon as I could. I wanted ter re'lize I war free, an' I couldn't, tell I got out er de sight and soun' ob ole Miss. When de war war ober an' de sogers war still stopping' yere, I made pies an' cakes, sole em to de sogers, an' jist made money han' ober fist. An' I kep' on a workin' an' a savin' till my ole man got back from de war wid his wages and his bounty money. I felt right set up an' mighty big wen we counted all dat money. We had neber seen so much money in our lives befo', let alone hab it fer ourselbs. An' I sez, 'John, you take dis money an' git a nice place wid it.' An' he sez, 'Dere's no use tryin', kase dey don't want ter sell us any lan'.' Ole Gundover said, 'fore he died, dat he would let de lan' grow up in trees 'fore he'd sell it to us. An' dere war Mr. Brayton; he buyed some lan' and sole it to some cullud folks, an' his ole frien's got so mad wid him dat dey wouldn't speak ter him, an' he war borned down yere. I tole ole Miss Anderson's daughter dat we wanted ter git some homes ob our ownselbs. She sez, 'Den you won't want ter work for us?' Jis' de same as ef we could eat an' drink our houses. I tell yer, Robby, dese white folks don't know eberything."

"That's a fact, Aunt Linda."

"Den I sez ter John, 'wen one door shuts anoder opens.' An' shore 'nough, ole Gundover died, an' his place war all in debt, an' had to be sole. Some Jews bought it, but dey didn't want to farm it, so dey gib us a chance to buy it. Dem Jews hez been right helpful to cullud people wen dey hab lan' to sell. I reckon dey don't keer who buys it so long as dey gits de money. Well, John didn't gib in at fust; didn't want to let on his wife knowed more dan he did, an' dat he war ruled ober by a woman. Yer know he is an' ole Firginian, an' some ob dem ole Firginians do so lub to rule a woman. But I kep' naggin at him, till I specs he got tired of my tongue, an' he went and buyed dis piece ob lan'. Dis house war on it, an' war all gwine to wrack. It used to belong to John's ole marster. His wife died right in dis house, an' arter dat her husband went right to de dorgs; an' now he's in de pore-house. My! but ain't dem tables turned. When we knowed it war our own, warn't my ole man proud! I seed it in him, but he wouldn't let on. Ain't you men powerful 'ceitful?"

"Oh, Aunt Linda, don't put me in with the rest!"

"I don't know 'bout dat. Put you all in de bag for 'ceitfulness, an' I don't know which would git out fust."

"Well, Aunt Linda, I suppose by this time you know how to read and write?"

"No, chile, sence freedom's com'd I'se bin scratchin' too hard to get a libin' to put my head down to de book."

"But, Aunt Linda, it would be such company when your husband is away, to take a book. Do you never get lonesome?"

"Chile, I ain't got no time ter get lonesome. Ef you had eber so many chickens to feed, an' pigs squealin' fer somethin' ter eat, an' yore ducks an' geese squakin' 'roun' yer, yer wouldn't hab time ter git lonesome."

"But, Aunt Linda, you might be sick for months, and think what a comfort it would be if you could read your Bible."

"Oh, I could hab prayin' and singin'. Dese people is mighty good 'bout prayin' by de sick. Why, Robby, I think it would gib me de hysterics ef I war to try to git book larnin' froo my pore ole head. How long is yer gwine to stay? An' whar is yer stoppin?"

"I got here to-day," said Robert, "but I expect to stay several days."

"Well, I wants yer to meet my ole man, an' talk 'bout ole times. Couldn't yer come an' stop wid me, or isn't my house sniptious 'nuff?"

"Yes, thank you; but there is a young lady in town whom I think is my niece, my sister's daughter, and I want to be with her all I can."

"Your niece! Whar did you git any niece from?"

"Don't you remember," asked Robert, "that my mother had a little daughter, when Mrs. Johnson sold her? Well, I believe this young lady is that daughter's child."

"Laws a marcy!" exclaimed Aunt Linda, "yer don't tell me so! Whar did yer ketch up wid her?"

"I met her first," said Robert, "at the hospital here, when our poor Tom was dying; and when I was wounded at Five Forks she attended me in the field hospital there. She was just as good as gold."

"Well, did I eber! You jis' fotch dat chile to see me, ef she ain't too fine. I'se pore, but I'se clean, an' I ain't forgot how ter git up good dinners. Now, I wants ter hab a good talk 'bout our feller-sarvants."

"Yes, and I," said Robert, "want to hear all about Uncle Daniel, and Jennie, and Uncle Ben Tunnel."

"Well, I'se got lots an' gobs ter tell yer. I'se kep' track

ob dem all. Aunt Katie died an' went ter hebben in a blaze ob glory. Uncle Dan'el stayed on de place till Marse Robert com'd back. When de war war ober he war smashed all ter pieces. I did pity him from de bottom ob my heart. When he went ter de war he looked so brave an' han'some; an' wen he com'd back he looked orful. 'Fore he went he gib Uncle Dan'el a bag full ob money ter take kere ob. 'An wen he com'd back Uncle Dan'el gibed him ebery cent ob it. It warn't ebery white pusson he could hab trusted wid it. 'Cause yer know, Bobby, money's a mighty temptin' thing. Dey tells me dat Marster Robert los' a heap ob property by de war; but Marse Robert war always mighty good ter Uncle Dan'el and Aunt Katie. He war wid her wen she war dyin' an' she got holt his han' an' made him promise dat he would meet her in glory. I neber seed anybody so happy in my life. She singed an' prayed ter de last. I tell you dis ole time religion is good 'nuff fer me. Mr. Robert didn't stay yere long arter her, but I beliebs he went all right. But 'fore he went he looked out fer Uncle Dan'el. Did you see dat nice little cabin down dere wid de green shutters an' nice little garden in front? Well, 'fore Marse Robert died he gib Uncle Dan'el dat place, an' Miss Mary and de chillen looks arter him yet; an' he libs jis' as snug as a bug in a rug. I'se gwine ter axe him ter take supper wid you. He'll be powerful glad ter see you."

"Do you ever go to see old Miss?" asked Robert.

"Oh, yes; I goes ebery now and den. But she's jis' fell froo. Ole Johnson jis' drunk hisself to death. He war de biggest guzzler I eber seed in my life. Why, dat man he drunk up ebery thing he could lay his han's on. Sometimes he would go 'roun' tryin' to borrer money from pore cullud folks. 'Twas rale drefful de way dat pore feller did frow hisself away. But drink did it all. I tell you, Bobby, dat drink's a drefful thing wen it gits de upper han' ob you. You'd better steer clar ob it."

"That's so," assented Robert.

"I know'd Miss Nancy's fadder and mudder. Dey war mighty rich. Some ob de real big bugs. Marse Jim used to know dem, an' come ober ter de plantation, an' eat an' drink wen he got ready, an' stay as long as he choose. Ole Cousins used to have wine at dere table ebery day, an' Marse Jim war mighty fon' ob dat wine, an' sometimes he would drink till he got quite boozy. Ole Cousins liked him bery well, till he foun' out he wanted his darter, an' den he didn't want him fer rags nor patches. But Miss Nancy war mighty headstrong, an' allers liked to hab her own way; an' dis time she got it. But didn't she step her foot inter it? Ole Johnson war mighty han'-some, but when dat war said all war said. She run'd off an' got married, but wen she got down she war too spunky to axe her pa for anything. Wen you war wid her, yer know she only took big bugs. But wen de war com'd 'roun' it tore her all ter pieces, an' now she's as pore as Job's turkey. I feel's right sorry fer her. Well, Robby, things is turned 'roun' mighty quare. Ole Mistus war up den, an' I war down; now, she's down, an' I'se up. But I pities her, 'cause she warn't so bad arter all. De wuss thing she eber did war to sell your mudder, an' she wouldn't hab done dat but she snatched de whip out ob her han' an gib her a lickin'. Now I belieb in my heart she war 'fraid ob your mudder arter dat. But we women had ter keep 'em from whippin' us, er dey'd all de time been libin' on our bones. She had no man ter whip us 'cept dat ole drunken husband ob hern, an' he war allers too drunk ter whip hisself. He jis' wandered off, an' I reckon he died in somebody's pore-house. He warn't no 'count nohow you fix it. Weneber I goes to town I carries her some garden sass, er a little milk an' butter. An' she's mighty glad ter git it. I ain't got nothin' agin her. She neber struck me a lick in her life, an' I belieb in praising de bridge dat carries me ober. Dem Yankees set me free, an' I thinks a powerful heap ob dem. But it does rile me ter see dese mean white men comin' down yere an' settin' up dere grog-shops, tryin' to fedder dere nests sellin' licker to pore culled people. Deys de bery kine ob men dat used ter keep dorgs to ketch de run-aways. I'd be chokin' fer a drink 'fore I'd eber spen' a cent wid dem, a spreadin' dere traps to git de black folks' money. You jis' go down town 'fore sun up to-morrer mornin' an' you see ef dey don't hab dem bars open to sell dere drams to dem hard workin' culled people 'fore dey goes ter work. I thinks some niggers is mighty big fools."

"Oh, Aunt Linda, don't run down your race. Leave that for the white people."

"I ain't runnin' down my people. But a fool's a fool, wether he's white or black. An' I think de nigger who will spen' his hard-earned money in dese yere new grog-shops is de biggest kine ob a fool, an' I sticks ter dat. You know we didn't hab all dese low places in slave times. An' what is dey fer, but to get the people's money. An' it's a shame how dey do sling de licker 'bout 'lection times."

"But don't the temperance people want the colored people to vote the temperance ticket?"

"Yes, but some ob de culled people gits mighty skittish ef dey tries to git em to vote dare ticket 'lection time, an' keeps dem at a proper distance wen de 'lection's ober. Some ob dem say dere's a trick behine it, an' don't want to tech it. Dese white folks could do a heap wid de culled folks ef dey'd only treat em right."

"When our people say there is a trick behind it," said Robert, "I only wish they could see the trick before it—the trick of worse than wasting their money, and of keeping themselves and families poorer and more ignorant than there is any need for them to be."

"Well, Bobby, I beliebs we might be a people ef it warn't for dat mizzable drink. An' Robby, I jis' tells yer what I wants; I wants some libe man to come down yere an' splain things ter dese people. I don't mean a politic man, but a man who'll larn dese people how to bring up dere chillen, to keep our gals straight, an' our boys from runnin' in de saloons an' gamblin' dens."

"Don't your preachers do that?" asked Robert.

"Well, some ob dem does, an' some ob dem doesn't. An' wen dey preaches, I want dem to practice wat dey preach. Some ob dem says dey's called, but I jis' thinks laziness called some ob dem. An' I thinks since freedom come deres some mighty pore sticks set up for preachers. Now dere's John Anderson, Tom's brudder; you 'member Tom."

"Yes; as brave a fellow and as honest as ever stepped in shoe leather."

"Well, his brudder war mighty diff'rent. He war down in de lower kentry wen de war war ober. He war mighty smart, an' had a good head-piece, an' a orful glib tongue. He set up store an' sole whisky, an' made a lot ob money. Den he wanted ter go to de legislatur. Now what

should he do but make out he'd got 'ligion, an' war called
to preach. He had no more 'ligion dan my ole dorg. But
he had money an' built a meetin' house, whar he could
hole meeting, an' hab funerals; an' you know cullud folks
is mighty great on funerals. Well dat jis' tuck wid de
people, an' he got 'lected to de legislatur. Den he got a
fine house, an' his ole wife warn't good 'nuff for him.
Den dere war a young school-teacher, an' he begun cuttin' his eyes at her. But she war as deep in de mud as
he war in de mire, an' he jis' gib up his ole wife and
married her, a fusty thing. He war a mean ole hypocrit,
an' I wouldn't sen' fer him to bury my cat. Robby, I'se
down on dese kine ob preachers like a thousand bricks."

"Well, Aunt Linda, all the preachers are not like
him."

"No; I knows dat; not by a jug full. We's got some
mighty good men down yere, an' we's glad when dey
comes, an' orful sorry when dey goes 'way. De las
preacher we had war a mighty good man. He didn't like
too much hollerin'."

"Perhaps," said Robert, "he thought it were best for
only one to speak at a time."

"I specs so. His wife war de nicest and sweetest lady
dat eber I did see. None ob yer airish, stuck up folks,
like a tarrapin carryin' eberything on its back. She used
ter hab meetins fer de mudders, na' larn us how to rise
our chillen, an' talk so putty to de chillen. I sartinly did
lub dat woman."

"Where is she now?" asked Robert.

"De Conference moved dem 'bout thirty miles from
yere. Deys gwine to hab a big meetin' ober dere next
Sunday. Don't you 'member dem meetins we used to hab
in de woods? We don't hab to hide like we did den. But
it don't seem as ef de people had de same good 'ligion
we had den. 'Pears like folks is took up wid makin'
money an' politics."

"Well, Aunt Linda, don't you wish those good old days
would come back?"

"No, chile; neber! neber! Wat fer you take me? I'd
ruther lib in a corn-crib. Freedom needn't keep me outer
heben; an' ef I'se sich a fool as ter lose my 'ligion cause
I'se free, I oughtn' ter git dere."

"But, Aunt Linda, if old Miss were able to take care of you, wouldn't you just as leave be back again?"

There was a faint quiver of indignation in Aunt Linda's voice, as she replied:—

"Don't yer want yer freedom? Well I wants ter pat my free foot. Halleluyah! But, Robby, I wants yer to go ter dat big meetin' de wuss kine."

"How will I get there?" asked Robert.

"Oh, dat's all right. My ole man's got two ob de nicest mules you eber set yer eyes on. It'll jis' do yer good ter look at dem. I 'spect you'll see some ob yer ole frens dere. Dere's a nice settlemen' of cullud folks ober dere, an' I wants yer to come an' bring dat young lady. I wants dem folks to see wat nice folks I kin bring to de meetin'. I hope's yer didn't lose all your 'ligion in de army."

"Oh, I hope not," replied Robert.

"Oh, chile, yer mus' be shore 'bout dat. I don't want yer to ride hope's hoss down to torment. Now be shore an' come to-morrer an' bring dat young lady, an' take supper wid me. I'se all on nettles to see dat chile."

CHAPTER XIX

Striking Contrasts

THE NEXT DAY, Robert, accompanied by Iola, went to the settlement to take supper with Aunt Linda, and a very luscious affair it was. Her fingers had not lost their skill since she had tasted the sweets of freedom. Her biscuits were just as light and flaky as ever. Her jelly was as bright as amber, and her preserves were perfectly delicious. After she had set the table she stood looking in silent admiration, chuckling to herself: "Ole Mistus can't set sich a table as dat. She ought'er be yere to see it. Specs 'twould make her mouf water. Well, I mus' let bygones be bygones. But dis yere freedom's mighty good."

Aunt Linda had invited Uncle Daniel, and, wishing to give him a pleasant surprise, she had refrained from telling him that Robert Johnson was the one she wished him to meet.

"Do you know dis gemmen?" said Aunt Linda to Uncle Daniel, when the latter arrived.

"Well, I can't say's I do. My eyes is gittin dim, an I disremembers him."

"Now jis' you look right good at him. Don't yer 'member him?"

Uncle Daniel looked puzzled and, slowly scanning Robert's features, said: "He do look like somebody I used ter know, but I can't make him out ter save my life. I don't know whar to place him. Who is de gemmen, ennyhow?"

"Why, Uncle Dan'el," replied Aunt Linda, "dis is Robby; Miss Nancy's bad, mischeebous Robby, dat war allers playin' tricks on me."

"Well, shore's I'se born, ef dis ain't our ole Bobby!" exclaimed Uncle Daniel, delightedly. "Why, chile, whar did yer come from? Thought you war dead an' buried long 'go."

"Why, Uncle Daniel, did you send anybody to kill me?" asked Robert, laughingly.

"Oh, no'n 'deed, chile! but I yeard dat you war killed in de battle, an' I never 'spected ter see you agin."

"Well, here I am," replied Robert, "large as life, and just as natural. And this young lady, Uncle Daniel, I believe is my niece." As he spoke he turned to Iola. "Do you remember my mother?"

"Oh, yes," said Uncle Daniel, looking intently at Iola as she stepped forward and cordially gave him her hand.

"Well, I firmly believe," continued Robert, "that this is the daughter of the little girl whom Miss Nancy sold away with my mother."

"Well, I'se rale glad ter see her. She puts me mighty much in mine ob dem days wen we war all young togedder; wen Miss Nancy sed, 'Harriet war too high fer her.' It jis' seems like yisterday wen I yeard Miss Nancy say, 'No house could flourish whar dere war two mistresses.' Well, Mr. Robert—"

"Oh, no, no, Uncle Daniel," interrupted Robert, "don't say that! Call me Robby or Bob, just as you used to."

"Well, Bobby, I'se glad klar from de bottom of my heart ter see yer."

"Even if you wouldn't go with us when we left?"

"Oh, Bobby, dem war mighty tryin' times. You boys didn't know it, but Marster Robert hab giben me a bag ob money ter take keer ob, an' I promised him I'd do it an' I had ter be ez good ez my word."

"Oh, Uncle Daniel, why didn't you tell us boys all about it? We could have helped you take care of it."

"Now, wouldn't dat hab bin smart ter let on ter you chaps, an' hab you huntin' fer it from Dan ter Barsheba? I specs some ob you would bin a rootin' fer it yit!"

"Well, Uncle Daniel, we were young then; I can't tell what we would have done if we had found it. But we are older now."

"Yes, yer older, but I wouldn't put it pas' yer eben now, ef yer foun' out whar it war."

"Yes," said Iola, laughing, "they say 'caution is the parent of safety.' "

"Money's a mighty tempting thing," said Robert, smiling.

"But, Robby, dere's nothin' like a klar conscience; a klar conscience, Robby!"

Just then Aunt Linda, who had been completing the preparations for her supper, entered the room with her husband, and said, "Salters, let me interdoos you ter my fren', Mr. Robert Johnson, an' his niece, Miss Leroy."

"Why, is it possible," exclaimed Robert, rising, and shaking hands, "that you are Aunt Linda's husband?"

"Dat's what de parson sed," replied Salters.

"I thought," pursued Robert, "that your name was John Andrews. It was such when you were in my company."

"All de use I'se got fer dat name is ter git my money wid it; an' wen dat's done, all's done. Got 'nuff ob my ole Marster in slave times, widout wearin' his name in freedom. Wen I got done wid him, I got done wid his name. Wen I 'listed, I war John Andrews; and wen I gits my pension, I'se John Andrews; but now Salters is my name, an' I likes it better."

"But how came you to be Aunt Linda's husband? Did you get married since the war?"

"Lindy an' me war married long 'fore de war. But my ole Marster sole me away from her an' our little gal, an' den sole her chile ter somebody else. Arter freedom, I hunted up our little gal, an' foun' her. She war a big woman den. Den I com'd right back ter dis place an' foun' Lindy. She hedn't married agin, nuther hed I; so we jis' let de parson marry us out er de book; an' we war mighty glad ter git togedder agin, an' feel hitched togedder fer life."

"Well, Uncle Daniel," said Robert, turning the conversation toward him, "you and Uncle Ben wouldn't go with us, but you came out all right at last."

"Yes, indeed," said Aunt Linda, "Ben got inter a stream of luck. Arter freedom com'd de people had a heap of fath in Ben; an' wen dey wanted some one to go ter Congress dey jist voted for Ben ter go. An' he went, too. An' wen Salters went to Washin'ton to git his pension, who should he see dere wid dem big men but our Ben, lookin' jist as big as any ob dem."

"An' it did my ole eyes good jist ter see it," broke in

Salters; "if I couldn't go dere myself, I war mighty glad to see some one ob my people dat could. I felt like de boy who, wen somebody said he war gwine to slap off his face, said, 'Yer kin slap off my face, but I'se got a big brudder, an' you can't slap off his face.' I went to see him 'fore I lef', and he war jist de same as he war wen we war boys togedder. He hadn't got de big head a bit."

"I reckon Mirandy war mighty sorry she didn't stay wid him. I know I should be," said Aunt Linda.

"Uncle Daniel," asked Robert, "are you still preaching?"

"Yes, chile, I'se still firing off de Gospel gun."

"I hear some of the Northern folks are down here teaching theology, that is, teaching young men how to preach. Why don't you study theology?"

"Look a yere, boy, I'se been a preachin' dese thirty years, an' you come yere a tellin' me 'bout studying yore ologies. I larn'd my 'ology at de foot ob de cross. You bin dar?"

"Dear Uncle Daniel," said Iola, "the moral aspect of the nation would be changed if it would learn at the same cross to subordinate the spirit of caste to the spirit of Christ."

"Does yer 'member Miss Nancy's Harriet," asked Aunt Linda, "dat she sole away kase she wouldn't let her whip her? Well, we think dis is Harriet's gran'chile. She war sole away from her mar, an' now she's a lookin' fer her."

"Well, I hopes she may fine her," replied Salters. "I war sole 'way from my mammy wen I war eighteen mont's ole, an' I wouldn't know her now from a bunch ob turnips."

"I," said Iola, "am on my way South seeking for my mother, and I shall not give up until I find her."

"Come," said Aunt Linda, "we mustn't stan' yer talkin', or de grub'll git cole. Come, frens, sit down, an' eat some ob my pore supper."

Aunt Linda sat at the table in such a flutter of excitement that she could hardly eat, but she gazed with intense satisfaction on her guests. Robert sat on her right hand, contrasting Aunt Linda's pleasant situation with the old days in Mrs. Johnson's kitchen, where he had played his pranks upon her, and told her the news of the war.

Over Iola there stole a spirit of restfulness. There was something so motherly in Aunt Linda's manner that it seemed to recall the bright, sunshiny days when she used to nestle in Mam Liza's arms, in her own happy home. The conversation was full of army reminiscences and recollections of the days of slavery. Uncle Daniel was much interested, and, as they rose from the table, exclaimed:—

"Robby, seein' yer an' hearin' yer talk, almos' puts new springs inter me. I feel 'mos' like I war gittin' younger."

After the supper, Salters and his guests returned to the front room, which Aunt Linda regarded with so much pride, and on which she bestowed so much care.

"Well, Captin," said Salters, "I neber 'spected ter see you agin. Do you know de las' time I seed yer? Well, you war on a stretcher, an' four ob us war carryin' you ter de hospital. War you much hurt?"

"No," replied Robert, "it was only a flesh wound; and this young lady nursed me so carefully that I soon got over it."

"Is dat de way you foun' her?"

"Yes, Andrews,"——

"Salters, ef you please," interrupted Salters. "I'se only Andrews wen I gits my money."

"Well, Salters," continued Robert, "our freedom was a costly thing. Did you know that Captain Sybil was killed in one of the last battles of the war? These young chaps, who are taking it so easy, don't know the hardships through which we older ones passed. But all the battles are not fought, nor all the victories won. The colored man has escaped from one slavery, and I don't want him to fall into another. I want the young folks to keep their brains clear, and their right arms strong, to fight the battles of life manfully, and take their places alongside of every other people in this country. And I cannot see what is to hinder them if they get a chance."

"I don't nuther," said Salters. "I don't see dat dey drinks any more dan anybody else, nor dat dere is any meanness or debilment dat a black man kin do dat a white man can't keep step wid him."

"Yes," assented Robert, "but while a white man is

stealing a thousand dollars, a black man is getting into trouble taking a few chickens."

"All that may be true," said Iola, "but there are some things a white man can do that we cannot afford to do."

"I beliebs eberybody, Norf and Souf, is lookin' at us; an' some ob dem ain't got no good blood fer us, nohow you fix it," said Salters.

"I specs cullud folks mus' hab done somethin'," interposed Aunt Linda.

"O, nonsense," said Robert. "I don't think they are any worse than the white people. I don't believe, if we had the power, we would do any more lynching, burning, and murdering than they do."

"Dat's so," said Aunt Linda, "it's rarely orful how our folks hab been murdered sence de war. But I don't think dese young folks is goin' ter take things as we's allers done."

"We war cowed down from the beginnin'," said Uncle Daniel, "but dese young folks ain't comin' up dat way."

"No," said Salters, "fer one night arter some ob our pore people had been killed, an' some ob our women had run'd away 'bout seventeen miles, my gran'son, looking me squar in de face, said: 'Ain't you got five fingers? Can't you pull a trigger as well as a white man?' I tell yer, Cap, dat jis' got to me, an' I made up my mine dat my boy should neber call me a coward."

"It is not to be expected," said Robert, "that these young people are going to put up with things as we did, when we weren't permitted to hold a meeting by ourselves, or to own a club or learn to read."

"I tried," said Salters, "to git a little out'er de book wen I war in de army. On Sundays I sometimes takes a book an' tries to make out de words, but my eyes is gittin' dim an' de letters all run togedder, an' I gits sleepy, an' ef yer wants to put me to sleep jis' put a book in my han'. But wen it comes to gittin' out a stan' ob cotton, an' plantin' corn, I'se dere all de time. But dat gran'son ob mine is smart as a steel trap. I specs he'll be a preacher."

Salters looked admiringly at his grandson, who sat grinning in the corner, munching a pear he had brought from the table.

"Yes," said Aunt Linda, "his fadder war killed by the

Secesh, one night, comin' home from a politic meetin', an' his pore mudder died a few weeks arter, an' we mean to make a man ob him."

"He's got to larn to work fust," said Salters, "an' den ef he's right smart I'se gwine ter sen' him ter college. An' ef he can't get a libin' one way, he kin de oder."

"Yes," said Iola, "I hope he will turn out an excellent young man, for the greatest need of the race is noble, earnest men, and true women."

"Job," said Salters, turning to his grandson, "tell Jake ter hitch up de mules, an' you stay dere an' help him. We's all gwine ter de big meetin'. Yore grandma hab set her heart on goin', an' it'll be de same as a spell ob sickness ef she don't hab a chance to show her bes' bib an' tucker. That ole gal's as proud as a peacock."

"Now, John Salters," exclaimed Aunt Linda, "ain't you 'shamed ob yourself? Allers tryin' to poke fun at yer pore wife. Never mine; wait till I'se gone, an' you'll miss me."

"Ef I war single," said Salters, "I could git a putty young gal, but it wouldn't be so easy wid you."

"Why not?" said Iola, smiling.

" 'Cause young men don't want ole hens, an' ole men want young pullets," was Salters' reply.

"Robby, honey," said Aunt Linda, "when you gits a wife, don't treat her like dat man treats me."

"Oh, his head's level," answered Robert; "at least it was in the army."

"Dat's jis' de way; you see dat, Miss Iola? One man takin' up for de oder. But I'll be eben wid you bof. I must go now an' git ready."

Iola laughed. The homely enjoyment of that evening was very welcome to her after the trying scenes through which she had passed. Further conversation was interrupted by the appearance of the wagon, drawn by two fine mules. John Salters stopped joking his wife to admire his mules.

"Jis' look at dem," he said. "Ain't dey beauties? I bought 'em out ob my bounty-money. Arter de war war ober I had a little money, an' I war gwine ter rent a plantation on sheers an' git out a good stan' ob cotton. Cotton war bringin' orful high prices den, but Lindy said to me, 'Now, John, you'se got a lot ob money, an' you'd better salt it down. I'd ruther lib on a little piece ob lan' ob my own dan a big piece ob somebody else's.' Well, I says to Lindy, I dun know nuthin' 'bout buyin' lan', an' I'se 'fraid arter I'se done buyed it an' put all de marrer ob dese bones in it, dat somebody's far-off cousin will come an' say de title ain't good, an' I'll lose it all."

"You're right thar, John," said Uncle Daniel. "White man's so unsartin, black man's nebber safe."

"But somehow," continued Salters, "Lindy warn't satisfied wid rentin', so I buyed a piece ob lan', an' I'se glad now I'se got it. Lindy's got a lot ob gumption; knows most as much as a man. She ain't got dat long head fer nuffin. She's got lots ob sense, but I don't like to tell her so."

"Why not?" asked Iola. "Do you think it would make her feel too happy?"

"Well, it don't do ter tell you women how much we thinks ob you. It sets you up too much. Ole Gundover's overseer war my marster, an' he used ter lib in dis bery house. I'se fixed it up sence I'se got it. Now I'se better off dan he is, 'cause he tuck to drink, an' all his frens is gone, an' he's in de pore-house."

Just then Linda came to the door with her baskets.

"Now, Lindy, ain't you ready yet? Do hurry up."

"Yes, I'se ready, but things wouldn't go right ef you didn't hurry me."

"Well, put your chicken fixins an' cake right in yere. Captin, you'll ride wid me, an' de young lady an' my ole woman'll take de back seat. Uncle Dan'el, dere's room for you ef you'll go."

"No, I thank you. It's time fer ole folks to go to bed. Good night! An', Bobby, I hopes to see you agin'."

CHAPTER XX

A Revelation

It was a lovely evening for the journey. The air was soft and balmy. The fields and hedges were redolent with flowers. Not a single cloud obscured the brightness of the moon or the splendor of the stars. The ancient trees were festooned with moss, which hung like graceful draperies. Ever and anon a startled hare glided over the path, and whip-poor-wills and crickets broke the restful silence of the night. Robert rode quietly along, quaffing the beauty of the scene and thinking of his boyish days, when he gathered nuts and wild plums in those woods; he also indulged pleasant reminiscences of later years, when, with Uncle Daniel and Tom Anderson, he attended the secret prayer-meetings. Iola rode along, conversing with Aunt Linda, amused and interested at the quaintness of her speech and the shrewdness of her intellect. To her the ride was delightful.

"Does yer know dis place, Robby?" asked Aunt Linda, as they passed an old resort.

"I should think I did," replied Robert. "It is the place where we held our last prayer-meeting."

"An' dere's dat ole broken pot we used, ter tell 'bout de war. But warn't ole Miss hoppin' wen she foun' out you war goin' to de war! I thought she'd go almos' wile. Now, own up, Robby, didn't you feel kine ob mean to go off widout eben biddin' her good bye? An' I ralely think ole Miss war fon' ob yer. Now, own up, honey, didn't yer feel a little down in de mouf wen yer lef' her."

"Not much," responded Robert. "I only thought she was getting paid back for selling my mother."

"Dat's so, Robby! yore mudder war a likely gal, wid long black hair, an' kine ob ginger-bread color. An' you neber hearn tell ob her sence dey sole her to Georgia?"

"Never," replied Robert, "but I would give everything

132

I have on earth to see her once more. I *do* hope, if she is living, that I may meet her before I die."

"You's right, boy, cause she lub'd you as she lub'd her own life. Many a time hes she set in my ole cabin an' cried 'bout yer wen you war fas' asleep. It's all ober now, but I'se gwine to hole up fer dem Yankees dat gib me my freedom, an' sent dem nice ladies from de Norf to gib us some sense. Some ob dese folks calls em nigger teachers, an' won't hab nuffin to do wid 'em, but I jis' thinks dey's splendid. But dere's some triflin' niggers down yere who'll sell der votes for almost nuffin. Does you 'member Jake Williams an' Gundover's Tom? Well dem two niggers is de las' ob pea-time. Dey's mighty small pertaters an' few in a hill."

"Oh, Aunt Linda," said Robert, "don't call them niggers. They are our own people."

"Dey ain't my kine ob people. I jis' calls em niggers, an' niggers I means; an' de bigges' kine ob niggers. An' if my John war sich a nigger I'd whip him an' leave him."

"An' what would I be a doin'," queried John, suddenly rousing up at the mention of his name.

"Standing still and taking it, I suppose," said Iola, who had been quietly listening to and enjoying the conversation.

"Yes, an' I'd ketch myself stan'in' still an' takin' it," was John's plucky response.

"Well, you oughter, ef you's mean enough to wote dat ticket ter put me back inter slavery," was Aunt Linda's parting shot. "Robby," she continued, "you 'member Miss Nancy's Jinnie?"

"Of course I do," said Robert.

"She married Mr. Gundover's Dick. Well, dere warn't much git up an' go 'bout him. So, wen 'lection time com'd, de man he war workin' fer tole him ef he woted de radical ticket he'd turn him off. Well, Jinnie war so 'fraid he'd do it, dat she jis' follered him fer days."

"Poor fellow!" exclaimed Robert. "How did he come out?"

"He certainly was between two fires," interposed Iola.

"Oh, Jinnie gained de day. She jis' got her back up, and said, 'Now ef yer wote dat ticket ter put me back inter slavery, you take yore rags an' go.' An' Dick jis' woted de radical ticket. Jake Williams went on de Secesh side, woted whar he thought he'd git his taters, but he got fooled es slick es greese."

"How was that?" asked Robert.

"Some ob dem folks, dat I 'spects buyed his wote, sent him some flour an' sugar. So one night his wife hab company ter tea. Dey made a big spread, an' put a lot ob sugar on de table fer supper, an' Tom jis' went fer dat sugar. He put a lot in his tea. But somehow it didn't tase right, an' wen dey come ter fine out what war de matter, dey hab sent him a barrel ob san' wid some sugar on top, an' wen de sugar war all gone de san' war dare. Wen I yeard it, I jis' split my sides a larfin. It war too good to keep; an' wen it got roun', Jake war as mad as a March hare. But it sarved him right."

"Well, Aunt Linda, you mustn't be too hard on Uncle Jake; you know he's getting old."

"Well he ain't too ole ter do right. He ain't no older dan Uncle Dan'el. An' I yered dey offered him $500 ef he'd go on dere side. An' Uncle Dan'el wouldn't tech it. An' dere's Uncle Job's wife; why didn't she go dat way? She war down on Job's meanness."

"What did she do?"

"Wen 'lection time 'rived, he com'd home bringing some flour an' meat; an' he says ter Aunt Polly, 'Ole woman, I got dis fer de wote.' She jis' picked up dat meat an' flour an' sent it sailin' outer doors, an' den com'd back an' gib him a good tongue-lashin'. 'Oder people,' she said, 'a wotin' ter lib good, an' you a sellin' yore wote! Ain't you got 'nuff ob ole Marster, an' ole Marster bin cuttin' you up? It shan't stay yere.' An' so she wouldn't let de things stay in de house."

"What did Uncle Job do?"

"He jis' stood dere an' cried."

"And didn't you feel sorry for him?" asked Iola.

"Not a bit! he hedn't no business ter be so shabby."

"But, Aunt Linda," pursued Iola, "if it were shabby for an ignorant colored man to sell his vote, wasn't it shabbier for an intelligent white man to buy it?"

"You see," added Robert, "all the shabbiness is not on our side."

"I knows dat," said Aunt Linda, "but I can't help it. I wants my people to wote right, an' to think somethin' ob demselves."

"Well, Aunt Linda, they say in every flock of sheep there will be one that's scabby," observed Iola.

"Dats so! But I ain't got no use fer scabby sheep."

"Lindy," cried John, "we's most dar! Don't you yere dat singin'? Dey's begun a'ready."

"Neber mine," said Aunt Linda, "sometimes de las' ob de wine is de bes'."

Thus discoursing they had beguiled the long hours of the night and made their long journey appear short.

Very soon they reached the church, a neat, commodious, frame building, with a blue ceiling, white walls within and without, and large windows with mahogany-colored facings. It was a sight full of pathetic interest to see that group which gathered from miles around. They had come to break bread with each other, relate their experiences, and tell of their hopes of heaven. In that meeting were remnants of broken families—mothers who had been separated from their children before the war, husbands who had not met their wives for years. After the bread had been distributed and the hand-shaking was nearly over, Robert raised the hymn which Iola had sung for him when he was recovering from his wounds, and Iola, with her clear, sweet tones, caught up the words and joined him in the strain. When the hymn was finished a dear old mother rose from her seat. Her voice was quite strong. With still a lingering light and fire in her eye, she said:—

"I rise, bredren an' sisters, to say I'm on my solemn march to glory."

"Amen!" "Glory!" came from a number of voices.

"I'se had my trials an' temptations, my ups an' downs; but I feels I'll soon be in one ob de many mansions. If it hadn't been for dat hope I 'spects I would have broken down long ago. I'se bin through de deep waters, but dey didn't overflow me; I'se bin in de fire, but de smell ob it isn't on my garments. Bredren an' sisters, it war a drefful time when I war tored away from my pore little chillen."

"Dat's so!" exclaimed a chorus of voices. Some of her hearers moaned, others rocked to and fro, as thoughts of similar scenes in their own lives arose before them.

"When my little girl," continued the speaker, "took hole ob my dress an' begged me ter let her go wid me, an' I couldn't do it, it mos' broke my heart. I had a little boy, an' wen my mistus sole me she kep' him. She carried on a boardin' house. Many's the time I hab stole out at night an' seen dat chile an' sleep'd wid him in my arms tell mos' day. Bimeby de people I libed wid got hard up fer money, an' dey sole me one way an' my pore little gal de oder; an' I neber laid my eyes on my pore chillen sence den. But, honeys, let de wind blow high or low, I 'spects to outwedder de storm an' anchor by'm bye in bright glory. But I'se bin a prayin' fer one thing, an' I beliebs I'll git it; an' dat is dat I may see my chillen 'fore I die. Pray fer me dat I may hole out an' hole on, an' neber make a shipwrack ob faith, an' at las' fine my way from earth to glory."

Having finished her speech, she sat down and wiped away the tears that flowed all the more copiously as she remembered her lost children. When she rose to speak her voice and manner instantly arrested Robert's attention. He found his mind reverting to the scenes of his childhood. As she proceeded his attention became riveted on her. Unbidden tears filled his eyes and great sobs shook his frame. He trembled in every limb. Could it be possible that after years of patient search through churches, papers, and inquiring friends, he had accidentally stumbled on his mother—the mother who, long years ago, had pillowed his head upon her bosom and left her parting kiss upon his lips? How should he reveal himself to her? Might not sudden joy do what years of sorrow had failed to accomplish? Controlling his feelings as best he could, he rose to tell his experience. He referred to the days when they used to hold their meetings in the lonely woods and gloomy swamps. How they had prayed for freedom and plotted to desert to the Union army; and continuing, he said: "Since then, brethren and sisters, I have had my crosses and trials, but I try to look at the mercies. Just think what it was then and what it is now! How many of us, since freedom has come, have been looking up our scattered relatives. I have just been over to visit my old mistress, Nancy Johnson, and to see if I could get some clue to my long-lost mother, who was sold from me nearly thirty years ago."

Again there was a chorus of moans.

On resuming, Robert's voice was still fuller of pathos. "When," he said, "I heard that dear old mother tell her experience it seemed as if some one had risen from the dead. She made me think of my own dear mother, who used to steal out at night to see me, fold me in her arms, and then steal back again to her work. After she was sold away I never saw her face again by daylight. I have been looking for her ever since the war, and I think at last I have got on the right track. If Mrs. Johnson, who kept the boarding-house in C——, is the one who sold that dear old mother from her son, then she is the one I am looking for, and I am the son she has been praying for."

The dear old mother raised her eyes. They were clear and tearless. An expression of wonder, hope, and love flitted over her face. It seemed as if her youth were suddenly renewed and, bounding from her seat, she rushed to the speaker in a paroxysm of joy. "Oh, Robby! Robby! is dis you? Is dat my pore, dear boy I'se been prayin' 'bout all dese years? Oh, glory! glory!" And overflowing with joyous excitement she threw her arms around him, looking the very impersonation of rapturous content. It was a happy time. Mothers whose children had been torn from them in the days of slavery knew how to rejoice in her joy. The young people caught the infection of the general happiness and rejoiced with them that rejoiced. There were songs of rejoicing and shouts of praise. The undertone of sadness which had so often mingled with their songs gave place to strains of exultation; and tears of tender sympathy flowed from eyes which had often been blurred by anguish. The child of many prayers and tears was restored to his mother.

Iola stood by the mother's side, smiling, and weeping tears of joy. When Robert's mother observed Iola, she said to Robert, "Is dis yore wife?"

"Oh, no," replied Robert, "but I believe she is your grandchild, the daughter of the little girl who was sold away from you so long ago. She is on her way to the farther South in search of her mother."

"Is she? Dear chile! I hope she'll fine her! She puts me in mine ob my pore little Marie. Well, I'se got one chile, an' I means to keep on prayin' tell I fine my daughter. I'm *so* happy! I feel's like a new woman!"

"My dear mother," said Robert, "now that I have found you, I mean to hold you fast just as long as you live. Ever since the war I have been trying to find out if you were living, but all efforts failed. At last, I thought I would come and hunt you myself and, now that I have found you, I am going to take you home to live with me, and to be as happy as the days are long. I am living in the North, and doing a good business there. I want you to see joy according to all the days wherein you have seen sorrow. I do hope this young lady will find *her* ma and that, when found, she will prove to be your daughter!"

"Yes, pore, dear chile! I specs her mudder's heart's mighty hungry fer her. I does hope she's my gran'chile."

Tenderly and caressingly Iola bent over the happy mother, with her heart filled with mournful memories of her own mother.

Aunt Linda was induced to stay until the next morning, and then gladly assisted Robert's mother in arranging for her journey northward. The friends who had given her a shelter in their hospitable home, learned to value her so much that it was with great reluctance they resigned her to the care of her son. Aunt Linda was full of bustling activity, and her spirits overflowed with good humor.

"Now, Harriet," she said, as they rode along on their return journey, "you mus' jis' thank me fer finin' yore chile, 'cause I got him to come to dat big meetin' wid me."

"Oh, Lindy," she cried, "I'se glad from de bottom ob my heart ter see you's all. I com'd out dere ter git a blessin', an' I'se got a double po'tion. De frens I war libin' wid war mighty good ter me. Dey lib'd wid me in de lower kentry, an' arter de war war ober I stopped wid 'em and helped take keer ob de chillen; an' when dey com'd up yere dey brought me wid 'em. I'se com'd a way I didn't know, but I'se mighty glad I'se com'd."

"Does you know dis place?" asked Aunt Linda, as they approached the settlement.

"No'n 'deed I don't. It's all new ter me."

"Well, dis is whar I libs. Ain't you mighty tired? I feels a little stiffish. Dese bones is gittin' ole."

"Dat's so! But I'se mighty glad I'se lib'd to see my

boy 'fore I crossed ober de riber. An' now I feel like ole Simeon."

"But, mother," said Robert, "if you are ready to go, I am not willing to let you. I want you to stay ever so long where I can see you."

A bright smile overspread her face. Robert's words reassured and gladdened her heart. She was well satisfied to have a pleasant aftermath from life on this side of the river.

After arriving home Linda's first thought was to prepare dinner for her guests. But, before she began her work of preparation, she went to the cupboard to get a cup of home-made wine.

"Here," she said, filling three glasses, "is some wine I made myself from dat grape-vine out dere. Don't it look nice and clar? Jist taste it. It's fus'-rate."

"No, thank you," said Robert. "I'm a temperance man, and never take anything which has alcohol in it."

"Oh, dis ain't got a bit ob alcohol in it. I made it myself."

"But, Aunt Linda, you didn't make the law which ferments grape-juice and makes it alcohol."

"But, Robby, ef alcohol's so bad, w'at made de Lord put it here?"

"Aunt Lindy," said Iola, "I heard a lady say that there were two things the Lord didn't make. One is sin, and the other alcohol."

"Why, Aunt Linda," said Robert, "there are numbers of things the Lord has made that I wouldn't touch with a pair of tongs."

"What are they?"

"Rattlesnakes, scorpions, and moccasins."

"Oh, sho!"

"Aunt Linda," said Iola, "the Bible says that the wine at last will bite like a serpent and sting like an adder."

"And, Aunt Linda," added Robert, "as I wouldn't wind a serpent around my throat, I don't want to put something inside of it which will bite like a serpent and sting as an adder."

"I reckon Robby's right," said his mother, setting down her glass and leaving the wine unfinished. "You young folks knows a heap more dan we ole folks."

"Well," declared Aunt Linda, "you all is temp'rence

to de backbone. But what could I do wid my wine ef we didn't drink it?"

"Let it turn to vinegar, and sign the temperance pledge," replied Robert.

"I don't keer 'bout it myself, but I don't 'spect John would be willin' ter let it go, 'cause he likes it a heap."

"Then you must give it up for his sake and Job's," said Robert. "They may learn to like it too well."

"You know, Aunt Linda," said Iola, "people don't get to be drunkards all at once. And you wouldn't like to feel, if Job should learn to drink, that you helped form his appetite."

"Dat' so! I beliebs I'll let dis turn to winegar, an' not make any more."

"That's right, Aunt Linda. I hope you'll hold to it," said Robert, encouragingly.

Very soon Aunt Linda had an excellent dinner prepared. After it was over Robert went with Iola to C——, where her friend, the bishop, was awaiting her return. She told him the wonderful story of Robert's finding his mother, and of her sweet, childlike faith.

The bishop, a kind, fatherly man, said, "Miss Iola, I hope that such happiness is in store for you. My dear child, still continue to pray and trust. I am old-fashioned enough to believe in prayer. I knew an old lady living in Illinois, who was a slave. Her son got a chance to come North and beg money to buy his mother. The mother was badly treated, and made up her mind to run away. But before she started she thought she would kneel down to pray. And something, she said, reasoned within her, and whispered, 'Stand still and see what I am going to do for you.' So real was it to her that she unpacked her bundle and desisted from her flight. Strange as it may appear to you, her son returned, bringing with him money enough to purchase her freedom, and she was redeemed from bondage. Had she persisted in running away she might have been lost in the woods and have died, exhausted by starvation. But she believed, she trusted, and was delivered. Her son took her North, where she could find a resting place for the soles of her feet."

That night Iola and the bishop left for the South.

CHAPTER XXI

A Home for Mother

AFTER IOLA HAD left the settlement, accompanied by Robert as far as the town, it was a pleasant satisfaction for the two old friends to settle themselves down, and talk of times past, departed friends, and long-forgotten scenes.

"What," said Mrs. Johnson, as we shall call Robert's mother, "hab become ob Miss Nancy's husband? Is he still a libin'?"

"Oh, he drunk hisself to death," responded Aunt Linda.

"He used ter be mighty handsome."

"Yes, but drink war his ruination."

"An' how's Miss Nancy?"

"Oh, she's com'd down migh'ly. She's pore as a church mouse. I thought 'twould com'd home ter her wen she sole yer 'way from yore chillen. Dere's nuffin goes ober de debil's back dat don't come under his belly. Do yo 'member Miss Nancy's fardder?"

"Ob course I does!"

"Well," said Aunt Linda, "he war a nice ole gemmen. Wen he died, I said de las' gemmen's dead, an' dere's noboddy ter step in his shoes."

"Pore Miss Nancy!" exclaimed Robert's mother. "I ain't nothin' agin her. But I wouldn't swap places wid her, 'cause I'se got my son; an' I beliebs he'll do a good part by me."

"Mother," said Robert, as he entered the room, "I've brought an old friend to see you. Do you remember Uncle Daniel?"

Uncle Daniel threw back his head, reached out his hand, and manifested his joy with "Well, Haryet! is dis you? I neber 'spected to see you in dese lower grouns! How does yer do? an' whar hab you bin all dis time?"

"O, I'se been tossin' roun' 'bout; but it's all com'd right at las'. I'se lib'd to see my boy 'fore I died."

"My wife an' boys is in glory," said Uncle Daniel. "But I 'spects to see 'em 'fore long. 'Cause I'se tryin' to dig deep, build sure, an' make my way from earth ter glory."

"Dat's de right kine ob talk, Dan'el. We ole folks ain't got long ter stay yere."

They chatted together until Job and Salters came home for supper. After they had eaten, Uncle Daniel said:—

"We'll hab a word ob prayer."

There, in that peaceful habitation, they knelt down, and mingled their prayers together, as they had done in bygone days, when they had met by stealth in lonely swamps or silent forests.

The next morning Robert and his mother started northward. They were well supplied with a bountiful luncheon by Aunt Linda, who had so thoroughly enjoyed their sojourn with her. On the next day he arrived in the city of P——, and took his mother to his boarding-house, until he could find a suitable home into which to install her. He soon came across one which just suited his taste, but when the agent discovered that Robert's mother was colored, he told him that the house had been previously engaged. In company with his mother he looked at several other houses in desirable neighborhoods, but they were constantly met with the answer, "The house is engaged," or, "We do not rent to colored people."

At length Robert went alone, and, finding a desirable house, engaged it, and moved into it. In a short time it was discovered that he was colored, and, at the behest of the local sentiment of the place, the landlord used his utmost endeavors to oust him, simply because he belonged to an unfashionable and unpopular race. At last he came across a landlord who was broad enough to rent him a good house, and he found a quiet resting place among a set of well-to-do and well-disposed people.

Further Lifting of the Veil

IN ONE OF those fearful conflicts by which the Mississippi was freed from Rebel intrusion and opened to commerce Harry was severely wounded, and forced to leave his place in the ranks for a bed in the hospital.

One day, as he lay in his bed, thinking of his former home in Mississippi and wondering if the chances of war would ever restore him to his loved ones, he fell into a quiet slumber. When he awoke he found a lady bending over him, holding in her hands some fruit and flowers. As she tenderly bent over Harry's bed their eyes met, and with a thrill of gladness they recognized each other.

"Oh, my son, my son!" cried Marie, trying to repress her emotion, as she took his wasted hand in hers, and kissed the pale cheeks that sickness and suffering had blanched. Harry was very weak, but her presence was a call to life. He returned the pressure of her hand, kissed it, and his eyes grew full of sudden light, as he murmured faintly, but joyfully:—

"Mamma; oh, mamma! have I found you at last?"

The effort was too much, and he immediately became unconscious.

Anxious, yet hopeful, Marie sat by the bedside of her son till consciousness was restored. Caressingly she bent over his couch, murmuring in her happiness the tenderest, sweetest words of motherly love. In Harry's veins flowed new life and vigor, calming the restlessness of his nerves.

As soon as possible Harry was carried to his mother's home; a home brought into the light of freedom by the victories of General Grant. Nursed by his mother's tender, loving care, he rapidly recovered, but, being too disabled to re-enter the army, he was honorably discharged.

Lorraine had taken Marie to Vicksburg, and there allowed her to engage in confectionery and preserving for the wealthy ladies of the city. He had at first attempted to refugee with her in Texas, but, being foiled in the attempt, he was compelled to enlist in the Confederate Army, and met his fate by being killed just before the surrender of Vicksburg.

"My dear son," Marie would say, as she bent fondly over him, "I am deeply sorry that you are wounded, but I am glad that the fortunes of war have brought us together. Poor Iola! I *do* wonder what has become of her? Just as soon as this war is over I want you to search the country all over. Poor child! How my heart has ached for her!"

Time passed on. Harry and his mother searched and inquired for Iola, but no tidings of her reached them.

Having fully recovered his health, and seeing the great need of education for the colored people, Harry turned his attention toward them, and joined the new army of Northern teachers.

He still continued his inquiries for his sister, not knowing whether or not she had succumbed to the cruel change in her life. He thought she might have passed into the white basis for the sake of bettering her fortunes. Hope deferred, which had sickened his mother's heart, had only roused him to renewed diligence.

A school was offered him in Georgia, and thither he repaired, taking his mother with him. They were soon established in the city of A——. In hope of finding Iola he visited all the conferences of the Methodist Church, but for a long time his search was in vain.

"Mamma," said Harry, one day during his vacation, "there is to be a Methodist Conference in this State in the city of S——, about one hundred and fifty miles from here. I intend to go and renew my search for Iola."

"Poor child!" burst out Marie, as the tears gathered in her eyes, "I wonder if she is living."

"I think so," said Harry, kissing the pale cheek of his mother; "I don't feel that Iola is dead. I believe we will find her before long."

"It seems to me my heart would burst with joy to see my dear child just once more. I am glad that you are going. When will you leave?"

"To-morrow morning."

"Well, my son, go, and my prayers will go with you," was Marie's tender parting wish.

Early next morning Harry started for the conference, and reached the church before the morning session was over. Near him sat two ladies, one fair, the other considerably darker. There was something in the fairer one that reminded him forcibly of his sister, but she was much older and graver than he imagined his sister to be. Instantly he dismissed the thought that had forced itself into his mind, and began to listen attentively to the proceedings of the conference.

When the regular business of the morning session was over the bishop arose and said:—

"I have an interesting duty to perform. I wish to introduce a young lady to the conference, who was the daughter of a Mississippi planter. She is now in search of her mother and brother, from whom she was sold a few months before the war. Her father married her mother in Ohio, where he had taken her to be educated. After his death they were robbed of their inheritance and enslaved by a distant relative named Lorraine. Miss Iola Leroy is the young lady's name. If any one can give the least information respecting the objects of her search it will be thankfully received."

"I can," exclaimed a young man, rising in the midst of the audience, and pressing eagerly, almost impetuously, forward. "I am her brother, and I came here to look for her."

Iola raised her eyes to his face, so flushed and bright with the glow of recognition, rushed to him, threw her arms around his neck, kissed him again and again, crying: "O, Harry!" Then she fainted from excitement. The women gathered around her with expressions of tender sympathy, and gave her all the care she needed. They called her the "dear child," for without any effort on her part she had slidden into their hearts and found a ready welcome in each sympathizing bosom.

Harry at once telegraphed the glad tidings to his mother, who waited their coming with joyful anticipation. Long before the cars reached the city, Mrs. Leroy was at the depot, restlessly walking the platform or ea-

gerly peering into the darkness to catch the first glimpse
of the train which was bearing her treasures.

At length the cars arrived, and, as Harry and Iola
alighted, Marie rushed forward, clasped Iola in her arms
and sobbed out her joy in broken words.

Very happy was the little family that sat together
around the supper-table for the first time for years. They
partook of that supper with thankful hearts and with eyes
overflowing with tears of joy. Very touching were the
prayers the mother uttered, when she knelt with her
children that night to return thanks for their happy reunion, and to seek protection through the slumbers of
the night.

The next morning, as they sat at the breakfast-table,
Marie said:—

"My dear child, you are so changed I do not think I
would have known you if I had met you in the street!"

"And I," said Harry, "can hardly realize that you are
our own Iola, whom I recognized as sister a half dozen
years ago."

"Am I so changed?" asked Iola, as a faint sigh escaped
her lips.

"Why, Iola," said Harry, "you used to be the most
harum-scarum girl I ever knew—laughing, dancing, and
singing from morning until night."

"Yes, I remember," said Iola. "It all comes back to
me like a dream. Oh, mamma! I have passed through a
fiery ordeal of suffering since then. But it is useless,"
and as she continued her face assumed a brighter look,
"to brood over the past. Let us be happy in the present.
Let me tell you something which will please you. Do you
remember telling me about your mother and brother?"

"Yes," said Marie, in a questioning tone.

"Well," continued Iola, with eyes full of gladness, "I
think I have found them."

"Can it be possible!" exclaimed Marie, in astonishment. "It is more than thirty years since we parted. I
fear you are mistaken."

"No, mamma; I have drawn my conclusions from good
circumstantial evidence. After I was taken from you, I
passed through a fearful siege of suffering, which would
only harrow up your soul to hear. I often shudder at the
remembrance. The last man in whose clutches I found

myself was mean, brutal, and cruel. I was in his power
when the Union army came into C——, where I was
living. A number of colored men stampeded to the Union
ranks, with a gentleman as a leader, whom I think is
your brother. A friend of his reported my case to the
commander of the post, who instantly gave orders for my
release. A place was given me as nurse in the hospital. I
attended that friend in his last illness. Poor fellow! he
was the best friend I had in all the time I have been
tossing about. The gentleman whom I think is your
brother appeared to be very anxious about his friend's
recovery, and was deeply affected by his death. In one
of the last terrible battles of the war, that of Five Forks,
he was wounded and put into the hospital ward where I
was an attendant. For a while he was delirious, and in
his delirium he would sometimes think that I was his
mother and at other times his sister. I humored his fancies, would often sing to him when he was restless, and
my voice almost invariably soothed him to sleep. One
day I sang to him that old hymn we used to sing on the
plantation:—

> "Drooping souls no longer grieve,
>   Heaven is propitious;
> If on Christ you do believe,
>   You will find Him precious."

"I remember," said Marie, with a sigh, as memories
of the past swept over her.

"After I had finished the hymn," continued Iola, "he
looked earnestly and inquiringly into my face, and asked,
'Where did you learn that hymn? I have heard my
mother sing it when I was a boy, but I have never heard
it since.' I think, mamma, the words, 'I was lost but now
I'm found; glory! glory! glory!' had imprinted themselves
on his memory, and that his mind was assuming a higher
state of intellectuality. He asked me to sing it again,
which I did, until he fell asleep. Then I noticed a marked
resemblance between him and Harry, and I thought,
'Suppose he should prove to be your long-lost brother?'
During his convalescence we found that we had a common ground of sympathy. We were anxious to be re-
united to our severed relations. We had both been

separated from our mothers. He told me of his little sister, with whom he used to play. She had a mole on her cheek which he called her beauty spot. He had the red spot on his forehead which you told me of."

CHAPTER XXIII

Delightful Reunions

VERY BRIGHT AND HAPPY was the home where Marie and her children were gathered under one roof. Mrs. Leroy's neighbors said she looked ten years younger. Into that peaceful home came no fearful forebodings of cruel separations. Harry and Iola were passionately devoted to their mother, and did all they could to flood her life with sunshine.

"Iola, dear," said Harry, one morning at the breakfast-table, "I have a new pleasure in store for you."

"What is it, brother mine?" asked Iola, assuming an air of interest.

"There is a young lady living in this city to whom I wish to introduce you. She is one of the most remarkable women I have ever met."

"Do tell me all about her," said Iola. "Is she young and handsome, brilliant and witty?"

"She," replied Harry, "is more than handsome, she is lovely; more than witty, she is wise; more than brilliant, she is excellent."

"Well, Harry," said Mrs. Leroy, smiling, "if you keep on that way I shall begin to fear that I shall soon be supplanted by a new daughter."

"Oh, no, mamma," replied Harry, looking slightly confused, "I did not mean that."

"Well, Harry," said Iola, amused, "go on with your description; I am becoming interested. Tax your powers of description to give me her likeness."

"Well, in the first place," continued Harry, "I suppose she is about twenty-five years old."

"Oh, the idea," interrupted Iola, "of a gentleman talking of a lady's age. That is a tabooed subject."

"Why, Iola, that adds to the interest of my picture. It

is her combination of earnestness and youthfulness which enhances her in my estimation."

"Pardon the interruption," said Iola; "I am anxious to hear more about her."

"Well, she is of medium height, somewhat slender, and well formed, with dark, expressive eyes, full of thought and feeling. Neither hair nor complexion show the least hint of blood admixture."

"I am glad of it," said Iola. "Every person of unmixed blood who succeeds in any department of literature, art, or science is a living argument for the capability which is in the race."

"Yes," responded Harry, "for it is not the white blood which is on trial before the world. Well, I will bring her around this evening."

In the evening Harry brought Miss Delany to call on his sister and mother. They were much pleased with their visitor. Her manner was a combination of suavity and dignity. During the course of the evening they learned that she was a graduate of the University of A——. One day she saw in the newspapers that colored women were becoming unfit to be servants for white people. She then thought that if they are not fit to be servants for white people, they are unfit to be mothers to their own children, and she conceived the idea of opening a school to train future wives and mothers. She began on a small scale, in a humble building, and her work was soon crowned with gratifying success. She had enlarged her quarters, increased her teaching force, and had erected a large and commodious school-house through her own exertions and the help of others.

Marie cordially invited her to call again, saying, as she rose to go: "I am very glad to have met you. Young women like you always fill my heart with hope for the future of our race. In you I see reflected some of the blessed possibilities which lie within us."

"Thank you," said Miss Delany, "I want to be classed among those of whom it is said, 'She has done what she could.'"

Very pleasant was the acquaintance which sprang up between Miss Delany and Iola. Although she was older than Iola, their tastes were so congenial, their views of life and duty in such unison, that their acquaintance soon ripened into strong and lasting friendship. There were no foolish rivalries and jealousies between them. Their lives were too full of zeal and earnestness for them to waste in selfishness their power to be moral and spiritual forces among a people who so much needed their helping hands. Miss Delany gave Iola a situation in her school; but before the term was quite over she was forced to resign, her health having been so undermined by the fearful strain through which she had passed, that she was quite unequal to the task. She remained at home, and did what her strength would allow in assisting her mother in the work of canning and preserving fruits.

In the meantime, Iola had been corresponding with Robert. She had told him of her success in finding her mother and brother, and had received an answer congratulating her on the glad fruition of her hopes. He also said that his business was flourishing, that his mother was keeping house for him, and, to use her own expression, was as happy as the days are long. She was firmly persuaded that Marie was her daughter, and she wanted to see her before she died.

"There is one thing," continued the letter, "that your mother may remember her by. It was a little handkerchief on which were a number of cats' heads. She gave one to each of us."

"I remember it well," said Marie, "she must, indeed, be my mother. Now, all that is needed to complete my happiness is her presence, and my brother's. And I intend, if I live long enough, to see them both."

Iola wrote Robert that her mother remembered the incident of the handkerchief, and was anxious to see them.

In the early fall Robert started for the South in order to clear up all doubts with respect to their relationship. He found Iola, Harry, and their mother living cosily together. Harry was teaching and was a leader among the rising young men of the State. His Northern education and later experience had done much toward adapting him to the work of the new era which had dawned upon the South.

Marie was very glad to welcome Robert to her home, but it was almost impossible to recognize her brother in that tall, handsome man, with dark-brown eyes and wealth of chestnut-colored hair, which he readily lifted to show the crimson spot which lay beneath it.

But as they sat together, and recalled the long-forgotten scenes of their childhood, they concluded that they were brother and sister.

"Marie," said Robert, "how would you like to leave the South?"

"I should like to go North, but I hate to leave Harry. He's a splendid young fellow, although I say it myself. He is so fearless and outspoken that I am constantly anxious about him, especially at election time."

Harry then entered the room, and, being introduced to Robert, gave him a cordial welcome. He had just returned from school.

"We were talking of you, my son," said Marie.

"What were you saying? Nothing of the absent but good?" asked Harry.

"I was telling your uncle, who wants me to come North, that I would go, but I am afraid that you will get into trouble and be murdered, as many others have been."

"Oh, well, mother, I shall not die till my time comes. And if I die helping the poor and needy, I shall die at my post. Could a man choose a better place to die?"

"Were you aware of the virulence of caste prejudice and the disabilities which surround the colored people when you cast your lot with them?" asked Robert.

"Not fully," replied Harry; "but after I found out that I was colored, I consulted the principal of the school, where I was studying, in reference to the future. He said that if I stayed in the North, he had friends whom he believed would give me any situation I could fill, and I could simply take my place in the rank of workers, the same as any other man. Then he told me of the army, and I made up my mind to enter it, actuated by a desire to find my mother and sister; and at any rate I wanted to avenge their wrongs. I do not feel so now. Since I have seen the fearful ravages of war, I have learned to pity and forgive. The principal said he thought I would be more apt to find my family if I joined a colored regiment in the West than if I joined one of the Maine companies. I confess at first I felt a shrinking from taking the step, but love for my mother overcame all repugnance on my part. Now that I have linked my fortunes to the race I intend to do all I can for its elevation."

As he spoke Robert gazed admiringly on the young face, lit up by noble purposes and lofty enthusiasm.

"You are right, Harry. I think it would be treason, not only to the race, but to humanity, to have you ignoring your kindred and masquerading as a white man."

"I think so, too," said Marie.

"But, sister, I am anxious for you all to come North. If Harry feels that the place of danger is the post of duty, let him stay, and he can spend his vacations with us. I think both you and Iola need rest and change. Mother longs to see you before she dies. She feels that we have been the children of many prayers and tears, and I want to make her last days as happy as possible. The South has not been a paradise to you all the time, and I should think you would be willing to leave it."

"Yes, that is so. Iola needs rest and change, and she would be such a comfort to mother. I suppose, for her sake, I will consent to have her go back with you, at least for a while."

In a few days, with many prayers and tears, Marie, half reluctantly, permitted Iola to start for the North in company with Robert Johnson, intending to follow as soon as she could settle her business and see Harry in a good boarding place.

Very joyful was the greeting of the dear grandmother. Iola soon nestled in her heart and lent additional sunshine to her once checkered life, and Robert, who had so long been robbed of kith and kin, was delighted with the new accession to his home life.

CHAPTER XXIV

Northern Experience

"UNCLE ROBERT," said Iola, after she had been North several weeks, "I have a theory that every woman ought to know how to earn her own living. I believe that a great amount of sin and misery springs from the weakness and inefficiency of women."

"Perhaps that's so, but what are you going to do about it?"

"I am going to join the great rank of bread-winners. Mr. Waterman has advertised for a number of saleswomen, and I intend to make application."

"When he advertises for help he means white women," said Robert.

"He said nothing about color," responded Iola.

"I don't suppose he did. He doesn't expect any colored girl to apply."

"Well, I think I could fill the place. At least I should like to try. And I do not think when I apply that I am in duty bound to tell him my great-grandmother was a negro."

"Well, child, there is no necessity for you to go out to work. You are perfectly welcome here, and I hope that you feel so."

"Oh, I certainly do. But still I would rather earn my own living."

That morning Iola applied for the situation, and, being prepossessing in her appearance, she obtained it.

For a while everything went as pleasantly as a marriage bell. But one day a young colored lady, well-dressed and well-bred in her manner, entered the store. It was an acquaintance which Iola had formed in the colored church which she attended. Iola gave her a few words of cordial greeting, and spent a few moments chatting with her. The attention of the girls who sold at the same counter was attracted, and their suspicion awakened. Iola was a stranger in that city. Who was she, and who were her people? At last it was decided that one of the girls should act as a spy, and bring what information she could concerning Iola.

The spy was successful. She found out that Iola was living in a good neighborhood, but that none of the neighbors knew her. The man of the house was very fair, but there was an old woman whom Iola called "Grandma," and she was unmistakably colored. The story was sufficient. If that were true, Iola must be colored, and she could be treated accordingly.

Without knowing the cause, Iola noticed a chill in the social atmosphere of the store, which communicated itself to the cash-boys, and they treated her so insolently that her situation became very uncomfortable. She saw the proprietor, resigned her position, and asked for and obtained a letter of recommendation to another merchant who had advertised for a saleswoman.

In applying for the place, she took the precaution to inform her employer that she was colored. It made no difference to him; but he said:—

"Don't say anything about it to the girls. They might not be willing to work with you."

Iola smiled, did not promise, and accepted the situation. She entered upon her duties, and proved quite acceptable as a saleswoman.

One day, during an interval in business, the girls began to talk of their respective churches, and the question was put to Iola:—

"Where do you go to church?"

"I go," she replied, "to Rev. River's church, corner of Eighth and L Streets."

"Oh, no; you must be mistaken. There is no church there except a colored one."

"That is where I go."

"Why do you go there?"

"Because I liked it when I came here, and joined it."

"A member of a colored church? What under heaven possessed you to do such a thing?"

"Because I wished to be with my own people."

Here the interrogator stopped, and looked surprised and pained, and almost instinctively moved a little farther from her. After the store was closed, the girls had an animated discussion, which resulted in the information being sent to Mr. Cohen that Iola was a colored girl, and that they protested against her being continued in his employ. Mr. Cohen yielded to the pressure, and informed Iola that her services were no longer needed.

When Robert came home in the evening, he found that Iola had lost her situation, and was looking somewhat discouraged.

"Well, uncle," she said, "I feel out of heart. It seems as if the prejudice pursues us through every avenue of life, and assigns us the lowest places."

"That is so," replied Robert, thoughtfully.

"And yet I am determined," said Iola, "to win for myself a place in the fields of labor. I have heard of a place in New England, and I mean to try for it, even if I only stay a few months."

"Well, if you *will* go, say nothing about your color."

"Uncle Robert, I see no necessity for proclaiming that fact on the house-top. Yet I am resolved that nothing shall tempt me to deny it. The best blood in my veins is African blood, and I am not ashamed of it."

"Hurrah for you!" exclaimed Robert, laughing heartily.

As Iola wished to try the world for herself, and so be prepared for any emergency, her uncle and grandmother were content to have her go to New England. The town to which she journeyed was only a few hours' ride from the city of P——, and Robert, knowing that there is no teacher like experience, was willing that Iola should have the benefit of her teaching.

Iola, on arriving in H——, sought the firm, and was informed that her services were needed. She found it a pleasant and lucrative position. There was only one drawback—her boarding place was too far from her work. There was an institution conducted by professed Christian women, which was for the special use of respectable young working girls. This was in such a desirable location that she called at the house to engage board.

The matron conducted her over the house, and grew so friendly in the interview that she put her arm around her, and seemed to look upon Iola as a desirable accession to the home. But, just as Iola was leaving, she said to the matron: "I must be honest with you; I am a colored woman."

Swift as light a change passed over the face of the matron. She withdrew her arm from Iola, and said: "I must see the board of managers about it."

When the board met, Iola's case was put before them, but they decided not to receive her. And these women, professors of a religion which taught, "If ye have respect to persons ye commit sin," virtually shut the door in her face because of the outcast blood in her veins.

Considerable feeling was aroused by the action of these women, who, to say the least, had not put their religion in the most favorable light.

Iola continued to work for the firm until she received letters from her mother and uncle, which informed her that her mother, having arranged her affairs in the South, was ready to come North. She then resolved to return to the city of P——, to be ready to welcome her mother on her arrival.

Iola arrived in time to see that everything was in order for her mother's reception. Her room was furnished neatly, but with those touches of beauty that womanly hands are such adepts in giving. A few charming pictures adorned the walls, and an easy chair stood waiting to receive the travel-worn mother. Robert and Iola met her at the depot; and grandma was on her feet at the first sound of the bell, opened the door, clasped Marie to her heart, and nearly fainted for joy.

"Can it be possible dat dis is my little Marie?" she exclaimed.

It did seem almost impossible to realize that this faded woman, with pale cheeks and prematurely whitened hair, was the rosy-cheeked child from whom she had been parted more than thirty years.

"Well," said Robert, after the first joyous greeting was over, "love is a very good thing, but Marie has had a long journey and needs something that will stick by the ribs. How about dinner, mother?"

"It's all ready," said Mrs. Johnson.

After Marie had gone to her room and changed her dress, she came down and partook of the delicious repast which her mother and Iola had prepared for her.

In a few days Marie was settled in the home, and was

well pleased with the change. The only drawback to her happiness was the absence of her son, and she expected him to come North after the closing of his school.

"Uncle Robert," said Iola, after her mother had been with them several weeks, "I am tired of being idle."

"What's the matter now?" asked Robert. "You are surely not going East again, and leave your mother?"

"Oh, I hope not," said Marie, anxiously. "I have been so long without you."

"No, mamma, I am not going East. I can get suitable employment here in the city of P——."

"But, Iola," said Robert, "you have tried, and been defeated. Why subject yourself to the same experience again?"

"Uncle Robert, I think that every woman should have some skill or art which would insure her at least a comfortable support. I believe there would be less unhappy marriages if labor were more honored among women."

"Well, Iola," said her mother, "what is your skill?"

"Nursing. I was very young when I went into the hospital, but I succeeded so well that the doctor said I must have been a born nurse. Now, I see by the papers, that a gentleman who has an invalid daughter wants some one who can be a nurse and companion for her, and I mean to apply for the situation. I do not think, if I do my part well in that position, that the blood in my veins will be any bar to my success."

A troubled look stole over Marie's face. She sighed faintly, but made no remonstrance. And so it was decided that Iola should apply for the situation.

Iola made application, and was readily accepted. Her patient was a frail girl of fifteen summers, who was ill with a low fever. Iola nursed her carefully, and soon had the satisfaction of seeing her restored to health. During her stay, Mr. Cloten, the father of the invalid, had learned some of the particulars of Iola's Northern experience as a bread-winner, and he resolved to give her employment in his store when her services were no longer needed in the house. As soon as a vacancy occurred he gave Iola a place in his store.

The morning she entered on her work he called his employees together, and told them that Miss Iola had colored blood in her veins, but that he was going to employ her and give her a desk. If any one objected to working with her, he or she could step to the cashier's desk and receive what was due. Not a man remonstrated, not a woman demurred; and Iola at last found a place in the great army of bread-winners, which the traditions of her blood could not affect.

"How did you succeed?" asked Mrs. Cloten of her husband, when he returned to dinner.

"Admirably! 'Everything is lovely and the goose hangs high.' I gave my employees to understand that they could leave if they did not wish to work with Miss Leroy. Not one of them left, or showed any disposition to rebel."

"I am very glad," said Mrs. Cloten. "I am ashamed of the way she has been treated in our city, when seeking to do her share in the world's work. I am glad that you were brave enough to face this cruel prejudice, and give her a situation."

"Well, my dear, do not make me a hero for a single act. I am grateful for the care Miss Leroy gave our Daisy. Money can buy services, but it cannot purchase tender, loving sympathy. I was also determined to let my employees know that I, not they, commanded my business. So, do not crown me a hero until I have won a niche in the temple of fame. In dealing with Southern prejudice against the negro, we Northerners could do it with better grace if we divested ourselves of our own. We irritate the South by our criticisms, and, while I confess that there is much that is reprehensible in their treatment of colored people, yet if our Northern civilization is higher than theirs we should 'criticise by creation.' We should stamp ourselves on the South, and not let the South stamp itself on us. When we have learned to treat men according to the complexion of their souls, and not the color of their skins, we will have given our best contribution towards the solution of the negro problem."

"I feel, my dear," said Mrs. Cloten, "that what you have done is a right step in the right direction, and I hope that other merchants will do the same. We have numbers of business men, rich enough to afford themselves the luxury of a good conscience."

CHAPTER XXV

An Old Friend

"GOOD-MORNING, MISS LEROY," said a cheery voice in tones of glad surprise, and, intercepting her path, Dr. Gresham stood before Iola, smiling, and reaching out his hand.

"Why, Dr. Gresham, is this you?" said Iola, lifting her eyes to that well-remembered face. "It has been several years since we met. How have you been all this time, and where?"

"I have been sick, and am just now recovering from malaria and nervous prostration. I am attending a medical convention in this city, and hope that I shall have the pleasure of seeing you again."

Iola hesitated, and then replied: "I should be pleased to have you call."

"It would give me great pleasure. Where shall I call?"

"My home is 1006 South Street, but I am only at home in the evenings."

They walked together a short distance till they reached Mr. Cloten's store; then, bidding the doctor good morning, Iola left him repeating to himself the words of his favorite poet:—

"Thou art too lovely and precious a gem
To be bound to their burdens and sullied by them."

No one noticed the deep flush on Iola's face as she entered the store, nor the subdued, quiet manner with which she applied herself to her tasks. She was living over again the past, with its tender, sad, and thrilling reminiscences.

In the evening Dr. Gresham called on Iola. She met him with a pleasant welcome. Dr. Gresham gazed upon her with unfeigned admiration, and thought that the years, instead of detracting from, had only intensified, her loveliness. He had thought her very beautiful in the hospital, in her gray dress and white collar, with her glorious wealth of hair drawn over her ears. But now, when he saw her with that hair artistically arranged, and her finely-proportioned form arrayed in a dark crimson dress, relieved by a shimmer of lace and a bow of white ribbon at her throat, he thought her superbly handsome. The lines which care had written upon her young face had faded away. There was no undertone of sorrow in her voice as she stood up before him in the calm loveliness of her ripened womanhood, radiant in beauty and gifted in intellect. Time and failing health had left their traces upon Dr. Gresham. His step was less bounding, his cheek a trifle paler, his manner somewhat graver than it was when he had parted from Iola in the hospital, but his meeting with her had thrilled his heart with unexpected pleasure. Hopes and sentiments which long had slept awoke at the touch of her hand and the tones of her voice, and Dr. Gresham found himself turning to the past, with its sad memories and disappointed hopes. No other face had displaced her image in his mind; no other love had woven itself around every tendril of his soul. His heart and hand were just as free as they were the hour they had parted.

"To see you again," said Dr. Gresham, "is a great and unexpected pleasure."

"You had not forgotten me, then?" said Iola, smiling.

"Forget you! I would just as soon forget my own existence. I do not think that time will ever efface the impressions of those days in which we met so often. When last we met you were intending to search for your mother. Have you been successful?"

"More than successful," said Iola, with a joyous ring in her voice. "I have found my mother, brother, grandmother, and uncle, and, except my brother, we are all living together, and we are so happy. Excuse me a few minutes," she said, and left the room. Iola soon returned, bringing with her her mother and grandmother.

"These," said Iola, introducing her mother and grandmother, "are the once-severed branches of our family; and this gentleman you have seen before," continued Iola, as Robert entered the room.

Dr. Gresham looked scrutinizingly at him and said: "Your face looks familiar, but I saw so many faces at the hospital that I cannot just now recall your name."

"Doctor," said Robert Johnson, "I was one of your last patients, and I was with Tom Anderson when he died."

"Oh, yes," replied Dr. Gresham; "it all comes back to me. You were wounded at the battle of Five Forks, were you not?"

"Yes," said Robert.

"I saw you when you were recovering. You told me that you thought you had a clue to your lost relatives, from whom you had been so long separated. How have you succeeded?"

"Admirably! I have been fortunate in finding my mother, my sister, and her children."

"Ah, indeed! I am delighted to hear it. Where are they?"

"They are right here. This is my mother," said Robert, bending fondly over her, as she returned his recognition with an expression of intense satisfaction; "and this," he continued, "is my sister, and Miss Leroy is my niece."

"Is it possible! I am very glad to hear it. It has been said that every cloud has its silver lining, and the silver lining of our war cloud is the redemption of a race and the reunion of severed hearts. War is a dreadful thing; but worse than the war was the slavery which preceded it."

"Slavery," said Iola, "was a fearful cancer eating into the nation's heart, sapping its vitality, and undermining its life."

"And war," said Dr. Gresham, "was the dreadful surgery by which the disease was eradicated. The cancer has been removed, but for years to come I fear that we will have to deal with the effects of the disease. But I believe that we have vitality enough to outgrow those effects."

"I think, Doctor," said Iola, "that there is but one remedy by which our nation can recover from the evil entailed upon her by slavery."

"What is that?" asked Robert.

"A fuller comprehension of the claims of the Gospel of Jesus Christ, and their application to our national life."

"Yes," said Robert; "while politicians are stumbling

on the barren mountains of fretful controversy, and asking what shall we do with the negro, I hold that Jesus answered that question nearly two thousand years ago, when he said, 'Whatsoever ye would that men should do to you, do ye even so to them.' "

"Yes," said Dr. Gresham; "the application of that rule in dealing with the negro would solve the whole problem."

"Slavery," said Mrs. Leroy, "is dead, but the spirit which animated it still lives; and I think that a reckless disregard for human life is more the outgrowth of slavery than any actual hatred of the negro."

"The problem of the nation," continued Dr. Gresham, "is not what men will do with the negro, but what will they do with the reckless, lawless white men who murder, lynch, and burn their fellow-citizens. To me these lynchings and burnings are perfectly alarming. Both races have reacted on each other—men fettered the slave, and cramped their own souls; denied him knowledge, and darkened their spiritual insight; subdued him to the pliancy of submission, and in their turn became the thralls of public opinion. The negro came here from the heathenism of Africa; but the young colonies could not take into their early civilization a stream of barbaric blood without being affected by its influence, and the negro, poor and despised as he is, has laid his hands on our Southern civilization and helped mould its character."

"Yes," said Mrs. Leroy; "the colored nurse could not nestle her master's child in her arms, hold up his baby footsteps on their floors, and walk with him through the impressible and formative period of his young life without leaving upon him the impress of her hand."

"I am glad," said Robert, "for the whole nation's sake, that slavery has been destroyed."

"And our work," said Dr. Gresham, "is to build over the desolations of the past a better and brighter future. The great distinction between savagery and civilization is the creation and maintenance of law. A people cannot habitually trample on law and justice without retrograding toward barbarism. But I am hopeful that time will bring us changes for the better; that, as we get farther away from the war, we will outgrow the animosities and prejudices engendered by slavery. The short-sightedness of our fathers linked the negro's destiny to ours. We are feeling the friction of the ligatures which bind us together, but I hope that the time will speedily come when the best members of both races will unite for the maintenance of law and order and the progress and prosperity of the country, and that the intelligence and virtue of the South will be strong to grapple effectually with its ignorance and vice."

"I hope that time will speedily come," said Marie. "My son is in the South, and I am always anxious for his safety. He is not only a teacher, but a leading young man in the community where he lives."

"Yes," said Robert, "and when I see the splendid work he is doing in the South, I am glad that, instead of trying to pass for a white man, he has cast his lot with us."

"But," answered Dr. Gresham, "he would possess advantages as a white man which he could not if he were known to be colored."

"Doctor," said Iola, decidedly, "he has greater advantages as a colored man."

"I do not understand you," said Dr. Gresham, looking somewhat puzzled.

"Doctor," continued Iola, "I do not think life's highest advantages are those that we can see with our eyes or grasp with our hands. To whom to-day is the world most indebted—to its millionaires or to its martyrs?"

"Taking it from the ideal standpoint," replied the doctor, "I should say its martyrs."

"To be," continued Iola, "the leader of a race to higher planes of thought and action, to teach men clearer views of life and duty, and to inspire their souls with loftier aims, is a far greater privilege than it is to open the gates of material prosperity and fill every home with sensuous enjoyment."

"And I," said Mrs. Leroy, her face aglow with fervid feeling, "would rather—ten thousand times rather—see Harry the friend and helper of the poor and ignorant than the companion of men who, under the cover of night, mask their faces and ride the country on lawless raids."

"Dr. Gresham," said Robert, "we ought to be the

leading nation of the earth, whose influence and example should give light to the world."

"Not simply," said Iola, "a nation building up a great material prosperity, founding magnificent cities, grasping the commerce of the world, or excelling in literature, art, and science, but a nation wearing sobriety as a crown and righteousness as the girdle of her loins."

Dr. Gresham gazed admiringly upon Iola. A glow of enthusiasm overspread her beautiful, expressive face. There was a rapt and far-off look in her eye, as if she were looking beyond the present pain to a brighter future for the race with which she was identified, and felt the grandeur of a divine commission to labor for its uplifting.

As Dr. Gresham was parting with Robert, he said: "This meeting has been a very unexpected pleasure. I have spent a delightful evening. I only regret that I had not others to share it with me. A doctor from the South, a regular Bourbon, is stopping at the hotel. I wish he could have been here to-night. Come down to the Concordia, Mr. Johnson, to-morrow night. If you know any colored man who is a strong champion of equal rights, bring him along. Good-night. I shall look for you," said the doctor, as he left the door.

When Robert returned to the parlor he said to Iola: "Dr. Gresham has invited me to come to his hotel to-morrow night, and to bring some wide-awake colored man with me. There is a Southerner whom he wishes me to meet. I suppose he wants to discuss the negro problem, as they call it. He wants some one who can do justice to the subject. I wonder whom I can take with me?"

"I will tell you who, I think, will be a capital one to take with you, and I believe he would go," said Iola.

"Who?" asked Robert.

"Rev. Carmicle, your pastor."

"He is just the one," said Robert, "courteous in his manner and very scholarly in his attainments. He is a man whom if everybody hated him no one could despise him."

CHAPTER XXVI

Open Questions

IN THE EVENING Robert and Rev. Carmicle called on Dr. Gresham, and found Dr. Latrobe, the Southerner, and a young doctor by the name of Latimer, already there. Dr. Gresham introduced Dr. Latrobe, but it was a new experience to receive colored men socially. His wits, however, did not forsake him, and he received the introduction and survived it.

"Permit me, now," said Dr. Gresham, "to introduce you to my friend, Dr. Latimer, who is attending our convention. He expects to go South and labor among the colored people. Don't you think that there is a large field of usefulness before him?"

"Yes," replied Dr. Latrobe, "if he will let politics alone."

"And why let politics alone?" asked Dr. Gresham.

"Because," replied Dr. Latrobe, "we Southerners will never submit to negro supremacy. We will never abandon our Caucasian civilization to an inferior race."

"Have you any reason," inquired Rev. Carmicle, "to dread that a race which has behind it the heathenism of Africa and the slavery of America, with its inheritance of ignorance and poverty, will be able, in less than one generation, to domineer over a race which has behind it ages of dominion, freedom, education, and Christianity?"

A slight shade of vexation and astonishment passed over the face of Dr. Latrobe. He hesitated a moment, then replied:—

"I am not afraid of the negro as he stands alone, but what I dread is that in some closely-contested election ambitious men will use him to hold the balance of power and make him an element of danger. He is ignorant, poor, and clannish, and they may impact him as their policy would direct."

"Any more," asked Robert, "than the leaders of the Rebellion did the ignorant, poor whites during our late conflict?"

"Ignorance, poverty, and clannishness," said Dr. Gresham, "are more social than racial conditions, which may be outgrown."

"And I think," said Rev. Carmicle, "that we are outgrowing them as fast as any other people would have done under the same conditions."

"The negro," replied Dr. Latrobe, "always has been and always will be an element of discord in our country."

"What, then, is your remedy?" asked Dr. Gresham.

"I would eliminate him from the politics of the country."

"As disfranchisement is a punishment for crime, is it just to punish a man before he transgresses the law?" asked Dr. Gresham.

"If," said Dr. Latimer, "the negro is ignorant, poor, and clannish, let us remember that in part of our land it was once a crime to teach him to read. If he is poor, for ages he was forced to bend to unrequited toil. If he is clannish, society has segregated him to himself."

"And even," said Robert, "has given him a negro pew in your churches and a negro seat at your communion table."

"Wisely, or unwisely," said Dr. Gresham, "the Government has put the ballot in his hands. It is better to teach him to use that ballot aright than to intimidate him by violence or vitiate his vote by fraud."

"To-day," said Dr. Latimer, "the negro is not plotting in beer-saloons against the peace and order of society. His fingers are not dripping with dynamite, neither is he spitting upon your flag, nor flaunting the red banner of anarchy in your face."

"Power," said Dr. Gresham, "naturally gravitates into the strongest hands. The class who have the best brain and most wealth can strike with the heaviest hand. I have too much faith in the inherent power of the white race to dread the competition of any other people under heaven."

"I think you Northerners fail to do us justice," said Dr. Latrobe. "The men into whose hands you put the ballot were our slaves, and we would rather die than submit to them. Look at the carpet-bag governments the wicked policy of the Government inflicted upon us. It was only done to humiliate us."

"Oh, no!" said Dr. Gresham, flushing, and rising to his feet. "We had no other alternative than putting the ballot in their hands."

"I will not deny," said Rev. Carmicle, "that we have made woeful mistakes, but with our antecedents it would have been miraculous if we had never committed any mistakes or made any blunders."

"They were allies in war," continued Dr. Gresham, "and I am sorry that we have not done more to protect them in peace."

"Protect them in peace!" said Robert, bitterly. "What protection does the colored man receive from the hands of the Government? I know of no civilized country outside of America where men are still burned for real or supposed crimes."

"Johnson," said Dr. Gresham, compassionately, "it is impossible to have a policeman at the back of each colored man's chair, and a squad of soldiers at each crossroad, to detect with certainty, and punish with celerity, each invasion of his rights. We tried provisional governments and found them a failure. It seemed like leaving our former allies to be mocked with the name of freedom and tortured with the essence of slavery. The ballot is our weapon of defense, and we gave it to them for theirs."

"And there," said Dr. Latrobe, emphatically, "is where you signally failed. We are numerically stronger in Congress to-day than when we went out. You made the law, but the administration of it is in our hands, and we are a unit."

"But, Doctor," said Rev. Carmicle, "you cannot willfully deprive the negro of a single right as a citizen without sending demoralization through your own ranks."

"I think," said Dr. Latrobe, "that we are right in suppressing the negro's vote. This is a white man's government, and a white man's country. We own nineteen-twentieths of the land, and have about the same ratio of intelligence. I am a white man, and, right or wrong, I go with my race."

"But, Doctor," said Rev. Carmicle, "there are rights

more sacred than the rights of property and superior intelligence."

"What are they?" asked Dr. Latrobe.

"The rights of life and liberty," replied Rev. Carmicle.

"That is true," said Dr. Gresham; "and your Southern civilization will be inferior until you shall have placed protection to those rights at its base, not in theory but in fact."

"But, Dr. Gresham, we have to live with these people, and the North is constantly irritating us by its criticisms."

"The world," said Dr. Gresham, "is fast becoming a vast whispering gallery, and lips once sealed can now state their own grievances and appeal to the conscience of the nation, and, as long as a sense of justice and mercy retains a hold upon the heart of our nation, you cannot practice violence and injustice without rousing a spirit of remonstrance. And if it were not so I would be ashamed of my country and of my race."

"You speak," said Dr. Latrobe, "as if we had wronged the negro by enslaving him and being unwilling to share citizenship with him. I think that slavery has been of incalculable value to the negro. It has lifted him out of barbarism and fetich worship, given him a language of civilization, and introduced him to the world's best religion. Think what he was in Africa and what he is in America!"

"The negro," said Dr. Gresham, thoughtfully, "is not the only branch of the human race which has been low down in the scale of civilization and freedom, and which has outgrown the measure of his chains. Slavery, polygamy, and human sacrifices have been practiced among Europeans in bygone days; and when Tyndall tells us that out of savages unable to count to the number of their fingers and speaking only a language of nouns and verbs, arise at length our Newtons and Shakespeares, I do not see that the negro could not have learned our language and received our religion without the intervention of ages of slavery."

"If," said Rev. Carmicle, "Mohammedanism, with its imperfect creed, is successful in gathering large numbers of negroes beneath the Crescent, could not a legitimate commerce and the teachings of a pure Christianity have done as much to plant the standard of the Cross over the ramparts of sin and idolatry in Africa? Surely we cannot concede that the light of the Crescent is greater than the glory of the Cross, that there is less constraining power in the Christ of Calvary than in the Prophet of Arabia? I do not think that I underrate the difficulties in your way when I say that you young men are holding in your hands golden opportunities which it would be madness and folly to throw away. It is your grand opportunity to help build up a new South, not on the shifting sands of policy and expediency, but on the broad basis of equal justice and universal freedom. Do this and you will be blessed, and will make your life a blessing."

After Robert and Rev. Carmicle had left the hotel, Drs. Latimer, Gresham, and Latrobe sat silent and thoughtful awhile, when Dr. Gresham broke the silence by asking Dr. Latrobe how he had enjoyed the evening.

"Very pleasantly," he replied. "I was quite interested in that parson. Where was he educated?"

"In Oxford, I believe. I was pleased to hear him say that he had no white blood in his veins."

"I should think not," replied Dr. Latrobe, "from his looks. But one swallow does not make a summer. It is the exceptions which prove the rule."

"Don't you think," asked Dr. Gresham, "that we have been too hasty in our judgment of the negro? He has come handicapped into life, and is now on trial before the world. But it is not fair to subject him to the same tests that you would a white man. I believe that there are possibilities of growth in the race which we have never comprehended."

"The negro," said Dr. Latrobe, "is perfectly comprehensible to me. The only way to get along with him is to let him know his place, and make him keep it."

"I think," replied Dr. Gresham, "every man's place is the one he is best fitted for."

"Why," asked Dr. Latimer, "should any place be assigned to the negro more than to the French, Irish, or German?"

"Oh," replied Dr. Latrobe, "they are all Caucasians."

"Well," said Dr. Gresham, "is all excellence summed up in that branch of the human race?"

"I think," said Dr. Latrobe, proudly, "that we belong to the highest race on earth and the negro to the lowest."

"And yet," said Dr. Latimer, "you have consorted with them till you have bleached their faces to the whiteness of your own. Your children nestle in their bosoms; they are around you as body servants, and yet if one of them should attempt to associate with you your bitterest scorn and indignation would be visited upon them."

"I think," said Dr. Latrobe, "that feeling grows out of our Anglo-Saxon regard for the marriage relation. These white negroes are of illegitimate origin, and we would scorn to share our social life with them. Their blood is tainted."

"Who tainted it?" asked Dr. Latimer, bitterly. "You give absolution to the fathers, and visit the misfortunes of the mothers upon the children."

"But, Doctor, what kind of society would we have if we put down the bars and admitted everybody to social equality?"

"This idea of social equality," said Dr. Latimer, "is only a bugbear which frightens well-meaning people from dealing justly with the negro. I know of no place on earth where there is perfect social equality, and I doubt if there is such a thing in heaven. The sinner who repents on his death-bed cannot be the equal of St. Paul or the Beloved Disciple."

"Doctor," said Dr. Gresham, "I sometimes think that the final solution of this question will be the absorption of the negro into our race."

"Never! never!" exclaimed Dr. Latrobe, vehemently. "It would be a death blow to American civilization."

"Why, Doctor," said Dr. Latimer, "you Southerners began this absorption before the war. I understand that in one decade the mixed bloods rose from one-ninth to one-eighth of the population, and that as early as 1663 a law was passed in Maryland to prevent English women from intermarrying with slaves; and, even now, your laws against miscegenation presuppose that you apprehend danger from that source."

"Doctor, it is no use talking," replied Dr. Latrobe, wearily. "There are niggers who are as white as I am, but the taint of blood is there and we always exclude it."

"How do you know it is there?" asked Dr. Gresham.

"Oh, there are tricks of blood which always betray them. My eyes are more practiced than yours. I can always tell them. Now, that Johnson is as white as any man; but I knew he was a nigger the moment I saw him. I saw it in his eye."

Dr. Latimer smiled at Dr. Latrobe's assertion, but did not attempt to refute it; and bade him good-night.

"I think," said Dr. Latrobe, "that our war was the great mistake of the nineteenth century. It has left us very serious complications. We cannot amalgamate with the negroes. We cannot expatriate them. Now, what are we to do with them?"

"Deal justly with them," said Dr. Gresham, "and let them alone. Try to create a moral sentiment in the nation, which will consider a wrong done to the weakest of them as a wrong done to the whole community. Whenever you find ministers too righteous to be faithless, cowardly, and time serving; women too. Christly to be scornful; and public men too noble to be tricky and too honest to pander to the prejudices of the people, stand by them and give them your moral support."

"Doctor," said Latrobe, "with your views you ought to be a preacher striving to usher in the millennium."

"It can't come too soon," replied Dr. Gresham.

CHAPTER XXVII

Diverging Paths

ON THE EVE of his departure from the city of P——, Dr. Gresham called on Iola, and found her alone. They talked awhile of reminiscences of the war and hospital life, when Dr. Gresham, approaching Iola, said:—

"Miss Leroy, I am glad the great object of your life is accomplished, and that you have found all your relatives. Years have passed since we parted, years in which I have vainly tried to get a trace of you and have been baffled, but I have found you at last!" Clasping her hand in his, he continued, "I would it were so that I should never lose you again! Iola, will you not grant me the privilege of holding this hand as mine all through the future of our lives? Your search for your mother is ended. She is well cared for. Are you not free at last to share with me my Northern home, free to be mine as nothing else on earth is mine." Dr. Gresham looked eagerly on Iola's face, and tried to read its varying expression. "Iola, I learned to love you in the hospital. I have tried to forget you, but it has been all in vain. Your image is just as deeply engraven on my heart as it was the day we parted."

"Doctor," she replied, sadly, but firmly, as she withdrew her hand from his, "I feel now as I felt then, that there is an insurmountable barrier between us."

"What is it, Iola?" asked Dr. Gresham, anxiously.

"It is the public opinion which assigns me a place with the colored people."

"But what right has public opinion to interfere with our marriage relations? Why should we yield to its behests?"

"Because it is stronger than we are, and we cannot run counter to it without suffering its penalties."

"And what are they, Iola? Shadows that you merely dread?"

"No! no! the penalties of social ostracism North and South, except here and there some grand and noble exceptions. I do not think that you fully realize how much prejudice against colored people permeates society, lowers the tone of our religion, and reacts upon the life of the nation. After freedom came, mamma was living in the city of A——, and wanted to unite with a Christian church there. She made application for membership. She passed her examination as a candidate, and was received as a church member. When she was about to make her first communion, she unintentionally took her seat at the head of the column. The elder who was administering the communion gave her the bread in the order in which she sat, but before he gave her the wine some one touched him on the shoulder and whispered a word in his ear. He then passed mamma by, gave the cup to others, and then returned to her. From that rite connected with the holiest memories of earth, my poor mother returned humiliated and depressed."

"What a shame!" exclaimed Dr. Gresham, indignantly.

"I have seen," continued Iola, "the same spirit manifested in the North. Mamma once attempted to do missionary work in this city. One day she found an outcast colored girl, whom she wished to rescue. She took her to an asylum for fallen women and made an application for her, but was refused. Colored girls were not received there. Soon after mamma found among the colored people an outcast white girl. Mamma's sympathies, unfettered by class distinction, were aroused in her behalf, and, in company with two white ladies, she went with the girl to that same refuge. For her the door was freely opened and admittance readily granted. It was as if two women were sinking in the quicksands, and on the solid land stood other women with life-lines in their hands, seeing the deadly sands slowly creeping up around the hapless victims. To one they readily threw the lines of deliverance, but for the other there was not one strand of salvation. Some time since, to the same asylum, came a poor fallen girl who had escaped from the clutches of a wicked woman. For her the door would have been opened, had not the vile woman from whom she was escaping followed her to that place of refuge and revealed the fact that she belonged to the colored race. That fact was enough to close the door upon her, and to send her back to sin and to suffer, and perhaps to die as a wretched outcast. And yet in this city where a number of charities are advertised, I do not think there is one of them which, in appealing to the public, talks more religion than the managers of this asylum. This prejudice against the colored race environs our lives and mocks our aspirations."

"Iola, I see no use in your persisting that you are colored when your eyes are as blue and complexion as white as mine."

"Doctor, were I your wife, are there not people who would caress me as a white woman who would shrink from me in scorn if they knew I had one drop of negro blood in my veins? When mistaken for a white woman I should hear things alleged against the race at which my blood would boil. No, Doctor, I am not willing to live under a shadow of concealment which I thoroughly hate as if the blood in my veins were an undetected crime of my soul."

"Iola, dear, surely you paint the picture too darkly."

"Doctor, I have painted it with my heart's blood. It is easier to outgrow the dishonor of crime than the disabilities of color. You have created in this country an aristocracy of color wide enough to include the South with its treason and Utah with its abominations, but too narrow to include the best and bravest colored man who bared his breast to the bullets of the enemy during your fratricidal strife. Is not the most arrant Rebel to-day more acceptable to you than the most faithful colored man?"

"No! no!" exclaimed Dr. Gresham, vehemently. "You are wrong. I belong to the Grand Army of the Republic. We have no separate State Posts for the colored people, and, were such a thing proposed, the majority of our members, I believe, would be against it. In Congress colored men have the same seats as white men, and the color line is slowly fading out in our public institutions."

"But how is it in the Church?" asked Iola.

"The Church is naturally conservative. It preserves old truths, even if it is somewhat slow in embracing new ideas. It has its social as well as its spiritual side. Society is woman's realm. The majority of church members are women, who are said to be the aristocratic element of our country. I fear that one of the last strongholds of this racial prejudice will be found beneath the shadow of some of our churches. I think, on account of this social question, that large bodies of Christian temperance women and other reformers, in trying to reach the colored people even for their own good, will be quicker to form separate associations than our National Grand Army, whose ranks are open to black and white, liberals and conservatives, saints and agnostics. But, Iola, we have drifted far away from the question. No one has a right to interfere with our marriage if we do not infringe on the rights of others."

"Doctor," she replied, gently, "I feel that our paths must diverge. My life-work is planned. I intend spending my future among the colored people of the South."

"My dear friend," he replied, anxiously, "I am afraid that you are destined to sad disappointment. When the novelty wears off you will be disillusioned, and, I fear, when the time comes that you can no longer serve them they will forget your services and remember only your failings."

"But, Doctor, they need me; and I am sure when I taught among them they were very grateful for my services."

"I think," he replied, "these people are more thankful than grateful."

"I do not think so; and if I did it would not hinder me from doing all in my power to help them. I do not expect all the finest traits of character to spring from the hot-beds of slavery and caste. What matters it if they do forget the singer, so they don't forget the song? No, Doctor, I don't think that I could best serve my race by forsaking them and marrying you."

"Iola," he exclaimed, passionately, "if you love your race, as you call it, work for it, live for it, suffer for it, and, if need be, die for it; but don't marry for it. Your education has unfitted you for social life among them."

"It was," replied Iola, "through their unrequited toil that I was educated, while they were compelled to live in ignorance. I am indebted to them for the power I have to serve them. I wish other Southern women felt as I do.

I think they could do so much to help the colored people at their doors if they would look at their opportunities in the light of the face of Jesus Christ. Nor am I wholly unselfish in allying myself with the colored people. All the rest of my family have done so. My dear grandmother is one of the excellent of the earth, and we all love her too much to ignore our relationship with her. I did not choose my lot in life, and the simplest thing I can do is to accept the situation and do the best I can."

"And is this your settled purpose?" he asked, sadly.

"It is, Doctor," she replied, tenderly but firmly. "I see no other. I must serve the race which needs me most."

"Perhaps you are right," he replied; "but I cannot help feeling sad that our paths, which met so pleasantly, should diverge so painfully. And yet, not only the freedmen, but the whole country, need such helpful, self-sacrificing teachers as you will prove; and if earnest prayers and holy wishes can brighten your path, your lines will fall in the pleasantest places."

As he rose to go, sympathy, love, and admiration were blended in the parting look he gave her; but he felt it was useless to attempt to divert her from her purpose. He knew that for the true reconstruction of the country something more was needed than bayonets and bullets, or the schemes of selfish politicians or plotting demagogues. He knew that the South needed the surrender of the best brain and heart of the country to build, above the wastes of war, more stately temples of thought and action.

CHAPTER XXVIII

Dr. Latrobe's Mistake

ON THE MORNING previous to their departure for their respective homes, Dr. Gresham met Dr. Latrobe in the parlor of the Concordia.

"How," asked Dr. Gresham, "did you like Dr. Latimer's paper?"

"Very much, indeed. It was excellant. He is a very talented young man. He sits next to me at lunch and I have conversed with him several times. He is very genial and attractive, only he seems to be rather cranky on the negro question. I hope if he comes South that he will not make the mistake of mixing up with the negroes. It would be throwing away his influence and ruining his prospects. He seems to be well versed in science and literature and would make a very delightful accession to our social life."

"I think," replied Dr. Gresham, "that he is an honor to our profession. He is one of the finest specimens of our young manhood."

Just then Dr. Latimer entered the room. Dr. Latrobe arose and, greeting him cordially, said: "I was delighted with your paper; it was full of thought and suggestion."

"Thank you," answered Dr. Latimer, "it was my aim to make it so."

"And you succeeded admirably," replied Dr. Latrobe. "I could not help thinking how much we owe to heredity and environment."

"Yes," said Dr. Gresham. "Continental Europe yearly sends to our shores subjects to be developed into citizens. Emancipation has given us millions of new citizens, and to them our influence and example should be a blessing and not a curse."

"Well," said Dr. Latimer, "I intend to go South, and

help those who so much need helpers from their own ranks."

"I hope," answered Dr. Latrobe, "that if you go South you will only sustain business relations with the negroes, and not commit the folly of equalizing yourself with them."

"Why not?" asked Dr. Latimer, steadily looking him in the eye.

"Because in equalizing yourself with them you drag us down; and our social customs must be kept intact."

"You have been associating with me at the convention for several days; I do not see that the contact has dragged you down, has it?"

"You! What has that got to do with associating with niggers?" asked Dr. Latrobe, curtly.

"The blood of that race is coursing through my veins. I am one of them," replied Dr. Latimer, proudly raising his head.

"You!" exclaimed Dr. Latrobe, with an air of profound astonishment and crimsoning face.

"Yes," interposed Dr. Gresham, laughing heartily at Dr. Latrobe's discomfiture. "He belongs to that negro race both by blood and choice. His father's mother made overtures to receive him as her grandson and heir, but he has nobly refused to forsake his mother's people and has cast his lot with them."

"And I," said Dr. Latimer, "would have despised myself if I had done otherwise."

"Well, well," said Dr. Latrobe, rising, "I was never so deceived before. Good morning!"

Dr. Latrobe had thought he was clear-sighted enough to detect the presence of negro blood when all physical traces had disappeared. But he had associated with Dr. Latimer for several days, and admired his talent, without suspecting for one moment his racial connection. He could not help feeling a sense of vexation at the signal mistake he had made.

Dr. Frank Latimer was the natural grandson of a Southern lady, in whose family his mother had been a slave. The blood of a proud aristocratic ancestry was flowing through his veins, and generations of blood admixture had effaced all trace of his negro lineage. His complexion was blonde, his eye bright and piercing, his lips firm and well moulded; his manner very affable; his intellect active and well stored with information. He was a man capable of winning in life through his rich gifts of inheritance and acquirements. When freedom came, his mother, like Hagar of old, went out into the wide world to seek a living for herself and child. Through years of poverty she labored to educate her child, and saw the glad fruition of her hopes when her son graduated as an M. D. from the University of P——.

After his graduation he met his father's mother, who recognized him by his resemblance to her dear, departed son. All the mother love in her lonely heart awoke, and she was willing to overlook "the missing link of matrimony," and adopt him as her heir, if he would ignore his identity with the colored race.

Before him loomed all the possibilities which only birth and blood can give a white man in our Democratic country. But he was a man of too much sterling worth of character to be willing to forsake his mother's race for the richest advantages his grandmother could bestow.

Dr. Gresham had met Dr. Latimer at the beginning of the convention, and had been attracted to him by his frank and genial manner. One morning, when conversing with him, Dr. Gresham had learned some of the salient points of his history, which, instead of repelling him, had only deepened his admiration for the young doctor. He was much amused when he saw the pleasant acquaintanceship between him and Dr. Latrobe, but they agreed to be silent about his racial connection until the time came when they were ready to divulge it; and they were hugely delighted at his signal blunder.

CHAPTER XXIX

Visitors from the South

"MAMMA IS NOT WELL," said Iola to Robert. "I spoke to her about sending for a doctor, but she objected and I did not insist."

"I will ask Dr. Latimer, whom I met at the Concordia, to step in. He is a splendid young fellow. I wish we had thousands like him."

In the evening the doctor called. Without appearing to make a professional visit he engaged Marie in conversation, watched her carefully, and came to the conclusion that her failing health proceeded more from mental than physical causes.

"I am so uneasy about Harry," said Mrs. Leroy. "He is so fearless and outspoken. I do wish the attention of the whole nation could be turned to the cruel barbarisms which are a national disgrace. I think the term 'bloody shirt' is one of the most heartless phrases ever invented to divert attention from cruel wrongs and dreadful outrages."

Just then Iola came in and was introduced by her uncle to Dr. Latimer, to whom the introduction was a sudden and unexpected pleasure.

After an interchange of courtesies, Marie resumed the conversation, saying: "Harry wrote me only last week that a young friend of his had lost his situation because he refused to have his pupils strew flowers on the streets through which Jefferson Davis was to pass."

"I think," said Dr. Latimer, indignantly, "that the Israelites had just as much right to scatter flowers over the bodies of the Egyptians, when the waves threw back their corpses on the shores of the Red Sea, as these children had to strew the path of Jefferson Davis with flowers. We want our boys to grow up manly citizens, and not cringing sycophants. When do you expect your son, Mrs. Leroy?"

"Some time next week," answered Marie.

"And his presence will do you more good than all the medicine in my chest."

"I hope, Doctor," said Mrs. Leroy, "that we will not lose sight of you, now that your professional visit is ended; for I believe your visit was the result of a conspiracy between Iola and her uncle."

Dr. Latimer laughed, as he answered, "Ah, Mrs. Leroy, I see you have found us all out."

"Oh, Doctor," exclaimed Iola, with pleasing excitement, "there is a young lady coming here to visit me next week. Her name is Miss Lucille Delany, and she is my ideal woman. She is grand, brave, intellectual, and religious."

"Is that so? She would make some man an excellent wife," replied Dr. Latimer.

"Now isn't that perfectly manlike," answered Iola, smiling. "Mamma, what do you think of that? Did any of you gentlemen ever see a young woman of much ability that you did not look upon as a flotsam all adrift until some man had appropriated her?"

"I think, Miss Leroy, that the world's work, if shared, is better done than when it is performed alone. Don't you think your life-work will be better done if some one shares it with you?" asked Dr. Latimer, slowly, and with a smile in his eyes.

"That would depend on the person who shared it," said Iola, faintly blushing.

"Here," said Robert, a few evenings after this conversation, as he handed Iola a couple of letters, "is something which will please you."

Iola took the letters, and, after reading one of them, said: "Miss Delany and Harry will be here on Wednesday; and this one is an invitation which also adds to my enjoyment."

"What is it?" asked Marie; "an invitation to a hop or a german?"

"No; but something which I value far more. We are all invited to Mr. Stillman's to a *conversazione.*"

"What is the object?"

"His object is to gather some of the thinkers and leaders of the race to consult on subjects of vital interest to our welfare. He has invited Dr. Latimer, Professor Gradnor, of North Carolina, Mr. Forest, of New York, Hon. Dugdale, Revs. Carmicle, Cantnor, Tunster, Professor Langhorne, of Georgia, and a few ladies, Mrs. Watson, Miss Brown, and others."

"I am glad that it is neither a hop nor a german," said Iola, "but something for which I have been longing."

"Why, Iola," asked Robert, "don't you believe in young people having a good time?"

"Oh, yes," answered Iola, seriously, "I believe in young people having amusements and recreations; but the times are too serious for us to attempt to make our lives a long holiday."

"Well, Iola," answered Robert, "this is the first holiday we have had in two hundred and fifty years, and you shouldn't be too exacting."

"Yes," replied Marie, "human beings naturally crave enjoyment, and if not furnished with good amusements they are apt to gravitate to low pleasures."

"Some one," said Robert, "has said that the Indian belongs to an old race and looks gloomily back to the past, and that the negro belongs to a young race and looks hopefully towards the future."

"If that be so," replied Marie, "our race-life corresponds more to the follies of youth than the faults of maturer years."

On Dr. Latimer's next visit he was much pleased to see a great change in Marie's appearance. Her eye had grown brighter, her step more elastic, and the anxiety had faded from her face. Harry had arrived, and with him came Miss Delany.

"Good evening, Dr. Latimer," said Iola, cheerily, as she entered the room with Miss Lucille Delany. "This is my friend, Miss Delany, from Georgia. Were she not present I would say she is one of the grandest women in America."

"I am very much pleased to meet you," said Dr. Latimer, cordially; "I have heard Miss Leroy speak of you. We were expecting you," he added, with a smile.

Just then Harry entered the room, and Iola presented him to Dr. Latimer, saying, "This is my brother, about whom mamma was so anxious."

"Had you a pleasant journey?" asked Dr. Latimer, after the first greetings were over.

"Not especially," answered Miss Delany. "Southern roads are not always very pleasant to travel. When Mr. Leroy entered the cars at A——, where he was known, had he taken his seat among the white people he would have been remanded to the colored car."

"But after awhile," said Harry, "as Miss Delany and myself were sitting together, laughing and chatting, a colored man entered the car, and, mistaking me for a white man, asked the conductor to have me removed, and I had to insist that I was colored in order to be permitted to remain. It would be ludicrous, if it were not vexatious, to be too white to be black, and too black to be white."

"Caste plays such fantastic tricks in this country," said Dr. Latimer.

"I tell Mr. Leroy," said Miss Delany, "that when he returns he must put a label on himself, saying, 'I am a colored man,' to prevent annoyance."

CHAPTER XXX

Friends in Council

ON THE FOLLOWING Friday evening, Mr. Stillman's pleasant, spacious parlors were filled to overflowing with a select company of earnest men and women deeply interested in the welfare of the race.

Bishop Tunster had prepared a paper on "Negro Emigration." Dr. Latimer opened the discussion by speaking favorably of some of the salient points, but said:—

"I do not believe self-exilement is the true remedy for the wrongs of the negro. Where should he go if he left this country?"

"Go to Africa," replied Bishop Tunster, in his bluff, hearty tones. "I believe that Africa is to be redeemed to civilization, and that the negro is to be gathered into the family of nations and recognized as a man and a brother."

"Go to Africa?" repeated Professor Langhorne, of Georgia. "Does the United States own one foot of African soil? And have we not been investing our blood in the country for ages?"

"I am in favor of missionary efforts," said Professor Gradnor, of North Carolina, "for the redemption of Africa, but I see no reason for expatriating ourselves because some persons do not admire the color of our skins."

"I do not believe," said Mr. Stillman, "in emptying on the shores of Africa a horde of ignorant, poverty-stricken people, as missionaries of civilization or Christianity. And while I am in favor of missionary efforts, there is need here for the best heart and brain to work in unison for justice and righteousness."

"America," said Miss Delany, "is the best field for human development. God has not heaped up our mountains with such grandeur, flooded our rivers with such majesty, crowned our valleys with such fertility, enriched our mines with such wealth, that they should only minister to grasping greed and sensuous enjoyment."

"Climate, soil, and physical environments," said Professor Gradnor, "have much to do with shaping national characteristics. If in Africa, under a tropical sun, the negro has lagged behind other races in the march of civilization, at least for once in his history he has, in this country, the privilege of using climatic advantages and developing under new conditions."

"Yes," replied Dr. Latimer, "and I do not wish our people to become restless and unsettled before they have tried one generation of freedom."

"I am always glad," said Mr. Forest, a tall, distinguished-looking gentleman from New York, "when I hear of people who are ill treated in one section of the country emigrating to another. Men who are deaf to the claims of mercy, and oblivious to the demands of justice, can feel when money is slipping from their pockets."

"The negro," said Hon. Dugdale, "does not present to my mind the picture of an effete and exhausted people, destined to die out before a stronger race. Gilbert Haven once saw a statue which suggested this thought, 'I am black, but comely; the sun has looked down upon me, but I will teach you who despise me to feel that I am your superior.' The men who are acquiring property and building up homes in the South show us what energy and determination may do even in that part of the country. I believe such men can do more to conquer prejudice than if they spent all their lives in shouting for their rights and ignoring their duties. No! as there are millions of us in this country, I think it best to settle down and work out our own salvation here."

"How many of us to-day," asked Professor Langhorne, "would be teaching in the South, if every field of labor in the North was as accessible to us as to the whites? It has been estimated that a million young white men have left the South since the war, and, had our chances been equal to theirs, would we have been any more willing to stay in the South with those who need us than they? But this prejudice, by impacting us together, gives us a common cause and brings our intellect in contact with the less favored of our race."

"I do not believe," said Miss Delany, "that the Southern white people themselves desire any wholesale exodus of the colored from their labor fields. It would be suicidal to attempt their expatriation."

"History," said Professor Langhorne, "tells that Spain was once the place where barbarian Europe came to light her lamp. Seven hundred years before there was a public lamp in London you might have gone through the streets of Cordova amid ten miles of lighted lamps, and stood there on solidly paved land, when hundreds of years afterwards, in Paris, on a rainy day you would have sunk to your ankles in the mud. But she who bore the name of the 'Terror of Nations,' and the 'Queen of the Ocean,' was not strong enough to dash herself against God's law of retribution and escape unscathed. She inaugurated a crusade of horror against a million of her best laborers and artisans. Vainly she expected the blessing of God to crown her work of violence. Instead of seeing the fruition of her hopes in the increased prosperity of her land, depression and paralysis settled on her trade and business. A fearful blow was struck at her agriculture; decay settled on her manufactories; money became too scarce to pay the necessary expenses of the king's exchequer; and that once mighty empire became a fallen kingdom, pierced by her crimes and dragged down by her transgressions."

"We did not," said Iola, "place the bounds of our habitation. And I believe we are to be fixtures in this country. But beyond the shadows I see the coruscation of a brighter day; and we can help usher it in, not by answering hate with hate, or giving scorn for scorn, but by striving to be more generous, noble, and just. It seems as if all creation travels to respond to the song of the Herald angels, 'Peace on earth, good-will toward men.' "

The next paper was on "Patriotism," by Rev. Cantnor. It was a paper in which the white man was extolled as the master race, and spoke as if it were a privilege for the colored man to be linked to his destiny and to live beneath the shadow of his power. He asserted that the white race of this country is the broadest, most Christian, and humane of that branch of the human family.

Dr. Latimer took exception to his position. "Law," he said, "is the pivot on which the whole universe turns; and obedience to law is the gauge by which a nation's strength or weakness is tried. We have had two evils by which our obedience to law has been tested—slavery and the liquor traffic. How have we dealt with them both? We have been weighed in the balance and found wanting. Millions of slaves and serfs have been liberated during this century, but not even in semi-barbaric Russia, heathen Japan, or Catholic Spain has slavery been abolished through such a fearful conflict as it was in the United States. The liquor traffic still sends its floods of ruin and shame to the habitations of men, and no political party has been found with enough moral power and numerical strength to stay the tide of death.''

"I think," said Professor Gradnor, "that what our country needs is truth more than flattery. I do not think that our moral life keeps pace with our mental development and material progress. I know of no civilized country on the globe, Catholic, Protestant, or Mohammedan, where life is less secure than it is in the South. Nearly eighteen hundred years ago the life of a Roman citizen in Palestine was in danger from mob violence. That pagan government threw around him a wall of living clay, consisting of four hundred and seventy men, when more than forty Jews had bound themselves with an oath that they would neither eat nor drink until they had taken the life of the Apostle Paul. Does not true patriotism demand that citizenship should be as much protected in Christian America as it was in heathen Rome?"

"I would have our people," said Miss Delany, "more interested in politics. Instead of forgetting the past, I would have them hold in everlasting remembrance our great deliverance. Hitherto we have never had a country with tender, precious memories to fill our eyes with tears, or glad reminiscences to thrill our hearts with pride and joy. We have been aliens and outcasts in the land of our birth. But I want my pupils to do all in their power to make this country worthy of their deepest devotion and loftiest patriotism. I want them to feel that its glory is their glory, its dishonor their shame."

"Our esteemed friend, Mrs. Watson," said Iola, "sends regrets that she cannot come, but has kindly favored us with a poem, called the 'Rallying Cry.' In her letter she says that, although she is no longer young, she feels that in the conflict for the right there's room for young as well as old. She hopes that we will here unite the enthusiasm of youth with the experience of age, and that we will have a pleasant and profitable conference. Is it your pleasure that the poem be read at this stage of our proceedings, or later on?"

"Let us have it now," answered Harry, "and I move that Miss Delany be chosen to lend to the poem the charm of her voice."

"I second the motion," said Iola, smiling, and handing the poem to Miss Delany.

Miss Delany took the poem and read it with fine effect. The spirit of the poem had entered her soul.

A Rallying Cry

Oh, children of the tropics,
    Amid our pain and wrong
Have you no other mission
    Than music, dance, and song?

When through the weary ages
    Our dripping tears still fall,
Is this a time to dally
    With pleasure's silken thrall?

Go, muffle all your viols;
    As heroes learn to stand,
With faith in God's great justice
    Nerve every heart and hand.

Dream not of ease nor pleasure,
    Nor honor, wealth, nor fame,
Till from the dust you've lifted
    Our long-dishonored name;

And crowned that name with glory
    By deeds of holy worth,
To shine with light emblazoned,
    The noblest name on earth.

Count life a dismal failure,
    Unblessing and unblest,
That seeks 'mid ease inglorious
    For pleasure or for rest.

With courage, strength, and valor
　　Your lives and actions brace;
Shrink not from toil or hardship,
　　And dangers bravely face.

Engrave upon your banners,
　　In words of golden light,
That honor, truth, and justice
　　Are more than godless might.

Above earth's pain and sorrow
　　Christ's dying face I see;
I hear the cry of anguish:—
　　"Why hast thou forsaken me?"

In the pallor of that anguish
　　I see the only light,
To flood with peace and gladness
　　Earth's sorrow, pain, and night.

Arrayed in Christly armor
　　'Gainst error, crime, and sin,
The victory can't be doubtful,
　　For God is sure to win.

The next paper was by Miss Iola Leroy, on the "Education of Mothers."

"I agree," said Rev. Eustace, of St. Mary's parish, "with the paper. The great need of the race is enlightened mothers."

"And enlightened fathers, too," added Miss Delany, quickly. "If there is anything I chafe to see it is a strong, hearty man shirking his burdens, putting them on the shoulders of his wife, and taking life easy for himself."

"I always pity such mothers," interposed Iola, tenderly.

"I think," said Miss Delany, with a flash in her eye and a ring of decision in her voice, "that such men ought to be drummed out of town!" As she spoke, there was an expression which seemed to say, "And I would like to help do it!"

Harry smiled, and gave her a quick glance of admiration.

"I do not think," said Mrs. Stillman, "that we can

begin too early to teach our boys to be manly and self-respecting, and our girls to be useful and self-reliant."

"You know," said Mrs. Leroy, "that after the war we were thrown upon the nation a homeless race to be gathered into homes, and a legally unmarried race to be taught the sacredness of the marriage relation. We must instill into our young people that the true strength of a race means purity in women and uprightness in men; who can say, with Sir Galahad:—

> 'My strength is the strength of ten,
> Because my heart is pure.'

And where this is wanting neither wealth nor culture can make up the deficiency."

"There is a field of Christian endeavor which lies between the school-house and the pulpit, which needs the hand of a woman more in private than in public," said Miss Delany.

"Yes, I have often felt the need of such work in my own parish. We need a union of women with the warmest hearts and clearest brains to help in the moral education of the race," said Rev. Eustace.

"Yes," said Iola, "if we would have the prisons empty we must make the homes more attractive."

"In civilized society," replied Dr. Latimer, "there must be restraint either within or without. If parents fail to teach restraint within, society has her check-reins without in the form of chain-gangs, prisons, and the gallows."

The closing paper was on the "Moral Progress of the Race," by Hon. Dugdale. He said: "The moral progress of the race was not all he could desire, yet he could not help feeling that, compared with other races, the outlook was not hopeless. I am so sorry to see, however, that in some States there is an undue proportion of colored people in prisons."

"I think," answered Professor Langhorne, of Georgia, "that this is owing to a partial administration of law in meting out punishment to colored offenders. I know red-handed murderers who walk in this Republic unwhipped of justice, and I have seen a colored woman sentenced to prison for weeks for stealing twenty-five cents. I knew a colored girl who was executed for murder when only a child in years. And it was through the intervention of a friend of mine, one of the bravest young men of the South, that a boy of fifteen was saved from the gallows."

"When I look," said Mr. Forest, "at the slow growth of modern civilization—the ages which have been consumed in reaching our present altitude, and see how we have outgrown slavery, feudalism, and religious persecutions, I cannot despair of the future of the race."

"Just now," said Dr. Latimer, "we have the fearful grinding and friction which comes in the course of an adjustment of the new machinery of freedom in the old ruts of slavery. But I am optimistic enough to believe that there will yet be a far higher and better Christian civilization than our country has ever known."

"And in that civilization I believe the negro is to be an important factor," said Rev. Cantnor.

"I believe it also," said Miss Delany, hopefully, "and this thought has been a blessed inspiration to my life. When I come in contact with Christless prejudices, I feel that my life is too much a part of the Divine plan, and invested with too much intrinsic worth, for me to be the least humiliated by indignities that beggarly souls can inflict. I feel more pitiful than resentful to those who do not know how much they miss by living mean, ignoble lives."

"My heart," said Iola, "is full of hope for the future. Pain and suffering are the crucibles out of which come gold more fine than the pavements of heaven, and gems more precious than the foundations of the Holy City."

"If," said Mrs. Leroy, "pain and suffering are factors in human development, surely we have not been counted too worthless to suffer."

"And is there," continued Iola, "a path which we have trodden in this country, unless it be the path of sin, into which Jesus Christ has not put His feet and left it luminous with the light of His steps? Has the negro been poor and homeless? The birds of the air had nests and the foxes had holes, but the Son of man had not where to lay His head. Has our name been a synonym for contempt? 'He shall be called a Nazarene.' Have we been despised and trodden under foot? Christ was despised and rejected of men. Have we been ignorant and unlearned? It was said of Jesus Christ, 'How knoweth this man letters, never having learned?' Have we been beaten and bruised in the prison-house of bondage? 'They took Jesus and scourged Him.' Have we been slaughtered, our bones scattered at the graves' mouth? He was spit upon by the mob, smitten and mocked by the rabble, and died as died Rome's meanest criminal slave. To-day that cross of shame is a throne of power. Those robes of scorn have changed to habiliments of light, and that crown of mockery to a diadem of glory. And never, while the agony of Gethsemane and the sufferings of Calvary have their hold upon my heart, will I recognize any religion as His which despises the least of His brethren."

As Iola finished, there was a ring of triumph in her voice, as if she were reviewing a path she had trodden with bleeding feet, and seen it change to lines of living light. Her soul seemed to be flashing through the rare loveliness of her face and etherealizing its beauty.

Every one was spell-bound. Dr. Latimer was entranced, and, turning to Hon. Dugdale, said, in a low voice and with deep-drawn breath, "She is angelic!"

Hon. Dugdale turned, gave a questioning look, then replied, "She is strangely beautiful! Do you know her?"

"Yes; I have met her several times. I accompanied her here to-night. The tones of her voice are like benedictions of peace; her words a call to higher service and nobler life."

Just then Rev. Carmicle was announced. He had been on a Southern tour, and had just returned.

"Oh, Doctor," exclaimed Mrs. Stillman, "I am delighted to see you. We were about to adjourn, but we will postpone action to hear from you."

"Thank you," replied Rev. Carmicle. "I have not the cue to the meeting, and will listen while I take breath."

"Pardon me," answered Mrs. Stillman. "I should have been more thoughtful than to press so welcome a guest into service before I had given him time for rest and refreshment; but if the courtesy failed on my lips it did not fail in my heart. I wanted our young folks to see one of our thinkers who had won distinction before the war."

"My dear friend," said Rev. Carmicle, smiling, "some of these young folks will look on me as a back number. You know the cry has already gone forth, 'Young men to the front.'"

"But we need old men for counsel," interposed Mr. Forest, of New York.

"Of course," said Rev. Carmicle, "we older men would rather retire gracefully than be relegated or hustled to a back seat. But I am pleased to see doors open to you which were closed to us, and opportunities which were denied us embraced by you."

"How," asked Hon. Dugdale, "do you feel in reference to our people's condition in the South?"

"Very hopeful, although at times I cannot help feeling anxious about their future. I was delighted with my visits to various institutions of learning, and surprised at the desire manifested among the young people to obtain an education. Where toil-worn mothers bent beneath their heavy burdens their more favored daughters are enjoying the privileges of education. Young people are making recitations in Greek and Latin where it was once a crime to teach their parents to read. I also became acquainted with colored professors and presidents of colleges. Saw young ladies who had graduated as doctors. Comfortable homes have succeeded old cabins of slavery. Vast crops have been raised by free labor. I read with interest and pleasure a number of papers edited by colored men. I saw it estimated that two millions of our people had learned to read, and I feel deeply grateful to the people who have supplied us with teachers who have stood their ground so nobly among our people."

"But," asked Mr. Forest, "you expressed fears about the future of our race. From whence do your fears arise?"

"From the unfortunate conditions which slavery has entailed upon that section of our country. I dread the results of that racial feeling which ever and anon breaks out into restlessness and crime. Also, I am concerned about the lack of home training for those for whom the discipline of the plantation has been exchanged for the penalties of prisons and chain-gangs. I am sorry to see numbers of our young men growing away from the influence of the church and drifting into prisons. I also fear that in some sections, as colored men increase in wealth and intelligence, there will be an increase of race rivalry and jealousy. It is said that savages, by putting their ears to the ground, can hear a far-off tread. So, to-day, I fear that there are savage elements in our civilization which hear the advancing tread of the negro and would retard his coming. It is the incarnation of these elements that I dread. It is their elimination I do so earnestly desire. Whether it be outgrown or not is our unsolved problem. Time alone will tell whether or not the virus of slavery and injustice has too fully permeated our Southern civilization for a complete recovery. Nations, honey-combed by vice, have fallen beneath the weight of their iniquities. Justice is always uncompromising in its claims and inexorable in its demands. The laws of the universe are never repealed to accommodate our follies."

"Surely," said Bishop Tunster, "the negro has a higher mission than that of aimlessly drifting through life and patiently waiting for death."

"We may not," answered Rev. Carmicle, "have the same dash, courage, and aggressiveness of other races, accustomed to struggle, achievement, and dominion, but surely the world needs something better than the results of arrogance, aggressiveness, and indomitable power. For the evils of society there are no solvents as potent as love and justice, and our greatest need is not more wealth and learning, but a religion replete with life and glowing with love. Let this be the impelling force in the race and it cannot fail to rise in the scale of character and condition."

"And," said Dr. Latimer, "instead of narrowing our sympathies to mere racial questions, let us broaden them to humanity's wider issues."

"Let us," replied Rev. Carmicle, "pass it along the lines, that to be willfully ignorant is to be shamefully criminal. Let us teach our people not to love pleasure or to fear death, but to learn the true value of life, and to do their part to eliminate the paganism of caste from our holy religion and the lawlessness of savagery from our civilization."

"How did you enjoy the evening, Marie?" asked Robert, as they walked homeward.

"I was interested and deeply pleased," answered Marie.

"I," said Robert, "was thinking of the wonderful changes that have come to us since the war. When I sat in those well-lighted, beautifully-furnished rooms, I was thinking of the meetings we used to have in bygone days. How we used to go by stealth into lonely woods and gloomy swamps, to tell of our hopes and fears, sorrows and trials. I hope that we will have many more of these gatherings. Let us have the next one here."

"I am sure," said Marie, "I would gladly welcome such a conference at any time. I think such meetings would be so helpful to our young people."

CHAPTER XXXI

Dawning Affections

"DOCTOR," said Iola, as they walked home from the *conversazione*, "I wish I could do something more for our people than I am doing. I taught in the South till failing health compelled me to change my employment. But, now that I am well and strong, I would like to do something of lasting service for the race."

"Why not," asked Dr. Latimer, "write a good, strong book which would be helpful to them? I think there is an amount of dormant talent among us, and a large field from which to gather materials for such a book."

"I would do it, willingly, if I could; but one needs both leisure and money to make a successful book. There is material among us for the broadest comedies and the deepest tragedies, but, besides money and leisure, it needs patience, perseverance, courage, and the hand of an artist to weave it into the literature of the country."

"Miss Leroy, you have a large and rich experience; you possess a vivid imagination and glowing fancy. Write, out of the fullness of your heart, a book to inspire men and women with a deeper sense of justice and humanity."

"Doctor," replied Iola, "I would do it if I could, not for the money it might bring, but for the good it might do. But who believes any good can come out of the black Nazareth?"

"Miss Leroy, out of the race must come its own thinkers and writers. Authors belonging to the white race have written good racial books, for which I am deeply grateful, but it seems to be almost impossible for a white man to put himself completely in our place. No man can feel the iron which enters another man's soul."

"Well, Doctor, when I write a book I shall take you for the hero of my story."

"Why, what have I done," asked Dr. Latimer, in a

surprised tone, "that you should impale me on your pen?"

"You have done nobly," answered Iola, "in refusing your grandmother's offer."

"I only did my duty," he modestly replied.

"But," said Iola, "when others are trying to slip out from the race and pass into the white basis, I cannot help admiring one who acts as if he felt that the weaker the race is the closer he would cling to it."

"My mother," replied Dr. Latimer, "faithful and true, belongs to that race. Where else should I be? But I know a young lady who could have cast her lot with the favored race, yet chose to take her place with the freed people, as their teacher, friend, and adviser. This young lady was alone in the world. She had been fearfully wronged, and to her stricken heart came a brilliant offer of love, home, and social position. But she bound her heart to the mast of duty, closed her ears to the syren song, and could not be lured from her purpose."

A startled look stole over Iola's face, and, lifting her eyes to his, she faltered:—

"Do you know her?"

"Yes, I know her and admire her; and she ought to be made the subject of a soul-inspiring story. Do you know of whom I speak?"

"How should I, Doctor? I am sure you have not made me your confidante," she responded, demurely; then she quickly turned and tripped up the steps of her home, which she had just reached.

After this conversation Dr. Latimer became a frequent visitor at Iola's home, and a firm friend of her brother. Harry was at that age when, for the young and inexperienced, vice puts on her fairest guise and most seductive smiles. Dr. Latimer's wider knowledge and larger experience made his friendship for Harry very valuable, and the service he rendered him made him a favorite and ever-welcome guest in the family.

"Are you all alone," asked Robert, one night, as he entered the cosy little parlor where Iola sat reading. "Where are the rest of the folks?"

"Mamma and grandma have gone to bed," answered Iola. "Harry and Lucille are at the concert. They are passionately fond of music, and find facilities here that they do not have in the South. They wouldn't go to hear a seraph where they must take a negro seat. I was too tired to go. Besides, 'two's company and three's a crowd,' " she added, significantly.

"I reckon you struck the nail on the head that time," said Robert, laughing. "But you have not been alone all the time. Just as I reached the corner I saw Dr. Latimer leaving the door. I see he still continues his visits. Who is his patient now?"

"Oh, Uncle Robert," said Iola, smiling and flushing, "he is out with Harry and Lucille part of the time, and drops in now and then to see us all."

"Well," said Robert, "I suppose the case is now an affair of the heart. But I cannot blame him for it," he added, looking fondly on the beautiful face of his niece, which sorrow had touched only to chisel into more loveliness. "How do you like him?"

"I must have within me," answered Iola, with unaffected truthfulness, "a large amount of hero worship. The characters of the Old Testament I most admire are Moses and Nehemiah. They were willing to put aside their own advantages for their race and country. Dr. Latimer comes up to my ideal of a high, heroic manhood."

"I think," answered Robert, smiling archly, "he would be delighted to hear your opinion of him."

"I tell him," continued Iola, "that he belongs to the days of chivalry. But he smiles and says, 'he only belongs to the days of hard-pan service.' "

"Some one," said Robert, "was saying to-day that he stood in his own light when he refused his grandmother's offer to receive him as her son."

"I think," said Iola, "it was the grandest hour of his life when he made that decision. I have admired him ever since I heard his story."

"But, Iola, think of the advantages he set aside. It was no sacrifice for me to remain colored, with my lack of education and race sympathies, but Dr. Latimer had doors open to him as a white man which are forever closed to a colored man. To be born white in this country is to be born to an inheritance of privileges, to hold in your hands the keys that open before you the doors of every occupation, advantage, opportunity, and achievement."

"I know that, uncle," answered Iola; "but even these advantages are too dearly bought if they mean loss of honor, true manliness, and self respect. He could not have retained these had he ignored his mother and lived under a veil of concealment, constantly haunted by a dread of detection. The gain would not have been worth the cost. It were better that he should walk the ruggedest paths of life a true man than tread the softest carpets a moral cripple."

"I am afraid," said Robert, laying his hand caressingly upon her head, "that we are destined to lose the light of our home."

"Oh, uncle, how you talk! I never dreamed of what you are thinking," answered Iola, half reproachfully.

"And how," asked Robert, "do you know what I am thinking about?"

"My dear uncle, I'm not blind."

"Neither am I," replied Robert, significantly, as he left the room.

Iola's admiration for Dr. Latimer was not a one-sided affair. Day after day she was filling a larger place in his heart. The touch of her hand thrilled him with emotion. Her lightest words were an entrancing melody to his ear. Her noblest sentiments found a response in his heart. In their desire to help the race their hearts beat in loving unison. One grand and noble purpose was giving tone and color to their lives and strengthening the bonds of affection between them.

CHAPTER XXXII

Wooing and Wedding

HARRY'S VACATION had been very pleasant. Miss Delany, with her fine conversational powers and ready wit, had added much to his enjoyment. Robert had given his mother the pleasantest room in the house, and in the evening the family would gather around her, tell her the news of the day, read to her from the Bible, join with her in thanksgiving for mercies received and in prayer for protection through the night. Harry was very grateful to Dr. Latimer for the kindly interest he had shown in accompanying Miss Delany and himself to places of interest and amusement. He was grateful, too, that in the city of P—— doors were open to them which were barred against them in the South.

The bright, beautiful days of summer were gliding into autumn, with its glorious wealth of foliage, and the time was approaching for the departure of Harry and Miss Delany to their respective schools, when Dr. Latimer received several letters from North Carolina, urging him to come South, as physicians were greatly needed there. Although his practice was lucrative in the city of P——, he resolved he would go where his services were most needed.

A few evenings before he started he called at the house, and made an engagement to drive Iola to the park.

At the time appointed he drove up to the door in his fine equipage. Iola stepped gracefully in and sat quietly by his side to enjoy the loveliness of the scenery and the gorgeous grandeur of the setting sun.

"I expect to go South," said Dr. Latimer, as he drove slowly along.

"Ah, indeed," said Iola, assuming an air of interest,

while a shadow flitted over her face. "Where do you expect to pitch your tent?"

"In the city of C——, North Carolina," he answered.

"Oh, I wish," she exclaimed, "that you were going to Georgia, where you could take care of that high-spirited brother of mine."

"I suppose if he were to hear you he would laugh, and say that he could take care of himself. But I know a better plan than that."

"What is it?" asked Iola, innocently.

"That you will commit yourself, instead of your brother, to my care."

"Oh, dear," replied Iola, drawing a long breath. "What would mamma say?"

"That she would willingly resign you, I hope."

"And what would grandma and Uncle Robert say?" again asked Iola.

"That they would cheerfully acquiesce. Now, what would I say if they all consent?"

"I don't know," modestly responded Iola.

"Well," replied Dr. Latimer, "I would say:—

> "Could deeds my love discover,
> Could valor gain thy charms,
> To prove myself thy lover
> I'd face a world in arms."

"And prove a good soldier," added Iola, smiling, "when there is no battle to fight."

"Iola, I am in earnest," said Dr. Latimer, passionately. "In the work to which I am devoted every burden will be lighter, every path smoother, if brightened and blessed with your companionship."

A sober expression swept over Iola's face, and, dropping her eyes, she said: "I must have time to think."

Quietly they rode along the river bank until Dr. Latimer broke the silence by saying:—

"Miss Iola, I think that you brood too much over the condition of our people."

"Perhaps I do," she replied, "but they never burn a man in the South that they do not kindle a fire around my soul."

"I am afraid," replied Dr. Latimer, "that you will

grow morbid and nervous. Most of our people take life easily—why shouldn't you?"

"Because," she answered, "I can see breakers ahead which they do not."

"Oh, give yourself no uneasiness. They will catch the fret and fever of the nineteenth century soon enough. I have heard several of our ministers say that it is chiefly men of disreputable characters who are made the subjects of violence and lynch-law."

"Suppose it is so," responded Iola, feelingly. "If these men believe in eternal punishment they ought to feel a greater concern for the wretched sinner who is hurried out of time with all his sins upon his head, than for the godly man who passes through violence to endless rest."

"That is true; and I am not counseling you to be selfish; but, Miss Iola, had you not better look out for yourself?"

"Thank you, Doctor, I am feeling quite well."

"I know it, but your devotion to study and work is too intense," he replied.

"I am preparing to teach, and must spend my leisure time in study. Mr. Cloten is an excellent employer, and treats his employees as if they had hearts as well as hands. But to be an expert accountant is not the best use to which I can put my life."

"As a teacher you will need strong health and calm nerves. You had better let me prescribe for you. You need," he added, with a merry twinkle in his eyes, "change of air, change of scene, and change of name."

"Well, Doctor," said Iola, laughing, "that is the newest nostrum out. Had you not better apply for a patent?"

"Oh," replied Dr. Latimer, with affected gravity, "you know you must have unlimited faith in your physician."

"So you wish me to try the faith cure?" asked Iola, laughing.

"Yes, faith in me," responded Dr. Latimer, seriously.

"Oh, here we are at home!" exclaimed Iola. "This has been a glorious evening, Doctor. I am indebted to you for a great pleasure. I am extremely grateful."

"You are perfectly welcome," replied Dr. Latimer. "The pleasure has been mutual, I assure you."

"Will you not come in?" asked Iola.

Tying his horse, he accompanied Iola into the parlor.

Seating himself near her, he poured into her ears words eloquent with love and tenderness.

"Iola," he said, "I am not an adept in courtly phrases. I am a plain man, who believes in love and truth. In asking you to share my lot, I am not inviting you to a life of ease and luxury, for year after year I may have to struggle to keep the wolf from the door, but your presence would make my home one of the brightest spots on earth, and one of the fairest types of heaven. Am I presumptuous in hoping that your love will become the crowning joy of my life?"

His words were more than a tender strain wooing her to love and happiness, they were a clarion call to a life of high and holy worth, a call which found a response in her heart. Her hand lay limp in his. She did not withdraw it, but, raising her lustrous eyes to his, she softly answered: "Frank, I love you."

After he had gone, Iola sat by the window, gazing at the splendid stars, her heart quietly throbbing with a delicious sense of joy and love. She had admired Dr. Gresham and, had there been no barrier in her way, she might have learned to love him; but Dr. Latimer had grown irresistibly upon her heart. There were depths in her nature that Dr. Gresham had never fathomed; aspirations in her soul with which he had never mingled. But as the waves leap up to the strand, so her soul went out to Dr. Latimer. Between their lives were no impeding barriers, no inclination impelling one way and duty compelling another. Kindred hopes and tastes had knit their hearts; grand and noble purposes were lighting up their lives; and they esteemed it a blessed privilege to stand on the threshold of a new era and labor for those who had passed from the old oligarchy of slavery into the new commonwealth of freedom.

On the next evening, Dr. Latimer rang the bell and was answered by Harry, who ushered him into the parlor, and then came back to the sitting-room, saying, "Iola, Dr. Latimer has called to see you."

"Has he?" answered Iola, a glad light coming into her eyes. "Come, Lucille, let us go into the parlor."

"Oh, no," interposed Harry, shrugging his shoulders and catching Lucille's hand. "He didn't ask for you.

When we went to the concert we were told three's a crowd. And I say one good turn deserves another."

"Oh, Harry, you are so full of nonsense. Let Lucille go!" said Iola.

"Indeed I will not. I want to have a good time as well as you," said Harry.

"Oh, you're the most nonsensical man I know," interposed Miss Delany. Yet she stayed with Harry.

"You're looking very bright and happy," said Dr. Latimer to Iola, as she entered.

"My ride in the park was so refreshing! I enjoyed it so much! The day was so lovely, the air delicious, the birds sang so sweetly, and the sunset was so magnificent."

"I am glad of it. Why, Iola, your home is so happy your heart should be as light as a school-girl's."

"Doctor," she replied, "I must be prematurely old. I have scarcely known what it is to be light-hearted since my father's death."

"I know it, darling," he answered, seating himself beside her, and drawing her to him. "You have been tried in the fire, but are you not better for the crucial test?"

"Doctor," she replied, "as we rode along yesterday, mingling with the sunshine of the present came the shadows of the past. I was thinking of the bright, joyous days of my girlhood, when I defended slavery, and of how the cup that I would have pressed to the lips of others was forced to my own. Yet, in looking over the mournful past, I would not change the Iola of then for the Iola of now."

"Yes," responded Dr. Latimer, musingly,

" 'Darkness shows us worlds of light
We never saw by day.' "

"Oh, Doctor, you cannot conceive what it must have been to be hurled from a home of love and light into the dark abyss of slavery; to be compelled to take your place among a people you have learned to look upon as inferiors and social outcasts; to be in the power of men whose presence would fill you with horror and loathing, and to know that there is no earthly power to protect you from the highest insults which brutal cowardice could shower upon you. I am so glad that no other woman of my race will suffer as I have done."

The flush deepened on her face, a mournful splendor beamed from her beautiful eyes, into which the tears had slowly gathered.

"Darling," he said, his voice vibrating with mingled feelings of tenderness and resentment, "you must forget the sad past. You are like a tender lamb snatched from the jaws of a hungry wolf, but who still needs protecting, loving care. But it must have been terrible," he added, in a painful tone.

"It was indeed! For a while I was like one dazed. I tried to pray, but the heavens seemed brass over my head. I was wild with agony, and had I not been placed under conditions which roused all the resistance of my soul, I would have lost my reason."

"Was it not a mistake to have kept you ignorant of your colored blood?"

"It was the great mistake of my father's life, but dear papa knew something of the cruel, crushing power of caste; and he tried to shield us from it."

"Yes, yes," replied Dr. Latimer, thoughtfully, "in trying to shield you from pain he plunged you into deeper suffering."

"I never blame him, because I know he did it for the best. Had he lived he would have taken us to France, where I should have had a life of careless ease and pleasure. But now my life has a much grander significance than it would have had under such conditions. Fearful as the awakening was, it was better than to have slept through life."

"Best for you and best for me," said Dr. Latimer. "There are souls that never awaken; but if they miss the deepest pain they also lose the highest joy."

Dr. Latimer went South, after his engagement, and through his medical skill and agreeable manners became very successful in his practice. In the following summer, he built a cosy home for the reception of his bride, and came North, where, with Harry and Miss Delany as attendants, he was married to Iola, amid a pleasant gathering of friends, by Rev. Carmicle.

CHAPTER XXXIII

Conclusion

IT WAS LATE in the summer when Dr. Latimer and his bride reached their home in North Carolina. Over the cottage porch were morning-glories to greet the first flushes of the rising day, and roses and jasmines to distill their fragrance on the evening air. Aunt Linda, who had been apprised of their coming, was patiently awaiting their arrival, and Uncle Daniel was pleased to know that "dat sweet young lady who had sich putty manners war comin' to lib wid dem."

As soon as they arrived, Aunt Linda rushed up to Iola, folded her in her arms, and joyfully exclaimed: "How'dy, honey! Ise so glad you's come. I seed it in a vision dat somebody fair war comin' to help us. An' wen I yered it war you, I larffed and jist rolled ober, and larffed and jist gib up."

"But, Aunt Linda, I am not very fair," replied Mrs. Latimer.

"Well, chile, you's fair to me. How's all yore folks in de up kentry?"

"All well. I expect them down soon to live here."

"What, Har'yet, and Robby, an' yer ma? Oh, dat is too good. I allers said Robby had san' in his craw, and war born for good luck. He war a mighty nice boy. Har'yet's in clover now. Well, ebery dorg has its day, and de cat has Sunday. I allers tole Har'yet ter keep a stiff upper lip; dat it war a long road dat had no turn."

Dr. Latimer was much gratified by the tender care Aunt Linda bestowed on Iola.

"I ain't goin' to let her do nuffin till she gits seasoned. She looks as sweet as a peach. I allers wanted some nice lady to come down yere and larn our gals some sense. I can't read myself, but I likes ter yere dem dat can."

"Well, Aunt Linda, I am going to teach in the Sunday-school, help in the church, hold mothers' meetings to help these boys and girls to grow up to be good men and women. Won't you get a pair of spectacles and learn to read?"

"Oh, yer can't git dat book froo my head, no way you fix it. I knows nuff to git to hebben, and dats all I wants to know." Aunt Linda was kind and obliging, but there was one place where she drew the line, and that was at learning to read.

Harry and Miss Delany accompanied Iola as far as her new home, and remained several days. The evening before their departure, Harry took Miss Delany a drive of several miles through the pine barrens.

"This thing is getting very monotonous," Harry broke out, when they had gone some distance.

"Oh, I enjoy it!" replied Miss Delany. "These stately pines look so grand and solemn, they remind me of a procession of hooded monks."

"What in the world are you talking about, Lucille?" asked Harry, looking puzzled.

"About those pine-trees," replied Miss Delany, in a tone of surprise.

"Pshaw, I wasn't thinking about them. I'm thinking about Iola and Frank."

"What about them?" asked Lucille.

"Why, when I was in P——, Dr. Latimer used to be first-rate company, but now it is nothing but what Iola wants, and what Iola says, and what Iola likes. I don't believe that there is a subject I could name to him, from spinning a top to circumnavigating the globe, that he wouldn't somehow contrive to bring Iola in. And I don't believe you could talk ten minutes to Iola on any subject, from dressing a doll to the latest discovery in science, that she wouldn't manage to lug in Frank."

"Oh, you absurd creature!" responded Lucille, "this is their honeymoon, and they are deeply in love with each other. Wait till you get in love with some one."

"I am in love now," replied Harry, with a serious air.

"With whom?" asked Lucille, archly.

"With you," answered Harry, trying to take her hand.

"Oh, Harry!" she exclaimed, playfully resisting. "Don't be so nonsensical! Don't you think the bride looked lovely, with that dress of spotless white and with those orange blossoms in her hair?"

"Yes, she did; that's a fact," responded Harry. "But, Lucille, I think there is a great deal of misplaced sentiment at weddings," he added, more seriously.

"How so?"

"Oh, here are a couple just married, and who are as happy as happy can be; and people will crowd around them wishing much joy; but who thinks of wishing joy to the forlorn old bachelors and restless old maids?"

"Well, Harry, if you want people to wish you much happiness, why don't you do as the doctor has done, get yourself a wife?"

"I will," he replied, soberly, "when you say so."

"Oh, Harry, don't be so absurd."

"Indeed there isn't a bit of absurdity about what I say. I am in earnest." There was something in the expression of Harry's face and the tone of his voice which arrested the banter on Lucille's lips.

"I think it was Charles Lamb," replied Lucille, "who once said that school-teachers are uncomfortable people, and, Harry, I would not like to make you uncomfortable by marrying you."

"You will make me uncomfortable by not marrying me."

"But," replied Lucille, "your mother may not prefer me for a daughter. You know, Harry, complexional prejudices are not confined to white people."

"My mother," replied Harry, with an air of confidence, "is too noble to indulge in such sentiments."

"And Iola, would she be satisfied?"

"Why, it would add to her satisfaction. She is not one who can't be white and won't be black."

"Well, then," replied Lucille, "I will take the question of your comfort into consideration."

The above promise was thoughtfully remembered by Lucille till a bridal ring and happy marriage were the result.

Soon after Iola had settled in C—— she quietly took her place in the Sunday-school as a teacher, and in the church as a helper. She was welcomed by the young pastor, who found in her a strong and faithful ally. Together they planned meetings for the especial benefit of mothers

and children. When the dens of vice are spreading their
snares for the feet of the tempted and inexperienced her
doors are freely opened for the instruction of the children
before their feet have wandered and gone far astray. She
has no carpets too fine for the tread of their little feet.
She thinks it is better to have stains on her carpet than
stains on their souls through any neglect of hers. In lowly
homes and windowless cabins her visits are always welcome. Little children love her. Old age turns to her for
comfort, young girls for guidance, and mothers for counsel. Her life is full of blessedness.

Doctor Latimer by his kindness and skill has won the
name of the "Good Doctor." But he is more than a
successful doctor; he is a true patriot and a good citizen.
Honest, just, and discriminating, he endeavors by pre-
cept and example to instill into the minds of others sentiments of good citizenship. He is a leader in every reform
movement for the benefit of the community; but his patriotism is not confined to race lines. "The world is his
country, and mankind his countrymen." While he abhors
their deeds of violence, he pities the short-sighted and
besotted men who seem madly intent upon laying magazines of power under the cradles of unborn generations.
He has great faith in the possibilities of the negro, and
believes that, enlightened and Christianized, he will sink
the old animosities of slavery into the new community of
interests arising from freedom; and that his influence
upon the South will be as the influence of the sun upon
the earth. As when the sun passes from Capricorn to
Cancer, beauty, greenness, and harmony spring up in his
path, so he hopes that the future career of the negro will
be a greater influence for freedom and social advancement than it was in the days of yore for slavery and its
inferior civilization.

Harry and Lucille are at the head of a large and flourishing school. Lucille gives her ripening experience to her
chosen work, to which she was too devoted to resign.
And through the school they are lifting up the homes of
the people. Some have pitied, others blamed, Harry for
casting his lot with the colored people, but he knows that
life's highest and best advantages do not depend on the
color of the skin or texture of the hair. He has his reward
in the improved condition of his pupils and the superb

manhood and noble life which he has developed in his much needed work.

Uncle Daniel still lingers on the shores of time, a cheery, lovable old man, loved and respected by all; a welcome guest in every home. Soon after Iola's marriage, Robert sold out his business and moved with his mother and sister to North Carolina. He bought a large plantation near C——, which he divided into small homesteads, and sold to poor but thrifty laborers, and his heart has been gladdened by their increased prosperity and progress. He has seen the one-roomed cabins change to comfortable cottages, in which cleanliness and order have supplanted the prolific causes of disease and death. Kind and generous, he often remembers Mrs. Johnson and sends her timely aid.

Marie's pale, spiritual face still bears traces of the beauty which was her youthful dower, but its bloom has been succeeded by an air of sweetness and dignity. Though frail in health, she is always ready to lend a helping hand wherever and whenever she can.

Grandmother Johnson was glad to return South and spend the remnant of her days with the remaining friends of her early life. Although feeble, she is in full sympathy with her children for the uplifting of the race. Marie and her mother are enjoying their aftermath of life, one by rendering to others all the service in her power, while the other, with her face turned toward the celestial city, is

> "Only waiting till the angels
> Open wide the mystic gate."

The shadows have been lifted from all their lives; and peace, like bright dew, has descended upon their paths. Blessed themselves, their lives are a blessing to others.

NOTE

FROM THREADS OF FACT and fiction I have woven a story whose mission will not be in vain if it awaken in the hearts of our countrymen a stronger sense of justice and a more Christlike humanity in behalf of those whom the fortunes of war threw, homeless, ignorant and poor, upon the threshold of a new era. Nor will it be in vain if it inspire the children of those upon whose brows God has poured the chrism of that new era to determine that they will embrace every opportunity, develop every faculty, and use every power God has given them to rise in the scale of character and condition, and to add their quota of good citizenship to the best welfare of the nation. There are scattered among us materials for mournful tragedies and mirth-provoking comedies, which some hand may yet bring into the literature of the country, glowing with the fervor of the tropics and enriched by the luxuriance of the Orient, and thus add to the solution of our unsolved American problem.

The race has not had very long to straighten its hands from the hoe, to grasp the pen and wield it as a power for good, and to erect above the ruined auction-block and slave-pen institutions of learning, but

> There is light beyond the darkness,
>   Joy beyond the present pain;
> There is hope in God's great justice
>   And the negro's rising brain.
> Though the morning seems to linger
>   O'er the hill-tops far away,
> Yet the shadows bear the promise
>   Of a brighter coming day.

The Marrow of Tradition

by

Charles W. Chesnutt

I like you and your book, ingenious Hone!
In whose capacious all-embracing leaves
The very marrow of tradition's shown.

CHARLES LAMB
To the Editor
of the Every-day Book

CHAPTER I

At Break of Day

"STAY HERE BESIDE HER, MAJOR. I shall not be needed for an hour yet. Meanwhile I'll go downstairs and snatch a bit of sleep, or talk to old Jane."

The night was hot and sultry. Though the windows of the chamber were wide open, and the muslin curtains looped back, not a breath of air was stirring. Only the shrill chirp of the cicada and the muffled croaking of the frogs in some distant marsh broke the night silence. The heavy scent of magnolias, overpowering even the strong smell of drugs in the sickroom, suggested death and funeral wreaths, sorrow and tears, the long home, the last sleep. The major shivered with apprehension as the slender hand which he held in his own contracted nervously and in a spasm of pain clutched his fingers with a viselike grip.

Major Carteret, though dressed in brown linen, had thrown off his coat for greater comfort. The stifling heat, in spite of the palm-leaf fan which he plied mechanically, was scarcely less oppressive than his own thoughts. Long ago, while yet a mere boy in years, he had come back from Appomattox to find his family, one of the oldest and proudest in the state, hopelessly impoverished by the war,—even their ancestral home swallowed up in the common ruin. His elder brother had sacrificed his life on the bloody altar of the lost cause, and his father, broken and chagrined, died not many years later, leaving the major the last of his line. He had tried in various pursuits to gain a foothold in the new life, but with indifferent success until he won the hand of Olivia Merkell, whom he had seen grow from a small girl to glorious womanhood. With her money he had founded the Morning Chronicle, which he had made the leading organ of his party and the most influential paper in the State. The fine old house in which they lived was hers. In this very room she had first drawn the breath of life; it had been their nuptial chamber; and here, too, within a few hours, she might die, for it seemed impossible that one could long endure such frightful agony and live.

One cloud alone had marred the otherwise perfect serenity of their happiness. Olivia was childless. To have children to perpetuate the name of which he was so proud, to write it still higher on the roll of honor, had been his dearest hope. His disappointment had been proportionately keen. A few months ago this dead hope had revived, and altered the whole aspect of their lives. But as time went on, his wife's age had begun to tell upon her, until even Dr. Price, the most cheerful and optimistic of physicians, had warned him, while hoping for the best, to be prepared for the worst. To add to the danger, Mrs. Carteret had only this day suffered from a nervous shock, which, it was feared, had hastened by several weeks the expected event.

Dr. Price went downstairs to the library, where a dim light was burning. An old black woman, dressed in a gingham frock, with a red bandana handkerchief coiled around her head by way of turban, was seated by an open window. She rose and curtsied as the doctor entered and dropped into a willow rocking-chair near her own.

"How did this happen, Jane?" he asked in a subdued voice, adding, with assumed severity, "You ought to have taken better care of your mistress."

"Now look a-hyuh, Doctuh Price," returned the old woman in an unctuous whisper, "you don' wanter come talkin' none er yo' foolishness 'bout my not takin' keer er Mis' 'Livy. *She* never would 'a' said sech a thing! Seven er eight mont's ago, w'en she sent fer me, I says ter her, says I:—

" 'Lawd, Lawd, honey! You don' tell me dat after all dese long w'ary years er waitin' de good Lawd is done heared yo' prayer an' is gwine ter sen' you de chile you be'n wantin' so long an' so bad? Bless his holy name! Will I come an' nuss yo' baby? Why, honey, I nussed you, an' nussed yo' mammy thoo her las' sickness, an' laid her out w'en she died. I wouldn' *let* nobody e'se nuss yo' baby; an' mo'over, I'm gwine ter come an' nuss you too. You're young side er me, Mis' 'Livy, but you're ove'ly ole ter be havin' yo' fus' baby, an' you'll need somebody roun', honey, w'at knows all 'bout de fam'ly, an' deir ways an' deir weaknesses, an' I don' know who dat'd be ef it wa'n't me.'

" ' 'Deed, Mammy Jane,' says she, 'dere ain' nobody e'se I'd have but you. You kin come ez soon ez you wanter an' stay ez long ez you mineter.'

"An huh I is, an' huh I'm gwine ter stay. Fer Mis' 'Livy is my ole mist'ess's daughter, an' my ole mis'tess wuz good ter me, an' dey ain' none er her folks gwine ter suffer ef ole Jane kin he'p it."

"Your loyalty does you credit, Jane," observed the doctor; "but you haven't told me yet what happened to Mrs. Carteret to-day. Did the horse run away, or did she see something that frightened her?"

"No, suh, de hoss didn' git skeered at nothin', but Mis' 'Livy did see somethin', er somebody; an' it wa'n't no fault er mine ner her'n neither,—it goes fu'ther back, suh, fu'ther dan dis day er dis year. Does you 'member de time w'en my ole mist'ess, Mis' 'Livy upstairs's mammy, died? No? Well, you wuz prob'ly 'way ter school den, studyin' ter be a doctuh. But I'll tell you all erbout it.

"W'en my ole mist'ess, Mis' 'Liz'beth Merkell,—an' a good mist'ess she wuz,—tuck sick fer de las' time, her sister Polly—ole Mis' Polly Ochiltree w'at is now—come ter de house ter he'p nuss her. Mis' 'Livy upstairs yander wuz erbout six years ole den, de sweetes' little angel you ever laid eyes on; an' on her dyin' bed Mis' 'Liz'beth ax' Miz' Polly fer ter stay hyuh an' take keer er her chile, an' Mis' Polly she promise'. She wuz a widder fer de secon' time, an' didn' have no child'en, an' could jes' as well come as not.

"But dere wuz trouble after de fune'al, an' it happen' right hyuh in dis lib'ary. Mars Sam wuz settin' by de table, w'en Mis' Polly come downstairs, slow an' solemn, an' stood dere in de middle er de flo', all in black, till Mars Sam sot a cheer fer her.

" 'Well, Samuel,' says she, 'now dat we've done all we can fer po' 'Liz'beth, it only 'mains fer us ter consider Olivia's future.'

"Mars Sam nodded his head, but didn' say nothin'.

" 'I don' need ter tell you,' says she, 'dat I am willin' ter carry out de wishes er my dead sister, an' sac'ifice my own comfo't, an' make myse'f yo' housekeeper an' yo' child's nuss, fer my dear sister's sake. It wuz her dyin' wish, an' on it I will ac', ef it is also yo'n.'

"Mars Sam didn' want Mis' Polly ter come, suh; fur he didn' like Mis' Polly. He wuz skeered er Miss Polly."

"I don't wonder," yawned the doctor, "if she was anything like she is now."

"Wuss, suh, fer she wuz younger, an' stronger. She always would have her say, no matter 'bout what, an' her own way, no matter who 'posed her. She had already be'n in de house fer a week, an' Mars Sam knowed ef she once come ter stay, she'd be de mist'ess of eve'ybody in it an' him too. But w'at could he do but say yas?

" 'Den it is unde'stood, is it,' says Mis' Polly, w'en he had spoke, 'dat I am ter take cha'ge er de house?'

" 'All right, Polly,' says Mars Sam, wid a deep sigh.

"Mis' Polly 'lowed he wuz sighin' fer my po' dead mist'ess, fer she didn' have no idee er his feelin's to'ds her,— she alluz did 'low dat all de gent'emen wuz in love wid 'er.

" 'You won' fin' much ter do,' Mars Sam went on, 'fer Julia is a good housekeeper, an' kin ten' ter mos' eve'ything, under yo' d'rections.'

"Mis' Polly stiffen' up like a ramrod. 'It mus' be unde'-stood, Samuel,' says she, 'dat w'en I 'sumes cha'ge er yo' house, dere ain' gwine ter be no 'vided 'sponsibility; an' as fer dis Julia, me an' her couldn' git 'long tergether nohow. Ef I stays, Julia goes.'

"W'en Mars Sam heared dat, he felt better, an' 'mence' ter pick up his courage. Mis' Polly had showed her han' too plain. My mist'ess had n' got col' yit, an' Mis' Polly, who 'd be'n a widder fer two years dis las' time, wuz already fig'rin' on takin' her place fer good, an' she didn' want no other woman roun' de house dat Mars Sam might take a' intrus' in.

" 'My dear Polly,' says Mars Sam, quite determine', 'I could n' possibly sen' Julia 'way. Fac' is, I couldn' git 'long widout Julia. She 'd be'n runnin' dis house like clockwo'k befo' you come, an' I likes her ways. My dear, dead 'Liz'beth sot a heap er sto' by Julia, an' I'm gwine ter keep her here fer 'Liz'beth's sake.'

"Mis' Polly's eyes flash' fire.

"'Ah,' says she, 'I see—I see! You perfers her housekeepin' ter mine, indeed! Dat is a fine way ter talk ter a lady! An' a heap er rispec' you is got fer de mem'ry er my po' dead sister!'

"Mars Sam knowed w'at she 'lowed she seed wa'n't so; but he didn' let on, fer it only made him de safer. He wuz willin' fer her ter 'magine w'at she please', jes' so long ez she kep' out er his house an' let him alone.

"'No, Polly,' says he, gittin' bolder ez she got madder, 'dere ain' no use talkin'. Nothin' in de worl' would make me part wid Julia.'

"Mis' Polly she r'ared an' she pitch', but Mars Sam helt on like grim death. Mis' Polly wouldn' give in nei-ther, an' so she fin'lly went away. Dey made some kind er 'rangement afterwa'ds, an' Miss Polly tuck Mis' 'Livy ter her own house. Mars Sam paid her bo'd an' 'lowed Mis' Polly somethin' fer takin' keer er her."

"And Julia stayed?"

"Julia stayed, suh, an' a couple er years later her chile wuz bawn, right here in dis house."

"But you said," observed the doctor, "that Mrs. Ochiltree was in error about Julia."

"Yas, suh, so she wuz, w'en my ole mist'ess died. But dis wuz two years after,—an' w'at has ter be has ter be. Julia had a easy time; she had a black gal ter wait on her, a buggy to ride in, an' eve'ything she wanted. Eve'ybody s'posed Mars Sam would give her a house an' lot, er leave her somethin' in his will. But he died suddenly, and didn' leave no will, an' Mis' Polly got herse'f 'pinted gyardeen ter young Mis' 'Livy, an' driv Julia an' her young un out er de house, an' lived here in dis house wid Mis' 'Livy till Mis' 'Livy ma'ied Majah Carteret."

"And what became of Julia?" asked Dr. Price.

Such relations, the doctor knew very well, had been all too common in the old slavery days, and not a few of them had been projected into the new era. Sins, like snakes, die hard. The habits and customs of a people were not to be changed in a day, nor by the stroke of a pen. As family physician, and father confessor by brevet, Dr. Price had looked upon more than one hidden skele-

ton; and no one in town had had better opportunities
than old Jane for learning the undercurrents in the lives
of the old families.

"Well," resumed Jane, "eve'ybody s'posed, after w'at
had happen', dat Julia 'd keep on livin' easy, fer she wuz
young an' good-lookin'. But she didn'. She tried ter make
a livin' sewin', but Mis' Polly wouldn' let de bes' w'ite
folks hire her. Den she tuck up washin', but didn' do no
better at dat; an' bimeby she got so discourage' dat she
ma'ied a shif'less yaller man, an' died er consumption
soon after,—an' wuz 'bout ez well off, fer dis man
couldn' hardly feed her nohow."

"And the child?"

"One er de No'the'n w'ite lady teachers at de mission
school tuck a likin' ter little Janet, an' put her thoo
school, an' den sent her off ter de No'th fer ter study ter
be a school teacher. W'en she come back, 'stead er
teachin' she ma'ied ole Adam Miller's son."

"The rich stevedore's son, Dr. Miller?"

"Yas, suh, dat's de man,—you knows 'im. Dis yer boy
wuz jes' gwine 'way fer ter study ter be a doctuh, an' he
ma'ied dis Janet, an' tuck her 'way wid 'im. Dey went
off ter Europe, er Irope, er Orope, er somewhere er
'nother, 'way off yander, an' come back here las' year
an' sta'ted dis yer horspital an' school fer ter train de
black gals fer nusses."

"He's a very good doctor, Jane, and is doing a useful
work. Your chapter of family history is quite interesting,—I knew part of it before, in a general way; but
you haven't yet told me what brought on Mrs. Carteret's
trouble."

"I'm jes' comin' ter dat dis minute, suh,—w'at I be'n
tellin' you is all a part of it. Dis yer Janet, w'at's Mis'
'Livy's half-sister, is ez much like her ez ef dey wuz twins.
Folks sometimes takes 'em fer one ernudder,—I s'pose
it tickles Janet mos' ter death, but it do make Mis' 'Livy
rippin'. An' den 'way back yander jes' after de wah, w'en
de ole Carteret mansion had ter be sol', Adam Miller
bought it, an' dis yer Janet an' her husban' is be'n livin'
in it ever sence ole Adam died, 'bout a year ago; an' dat
makes de majah mad, 'ca'se he don' wanter see cullud
folks livin' in de ole fam'ly mansion w'at he wuz bawn
in. An' mo'over, an' dat 's de wust of all, w'iles Mis'

'Livy ain' had no child'en befo', dis yer sister er her'n is got a fine-lookin' little yaller boy, w'at favors de fam'ly so dat ef Mis' 'Livy'd see de chile anywhere, it 'd mos' break her heart fer ter think 'bout her not havin' no child'en herse'f. So ter-day, w'en Mis' 'Livy wuz out ridin' an' met dis yer Janet wid her boy, an' w'en Mis' 'Livy got ter studyin' 'bout her own chances, an' how she mought not come thoo safe, she jes' had a fit er hysterics right dere in de buggy. She wuz mos' home, an' William got her here, an' you know de res'."

Major Carteret, from the head of the stairs, called the doctor anxiously.

"You had better come along up now, Jane," said the doctor.

For two long hours they fought back the grim spectre that stood by the bedside. The child was born at dawn. Both mother and child, the doctor said, would live.

"Bless its 'ittle hea't!" exclaimed Mammy Jane, as she held up the tiny mite, which bore as much resemblance to mature humanity as might be expected of an infant which had for only a few minutes drawn the breath of life. "Bless its 'ittle hea't! it's de ve'y spit an' image er its pappy!"

The doctor smiled. The major laughed aloud. Jane's unconscious witticism, or conscious flattery, whichever it might be, was a welcome diversion from the tense strain of the last few hours.

"Be that as it may," said Dr. Price cheerfully, "and I'll not dispute it, the child is a very fine boy,—a very fine boy, indeed! Take care of it, major," he added with a touch of solemnity, "for your wife can never bear another."

With the child's first cry a refreshing breeze from the distant ocean cooled the hot air of the chamber; the heavy odor of the magnolias, with its mortuary suggestiveness, gave place to the scent of rose and lilac and honeysuckle. The birds in the garden were singing lustily.

All these sweet and pleasant things found an echo in the major's heart. He stood by the window, and looking toward the rising sun, breathed a silent prayer of thanksgiving. All nature seemed to rejoice in sympathy with his happiness at the fruition of this long-deferred hope, and to predict for this wonderful child a bright and glorious future.

Old Mammy Jane, however, was not entirely at ease concerning the child. She had discovered, under its left ear, a small mole, which led her to fear that the child was born for bad luck. Had the baby been black, or yellow, or poor-white, Jane would unhesitatingly have named, as his ultimate fate, a not uncommon form of taking off, usually resultant upon the infraction of certain laws, or, in these swift modern days, upon too violent a departure from established social customs. It was manifestly impossible that a child of such high quality as the grandson of her old mistress should die by judicial strangulation; but nevertheless the warning was a serious thing, and not to be lightly disregarded.

Not wishing to be considered as a prophet of evil omen, Jane kept her own counsel in regard to this significant discovery. But later, after the child was several days old, she filled a small vial with water in which the infant had been washed, and took it to a certain wise old black woman, who lived on the farther edge of the town and was well known to be versed in witchcraft and conjuration. The conjure woman added to the contents of the bottle a bit of calamus root, and one of the cervical vertebræ from the skeleton of a black cat, with several other mysterious ingredients, the nature of which she did not disclose. Following instructions given her, Aunt Jane buried the bottle in Carteret's back yard, one night during the full moon, as a good-luck charm to ward off evil from the little grandson of her dear mistress, so long since dead and gone to heaven.

CHAPTER II

The Christening Party

THEY NAMED THE Carteret baby Theodore Felix. Theodore was a family name, and had been borne by the eldest son for several generations, the major himself being a second son. Having thus given the child two beautiful names, replete with religious and sentimental significance, they called him—"Dodie."

The baby was christened some six weeks after its birth, by which time Mrs. Carteret was able to be out. Old Mammy Jane, who had been brought up in the church, but who, like some better informed people in all ages, found religion not inconsistent with a strong vein of superstition, felt her fears for the baby's future much relieved when the rector had made the sign of the cross and sprinkled little Dodie with the water from the carved marble font, which had come from England in the reign of King Charles the Martyr, as the ill-fated son of James I. was known to St. Andrew's. Upon this special occasion Mammy Jane had been provided with a seat downstairs among the white people, to her own intense satisfaction, and to the secret envy of a small colored attendance in the gallery, to whom she was ostentatiously pointed out by her grandson Jerry, porter at the Morning Chronicle office, who sat among them in the front row.

On the following Monday evening the major gave a christening party in honor of this important event. Owing to Mrs. Carteret's still delicate health, only a small number of intimate friends and family connections were invited to attend. These were the rector of St. Andrew's; old Mrs. Polly Ochiltree, the godmother; old Mr. Delamere, a distant relative and also one of the sponsors; and his grandson, Tom Delamere. The major had also invited Lee Ellis, his young city editor, for whom he had a great liking apart from his business value, and who was a frequent visitor at the house. These, with the family itself, which consisted of the major, his wife, and his half-sister, Clara Pemberton, a young woman of about eighteen, made up the eight persons for whom covers were laid.

Ellis was the first to arrive, a tall, loose-limbed young man, with a slightly freckled face, hair verging on auburn, a firm chin, and honest gray eyes. He had come half an hour early, and was left alone for a few minutes in the parlor, a spacious, high-ceilinged room, with large windows, and fitted up in excellent taste, with stately reminiscences of a past generation. The walls were hung with figured paper. The ceiling was whitewashed, and decorated in the middle with a plaster centre-piece, from which hung a massive chandelier sparkling with prismatic rays from a hundred crystal pendants. There was a handsome mantel, set with terra-cotta tiles, on which fauns and satyrs, nymphs and dryads, disported themselves in idyllic abandon. The furniture was old, and in keeping with the room.

At seven o'clock a carriage drove up, from which alighted an elderly gentleman, with white hair and mustache, and bowed somewhat with years. Short of breath and painfully weak in the legs, he was assisted from the carriage by a colored man, apparently about forty years old, to whom short side-whiskers and spectacles imparted an air of sobriety. This attendant gave his arm respectfully to the old gentleman, who leaned upon it heavily, but with as little appearance of dependence as possible. The servant, assuming a similar unconsciousness of the weight resting upon his arm, assisted the old gentleman carefully up the steps.

"I'm all right now, Sandy," whispered the gentleman as soon as his feet were planted firmly on the piazza. "You may come back for me at nine o'clock."

Having taken his hand from his servant's arm, he advanced to meet a lady who stood in the door awaiting him, a tall, elderly woman, gaunt and angular of frame, with a mottled face, and high cheekbones partially covered by bands of hair entirely too black and abundant for a person of her age, if one might judge from the lines of her mouth, which are rarely deceptive in such matters.

"Perhaps you'd better not send your man away, Mr. Delamere," observed the lady, in a high shrill voice, which grated upon the old gentleman's ears. He was slightly hard of hearing, but, like most deaf people, resented being screamed at. "You might need him before nine o'clock. One never knows what may happen after one has had the second stroke. And moreover, our butler has fallen down the back steps—negroes are so careless!—and sprained his ankle so that he can't stand. I'd like to have Sandy stay and wait on the table in Peter's place, if you don't mind."

"I thank you, Mrs. Ochiltree, for your solicitude," replied Mr. Delamere, with a shade of annoyance in his voice, "but my health is very good just at present, and I do not anticipate any catastrophe which will require my servant's presence before I am ready to go home. But I have no doubt, madam," he continued, with a courteous inclination, "that Sandy will be pleased to serve you, if you desire it, to the best of his poor knowledge."

"I shill be honored, ma'am," assented Sandy, with a bow even deeper than his master's, "only I'm 'feared I ain't rightly dressed fer ter wait on table. I wuz only goin' ter pra'r-meetin', an' so I didn' put on my bes' clo's. Ef Mis' Ochiltree ain' gwine ter neeJ me fer de nex' fifteen minutes, I kin ride back home in de ca'ige an' dress myse'f suitable fer de occasion, suh."

"If you think you'll wait on the table any better," said Mrs. Ochiltree, "you may go along and change your clothes; but hurry back, for it is seven now, and dinner will soon be served."

Sandy retired with a bow. While descending the steps to the carriage, which had waited for him, he came face to face with a young man just entering the house.

"Am I in time for dinner, Sandy?" asked the newcomer.

"Yas, Mistuh Tom, you're in plenty er time. Dinner won't be ready till *I* git back, which won' be fer fifteen minutes er so yit."

Throwing away the cigarette which he held between his fingers, the young man crossed the piazza with a light step, and after a preliminary knock, for an answer to which he did not wait, entered the house with the air of one thoroughly at home. The lights in the parlor had been lit, and Ellis, who sat talking to Major Carteret when the newcomer entered, covered him with a jealous glance.

Slender and of medium height, with a small head of almost perfect contour, a symmetrical face, dark almost to swarthiness, black eyes, which moved somewhat restlessly, curly hair of raven tint, a slight mustache, small hands and feet, and fashionable attire, Tom Delamere, the grandson of the old gentleman who had already arrived, was easily the handsomest young man in Wellington. But no discriminating observer would have characterized his beauty as manly. It conveyed no impression of strength, but did possess a certain element, feline rather than feminine, which subtly negatived the idea of manliness.

He gave his hand to the major, nodded curtly to Ellis, saluted his grandfather respectfully, and inquired for the ladies.

"Olivia is dressing for dinner," replied the major; "Mrs. Ochiltree is in the kitchen, struggling with the servants. Clara— Ah, here she comes now!"

Ellis, whose senses were preternaturally acute where Clara was concerned, was already looking toward the hall and was the first to see her. Clad in an evening gown of simple white, to the close-fitting corsage of which she had fastened a bunch of pink roses, she was to Ellis a dazzling apparition. To him her erect and well-moulded form was the embodiment of symmetry, her voice sweet music, her movements the perfection of grace; and it scarcely needed a lover's imagination to read in her fair countenance a pure heart and a high spirit,—the truthfulness that scorns a lie, the pride which is not haughtiness. There were suggestive depths of tenderness, too, in the curl of her lip, the droop of her long lashes, the glance of her blue eyes,—depths that Ellis had long since divined, though he had never yet explored them. She gave Ellis a friendly nod as she came in, but for the smile with which she greeted Delamere, Ellis would have given all that he possessed,—not a great deal, it is true, but what could a man do more?

"You are the last one, Tom," she said reproachfully. "Mr. Ellis has been here half an hour."

Delamere threw a glance at Ellis which was not exactly friendly. Why should this fellow always be on hand to emphasize his own shortcomings?

"The rector is not here," answered Tom triumphantly. "You see I am not the last."

"The rector," replied Clara, "was called out of town at six o'clock this evening, to visit a dying man, and so cannot be here. You are the last, Tom, and Mr. Ellis was the first."

Ellis was ruefully aware that this comparison in his favor was the only visible advantage that he had gained from his early arrival. He had not seen Miss Pemberton a moment sooner by reason of it. There had been a certain satisfaction in being in the same house with her, but Delamere had arrived in time to share or, more correctly, to monopolize, the sunshine of her presence.

Delamere gave a plausible excuse which won Clara's pardon and another enchanting smile, which pierced Ellis like a dagger. He knew very well that Delamere's excuse was a lie. Ellis himself had been ready as early as six o'clock, but judging this to be too early, had stopped in at the Clarendon Club for half an hour, to look over the magazines. While coming out he had glanced into the card-room, where he had seen his rival deep in a game of cards, from which Delamere had evidently not been able to tear himself until the last moment. He had accounted for his lateness by a story quite inconsistent with these facts.

The two young people walked over to a window on the opposite side of the large room, where they stood talking to one another in low tones. The major had left the room for a moment. Old Mr. Delamere, who was watching his grandson and Clara with an indulgent smile, proceeded to rub salt into Ellis's wounds.

"They make a handsome couple," he observed. "I remember well when her mother, in her youth an ideally beautiful woman, of an excellent family, married Daniel Pemberton, who was not of so good a family, but had made money. The major, who was only a very young man then, disapproved of the match; he considered that his mother, although a widow and nearly forty, was marrying beneath her. But he has been a good brother to Clara, and a careful guardian of her estate. Ah, young gentleman, you cannot appreciate, except in imagination, what it means, to one standing on the brink of eternity, to feel sure that he will live on in his children and his children's children!"

Ellis was appreciating at that moment what it meant, in cold blood, with no effort of the imagination, to see the girl whom he loved absorbed completely in another man. She had looked at him only once since Tom Delamere had entered the room, and then merely to use him as a spur with which to prick his favored rival.

"Yes, sir," he returned mechanically, "Miss Clara is a beautiful young lady."

"And Tom is a good boy—a fine boy," returned the old gentleman. "I am very well pleased with Tom, and shall be entirely happy when I see them married."

Ellis could not echo this sentiment. The very thought of this marriage made him miserable. He had always understood that the engagement was merely tentative, a sort of family understanding, subject to confirmation after Delamere should have attained his majority, which was still a year off, and when the major should think Clara old enough to marry. Ellis saw Delamere with the eye of a jealous rival, and judged him mercilessly,—whether correctly or not the sequel will show. He did not at all believe that Tom Delamere would make a fit husband for Clara Pemberton; but his opinion would have had no weight,—he could hardly have expressed it without showing his own interest. Moreover, there was no element of the sneak in Lee Ellis's make-up. The very fact that he might profit by the other's discomfiture left Delamere secure, so far as he could be affected by anything that Ellis might say. But Ellis did not shrink from a fair fight, and though in this one the odds were heavily against him, yet so long as this engagement remained indefinite, so long, indeed, as the object of his love was still unwed, he would not cease to hope. Such a sacrifice as this marriage clearly belonged in the catalogue of impossibilities. Ellis had not lived long enough to learn that impossibilities are merely things of which we have not learned, or which we do not wish to happen.

Sandy returned at the end of a quarter of an hour, and dinner was announced. Mr. Delamere led the way to the dining-room with Mrs. Ochiltree. Tom followed with Clara. The major went to the head of the stairs and came down with Mrs. Carteret upon his arm, her beauty rendered more delicate by the pallor of her countenance and more complete by the happiness with which it glowed. Ellis went in alone. In the rector's absence it was practically a family party which sat down, with the exception of Ellis, who, as we have seen, would willingly have placed himself in the same category.

The table was tastefully decorated with flowers, which grew about the house in lavish profusion. In warm climates nature adorns herself with true feminine vanity.

"What a beautiful table!" exclaimed Tom, before they were seated.

"The decorations are mine," said Clara proudly. "I cut the flowers and arranged them all myself."

"Which accounts for the admirable effect," rejoined Tom with a bow, before Ellis, to whom the same thought had occurred, was able to express himself. He had always counted himself the least envious of men, but for this occasion he coveted Tom Delamere's readiness.

"The beauty of the flowers," observed old Mr. Delamere, with sententious gallantry, "is reflected upon all around them. It is a handsome company."

Mrs. Ochiltree beamed upon the table with a dry smile.

"I don't perceive any effect that it has upon you or me," she said. "And as for the young people, 'Handsome is as handsome does.' If Tom here, for instance, were as good as he looks"—

"You flatter me, Aunt Polly," Tom broke in hastily, anticipating the crack of the whip; he was familiar with his aunt's conversational idiosyncrasies.

"If you are as good as you look," continued the old lady, with a cunning but indulgent smile, "some one has been slandering you."

"Thanks, Aunt Polly! Now you don't flatter me."

"There is Mr. Ellis," Mrs. Ochiltree went on, "who is not half so good-looking, but is steady as a clock, I dare say."

"Now, Aunt Polly," interposed Mrs. Carteret, "let the gentlemen alone."

"She doesn't mean half what she says," continued Mrs. Carteret apologetically, "and only talks that way to people whom she likes."

Tom threw Mrs. Carteret a grateful glance. He had

been apprehensive, with the sensitiveness of youth, lest his old great-aunt should make a fool of him before Clara's family. Nor had he relished the comparison with Ellis, who was out of place, anyway, in this family party. He had never liked the fellow, who was too much of a plodder and a prig to make a suitable associate for a whole-souled, generous-hearted young gentleman. He tolerated him as a visitor at Carteret's and as a member of the Clarendon Club, but that was all.

"Mrs. Ochiltree has a characteristic way of disguising her feelings," observed old Mr. Delamere, with a touch of sarcasm.

Ellis had merely flushed and felt uncomfortable at the reference to himself. The compliment to his character hardly offset the reflection upon his looks. He knew he was not exactly handsome, but it was not pleasant to have the fact emphasized in the presence of the girl he loved; he would like at least fair play, and judgment upon the subject left to the young lady.

Mrs. Ochiltree was quietly enjoying herself. In early life she had been accustomed to impale fools on epigrams, like flies on pins, to see them wriggle. But with advancing years she had lost in some measure the faculty of nice discrimination,—it was pleasant to see her victims squirm, whether they were fools or friends. Even one's friends, she argued, were not always wise, and were sometimes the better for being told the truth. At her niece's table she felt at liberty to speak her mind, which she invariably did, with a frankness that sometimes bordered on brutality. She had long ago outgrown the period where ambition or passion, or its partners, envy and hatred, were springs of action in her life, and simply retained a mild enjoyment in the exercise of an old habit, with no active malice whatever. The ruling passion merely grew stronger as the restraining faculties decreased in vigor.

A diversion was created at this point by the appearance of old Mammy Jane, dressed in a calico frock, with clean white neckerchief and apron, carrying the wonderful baby in honor of whose naming this feast had been given. Though only six weeks old, the little Theodore had grown rapidly, and Mammy Jane declared was already quite large for his age, and displayed signs of an unusually precocious intelligence. He was passed around the table and duly admired. Clara thought his hair was fine. Ellis inquired about his teeth. Tom put his finger in the baby's fist to test his grip. Old Mr. Delamere was unable to decide as yet whether he favored most his father or his mother. The object of these attentions endured them patiently for several minutes, and then protested with a vocal vigor which led to his being taken promptly back upstairs. Whatever fate might be in store for him, he manifested no sign of weak lungs.

"Sandy," said Mrs. Carteret when the baby had retired, "pass that tray standing upon the side table, so that we may all see the presents."

Mr. Delamere had brought a silver spoon, and Tom a napkin ring. Ellis had sent a silver watch; it was a little premature, he admitted, but the boy would grow to it, and could use it to play with in the mean time. It had a glass back, so that he might see the wheels go round. Mrs. Ochiltree's present was an old and yellow ivory rattle, with a handle which the child could bite while teething, and a knob screwed on at the end to prevent the handle from slipping through the baby's hand.

"I saw that in your cedar chest, Aunt Polly," said Clara, "when I was a little girl, and you used to pull the chest out from under your bed to get me a dime."

"You kept the rattle in the right-hand corner of the chest," said Tom, "in the box with the red silk purse, from which you took the gold piece you gave me every Christmas."

A smile shone on Mrs. Ochiltree's severe features at this appreciation, like a ray of sunlight on a snowbank.

"Aunt Polly's chest is like the widow's cruse," said Mrs. Carteret, "which was never empty."

"Or Fortunatus's purse, which was always full," added old Mr. Delamere, who read the Latin poets, and whose allusions were apt to be classical rather than scriptural.

"It will last me while I live," said Mrs. Ochiltree, adding cautiously, "but there'll not be a great deal left. It won't take much to support an old woman for twenty years."

Mr. Delamere's man Sandy had been waiting upon the table with the decorum of a trained butler, and a gravity all his own. He had changed his suit of plain gray for a long blue coat with brass buttons, which dated back to the fashion of a former generation, with which he wore a pair of plaid trousers of strikingly modern cut and pattern. With his whiskers, his spectacles, and his solemn air of responsibility, he would have presented, to one unfamiliar with the negro type, an amusingly impressive appearance. But there was nothing incongruous about Sandy to this company, except perhaps to Tom Delamere, who possessed a keen eye for contrasts and always regarded Sandy, in that particular rig, as a very comical darkey.

"Is it quite prudent, Mrs. Ochiltree," suggested the major at a moment when Sandy, having set down the tray, had left the room for a little while, "to mention, in the presence of the servants, that you keep money in the house?"

"I beg your pardon, major," observed old Mr. Delamere, with a touch of stiffness. "The only servant in hearing of the conversation has been my own; and Sandy is as honest as any man in Wellington."

"You mean, sir," replied Carteret, with a smile, "as honest as any *negro* in Wellington."

"I make no exceptions, major," returned the old gentleman, with emphasis. "I would trust Sandy with my life,—he saved it once at the risk of his own."

"No doubt," mused the major, "the negro is capable of a certain doglike fidelity,—I make the comparison in a kindly sense,—a certain personal devotion which is admirable in itself, and fits him eminently for a servile career. I should imagine, however, that one could more safely trust his life with a negro than his portable property."

"Very clever, major! I read your paper, and know that your feeling is hostile toward the negro, but"—

The major made a gesture of dissent, but remained courteously silent until Mr. Delamere had finished.

"For my part," the old gentleman went on, "I think they have done very well, considering what they started from, and their limited opportunities. There was Adam Miller, for instance, who left a comfortable estate. His son George carries on the business, and the younger boy, William, is a good doctor and stands well with his profession. His hospital is a good thing, and if my estate were clear, I should like to do something for it."

"You are mistaken, sir, in imagining me hostile to the negro," explained Carteret. "On the contrary, I am friendly to his best interests. I give him employment; I pay taxes for schools to educate him, and for courthouses and jails to keep him in order. I merely object to being governed by an inferior and servile race."

Mrs. Carteret's face wore a tired expression. This question was her husband's hobby, and therefore her own nightmare. Moreover, she had her personal grievance against the negro race, and the names mentioned by old Mr. Delamere had brought it vividly before her mind. She had no desire to mar the harmony of the occasion by the discussion of a distasteful subject.

Mr. Delamere, glancing at his hostess, read something of this thought, and refused the challenge to further argument.

"I do not believe, major," he said, "that Olivia relishes the topic. I merely wish to say that Sandy is an exception to any rule which you may formulate in derogation of the negro. Sandy is a gentleman in ebony!"

Tom could scarcely preserve his gravity at this characterization of old Sandy, with his ridiculous air of importance, his long blue coat, and his loud plaid trousers. That suit would make a great costume for a masquerade. He would borrow it some time,—there was nothing in the world like it.

"Well, Mr. Delamere," returned the major good-humoredly, "no doubt Sandy is an exceptionally good negro,—he might well be, for he has had the benefit of your example all his life,—and we know that he is a faithful servant. But nevertheless, if I were Mrs. Ochiltree, I should put my money in the bank. Not all negroes are as honest as Sandy, and an elderly lady might not prove a match for a burly black burglar."

"Thank you, major," retorted Mrs. Ochiltree, with spirit, "I'm not yet too old to take care of myself. That cedar chest has been my bank for forty years, and I shall not change my habits at my age."

At this moment Sandy reentered the room. Carteret made a warning gesture, which Mrs. Ochiltree chose not to notice.

"I've proved a match for two husbands, and am not afraid of any man that walks the earth, black or white, by day or night. I have a revolver, and know how to use it. Whoever attempts to rob me will do so at his peril."

After dinner Clara played the piano and sang duets with Tom Delamere. At nine o'clock Mr. Delamere's carriage came for him, and he went away accompanied by Sandy. Under cover of the darkness the old gentleman leaned on his servant's arm with frank dependence, and Sandy lifted him into the carriage with every mark of devotion.

Ellis had already excused himself to go to the office and look over the late proofs for the morning paper. Tom remained a few minutes longer than his grandfather, and upon taking his leave went round to the Clarendon Club, where he spent an hour or two in the card-room with a couple of congenial friends. Luck seemed to favor him, and he went home at midnight with a comfortable balance of winnings. He was fond of excitement, and found a great deal of it in cards. To lose was only less exciting than to win. Of late he had developed into a very successful player,—so successful, indeed, that several members of the club generally found excuses to avoid participating in a game where he made one.

CHAPTER III

The Editor at Work

TO GO BACK A LITTLE, for several days after his child's birth Major Carteret's chief interest in life had been confined to the four walls of the chamber where his pale wife lay upon her bed of pain, and those of the adjoining room where an old black woman crooned lovingly over a little white infant. A new element had been added to the major's consciousness, broadening the scope and deepening the strength of his affections. He did not love Olivia the less, for maternity had crowned her wifehood with an added glory; but side by side with this old and tried attachment was a new passion, stirring up dormant hopes and kindling new desires. His regret had been more than personal at the thought that with himself an old name should be lost to the State; and now all the old pride of race, class, and family welled up anew, and swelled and quickened the current of his life.

Upon the major's first appearance at the office, which took place the second day after the child's birth, he opened a box of cigars in honor of the event. The word had been passed around by Ellis, and the whole office force, including reporters, compositors, and pressmen, came in to congratulate the major and smoke at his expense. Even Jerry, the colored porter,—Mammy Jane's grandson and therefore a protégé of the family,—presented himself among the rest, or rather, after the rest. The major shook hands with them all except Jerry, though he acknowledged the porter's congratulations with a kind nod and put a good cigar into his outstretched palm, for which Jerry thanked him without manifesting any consciousness of the omission. He was quite aware that under ordinary circumstances the major would not have shaken hands with white workingmen, to say nothing of negroes; and he had merely hoped that in the pleasurable distraction of the moment the major might also overlook the distinction of color. Jerry's hope had been shattered, though not rudely; for the major had spoken pleasantly and the cigar was a good one. Mr. Ellis had once shaken hands with Jerry,—but Mr. Ellis was a young man, whose Quaker father had never owned any slaves, and he could not be expected to have as much pride as one of the best "quality," whose families had possessed land and negroes for time out of mind. On the whole, Jerry preferred the careless nod of the editor-in-chief to the more familiar greeting of the subaltern.

Having finished this pleasant ceremony, which left him with a comfortable sense of his new dignity, the major turned to his desk. It had been much neglected during the week, and more than one matter claimed his attention; but as typical of the new trend of his thoughts, the first subject he took up was one bearing upon the future of his son. Quite obviously the career of a Carteret must not be left to chance,—it must be planned and worked out with a due sense of the value of good blood.

There lay upon his desk a letter from a well-known promoter, offering the major an investment which promised large returns, though several years must elapse before the enterprise could be put upon a paying basis. The element of time, however, was not immediately important. The Morning Chronicle provided him an ample income. The money available for this investment was part of his wife's patrimony. It was invested in a local cotton mill, which was paying ten per cent, but this was a beggarly return compared with the immense profits promised by the offered investment,—profits which would enable his son, upon reaching manhood, to take a place in the world commensurate with the dignity of his ancestors, one of whom, only a few generations removed, had owned an estate of ninety thousand acres of land and six thousand slaves.

This letter having been disposed of by an answer accepting the offer, the major took up his pen to write an editorial. Public affairs in the state were not going to his satisfaction. At the last state election his own party, after an almost unbroken rule of twenty years, had been defeated by the so-called "Fusion" ticket, a combination of Republicans and Populists. A clean sweep had been made of the offices in the state, which were now filled by new men. Many of the smaller places had gone to colored men, their people having voted almost solidly for the Fusion ticket. In spite of the fact that the population of Wellington was two thirds colored, this state of things was gall and wormwood to the defeated party, of which the Morning Chronicle was the acknowledged organ. Major Carteret shared this feeling. Only this very morning, while passing the city hall, on his way to the office, he had seen the steps of that noble building disfigured by a fringe of job-hunting negroes, for all the world—to use a local simile—like a string of buzzards sitting on a rail, awaiting their opportunity to batten upon the helpless corpse of a moribund city.

Taking for this theme the unfitness of the negro to participate in government,—an unfitness due to his limited education, his lack of experience, his criminal tendencies, and more especially to his hopeless mental and physical inferiority to the white race,—the major had demonstrated, it seemed to him clearly enough, that the ballot in the hands of the negro was a menace to the commonwealth. He had argued, with entire conviction, that the white and black races could never attain social and political harmony by commingling their blood; he had proved by several historical parallels that no two unassimilable races could ever live together except in the relation of superior and inferior; and he was just dipping his gold pen into the ink to indite his conclusions from the premises thus established, when Jerry, the porter, announced two visitors.

"Gin'l Belmont an' Cap'n McBane would like ter see you, suh."

"Show them in, Jerry."

The man who entered first upon this invitation was a dapper little gentleman with light-blue eyes and a Vandyke beard. He wore a frock coat, patent leather shoes, and a Panama hat. There were crow's-feet about his eyes, which twinkled with a hard and, at times, humorous shrewdness. He had sloping shoulders, small hands and feet, and walked with the leisurely step characteristic of those who have been reared under hot suns.

Carteret gave his hand cordially to the gentleman thus described.

"How do you do, Captain McBane," he said, turning to the second visitor.

The individual thus addressed was strikingly different in appearance from his companion. His broad shoulders, burly form, square jaw, and heavy chin betokened strength, energy, and unscrupulousness. With the exception of a small, bristling mustache, his face was clean shaven, with here and there a speck of dried blood due to a carelessly or unskillfully handled razor. A single deep-set gray eye was shadowed by a beetling brow, over which a crop of coarse black hair, slightly streaked with gray, fell almost low enough to mingle with his black, bushy eyebrows. His coat had not been brushed for several days, if one might judge from the accumulation of dandruff upon the collar, and his shirt-front, in the middle of which blazed a showy diamond, was plentifully stained with tobacco juice. He wore a large slouch hat, which, upon entering the office, he removed and held in his hand.

Having greeted this person with an unconscious but quite perceptible diminution of the warmth with which he had welcomed the other, the major looked around the room for seats for his visitors, and perceiving only one chair, piled with exchanges, and a broken stool propped against the wall, pushed a button, which rang a bell in the hall, summoning the colored porter to his presence.

"Jerry," said the editor when his servant appeared, "bring a couple of chairs for these gentlemen."

While they stood waiting, the visitors congratulated the major on the birth of his child, which had been announced in the Morning Chronicle, and which the prominence of the family made in some degree a matter of public interest.

"And now that you have a son, major," remarked the gentleman first described, as he lit one of the major's cigars, "you'll be all the more interested in doing something to make this town fit to live in, which is what we came up to talk about. Things are in an awful condition! A negro justice of the peace has opened an office on Market Street, and only yesterday summoned a white man to appear before him. Negro lawyers get most of the business in the criminal court. Last evening a group of young white ladies, going quietly along the street arm-in-arm, were forced off the sidewalk by a crowd of negro girls. Coming down the street just now, I saw a spectacle of social equality and negro domination that made my blood boil with indignation,—a white and a black convict, chained together, crossing the city in charge of a negro officer! We cannot stand that sort of thing, Carteret,—it is the last straw! Something must be done, and that quickly!"

The major thrilled with responsive emotion. There was something prophetic in this opportune visit. The matter was not only in his own thoughts, but in the air; it was the spontaneous revulsion of white men against the rule of an inferior race. These were the very men, above all others in the town, to join him in a movement to change these degrading conditions.

General Belmont, the smaller of the two, was a man of good family, a lawyer by profession, and took an active part in state and local politics. Aristocratic by birth and instinct, and a former owner of slaves, his conception of the obligations and rights of his caste was nevertheless somewhat lower than that of the narrower but more sincere Carteret. In serious affairs Carteret desired the approval of his conscience, even if he had to trick that docile organ into acquiescence. This was not difficult to do in politics, for he believed in the divine right of white men and gentlemen, as his ancestors had believed in and died for the divine right of kings. General Belmont was not without a gentleman's distaste for meanness, but he permitted no fine scruples to stand in the way of success. He had once been minister, under a Democratic administration, to a small Central American state. Political rivals had characterized him as a tricky demagogue, which may of course have been a libel. He had an amiable disposition, possessed the gift of eloquence, and was a prime social favorite.

Captain George McBane had sprung from the poor-white class, to which, even more than to the slaves, the abolition of slavery had opened the door of opportunity. No longer overshadowed by a slaveholding caste, some of this class had rapidly pushed themselves forward. Some had made honorable records. Others, foremost in negro-baiting and election frauds, had done the dirty work of politics, as their fathers had done that of slavery, seeking their reward at first in minor offices,—for which men of gentler breeding did not care,—until their ambition began to reach out for higher honors.

Of this class McBane—whose captaincy, by the way, was merely a polite fiction—had been one of the most successful. He had held, until recently, as the reward of questionable political services, a contract with the State for its convict labor, from which in a few years he had realized a fortune. But the methods which made his contract profitable had not commended themselves to humane people, and charges of cruelty and worse had been preferred against him. He was rich enough to escape serious consequences from the investigation which followed, but when the Fusion ticket carried the state he lost his contract, and the system of convict labor was abolished. Since then McBane had devoted himself to politics: he was ambitious for greater wealth, for office, and for social recognition. A man of few words and self-engrossed, he seldom spoke of his aspirations except where speech might favor them, preferring to seek his ends by secret "deals" and combinations rather than to challenge criticism and provoke rivalry by more open methods.

At sight, therefore, of these two men, with whose careers and characters he was entirely familiar, Carteret felt sweep over his mind the conviction that now was the time and these the instruments with which to undertake the redemption of the state from the evil fate which had befallen it.

Jerry, the porter, who had gone downstairs to the counting-room to find two whole chairs, now entered with one in each hand. He set a chair for the general, who gave him an amiable nod, to which Jerry responded with a bow and a scrape. Captain McBane made no acknowledgment, but fixed Jerry so fiercely with his single eye that upon placing the chair Jerry made his escape from the room as rapidly as possible.

"I don' like dat Cap'n McBane," he muttered, upon reaching the hall. "Dey says he got dat eye knock' out tryin' ter whip a cullud 'oman, when he wuz a boy, an' dat he ain' never had no use fer niggers sence,—'cep'n' fer what he could make outen 'em wid his convic' labor contrac's. His daddy wuz a' overseer befo' 'im, an' it come nachul fer him ter be a nigger-driver. I don' want dat one eye er his'n restin' on me no longer 'n I kin he'p, an' I don' know how I'm gwine ter like dis job ef he 's gwine ter be comin' roun' here. He ain' nothin' but po' w'ite trash nohow; but Lawd! Lawd! look at de money he 's got,—livin' at de hotel, wearin' di'mon's, an' collo-guin' wid de bes' quality er dis town! 'Pears ter me de bottom rail is gittin' mighty close ter de top. Well, I s'pose it all comes f'm bein' w'ite. I wush ter Gawd I wuz w'ite!"

After this fervent aspiration, having nothing else to do for the time being, except to remain within call, and having caught a few words of the conversation as he went in with the chairs, Jerry, who possessed a certain amount of curiosity, placed close to the wall the broken stool upon which he sat while waiting in the hall, and applied his ear to a hole in the plastering of the hallway. There was a similar defect in the inner wall, between the same two pieces of studding, and while this inner opening was not exactly opposite the outer, Jerry was enabled, through the two, to catch in a more or less fragmentary way what was going on within.

He could hear the major, now and then, use the word "negro," and McBane's deep voice was quite audible when he referred, it seemed to Jerry with alarming frequency, to "the damned niggers," while the general's suave tones now and then pronounced the word "nig-gro,"—a sort of compromise between ethnology and the vernacular. That the gentlemen were talking politics seemed quite likely, for gentlemen generally talked politics when they met at the Chronicle office. Jerry could hear the words "vote," "franchise," "eliminate," "constitution," and other expressions which marked the general tenor of the talk, though he could not follow it all,—partly because he could not hear everything distinctly, and partly because of certain limitations which nature had placed in the way of Jerry's understanding anything very difficult or abstruse.

He had gathered enough, however, to realize, in a vague way, that something serious was on foot, involving his own race, when a bell sounded over his head, at which he sprang up hastily and entered the room where the gentlemen were talking.

"Jerry," said the major, "wait on Captain McBane."

"Yas, suh," responded Jerry, turning toward the captain, whose eye he carefully avoided meeting directly.

"Take that half a dollar, boy," ordered McBane, "an' go 'cross the street to Mr. Sykes's, and tell him to send me three whiskies. Bring back the change, and make has'e."

The captain tossed the half dollar at Jerry, who, looking to one side, of course missed it. He picked the money up, however, and backed out of the room. Jerry did not like Captain McBane, to begin with, and it was clear that the captain was no gentleman, or he would not have thrown the money at him. Considering the source, Jerry might have overlooked this discourtesy had it not been coupled with the remark about the change, which seemed to him in very poor taste.

Returning in a few minutes with three glasses on a tray, he passed them round, handed Captain McBane his change, and retired to the hall.

"Gentlemen," exclaimed the captain, lifting his glass, "I propose a toast: 'No nigger domination.' "

"Amen!" said the others, and three glasses were solemnly drained.

"Major," observed the general, smacking his lips, "*I* should like to use Jerry for a moment, if you will permit me."

Jerry appeared promptly at the sound of the bell. He had remained conveniently near,—calls of this sort were apt to come in sequence.

"Jerry," said the general, handing Jerry half a dollar, "go over to Mr. Brown's,—I get my liquor there,—and tell them to send me three glasses of my special mixture. And, Jerry,—you may keep the change!"

"Thank y', gin'l, thank y', marster," replied Jerry, with unctuous gratitude, bending almost double as he backed out of the room.

"Dat 's a gent'eman, a rale ole-time gent'eman," he said to himself when he had closed the door. "But dere 's somethin' gwine on in dere,—dere sho' is! 'No nigger damnation!' Dat soun's all right,—I'm sho' dere ain' no nigger I knows w'at wants damnation, do' dere 's lots of 'em w'at deserves it; but ef dat one-eyed Cap'n McBane got anything ter do wid it, w'atever it is, it don' mean no good fer de niggers,—damnation 'd be better fer 'em dan dat Cap'n McBane! He look at a nigger lack he could jes' eat 'im alive."

"This mixture, gentlemen," observed the general when Jerry had returned with the glasses, "was originally compounded by no less a person than the great John C. Calhoun himself, who confided the recipe to my father over the convivial board. In this nectar of the gods, gentlemen, I drink with you to 'White Supremacy!' "

"White Supremacy everywhere!" added McBane with fervor.

"Now and forever!" concluded Carteret solemnly.

When the visitors, half an hour later, had taken their departure, Carteret, inspired by the theme, and in less degree by the famous mixture of the immortal Calhoun, turned to his desk and finished, at a white heat, his famous editorial in which he sounded the tocsin of a new crusade.

At noon, when the editor, having laid down his pen, was leaving the office, he passed Jerry in the hall without a word or a nod. The major wore a rapt look, which Jerry observed with a vague uneasiness.

"He looks jes' lack he wuz walkin' in his sleep," muttered Jerry uneasily. "Dere's somethin' up, sho 's you bawn! 'No nigger damnation!' Anybody 'd 'low dey wuz all gwine ter heaven; but I knows better! W'en a passel er w'ite folks gits ter talkin' 'bout de niggers lack dem in yander, it's mo' lackly dey 're gwine ter ketch somethin' e'se dan heaven! I got ter keep my eyes open an' keep up wid w'at 's happenin'. Ef dere 's gwine ter be anudder flood 'roun' here, I wants ter git in de ark wid de w'ite folks,—I may haf ter be anudder Ham, an' sta't de cullud race all over ag'in."

CHAPTER IV

Theodore Felix

THE YOUNG HEIR of the Carterets had thriven apace, and at six months old was, according to Mammy Jane, whose experience qualified her to speak with authority, the largest, finest, smartest, and altogether most remarkable baby that had ever lived in Wellington. Mammy Jane had recently suffered from an attack of inflammatory rheumatism, as the result of which she had returned to her own home. She nevertheless came now and then to see Mrs. Carteret. A younger nurse had been procured to take her place, but it was understood that Jane would come whenever she might be needed.

"You really mean that about Dodie, do you, Mammy Jane?" asked the delighted mother, who never tired of hearing her own opinion confirmed concerning this wonderful child, which had come to her like an angel from heaven.

"Does I mean it!" exclaimed Mammy Jane, with a tone and an expression which spoke volumes of reproach. "Now, Mis' 'Livy, what is I ever uttered er said er spoke er done dat would make you s'pose I could tell you a lie 'bout yo' own chile?"

"No, Mammy Jane, I'm sure you wouldn't."

" 'Deed, ma'am, I'm tellin' you de Lawd's truf. I don' haf ter tell no lies ner strain no p'ints 'bout my ole mist'ess's gran'chile. Dis yer boy is de ve'y spit an' image er yo' brother, young Mars Alick, w'at died w'en he wuz 'bout eight mont's ole, w'iles I wuz laid off havin' a baby er my own, an' couldn' be roun' ter look after 'im. An' dis chile is a rale quality chile, he is,—I never seed a baby wid sech fine hair fer his age, ner sech blue eyes, ner sech a grip, ner sech a heft. W'y, dat chile mus' weigh 'bout twenty-fo' poun's, an' he not but six mont's

244

ole. Does dat gal w'at does de nussin' w'iles I'm gone ten' ter dis chile right, Mis' 'Livy?"

"She does fairly well, Mammy Jane, but I could hardly expect her to love the baby as you do. There's no one like you, Mammy Jane."

" 'Deed dere ain't, honey; you is talkin' de gospel truf now! None er dese yer young folks ain' got de trainin' my ole mist'ess give me. Dese yer newfangle' schools don' l'arn 'em nothin' ter compare wid it. I'm jes' gwine ter give dat gal a piece er my min', befo' I go, so she'll ten' ter dis chile right."

The nurse came in shortly afterwards, a neat-looking brown girl, dressed in a clean calico gown, with a nurse's cap and apron.

"Look a-here, gal," said Mammy Jane sternly, "I wants you ter understan' dat you got ter take good keer er dis chile; fer I nussed his mammy dere, an' his gran'-mammy befo' 'im, an' you is got a priv'lege dat mos' lackly you don' 'preciate. I wants you to 'member, in yo' incomin's an' outgoin's, dat I got my eye on you, an' am gwine ter see dat you does yo' wo'k right."

"Do you need me for anything, ma'am?" asked the young nurse, who had stood before Mrs. Carteret, giving Mammy Jane a mere passing glance, and listening impassively to her harangue. The nurse belonged to the younger generation of colored people. She had graduated from the mission school, and had received some instruction in Dr. Miller's class for nurses. Standing, like most young people of her race, on the border line between two irreconcilable states of life, she had neither the picturesqueness of the slave, nor the unconscious dignity of those whom freedom has been the immemorial birthright; she was in what might be called the chip-on-the-shoulder stage, through which races as well as individuals must pass in climbing the ladder of life,—not an interesting, at least not an agreeable stage, but an inevitable one, and for that reason entitled to a paragraph in a story of Southern life, which, with its as yet imperfect blending of old with new, of race with race, of slavery with freedom, is like no other life under the sun.

Had this old woman, who had no authority over her, been a little more polite, or a little less offensive, the nurse might have returned her a pleasant answer. These old-time negroes, she said to herself, made her sick with their slavering over the white folks, who, she supposed, favored them and made much of them because they had once belonged to them,—much the same reason why they fondled their cats and dogs. For her own part, they gave her nothing but her wages, and small wages at that, and she owed them nothing more than equivalent service. It was purely a matter of business; she sold her time for their money. There was no question of love between them.

Receiving a negative answer from Mrs. Carteret, she left the room without a word, ignoring Mammy Jane completely, and leaving that venerable relic of ante-bellum times gasping in helpless astonishment.

"Well, I nevuh!" she ejaculated, as soon as she could get her breath, "ef dat ain' de beatinis' pe'fo'mance I ever seed er heared of! Dese yer young niggers ain' got de manners dey wuz bawned wid! I don' know w'at dey're comin' to, w'en dey ain' got no mo' rispec' fer ole age—I don' know—I don' know!"

"Now what are you croaking about, Jane?" asked Major Carteret, who came into the room and took the child into his arms.

Mammy Jane hobbled to her feet and bobbed a curtsy. She was never lacking in respect to white people of proper quality; but Major Carteret, the quintessence of aristocracy, called out all her reserves of deference. The major was always kind and considerate to these old family retainers, brought up in the feudal atmosphere now so rapidly passing away. Mammy Jane loved Mrs. Carteret; toward the major she entertained a feeling bordering upon awe.

"Well, Jane," returned the major sadly, when the old nurse had related her grievance, "the old times have vanished, the old ties have been ruptured. The old relations of dependence and loyal obedience on the part of the colored people, the responsibility of protection and kindness upon that of the whites, have passed away forever. The young negroes are too self-assertive. Education is spoiling them, Jane; they have been badly taught. They are not content with their station in life. Some time they will overstep the mark. The white people are patient, but there is a limit to their endurance."

"Dat's w'at I tells dese young niggers," groaned Mammy

Jane, with a portentous shake of her turbaned head, "w'en I hears 'em gwine on wid deir foolishniss; but dey don' min' me. Dey 'lows dey knows mo' d'n I does, 'ca'se dey be'n l'arnt ter look in a book. But, pshuh! my ole mist'ess showed me mo' d'n dem niggers'll l'arn in a thousan' years! I's fetch' my gran'son' Jerry up ter be 'umble, an' keep in 'is place. An' I tells dese other niggers dat ef dey 'd do de same, an' not crowd de w'ite folks, dey 'd git ernuff ter eat, an' live out deir days in peace an' comfo't. But dey don' min' me—dey don' min' me!"

"If all the colored people were like you and Jerry, Jane," rejoined the major kindly, "there would never be any trouble. You have friends upon whom, in time of need, you can rely implicitly for protection and succor. You served your mistress faithfully before the war; you remained by her when the other negroes were running hither and thither like sheep without a shepherd; and you have transferred your allegiance to my wife and her child. We think a great deal of you, Jane."

"Yes, indeed, Mammy Jane," assented Mrs. Carteret, with sincere affection, glancing with moist eyes from the child in her husband's arms to the old nurse, whose dark face was glowing with happiness at these expressions of appreciation, "you shall never want so long as we have anything. We would share our last crust with you."

"Thank y', Mis' 'Livy," said Jane with reciprocal emotion, "I knows who my frien's is, an' I ain' gwine ter let nothin' worry me. But fer de Lawd's sake, Mars Philip, gimme dat chile, an' lemme pat 'im on de back, er he 'll choke hisse'f ter death!"

The old nurse had been the first to observe that little Dodie, for some reason, was gasping for breath. Catching the child from the major's arms, she patted it on the back, and shook it gently. After a moment of this treatment, the child ceased to gasp, but still breathed heavily, with a strange, whistling noise.

"Oh, my child!" exclaimed the mother, in great alarm, taking the baby in her arms, "what can be the matter with him, Mammy Jane?"

"Fer de Lawd's sake, ma'am, I don' know, 'less he 's swallered somethin'; an' he ain' had nothin' in his han's but de rattle Mis' Polly give 'im."

Mrs. Carteret caught up the ivory rattle, which hung suspended by a ribbon from the baby's neck.

"He has swallowed the little piece off the end of the handle," she cried, turning pale with fear, "and it has lodged in his throat. Telephone Dr. Price to come immediately, Philip, before my baby chokes to death! Oh, my baby, my precious baby!"

An anxious half hour passed, during which the child lay quiet, except for its labored breathing. The suspense was relieved by the arrival of Dr. Price, who examined the child carefully.

"It's a curious accident," he announced at the close of his inspection. "So far as I can discover, the piece of ivory has been drawn into the trachea, or windpipe, and has lodged in the mouth of the right bronchus. I'll try to get it out without an operation, but I can't guarantee the result."

At the end of another half hour Dr. Price announced his inability to remove the obstruction without resorting to more serious measures.

"I do not see," he declared, "how an operation can be avoided."

"Will it be dangerous?" inquired the major anxiously, while Mrs. Carteret shivered at the thought.

"It will be necessary to cut into his throat from the outside. All such operations are more or less dangerous, especially on small children. If this were some other child, I might undertake the operation unassisted; but I know how you value this one, major, and I should prefer to share the responsibility with a specialist."

"Is there one in town?" asked the major.

"No, but we can get one from out of town."

"Send for the best one in the country," said the major, "who can be got here in time. Spare no expense, Dr. Price. We value this child above any earthly thing."

"The best is the safest," replied Dr. Price. "I will send for Dr. Burns, of Philadelphia, the best surgeon in that line in America. If he can start at once, he can reach here in sixteen or eighteen hours, and the case can wait even longer, if inflammation does not set in."

The message was dispatched forthwith. By rare good fortune the eminent specialist was able to start within an hour or two after the receipt of Dr. Price's telegram. Meanwhile the baby remained restless and uneasy, the doctor spending most of his time by its side. Mrs. Carteret, who had never been quite strong since the child's birth, was a prey to the most agonizing apprehensions.

Mammy Jane, while not presuming to question the opinion of Dr. Price, and not wishing to add to her mistress's distress, was secretly oppressed by forebodings which she was unable to shake off. The child was born for bad luck. The mole under its ear, just at the point where the hangman's knot would strike, had foreshadowed dire misfortune. She had already observed several little things which had rendered her vaguely anxious.

For instance, upon one occasion, on entering the room where the baby had been left alone, asleep in his crib, she had met a strange cat hurrying from the nursery, and, upon examining closely the pillow upon which the child lay, had found a depression which had undoubtedly been due to the weight of the cat's body. The child was restless and uneasy, and Jane had ever since believed that the cat had been sucking little Dodie's breath, with what might have been fatal results had she not appeared just in the nick of time.

This untimely accident of the rattle, a fatality for which no one could be held responsible, had confirmed the unlucky omen. Jane's duties in the nursery did not permit her to visit her friend the conjure woman; but she did find time to go out in the back yard at dusk, and to dig up the charm which she had planted there. It had protected the child so far; but perhaps its potency had become exhausted. She picked up the bottle, shook it vigorously, and then laid it back, with the other side up. Refilling the hole, she made a cross over the top with the thumb of her left hand, and walked three times around it.

What this strange symbolism meant, or whence it derived its origin, Aunt Jane did not know. The cross was there, and the Trinity, though Jane was scarcely conscious of these, at this moment, as religious emblems. But she hoped, on general principles, that this performance would strengthen the charm and restore little Dodie's luck. It certainly had its moral effect upon Jane's own mind, for she was able to sleep better, and contrived to impress Mrs. Carteret with her own hopefulness.

CHAPTER V

A Journey Southward

As THE SOUTH-BOUND train was leaving the station at Philadelphia, a gentleman took his seat in the single sleeping-car attached to the train, and proceeded to make himself comfortable. He hung up his hat and opened his newspaper, in which he remained absorbed for a quarter of an hour. When the train had left the city behind, he threw the paper aside, and looked around at the other occupants of the car. One of these, who had been on the car since it had left New York, rose from his seat upon perceiving the other's glance, and came down the aisle.

"How do you do, Dr. Burns?" he said, stopping beside the seat of the Philadelphia passenger.

The gentleman looked up at the speaker with an air of surprise, which, after the first keen, incisive glance, gave place to an expression of cordial recognition.

"Why, it's Miller!" he exclaimed, rising and giving the other his hand, "William Miller—Dr. Miller, of course. Sit down, Miller, and tell me all about yourself,—what you're doing, where you've been, and where you're going. I'm delighted to meet you, and to see you looking so well—and so prosperous."

"I deserve no credit for either, sir," returned the other, as he took the proffered seat, "for I inherited both health and prosperity. It is a fortunate chance that permits me to meet you."

The two acquaintances, thus opportunely thrown together so that they might while away in conversation the tedium of their journey, represented very different and yet very similar types of manhood. A celebrated traveler, after many years spent in barbarous or savage lands, has said that among all varieties of mankind the similarities are vastly more important and fundamental than the differences. Looking at these two men with the American eye, the differences would perhaps be the more striking, or at least the more immediately apparent, for the first was white and the second black, or, more correctly speaking, brown; it was even a light brown, but both his swarthy complexion and his curly hair revealed what has been described in the laws of some of our states as a "visible admixture" of African blood.

Having disposed of this difference, and having observed that the white man was perhaps fifty years of age and the other not more than thirty, it may be said that they were both tall and sturdy, both well dressed, the white man with perhaps a little more distinction; both seemed from their faces and their manners to be men of culture and accustomed to the society of cultivated people. They were both handsome men, the elder representing a fine type of Anglo-Saxon, as the term is used in speaking of our composite white population; while the mulatto's erect form, broad shoulders, clear eyes, fine teeth, and pleasingly moulded features showed nowhere any sign of that degeneration which the pressimist so sadly maintains is the inevitable heritage of mixed races.

As to their personal relations, it has already appeared that they were members of the same profession. In past years they had been teacher and pupil. Dr. Alvin Burns was professor in the famous medical college where Miller had attended lectures. The professor had taken an interest in his only colored pupil, to whom he had been attracted by his earnestness of purpose, his evident talent, and his excellent manners and fine physique. It was in part due to Dr. Burns's friendship that Miller had won a scholarship which had enabled him, without drawing too heavily upon his father's resources, to spend in Europe, studying in the hospitals of Paris and Vienna, the two most delightful years of his life. The same influence had strengthened his natural inclination toward operative surgery, in which Dr. Burns was a distinguished specialist of national reputation.

Miller's father, Adam Miller, had been a thrifty colored man, the son of a slave, who, in the olden time, had bought himself with money which he had earned and saved, over and above what he had paid his master for his time. Adam Miller had inherited his father's thrift, as well as his trade, which was that of a stevedore, or contractor for the loading and unloading of vessels at the port of Wellington. In the flush turpentine days following a few years after the civil war, he had made money. His savings, shrewdly invested, had by constant accessions become a competence. He had brought up his eldest son to the trade; the other he had given a professional education, in the proud hope that his children or his grandchildren might be gentlemen in the town where their ancestors had once been slaves.

Upon his father's death, shortly after Dr. Miller's return from Europe, and a year or two before the date at which this story opens, he had promptly spent part of his inheritance in founding a hospital, to which was to be added a training school for nurses, and in time perhaps a medical college and a school of pharmacy. He had been strongly tempted to leave the South, and seek a home for his family and a career for himself in the freer North, where race antagonism was less keen, or at least less oppressive, or in Europe, where he had never found his color work to his disadvantage. But his people had needed him, and he had wished to help them, and had sought by means of this institution to contribute to their uplifting. As he now informed Dr. Burns, he was returning from New York, where he had been in order to purchase equipment for his new hospital, which would soon be ready for the reception of patients.

"How much I can accomplish I do not know," said Miller, "but I'll do what I can. There are eight or nine million of us, and it will take a great deal of learning of all kinds to leaven that lump."

"It is a great problem, Miller, the future of your race," returned the other, "a tremendously interesting problem. It is a serial story which we are all reading, and which grows in vital interest with each successive installment. It is not only your problem, but ours. Your race must come up or drag ours down."

"We shall come up," declared Miller; "slowly and painfully, perhaps, but we shall win our way. If our race had made as much progress everywhere as they have made in Wellington, the problem would be well on the way toward solution."

"Wellington?" exclaimed Dr. Burns. "That's where

I'm going. A Dr. Price, of Wellington, has sent for me to perform an operation on a child's throat. Do you know Dr. Price?"

"Quite well," replied Miller, "he is a friend of mine."

"So much the better. I shall want you to assist me. I read in the Medical Gazette, the other day, an account of a very interesting operation of yours. I felt proud to number you among my pupils. It was a remarkable case—a rare case. I must certainly have you with me in this one."

"I shall be delighted, sir," returned Miller, "if it is agreeable to all concerned."

Several hours were passed in pleasant conversation while the train sped rapidly southward. They were already far down in Virginia, and had stopped at a station beyond Richmond, when the conductor entered the car.

"All passengers," he announced, "will please transfer to the day coaches ahead. The sleeper has a hot box, and must be switched off here."

Dr. Burns and Miller obeyed the order, the former leading the way into the coach immediately in front of the sleeping-car.

"Let's sit here, Miller," he said, having selected a seat near the rear of the car and deposited his suitcase in a rack. "It's on the shady side."

Miller stood a moment hesitatingly, but finally took the seat indicated, and a few minutes later the journey was again resumed.

When the train conductor made his round after leaving the station, he paused at the seat occupied by the two doctors, glanced interrogatively at Miller, and then spoke to Dr. Burns, who sat in the end of the seat nearest the aisle.

"This man is with you?" he asked, indicating Miller with a slight side movement of his head, and a keen glance in his direction.

"Certainly," replied Dr. Burns curtly, and with some surprise. "Don't you see that he is?"

The conductor passed on. Miller paid no apparent attention to this little interlude, though no syllable had escaped him. He resumed the conversation where it had been broken off, but nevertheless followed with his eyes the conductor, who stopped at a seat near the forward end of the car, and engaged in conversation with a man whom Miller had not hitherto noticed.

As this passenger turned his head and looked back toward Miller, the latter saw a broad-shouldered, burly white man, and recognized in his square-cut jaw, his coarse, firm mouth, and the single gray eye with which he swept Miller for an instant with a scornful glance, a well-known character of Wellington, with whom the reader has already made acquaintance in these pages. Captain McBane wore a frock coat and a slouch hat; several buttons of his vest were unbuttoned, and his solitaire diamond blazed in his soiled shirt-front like the headlight of a locomotive.

The conductor in his turn looked back at Miller, and retraced his steps. Miller braced himself for what he feared was coming, though he had hoped, on account of his friend's presence, that it might be avoided.

"Excuse me, sir," said the conductor, addressing Dr. Burns, "but did I understand you to say that this man was your servant?"

"No, indeed!" replied Dr. Burns indignantly. "The gentleman is not my servant, nor anybody's servant, but is my friend. But, by the way, since we are on the subject, may I ask what affair it is of yours?"

"It's very much my affair," returned the conductor, somewhat nettled at this questioning of his authority. "I'm sorry to part *friends*, but the law of Virginia does not permit colored passengers to ride in the white cars. You'll have to go forward to the next coach," he added, addressing Miller this time.

"I have paid my fare on the sleeping-car, where the separate-car law does not apply," remonstrated Miller.

"I can't help that. You can doubtless get your money back from the sleeping-car company. But this is a day coach, and is distinctly marked 'White,' as you must have seen before you sat down here. The sign is put there for that purpose."

He indicated a large card neatly framed and hung at the end of the car, containing the legend, "White," in letters about a foot long, painted in white upon a dark background, typical, one might suppose, of the distinction thereby indicated.

"You shall not stir a step, Miller," exclaimed Dr.

Burns wrathfully. "This is an outrage upon a citizen of a free country. You shall stay right here."

"I'm sorry to discommode you," returned the conductor, "but there's no use kicking. It's the law of Virginia, and I am bound by it as well as you. I have already come near losing my place because of not enforcing it, and I can take no more such chances, since I have a family to support."

"And my friend has his rights to maintain," returned Dr. Burns with determination. "There is a vital principle at stake in the matter."

"Really, sir," argued the conductor, who was a man of peace and not fond of controversy, "there's no use talking—he absolutely cannot ride in this car."

"How can you prevent it?" asked Dr. Burns, lapsing into the argumentative stage.

"The law gives me the right to remove him by force. I can call on the train crew to assist me, or on the other passengers. If I should choose to put him off the train entirely, in the middle of a swamp, he would have no redress—the law so provides. If I did not wish to use force, I could simply switch this car off at the next siding, transfer the white passengers to another, and leave you and your friend in possession until you were arrested and fined or imprisoned."

"What he says is absolutely true, doctor," interposed Miller at this point. "It is the law, and we are powerless to resist it. If we made any trouble, it would merely delay your journey and imperil a life at the other end. I'll go into the other car."

"You shall not go alone," said Dr. Burns stoutly, rising in his turn. "A place that is too good for you is not good enough for me. I will sit wherever you do."

"I'm sorry again," said the conductor, who had quite recovered his equanimity, and calmly conscious of his power, could scarcely restrain an amused smile; "I dislike to interfere, but white passengers are not permitted to ride in the colored car."

"This is an outrage," declared Dr. Burns, "a d——d outrage! You are curtailing the rights, not only of colored people, but of white men as well. I shall sit where I please!"

"I warn you, sir," rejoined the conductor, hardening

again, "that the law will be enforced. The beauty of the system lies in its strict impartiality—it applies to both races alike."

"And is equally infamous in both cases," declared Dr. Burns. "I shall immediately take steps"—

"Never mind, doctor," interrupted Miller, soothingly, "it's only for a little while. I'll reach my destination just as surely in the other car, and we can't help it, anyway. I'll see you again at Wellington."

Dr. Burns, finding resistance futile, at length acquiesced and made way for Miller to pass him.

The colored doctor took up his valise and crossed the platform to the car ahead. It was an old car, with faded upholstery, from which the stuffing projected here and there through torn places. Apparently the floor had not been swept for several days. The dust lay thick upon the window sills, and the water-cooler, from which he essayed to get a drink, was filled with stale water which had made no recent acquaintance with ice. There was no other passenger in the car, and Miller occupied himself in making a rough calculation of what it would cost the Southern railroads to haul a whole car for every colored passenger. It was expensive, to say the least; it would be cheaper, and quite as considerate of their feelings, to make the negroes walk.

The car was conspicuously labeled at either end with large cards, similar to those in the other car, except that they bore the word "Colored" in black letters upon a white background. The author of this piece of legislation had contrived, with an ingenuity worthy of a better cause, that not merely should the passengers be separated by the color line, but that the reason for this division should be kept constantly in mind. Lest a white man should forget that he was white,—not a very likely contingency,—these cars would keep him constantly admonished of the fact; should a colored person endeavor, for a moment, to lose sight of his disability, these staring signs would remind him continually that between him and the rest of mankind not of his own color, there was by law a great gulf fixed.

Having composed himself, Miller had opened a newspaper, and was deep in an editorial which set forth in glowing language the inestimable advantages which would follow to certain recently acquired islands by the introduction of American liberty, when the rear door of the car opened to give entrance to Captain George McBane, who took a seat near the door and lit a cigar. Miller knew him quite well by sight and by reputation, and detested him as heartily. He represented the aggressive, offensive element among the white people of the New South, who made it hard for a negro to maintain his self-respect or to enjoy even the rights conceded to colored men by Southern laws. McBane had undoubtedly identified him to the conductor in the other car. Miller had no desire to thrust himself upon the society of white people, which, indeed, to one who had traveled so much and so far, was no novelty; but he very naturally resented being at this late day—the law had been in operation only a few months—branded and tagged and set apart from the rest of mankind upon the public highways, like an unclean thing. Nevertheless, he preferred even this to the exclusive society of Captain George McBane.

"Porter," he demanded of the colored train attaché who passed through the car a moment later, "is this a smoking car for white men?"

"No, suh," replied the porter, "but they comes in here sometimes, when they ain' no cullud ladies on the kyar."

"Well, I have paid first-class fare, and I object to that man's smoking in here. You tell him to go out."

"I'll tell the conductor, suh," returned the porter in a low tone. "I'd jus' as soon talk ter the devil as ter that man."

The white man had spread himself over two seats, and was smoking vigorously, from time to time spitting carelessly in the aisle, when the conductor entered the compartment.

"Captain," said Miller, "this car is plainly marked 'Colored.' I have paid first-class fare, and I object to riding in a smoking car."

"All right," returned the conductor, frowning irritably. "I'll speak to him."

He walked over to the white passenger, with whom he was evidently acquainted, since he addressed him by name.

"Captain McBane," he said, "it's against the law for you to ride in the nigger car."

"Who are you talkin' to?" returned the other. "I'll ride where I damn please."

"Yes, sir, but the colored passenger objects. I'm afraid I'll have to ask you to go into the smoking-car."

"The hell you say!" rejoined McBane. "I'll leave this car when I get good and ready, and that won't be till I've finished this cigar. See?"

He was as good as his word. The conductor escaped from the car before Miller had time for further expostulation. Finally McBane, having thrown the stump of his cigar into the aisle and added to the floor a finishing touch in the way of expectoration, rose and went back into the white car.

Left alone in his questionable glory, Miller buried himself again in his newspaper, from which he did not look up until the engine stopped at a tank station to take water.

As the train came to a standstill, a huge negro, covered thickly with dust, crawled off one of the rear trucks unobserved, and ran round the rear end of the car to a watering-trough by a neighboring well. Moved either by extreme thirst or by the fear that his time might be too short to permit him to draw a bucket of water, he threw himself down by the trough, drank long and deep, and plunging his head into the water, shook himself like a wet dog, and crept furtively back to his dangerous perch.

Miller, who had seen this man from the car window, had noticed a very singular thing. As the dusty tramp passed the rear coach, he cast toward it a glance of intense ferocity. Up to that moment the man's face, which Miller had recognized under its grimy coating, had been that of an ordinarily good-natured, somewhat reckless, pleasure-loving negro, at present rather the worse for wear. The change that now came over it suggested a concentrated hatred almost uncanny in its murderousness. With awakened curiosity Miller followed the direction of the negro's glance, and saw that it rested upon a window where Captain McBane sat looking out. When Miller looked back, the negro had disappeared.

At the next station a Chinaman, of the ordinary laundry type, boarded the train, and took his seat in the white car without objection. At another point a colored nurse found a place with her mistress.

"White people," said Miller to himself, who had seen these passengers from the window, "do not object to the negro as a servant. As the traditional negro,—the servant,—he is welcomed; as an equal, he is repudiated."

Miller was something of a philosopher. He had long ago had the conclusion forced upon him that an educated man of his race, in order to live comfortably in the United States, must be either a philosopher or a fool; and since he wished to be happy, and was not exactly a fool, he had cultivated philosophy. By and by he saw a white man, with a dog, enter the rear coach. Miller wondered whether the dog would be allowed to ride with his master, and if not, what disposition would be made of him. He was a handsome dog, and Miller who was fond of animals, would not have objected to the company of a dog, as a dog. He was nevertheless conscious of a queer sensation when he saw the porter take the dog by the collar and start in his own direction, and felt consciously relieved when the canine passenger was taken on past him into the baggage-car ahead. Miller's hand was hanging over the arm of his seat, and the dog, an intelligent shepherd, licked it as he passed. Miller was not entirely sure that he would not have liked the porter to leave the dog there; he was a friendly dog, and seemed inclined to be sociable.

Toward evening the train drew up at a station where quite a party of farm laborers, fresh from their daily toil, swarmed out from the conspicuously labeled colored waiting-room, and into the car with Miller. They were a jolly, good-natured crowd, and, free from the embarrassing presence of white people, proceeded to enjoy themselves after their own fashion. Here an amorous fellow sat with his arm around a buxom girl's waist. A musically inclined individual—his talents did not go far beyond inclination—produced a mouth-organ and struck up a tune, to which a limber-legged boy danced in the aisle. They were noisy, loquacious, happy, dirty, and malodorous. For a while Miller was amused and pleased. They were his people, and he felt a certain expansive warmth toward them in spite of their obvious shortcomings. By and by, however, the air became too close, and he went out upon the platform. For the sake of the democratic ideal, which meant so much to his race, he might have endured the affliction. He could easily imagine that people of refinement, with the power in their hands, might be tempted to strain the democratic ideal in order to avoid such contact; but personally, and apart from the mere matter of racial sympathy, these people were just as offensive to him as to the whites in the other end of the train. Surely, if a classification of passengers on trains was at all desirable, it might be made upon some more logical and considerate basis than a mere arbitrary, tactless, and, by the very nature of things, brutal drawing of a color line. It was a veritable bed of Procrustes, this standard which the whites had set for the negroes. Those who grew above it must have their heads cut off, figuratively speaking,—must be forced back to the level assigned to their race; those who fell beneath the standard set had their necks stretched, literally enough, as the ghastly record in the daily papers gave conclusive evidence.

Miller breathed more freely when the lively crowd got off at the next station, after a short ride. Moreover, he had a light heart, a conscience void of offense, and was only thirty years old. His philosophy had become somewhat jaded on this journey, but he pulled it together for a final effort. Was it not, after all, a wise provision of nature that had given to a race, destined to a long servitude and a slow emergence therefrom, a cheerfulness of spirit which enabled them to catch pleasure on the wing, and endure with equanimity the ills that seemed inevitable? The ability to live and thrive under adverse circumstances is the surest guaranty of the future. The race which at the last shall inherit the earth—the residuary legatee of civilization—will be the race which remains longest upon it. The negro was here before the Anglo-Saxon was evolved, and his thick lips and heavy-lidded eyes looked out from the inscrutable face of the Sphinx across the sands of Egypt while yet the ancestors of those who now oppress him were living in caves, practicing human sacrifice, and painting themselves with woad—and the negro is here yet.

" 'Blessed are the meek,' " quoted Miller at the end of these consoling reflections, " 'for they shall inherit the earth.' If this be true, the negro may yet come into his estate, for meekness seems to be set apart as his portion."

The journey came to an end just as the sun had sunk into the west.

Simultaneously with Miller's exit from the train, a great black figure crawled off the trucks of the rear car, on the side opposite the station platform. Stretching and shaking himself with a free gesture, the black man, seeing himself unobserved, moved somewhat stiffly round the end of the car to the station platform.

" 'Fo de Lawd!" he muttered, "ef I hadn' had a cha'm' life, I'd 'a' never got here on dat ticket, an' dat's a fac'— it sho' am! I kind er 'lowed I wuz gone a dozen times, ez it wuz. But I got my job ter do in dis worl', an' I knows I ain' gwine ter die 'tel I've 'complished it. I jes' want one mo' look at dat man, an' den I'll haf ter git somethin' ter eat; fer two raw turnips in twelve hours is slim pickin's fer a man er my size!"

CHAPTER VI

Janet

As THE TRAIN drew up at the station platform, Dr. Price came forward from the white waiting-room, and stood expectantly by the door of the white coach. Miller, having left his car, came down the platform in time to intercept Burns as he left the train, and to introduce him to Dr. Price.

"My carriage is in waiting," said Dr. Price. "I should have liked to have you at my own house, but my wife is out of town. We have a good hotel, however, and you will doubtless find it more convenient."

"You are very kind, Dr. Price. Miller, won't you come up and dine with me?"

"Thank you, no," said Miller, "I am expected at home. My wife and child are waiting for me in the buggy yonder by the platform."

"Oh, very well; of course you must go; but don't forget our appointment. Let's see, Dr. Price, I can eat and get ready in half an hour—that will make it"—

"I have asked several of the local physicians to be present at eight o'clock," said Dr. Price. "The case can safely wait until then."

"Very well, Miller, be on hand at eight. I shall expect you without fail. Where shall he come, Dr. Price?"

"To the residence of Major Philip Carteret, on Vine Street."

"I have invited Dr. Miller to be present and assist in the operation," Dr. Burns continued, as they drove toward the hotel. "He was a favorite pupil of mine, and is a credit to the profession. I presume you saw his article in the Medical Gazette?"

"Yes, and I assisted him in the case," returned Dr. Price. "It was a colored lad, one of his patients, and he called me in to help him. He is a capable man, and very much liked by the white physicians."

Miller's wife and child were waiting for him in fluttering anticipation. He kissed them both as he climbed into the buggy.

"We came at four o'clock," said Mrs. Miller, a handsome young woman, who might be anywhere between twenty-five and thirty, and whose complexion, in the twilight, was not distinguishable from that of a white person, "but the train was late two hours, they said. We came back at six, and have been waiting ever since."

"Yes, papa," piped the child, a little boy of six or seven, who sat between them, "and I am very hungry."

Miller felt very much elated as he drove homeward through the twilight. By his side sat the two persons whom he loved best in all the world. His affairs were prosperous. Upon opening his office in the city, he had been received by the members of his own profession with a cordiality generally frank, and in no case much reserved. The colored population of the city was large, but in the main poor, and the white physicians were not unwilling to share this unprofitable practice with a colored doctor worthy of confidence. In the intervals of the work upon his hospital, he had built up a considerable practice among his own people; but except in the case of some poor unfortunate whose pride had been lost in poverty or sin, no white patient had ever called upon him for treatment. He knew very well the measure of his powers,—a liberal education had given him opportunity to compare himself with other men,—and was secretly conscious that in point of skill and knowledge he did not suffer by comparison with any other physician in the town. He liked to believe that the race antagonism which hampered his progress and that of his people was a mere temporary thing, the outcome of former conditions, and bound to disappear in time, and that when a colored man should demonstrate to the community in which he lived that he possessed character and power, that community would find a way in which to enlist his services for the public good.

He had already made himself useful, and had received many kind words and other marks of appreciation. He was now offered a further confirmation of his theory:

having recognized his skill, the white people were now ready to take advantage of it. Any lurking doubt he may have felt when first invited by Dr. Burns to participate in the operation, had been dispelled by Dr. Price's prompt acquiescence.

On the way homeward Miller told his wife of this appointment. She was greatly interested; she was herself a mother, with an only child. Moreover, there was a stronger impulse than mere humanity to draw her toward the stricken mother. Janet had a tender heart, and could have loved this white sister, her sole living relative of whom she knew. All her life long she had yearned for a kind word, a nod, a smile, the least thing that imagination might have twisted into a recognition of the tie between them. But it had never come.

And yet Janet was not angry. She was of a forgiving temper; she could never bear malice. She was educated, had read many books, and appreciated to the full the social forces arrayed against any such recognition as she had dreamed of. Of the two barriers between them a man might have forgiven the one; a woman would not be likely to overlook either the bar sinister or the difference of race, even to the slight extent of a silent recognition. Blood is thicker than water, but, if it flow too far from conventional channels, may turn to gall and wormwood. Nevertheless, when the heart speaks, reason falls into the background, and Janet would have worshiped this sister, even afar off, had she received even the slightest encouragement. So strong was this weakness that she had been angry with herself for her lack of pride, or even of a decent self-respect. It was, she sometimes thought, the heritage of her mother's race, and she was ashamed of it as part of the taint of slavery. She had never acknowledged, even to her husband, from whom she concealed nothing else, her secret thoughts upon this lifelong sorrow. This silent grief was nature's penalty, or society's revenge, for whatever heritage of beauty or intellect or personal charm had come to her with her father's blood. For she had received no other inheritance. Her sister was rich by right of her birth; if Janet had been fortunate, her good fortune had not been due to any provision made for her by her white father.

She knew quite well how passionately, for many years,

her proud sister had longed and prayed in vain for the child which had at length brought joy into her household, and she could feel, by sympathy, all the sickening suspense with which the child's parents must await the result of this dangerous operation.

"O Will," she adjured her husband anxiously, when he had told her of the engagement, "you must be very careful. Think of the child's poor mother! Think of our own dear child, and what it would mean to lose him!"

CHAPTER VII

The Operation

DR. PRICE was not entirely at ease in his mind as the two doctors drove rapidly from the hotel to Major Carteret's. Himself a liberal man, from his point of view, he saw no reason why a colored doctor might not operate upon a white male child,—there are fine distinctions in the application of the color line,—but several other physicians had been invited, some of whom were men of old-fashioned notions, who might not relish such an innovation.

This, however, was but a small difficulty compared with what might be feared from Major Carteret himself. For he knew Carteret's unrelenting hostility to anything that savored of recognition of the negro as the equal of white men. It was traditional in Wellington that no colored person had ever entered the front door of the Carteret residence, and that the luckless individual who once presented himself there upon alleged business and resented being ordered to the back door had been unceremoniously thrown over the piazza railing into a rather thorny clump of rose-bushes below. If Miller were going as a servant, to hold a basin or a sponge, there would be no difficulty; but as a surgeon—well, he wouldn't borrow trouble. Under the circumstances the major might yield a point.

But as they neared the house the major's unyielding disposition loomed up formidably. Perhaps if the matter were properly presented to Dr. Burns, he might consent to withdraw the invitation. It was not yet too late to send Miller a note.

"By the way, Dr. Burns," he said, "I'm very friendly to Dr. Miller, and should personally like to have him with us to-night. But—I ought to have told you this before, but I couldn't very well do so, on such short notice, in Miller's presence—we are a conservative people, and our local customs are not very flexible. We jog along in much the same old way our fathers did. I'm not at all sure that Major Carteret or the other gentlemen would consent to the presence of a negro doctor."

"I think you misjudge your own people," returned Dr. Burns, "they are broader than you think. We have our prejudices against the negro at the North, but we do not let them stand in the way of anything that *we* want. At any rate, it is too late now, and I will accept the responsibility. If the question is raised, I will attend to it. When I am performing an operation I must be *aut Caesar, aut nullus.*"

Dr. Price was not reassured, but he had done his duty and felt the reward of virtue. If there should be trouble, he would not be responsible. Moreover, there was a large fee at stake, and Dr. Burns was not likely to prove too obdurate.

They were soon at Carteret's, where they found assembled the several physicians invited by Dr. Price. These were successively introduced as Drs. Dudley, Hooper, and Ashe, all of whom were gentlemen of good standing, socially and in their profession, and considered it a high privilege to witness so delicate an operation at the hands of so eminent a member of their profession.

Major Carteret entered the room and was duly presented to the famous specialist. Carteret's anxious look lightened somewhat at sight of the array of talent present. It suggested, of course, the gravity of the impending event, but gave assurance of all the skill and care which science could afford.

Dr. Burns was shown to the nursery, from which he returned in five minutes.

"The case is ready," he announced. "Are the gentlemen all present?"

"I believe so," answered Dr. Price quickly.

Miller had not yet arrived. Perhaps, thought Dr. Price, a happy accident, or some imperative call, had detained him. This would be fortunate indeed. Dr. Burns's square jaw had a very determined look. It would be a pity if any acrimonious discussion should arise on the eve of a delicate operation. If the clock on the mantel would only move faster, the question might never come up.

"I don't see Dr. Miller," observed Dr. Burns, looking

around the room. "I asked him to come at eight. There are ten minutes yet."

Major Carteret looked up with a sudden frown.

"May I ask to whom you refer?" he inquired, in an ominous tone.

The other gentlemen showed signs of interest, not to say emotion. Dr. Price smiled quizzically.

"Dr. Miller, of your city. He was one of my favorite pupils. He is also a graduate of the Vienna hospitals, and a surgeon of unusual skill. I have asked him to assist in the operation."

Every eye was turned toward Carteret, whose crimsoned face had set in a look of grim determination.

"The person to whom you refer is a negro, I believe?" he said.

"He is a colored man, certainly," returned Dr. Burns, "though one would never think of his color after knowing him well."

"I do not know, sir," returned Carteret, with an effort at self-control, "what the customs of Philadelphia or Vienna may be; but in the South we do not call negro doctors to attend white patients. I could not permit a negro to enter my house upon such an errand."

"I am here, sir," replied Dr. Burns with spirit, "to perform a certain operation. Since I assume the responsibility, the case must be under my entire control. Otherwise I cannot operate."

"Gentlemen," interposed Dr. Price, smoothly, "I beg of you both—this is a matter for calm discussion, and any asperity is to be deplored. The life at stake here should not be imperiled by any consideration of minor importance."

"Your humanity does you credit, sir," retorted Dr. Burns. "But other matters, too, are important. I have invited this gentleman here. My professional honor is involved, and I merely invoke my rights to maintain it. It is a matter of principle, which ought not to give way to a mere prejudice."

"That also states the case for Major Carteret," rejoined Dr. Price, suavely. "He has certain principles,— call them prejudices, if you like,—certain inflexible rules of conduct by which he regulates his life. One of these, which he shares with us all in some degree, forbids the recognition of the negro as a social equal."

"I do not know what Miller's social value may be," replied Dr. Burns, stoutly, "or whether you gain or lose by your attitude toward him. I have invited him here in a strictly professional capacity, with which his color is not at all concerned."

"Dr. Burns does not quite appreciate Major Carteret's point of view," said Dr. Price. "This is not with him an unimportant matter, or a mere question of prejudice, or even of personal taste. It is a sacred principle, lying at the very root of our social order, involving the purity and prestige of our race. You Northern gentlemen do not quite appreciate our situation; if you lived here a year or two you would act as we do. Of course," he added, diplomatically, "if there were no alternative—if Dr. Burns were willing to put Dr. Miller's presence on the ground of imperative necessity"—

"I do nothing of the kind, sir," retorted Dr. Burns with some heat. "I have not come all the way from Philadelphia to undertake an operation which I cannot perform without the aid of some particular physician. I merely stand upon my professional rights."

Carteret was deeply agitated. The operation must not be deferred; his child's life might be endangered by delay. If the negro's presence were indispensable he would even submit to it, though in order to avoid so painful a necessity, he would rather humble himself to the Northern doctor. The latter course involved merely a personal sacrifice—the former a vital principle. Perhaps there was another way of escape. Miller's presence could not but be distasteful to Mrs. Carteret for other reasons. Miller's wife was the living evidence of a painful episode in Mrs. Carteret's family, which the doctor's presence would inevitably recall. Once before, Mrs. Carteret's life had been endangered by encountering, at a time of great nervous strain, this ill-born sister and her child. She was even now upon the verge of collapse at the prospect of her child's suffering, and should be protected from the intrusion of any idea which might add to her distress.

"Dr. Burns," he said, with the suave courtesy which was part of his inheritance, "I beg your pardon for my heat, and throw myself upon your magnanimity, as between white men"—

"I am a gentleman, sir, before I am a white man," interposed Dr. Burns, slightly mollified, however, by Carteret's change of manner.

"The terms should be synonymous," Carteret could not refrain from saying. "As between white men, and gentlemen, I say to you, frankly, that there are vital, personal reasons, apart from Dr. Miller's color, why his presence in this house would be distasteful. With this statement, sir, I throw myself upon your mercy. My child's life is worth more to me than any earthly thing, and I must be governed by your decision."

Dr. Burns was plainly wavering. The clock moved with provoking slowness. Miller would be there in five minutes.

"May I speak with you privately a moment, doctor?" asked Dr. Price.

They withdrew from the room and were engaged in conversation for a few moments. Dr. Burns finally yielded.

"I shall nevertheless feel humiliated when I meet Miller again," he said, "but of course if there is a personal question involved, that alters the situation. Had it been merely a matter of color, I should have maintained my position. As things stand, I wash my hands of the whole affair, so far as Miller is concerned, like Pontius Pilate—yes, indeed, sir, I feel very much like that individual."

"I'll explain the matter to Miller," returned Dr. Price, amiably, "and make it all right with him. We Southern people understand the negroes better than you do, sir. Why should we not? They have been constantly under our interested observation for several hundred years. You feel this vastly more than Miller will. He knows the feeling of the white people, and is accustomed to it. He wishes to live and do business here, and is quite too shrewd to antagonize his neighbors or come where he is not wanted. He is in fact too much of a gentleman to do so."

"I shall leave the explanation to you entirely," rejoined Dr. Burns, as they reentered the other room.

Carteret led the way to the nursery, where the operation was to take place. Dr. Price lingered for a moment. Miller was not likely to be behind the hour, if he came at all, and it would be well to head him off before the operation began.

Scarcely had the rest left the room when the doorbell sounded, and a servant announced Dr. Miller.

Dr. Price stepped into the hall and met Miller face to face.

He had meant to state the situation to Miller frankly, but now that the moment had come he wavered. He was a fine physician, but he shrank from strenuous responsibilities. It had been easy to theorize about the negro; it was more difficult to look this man in the eyes—whom at this moment he felt to be as essentially a gentleman as himself—and tell him the humiliating truth.

As a physician his method was to ease pain—he would rather take the risk of losing a patient from the use of an anæsthetic than from the shock of an operation. He liked Miller, wished him well, and would not wittingly wound his feelings. He really thought him too much of a gentleman for the town, in view of the restrictions with which he must inevitably be hampered. There was something melancholy, to a cultivated mind, about a sensitive, educated man who happened to be off color. Such a person was a sort of social misfit, an odd quantity, educated out of his own class, with no possible hope of entrance into that above it. He felt quite sure that if he had been in Miller's place, he would never have settled in the South—he would have moved to Europe, or to the West Indies, or some Central or South American state where questions of color were not regarded as vitally important.

Dr. Price did not like to lie, even to a negro. To a man of his own caste, his word was his bond. If it were painful to lie, it would be humiliating to be found out. The principle of *noblesse oblige* was also involved in the matter. His claim of superiority to the colored doctor rested fundamentally upon the fact that he was white and Miller was not; and yet this superiority, for which he could claim no credit, since he had not made himself, was the very breath of his nostrils,—he would not have changed places with the other for wealth untold; and as a gentleman, he would not care to have another gentleman, even a colored man, catch him in a lie. Of this, however, there was scarcely any danger. A word to the other surgeons would insure their corroboration of whatever he might tell Miller. No one of them would willingly wound Dr. Miller or embarrass Dr. Price; indeed, they need not know that Miller had come in time for the operation.

"I'm sorry, Miller," he said with apparent regret, "but we were here ahead of time, and the case took a turn which would admit of no delay, so the gentlemen went in. Dr. Burns is with the patient now, and asked me to explain why we did not wait for you."

"I'm sorry too," returned Miller, regretfully, but nothing doubting. He was well aware that in such cases danger might attend upon delay. He had lost his chance, through no fault of his own or of any one else.

"I hope that all is well?" he said, hesitatingly, not sure whether he would be asked to remain.

"All is well, so far. Step round to my office in the morning, Miller, or come in when you're passing, and I'll tell you the details."

This was tantamount to a dismissal, so Miller took his leave. Descending the doorsteps, he stood for a moment, undecided whether to return home or to go to the hotel and await the return of Dr. Burns, when he heard his name called from the house in a low tone.

"Oh, doctuh!"

He stepped back toward the door, outside of which stood the colored servant who had just let him out.

"Dat's all a lie, doctuh," he whispered, " 'bout de operation bein' already pe'fo'med. Dey-all had jes' gone in de minute befo' you come—Doctuh Price hadn' even got out'n de room. Dey be'n quollin' 'bout you fer de las' ha'f hour. Majah Ca'te'et say he wouldn' have you, an' de No'then doctuh say he wouldn't do nothin' widout you, an' Doctuh Price he j'ined in on bofe sides, an' dey had it hot an' heavy, nip an' tuck, till bimeby Majah Ca'te'et up an' say it wa'n't altogether yo' color he objected to, an' wid dat de No'then doctuh give in. He's a fine man, suh, but dey wuz too much fer 'im!"

"Thank you, Sam, I'm much obliged," returned Miller mechanically. "One likes to know the truth."

Truth, it has been said, is mighty, and must prevail; but it sometimes leaves a bad taste in the mouth. In the ordinary course of events Miller would not have anticipated such an invitation, and for that reason had appreciated it all the more. The rebuff came with a corresponding shock. He had the heart of a man, the sensibilities of a cultivated gentleman; the one was sore, the other deeply wounded. He was not altogether sure, upon reflection, whether he blamed Dr. Price very much for the amiable lie, which had been meant to spare his feelings, or thanked Sam a great deal for the unpalatable truth.

Janet met him at the door. "How is the baby?" she asked excitedly.

"Dr. Price says he is doing well."

"What is the matter, Will, and why are you back so soon?"

He would have spared her the story, but she was a woman, and would have it. He was wounded, too, and wanted sympathy, of which Janet was an exhaustless fountain. So he told her what had happened. She comforted him after the manner of a loving woman, and felt righteously indignant toward her sister's husband, who had thus been instrumental in the humiliation of her own. Her anger did not embrace her sister, and yet she felt obscurely that their unacknowledged relationship had been the malignant force which had given her husband pain, and defeated his honorable ambition.

When Dr. Price entered the nursery, Dr. Burns was leaning attentively over the operating table. The implements needed for the operation were all in readiness—the knives, the basin, the sponge, the materials for dressing the wound—all the ghastly paraphernalia of vivisection.

Mrs. Carteret had been banished to another room, where Clara vainly attempted to soothe her. Old Mammy Jane, still burdened by her fears, fervently prayed the good Lord to spare the life of the sweet little grandson of her dear old mistress.

Dr. Burns had placed his ear to the child's chest, which had been bared for the incision. Dr. Price stood ready to administer the anæsthetic. Little Dodie looked up with a faint expression of wonder, as if dimly conscious of some unusual event. The major shivered at the thought of what the child must undergo.

"There's a change in his breathing," said Dr. Burns, lifting his head. "The whistling noise is less pronounced, and he breathes easier. The obstruction seems to have shifted."

Applying his ear again to the child's throat, he listened for a moment intently, and then picking the baby up from the table, gave it a couple of sharp claps between the shoulders. Simultaneously a small object shot out from the child's mouth, struck Dr. Price in the neighborhood of his waistband, and then rattled lightly against the floor. Whereupon the baby, as though conscious of his narrow escape, smiled and gurgled, and reaching upward clutched the doctor's whiskers with his little hand, which, according to old Jane, had a stronger grip than any other infant's in Wellington.

CHAPTER VIII

The Campaign Drags

THE CAMPAIGN FOR white supremacy was dragging. Carteret had set out, in the columns of the Morning Chronicle, all the reasons why this movement, inaugurated by the three men who had met, six months before, at the office of the Chronicle, should be supported by the white public. Negro citizenship was a grotesque farce—Sambo and Dinah raised from the kitchen to the cabinet were a spectacle to make the gods laugh. The laws by which it had been sought to put the negroes on a level with the whites must be swept away in theory, as they had failed in fact. If it were impossible, without a further education of public opinion, to secure the repeal of the fifteenth amendment, it was at least the solemn duty of the state to endeavor, through its own constitution, to escape from the domination of a weak and incompetent electorate and confine the negro to that inferior condition for which nature had evidently designed him.

In spite of the force and intelligence with which Carteret had expressed these and similar views, they had not met the immediate response anticipated. There were thoughtful men, willing to let well enough alone, who saw no necessity for such a movement. They believed that peace, prosperity, and popular education offered a surer remedy for social ills than the reopening of issues supposed to have been settled. There were timid men who shrank from civic strife. There were busy men, who had something else to do. There were a few fair men, prepared to admit, privately, that a class constituting half to two thirds of the population were fairly entitled to some representation in the law-making bodies. Perhaps there might have been found, somewhere in the state, a single white man ready to concede that all men were entitled to equal rights before the law.

That there were some white men who had learned little and forgotten nothing goes without saying, for knowledge and wisdom are not impartially distributed among even the most favored race. There were ignorant and vicious negroes, and they had a monopoly of neither ignorance nor crime, for there were prosperous negroes and poverty-stricken whites. Until Carteret and his committee began their baleful campaign the people of the state were living in peace and harmony. The anti-negro legislation in more southern states, with large negro majorities, had awakened scarcely an echo in this state, with a population two thirds white. Even the triumph of the Fusion party had not been regarded as a race issue. It remained for Carteret and his friends to discover, with inspiration from whatever supernatural source the discriminating reader may elect, that the darker race, docile by instinct, humble by training, patiently waiting upon its as yet uncertain destiny, was an incubus, a corpse chained to the body politic, and that the negro vote was a source of danger to the state, no matter how cast or by whom directed.

To discuss means for counteracting this apathy, a meeting of the "Big Three," as they had begun to designate themselves jocularly, was held at the office of the "Morning Chronicle," on the next day but one after little Dodie's fortunate escape from the knife.

"It seems," said General Belmont, opening the discussion, "as though we had undertaken more than we can carry through. It is clear that we must reckon on opposition, both at home and abroad. If we are to hope for success, we must extend the lines of our campaign. The North, as well as our own people, must be convinced that we have right upon our side. We are conscious of the purity of our motives, but we should avoid even the appearance of evil."

McBane was tapping the floor impatiently with his foot during this harangue.

"I don't see the use," he interrupted, "of so much beating about the bush. We may as well be honest about this thing. We are going to put the niggers down because we want to, and think we can; so why waste our time in mere pretense? I'm no hypocrite myself,—if I want a thing I take it, provided I'm strong enough."

"My dear captain," resumed the general, with biting suavity, "your frankness does you credit,—'an honest man 's the noblest work of God,'—but we cannot carry on politics in these degenerate times without a certain amount of diplomacy. In the good old days when your father was alive, and perhaps nowadays in the discipline of convicts, direct and simple methods might be safely resorted to; but this is a modern age, and in dealing with so fundamental a right as the suffrage we must profess a decent regard for the opinions of even that misguided portion of mankind which may not agree with us. This is the age of crowds, and we must have the crowd with us."

The captain flushed at the allusion to his father's calling, at which he took more offense than at the mention of his own. He knew perfectly well that these old aristocrats, while reaping the profits of slavery, had despised the instruments by which they were attained—the poor-white overseer only less than the black slave. McBane was rich; he lived in Wellington, but he had never been invited to the home of either General Belmont or Major Carteret, nor asked to join the club of which they were members. His face, therefore, wore a distinct scowl, and his single eye glowed ominously. He would help those fellows carry the state for white supremacy, and then he would have his innings,—he would have more to say than they dreamed, as to who should fill the offices under the new deal. Men of no better birth or breeding than he had represented Southern states in Congress since the war. Why should he not run for governor, representative, whatever he chose? He had money enough to buy out half a dozen of these broken-down aristocrats, and money was all-powerful.

"You see, captain," the general went on, looking McBane smilingly and unflinchingly in the eye, "we need white immigration—we need Northern capital. 'A good name is better than great riches,' and we must prove our cause a righteous one."

"We must be armed at all points," added Carteret, "and prepared for defense as well as for attack,—we must make our campaign a national one."

"For instance," resumed the general, "you, Carteret, represent the Associated Press. Through your hands passes all the news of the state. What more powerful medium for the propagation of an idea? The man who would govern a nation by writing its songs was a blethering idiot beside the fellow who can edit its news dispatches. The negroes are playing into our hands,—every crime that one of them commits is reported by us. With the latitude they have had in this state they are growing more impudent and self-assertive every day. A yellow demagogue in New York made a speech only a few days ago, in which he deliberately, and in cold blood, advised negroes to defend themselves to the death when attacked by white people! I remember well the time when it was death for a negro to strike a white man."

"It's death now, if he strikes the right one," interjected McBane, restored to better humor by this mention of a congenial subject.

The general smiled a fine smile. He had heard the story of how McBane had lost his other eye.

"The local negro paper is quite outspoken, too," continued the general, "if not impudent. We must keep track of that; it may furnish us some good campaign material."

"Yes," returned Carteret, "we must see to that. I threw a copy into the waste-basket this morning, without looking at it. Here it is now!"

CHAPTER IX

A White Man's "Nigger"

CARTERET FISHED FROM the depths of the waste-basket and handed to the general an eighteen by twenty-four sheet, poorly printed on cheap paper, with a "patent" inside, a number of advertisements of proprietary medicines, quack doctors, and fortune-tellers, and two or three columns of editorial and local news. Candor compels the admission that it was not an impressive sheet in any respect, except when regarded as the first local effort of a struggling people to make public expression of their life and aspirations. From this point of view it did not speak at all badly for a class to whom, a generation before, newspapers, books, and learning had been forbidden fruit.

"It's an elegant specimen of journalism, isn't it?" laughed the general, airily. "Listen to this 'ad':—

" 'Kinky, curly hair made straight by one application of our specific. Our face bleach will turn the skin of a black or brown person four or five shades lighter, and of a mulatto perfectly white. When you get the color you wish, stop using the preparation.'

"Just look at those heads!—'Before using' and 'After using.' We'd better hurry, or there'll be no negroes to disfranchise! If they don't stop till they get the color they desire, and the stuff works according to contract, they'll all be white. Ah! what have we here? This looks as though it might be serious."

Opening the sheet the general read aloud an editorial article, to which Carteret listened intently, his indignation increasing in strength from the first word to the last, while McBane's face grew darkly purple with anger.

The article was a frank and somewhat bold discussion of lynching and its causes. It denied that most lynchings were for the offense most generally charged as their justification, and declared that, even of those seemingly traced to this cause, many were not for crimes at all, but for voluntary acts which might naturally be expected to follow from the miscegenation laws by which it was sought, in all the Southern States, to destroy liberty of contract, and, for the purpose of maintaining a fanciful purity of race, to make crimes of marriages to which neither nature nor religion nor the laws of other states interposed any insurmountable barrier. Such an article in a Northern newspaper would have attracted no special attention, and might merely have furnished food to an occasional reader for serious thought upon a subject not exactly agreeable; but coming from a colored man, in a Southern city, it was an indictment of the laws and social system of the South that could not fail of creating a profound sensation.

"Infamous—infamous!" exclaimed Carteret, his voice trembling with emotion. "The paper should be suppressed immediately."

"The impudent nigger ought to be horsewhipped and run out of town," growled McBane.

"Gentlemen," said the general soothingly, after the first burst of indignation had subsided, "I believe we can find a more effective use for this article, which, by the way, will not bear too close analysis,—there's some truth in it, at least there's an argument."

"That is not the point," interrupted Carteret.

"No," interjected McBane with an oath, "that ain't at all the point. Truth or not, no damn nigger has any right to say it."

"This article," said Carteret, "violates an unwritten law of the South. If we are to tolerate this race of weaklings among us, until they are eliminated by the stress of competition, it must be upon terms which we lay down. One of our conditions is violated by this article, in which our wisdom is assailed, and our women made the subject of offensive comment. We must make known our disapproval."

"I say lynch the nigger, break up the press, and burn down the newspaper office," McBane responded promptly.

"Gentlemen," interposed the general, "would you mind suspending the discussion for a moment, while I send Jerry across the street? I think I can then suggest a better plan."

Carteret rang the bell for Jerry, who answered promptly. He had been expecting such a call ever since the gentlemen had gone in.

"Jerry," said the general, "step across to Brown's and tell him to send me three Calhoun cocktails. Wait for them,—here's the money."

"Yas, suh," replied Jerry, taking the proffered coin.

"And make has'e, charcoal," added McBane, "for we're gettin' damn dry."

A momentary cloud of annoyance darkened Carteret's brow. McBane had always grated upon his aristocratic susceptibilities. The captain was an upstart, a product of the democratic idea operating upon the poor white man, the descendant of the indentured bondservant and the socially unfit. He had wealth and energy, however, and it was necessary to make use of him; but the example of such men was a strong incentive to Carteret in his campaign against the negro. It was distasteful enough to rub elbows with an illiterate and vulgar white man of no ancestry,—the risk of similar contact with negroes was to be avoided at any cost. He could hardly expect McBane to be a gentleman, but when among men of that class he might at least try to imitate their manners. A gentleman did not order his own servants around offensively, to say nothing of another's.

The general had observed Carteret's annoyance, and remarked pleasantly while they waited for the servant's return:—

"Jerry, now, is a very good negro. He's not one of your new negroes, who think themselves as good as white men, and want to run the government. Jerry knows his place,—he is respectful, humble, obedient, and content with the face and place assigned to him by nature."

"Yes, he's one of the best of 'em," sneered McBane. "He'll call any man 'master' for a quarter, or 'God' for half a dollar; for a dollar he'll grovel at your feet, and for a cast-off coat you can buy an option on his immortal soul,—if he has one! I've handled niggers for ten years, and I know 'em from the ground up. They're all alike,—they're a scrub race, an affliction to the country, and the quicker we're rid of 'em all the better."

Carteret had nothing to say by way of dissent. McBane's sentiments, in their last analysis, were much the same as his, though he would have expressed them less brutally.

"The negro," observed the general, daintily flicking the ash from his cigar, "is all right in his place and very useful to the community. We lived on his labor for quite a long time, and lived very well. Nevertheless we are better off without slavery, for we can get more out of the free negro, and with less responsibility. I really do not see how we could get along without the negroes. If they were all like Jerry, we'd have no trouble with them."

Having procured the drinks, Jerry, the momentary subject of the race discussion which goes on eternally in the South, was making his way back across the street, somewhat disturbed in mind.

"O Lawd!" he groaned, "I never troubles trouble till trouble troubles me; but w'en I got dem drinks befo', Gin'l Belmont gimme half a dollar an' tol' me ter keep de change. Dis time he did n' say nothin' 'bout de change. I s'pose he jes' fergot erbout it, but w'at is a po' nigger gwine ter do w'en he has ter conten' wid w'ite folks's fergitfulniss? I don' see no way but ter do some fergittin' myse'f. I'll jes' stan' outside de do' here till dey gits so wrop' up in deir talk dat dey won' 'member nothin' e'se, an' den at de right minute I'll han' de glasses 'roun, an' mos' lackly de gin'l 'll fergit all 'bout de change."

While Jerry stood outside, the conversation within was plainly audible, and some inkling of its purport filtered through his mind.

"Now, gentlemen," the general was saying, "here's my plan. That editorial in the negro newspaper is good campaign matter, but we should reserve it until it will be most effective. Suppose we just stick it in a pigeon-hole, and let the editor,—what's his name?"

"The nigger's name is Barber," replied McBane. "I'd like to have him under me for a month or two; he'd write no more editorials."

"Let Barber have all the rope he wants," resumed the general, "and he'll be sure to hang himself. In the mean time we will continue to work up public opinion,—we can use this letter privately for that purpose,—and when the state campaign opens we'll print the editorial, with suitable comment, scatter it broadcast throughout the state, fire the Southern heart, organize the white people on the color line, have a little demonstration with red shirts and shotguns, scare the negroes into fits, win the state for white supremacy, and teach our colored fellow citizens that we are tired of negro domination and have put an end to it forever. The Afro-American Banner will doubtless die about the same time."

"And so will the editor!" exclaimed McBane ferociously; "I'll see to that. But I wonder where that nigger is with them cocktails? I'm so thirsty I could swallow blue blazes."

"Here's yo' drinks, gin'l," announced Jerry, entering with the glasses on a tray.

The gentlemen exchanged compliments and imbibed—McBane at a gulp, Carteret with more deliberation, leaving about half the contents of his glass.

The general drank slowly, with every sign of appreciation. "If the illustrious statesmen," he observed, "whose name this mixture bears, had done nothing more than invent it, his fame would still deserve to go thundering down the endless ages."

"It ain't bad liquor," assented McBane, smacking his lips.

Jerry received the empty glasses on the tray and left the room. He had scarcely gained the hall when the general called him back.

"O Lawd!" groaned Jerry, "he's gwine ter ax me fer de change. Yas, suh, yas, suh; comin', gin'l, comin, suh!"

"You may keep the change, Jerry," said the general.

Jerry's face grew radiant at this announcement. "Yas, suh, gin'l; thank y', suh; much obleedzed, suh. I wuz jus' gwine ter fetch it in, suh, w'en I had put de tray down. Thank y', suh, truly, suh!"

Jerry backed and bowed himself out into the hall.

"Dat wuz a close shave," he muttered, as he swallowed the remaining contents of Major Carteret's glass. "I 'lowed dem twenty cents wuz gone dat time,— an' whar I wuz gwine ter git de money ter take my gal ter de chu'ch fetibal ter-night, de Lawd only knows!—'less'n I borried it off'n Mr. Ellis, an' I owes him sixty cents a'ready. But I wonduh w'at dem w'ite folks in dere is up ter? Dere's one thing sho',—dey're gwine ter git after de niggers some way er 'nuther, an' w'en dey does, whar is Jerry gwine ter be? Dat's de mos' impo'tantes' question. I'm gwine ter look at dat newspaper dey be'n talkin' 'bout, an' 'les'n my min' changes mightily, I'm gwine ter keep my mouf shet an' stan' in wid de Angry-Saxon race,—ez dey calls deyse'ves nowadays,—an' keep on de right side er my bread an' meat. W'at nigger ever give me twenty cents in all my bawn days?"

"By the way, major," said the general, who lingered behind McBane as they were leaving, "is Miss Clara's marriage definitely settled upon?"

"Well, general, not exactly; but it's the understanding that they will marry when they are old enough."

"I was merely thinking," the general went on, "that if I were you I'd speak to Tom about cards and liquor. He gives more time to both than a young man can afford. I'm speaking in his interest and in Miss Clara's,—we of the old families ought to stand together."

"Thank you, general, for the hint. I'll act upon it."

This political conference was fruitful in results. Acting upon the plans there laid out, McBane traveled extensively through the state, working up sentiment in favor of the new movement. He possessed a certain forceful eloquence; and white supremacy was so obviously the divine intention that he had merely to affirm the doctrine in order to secure adherents.

General Belmont, whose business required him to spend much of the winter in Washington and New York, lost no opportunity to get the ear of lawmakers, editors, and other leaders of national opinion, and to impress upon them, with persuasive eloquence, the impossibility of maintaining existing conditions, and the tremendous blunder which had been made in conferring the franchise upon the emancipated race.

Carteret conducted the press campaign, and held out to the Republicans of the North the glittering hope that, with the elimination of the negro vote, and a proper deference to Southern feeling, a strong white Republican party might be built up in the New South. How well the bait took is a matter of history,—but the promised result is still in the future. The disfranchisement of the negro has merely changed the form of the same old problem.

The negro had no vote before the rebellion, and few other rights, and yet the negro question was, for a century, the pivot of American politics. It plunged the nation into a bloody war, and it will trouble the American government and the American conscience until a sustained attempt is made to settle it upon principles of justice and equity.

The personal ambitions entertained by the leaders of this movement are but slightly involved in this story. McBane's aims have been touched upon elsewhere. The general would have accepted the nomination for governor of the state, with a vision of a senatorship in the future. Carteret hoped to vindicate the supremacy of his race, and make the state fit for his son to live in, and, incidentally, he would not refuse any office, worthy of his dignity, which a grateful people might thrust upon him.

So powerful a combination of bigot, self-seeking demagogue, and astute politician was fraught with grave menace to the peace of the state and the liberties of the people,—by which is meant the whole people, and not any one class, sought to be built up at the expense of another.

CHAPTER X

Delamere Plays a Trump

CARTERET DID NOT forget what General Belmont had said in regard to Tom. The major himself had been young, not so very long ago, and was inclined toward indulgence for the foibles of youth. A young gentleman should have a certain knowledge of life,—but there were limits. Clara's future happiness must not be imperiled.

The opportunity to carry out this purpose was not long delayed. Old Mr. Delamere wished to sell some timber which had been cut at Belleview, and sent Tom down to the Chronicle office to leave an advertisement. The major saw him at the desk, invited him into his sanctum, and delivered him a mild lecture. The major was kind, and talked in a fatherly way about the danger of extremes, the beauty of moderation, and the value of discretion as a rule of conduct. He mentioned collaterally the unblemished honor of a fine old family, its contemplated alliance with his own, and dwelt upon the sweet simplicity of Clara's character. The major was a man of feeling and of tact, and could not have put the subject in a way less calculated to wound the *amour propre* of a very young man.

Delamere had turned red with anger while the major was speaking. He was impulsive, and an effort was required to keep back the retort that sprang once or twice to his lips; but his conscience was not clear, and he could not afford hard words with Clara's guardian and his grandfather's friend. Clara was rich, and the most beautiful girl in town; they were engaged; he loved her as well as he could love anything of which he seemed sure; and he did not mean that any one else should have her. The major's mild censure disturbed slightly his sense of security; and while the major's manner did not indicate that he knew anything definite against him, it would be best to let well enough alone.

"Thank you, major," he said, with well-simulated frankness. "I realize that I may have been a little careless, more from thoughtlessness than anything else; but my heart is all right, sir, and I am glad that my conduct has been brought to your attention, for what you have said enables me to see it in a different light. I will be more careful of my company hereafter; for I love Clara, and mean to try to be worthy of her. Do you know whether she will be at home this evening?"

"I have heard nothing to the contrary," replied the major warmly. "Call her up by telephone and ask—or come up and see. You're always welcome, my boy."

Upon leaving the office, which was on the second floor, Tom met Ellis coming up the stairs. It had several times of late occurred to Tom that Ellis had a sneaking fondness for Clara. Panoplied in his own engagement, Tom had heretofore rather enjoyed the idea of a hopeless rival. Ellis was such a solemn prig, and took life so seriously, that it was a pleasure to see him sit around sighing for the unattainable. That he should be giving pain to Ellis added a certain zest to his own enjoyment.

But this interview with the major had so disquieted him that upon meeting Ellis upon the stairs he was struck by a sudden suspicion. He knew that Major Carteret seldom went to the Clarendon Club, and that he must have got his information from some one else. Ellis was a member of the club, and a frequent visitor. Who more likely than he to try to poison Clara's mind, or the minds of her friends, against her accepted lover? Tom did not think that the world was using him well of late; bad luck had pursued him, in cards and other things, and despite his assumption of humility, Carteret's lecture had left him in an ugly mood. He nodded curtly to Ellis without relaxing the scowl that disfigured his handsome features.

"That's the damned sneak who's been giving me away," he muttered. "I'll get even with him yet for this."

Delamere's suspicions with regard to Ellis's feelings were not, as we have seen, entirely without foundation. Indeed, he had underestimated the strength of this rivalry and its chances of success. Ellis had been watching Delamere for a year. There had been nothing surreptitious about it, but his interest in Clara had led him to note things about his favored rival which might have escaped the attention of others less concerned.

Ellis was an excellent judge of character, and had formed a very decided opinion of Tom Delamere. To Ellis, unbiased by ancestral traditions, biased perhaps by jealousy, Tom Delamere was a type of the degenerate aristocrat. If, as he had often heard, it took three or four generations to make a gentleman, and as many more to complete the curve and return to the base from which it started, Tom Delamere belonged somewhere on the downward slant, with large possibilities of further decline. Old Mr. Delamere, who might be taken as the apex of an ideal aristocratic development, had been distinguished, during his active life, as Ellis had learned, for courage and strength of will, courtliness of bearing, deference to his superiors, of whom there had been few, courtesy to his equals, kindness and consideration for those less highly favored, and above all, a scrupulous sense of honor; his grandson Tom was merely the shadow without the substance, the empty husk without the grain. Of grace he had plenty. In manners he could be perfect, when he so chose. Courage and strength he had none. Ellis had seen this fellow, who boasted of his descent from a line of cavaliers, turn pale with fright and spring from a buggy to which was harnessed a fractious horse, which a negro stable-boy drove fearlessly. A valiant carpet-knight, skilled in all parlor exercises, great at whist or euchre, a dream of a dancer, unexcelled in cakewalk or "coon" impersonations, for which he was in large social demand, Ellis had seen him kick an inoffensive negro out of his path and treat a poor-white man with scant courtesy. He suspected Delamere of cheating at cards, and knew that others entertained the same suspicion. For while regular in his own habits,—his poverty would not have permitted him any considerable extravagance,—Ellis's position as a newspaper man kept him in touch with what was going on about town. He was a member, proposed by Carteret, of the Clarendon Club, where cards were indulged in within reasonable limits, and a certain set were known to bet dollars in terms of dimes.

Delamere was careless, too, about money matters. He

had a habit of borrowing, right and left, small sums which might be conveniently forgotten by the borrower, and for which the lender would dislike to ask. Ellis had a strain of thrift, derived from a Scotch ancestry, and a tenacious memory for financial details. Indeed, he had never had so much money that he could lose track of it. He never saw Delamere without being distinctly conscious that Delamere owed him four dollars, which he had lent at a time when he could ill afford to spare it. It was a prerogative of aristocracy, Ellis reflected, to live upon others, and the last privilege which aristocracy in decay would willingly relinquish. Neither did the aristocratic memory seem able to retain the sordid details of a small pecuniary transaction.

No doubt the knowledge that Delamere was the favored lover of Miss Pemberton lent a touch of bitterness to Ellis's reflections upon his rival. Ellis had no grievance against the "aristocracy" of Wellington. The "best people" had received him cordially, though his father had not been of their caste; but Ellis hated a hypocrite, and despised a coward, and he felt sure that Delamere was both. Otherwise he would have struggled against his love for Clara Pemberton. His passion for her had grown with his appreciation of Delamere's unworthiness. As a friend of the family, he knew the nature and terms of the engagement, and that if the marriage took place at all, it would not be for at least a year. This was a long time,—many things might happen in a year, especially to a man like Tom Delamere. If for any reason Delamere lost his chance, Ellis meant to be next in the field. He had not made love to Clara, but he had missed no opportunity of meeting her and making himself quietly and unobtrusively agreeable.

On the day after this encounter with Delamere on the stairs of the Chronicle office, Ellis, while walking down Vine Street, met old Mrs. Ochiltree. She was seated in her own buggy, which was of ancient build and pattern, driven by her colored coachman and man of all work.

"Mr. Ellis," she called in a shrill voice, having directed her coachman to draw up at the curb as she saw the young man approaching, "come here. I want to speak to you."

Ellis came up to the buggy and stood uncovered beside it.

"People are saying," said Mrs. Ochiltree, "that Tom Delamere is drinking hard, and has to be carried home intoxicated, two or three times a week, by old Mr. Delamere's man Sandy. Is there any truth in the story?"

"My dear Mrs. Ochiltree, I am not Tom Delamere's keeper. Sandy could tell you better than I."

"You are dodging my question, Mr. Ellis. Sandy wouldn't tell me the truth, and I know that you wouldn't lie,—you don't look like a liar. They say Tom is gambling scandalously. What do you know about that?"

"You must excuse me, Mrs. Ochiltree. A great deal of what we hear is mere idle gossip, and the truth is often grossly exaggerated. I'm a member of the same club with Delamere, and gentlemen who belong to the same club are not in the habit of talking about one another. As long as a man retains his club membership, he's presumed to be a gentleman. I wouldn't say anything against Delamere if I could."

"You don't need to," replied the old lady, shaking her finger at him with a cunning smile. "You are a very open young man, Mr. Ellis, and I can read you like a book. You are much smarter than you look, but you can't fool me. Good-morning."

Mrs. Ochiltree drove immediately to her niece's, where she found Mrs. Carteret and Clara at home. Clara was very fond of the baby, and was holding him in her arms. He was a fine baby, and bade fair to realize the bright hopes built upon him.

"You hold a baby very naturally, Clara," chuckled the old lady. "I suppose you are in training. But you ought to talk to Tom. I have just learned from Mr. Ellis that Tom is carried home drunk two or three times a week, and that he is gambling in the most reckless manner imaginable."

Clara's eyes flashed indignantly. Ere she could speak, Mrs. Carteret exclaimed:—

"Why, Aunt Polly! did Mr. Ellis say that?"

"I got it from Dinah," she replied, "who heard it from her husband, who learned it from a waiter at the club. And"—

"Pshaw!" said Mrs. Carteret, "mere servants' gossip."

"No, it isn't, Olivia. I met Mr. Ellis on the street, and asked him point blank, and he didn't deny it. He's a member of the club, and ought to know."

"Well, Aunt Polly, it can't be true. Tom is here every other night, and how could he carry on so without showing the signs of it? and where would he get the money? You know he has only a moderate allowance."

"He may win it at cards,—it's better to be born lucky than rich," returned Mrs. Ochiltree. "Then he has expectations, and can get credit. There's no doubt that Tom is going on shamefully."

Clara's indignation had not yet found vent in speech; Olivia had said all that was necessary, but she had been thinking rapidly. Even if all this had been true, why should Mr. Ellis have said it? Or, if he had not stated it directly, he had left the inference to be drawn. It seemed a most unfair and ungentlemanly thing. What motive could Ellis have for such an act?

She was not long in reaching a conclusion which was not flattering to Ellis. Mr. Ellis came often to the house, and she had enjoyed his society in a friendly way. That he had found her pleasant company had been very evident. She had never taken his attentions seriously, however, or regarded his visits as made especially to her, nor had the rest of the family treated them from that point of view. Her engagement to Tom Delamere, though not yet formally ratified, was so well understood by the world of Wellington that Mr. Ellis would scarcely have presumed to think of her as anything more than a friend.

This revelation of her aunt's, however, put a different face upon his conduct. Certain looks and sighs and enigmatical remarks of Ellis, to which she had paid but casual attention and attached no particular significance, now recurred to her memory with a new meaning. He had now evidently tried, in a roundabout way, to besmirch Tom's character and undermine him in her regard. While loving Tom, she had liked Ellis well enough, as a friend; but he had abused the privileges of friendship, and she would teach him a needed lesson.

Nevertheless, Mrs. Ochiltree's story had given Clara food for thought. She was uneasily conscious, after all, that there might be a grain of truth in what had been said, enough, at least, to justify her in warning Tom to be careful, lest his enemies should distort some amiable weakness into a serious crime.

She put this view of the case to Tom at their next meeting, assuring him, at the same time, of her unbounded faith and confidence. She did not mention Ellis's name, lest Tom, in righteous indignation, might do something rash, which he might thereafter regret. If any subtler or more obscure motive kept her silent as to Ellis, she was not aware of it; for Clara's views of life were still in the objective stage, and she had not yet fathomed the deepest recesses of her own consciousness.

Delamere had the cunning of weakness. He knew, too, better than any one else could know, how much truth there was in the rumors concerning him, and whether or not they could be verified too easily for him to make an indignant denial. After a little rapid reflection, he decided upon a different course.

"Clara," he said with a sigh, taking the hand which she generously yielded to soften any suggestion of reproach which he may have read into her solicitude, "you are my guardian angel. I do not know, of course, who has told you this pack of lies,—for I can see that you have heard more than you have told me,—but I think I could guess the man they came from. I am not perfect, Clara, though I have done nothing of which a gentleman should be ashamed. There is one sure way to stop the tongue of calumny. My home life is not ideal,—grandfather is an old, weak man, and the house needs the refining and softening influence of a lady's presence. I do not love club life; its ideals are not elevating. With you by my side, dearest, I should be preserved from every influence except the purest and the best. Don't you think, dearest, that the major might be induced to shorten our weary term of waiting?"

"Oh, Tom," she demurred blushingly. "I shall be young enough at eighteen; and you are barely twenty-one."

But Tom proved an eloquent pleader, and love a still more persuasive advocate. Clara spoke to the major the same evening, who looked grave at the suggestion, and said he would think about it. They were both very young; but where both parties were of good family, in good health and good circumstances, an early marriage might not be undesirable. Tom was perhaps a little unsettled, but blood would tell in the long run, and marriage always exercised a steadying influence.

The only return, therefore, which Ellis received for his well-meant effort to ward off Mrs. Ochiltree's embarrassing inquiries was that he did not see Clara upon his next visit, which was made one afternoon while he was on night duty at the office. In conversation with Mrs. Carteret he learned that Clara's marriage had been definitely agreed upon, and the date fixed,—it was to take place in about six months. Meeting Miss Pemberton on the street the following day, he received the slightest of nods. When he called again at the house, after a week of misery, she treated him with a sarcastic coolness which chilled his heart.

"How have I offended you, Miss Clara?" he demanded desperately, when they were left alone for a moment.

"Offended me?" she replied, lifting her eyebrows with an air of puzzled surprise. "Why, Mr. Ellis! What could have put such a notion into your head? Oh dear, I think I hear Dodie,—I know you'll excuse me, Mr. Ellis, won't you? Sister Olivia will be back in a moment; and we're expecting Aunt Polly this afternoon,—if you'll stay awhile she'll be glad to talk to you! You can tell her all the interesting news about your friends!"

CHAPTER XI

The Baby and the Bird

WHEN ELLIS, after this rebuff, had disconsolately taken his leave, Clara, much elated at the righteous punishment she had inflicted upon the slanderer, ran upstairs to the nursery, and, snatching Dodie from Mammy Jane's arms, began dancing gayly with him round the room.

"Look a-hyuh, honey," said Mammy Jane, "you better be keerful wid dat chile, an' don' drap 'im on de flo'. You might let him fall on his head an' break his neck. My, my! but you two does make a pretty pictur'! You'll be wantin' ole Jane ter come an' nuss yo' child'en some er dese days," she chuckled unctuously.

Mammy Jane had been very much disturbed by the recent dangers through which little Dodie had passed; and his escape from strangulation, in the first place, and then from the knife had impressed her as little less than miraculous. She was not certain whether this result had been brought about by her manipulation of the buried charm, or by the prayers which had been offered for the child, but was inclined to believe that both had cooperated to avert the threatened calamity. The favorable outcome of this particular incident had not, however, altered the general situation. Prayers and charms, after all, were merely temporary things, which must be constantly renewed, and might be forgotten or overlooked; while the mole, on the contrary, neither faded nor went away. If its malign influence might for a time seem to disappear, it was merely lying dormant, like the germs of some deadly disease, awaiting its opportunity to strike at an unguarded spot.

Clara and the baby were laughing in great glee, when a mockingbird, perched on the topmost bough of a small tree opposite the nursery window, burst suddenly into song, with many a trill and quaver. Clara, with the child in her arms, sprang to the open window.

"Sister Olivia," she cried, turning her face toward Mrs. Carteret, who at that moment entered the room, "come and look at Dodie."

The baby was listening intently to the music, meanwhile gurgling with delight, and reaching his chubby hands toward the source of this pleasing sound. It seemed as though the mockingbird were aware of his appreciative audience, for he ran through the songs of a dozen different birds, selecting, with the discrimination of a connoisseur and entire confidence in his own powers, those which were most difficult and most alluring.

Mrs. Carteret approached the window, followed by Mammy Jane, who waddled over to join the admiring party. So absorbed were the three women in the baby and the bird that neither one of them observed a neat top buggy, drawn by a sleek sorrel pony, passing slowly along the street before the house. In the buggy was seated a lady, and beside her a little boy, dressed in a child's sailor suit and a straw hat. The lady, with a wistful expression, was looking toward the party grouped in the open window.

Mrs. Carteret, chancing to lower her eyes for an instant, caught the other woman's look directed toward her and her child. With a glance of cold aversion she turned away from the window.

Old Mammy Jane had observed this movement, and had divined the reason for it. She stood beside Clara, watching the retreating buggy.

"Uhhuh!" she said to herself, "it's huh sister Janet! She ma'ied a doctuh, an' all dat, an' she lives in a big house, an' she's be'n roun' de worl' an de Lawd knows where e'se; but Mis' 'Livy don' like de sight er her, an' never will, ez long ez de sun rises an' sets. Dey ce't'nly does favor one anudder,—anybody mought 'low dey wuz twins, ef dey did n' know better. Well, well! Fo'ty yeahs ago who'd 'a' ever expected ter see a nigger gal ridin' in her own buggy? My, my! but I don' know,—I don' know! It don' look right, an' it ain' gwine ter las'!—you can't make me b'lieve!"

Meantime Janet, stung by Mrs. Carteret's look,—the nearest approach she had ever made to a recognition of her sister's existence,—had turned away with hardening face. She had struck her pony sharply with the whip, much to the gentle creature's surprise, when the little boy, who was still looking back, caught his mother's sleeve and exclaimed excitedly:—

"Look, look, mama! The baby,—the baby!"

Janet turned instantly, and with a mother's instinct gave an involuntary cry of alarm.

At the moment when Mrs. Carteret had turned away from the window, and while Mammy Jane was watching Janet, Clara had taken a step forward, and was leaning against the window-sill. The baby, convulsed with delight, had given a spasmodic spring and slipped from Clara's arms. Instinctively the young woman gripped the long skirt as it slipped through her hands, and held it tenaciously, though too frightened for an instant to do more. Mammy Jane, ashen with sudden dread, uttered an inarticulate scream, but retained self-possession enough to reach down and draw up the child, which hung dangerously suspended, head downward, over the brick pavement below.

"Oh, Clara, Clara, how could you!" exclaimed Mrs. Carteret reproachfully; "you might have killed my child!"

She had snatched the child from Jane's arms, and was holding him closely to her own breast. Struck by a sudden thought, she drew near the window and looked out. Twice within a few weeks her child had been in serious danger, and upon each occasion a member of the Miller family had been involved, for she had heard of Dr. Miller's presumption in trying to force himself where he must have known he would be unwelcome.

Janet was just turning her head away as the buggy moved slowly off. Olivia felt a violent wave of antipathy sweep over her toward this baseborn sister who had thus thrust herself beneath her eyes. If she had not cast her brazen glance toward the window, she herself would not have turned away and lost sight of her child. To this shameless intrusion, linked with Clara's carelessness, had been due the catastrophe, so narrowly averted, which might have darkened her own life forever. She took to her bed for several days, and for a long time was cold toward Clara, and did not permit her to touch the child.

Mammy Jane entertained a theory of her own about the accident, by which the blame was placed, in another way, exactly where Mrs. Carteret had laid it. Julia's daughter, Janet, had been looking intently toward the window just before little Dodie had sprung from Clara's arms. Might she not have cast the evil eye upon the baby, and sought thereby to draw him out of the window? One would not ordinarily expect so young a woman to possess such a power, but she might have acquired it, for this very purpose, from some more experienced person. By the same reasoning, the mockingbird might have been a familiar of the witch, and the two might have conspired to lure the infant to destruction. Whether this were so or not, the transaction at least wore a peculiar look. There was no use telling Mis' 'Livy about it, for she didn't believe, or pretended not to believe, in witchcraft and conjuration. But one could not be too careful. The child was certainly born to be exposed to great dangers,—the mole behind the left ear was an unfailing sign,—and no precaution should be omitted to counteract its baleful influence.

While adjusting the baby's crib, a few days later, Mrs. Carteret found fastened under one of the slats a small bag of cotton cloth, about half an inch long and tied with a black thread, upon opening which she found a few small roots or fibres and a pinch of dried and crumpled herbs. It was a good-luck charm which Mammy Jane had placed there to ward off the threatened evil from the grandchild of her dear old mistress. Mrs. Carteret's first impulse was to throw the bag into the fire, but on second thoughts she let it remain. To remove it would give unnecessary pain to the old nurse. Of course these old negro superstitions were absurd,—but if the charm did no good, it at least would do no harm.

CHAPTER XII

Another Southern Product

ONE MORNING SHORTLY after the opening of the hospital, while Dr. Miller was making his early rounds, a new patient walked in with a smile on his face and a broken arm hanging limply by his side. Miller recognized in him a black giant by the name of Josh Green, who for many years had worked on the docks for Miller's father,—and simultaneously identified him as the dust-begrimed negro who had stolen a ride to Wellington on the trucks of a passenger car.

"Well, Josh," asked the doctor, as he examined the fracture, "how did you get this? Been fighting again?"

"No, suh, I don' s'pose you could ha'dly call it a fight. One er dem dagoes off'n a Souf American boat gimme some er his jaw, an' I give 'im a back answer, an' here I is wid a broken arm. He got holt er a belayin'-pin befo' I could hit 'im."

"What became of the other man?" demanded Miller suspiciously. He perceived, from the indifference with which Josh bore the manipulation of the fractured limb, that such an accident need not have interfered seriously with the use of the remaining arm, and he knew that Josh had a reputation for absolute fearlessness.

"Lemme see," said Josh reflectively, "ef I kin 'member w'at *did* become er him! Oh, yes, I 'member now! Dey tuck him ter de Marine Horspittle in de amberlance, 'cause his leg wuz broke, an' I reckon somethin' must 'a' accident'ly hit 'im in de jaw, fer he wuz scatt'rin' teeth all de way 'long de street. I didn' wan' ter kill de man, fer he might have somebody dependin' on 'im, an' I knows how dat'd be ter dem. But no man kin call me a damn' low-down nigger and keep on enjoyin' good health right along."

"It was considerate of you to spare his life," said Miller

dryly, "but you'll hit the wrong man some day. These are bad times for bad negroes. You'll get into a quarrel with a white man, and at the end of it there'll be a lynching, or a funeral. You'd better be peaceable and endure a little injustice, rather than run the risk of a sudden and violent death."

"I expec's ter die a vi'lent death in a quarrel wid a w'ite man," replied Josh, in a matter-of-fact tone, "an' fu'thermo', he's gwine ter die at the same time, er a little befo'. I be'n takin' my own time 'bout killin' 'im; I ain' be'n crowdin' de man, but I'll be ready after a w'ile, an' den he kin look out!"

"And I suppose you 're merely keeping in practice on these other fellows who come your way. When I get your arm dressed, you'd better leave town till that fellow's boat sails; it may save you the expense of a trial and three months in the chain-gang. But this talk about killing a man is all nonsense. What has any man in this town done to you, that you should thirst for his blood?"

"No, suh, it ain' nonsense,—it's straight, solem' fac'. I'm gwine ter kill dat man as sho' as I 'm settin' in dis cheer; an' dey ain't nobody kin say I ain' got a right ter kill 'im. Does you 'member de Ku-Klux?"

"Yes, but I was a child at the time, and recollect very little about them. It is a page of history which most people are glad to forget."

"Yas, suh; I was a chile, too, but I wuz right in it, an' so I 'members mo' erbout it 'n you does. My mammy an' daddy lived 'bout ten miles f'm here, up de river. One night a crowd er w'ite men come ter ou' house an' tuck my daddy out an' shot 'im ter death, an' skeered my mammy so she ain' be'n herse'f f'm dat day ter dis. I wa'n't mo' 'n ten years ole at de time, an' w'en my mammy seed de w'ite men comin', she tol' me ter run. I hid in de bushes an' seen de whole thing, an' it wuz branded on my mem'ry, suh, like a red-hot iron bran's de skin. De w'ite folks had masks on, but one of 'em fell off,—he wuz de boss, he wuz de head man, an' tol' de res' w'at ter do,—an' I seen his face. It wuz a easy face ter 'member; an' I swo' den, 'way down deep in my hea't, little ez I wuz, dat some day er 'nother I'd kill dat man. I ain't never had no doubt erbout it; it's jus' w'at I'm livin' fer, an' I know I ain' gwine ter die till I've done it. Some lives fer one thing an' some fer another, but dat's my job. I ain' be'n in no has'e, fer I'm not ole yit, an' dat man is in good health. I'd like ter see a little er de worl' befo' I takes chances on leavin' it sudden; an', mo'over, somebody's got ter take keer er de ole 'oman. But her time'll come some er dese days, an den *his* time'll be come—an' prob'ly mine. But I ain' keerin' 'bout myse'f: w'en I git thoo wid him, it won' make no dif-f'ence 'bout me."

Josh was evidently in dead earnest. Miller recalled, very vividly, the expression he had seen twice on his patient's face, during the journey to Wellington. He had often seen Josh's mother, old Aunt Milly,—"Silly Milly," the children called her,—wandering aimlessly about the street, muttering to herself incoherently. He had felt a certain childish awe at the sight of one of God's creatures who had lost the light of reason, and he had always vaguely understood that she was the victim of human cruelty, though he had dated it farther back into the past. This was his first knowledge of the real facts of the case.

He realized, too, for a moment, the continuity of life, how inseparably the present is woven with the past, how certainly the future will be but the outcome of the present. He had supposed this old wound healed. The negroes were not a vindictive people. If, swayed by passion or emotion, they sometimes gave way to gusts of rage, these were of brief duration. Absorbed in the contemplation of their doubtful present and their uncertain future, they gave little thought to the past,—it was a dark story, which they would willingly forget. He knew the timeworn explanation that the Ku-Klux movement, in the main, was merely an ebullition of boyish spirits, begun to amuse young white men by playing upon the fears and superstitions of ignorant negroes. Here, however, was its tragic side,—the old wound still bleeding, the fruit of one tragedy, the seed of another. He could not approve of Josh's application of the Mosaic law of revenge, and yet the incident was not without significance. Here was a negro who could remember an injury, who could shape his life to a definite purpose, if not a high or holy one. When his race reached the point where they would resent a wrong, there was hope that they might soon attain the stage where they would try, and, if need be, die, to defend a right. This man, too, had a purpose in life, and was willing to die that he might accomplish it. Miller was willing to give up his life to a cause. Would he be equally willing, he asked himself, to die for it? Miller had no prophetic instinct to tell him how soon he would have the opportunity to answer his own question. But he could not encourage Josh to carry out this dark and revengeful purpose. Every worthy consideration required him to dissuade his patient from such a desperate course.

"You had better put away these murderous fancies, Josh," he said seriously. "The Bible says that we should 'forgive our enemies, bless them that curse us, and do good to them that despitefully use us.' "

"Yas, suh, I've l'arnt all dat in Sunday-school, an' I've heared de preachers say it time an' time ag'in. But it 'pears ter me dat dis fergitfulniss an' fergivniss is mighty one-sided. De w'ite folks don' fergive nothin' de niggers does. Dey got up de Ku-Klux, dey said, on 'count er de kyarpit-baggers. Dey be'n talkin' 'bout de kyarpit-baggers ever sence, an' dey 'pears ter fergot all 'bout de Ku-Klux. But I ain' fergot. De niggers is be'n train' ter fergiveniss; an' fer fear dey might fergit how ter fergive, de w'ite folks gives 'em somethin' new ev'y now an' den, ter practice on. A w'ite man kin do w'at he wants ter a nigger, but de minute de nigger gits back at 'im, up goes de nigger, an' don' come down tell somebody cuts 'im down. If a nigger gits a' office, er de race 'pears ter be prosperin' too much, de w'ite folks up an' kills a few, so dat de res' kin keep on fergivin' an' bein' thankful dat dey're lef' alive. Don' talk ter me 'bout dese w'ite folks,—I knows 'em, I does! Ef a nigger wants ter git down on his marrow-bones, an' eat dirt, an' call 'em 'marster,' *he's* a good nigger, dere's room fer *him*. But I ain' no w'ite folks' nigger, I ain'. I don' call no man 'marster.' I don' wan' nothin' but w'at I wo'k fer, but I wants all er dat. I never moles's no w'ite man, 'less 'n he moles's me fus'. But w'en de ole 'oman dies, doctuh, an' I gits a good chance at dat w'ite man,—dere ain' no use talkin', suh!—dere's gwine ter be a mix-up, an' a fune'al, er two fune'als—er may be mo', ef anybody is keerliss enough to git in de way."

"Josh," said the doctor, laying a cool hand on the other's brow, "you 're feverish, and don't know what you're talking about. I shouldn't let my mind dwell on such things, and you must keep quiet until this arm is well, or you may never be able to hit any one with it again."

Miller determined that when Josh got better he would talk to him seriously and dissuade him from this dangerous design. He had not asked the name of Josh's enemy, but the look of murderous hate which the dust-begrimed tramp of the railway journey had cast at Captain George McBane rendered any such question superfluous. McBane was probably deserving of any evil fate which might befall him; but such a revenge would do no good, would right no wrong; while every such crime, committed by a colored man, would be imputed to the race, which was already staggering under a load of obloquy because, in the eyes of a prejudiced and undiscriminating public, it must answer as a whole for the offenses of each separate individual. To die in defense of the right was heroic. To kill another for revenge was pitifully human and weak: "Vengeance is mine, I will repay," saith the Lord.

CHAPTER XIII

The Cakewalk

OLD MR. DELAMERE's servant, Sandy Campbell, was in deep trouble.

A party of Northern visitors had been staying for several days at the St. James Hotel. The gentlemen of the party were concerned in a projected cotton mill, while the ladies were much interested in the study of social conditions, and especially in the negro problem. As soon as their desire for information became known, they were taken courteously under the wing of prominent citizens and their wives, who gave them, at elaborate luncheons, the Southern white man's views of the negro, sighing sentimentally over the disappearance of the good old negro of before the war, and gravely deploring the degeneracy of his descendants. They enlarged upon the amount of money the Southern whites had spent for the education of the negro, and shook their heads over the inadequate results accruing from this unexampled generosity. It was sad, they said, to witness this spectacle of a dying race, unable to withstand the competition of a superior type. The severe reprisals taken by white people for certain crimes committed by negroes were of course not the acts of the best people, who deplored them; but still a certain charity should be extended towards those who in the intense and righteous anger of the moment should take the law into their own hands and deal out rough but still substantial justice; for no negro was ever lynched without incontestable proof of his guilt. In order to be perfectly fair, and give their visitors an opportunity to see both sides of the question, they accompanied the Northern visitors to a colored church where they might hear a colored preacher, who had won a jocular popularity throughout the whole country by an oft-repeated sermon intended to demonstrate

303

that the earth was flat like a pancake. This celebrated divine could always draw a white audience, except on the days when his no less distinguished white rival in the field of sensationalism preached his equally famous sermon to prove that hell was exactly one half mile, linear measure, from the city limits of Wellington. Whether accidentally or not, the Northern visitors had no opportunity to meet or talk alone with any colored person in the city except the servants at the hotel. When one of the party suggested a visit to the colored mission school, a Southern friend kindly volunteered to accompany them.

The visitors were naturally much impressed by what they learned from their courteous hosts, and felt inclined to sympathize with the Southern people, for the negro is not counted as a Southerner, except to fix the basis of congressional representation. There might of course be things to criticise here and there, certain customs for which they did not exactly see the necessity, and which seemed in conflict with the highest ideals of liberty but surely these courteous, soft-spoken ladies and gentlemen, entirely familiar with local conditions, who descanted so earnestly and at times pathetically upon the grave problems confronting them, must know more about it than people in the distant North, without their means of information. The negroes who waited on them at the hotel seemed happy enough, and the teachers whom they had met at the mission school had been well-dressed, well-mannered, and apparently content with their position in life. Surely a people who made no complaints could not be very much oppressed.

In order to give the visitors, ere they left Wellington, a pleasing impression of Southern customs, and particularly of the joyous, happy-go-lucky disposition of the Southern darky and his entire contentment with existing conditions, it was decided by the hotel management to treat them, on the last night of their visit, to a little diversion, in the shape of a genuine negro cakewalk.

On the afternoon of this same day Tom Delamere strolled into the hotel, and soon gravitated to the bar, where he was a frequent visitor. Young men of leisure spent much of their time around the hotel, and no small part of it in the bar. Delamere had been to the club, but had avoided the card-room. Time hanging heavy on his hands, he had sought the hotel in the hope that some form of distraction might present itself.

"Have you heard the latest, Mr. Delamere?" asked the bartender, as he mixed a cocktail for his customer.

"No, Billy; what is it?"

"There's to be a big cakewalk upstairs to-night. The No'the'n gentlemen an' ladies who are down here to see about the new cotton fact'ry want to study the nigger some more, and the boss has got up a cakewalk for 'em, 'mongst the waiters and chambermaids, with a little outside talent."

"Is it to be public?" asked Delamere.

"Oh, no, not generally, but friends of the house won't be barred out. The clerk'll fix it for you. Ransom, the head waiter, will be floor manager."

Delamere was struck with a brilliant idea. The more he considered it, the brighter it seemed. Another cocktail imparted additional brilliancy to the conception. He had been trying, after a feeble fashion, to keep his promise to Clara, and was really suffering from lack of excitement.

He left the bar-room, found the head waiter, held with him a short conversation, and left in his intelligent and itching palm a piece of money.

The cakewalk was a great success. The most brilliant performer was a late arrival, who made his appearance just as the performance was about to commence. The newcomer was dressed strikingly, the conspicuous features of his attire being a long blue coat with brass buttons and a pair of plaid trousers. He was older, too, than the other participants, which made his agility the more remarkable. His partner was a new chambermaid, who had just come to town, and whom the head waiter introduced to the newcomer upon his arrival. The cake was awarded to this couple by a unanimous vote. The man presented it to his partner with a grandiloquent flourish, and returned thanks in a speech which sent the Northern visitors into spasms of delight at the quaintness of the darky dialect and the darky wit. To cap the climax, the winner danced a buck dance with a skill and agility that brought a shower of complimentary silver, which he gathered up and passed to the head waiter.

Ellis was off duty for the evening. Not having ventured to put in an appearance at Carteret's since his last rebuff, he found himself burdened with a superfluity of leisure, from which he essayed to find relief by dropping into the hotel office at about nine o'clock. He was invited up to see the cakewalk, which he rather enjoyed, for there was some graceful dancing and posturing. But the grotesque contortions of one participant had struck him as somewhat overdone, even for the comical type of negro. He recognized the fellow, after a few minutes' scrutiny, as the body-servant of old Mr. Delamere. The man's present occupation, or choice of diversion, seemed out of keeping with his employment as attendant upon an invalid old gentleman, and strangely inconsistent with the gravity and decorum which had been so noticeable when this agile cakewalker had served as butler at Major Carteret's table, upon the occasion of the christening dinner. There was a vague suggestion of unreality about this performance, too, which Ellis did not attempt to analyze, but which recurred vividly to his memory upon a subsequent occasion.

Ellis had never pretended to that intimate knowledge of negro thought and character by which some of his acquaintances claimed the ability to fathom every motive of a negro's conduct, and predict in advance what any one of the darker race would do under a given set of circumstances. He would not have believed that a white man could possess two so widely varying phases of character; but as to negroes, they were as yet a crude and undeveloped race, and it was not safe to make predictions concerning them. No one could tell at what moment the thin veneer of civilization might peel off and reveal the underlying savage.

The champion cakewalker, much to the surprise of his sable companions, who were about equally swayed by admiration and jealousy, disappeared immediately after the close of the performance. Any one watching him on his way home through the quiet streets to old Mr. Delamere's would have seen him now and then shaking with laughter. It had been excellent fun. Nevertheless, as he neared home, a certain aspect of the affair, hitherto unconsidered, occurred to him, and it was in a rather serious frame of mind that he cautiously entered the house and sought his own room.

*   *   *

The cakewalk had results which to Sandy were very serious. The following week he was summoned before the disciplinary committee of his church and charged with unchristian conduct, in the following particulars, to wit: dancing, and participating in a sinful diversion called a cakewalk, which was calculated to bring the church into disrepute and make it the mockery of sinners.

Sandy protested his innocence vehemently, but in vain. The proof was overwhelming. He was positively identified by Sister 'Manda Patterson, the hotel cook, who had watched the whole performance from the hotel corridor for the sole, single, solitary, and only purpose, she averred, of seeing how far human wickedness could be carried by a professing Christian. The whole thing had been shocking and offensive to her, and only a stern sense of duty had sustained her in looking on, that she might be qualified to bear witness against the offender. She had recognized his face, his clothes, his voice, his walk—there could be no shadow of doubt that it was Brother Sandy. This testimony was confirmed by one of the deacons, whose son, a waiter at the hotel, had also seen Sandy at the cakewalk.

Sandy stoutly insisted that he was at home the whole evening; that he had not been near the hotel for three months; that he had never in his life taken part in a cakewalk, and that he did not know how to dance. It was replied that wickedness, like everything else, must have a beginning; that dancing was an art that could be acquired in secret, and came natural to some people. In the face of positive proof, Sandy's protestations were of no avail; he was found guilty, and suspended from church fellowship until he should have repented and made full confession.

Sturdily refusing to confess a fault of which he claimed to be innocent, Sandy remained in contumacy, thereby falling somewhat into disrepute among the members of his church, the largest in the city. The effect of a bad reputation being subjective as well as objective, and poor human nature arguing that one may as well have the game as the name, Sandy insensibly glided into habits of which the church would not have approved, though he took care that they should not interfere with his duties to Mr. Delamere. The consolation thus afforded, however, followed as it was by remorse of conscience, did not compensate him for the loss of standing in the church, which to him was a social club as well as a religious temple. At times, in conversation with young Delamere, he would lament his hard fate.

Tom laughed until he cried at the comical idea which Sandy's plaint always brought up, of half-a-dozen negro preachers sitting in solemn judgment upon that cakewalk,—it had certainly been a good cakewalk!—and sending poor Sandy to spiritual Coventry.

"Cheer up, Sandy, cheer up!" he would say when Sandy seemed most depressed. "Go into my room and get yourself a good drink of liquor. The devil's church has a bigger congregation than theirs, and we have the consolation of knowing that when we die, we'll meet all our friends on the other side. Brace up, Sandy, and be a man, or, if you can't be a man, be as near a man as you can!"

Hoping to revive his drooping spirits, Sandy too often accepted the proffered remedy.

CHAPTER XIV

The Maunderings
of Old Mrs. Ochiltree

WHEN MRS. CARTERET had fully recovered from the shock attendant upon the accident at the window, where little Dodie had so narrowly escaped death or serious injury, she ordered her carriage one afternoon and directed the coachman to drive her to Mrs. Ochiltree's.

Mrs. Carteret had discharged her young nurse only the day before, and had sent for Mammy Jane, who was now recovered from her rheumatism, to stay until she could find another girl. The nurse had been ordered not to take the child to negroes' houses. Yesterday, in driving past the old homestead of her husband's family, now occupied by Dr. Miller and his family, Mrs. Carteret had seen her own baby's carriage standing in the yard.

When the nurse returned home, she was immediately discharged. She offered some sort of explanation, to the effect that her sister worked for Mrs. Miller, and that some family matter had rendered it necessary for her to see her sister. The explanation only aggravated the offense: if Mrs. Carteret could have overlooked the disobedience, she would by no means have retained in her employment a servant whose sister worked for the Miller woman.

Old Mrs. Ochiltree had within a few months begun to show signs of breaking up. She was over seventy years old, and had been of late, by various afflictions, confined to the house much of the time. More than once within the year, Mrs. Carteret had asked her aunt to come and live with her; but Mrs. Ochiltree, who would have regarded such a step as an acknowledgment of weakness, preferred her lonely independence. She resided in a small, old-fashioned house, standing back in the middle of a garden on a quiet street. Two old servants made up her modest household.

This refusal to live with her niece had been lightly borne, for Mrs. Ochiltree was a woman of strong individuality, whose comments upon her acquaintance, present or absent, were marked by a frankness at times no less than startling. This characteristic caused her to be more or less avoided. Mrs. Ochiltree was aware of this sentiment on the part of her acquaintance, and rather exulted in it. She hated fools. Only fools ran away from her, and that because they were afraid she would expose their folly. If most people were fools, it was no fault of hers, and she was not obliged to indulge them by pretending to believe that they knew anything. She had once owned considerable property, but was reticent about her affairs, and told no one how much she was worth, though it was supposed that she had considerable ready money, besides her house and some other real estate. Mrs. Carteret was her nearest living relative, though her grand-nephew Tom Delamere had been a great favorite with her. If she did not spare him her tongue-lashings, it was nevertheless expected in the family that she would leave him something handsome in her will.

Mrs. Ochiltree had shared in the general rejoicing upon the advent of the Carteret baby. She had been one of his godmothers, and had hinted at certain intentions held by her concerning him. During Mammy Jane's administration she had tried the old nurse's patience more or less by her dictatorial interference. Since her partial confinement to the house, she had gone, when her health and the weather would permit, to see the child, and at other times had insisted that it be sent to her in charge of the nurse at least every other day.

Mrs. Ochiltree's faculties had shared insensibly in the decline of her health. This weakness manifested itself by fits of absent-mindedness, in which she would seemingly lose connection with the present, and live over again, in imagination, the earlier years of her life. She had buried two husbands, had tried in vain to secure a third, and had never borne any children. Long ago she had petrified into a character which nothing under heaven could change, and which, if death is to take us as it finds us, and the future life to keep us as it takes us, promised anything but eternal felicity to those with whom she might associate after this life. Tom Delamere had been heard to say, profanely, that if his Aunt Polly went to heaven, he would let his mansion in the skies on a long lease, at a low figure.

When the carriage drove up with Mrs. Carteret, her aunt was seated on the little front piazza, with her wrinkled hands folded in her lap, dozing the afternoon away in fitful slumber.

"Tie the horse, William," said Mrs. Carteret, "and then go in and wake Aunt Polly, and tell her I want her to come and drive with me."

Mrs. Ochiltree had not observed her niece's approach, nor did she look up when William drew near. Her eyes were closed, and she would let her head sink slowly forward, recovering it now and then with a spasmodic jerk.

"Colonel Ochiltree," she muttered, "was shot at the battle of Culpepper Court House, and left me a widow for the second time. But I would not have married any man on earth after him."

"Mis' Ochiltree!" cried William, raising his voice, "oh, Mis' Ochiltree!"

"If I had found a man,—a real man,—I might have married again. I did not care for weaklings. I could have married John Delamere if I had wanted him. But pshaw! I could have wound him round"—

"Go round to the kitchen, William," interrupted Mrs. Carteret impatiently, "and tell Aunt Dinah to come and wake her up."

William returned in a few moments with a fat, comfortable looking black woman, who curtsied to Mrs. Carteret at the gate, and then going up to her mistress seized her by the shoulder and shook her vigorously.

"Wake up dere, Mis' Polly," she screamed, as harshly as her mellow voice would permit. "Mis' 'Livy wants you ter go drivin' wid 'er!"

"Dinah," exclaimed the old lady, sitting suddenly upright with a defiant assumption of wakefulness, "why do you take so long to come when I call? Bring me my bonnet and shawl. Don't you see my niece waiting for me at the gate?"

"Hyuh dey is, hyuh dey is!" returned Dinah, producing the bonnet and shawl, and assisting Mrs. Ochiltree to put them on.

Leaning on William's arm, the old lady went slowly down the walk, and was handed to the rear seat with Mrs. Carteret.

"How's the baby to-day, Olivia, and why didn't you bring him?"

"He has a cold to-day, and is a little hoarse," replied Mrs. Carteret, "so I thought it best not to bring him out. Drive out the Weldon road, William, and back by Pine Street."

The drive led past an eminence crowned by a handsome brick building of modern construction, evidently an institution of some kind, surrounded on three sides by a grove of venerable oaks.

"Hugh Poindexter," Mrs. Ochiltree exclaimed explosively, after a considerable silence, "has been building a new house, in place of the old family mansion burned during the war."

"It isn't Mr. Poindexter's house, Aunt Polly. That is the new colored hospital built by the colored doctor."

"The new colored hospital, indeed, and the colored doctor! Before the war the negroes were all healthy, and when they got sick we took care of them ourselves! Hugh Poindexter has sold the graves of his ancestors to a negro,—I should have starved first!"

"He had his grandfather's grave opened, and there was nothing to remove, except a few bits of heart-pine from the coffin. All the rest had crumbled into dust."

"And he sold the dust to a negro! The world is upside down."

"He had the tombstone transferred to the white cemetery, Aunt Polly, and he has moved away."

"Esau sold his birthright for a mess of pottage. When I die, if you outlive me, Olivia, which is not likely, I shall leave my house and land to this child! He is a Carteret,—he would never sell them to a negro. I can't trust Tom Delamere, I'm afraid."

The carriage had skirted the hill, passing to the rear of the new building.

"Turn to the right, William," ordered Mrs. Carteret, addressing the coachman, "and come back past the other side of the hospital."

A turn to the right into another road soon brought them to the front of the building, which stood slightly back from the street, with no intervening fence or inclosure. A sorrel pony in a light buggy was fastened to a hitching-post near the entrance. As they drove past, a lady came out of the front door and descended the steps, holding by the hand a very pretty child about six years old.

"Who is that woman, Olivia?" asked Mrs. Ochiltree abruptly, with signs of agitation.

The lady coming down the steps darted at the approaching carriage a look which lingered involuntarily.

Mrs. Carteret, perceiving this glance, turned away coldly.

With a sudden hardening of her own features the other woman lifted the little boy into the buggy and drove sharply away in the direction opposite to that taken by Mrs. Carteret's carriage.

"Who is that woman, Olivia?" repeated Mrs. Ochiltree, with marked emotion.

"I have not the honor of her acquaintance," returned Mrs. Carteret sharply. "Drive faster, William."

"I want to know who that woman is," persisted Mrs. Ochiltree querulously. "William," she cried shrilly, poking the coachman in the back with the end of her cane, "who is that woman?"

"Dat's Mis' Miller, ma'am," returned the coachman, touching his hat; "Doctuh Miller's wife."

"What was her mother's name?"

"Her mother's name wuz Julia Brown. She's be'n dead dese twenty years er mo'. Why, you knowed Julia, Mis' Polly!—she used ter b'long ter yo' own father befo' de wah; an' after de wah she kep' house fer"—

"Look to your horses, William!" exclaimed Mrs. Carteret sharply.

"It's that hussy's child," said Mrs. Ochiltree, turning to her niece with great excitement. "When your father died, I turned the mother and the child out into the street. The mother died and went to—the place provided for such as she. If I hadn't been just in time, Olivia, they would have turned you out. I saved the property for you and your son! You can thank me for it all!"

"Hush, Aunt Polly, for goodness' sake! William will hear you. Tell me about it when you get home."

Mrs. Ochiltree was silent, except for a few incoherent mumblings. What she might say, what distressing family secret she might repeat in William's hearing, should she take another talkative turn, was beyond conjecture.

Olivia looked anxiously around for something to distract her aunt's attention, and caught sight of a colored man, dressed in sober gray, who was coming toward the carriage.

"There's Mr. Delamere's Sandy!" exclaimed Mrs. Carteret, touching her aunt on the arm. "I wonder how his master is? Sandy, oh, Sandy!"

Sandy approached the carriage, lifting his hat with a slight exaggeration of Chesterfieldian elegance. Sandy, no less than his master, was a survival of an interesting type. He had inherited the feudal deference for his superiors in position, joined to a certain self-respect which saved him from sycophancy. His manners had been formed upon those of old Mr. Delamere, and were not a bad imitation; for in the man, as in the master, they were the harmonious reflection of a mental state.

"How is Mr. Delamere, Sandy?" asked Mrs. Carteret, acknowledging Sandy's salutation with a nod and a smile.

"He ain't ez peart ez he has be'n, ma'am," replied Sandy, "but he's doin' tol'able well. De doctuh say he's good fer a dozen years yit, ef he'll jes' take good keer of hisse'f an' keep f'm gittin' excited; fer sence dat secon' stroke, excitement is dange'ous fer 'im."

"I'm sure you take the best care of him," returned Mrs. Carteret kindly.

"You can't do anything for him, Sandy," interposed old Mrs. Ochiltree, shaking her head slowly to emphasize her dissent. "All the doctors in creation couldn't keep him alive another year. I shall outlive him by twenty years, though we are not far from the same age."

"Lawd, ma'am!" exclaimed Sandy, lifting his hands in affected amazement,—his study of gentle manners had been more than superficial,—"whoever would 'a' s'picion' dat you an' Mars John wuz nigh de same age? I'd 'a' 'lowed you wuz ten years younger 'n him, easy, ef you wuz a day!"

"Give my compliments to the poor old gentleman,"

returned Mrs. Ochiltree, with a simper of senile vanity, though her back was weakening under the strain of the effort to sit erect that she might maintain this illusion of comparative youthfulness. "Bring him to see me some day when he is able to walk."

"Yas 'm, I will," rejoined Sandy. "He's gwine out ter Belleview nex' week, fer ter stay a mont' er so, but I'll fetch him 'roun' w'en he comes back. I'll tell 'im dat you ladies 'quired fer 'im."

Sandy made another deep bow, and held his hat in his hand until the carriage had moved away. He had not condescended to notice the coachman at all, who was one of the young negroes of the new generation; while Sandy regarded himself as belonging to the quality, and seldom stooped to notice those beneath him. It would not have been becoming in him, either, while conversing with white ladies, to have noticed a colored servant. Moreover, the coachman was a Baptist, while Sandy was a Methodist, though under a cloud, and considered a Methodist in poor standing as better than a Baptist of any degree or sanctity.

"Lawd, Lawd!" chuckled Sandy, after the carriage had departed, "I never seed nothin' lack de way dat ole lady do keep up her temper! Wid one foot in de grave, an' de other hov'rin' on de edge, she talks 'bout my ole marster lack he wuz in his secon' chil'hood. But I'm jes' willin' ter bet dat he'll outlas' her! She ain't half de woman she wuz dat night I waited on de table at de christenin' pa'ty, w'en she 'lowed she wuz n' feared er no man livin'."

CHAPTER XV

Mrs. Carteret
Seeks an Explanation

As a STONE dropped into a pool of water sets in motion
a series of concentric circles which disturb the whole
mass in varying degree, so Mrs. Ochiltree's enigmatical
remark had started in her niece's mind a disturbing train
of thought. Had her words, Mrs. Carteret asked herself,
any serious meaning, or were they the mere empty babblings of a clouded intellect?

"William," she said to the coachman when they
reached Mrs. Ochiltree's house, "you may tie the horse
and help us out. I shall be here a little while."

William helped the ladies down, assisted Mrs. Ochiltree
into the house, and then went round to the kitchen.
Dinah was an excellent hand at potato-pone and other
culinary delicacies dear to the Southern heart, and William was a welcome visitor in her domain.

"Now, Aunt Polly," said Mrs. Carteret resolutely, as
soon as they were alone, "I want to know what you
meant by what you said about my father and Julia, and
this—this child of hers?"

The old woman smiled cunningly, but her expression
soon changed to one more grave.

"Why do you want to know?" she asked suspiciously.
"You've got the land, the houses, and the money.
You've nothing to complain of. Enjoy yourself, and be
thankful!"

"I'm thankful to God," returned Olivia, "for all his
good gifts,—and He has blessed me abundantly,—but
why should I be thankful to *you* for the property my
father left me?"

"Why should you be thankful to me?" rejoined Mrs.
Ochiltree with querulous indignation. "You'd better ask

why *shouldn't* you be thankful to me. What have I not done for you?"

"Yes, Aunt Polly, I know you've done a great deal. You reared me in your own house when I had been cast out of my father's; you have been a second mother to me, and I am very grateful,—you can never say that I have not shown my gratitude. But if you have done anything else for me, I wish to know it. Why should I thank you for my inheritance?"

"Why should you thank me? Well, because I drove that woman and her brat away."

"But she had no right to stay, Aunt Polly, after father died. Of course she had no moral right before, but it was his house, and he could keep her there if he chose. But after his death she surely had no right."

"Perhaps not so surely as you think,—if she had not been a negro. Had she been white, there might have been a difference. When I told her to go, she said"—

"What did she say, Aunt Polly," demanded Olivia eagerly.

It seemed for a moment as though Mrs. Ochiltree would speak no further: but her once strong will, now weakened by her bodily infirmities, yielded to the influence of her niece's imperious demand.

"I'll tell you the whole story," she said, "and then you'll know what I did for you and yours."

Mrs. Ochiltree's eyes assumed an introspective expression, and her story, as it advanced, became as keenly dramatic as though memory had thrown aside the veil of intervening years and carried her back directly to the events which she now described.

"Your father," she said, "while living with that woman, left home one morning the picture of health. Five minutes later he tottered into the house groaning with pain, stricken unto death by the hand of a just God, as a punishment for his sins."

Olivia gave a start of indignation, but restrained herself.

"I was at once informed of what had happened, for I had means of knowing all that took place in the household. Old Jane—she was younger then—had come with you to my house; but her daughter remained, and through her I learned all that went on.

"I hastened immediately to the house, entered without knocking, and approached Mr. Merkell's bedroom, which was on the lower floor and opened into the hall. The door was ajar, and as I stood there for a moment I heard your father's voice.

" 'Listen, Julia,' he was saying. 'I shall not live until the doctor comes. But I wish you to know, *dear* Julia!'—he called her 'dear Julia!'—'before I die, that I have kept my promise. You did me one great service, Julia,—you saved me from Polly Ochiltree!' Yes, Olivia, that is what he said! 'You have served me faithfully and well, and I owe you a great deal, which I have tried to pay.'

" 'Oh, Mr. Merkell, dear Mr. Merkell,' cried the hypocritical hussy, falling to her knees by his bedside, and shedding her crocodile tears, 'you owe me nothing. You have done more for me than I could ever repay. You will not die and leave me,—no, no, it cannot be!'

" 'Yes, I am going to die,—I am dying now, Julia. But listen,—compose yourself and listen, for this is a more important matter. Take the keys from under my pillow, open the desk in the next room, look in the second drawer on the right, and you will find an envelope containing three papers: one of them is yours, one is the paper I promised to make, and the third is a letter which I wrote last night. As soon as the breath has left my body, deliver the envelope to the address indorsed upon it. Do not delay one moment, or you may live to regret it. Say nothing until you have delivered the package, and then be guided by the advice which you receive,—it will come from a friend of mine who will not see you wronged.'

"I slipped away from the door without making my presence known and entered, by a door from the hall, the room adjoining the one where Mr. Merkell lay. A moment later there was a loud scream. Returning quickly to the hall, I entered Mr. Merkell's room as though just arrived.

" 'How is Mr. Merkell?' I demanded, as I crossed the threshold.

" 'He is dead,' sobbed the woman, without lifting her head,—she had fallen on her knees by the bedside. She had good cause to weep, for my time had come.

" 'Get up,' I said. 'You have no right here. You pollute Mr. Merkell's dead body by your touch. Leave the house immediately,—your day is over!'

" 'I will not!' she cried, rising to her feet and facing me with brazen-faced impudence. 'I have a right to stay,—he has given me the right!'

" 'Ha, ha!' I laughed. 'Mr. Merkell is dead, and I am mistress here henceforth. Go, and go at once,—do you hear?'

" 'I hear, but I shall not heed. I can prove my rights! I shall not leave!'

" 'Very well,' I replied, 'we shall see. The law will decide.'

"I left the room, but did not leave the house. On the contrary, I concealed myself where I could see what took place in the room adjoining the death-chamber.

"She entered the room a moment later, with her child on one arm and the keys in the other hand. Placing the child on the floor, she put the key in the lock, and seemed surprised to find the desk already unfastened. She opened the desk, picked up a roll of money and a ladies' watch, which first caught her eye, and was reaching toward the drawer upon the right, when I interrupted her:—

" 'Well, thief, are you trying to strip the house before you leave it?'

"She gave an involuntary cry, clasped one hand to her bosom and with the other caught up her child, and stood like a wild beast at bay.

" 'I am not a thief,' she panted. 'The things are mine!'

" 'You lie,' I replied. 'You have no right to them,— no more right than you have to remain in this house!'

" 'I have a right,' she persisted, 'and I can prove it!'

"She turned toward the desk, seized the drawer, and drew it open. Never shall I forget her look,—never shall I forget that moment; it was the happiest of my life. The drawer was empty!

"Pale as death she turned and faced me.

" 'The papers!' she shrieked, 'the papers! *You* have stolen them!'

" 'Papers?' I laughed, 'what papers? Do you take me for a thief, like yourself?'

" 'There were papers here,' she cried, 'only a minute since. They are mine,—give them back to me!'

" 'Listen, woman,' I said sternly, 'you are lying—or dreaming. My brother-in-law's papers are doubtless in his safe at his office, where they ought to be. As for the rest,—you are a thief.'

" 'I am not,' she screamed; 'I am his wife. He married me, and the papers that were in the desk will prove it.'

" 'Listen,' I exclaimed, when she finished,—'listen carefully, and take heed to what I say. You are a liar. You have no proofs,—there never were any proofs of what you say, because it never happened,—it is absurd upon the face of it. Not one person in Wellington would believe it. Why should he marry you? He did not need to! You are merely lying,—you are not even self-deceived. If he had really married you, you would have made it known long ago. That you did not is proof that your story is false.'

"She was hit so hard that she trembled and sank into a chair. But I had no mercy—she had saved your father from *me*—'dear Julia,' indeed!

" 'Stand up,' I ordered. 'Do not dare to sit down in my presence. I have you on the hip, my lady, and will teach you your place.'

"She struggled to her feet, and stood supporting herself with one hand on the chair. I could have killed her, Olivia! She had been my father's slave; if it had been before the war, I would have had her whipped to death.

" 'You are a thief,' I said, 'and of that there *are* proofs. I have caught you in the act. The watch in your bosom is my own, the money belongs to Mr. Merkell's estate, which belongs to my niece, his daughter Olivia. I saw you steal them. My word is worth yours a hundred times over, for I am a lady, and you are—what? And now hear me: if ever you breathe to a living soul one word of this preposterous story, I will charge you with the theft, and have you sent to the penitentiary. Your child will be taken from you, and you shall never see it again. I will give you now just ten minutes to take your brat and your rags out of this house forever. But before you go, put down your plunder there upon the desk!'

"She laid down the money and the watch, and a few minutes later left the house with the child in her arms.

"And now, Olivia, you know how I saved your estate, and why you should be grateful to me."

Olivia had listened to her aunt's story with intense interest. Having perceived the old woman's mood, and fearful lest any interruption might break the flow of her narrative, she had with an effort kept back the one question which had been hovering upon her lips, but which could now no longer be withheld.

"What became of the papers, Aunt Polly?"

"Ha, ha!" chuckled Mrs. Ochiltree with a cunning look, "did I not tell you that she found no papers?"

A change had come over Mrs. Ochiltree's face, marking the reaction from her burst of energy. Her eyes were half closed, and she was muttering incoherently. Olivia made some slight effort to arouse her, but in vain, and realizing the futility of any further attempt to extract information from her aunt at this time, she called William and drove homeward.

CHAPTER XVI

Ellis Takes a Trick

LATE ONE AFTERNOON a handsome trap, drawn by two spirited bays, drove up to Carteret's gate. Three places were taken by Mrs. Carteret, Clara, and the major, leaving the fourth seat vacant.

"I've asked Ellis to drive out with us," said the major, as he took the lines from the colored man who had the trap in charge. "We'll go by the office and pick him up."

Clara frowned, but perceiving Mrs. Carteret's eye fixed upon her, restrained any further expression of annoyance.

The major's liking for Ellis had increased within the year. The young man was not only a good journalist, but possessed sufficient cleverness and tact to make him excellent company. The major was fond of argument, but extremely tenacious of his own opinions. Ellis handled the foils of discussion with just the requisite skill to draw out the major, permitting himself to be vanquished, not too easily, but, as it were, inevitably, by the major's incontrovertible arguments.

Olivia had long suspected Ellis of feeling a more than friendly interest in Clara. Herself partial to Tom, she had more than once thought it hardly fair to Delamere, or even to Clara, who was young and impressionable, to have another young man constantly about the house. True, there had seemed to be no great danger, for Ellis had neither the family nor the means to make him a suitable match for the major's sister; nor had Clara made any secret of her dislike for Ellis, or of her resentment for his supposed depreciation of Delamere. Mrs. Carteret was inclined to a more just and reasonable view of Ellis's conduct in this matter, but nevertheless did not deem it wise to undeceive Clara. Dislike was a stout barrier, which remorse might have broken down. The major, absorbed in schemes of empire and dreams of his child's future, had not become cognizant of the affair. His wife, out of friendship for Tom, had refrained from mentioning it; while the major, with a delicate regard for Clara's feelings, had said nothing at home in regard to his interview with her lover.

At the Chronicle office Ellis took the front seat beside the major. After leaving the city pavements, they bowled along merrily over an excellent toll-road, built of oyster shells from the neighboring sound, stopping at intervals to pay toll to the gate-keepers, most of whom were white women with tallow complexions and snuff-stained lips,— the traditional "poor-white." For part of the way the road was bordered with a growth of scrub oak and pine, interspersed with stretches of cleared land, white with the opening cotton or yellow with ripening corn. To the right, along the distant river-bank, were visible here and there groups of turpentine pines, though most of this growth had for some years been exhausted. Twenty years before, Wellington had been the world's greatest shipping port for naval stores. But as the turpentine industry had moved southward, leaving a trail of devastated forests in its rear, the city had fallen to a poor fifth or sixth place in this trade, relying now almost entirely upon cotton for its export business.

Occasionally our party passed a person, or a group of persons,—mostly negroes approximating the pure type, for those of lighter color grew noticeably scarcer as the town was left behind. Now and then one of these would salute the party respectfully, while others glanced at them indifferently or turned away. There would have seemed, to a stranger, a lack of spontaneous friendliness between the people of these two races, as though each felt that it had no part or lot in the other's life. At one point the carriage drew near a party of colored folks who were laughing and jesting among themselves with great glee. Paying no attention to the white people, they continued to laugh and shout boisterously as the carriage swept by.

Major Carteret's countenance wore an angry look.

"The negroes around this town are becoming absolutely insufferable," he averred. "They are sadly in need of a lesson in manners."

Half an hour later they neared another group, who were also making merry. As the carriage approached, they became mute and silent as the grave until the major's party had passed.

"The negroes are a sullen race," remarked the major thoughtfully. "They will learn their lesson in a rude school, and perhaps much sooner than they dream. By the way," he added, turning to the ladies, "what was the arrangement with Tom? Was he to come out this evening?"

"He came out early in the afternoon," replied Clara, "to go a-fishing. He is to join us at the hotel."

After an hour's drive they reached the hotel, in front of which stretched the beach, white and inviting, along the shallow sound. Mrs. Carteret and Clara found seats on the veranda. Having turned the trap over to a hostler, the major joined a group of gentlemen, among whom was General Belmont, and was soon deep in the discussion of the standing problem of how best to keep the negroes down.

Ellis remained by the ladies. Clara seemed restless and ill at ease. Half an hour elapsed and Delamere had not appeared.

"I wonder where Tom is," said Mrs. Carteret.

"I guess he hasn't come in yet from fishing," said Clara. "I wish he would come. It's lonesome here. Mr. Ellis, would you mind looking about the hotel and seeing if there's any one here that we know?"

For Ellis the party was already one too large. He had accepted this invitation eagerly, hoping to make friends with Clara during the evening. He had never been able to learn definitely the reason of her coldness, but had dated it from his meeting with old Mrs. Ochiltree, with which he felt it was obscurely connected. He had noticed Delamere's scowling look, too, at their last meeting. Clara's injustice, whatever its cause, he felt keenly. To Delamere's scowl he had paid little attention,—he despised Tom so much that, but for his engagement to Clara, he would have held his opinions in utter contempt.

He had even wished that Clara might make some charge against him,—he would have preferred that to her attitude of studied indifference, the only redeeming feature about which was that it *was* studied, showing that she, at least, had him in mind. The next best thing, he reasoned, to having a woman love you, is to have her dislike you violently,—the main point is that you should be kept in mind, and made the subject of strong emotions. He thought of the story of Hall Caine's, where the woman, after years of persecution at the hands of an unwelcome suitor, is on the point of yielding, out of sheer irresistible admiration for the man's strength and persistency, when the lover, unaware of his victory and despairing of success, seizes her in his arms and, springing into the sea, finds a watery grave for both. The analogy of this case with his own was, of course, not strong. He did not anticipate any tragedy in their relations; but he was glad to be thought of upon almost any terms. He would not have done a mean thing to make her think of him; but if she did so because of a misconception, which he was given no opportunity to clear up, while at the same time his conscience absolved him from evil and gave him the compensating glow of martyrdom, it was at least better than nothing.

He would, of course, have preferred to be upon a different footing. It had been a pleasure to have her speak to him during the drive,—they had exchanged a few trivial remarks in the general conversation. It was a greater pleasure to have her ask a favor of him,—a pleasure which, in this instance, was partly offset when he interpreted her request to mean that he was to look for Tom Delamere. He accepted the situation gracefully, however, and left the ladies alone.

Knowing Delamere's habits, he first went directly to the bar-room,—the atmosphere would be congenial, even if he were not drinking. Delamere was not there. Stepping next into the office, he asked the clerk if young Mr. Delamere had been at the hotel.

"Yes, sir," returned the man at the desk, "he was here at luncheon, and then went out fishing in a boat with several other gentlemen. I think they came back about three o'clock. I'll find out for you."

He rang the bell, to which a colored boy responded.

"Front," said the clerk, "see if young Mr. Delamere's upstairs. Look in 255 or 256, and let me know at once."

The bell-boy returned in a moment.

"Yas, suh," he reported, with a suppressed grin, "he's

in 256, suh. De do' was open, an' I seed 'im from de hall, suh."

"I wish you'd go up and tell him," said Ellis, "that— What are you grinning about?" he asked suddenly, noticing the waiter's expression.

"Nothin', suh, nothin' at all, suh," responded the negro, lapsing into the stolidity of a wooden Indian. "What shall I tell Mr. Delamere, suh?"

"Tell him," resumed Ellis, still watching the boy suspiciously,—"no, I'll tell him myself."

He ascended the broad stair to the second floor. There was an upper balcony and a parlor, with a piano for the musically inclined. To reach these one had to pass along the hall upon which the room mentioned by the bell-boy opened. Ellis was quite familiar with the hotel. He could imagine circumstances under which he would not care to speak to Delamere; he would merely pass through the hall and glance into the room casually, as any one else might do, and see what the darky downstairs might have meant by his impudence.

It required but a moment to reach the room. The door was not wide open, but far enough ajar for him to see what was going on within.

Two young men, members of the fast set at the Clarendon Club, were playing cards at a small table, near which stood another, decorated with an array of empty bottles and glasses. Sprawling on a lounge, with flushed face and disheveled hair, his collar unfastened, his vest buttoned awry, lay Tom Delamere, breathing stertorously, in what seemed a drunken sleep. Lest there should be any doubt of the cause of his condition, the fingers of his right hand had remained clasped mechanically around the neck of a bottle which lay across his bosom.

Ellis turned away in disgust, and went slowly back to the ladies.

"There seems to be no one here yet," he reported. "We came a little early for the evening crowd. The clerk says Tom Delamere was here to luncheon, but he hasn't seen him for several hours."

"He's not a very gallant cavalier," said Mrs. Carteret severely. "He ought to have been waiting for us."

Clara was clearly disappointed, and made no effort to

conceal her displeasure, leaving Ellis in doubt as to whether or not he were its object. Perhaps she suspected him of not having made a very thorough search. Her next remark might have borne such a construction.

"Sister Olivia," she said pettishly, "let's go up to the parlor. I can play the piano anyway, if there's no one to talk to."

"I find it very comfortable here, Clara," replied her sister placidly. "Mr. Ellis will go with you. You'll probably find some one in the parlor, or they'll come when you begin to play."

Clara's expression was not cordial, but she rose as if to go. Ellis was in a quandary. If she went through the hall, the chances were at least even that she would see Delamere. He did not care a rap for Delamere,—if he chose to make a public exhibition of himself, it was his own affair; but to see him would surely spoil Miss Pemberton's evening, and, in her frame of mind, might lead to the suspicion that Ellis had prearranged the exposure. Even if she should not harbor this unjust thought, she would not love the witness of her discomfiture. We had rather not meet the persons who have seen, even though they never mention, the skeletons in our closets. Delamere had disposed of himself for the evening. Ellis would have a fairer field with Delamere out of sight and unaccounted for, than with Delamere in evidence in his present condition.

"Wouldn't you rather take a stroll on the beach, Miss Clara?" he asked, in the hope of creating a diversion.

"No, I'm going to the parlor. *You* needn't come, Mr. Ellis, if you'd rather go down to the beach. I can quite as well go alone."

"I'd rather go with you," he said meekly.

They were moving toward the door opening into the hall, from which the broad staircase ascended. Ellis, whose thoughts did not always respond quickly to a sudden emergency, was puzzling his brain as to how he should save her from any risk of seeing Delamere. Through the side door leading from the hall into the office, he saw the bell-boy to whom he had spoken seated on the bench provided for the servants.

"Won't you wait for me just a moment, Miss Clara,

"while I step into the office? I'll be with you in an instant."

Clara hesitated.

"Oh, certainly," she replied nonchalantly.

Ellis went direct to the bell-boy. "Sit right where you are," he said, "and don't move a hair. What is the lady in the hall doing?"

"She's got her back tu'ned this way, suh. I 'spec' she's lookin' at the picture on the opposite wall, suh."

"All right," whispered Ellis, pressing a coin into the servant's hand. "I'm going up to the parlor with the lady. You go up ahead of us, and keep in front of us along the hall. Don't dare to look back. I shall keep on talking to the lady, so that you can tell by my voice where we are. When you get to room 256, go in and shut the door behind you: pretend that you were called,—ask the gentlemen what they want,—tell any kind of a lie you like,— but keep the door shut until you're sure we've got by. Do you hear?"

"Yes, suh," replied the negro intelligently.

The plan worked without a hitch. Ellis talked steadily, about the hotel, the furnishings, all sorts of irrelevant subjects, to which Miss Pemberton paid little attention. She was angry with Delamere, and took no pains to conceal her feelings. The bell-boy entered room 256 just before they reached the door. Ellis had heard loud talking as they approached, and as they were passing there was a crash of broken glass, as though some object had been thrown at the door.

"What is the matter there?" exclaimed Clara, quickening her footsteps and instinctively drawing closer to Ellis.

"Some one dropped a glass, I presume," replied Ellis calmly.

Miss Pemberton glanced at him suspiciously. She was in a decidedly perverse mood. Seating herself at the piano, she played brilliantly for a quarter of an hour. Quite a number of couples strolled up to the parlor, but Delamere was not among them.

"Oh dear!" exclaimed Miss Pemberton, as she let her fingers fall upon the keys with a discordant crash, after the last note, "I don't see why we came out here tonight. Let's go back downstairs."

Ellis felt despondent. He had done his utmost to serve and to please Miss Pemberton, but was not likely, he foresaw, to derive much benefit from his opportunity. Delmare was evidently as much or more in her thoughts by reason of his absence than if he had been present. If the door should have been opened, and she should see him from the hall upon their return, Ellis could not help it. He took the side next to the door, however, meaning to hurry past the room so that she might not recognize Delamere.

Fortunately the door was closed and all quiet within the room. On the stairway they met the bell-boy, rubbing his head with one hand and holding a bottle of seltzer upon a tray in the other. The boy was well enough trained to give no sign of recognition, though Ellis guessed the destination of the bottle.

Ellis hardly knew whether to feel pleased or disappointed at the success of his manœuvres. He had spared Miss Pemberton some mortification, but he had saved Tom Delamere from merited exposure. Clara ought to know the truth, for her own sake.

On the beach, a few rods away, fires were burning, around which several merry groups had gathered. The smoke went mostly to one side, but a slight whiff came now and then to where Mrs. Carteret sat awaiting them.

"They're roasting oysters," said Mrs. Carteret. "I wish you'd bring me some, Mr. Ellis."

Ellis strolled down to the beach. A large iron plate, with a turned-up rim like a great baking-pan, supported by legs which held it off the ground, was set over a fire built upon the sand. This primitive oven was heaped with small oysters in the shell, taken from the neighboring sound, and hauled up to the hotel by a negro whose pony cart stood near by. A wet coffee-sack of burlaps was spread over the oysters, which, when steamed sufficiently, were opened by a colored man and served gratis to all who cared for them.

Ellis secured a couple of plates of oysters, which he brought to Mrs. Carteret and Clara; they were small, but finely flavored.

Meanwhile Delamere, who possessed a remarkable faculty of recuperation from the effects of drink, had waked from his sleep, and remembering his engagement, had exerted himself to overcome the ravages of the afternoon's debauch. A dash of cold water braced him up somewhat. A bottle of seltzer and a big cup of strong coffee still further strengthened his nerves.

When Ellis returned to the veranda, after having taken away the plates, Delamere had joined the ladies and was explaining the cause of his absence.

He had been overcome by the heat, he said, while out fishing, and had been lying down ever since. Perhaps he ought to have sent for a doctor, but the fellows had looked after him. He hadn't sent word to his friends because he hadn't wished to spoil their evening.

"That was very considerate of you, Tom," said Mrs. Carteret dryly, "but you ought to have let us know. We have been worrying about you very much. Clara has found the evening dreadfully dull."

"Indeed, no, sister Olivia," said the young lady cheerfully, "I've been having a lovely time. Mr. Ellis and I have been up in the parlor; I played the piano; and we've been eating oysters and having a most delightful time. Won't you take me down there to the beach, Mr. Ellis? I want to see the fires. Come on."

"Can't I go?" asked Tom jealously.

"No, indeed, you mustn't stir a foot! You must not overtax yourself so soon; it might do you serious injury. Stay here with sister Olivia."

She took Ellis's arm with exaggerated cordiality. Delamere glared after them angrily. Ellis did not stop to question her motives, but took the goods the gods provided. With no very great apparent effort, Miss Pemberton became quite friendly, and they strolled along the beach, in sight of the hotel, for nearly half an hour. As they were coming up she asked him abruptly,—

"Mr. Ellis, did you know Tom was in the hotel?"

Ellis was looking across the sound, at the lights of a distant steamer which was making her way toward the harbor.

"I wonder," he said musingly, as though he had not heard her question, "if that is the Ocean Belle?"

"And was he really sick?" she demanded.

"She's later than usual this trip," continued Ellis, pursuing his thought. "She was due about five o'clock."

Miss Pemberton, under cover of the darkness, smiled

a fine smile, which foreboded ill for some one. When they joined the party on the piazza, the major had come up and was saying that it was time to go. He had been engaged in conversation, for most of the evening, with General Belmont and several other gentlemen.

"Here comes the general now. Let me see. There are five of us. The general has offered me a seat in his buggy, and Tom can go with you-all."

The general came up and spoke to the ladies. Tom murmured his thanks; it would enable him to make up a part of the delightful evening he had missed.

When Mrs. Carteret had taken the rear seat, Clara promptly took the place beside her. Ellis and Delamere sat in front. When Delamere, who had offered to drive, took the reins, Ellis saw that his hands were shaking.

"Give me the lines," he whispered. "Your nerves are unsteady and the road is not well lighted."

Delamere prudently yielded the reins. He did not like Ellis's tone, which seemed sneering rather than expressive of sympathy with one who had been suffering. He wondered if the beggar knew anything about his illness. Clara had been acting strangely. It would have been just like Ellis to have slandered him. The upstart had no business with Clara, anyway. He would cheerfully have strangled Ellis, if he could have done so with safety to himself and no chance of discovery.

The drive homeward through the night was almost a silent journey. Mrs. Carteret was anxious about her baby. Clara did not speak, except now and then to Ellis with reference to some object in or near the road. Occasionally they passed a vehicle in the darkness, sometimes barely avoiding a collision. Far to the north the sky was lit up with the glow of a forest fire. The breeze from the Sound was deliciously cool. Soon the last toll-gate was passed and the lights of the town appeared.

Ellis threw the lines to William, who was waiting, and hastened to help the ladies out.

"Good-night, Mr. Ellis," said Clara sweetly, as she gave Ellis her hand. "Thank you for a very pleasant evening. Come up and see us soon."

She ran into the house without a word to Tom.

CHAPTER XVII

The Social Aspirations
of Captain McBane

IT WAS ONLY eleven o'clock, and Delamere, not being at all sleepy, and feeling somewhat out of sorts as the combined results of his afternoon's debauch and the snubbing he had received at Clara's hands, directed the major's coachman, who had taken charge of the trap upon its arrival, to drive him to the St. James Hotel before returning the horses to the stable. First, however, the coachman left Ellis at his boarding-house, which was near by. The two young men parted with as scant courtesy as was possible without an open rupture.

Delamere hoped to find at the hotel some form of distraction to fill in an hour or two before going home. Ill fortune favored him by placing in his way the burly form of Captain George McBane, who was sitting in an armchair alone, smoking a midnight cigar, under the hotel balcony. Upon Delamere's making known his desire for amusement, the captain proposed a small game of poker in his own room.

McBane had been waiting for some such convenient opportunity. We have already seen that the captain was desirous of social recognition, which he had not yet obtained beyond the superficial acquaintance acquired by association with men about town. He had determined to assault society in its citadel by seeking membership in the Clarendon Club, of which most gentlemen of the best families of the city were members.

The Clarendon Club was a historic institution, and its membership a social cult, the temple of which was located just off the main street of the city, in a dignified old colonial mansion which had housed it for the nearly one hundred years during which it had maintained its existence unbroken. There had grown up around it many traditions and special usages. Membership in the Clarendon was the *sine qua non* of high social standing, and was conditional upon two of three things,—birth, wealth, and breeding. Breeding was the prime essential, but, with rare exceptions, must be backed by either birth or money.

Having decided, therefore, to seek admission into this social arcanum, the captain, who had either not quite appreciated the standard of the Clarendon's membership, or had failed to see that he fell beneath it, looked about for an intermediary through whom to approach the object of his desire. He had already thought of Tom Delamere in this connection, having with him such an acquaintance as one forms around a hotel, and having long ago discovered that Delamere was a young man of superficially amiable disposition, vicious instincts, lax principles, and a weak will, and, which was quite as much to the purpose, a member of the Clarendon Club. Possessing mental characteristics almost entirely opposite, Delamere and the captain had certain tastes in common, and had smoked, drunk, and played cards together more than once.

Still more to his purpose, McBane had detected Delamere trying to cheat him at cards. He had said nothing about this discovery, but had merely noted it as something which at some future time might prove useful. The captain had not suffered by Delamere's deviation from the straight line of honor, for while Tom was as clever with the cards as might be expected of a young man who had devoted most of his leisure for several years to handling them, McBane was past master in their manipulation. During a stormy career he had touched more or less pitch, and had escaped few sorts of defilement.

The appearance of Delamere at a late hour, unaccompanied, and wearing upon his countenance an expression in which the captain read aright the craving for mental and physical excitement, gave him the opportunity for which he had been looking. McBane was not the man to lose an opportunity, nor did Delamere require a second invitation. Neither was it necessary, during the progress of the game, for the captain to press upon his guest the contents of the decanter which stood upon the table within convenient reach.

The captain permitted Delamere to win from him several small amounts, after which he gradually increased the stakes and turned the tables.

Delamere, with every instinct of a gamester, was no more a match for McBane in self-control than in skill. When the young man had lost all his money, the captain expressed his entire willingness to accept notes of hand, for which he happened to have convenient blanks in his apartment.

When Delamere, flushed with excitement and wine, rose from the gaming table at two o'clock, he was vaguely conscious that he owed McBane a considerable sum, but could not have stated how much. His opponent, who was entirely cool and collected, ran his eye carelessly over the bits of paper to which Delamere had attached his signature.

"Just one thousand dollars even," he remarked.

The announcement of this total had as sobering an effect upon Delamere as though he had been suddenly deluged with a shower of cold water. For a moment he caught his breath. He had not a dollar in the world with which to pay this sum. His only source of income was an allowance from his grandfather, the monthly installment of which, drawn that very day, he had just lost to McBane, before starting in upon the notes of hand.

"I'll give you your revenge another time," said McBane, as they rose. "Luck is against you to-night, and I'm unwilling to take advantage of a clever young fellow like you. Meantime," he added, tossing the notes of hand carelessly on a bureau, "don't worry about these bits of paper. Such small matters shouldn't cut any figure between friends; but if you are around the hotel to-morrow, I should like to speak to you upon another subject."

"Very well, captain," returned Tom somewhat ungraciously.

Delamere had been completely beaten with his own weapons. He had tried desperately to cheat McBane. He knew perfectly well that McBane had discovered his efforts and had cheated him in turn, for the captain's play had clearly been gauged to meet his own. The biter had been bit, and could not complain of the outcome.

*   *   *

The following afternoon McBane met Delamere at the hotel, and bluntly requested the latter to propose him for membership in the Clarendon Club.

Delamere was annoyed at this request. His aristocratic gorge rose at the presumption of this son of an overseer and ex-driver of convicts. McBane was good enough to win money from, or even to lose money to, but not good enough to be recognized as a social equal. He would instinctively have blackballed McBane had he been proposed by some one else; with what grace could he put himself forward as the sponsor for this impossible social aspirant? Moreover, it was clearly a vulgar, cold-blooded attempt on McBane's part to use his power over him for a personal advantage.

"Well, now, Captain McBane," returned Delamere diplomatically, "I've never put any one up yet, and it's not regarded as good form for so young a member as myself to propose candidates. I'd much rather you'd ask some older man."

"Oh, well," replied McBane, "just as you say, only I thought you had cut your eye teeth."

Delamere was not pleased with McBane's tone. His remark was not acquiescent, though couched in terms of assent. There was a sneering savagery about it, too, that left Delamere uneasy. He was, in a measure, in McBane's power. He could not pay the thousand dollars, unless it fell from heaven, or he could win it from some one else. He would not dare go to his grandfather for help. Mr. Delamere did not even know that his grandson gambled. He might not have objected, perhaps, to a gentleman's game, with moderate stakes, but he would certainly, Tom knew very well, have looked upon a thousand dollars as a preposterous sum to be lost at cards by a man who had nothing with which to pay it. It was part of Mr. Delamere's creed that a gentleman should not make debts that he was not reasonably able to pay.

There was still another difficulty. If he had lost the money to a gentleman, and it had been his first serious departure from Mr. Delamere's perfectly well understood standard of honor, Tom might have risked a confession and thrown himself on his grandfather's mercy; but he owed other sums here and there, which, to his just now much disturbed imagination, loomed up in alarming number and amount. He had recently observed signs of coldness, too, on the part of certain members of the club. Moreover, like most men with one commanding vice, he was addicted to several subsidiary forms of iniquity, which in case of a scandal were more than likely to come to light. He was clearly and most disagreeably caught in the net of his own hypocrisy. His grandfather believed him a model of integrity, a pattern of honor; he could not afford to have his grandfather undeceived.

He thought of old Mrs. Ochiltree. If she were a liberal soul, she could give him a thousand dollars now, when he needed it, instead of making him wait until she died, which might not be for ten years or more, for a legacy which was steadily growing less and might be entirely exhausted if she lived long enough,—some old people were very tenacious of life! She was a careless old woman, too, he reflected, and very foolishly kept her money in the house. Latterly she had been growing weak and childish. Some day she might be robbed, and then his prospective inheritance from that source would vanish into thin air!

With regard to this debt to McBane, if he could not pay it, he could at least gain a long respite by proposing the captain at the club. True, he would undoubtedly be blackballed, but before this inevitable event his name must remain posted for several weeks, during which interval McBane would be conciliatory. On the other hand, to propose McBane would arouse suspicion of his own motives; it might reach his grandfather's ears, and lead to a demand for an explanation, which it would be difficult to make. Clearly, the better plan would be to temporize with McBane, with the hope that something might intervene to remove this cursed obligation.

"Suppose, captain," he said affably, "we leave the matter open for a few days. This is a thing that can't be rushed. I'll feel the pulse of my friends and yours, and when we get the lay of the land, the affair can be accomplished much more easily."

"Well, that's better," returned McBane, somewhat mollified,—"*if* you'll do that."

"To be sure I will," replied Tom easily, too much relieved to resent, if not too preoccupied to perceive, the implied doubt of his veracity.

McBane ordered and paid for more drinks, and they parted on amicable terms.

"We'll let these notes stand for the time being, Tom," said McBane, with significant emphasis, when they separated.

Delamere winced at the familiarity. He had reached that degree of moral deterioration where, while principles were of little moment, the externals of social intercourse possessed an exaggerated importance. McBane had never before been so personal. He had addressed the young aristocrat first as "Mr. Delamere," then, as their acquaintance advanced, as "Delamere." He had now reached the abbreviated Christian name stage of familiarity. There was no lower depth to which Tom could sink, unless McBane should invent a nickname by which to address him.

He did not like McBane's manner,—it was characterized by a veiled insolence which was exceedingly offensive. He would go over to the club and try his luck with some honest player,—perhaps something might turn up to relieve him from his embarrassment.

He put his hand in his pocket mechanically,—and found it empty! In the present state of his credit, he could hardly play without money.

A thought struck him. Leaving the hotel, he hastened home, where he found Sandy dusting his famous suit of clothes on the back piazza. Mr. Delamere was not at home, having departed for Belleview about two o'clock, leaving Sandy to follow him in the morning.

"Hello, Sandy," exclaimed Tom, with an assumed jocularity which he was very far from feeling, "what are you doing with those gorgeous garments?"

"I'm a-dustin' of 'em, Mistuh Tom, dat's w'at I'm a-doin'. Dere's somethin' wrong 'bout dese clo's er mine—I don' never seem ter be able ter keep 'em clean no mo'. Ef I b'lieved in dem ole-timey sayin's, I'd 'low dere wuz a witch come here eve'y night an' tuk 'em out an' wo' 'em, er tuk me out an' rid me in 'em. Dere wuz somethin' wrong 'bout dat cakewalk business, too, dat I ain' never unde'stood an' don' know how ter 'count fer, 'less dere wuz some kin' er dev'lishness goin' on dat don' show on de su'face."

"Sandy," asked Tom irrelevantly, "have you any money in the house?"

"Yas, suh, I got de money Mars John give me ter git dem things ter take out ter Belleview in de mawnin'."

"I mean money of your own."

"I got a qua'ter ter buy terbacker wid," returned Sandy cautiously.

"Is that all? Haven't you some saved up?"

"Well, yas, Mistuh Tom," returned Sandy, with evident reluctance, "dere's a few dollahs put away in my bureau drawer fer a rainy day,—not much, suh."

"I'm a little short this afternoon, Sandy, and need some money right away. Grandfather isn't here, so I can't get any from him. Let me take what you have for a day or two, Sandy, and I'll return it with good interest."

"Now, Mistuh Tom," said Sandy seriously, "I don' min' lettin' you take my money, but I hopes you ain' gwine ter use it fer none er dem rakehelly gwines-on er yo'n,—gamblin' an' bettin' an' so fo'th. Yo' grandaddy'll fin' out 'bout you yit, ef you don' min' yo' P's an' Q's. I does my bes' ter keep yo' misdoin's f'm 'im, an' sense I b'en tu'ned out er de chu'ch—thoo no fault er my own, God knows!—I've tol' lies 'nuff 'bout you ter sink a ship. But it ain' right, Mistuh Tom, it ain't right! an' I only does it fer de sake er de fam'ly honuh, dat Mars John sets so much sto' by, an' ter save his feelin's; fer de doctuh says he mus'n' git ixcited 'bout nothin', er it mought bring on another stroke."

"That's right, Sandy," replied Tom approvingly; "but the family honor is as safe in my hands as in grandfather's own, and I'm going to use the money for an excellent purpose, in fact to relieve a case of genuine distress; and I'll hand it back to you in a day or two,—perhaps to-morrow. Fetch me the money, Sandy,—that's a good darky!"

"All right, Mistuh Tom, you shill have de money; but I wants ter tell you, suh, dat in all de yeahs I has wo'ked fer yo' gran'daddy, he has never called me a 'darky' ter my face, suh. Co'se I knows dere's w'ite folks an' black folks,—but dere's manners, suh, dere's manners, an' gent'emen oughter be de ones ter use 'em, suh, ef dey ain't ter be fergot enti'ely!"

"There, there, Sandy," returned Tom in a conciliatory

tone, "I beg your pardon! I've been associating with some Northern white folks at the hotel, and picked up the word from them. You're a high-toned colored gentleman, Sandy,—the finest one on the footstool."

Still muttering to himself, Sandy retired to his own room, which was in the house, so that he might be always near his master. He soon returned with a time-stained leather pocket-book and a coarse-knit cotton sock, from which two receptacles he painfully extracted a number of bills and coins.

"You count dat, Mistuh Tom, so I'll know how much I'm lettin' you have."

"This isn't worth anything," said Tom, pushing aside one roll of bills. "It's Confederate money."

"So it is, suh. It ain't wuth nothin' now; but it has be'n money, an' who kin tell but what it mought be money agin? De rest er dem bills is greenbacks,—dey'll pass all right, I reckon."

The good money amounted to about fifty dollars, which Delamere thrust eagerly into his pocket.

"You won't say anything to grandfather about this, will you, Sandy," he said, as he turned away.

"No, suh, co'se I won't! Does I ever tell 'im 'bout yo' gwines-on? Ef I did," he added to himself, as the young man disappeared down the street, "I wouldn' have time ter do nothin' e'se ha'dly. I don' know whether I'll ever see dat money agin er no, do' I 'magine de ole gent'eman wouldn' lemme lose it ef he knowed. But I ain' gwine ter tell him, whether I git my money back er no, fer he is jes' so wrop' up in dat boy dat I b'lieve it'd jes' break his hea't ter fin' out how he's be'n gwine on. Doctuh Price has tol' me not ter let de ole gent'eman git ixcited, er e'se dere's no tellin' w'at mought happen. He's be'n good ter me, he has, an' I'm gwine ter take keer er him,—dat's w'at I is, ez long ez I has de chance."

Delamere went directly to the club, and soon lounged into the card-room, where several of the members were engaged in play. He sauntered here and there, too much absorbed in his own thoughts to notice that the greetings he received were less cordial than those usually exchanged between the members of a small and select social club. Finally, when Augustus, commonly and more

appropriately called "Gus," Davidson came into the
room, Tom stepped toward him.

"Will you take a hand in a game, Gus?"

"Don't care if I do," said the other. "Let's sit over
here."

Davidson led the way to a table near the fireplace,
near which stood a tall screen, which at times occupied
various places in the room. Davidson took the seat opposite the fireplace, leaving Delamere with his back to the
screen.

Delamere staked half of Sandy's money, and lost. He
staked the rest, and determined to win, because he could
not afford to lose. He had just reached out his hand to
gather in the stakes, when he was charged with cheating
at cards, of which two members, who had quietly entered
the room and posted themselves behind the screen, had
secured specific proof.

A meeting of the membership committee was hastily
summoned, it being an hour at which most of them might
be found at the club. To avoid a scandal, and to save
the feelings of a prominent family, Delamere was given
an opportunity to resign quietly from the club, on condition that he paid all his gambling debts within three days,
and took an oath never to play cards again for money.
This latter condition was made at the suggestion of an
elderly member, who apparently believed that a man
who would cheat at cards would stick at perjury.

Delamere acquiesced very promptly. The taking of the
oath was easy. The payment of some fifteen hundred
dollars of debts was a different matter. He went away
from the club thoughtfully, and it may be said, in full
justice to a past which was far from immaculate, that in
his present thoughts he touched a depth of scoundrelism
far beyond anything of which he had as yet deemed himself capable. When a man of good position, of whom
much is expected, takes to evil courses, his progress is
apt to resemble that of a well-bred woman who had
started on the downward path,—the pace is all the swifter
because of the distance which must be traversed to reach
the bottom. Delamere had made rapid headway; having
hitherto played with sin, his servant had now become his
master, and held him in an iron grip.

CHAPTER XVIII

Sandy Sees His Own Ha'nt

HAVING FINISHED CLEANING his clothes, Sandy went out to the kitchen for supper, after which he found himself with nothing to do. Mr. Delamere's absence relieved him from attendance at the house during the evening. He might have smoked his pipe tranquilly in the kitchen until bedtime, had not the cook intimated, rather pointedly, that she expected other company. To a man of Sandy's tact a word was sufficient, and he resigned himself to seeking companionship elsewhere.

Under normal circumstances, Sandy would have attended prayer-meeting on this particular evening of the week; but being still in contumacy, and cherishing what he considered the just resentment of a man falsely accused, he stifled the inclination which by long habit led him toward the church, and set out for the house of a friend with whom it occurred to him that he might spend the evening pleasantly. Unfortunately, his friend proved to be not at home, so Sandy turned his footsteps toward the lower part of the town, where the streets were well lighted, and on pleasant evenings quite animated. On the way he met Josh Green, whom he had known for many years, though their paths did not often cross. In his loneliness Sandy accepted an invitation to go with Josh and have a drink,—a single drink.

When Sandy was going home about eleven o'clock, three sheets in the wind, such was the potent effect of the single drink and those which had followed it, he was scared almost into soberness by a remarkable apparition. As it seemed to Sandy, he saw himself hurrying along in front of himself toward the house. Possibly the muddled condition of Sandy's intellect had so affected his judgment as to vitiate any conclusion he might draw, but Sandy was quite sober enough to perceive that the figure

341

ahead of him wore his best clothes and looked exactly like him, but seemed to be in something more of a hurry, a discrepancy which Sandy at once corrected by quickening his own pace so as to maintain as nearly as possible an equal distance between himself and his double. The situation was certainly an incomprehensible one, and savored the supernatural.

"Ef dat's me gwine 'long in front," mused Sandy, in vinous perplexity, "den who is dis behin' here? Dere ain' but one er me, an' my ha'nt wouldn' leave my body 'tel I wuz dead. Ef dat's me in front, den I mus' be my own ha'nt; an' whichever one of us is de ha'nt, de yuther must be dead an' don' know it. I don' know what ter make er no sech gwines-on, I don't. Maybe it ain' me after all, but it certainly do look lack me."

When the apparition disappeared in the house by the side door, Sandy stood in the yard for several minutes, under the shade of an elm-tree, before he could make up his mind to enter the house. He took courage, however, upon the reflection that perhaps, after all, it was only the bad liquor he had drunk. Bad liquor often made people see double.

He entered the house. It was dark, except for a light in Tom Delamere's room. Sandy tapped softly at the door.

"Who's there?" came Delamere's voice, in a somewhat startled tone, after a momentary silence.

"It's me, suh; Sandy."

They both spoke softly. It was the rule of the house when Mr. Delamere had retired, and though he was not at home, habit held its wonted sway.

"Just a moment, Sandy."

Sandy waited patiently in the hall until the door was opened. If the room showed any signs of haste or disorder, Sandy was too full of his own thoughts—and other things—to notice them.

"What do you want, Sandy," asked Tom.

"Mistuh Tom," asked Sandy solemnly, "ef I wuz in yo' place, an' you wuz in my place, an' we wuz bofe in de same place, whar would I be?"

Tom looked at Sandy keenly, with a touch of apprehension. Did Sandy mean anything in particular by this enigmatical inquiry, and if so, what? But Sandy's face clearly indicated a state of mind in which consecutive thought was improbable; and after a brief glance Delamere breathed more freely.

"I give it up, Sandy," he responded lightly. "That's too deep for me."

" 'Scuse me, Mistuh Tom, but is you heared er seed anybody er anything come in de house fer de las' ten minutes?"

"Why, no, Sandy, I haven't heard any one. I came from the club an hour ago. I had forgotten my key, and Sally got up and let me in, and then went back to bed. I've been sitting here reading ever since. I should have heard any one who came in."

"Mistuh Tom," inquired Sandy anxiously, "would you 'low dat I'd be'n drinkin' too much?"

"No, Sandy, I should say you were sober enough, though of course you may have had a few drinks. Perhaps you'd like another? I've got something good here."

"No, suh, Mistuh Tom, no, suh! No mo' liquor fer me, suh, never! When liquor kin make a man see his own ha'nt, it's 'bout time fer dat man ter quit drinkin', it sho' is! Good-night, Mistuh Tom."

As Sandy turned to go, Delamere was stuck by a sudden and daring thought. The creature of impulse, he acted upon it immediately.

"By the way, Sandy," he exclaimed carelessly, "I can pay you back that money you were good enough to lend me this afternoon. I think I'll sleep better if I have the debt off my mind, and I shouldn't wonder if you would. You don't mind having it in gold, do you?"

"No, indeed, suh," replied Sandy. "I ain' seen no gol' fer so long dat de sight er it'd be good fer my eyes."

Tom counted out ten five-dollar gold pieces upon the table at his elbow.

"And here's another, Sandy," he said, adding an eleventh, "as interest for the use of it."

"Thank y', Mistuh Tom. I didn't spec' no intrus', but I don' never 'fuse gol' w'en I kin git it."

"And here," added Delamere, reaching carelessly into a bureau drawer, "is a little old silk purse that I've had since I was a boy. I'll put the gold in it, Sandy; it will hold it very nicely."

"Thank y', Mistuh Tom. You're a gentleman, suh, an' wo'thy er de fam'ly name. Good-night, suh, an' I hope yo' dreams'll be pleasanter 'n' mine. Ef it wa'n't fer dis gol' kinder takin' my min' off'n dat ha'nt, I don' s'pose I'd be able to do much sleepin' ter-night. Good-night, suh."

"Good-night, Sandy."

Whether or not Delamere slept soundly, or was troubled by dreams, pleasant or unpleasant, it is nevertheless true that he locked his door, and sat up an hour later, looking through the drawers of his bureau, and burning several articles in the little iron stove which constituted part of the bedroom furniture.

It is also true that he rose very early, before the household was stirring. The cook slept in a room off the kitchen, which was in an outhouse in the back yard. She was just stretching herself, preparatory to getting up, when Tom came to her window and said that he was going off fishing, to be gone all day, and that he would not wait for breakfast.

CHAPTER XIX

A Midnight Walk

ELLIS LEFT THE OFFICE of the Morning Chronicle about eleven o'clock the same evening and set out to walk home. His boarding-house was only a short distance beyond old Mr. Delamere's residence, and while he might have saved time and labor by a slightly shorter route, he generally selected this one because it led also by Major Carteret's house. Sometimes there would be a ray of light from Clara's room, which was on one of the front corners; and at any rate he would have the pleasure of gazing at the outside of the casket that enshrined the jewel of his heart. It was true that this purely sentimental pleasure was sometimes dashed with bitterness at the thought of his rival; but one in love must take the bitter with the sweet, and who would say that a spice of jealousy does not add a certain zest to love? On this particular evening, however, he was in a hopeful mood. At the Clarendon Club, where he had gone, a couple of hours before, to verify a certain news item for the morning paper, he had heard a story about Tom Delamere which, he imagined, would spike that gentleman's guns for all time, so far as Miss Pemberton was concerned. So grave an affair as cheating at cards could never be kept secret,—it was certain to reach her ears; and Ellis was morally certain that Clara would never marry a man who had been proved dishonorable. In all probability there would be no great sensation about the matter. Delamere was too well connected; too many prominent people would be involved,—even Clara, and the editor himself, of whom Delamere was a distant cousin. The reputation of the club was also to be considered. Ellis was not the man to feel a malicious delight in the misfortunes of another, nor was he a pessimist who welcomed scandal and disgrace with open arms, as confirming a gloomy theory of human life. But, with the best intentions in the world, it was no more than human nature that he should feel a certain elation in the thought that his rival had been practically disposed of, and the field left clear; especially since this good situation had been brought about merely by the unmasking of a hypocrite, who had held him at an unfair disadvantage in the race for Clara's favor.

The night was quiet, except for the faint sound of distant music now and then, or the mellow laughter of some group of revelers. Ellis met but few pedestrians, but as he neared old Mr. Delamere's, he saw two men walking in the same direction as his own, on the opposite side of the street. He had observed that they kept at about an equal distance apart, and that the second, from the stealthy manner in which he was making his way, was anxious to keep the first in sight, without disclosing his own presence. This aroused Ellis's curiosity, which was satisfied in some degree when the man in advance stopped beneath a lamp-post and stood for a moment looking across the street, with his face plainly visible in the yellow circle of light. It was a dark face, and Ellis recognized it instantly as that of old Mr. Delamere's body servant, whose personal appearance had been very vividly impressed upon Ellis at the christening dinner at Major Carteret's. He had seen Sandy once since, too, at the hotel cakewalk. The negro had a small bundle in his hand, the nature of which Ellis could not make out.

When Sandy had stopped beneath the lamp-post, the man who was following him had dodged behind a tree-trunk. When Sandy moved on, Ellis, who had stopped in turn, saw the man in hiding come out and follow Sandy. When this second man came in range of the light, Ellis wondered that there should be two men so much alike. The first of the two had undoubtedly been Sandy. Ellis had recognized the peculiar, old-fashioned coat that Sandy had worn upon the two occasions when he had noticed him. Barring this difference, and the somewhat unsteady gait of the second man, the two were as much alike as twin brothers.

When they had entered Mr. Delamere's house, one after the other,—in the stillness of the night Ellis could perceive that each of them tried to make as little noise as possible,—Ellis supposed that they were probably rel-

atives, both employed as servants, or that some younger
negro, taking Sandy for a model, was trying to pattern
himself after his superior. Why all this mystery, of course
he could not imagine, unless the younger man had been
out without permission and was trying to avoid the accus-
ing eye of Sandy. Ellis was vaguely conscious that he had
seen the other negro somewhere, but he could not for
the moment place him,—there were so many negroes,
nearly three negroes to one white man in the city of
Wellington!

The subject, however, while curious, was not important as compared with the thoughts of his sweetheart
which drove it from his mind. Clara had been kind to
him the night before,—whatever her motive, she had
been kind, and could not consistently return to her attitude of coldness. With Delamere hopelessly discredited,
Ellis hoped to have at least fair play,—with fair play, he
would take his chances of the outcome.

CHAPTER XX

A Shocking Crime

ON FRIDAY MORNING, when old Mrs. Ochiltree's cook Dinah went to wake her mistress, she was confronted with a sight that well-nigh blanched her ebony cheek and caused her eyes almost to start from her head with horror. As soon as she could command her trembling limbs sufficiently to make them carry her, she rushed out of the house and down the street, bareheaded, covering in an incredibly short time the few blocks that separated Mrs. Ochiltree's residence from that of her niece.

She hastened around the house, and finding the back door open and the servants stirring, ran into the house and up the stairs with the familiarity of an old servant, not stopping until she reached the door of Mrs. Carteret's chamber, at which she knocked in great agitation.

Entering in response to Mrs. Carteret's invitation, she found the lady, dressed in a simple wrapper, superintending the morning toilet of little Dodie, who was a wakeful child, and insisted upon rising with the birds, for whose music he still showed a great fondness, in spite of his narrow escape while listening to the mockingbird.

"What is it, Dinah?" asked Mrs. Carteret, alarmed at the frightened face of her aunt's old servitor.

"O my Lawd, Mis' 'Livy, my Lawd, my Lawd! My legs is trim'lin' so dat I can't ha'dly hol' my han's stiddy 'nough ter say w'at I got ter say! O Lawd have mussy on us po' sinners! W'atever is gwine ter happen in dis worl' er sin an' sorrer!"

"What in the world is the matter, Dinah?" demanded Mrs. Carteret, whose own excitement had increased with the length of this preamble. "Has anything happened to Aunt Polly?"

"Somebody done broke in de house las' night, Mis' 'Livy, an' kill' Mis' Polly, an' lef' her layin' dead on de

348

flo', in her own blood, wid her cedar chis' broke' open, an' eve'thing scattered roun' de flo'! O my Lawd, my Lawd, my Lawd, my Lawd!"

Mrs. Carteret was shocked beyond expression. Perhaps the spectacle of Dinah's unrestrained terror aided her to retain a greater measure of self-control than she might otherwise have been capable of. Giving the nurse some directions in regard to the child, she hastily descended the stairs, and seizing a hat and jacket from the rack in the hall, ran immediately with Dinah to the scene of the tragedy. Before the thought of this violent death all her aunt's faults faded into insignificance, and only her good qualities were remembered. She had reared Olivia; she had stood up for the memory of Olivia's mother when others had seemed to forget what was due to it. To her niece she had been a second mother, and had never been lacking in affection.

More than one motive, however, lent wings to Mrs. Carteret's feet. Her aunt's incomplete disclosures on the day of the drive past the hospital had been weighing upon Mrs. Carteret's mind, and she had intended to make another effort this very day, to get an answer to her question about the papers which the woman had claimed were in existence. Suppose her aunt had really found such papers,—papers which would seem to prove the preposterous claim made by her father's mulatto mistress? Suppose that, with the fatuity which generally leads human beings to keep compromising documents, her aunt had preserved these papers? If they should be found there in the house, there might be a scandal, if nothing worse, and this was to be avoided at all hazards.

Guided by some fortunate instinct, Dinah had as yet informed no one but Mrs. Carteret of her discovery. If they could reach the house before the murder became known to any third person, she might be the first to secure access to the remaining contents of the cedar chest, which would be likely to be held as evidence in case the officers of the law forestalled her own arrival.

They found the house wrapped in the silence of death. Mrs. Carteret entered the chamber of the dead woman. Upon the floor, where it had fallen, lay the body in a pool of blood, the strongly marked countenance scarcely more grim in the rigidity of death than it had been in

life. A gaping wound in the head accounted easily for
the death. The cedar chest stood open, its strong fasten-
ings having been broken by a steel bar which still lay
beside it. Near it were scattered pieces of old lace, anti-
quated jewelry, tarnished silverware,—the various mute
souvenirs of the joys and sorrows of a long and active
life.

Kneeling by the open chest, Mrs. Carteret glanced hurriedly through its contents. There were no papers there
except a few old deeds and letters. She had risen with a
sigh of relief, when she perceived the end of a paper
projecting from beneath the edge of a rug which had
been carelessly rumpled, probably by the burglar in his
hasty search for plunder. This paper, or sealed envelope
as it proved to be, which evidently contained some inclosure, she seized, and at the sound of approaching footsteps thrust hastily into her own bosom.

The sight of two agitated women rushing through the
quiet streets at so early an hour in the morning had attracted attention and aroused curiosity, and the story of
the murder, having once become known, spread with the
customary rapidity of bad news. Very soon a policeman,
and a little later a sheriff's officer, arrived at the house
and took charge of the remains to await the arrival of
the coroner.

By nine o'clock a coroner's jury had been summoned,
who, after brief deliberation, returned a verdict of willful
murder at the hands of some person or persons unknown,
while engaged in the commission of a burglary.

No sooner was the verdict announced than the community, or at least the white third of it, resolved itself spontaneously into a committee of the whole to discover the
perpetrator of this dastardly crime, which, at this stage
of the affair, seemed merely one of robbery and murder.

Suspicion was at once directed toward the negroes, as
it always is when an unexplained crime is committed in
a Southern community. The suspicion was not entirely
an illogical one. Having been, for generations, trained
up to thriftlessness, theft, and immorality, against which
only thirty years of very limited opportunity can be offset, during which brief period they have been denied in
large measure the healthful social stimulus and sympathy
which holds most men in the path of rectitude, colored

people might reasonably be expected to commit at least a share of crime proportionate to their numbers. The population of the town was at least two thirds colored. The chances were, therefore, in the absence of evidence, at least two to one that a man of color had committed the crime. The Southern tendency to change the negroes with all the crime and immorality of that region, unjust and exaggerated as the claim may be, was therefore not without a logical basis to the extent above indicated.

It must not be imagined that any logic was needed, or any reasoning consciously worked out. The mere suggestion that the crime had been committed by a negro was equivalent to proof against any negro that might be suspected and could not prove his innocence. A committee of white men was hastily formed. Acting independently of the police force, which was practically ignored as likely to favor the negroes, this committee set to work to discover the murderer.

The spontaneous activity of the whites was accompanied by a visible shrinkage of the colored population. This could not be taken as any indication of guilt, but was merely a recognition of the palpable fact that the American habit of lynching had so whetted the thirst for black blood that a negro suspected of crime had to face at least the possibility of a short shrift and a long rope, not to mention more gruesome horrors, without the intervention of judge or jury. Since to have a black face at such a time was to challenge suspicion, and since there was neither the martyr's glory nor the saint's renown in being killed for some one else's crime, and very little hope of successful resistance in case of an attempt at lynching, it was obviously the part of prudence for those thus marked to seek immunity in a temporary disappearance from public view.

CHAPTER XXI

The Necessity
of an Example

ABOUT TEN O'CLOCK on the morning of the discovery of the murder, Captain McBane and General Belmont, as though moved by a common impulse, found themselves at the office of the Morning Chronicle. Carteret was expecting them, though there had been no appointment made. These three resourceful and energetic minds, representing no organized body, and clothed with no legal authority, had so completely arrogated to themselves the leadership of white public sentiment as to come together instinctively when an event happened which concerned the public, and, as this murder presumably did, involved the matter of race.

"Well, gentlemen," demanded McBane impatiently, "what are we going to do with the scoundrel when we catch him?"

"They've got the murderer," announced a reporter, entering the room.

"Who is he?" they demanded in a breath.

"A nigger by the name of Sandy Campbell, a servant of old Mr. Delamere."

"How did they catch him?"

"Our Jerry saw him last night, going toward Mrs. Ochiltree's house, and a white man saw him coming away, half an hour later."

"Has he confessed?"

"No, but he might as well. When the posse went to arrest him, they found him cleaning the clothes he had worn last night, and discovered in his room a part of the plunder. He denies it strenuously, but it seems a clear case."

"There can be no doubt," said Ellis, who had come

into the room behind the reporter. "I saw the negro last night, at twelve o'clock, going into Mr. Delamere's yard, with a bundle in his hand."

"He is the last negro I should have suspected," said Carteret. "Mr. Delamere had implicit confidence in him."

"All niggers are alike," remarked McBane sententiously. "The only way to keep them from stealing is not to give them the chance. A nigger will steal a cent off a dead man's eye. He has assaulted and murdered a white woman,—an example should be made of him."

Carteret recalled very distinctly the presence of this negro at his own residence on the occasion of little Theodore's christening dinner. He remembered having questioned the prudence of letting a servant know that Mrs. Ochiltree kept money in the house. Mr. Delamere had insisted strenuously upon the honesty of this particular negro. The whole race, in the major's opinion, was morally undeveloped, and only held within bounds by the restraining influence of the white people. Under Mr. Delamere's thumb this Sandy had been a model servant,—faithful, docile, respectful, and self-respecting; but Mr. Delamere had grown old, and had probably lost in a measure his moral influence over his servant. Left to his own degraded ancestral instincts, Sandy had begun to deteriorate, and a rapid decline had culminated in this robbery and murder,—and who knew what other horror? The criminal was a negro, the victim a white woman;— it was only reasonable to expect the worst.

"He'll swing for it," observed the general.

Ellis went into another room, where his duty called him.

"He should burn for it," averred McBane. "I say, burn the nigger."

"This," said Carteret, "is something more than an ordinary crime, to be dealt with by the ordinary processes of law. It is a murderous and fatal assault upon a woman of our race,—upon our race in the person of its womanhood, its crown and flower. If such crimes are not punished with swift and terrible directness, the whole white womanhood of the South is in danger."

"Burn the nigger," repeated McBane automatically.

"Neither is this a mere sporadic crime," Carteret went

on. "It is symptomatic; it is the logical and inevitable result of the conditions which have prevailed in this town for the past year. It is the last straw."

"Burn the nigger," reiterated McBane. "We seem to have the right nigger, but whether we have or not, burn *a* nigger. It is an assault upon the white race, in the person of old Mrs. Ochiltree, committed by the black race, in the person of some nigger. It would justify the white people in burning *any* nigger. The example would be all the more powerful if we got the wrong one. It would serve notice on the niggers that we shall hold the whole race responsible for the misdeeds of each individual."

"In ancient Rome," said the general, "when a master was killed by a slave, all his slaves were put to the sword."

"We couldn't afford that before the war," said McBane, "but the niggers don't belong to anybody now, and there's nothing to prevent our doing as we please with them. A dead nigger is no loss to any white man. I say, burn the nigger."

"I do not believe," said Carteret, who had gone to the window and was looking out,—"I do not believe that we need trouble ourselves personally about his punishment. I should judge, from the commotion in the street, that the public will take the matter into its own hands. I, for one, would prefer that any violence, however justifiable, should take place without my active intervention."

"It won't take place without mine, if I know it," exclaimed McBane, starting for the door.

"Hold on a minute, captain," exclaimed Carteret. "There's more at stake in this matter than the life of a black scoundrel. Wellington is in the hands of negroes and scalawags. What better time to rescue it?"

"It's a trifle premature," replied the general. "I should have preferred to have this take place, if it was to happen, say three months hence, on the eve of the election,—but discussion always provokes thirst with me; I wonder if I could get Jerry to bring us some drinks?"

Carteret summoned the porter. Jerry's usual manner had taken on an element of self-importance, resulting in what one might describe as a sort of condescending obsequiousness. Though still a porter, he was also a hero, and wore his aureole.

"Jerry," said the general kindly, "the white people are very much pleased with the assistance you have given them in apprehending this scoundrel Campbell. You have rendered a great public service, Jerry, and we wish you to know that it is appreciated."

"Thank y', gin'l, thank y', suh! I alluz tries ter do my duty, suh, an' stan' by dem dat stan's by me. Dat low-down nigger oughter be lynch', suh, don't you think, er e'se bu'nt? Dere ain' nothin' too bad ter happen ter 'im."

"No doubt he will be punished as he deserves, Jerry," returned the general, "and we will see that you are suitably rewarded. Go across the street and get me three Calhoun cocktails. I seem to have nothing less than a two-dollar bill, but you may keep the change, Jerry,—all the change."

Jerry was very happy. He had distinguished himself in the public view, for to Jerry, as to the white people themselves, the white people were the public. He had won the goodwill of the best people, and had already begun to reap a tangible reward. It is true that several strange white men looked at him with lowering brows as he crossed the street, which was curiously empty of colored people; but he nevertheless went firmly forward, panoplied in the consciousness of his own rectitude, and serenely confident of the protection of the major and the major's friends.

"Jerry is about the only negro I have seen since nine o'clock," observed the general when the porter had gone. "If this were election day, where would the negro vote be?"

"In hiding, where most of the negro population is to-day," answered McBane. "It's a pity, if old Mrs. Ochiltree had to go this way, that it couldn't have been deferred a month or six weeks."

Carteret frowned at this remark, which, coming from McBane, seemed lacking in human feeling, as well as in respect to his wife's dead relative.

"But," resumed the general, "if this negro is lynched, as he well deserves to be, it will not be without its effect. We still have in reserve for the election a weapon which this affair will only render more effective. What became of the piece in the negro paper?"

"I have it here," answered Carteret. "I was just about to use it as the text for an editorial."

"Save it awhile longer," responded the general. "This crime itself will give you text enough for a four-volume work."

When this conference ended, Carteret immediately put into press an extra edition of the Morning Chronicle, which was soon upon the streets, giving details of the crime, which was characterized as an atrocious assault upon a defenseless old lady, whose age and sex would have protected her from harm at the hands of any one but a brute in the lowest human form. This event, the Chronicle suggested, had only confirmed the opinion, which had been of late growing upon the white people, that drastic efforts were necessary to protect the white women of the South against brutal, lascivious, and murderous assaults at the hands of negro men. It was only another significant example of the results which might have been foreseen from the application of a false and pernicious political theory, by which ignorance, clothed in a little brief authority, was sought to be exalted over knowledge, vice over virtue, an inferior and degraded race above the heaven-crowned Anglo-Saxon. If an outraged people, justly infuriated, and impatient of the slow processes of the courts, should assert their inherent sovereignty, which the law after all were merely intended to embody, and should choose, in obedience to the higher law, to set aside, temporarily, the ordinary judicial procedure, it would serve as a warning and an example to the vicious elements of the community, of the swift and terrible punishment which would fall, like the judgment of God, upon any one who laid sacrilegious hands upon white womanhood.

How Not
to Prevent a Lynching

DR. MILLER, who had sat up late the night before with a difficult case at the hospital, was roused, about eleven o'clock, from a deep and dreamless sleep. Struggling back into consciousness, he was informed by his wife, who stood by his bedside, that Mr. Watson, the colored lawyer, wished to see him upon a matter of great importance.

"Nothing but a matter of life and death would make me get up just now," he said with a portentous yawn.

"This *is* a matter of life and death," replied Janet. "Old Mrs. Polly Ochiltree was robbed and murdered last night, and Sandy Campbell has been arrested for the crime,—and they are going to lynch him!"

"Tell Watson to come right up," exclaimed Miller, springing out of bed. "We can talk while I'm dressing."

While Miller made a hasty toilet Watson explained the situation. Campbell had been arrested on the charge of murder. He had been seen, during the night, in the neighborhood of the scene of the crime, by two different persons, a negro and a white man, and had been identified later while entering Mr. Delamere's house, where he lived, and where damning proofs of his guilt had been discovered; the most important item of which was an old-fashioned knit silk purse, recognized as Mrs. Ochiltree's, and several gold pieces of early coinage, of which the murdered woman was known to have a number. Watson brought with him one of the first copies procurable of the extra edition of the Chronicle, which contained these facts and further information.

They were still talking when Mrs. Miller, knocking at the door, announced that big Josh Green wished to see the doctor about Sandy Campbell. Miller took his collar and necktie in his hand and went downstairs, where Josh saw waiting.

"Doctuh," said Green, "de w'ite folks is talkin' 'bout lynchin' Sandy Campbell fer killin' ole Mis' Ochiltree. He never done it, an' dey oughtn' ter be 'lowed ter lynch 'im."

"They ought not to lynch him, even if he committed the crime," returned Miller, "but still less if he didn't. What do you know about it?"

"I know he was wid me, suh, las' night, at de time when dey say ole Mis' Ochiltree wuz killed. We wuz down ter Sam Taylor's place, havin' a little game of kyards an' a little liquor. Den we lef dere an' went up ez fur ez de corner er Main an' Vine Streets, where we pa'ted, an' Sandy went 'long to'ds home. Mo'over, dey say he had on check' britches an' a blue coat. When Sandy wuz wid me he had on gray clo's, an' when we sep'rated he wa'n't in no shape ter be changin' his clo's, let 'lone robbin' er killin' anybody."

"Your testimony ought to prove an alibi for him," declared Miller.

"Dere ain' gwine ter be no chance ter prove nothin', 'less'n we kin do it mighty quick! Dey say dey 're gwine ter lynch 'im ter-night,—some on 'em is talkin' 'bout burnin' 'im. My idee is ter hunt up de niggers an' git 'em ter stan' tergether an' gyard de jail."

"Why shouldn't we go to the principal white people of the town and tell them Josh's story, and appeal to them to stop this thing until Campbell can have a hearing?"

"It wouldn't do any good," said Watson despondently; "their blood is up. It seems that some colored man attacked Mrs. Ochiltree,—and he was a murderous villain, whoever he may be. To quote Josh would destroy the effect of his story,—we know he never harmed any one but himself"—

"An' a few keerliss people w'at got in my way," corrected Josh.

"He has been in court several times for fighting,—and that's against him. To have been at Sam Taylor's place is against Sandy, too, rather than in his favor. No, Josh, the white people would believe that you were trying to shield Sandy, and you would probably be arrested as an accomplice."

"But look a-here, Mr. Watson,—Dr. Miller, is we-all jes' got ter set down here, widout openin' ou' mouths, an' let des w'ite folks hang er bu'n a man w'at we *know* ain' guilty? Dat ain' no law, ner jestice, ner nothin'! Ef you-all won't he'p, I'll do somethin' myse'f! Dere's two niggers ter one white man in dis town, an' I'm sho' I kin fin' fifty of 'em w'at'll fight, ef dey kin fin' anybody ter lead 'em."

"Now hold on, Josh," argued Miller; "what is to be gained by fighting? Suppose you got your crowd together and surrounded the jail,—what then?"

"There'd be a clash," declared Watson, "and instead of one dead negro there'd be fifty. The white people are claiming now that Campbell didn't stop with robbery and murder. A special edition of the Morning Chronicle, just out, suggests a further purpose, and has all the old shop-worn cant about race purity and supremacy and imperative necessity, which always comes to the front whenever it is sought to justify some outrage on the colored folks. The blood of the whites is up, I tell you!"

"Is there anything to that suggestion?" asked Miller incredulously.

"It doesn't matter whether there is or not," returned Watson. "Merely to suggest it proves it. Nothing was said about this feature until the paper came out,—and even its statement is vague and indefinite,—but now the claim is in every mouth. I met only black looks as I came down the street. White men with whom I have long been on friendly terms passed me without a word. A negro has been arrested on suspicion,—the entire race is condemned on general principles."

"The whole thing is profoundly discouraging," said Miller sadly. "Try as we may to build up the race in the essentials of good citizenship and win the good opinion of the best people, some black scoundrel comes along, and by a single criminal act, committed in the twinkling of an eye, neutralizes the effect of a whole year's work."

"It's mighty easy neut'alize', er whatever you call it," said Josh sullenly. "De w'ite folks don' want too good an opinion er de niggers,—ef dey had a good opinion of 'em, dey wouldn' have no excuse fer 'busin' an' hangin' an' burnin' 'em. But ef dey can't keep from doin' it, let 'em git de right man! Dis way er pickin' up de fus' nigger dey comes across, an' stringin' 'im up rega'dliss, ought ter be stop', an' stop' right now!"

"Yes, that's the worst of lynch law," said Watson; "but we are wasting valuable time,—it's hardly worthwhile for us to discuss a subject we are all agreed upon. One of our race, accused of certain acts, is about to be put to death without judge or jury, ostensibly because he committed a crime,—really because he is a negro, for if he were white he would not be lynched. It is thus made a race issue, on the one side as well as on the other. What can we do to protect him?"

"We kin fight, ef we haf ter," replied Josh resolutely.

"Well, now, let us see. Suppose the colored people armed themselves? Messages would at once be sent to every town and county in the neighborhood. White men from all over the state, armed to the teeth, would at the slightest word pour into town on every railroad train, and extras would be run for their benefit."

"They're already coming in," said Watson.

"We might go to the sheriff," suggested Miller, "and demand that he telegraph the governor to call out the militia."

"I spoke to the sheriff an hour ago," replied Watson. "He has a white face and a whiter liver. He does not dare call out the militia to protect a negro charged with such a brutal crime;—and if he did, the militia are white men, and who can say that their efforts would not be directed to keeping the negroes out of the way, in order that the white devils might do their worst? The whole machinery of the state is in the hands of white men, elected partly by our votes. When the color line is drawn, if they choose to stand together with the rest of their race against us, or to remain passive and let the others work their will, we are helpless,—our cause is hopeless."

"We might call on the general government," said Miller. "Surely the President would intervene."

"Such a demand would be of no avail," returned Watson. "The government can only intervene under certain conditions, of which it must be informed through designated channels. It never sees anything that is not officially called to its attention. The whole negro population of the South might be slaughtered before the necessary red tape could be spun out to inform the President that a state of anarchy prevailed. There's no hope there.''

"Den w'at we gwine ter do?" demanded Josh indignantly; "jes' set here an' let 'em hang Sandy, er bu'n 'im?"

"God knows!" exclaimed Miller. "The outlook is dark, but we should at least try to do something. There must be *some* white men in the town who would stand for law and order,—there's no possible chance for Sandy to escape hanging by due process of law, if he is guilty. We might at least try half a dozen gentlemen."

"We'd better leave Josh here," said Watson. "He's too truculent. If he went on the street he'd make trouble, and if he accompanied us he'd do more harm than good. Wait for us here, Josh, until we've seen what we can do. We'll be back in half an hour."

In half an hour they had both returned.

"It's no use," reported Watson gloomily. "I called at the mayor's office and found it locked. He is doubtless afraid on his own account, and would not dream of asserting his authority. I then looked up Judge Everton, who has always seemed to be fair. My reception was cold. He admitted that lynching was, as a rule, unjustifiable, but maintained that there were exceptions to all rules,—that laws were made, after all, to express the will of the people in regard to the ordinary administration of justice, but that in an emergency the sovereign people might assert itself and take the law into its own hands,— the creature was not greater than the creator. He laughed at my suggestion that Sandy was innocent. 'If he is innocent,' he said, 'then produce the real criminal. You negroes are standing in your own light when you try to protect such dastardly scoundrels as this Campbell, who is an enemy of society and not fit to live. I shall not move in the matter. If a negro wants the protection of the law, let him obey the law.' A wise judge,—a second Daniel come to judgment! If this were the law, there would be no need of judges or juries."

"I called on Dr. Price," said Miller, "my good friend Dr. Price, who would rather lie than hurt my feelings. 'Miller,' he declared, 'this is no affair of mine, or yours. I have too much respect for myself and my profession to interfere in such a matter, and you will accomplish nothing, and only lessen your own influence, by having anything to say.' 'But the man may be innocent,' I replied; 'there is every reason to believe that he is.' He shook his head pityingly. 'You are self-deceived, Miller; your prejudice has warped your judgment. The proof is overwhelming that he robbed this old lady, laid violent hands upon her, and left her dead. If he did no more, he has violated the written and unwritten law of the Southern States. I could not save him if I would, Miller, and frankly, I would not if I could. If he is innocent, his people can console themselves with the reflection that Mrs. Ochiltree was also innocent, and balance one crime against the other, the white against the black. Of course I shall take no part in whatever may be done,—but it is not my affair, nor yours. Take my advice, Miller, and keep out of it.'

"That is the situation," added Miller, summing up. "Their friendship for us, a slender stream at the best, dries up entirely when it strikes their prejudices. There is seemingly not one white man in Wellington who will speak a word for law, order, decency, or humanity. Those who do not participate will stand idly by and see an untried man deliberately and brutally murdered. Race prejudice is the devil unchained."

"Well, den, suh," said Josh, "where does we stan' now? W'at is we gwine ter do? I wouldn' min' fightin', fer my time ain't come yit,—I feels dat in my bones. W'at we gwine ter do, dat's w'at I wanter know."

"What does old Mr. Delamere have to say about the matter?" asked Miller suddenly. "Why haven't we thought of him before? Has he been seen?"

"No," replied Watson gloomily, "and for a good reason,—he is not in town. I came by the house just now, and learned that he went out to his country place yesterday afternoon, to remain a week. Sandy was to have followed him out there this morning,—it's a pity he didn't go yesterday. The old gentleman has probably heard nothing about the matter."

"How about young Delamere?"

"He went away early this morning, down the river, to fish. He'll probably not hear of it before night, and he's only a boy anyway, and could very likely do nothing," said Watson.

Miller looked at his watch.

"Belleview is ten miles away," he said. "It is now eleven o'clock. I can drive out there in an hour and a half at the farthest. I'll go and see Mr. Delamere,—he can do more than any living man, if he is able to do anything at all. There's never been a lynching here, and one good white man, if he choose, may stem the flood long enough to give justice a chance. Keep track of the white people while I'm gone, Watson; and you, Josh, learn what the colored folks are saying, and do nothing rash until I return. In the meantime, do all that you can to find out who did commit this most atrocious murder."

CHAPTER XXIII

Belleview

MILLER DID NOT reach his destination without interruption. At one point a considerable stretch of the road was under repair, which made it necessary for him to travel slowly. His horse cast a shoe, and threatened to go lame; but in the course of time he arrived at the entrance gate of Belleview, entering which he struck into a private road, bordered by massive oaks, whose multitudinous branches, hung with long streamers of trailing moss, formed for much of the way a thick canopy above his head. It took him only a few minutes to traverse the quarter of a mile that lay between the entrance gate and the house itself.

This old colonial plantation, rich in legendary lore and replete with historic distinction, had been in the Delamere family for nearly two hundred years. Along the bank of the river which skirted its domain the famous pirate Blackbeard had held high carnival, and was reputed to have buried much treasure, vague traditions of which still lingered among the negroes and poor-whites of the country roundabout. The beautiful residence, rising white and stately in a grove of ancient oaks, dated from 1750, and was built of brick which had been brought from England. Enlarged and improved from generation to generation, it stood, like a baronial castle, upon a slight eminence from which could be surveyed the large demesne still belonging to the estate, which had shrunk greatly from its colonial dimensions. While still embracing several thousand acres, part forest and part cleared land, it had not of late years been profitable; in spite of which Mr. Delamere, with the conservatism of his age and caste, had never been able to make up his mind to part with any considerable portion of it. His grandson, he imagined, could make the estate pay and yet preserve it in its integrity. Here, in pleasant weather, surrounded by the scenes which he loved, old Mr. Delamere spent much of the time during his declining years.

Dr. Miller had once passed a day at Belleview, upon Mr. Delamere's invitation. For this old-fashioned gentleman, whose ideals not even slavery had been able to spoil, regarded himself as a trustee for the great public, which ought, in his opinion, to take as much pride as he in the contemplation of this historic landmark. In earlier years Mr. Delamere had been a practicing lawyer, and had numbered Miller's father among his clients. He had always been regarded as friendly to the colored people, and, until age and ill health had driven him from active life, had taken a lively interest in their advancement since the abolition of slavery. Upon the public opening of Miller's new hospital, he had made an effort to be present, and had made a little speech of approval and encouragement which had manifested his kindliness and given Miller much pleasure.

It was with the consciousness, therefore, that he was approaching a friend, as well as Sandy's master, that Miller's mind was chiefly occupied as his tired horse, scenting the end of his efforts, bore him with a final burst of speed along the last few rods of the journey; for the urgency of Miller's errand, involving as it did the issues of life and death, did not permit him to enjoy the charm of mossy oak or forest reaches, or even to appreciate the noble front of Belleview House when it at last loomed up before him.

"Well, William," said Mr. Delamere, as he gave his hand to Miller from the armchair in which he was seated under the broad and stately portico. "I didn't expect to see you out here. You'll excuse my not rising,—I'm none too firm on my legs. Did you see anything of my man Sandy back there on the road? He ought to have been here by nine o'clock, and it's now one. Sandy is punctuality itself, and I don't know how to account for his delay."

Clearly there need be no time wasted in preliminaries. Mr. Delamere had gone directly to the subject in hand.

"He will not be here to-day, sir," replied Miller. "I have come to you on his account."

In a few words Miller stated the situation.

"Preposterous!" exclaimed the old gentleman, with

more vigor than Miller had supposed him to possess. "Sandy is absolutely incapable of such a crime as robbery, to say nothing of murder; and as for the rest, that is absurd upon the face of it! And so the poor old woman is dead! Well, well, well! she could not have lived much longer anyway; but Sandy did not kill her,—it's simply impossible! Why, *I* raised that boy! He was born on my place. I'd as soon believe such a thing of my own grandson as of Sandy! No negro raised by a Delamere would ever commit such a crime. I really believe, William, that Sandy has the family honor of the Delameres quite as much at heart as I have. Just tell them I say Sandy is innocent, and it will be all right."

"I'm afraid, sir," rejoined Miller, who kept his voice up so that the old gentleman could understand without having it suggested that Miller knew he was hard of hearing, "that you don't quite appreciate the situation. *I* believe Sandy innocent; *you* believe him innocent; but there are suspicious circumstances which do not explain themselves, and the white people of the city believe him guilty, and are going to lynch him before he has a chance to clear himself."

"Why doesn't he explain the suspicious circumstances?" asked Mr. Delamere. "Sandy is truthful and can be believed. I would take Sandy's word as quickly as another man's oath."

"He has no chance to explain," said Miller. "The case is prejudged. A crime has been committed. Sandy is charged with it. He is black, and therefore he is guilty. No colored lawyer would be allowed in the jail, if one should dare to go there. No white lawyer will intervene. He'll be lynched to-night, without judge, jury, or preacher, unless we can stave the thing off for a day or two."

"Have you seen my grandson?" asked the old gentleman. "Is he not looking after Sandy?"

"No, sir. It seems he went down the river this morning to fish, before the murder was discovered; no one knows just where he has gone, or at what hour he will return."

"Well, then," said Mr. Delamere, rising from his chair with surprising vigor, "I shall have to go myself. No faithful servant of mine shall be hanged for a crime he didn't commit, so long as I have a voice to speak or a dollar to spend. There'll be no trouble after I get there,

William. The people are naturally wrought up at such a crime. A fine old woman,—she had some detestable traits, and I was always afraid she wanted to marry me, but she was of an excellent family and had many good points,—an old woman of one of the best families, struck down by the hand of a murderer! You must remember, William, that blood is thicker than water, and that the provocation is extreme, and that a few hotheads might easily lose sight of the great principles involved and seek immediate vengeance, without too much discrimination. But they are good people, William, and when I have spoken, and they have an opportunity for the sober second thought, they will do nothing rashly, but will wait for the operation of the law, which will, of course, clear Sandy."

"I'm sure I hope so," returned Miller. "Shall I try to drive you back, sir, or will you order your own carriage?"

"My horses are fresher, William, and I'll have them brought around. You can take the reins, if you will,—I'm rather old to drive,—and my man will come behind with your buggy."

In a few minutes they set out along the sandy road. Having two fresh horses, they made better headway than Miller had made coming out, and reached Wellington easily by three o'clock.

"I think, William," said Mr. Delamere, as they drove into the town, "that I had first better talk with Sandy. He may be able to explain away the things that seem to connect him with this atrocious affair; and that will put me in a better position to talk to other people about it."

Miller drove directly to the county jail. Thirty or forty white men, who seemed to be casually gathered near the door, closed up when the carriage approached. The sheriff, who had seen them from the inside, came to the outer door and spoke to the visitor through a grated wicket.

"Mr. Wemyss," said Mr. Delamere, when he had made his way to the entrance with the aid of his cane, "I wish to see my servant, Sandy Campbell, who is said to be in your custody."

The sheriff hesitated. Meantime there was some parleying in low tones among the crowd outside. No one interfered, however, and in a moment the door opened sufficiently to give entrance to the old gentleman, after which it closed quickly and clangorously behind him.

Feeling no desire to linger in the locality, Miller, having seen his companion enter the jail, drove the carriage round to Mr. Delamere's house, and leaving it in charge of a servant with instructions to return for his master in a quarter of an hour, hastened to his own home to meet Watson and Josh and report the result of his efforts.

CHAPTER XXIV

Two Southern Gentlemen

THE IRON BOLT rattled in the lock, the door of a cell swung open, and when Mr. Delamere had entered was quickly closed again.

"Well, Sandy!"

"Oh, Mars John! Is you fell from hebben ter he'p me out er here? I prayed de Lawd ter sen' you, an' He answered my prayer, an' here you is, Mars John,—here you is! Oh, Mars John, git me out er dis place!"

"Tut, tut, Sandy!" answered his master; "of course I'll get you out. That's what I've come for. How in the world did such a mistake ever happen? You would no more commit such a crime than I would!"

"No, suh, 'deed I wouldn', an' you know I wouldn'! I wouldn' want ter bring no disgrace on de fam'ly dat raise' me, ner ter make no trouble fer you, suh; but here I is, suh, lock' up in jail, an' folks talkin' 'bout hangin' me fer somethin' dat never entered my min', suh. I swea' ter God I never thought er sech a thing!"

"Of course you didn't, Sandy," returned Mr. Delamere soothingly; "and now the next thing, and the simplest thing, is to get you out of this. I'll speak to the officers, and at the preliminary hearing to-morrow I'll tell them all about you, and they will let you go. You won't mind spending one night in jail for your sins."

"No, suh, ef I wuz sho' I'd be 'lowed ter spen' it here. But dey say dey're gwine ter lynch me ternight,—I kin hear 'em talkin' f'm de winders er de cell, suh."

"Well, *I* say, Sandy, that they shall do no such thing! Lynch a man brought up by a Delamere, for a crime of which he is innocent? Preposterous! I'll speak to the authorities and see that you are properly protected until this mystery is unraveled. If Tom had been here, he would have had you out before now, Sandy. My grandson is a genuine Delamere, is he not, Sandy?"

"Yas, suh, yas, suh," returned Sandy, with a lack of enthusiasm which he tried to conceal from his master. "An' I s'pose ef he hadn' gone fishin' so soon dis mawnin', he'd 'a' be'n lookin' after me, suh."

"It has been my love for him and your care of me, Sandy," said the old gentleman tremulously, "that have kept me alive so long; but now explain to me everything concerning this distressing matter, and I shall then be able to state your case to better advantage."

"Well, suh," returned Sandy, "I mought's well tell de whole tale an' not hol' nothin' back. I wuz kind er lonesome las' night, an' sence I be'n tu'ned outen de chu'ch on account er dat cakewalk I didn' go ter, so he'p me God! I didn' feel like gwine ter prayer-meetin', so I went roun' ter see Solomon Williams, an' he wa'n't home, an' den I walk' down street an' met Josh Green, an' he ax' me inter Sam Taylor's place, an' I sot roun' dere wid Josh till 'bout 'leven o'clock, w'en I sta'ted back home. I went straight ter de house, suh, an' went ter bed an' ter sleep widout sayin' a wo'd ter a single soul excep' Mistuh Tom, who wuz settin' up readin' a book w'en I come in. I wish I may drap dead in my tracks, suh, ef dat ain't de God's truf, suh, eve'y wo'd of it!"

"I believe every word of it, Sandy; now tell me about the clothes that you are said to have been found cleaning, and the suspicious articles that were found in your room?"

"Dat's w'at beats me, Mars John," replied Sandy, shaking his head mournfully. "W'en I lef' home las' night after supper, my clo's wuz all put erway in de closet in my room, folded up on de she'f ter keep de moths out. Dey wuz my good clo's,—de blue coat dat you wo' ter de weddin' fo'ty years ago, an' dem dere plaid pants I gun Mistuh Cohen fo' dollars fer three years ago; an' w'en I looked in my closet dis mawnin', suh, befo' I got ready ter sta't fer Belleview, dere wuz my clo's layin' on de flo', all muddy an' crumple' up, des lack somebody had wo' 'em in a fight! Somebody e'se had wo' my clo's,—er e'se dere 'd be'n some witchcraf', er some sort er devilment gwine on dat I can't make out, suh, ter save my soul!"

"There was no witchcraft, Sandy, but that there was some deviltry might well be. Now, what other negro, who might have been mistaken for you, could have taken your clothes? Surely no one about the house?"

"No, suh, no, suh. It couldn't 'a' be'n Jeff, fer he wuz at Belleview wid you; an' it couldn't 'a' be'n Billy, fer he wuz too little ter wear my clo's; an' it couldn't 'a' be'n Sally, fer she's a 'oman. It's a myst'ry ter me, suh!"

"Have you no enemies? Is there any one in Wellington whom you imagine would like to do you an injury?"

"Not a livin' soul dat I knows of, suh. I've be'n tu'ned out'n de chu'ch, but I don' know who my enemy is dere, er ef it wuz all a mistake, like dis yer jailin' is; but de Debbil is in dis somewhar, Mars John,—an' I got my reasons fer sayin' so."

"What do you mean, Sandy?"

Sandy related his experience of the preceding evening: how he had seen the apparition preceding him to the house, and how he had questioned Tom upon the subject.

"There's some mystery here, Sandy," said Mr. Delamere reflectively. "Have you told me all, now, upon your honor? I am trying to save your life, Sandy, and I must be able to trust your word implicitly. You must tell me every circumstance; a very little and seemingly unimportant bit of evidence may sometimes determine the issue of a great lawsuit. There is one thing especially, Sandy: where did you get the gold which was found in your trunk?"

Sandy's face lit up with hopefulness.

"Why, Mars John, I kin 'splain dat part easy. Dat wuz money I had lent out, an' I got back f'm—But no, suh, I promise' not ter tell."

"Circumstances absolve you from your promise, Sandy. Your life is of more value to you than any other thing. If you will explain where you got the gold, and the silk purse that contained it, which is said to be Mrs. Ochiltree's, you will be back home before night."

Old Mr. Delamere's faculties, which had been waning somewhat in sympathy with his health, were stirred to unusual acuteness by his servant's danger. He was watching Sandy with all the awakened instincts of the trial lawyer. He could see clearly enough that, in beginning

to account for the possession of the gold, Sandy had
started off with his explanation in all sincerity. At the
mention of the silk purse, however, his face had blanched
to an ashen gray, and the words had frozen upon his lips.

A less discerning observer might have taken these
things as signs of guilt, but not so Mr. Delamere.

"Well, Sandy," said his master encouragingly, "go on.
You got the gold from"—

Sandy remained silent. He had had a great shock, and
had taken a great resolution.

"Mars John," he asked dreamily, "you don' b'lieve dat
I done dis thing?"

"Certainly not, Sandy, else why should I be here?"

"An' nothin' wouldn' make you b'lieve it, suh?"

"No, Sandy,—I could not believe it of you. I've known
you too long and too well."

"An' you wouldn' b'lieve it, not even ef I wouldn' say
one wo'd mo' about it?"

"No, Sandy, I believe you no more capable of this
crime than I would be,—or my grandson, Tom. I wish
Tom were here, that he might help me overcome your
stubbornness; but you'll not be so foolish, so absurdly
foolish, Sandy, as to keep silent and risk your life merely
to shield some one else, when by speaking you might
clear up this mystery and be restored at once to liberty.
Just tell me where you got the gold," added the old gentleman persuasively. "Come, now, Sandy, that's a good
fellow!"

"Mars John," asked Sandy softly, "w'en my daddy,
'way back yander befo' de wah, wuz about ter be sol'
away f'm his wife an' child'en, you bought him an' dem,
an' kep' us all on yo' place tergether, didn't you, suh?"

"Yes, Sandy, and he was a faithful servant, and proved
worthy of all I did for him."

"And w'en he had wo'ked fer you ten years, suh, you
sot 'im free?"

"Yes, Sandy, he had earned his freedom."

"An' w'en de wah broke out, an' my folks wuz scattered, an' I didn' have nothin' ter do ner nowhar ter go,
you kep' me on yo' place, and tuck me ter wait on you,
suh, didn't you?"

"Yes, Sandy, and you have been a good servant and
a good friend; but tell me now about this gold, and I'll

go and get you out of this, right away, for I need you, Sandy, and you'll not be of any use to me shut up here!"

"Jes' hol' on a minute befo' you go, Mars John; fer ef dem people outside should git holt er me befo' you *does* git me out er here, I may never see you no mo', suh, in dis worl'. W'en Mars Billy McLean shot me by mistake, w'ile we wuz out huntin' dat day, who wuz it boun' up my woun's an' kep' me from bleedin' ter def, an' kyar'ed me two miles on his own shoulders ter a doctuh?"

"Yes, Sandy, and when black Sally ran away with your young mistress and Tom, when Tom was a baby, who stopped the runaway, and saved their lives at the risk of his own?"

"Dat wa'n't nothin' suh; anybody could 'a' done dat, w'at wuz strong ernuff an' swif' ernuff. You is be'n good ter me, suh, all dese years, an' I've tried ter do my duty by you, suh, an' by Mistuh Tom, who wuz yo' own gran'-son, an' de las' one er de fam'ly."

"Yes, you have, Sandy, and when I am gone, which will not be very long, Tom will take care of you, and see that you never want. But we are wasting valuable time, Sandy, in these old reminiscences. Let us get back to the present. Tell me about the gold, now, so that I may at once look after your safety. It may not even be necessary for you to remain here all night."

"Jes' one wo'd mo', Mars John, befo' you go! I know you're gwine ter do de bes' you kin fer me, an' I'm sorry I can't he'p you no mo' wid it; but ef dere should be any accident, er ef you *can't* git me out er here, don' bother yo' min' 'bout it no mo', suh, an' don' git yo'se'f ixcited, fer you know de doctuh says, suh, dat you can't stan' ixcitement; but jes' leave me in de han's er de Lawd, suh,—*He'll* look after me, here er hereafter. I know I've fell f'm grace mo' d'n once, but I've done made my peace wid Him in dis here jail-house, suh, an' I ain't 'feared ter die—ef I haf ter. I ain' got no wife ner child'n ter mo'n fer me, an' I'll die knownin' dat I've done my duty ter dem dat hi'ed me, an' trusted me, an' had claims on me. Fer I wuz raise' by a Delamere, suh, an' all de ole Delameres wuz gent'emen, an' deir principles spread ter de niggers 'round 'em, suh; an' ef I has ter die fer so-methin' I did n' do,—I kin die, suh, like a gent'eman!

But ez fer dat gol', suh, I ain' gwine ter say one wo'd mo' 'bout it ter nobody in dis worl'!"

Nothing could shake Sandy's determination. Mr. Delamere argued, expostulated, but all in vain. Sandy would not speak.

More and more confident of some mystery, which would come out in time, if properly investigated, Mr. Delamere, strangely beset by a vague sense of discomfort over and beyond that occasioned by his servant's danger, hurried away upon his errand of mercy. He felt less confident of the outcome than when he had entered the jail, but was quite as much resolved that no effort should be spared to secure protection for Sandy until there had been full opportunity for the truth to become known.

"Take good care of your prisoner, sheriff," he said sternly, as he was conducted to the door. "He will not be long in your custody, and I shall see that you are held strictly accountable for his safety."

"I'll do what I can, sir," replied the sheriff in an even tone and seemingly not greatly impressed by this warning. "If the prisoner is taken from me, it will be because the force that comes for him is too strong for resistance."

"There should be no force too strong for an honest man in your position to resist,—whether successfully or not is beyond the question. The officer who is intimidated by threats, or by his own fears, is recreant to his duty, and no better than the mob which threatens him. But you will have no such test, Mr. Wemyss! I shall see to it myself that there is no violence!"

CHAPTER XXV

The Honor of a Family

MR. DELAMERE'S COACHMAN, who, in accordance with instructions left by Miller, had brought the carriage around to the jail and was waiting anxiously at the nearest corner, drove up with some trepidation as he saw his master emerge from the prison. The old gentleman entered the carriage and gave the order to be driven to the office of the Morning Chronicle. According to Jerry, the porter, whom he encountered at the door, Carteret was in his office, and Mr. Delamere, with the aid of his servant, climbed the stairs painfully and found the editor at his desk.

"Carteret," exclaimed Mr. Delamere, "what is all this talk about lynching my man for murder and robbery and criminal assault! It's perfectly absurd! The man was raised by me; he had lived in my house forty years. He has been honest, faithful, and trustworthy. He would no more be capable of this crime than you would, or my grandson Tom. Sandy has too much respect for the family to do anything that would reflect disgrace upon it."

"My dear Mr. Delamere," asked Carteret, with an indulgent smile, "how could a negro possibly reflect discredit upon a white family? I should really like to know."

"How, sir? A white family raised him. Like all the negroes, he has been clay in the hands of the white people. They are what we have made them, or permitted them to become."

"We are not God, Mr. Delamere! We do not claim to have created these—masterpieces."

"No; but we thought to overrule God's laws, and we enslaved these people for our greed, and sought to escape the manstealer's curse by laying to our souls the flattering unction that we were making of barbarous negroes civilized and Christian men. If we did not, if in-

stead of making them Christians we have made some of
them brutes, we have only ourselves to blame, and if
these prey upon society, it is our just punishment! But
my negroes, Carteret, were well raised and well behaved.
This man is innocent of this offense, I solemnly affirm,
and I want your aid to secure his safety until a fair trial
can be had."

"On your bare word, sir?" asked Carteret, not at all
moved by this outburst.

Old Mr. Delamere trembled with anger, and his with-
ered cheek flushed darkly, but he restrained his feelings,
and answered with an attempt at calmness:—

"Time was, sir, when the word of a Delamere was held
as good as his bond, and those who questioned it were
forced to maintain their skepticism upon the field of
honor. Time was, sir, when the law was enforced in this
state in a manner to command the respect of the world!
Our lawyers, our judges, our courts, were a credit to
humanity and civilization. I fear I have outlasted my
epoch,—I have lived to hear of white men, the most
favored of races, the heirs of civilization, the conserva-
tors of liberty, howling like red Indians around a human
being slowly roasting at the stake."

"My dear sir," said Carteret soothingly, "you should
undeceive yourself. This man is no longer your property.
The negroes are no longer under our control, and with
their emancipation ceased our responsibility. Their insolence and disregard for law have reached a point where
they must be sternly rebuked."

"The law," retorted Mr. Delamere, "furnishes a sufficient penalty for any crime, however heinous, and our
code is by no means lenient. To my old-fashioned notions, death would seem an adequate punishment for any
crime, and torture has been abolished in civilized coun-
tries for a hundred years. It would be better to let a
crime go entirely unpunished, than to use it as a pretext
for turning the whole white population into a mob of
primitive savages, dancing in hellish glee around the
mangled body of a man who has never been tried for a
crime. All this, however, is apart from my errand, which
is to secure your assistance in heading off this mob until
Sandy can have a fair hearing and an opportunity to
prove his innocence."

"How can I do that, Mr. Delamere?"

"You are editor of the Morning Chronicle. The Chronicle is the leading newspaper of the city. This morning's issue practically suggested the mob; the same means will stop it. I will pay the expense of an extra edition, calling off the mob, on the ground that newly discovered evidence has shown the prisoner's innocence."

"But where is the evidence?" asked Carteret.

Again Mr. Delamere flushed and trembled. "*My* evidence, sir! I say the negro was morally incapable of the crime. A man of forty-five does not change his nature over-night. He is no more capable of a disgraceful deed than my grandson would be!"

Carteret smiled sadly.

"I am sorry, Mr. Delamere," he said, "that you should permit yourself to be so exercised about a worthless scoundrel who has forfeited his right to live. The proof against him is overwhelming. As to his capability of crime, we will apply your own test. You have been kept in the dark too long, Mr. Delamere,—indeed, we all have,—about others as well as this negro. Listen, sir: last night, at the Clarendon Club, Tom Delamere was caught cheating outrageously at cards. He had been suspected for some time; a trap was laid for him, and he fell into it. Out of regard for you and for my family, he has been permitted to resign quietly, with the understanding that he first pay off his debts, which are considerable."

Mr. Delamere's face, which had taken on some color in the excitement of the interview, had gradually paled to a chalky white while Carteret was speaking. His head sunk forward; already an old man, he seemed to have aged ten years in but little more than as many seconds.

"Can this be true?" he demanded in a hoarse whisper. "Is it—entirely authentic?"

"True as gospel; true as it is that Mrs. Ochiltree has been murdered, and that this negro killed her. Ellis was at the club a few minutes after the affair happened, and learned the facts from one of the participants. Tom made no attempt at denial. We have kept the matter out of the others papers, and I would have spared your feelings,—I surely would not wish to wound them,—but the temptation proved too strong for me, and it seemed the only way to convince you: it was your own test. If a gentleman of a distinguished name and an honorable ancestry, with all the restraining forces of social position surrounding him, to hold him in check, can stoop to dishonor, what is the improbability of an illiterate negro's being at least *capable* of crime?"

"Enough, sir," said the old gentleman. "You have proved enough. My grandson may be a scoundrel,—I can see, in the light of this revelation, how he might be; and he seems not to have denied it. I maintain, nevertheless, that my man Sandy is innocent of the charge against him. He *has* denied it, and it has not been proved. Carteret, I owe that negro my life; he, and his father before him, have served me and mine faithfully and well. I cannot see him killed like a dog, without judge or jury,—no, not even if he were guilty, which I do not believe!"

Carteret felt a twinge of remorse for the pain he had inflicted upon this fine old man, this ideal gentleman of the ideal past,—the past which he himself so much admired and regretted. He would like to spare his old friend any further agitation; he was in a state of health where too great excitement might prove fatal. But how could he? The negro was guilty, and sure to die sooner or later. He had not meant to interfere, and his intervention might be fruitless.

"Mr. Delamere," he said gently, "there is but one way to gain time. You say the negro is innocent. Appearances are against him. The only way to clear him is to produce the real criminal, or prove an alibi. If you, or some other white man of equal standing, could swear that the negro was in your presence last night at any hour when this crime could have taken place, it might be barely possible to prevent the lynching for the present; and when he is tried, which will probably be not later than next week, he will have every opportunity to defend himself, with you to see that he gets no less than justice. I think it can be managed, though there is still a doubt. I will do my best, for your sake, Mr. Delamere,—solely for your sake, be it understood, and not for that of the negro, in whom you are entirely deceived."

"I shall not examine your motives, Carteret," replied the other, "if you can bring about what I desire."

"Whatever is done," added Carteret, "must be done quickly. It is now four o'clock; no one can answer for what may happen after seven. If he can prove an alibi, there may yet be time to save him. White men might lynch a negro on suspicion; they would not kill a man who was proven, by the word of white men, to be entirely innocent."

"I do not know," returned Mr. Delamere, shaking his head sadly. "After what you have told me, it is no longer safe to assume what white men will or will not do;—what I have learned here has shaken my faith in humanity. I am going away, but shall return in a short time. Shall I find you here?"

"I will await your return," said Carteret.

He watched Mr. Delamere pityingly as the old man moved away on the arm of the coachman waiting in the hall. He did not believe that Mr. Delamere could prove an alibi for his servant, and without some positive proof the negro would surely die,—as he well deserved to die.

CHAPTER XXVI

The Discomfort of Ellis

MR. ELLIS WAS vaguely uncomfortable. In the first excitement following the discovery of the crime, he had given his bit of evidence, and had shared the universal indignation against the murderer. When public feeling took definite shape in the intention to lynch the prisoner, Ellis felt a sudden sense of responsibility growing upon himself. When he learned, an hour later, that it was proposed to burn the negro, his part in the affair assumed a still graver aspect; for his had been the final word to fix the prisoner's guilt.

Ellis did not believe in lynch law. He had argued against it, more than once, in private conversation, and had written several editorials against the practice, while in charge of the Morning Chronicle during Major Carteret's absence. A young man, however, and merely representing another, he had not set up as a reformer, taking rather the view that this summary method of punishing crime, with all its possibilities of error, to say nothing of the resulting disrespect of the law and contempt for the time-honored methods of establishing guilt, was a mere temporary symptom of the unrest caused by the unsettled relations of the two races at the South. There had never before been any special need for any vigorous opposition to lynch law, so far as the community was concerned, for there had not been a lynching in Wellington since Ellis had come there, eight years before, from a smaller town, to seek a place for himself in the world of action. Twenty years before, indeed, there had been wild doings, during the brief Ku-Klux outbreak, but that was before Ellis's time,—or at least when he was but a child. He had come of a Quaker family,—the modified Quakers of the South,—and while sharing in a general way the Southern prejudice against the negro, his prejudices had been tempered by the peaceful tenets of his father's sect. His father had been a Whig, and a non-slaveholder; and while he had gone with the South in the civil war so far as a man of peace could go, he had not done so for love of slavery.

As the day wore on, Ellis's personal responsibility for the intended *auto-da-fé* bore more heavily upon him. Suppose he had been wrong? He had seen the accused negro; he had recognized him by his clothes, his whiskers, his spectacles, and his walk; but he had also seen another man, who resembled Sandy so closely that but for the difference in their clothes, he was forced to acknowledge, he could not have told them apart. Had he not seen the first man, he would have sworn with even greater confidence that the second was Sandy. There had been, he recalled, about one of the men—he had not been then nor was he now able to tell which—something vaguely familiar, and yet seemingly discordant to whichever of the two it was, or, as it seemed to him now, to any man of that race. His mind reverted to the place where he had last seen Sandy, and then a sudden wave of illumination swept over him, and filled him with a thrill of horror. The cakewalk,—the dancing,—the speech,—they were not Sandy's at all, nor any negro's! It was a white man who had stood in the light of the street lamp, so that the casual passer-by might see and recognize in him old Mr. Delamere's servant. The scheme was a dastardly one, and worthy of a heart that was something worse than weak and vicious.

Ellis resolved that the negro should not, if he could prevent it, die for another's crime; but what proof had he himself to offer in support of his theory? Then again, if he denounced Tom Delamere as the murderer, it would involve, in all probability, the destruction of his own hopes with regard to Clara. Of course she could not marry Delamere after the disclosure,—the disgraceful episode at the club would have been enough to make that reasonably certain; it had put a nail in Delamere's coffin, but this crime had driven it in to the head and clinched it. On the other hand, would Miss Pemberton ever speak again to the man who had been the instrument of bringing disgrace upon the family? Spies, detectives, police officers, may be useful citizens, but they are rarely pleasant company for other people. We fee the executioner, but we do not touch his bloody hand. We might feel a certain tragic admiration for Brutus condemning his sons to death, but we would scarcely invite Brutus to dinner after the event. It would harrow our feelings too much.

Perhaps, thought Ellis, there might be a way out of the dilemma. It might be possible to save this innocent negro without, for the time being, involving Delamere. He believed that murder will out, but it need not be through his initiative. He determined to go to the jail and interview the prisoner, who might give such an account of himself as would establish his innocence beyond a doubt. If so, Ellis would exert himself to stem the tide of popular fury. If, as a last resort, he could save Sandy only by denouncing Delamere, he would do his duty, let it cost him what it might.

The gravity of his errand was not lessened by what he saw and heard on the way to the jail. The anger of the people was at a white heat. A white woman had been assaulted and murdered by a brutal negro. Neither advanced age, nor high social standing, had been able to protect her from the ferocity of a black savage. Her sex, which should have been her shield and buckler, had made her an easy mark for the villainy of a black brute. To take the time to try him would be a criminal waste of public money. To hang him would be too slight a punishment for so dastardly a crime. An example must be made.

Already the preparations were under way for the impending execution. A T-rail from the railroad yard had been procured, and men were burying it in the square before the jail. Others were bringing chains, and a load of pine wood was piled in convenient proximity. Some enterprising individual had begun the erection of seats from which, for a pecuniary consideration, the spectacle might be the more easily and comfortably viewed.

Ellis was stopped once or twice by persons of his acquaintance. From one he learned that the railroads would run excursions from the neighboring towns in order to bring spectators to the scene; from another that the burning was to take place early in the evening, so that the children might not be kept up beyond their usual bedtime. In one group that he passed he heard several young men discussing the question of which portions of the negro's body they would prefer for souvenirs. Ellis shuddered and hastened forward. Whatever was to be done must be done quickly, or it would be too late. He saw that already it would require a strong case in favor of the accused to overcome the popular verdict.

Going up the steps of the jail, he met Mr. Delamere, who was just coming out, after a fruitless interview with Sandy.

"Mr. Ellis," said the old gentleman, who seemed greatly agitated, "this is monstrous!"

"It is indeed, sir!" returned the younger man. "I mean to stop it if I can. The negro did not kill Mrs. Ochiltree."

Mr. Delamere looked at Ellis keenly, and, as Ellis recalled afterwards, there was death in his eyes. Unable to draw a syllable from Sandy, he had found his servant's silence more eloquent than words. Ellis felt a presentiment that this affair, however it might terminate, would be fatal to this fine old man, whom the city could ill spare, in spite of his age and infirmities.

"Mr. Ellis," asked Mr. Delamere, in a voice which trembled with ill-suppressed emotion, "do you know who killed her?"

Ellis felt a surging pity for his old friend; but every step that he had taken toward the jail had confirmed and strengthened his own resolution that this contemplated crime, which he dimly felt to be far more atrocious than that of which Sandy was accused, in that it involved a whole community rather than one vicious man, should be stopped at any cost. Deplorable enough had the negro been guilty, it became, in view of his certain innocence, an unspeakable horror, which for all time would cover the city with infamy.

"Mr. Delamere," he replied, looking the elder man squarely in the eyes, "I think I do,—and I am very sorry."

"And who was it, Mr. Ellis?"

He put the question hopelessly, as though the answer were a foregone conclusion.

"I do not wish to say at present," replied Ellis, with a remorseful pang, "unless it becomes absolutely necessary, to save the negro's life. Accusations are dangerous,—as this case proves,—unless the proof be certain."

For a moment it seemed as though Mr. Delamere would collapse upon the spot. Rallying almost instantly, however, he took the arm which Ellis involuntarily offered, and said with an effort:—

"Mr. Ellis, you are a gentleman whom it is an honor to know. If you have time, I wish you would go with me to my house,—I can hardly trust myself alone,—and thence to the Chronicle office. This thing shall be stopped, and you will help me stop it."

It required but a few minutes to cover the half mile that lay between the prison and Mr. Delamere's residence.

CHAPTER XXVII

The Vagaries
of the Higher Law

MR. DELAMERE WENT immediately to his grandson's room, which he entered alone, closing and locking the door behind him. He had requested Ellis to wait in the carriage.

The bed had been made, and the room was apparently in perfect order. There was a bureau in the room, through which Mr. Delamere proceeded to look thoroughly. Finding one of the drawers locked, he tried it with a key of his own, and being unable to unlock it, took a poker from beside the stove and broke it ruthlessly open.

The contents served to confirm what he had heard concerning his grandson's character. Thrown together in disorderly confusion were bottles of wine and whiskey; soiled packs of cards; a dice-box with dice; a box of poker chips, several revolvers, and a number of photographs and paper-covered books at which the old gentleman glanced to ascertain their nature.

So far, while his suspicion had been strengthened, he had found nothing to confirm it. He searched the room more carefully, and found, in the wood-box by the small heating-stove which stood in the room, a torn and crumpled bit of paper. Stooping to pick this up, his eye caught a gleam of something yellow beneath the bureau, which lay directly in his line of vision.

First he smoothed out the paper. It was apparently the lower half of a label, or part of the cover of a small box, torn diagonally from corner to corner. From the business card at the bottom, which gave the name of a firm of manufacturers of theatrical supplies in a Northern city, and from the letters remaining upon the upper and narrower half, the bit of paper had plainly formed part of the wrapper of a package of burnt cork.

Closing his fingers spasmodically over this damning piece of evidence, Mr. Delamere knelt painfully, and with the aid of his cane drew out from under the bureau the yellow object which had attracted his attention. It was a five-dollar gold piece of a date back toward the beginning of the century.

To make assurance doubly sure, Mr. Delamere summoned the cook from the kitchen in the back yard. In answer to her master's questions, Sally averred that Mr. Tom had got up very early, had knocked at her window,—she slept in a room off the kitchen in the yard,— and had told her that she need not bother about breakfast for him, as he had had a cold bite from the pantry; that he was going hunting and fishing, and would be gone all day. According to Sally, Mr. Tom had come in about ten o'clock the night before. He had forgotten his night-key, Sandy was out, and she had admitted him with her own key. He had said that he was very tired and was going immediately to bed.

Mr. Delamere seemed perplexed; the crime had been committed later in the evening than ten o'clock. The cook cleared up the mystery.

"I reckon he must 'a' be'n dead ti'ed, suh, fer I went back ter his room fifteen er twenty minutes after he come in fer ter fin' out w'at he wanted fer breakfus'; an' I knock' two or three times, rale ha'd, an' Mistuh Tom did n' wake up no mo' d'n de dead. He sho'ly had a good sleep, er he'd never 'a' got up so ea'ly."

"Thank you, Sally," said Mr. Delamere, when the woman had finished, "that will do."

"Will you be home ter suppah, suh?" asked the cook. "Yes."

It was a matter of the supremest indifference to Mr. Delamere whether he should ever eat again, but he would not betray his feelings to a servant. In a few minutes he was driving rapidly with Ellis toward the office of the Morning Chronicle. Ellis could see that Mr. Delamere had discovered something of tragic import. Neither spoke. Ellis gave all his attention to the horses, and Mr. Delamere remained wrapped in his own sombre reflections.

When they reached the office, they were informed by Jerry that Major Carteret was engaged with General Belmont and Captain McBane. Mr. Delamere knocked peremptorily at the door of the inner office, which was opened by Carteret in person.

"Oh, it is you, Mr. Delamere."

"Carteret," exclaimed Mr. Delamere, "I must speak to you immediately, and alone."

"Excuse me a moment, gentlemen," said Carteret, turning to those within the room. "I'll be back in a moment—don't go away."

Ellis had left the room, closing the door behind him. Mr. Delamere and Carteret were quite alone.

"Carteret," declared the old gentleman, "this murder must not take place."

" 'Murder' is a hard word," replied the editor, frowning slightly.

"It is the right word," rejoined Mr. Delamere, decidedly. "It would be a foul and most unnatural murder, for Sandy did not kill Mrs. Ochiltree."

Carteret with difficulty restrained a smile of pity. His old friend was very much excited, as the tremor in his voice gave proof. The criminal was his trusted servant, who had proved unworthy of confidence. No one could question Mr. Delamere's motives; but he was old, his judgment was no longer to be relied upon. It was a great pity that he should so excite and overstrain himself about a worthless negro, who had forfeited his life for a dastardly crime. Mr. Delamere had had two paralytic strokes, and a third might prove fatal. He must be dealt with gently.

"Mr. Delamere," he said, with patient tolerance, "I think you are deceived. There is but one sure way to stop this execution. If your servant is innocent, you must produce the real criminal. If the negro, with such overwhelming proofs against him, is not guilty, who is?"

"I will tell you who is," replied Mr. Delamere. "The murderer is"—the words came with a note of anguish, as though torn from his very heart—"the murderer is Tom Delamere, my own grandson!"

"Impossible, sir!" exclaimed Carteret, starting back involuntarily. "That could not be! The man was seen leaving the house, and he was black!"

"All cats are gray in the dark, Carteret; and moreover, nothing is easier than for a white man to black his face. God alone knows how many crimes have been done in this guise! Tom Delamere, to get the money to pay his gambling debts, committed this foul murder, and then tried to fasten it upon as honest and faithful a soul as ever trod the earth."

Carteret, though at first overwhelmed by this announcement, perceived with quick intuition that it might easily be true. It was but a step from fraud to crime, and in Delamere's need of money there lay a palpable notice for robbery,—the murder may have been an afterthought. Delamere knew as much about the cedar chest as the negro could have known, and more.

But a white man must not be condemned without proof positive.

"What foundation is there, sir," he asked, "for this astounding charge?"

Mr. Delamere related all that had taken place since he had left Belleview a couple of hours before, and as he proceeded, step by step, every word carried conviction to Carteret. Tom Delamere's skill as a mimic and a negro impersonator was well known; he had himself laughed at more than one of his performances. There had been a powerful motive, and Mr. Delamere's discoveries had made clear the means. Tom's unusual departure, before breakfast, on a fishing expedition was a suspicious circumstance. There was a certain devilish ingenuity about the affair which he would hardly have expected of Tom Delamere, but for which the reason was clear enough. One might have thought that Tom would have been satisfied with merely blacking his face, and leaving to chance the identification of the negro who might be apprehended. He would hardly have implicated, out of pure malignity, his grandfather's old servant, who had been his own care-taker for many years. Here, however, Carteret could see where Tom's own desperate position operated to furnish a probable motive for the crime. The surest way to head off suspicion from himself was to direct it strongly toward some particular person, and this he had been able to do conclusively by his access to Sandy's clothes, his skill in making up to resemble him, and by the episode of the silk purse. By placing himself beyond reach during the next day, he would not be called upon to corroborate or deny any inculpating statements which Sandy might make, and in the very probable case that the crime should be summarily avenged, any such statements on Sandy's part would be regarded as mere desperate subterfuges of the murderer to save his own life. It was a bad affair.

"The case seems clear," said Carteret reluctantly but conclusively. "And now, what shall we do about it?"

"I want you to print a handbill," said Mr. Delamere, "and circulate it through the town, stating that Sandy Campbell is innocent and Tom Delamere guilty of this crime. If this is not done, I will go myself and declare it to all who will listen, and I will publicly disown the villain who is no more grandson of mine. There is no deeper sink of iniquity into which he could fall."

Carteret's thoughts were chasing one another tumultuously. There could be no doubt that the negro was innocent, from the present aspect of affairs, and he must not be lynched; but in what sort of position would the white people be placed, if Mr. Delamere carried out his Spartan purpose of making the true facts known? The white people of the city had raised the issue of their own superior morality, and had themselves made this crime a race question. The success of the impending "revolution," for which he and his *confrères* had labored so long, depended in large measure upon the maintenance of their race prestige, which would be injured in the eyes of the world by such a fiasco. While they might yet win by sheer force, their cause would suffer in the court of morals, where they might stand convicted as pirates, instead of being applauded as patriots. Even the negroes would have the laugh on them,—the people whom they hoped to make approve and justify their own despoilment. To be laughed at by the negroes was a calamity only less terrible than failure or death.

Such an outcome of an event which had already been heralded to the four corners of the earth would throw a cloud of suspicion upon the stories of outrage which had gone up from the South for so many years, and had done so much to win the sympathy of the North for the white South and to alienate it from the colored people. The reputation of the race was threatened. They must not lynch the negro, and yet, for the credit of the town, its aristocracy, and the race, the truth of this ghastly story must not see the light,—at least not yet.

"Mr. Delamere," he exclaimed, "I am shocked and humiliated. The negro must be saved, of course, but— consider the family honor."

"Tom is no longer a member of my family. I disown him. He has covered the family name—my name, sir— with infamy. We have no longer a family honor. I wish never to hear his name spoken again!"

For several minutes Carteret argued with his old friend. Then he went into the other room and consulted with General Belmont.

As a result of these conferences, and of certain urgent messages sent out, within half an hour thirty or forty of the leading citizens of Wellington were gathered in the Morning Chronicle office. Several other curious persons, observing that there was something in the wind, and supposing correctly that it referred to the projected event of the evening, crowded in with those who had been invited.

Carteret was in another room, still arguing with Mr. Delamere. "It's a mere formality, sir," he was saying suavely, "accompanied by a mental reservation. We know the facts; but this must be done to justify us, in the eyes of the mob, in calling them off before they accomplish their purpose."

"Carteret," said the old man, in a voice eloquent of the struggle through which he had passed, "I would not perjure myself to prolong my own miserable existence another day, but God will forgive a sin committed to save another's life. Upon your head be it, Carteret, and not on mine!"

"Gentlemen," said Carteret, entering with Mr. Delamere the room where the men were gathered, and raising his hand for silence, "the people of Wellington were on the point of wreaking vengeance upon a negro who was supposed to have been guilty of a terrible crime. The white men of this city, impelled by the highest and holiest sentiments, were about to take steps to defend their hearthstones and maintain the purity and ascendency of their race. Your purpose sprung from hearts wounded in their tenderest susceptibilities."

" 'Rah, 'rah!" shouted a tipsy sailor, who had edged in with the crowd.

"But this same sense of justice," continued Carteret oratorically, "which would lead you to visit swift and terrible punishment upon the guilty, would not permit you to slay an innocent man. Even a negro, as long as he behaves himself and keeps in his place, is entitled to the protection of the law. We may be stern and unbending in the punishment of crime, as befits our masterful race, but we hold the scales of justice with even and impartial hand."

" 'Rah f' 'mpa'tial han'!" cried the tipsy sailor, who was immediately ejected with slight ceremony.

"We have discovered, beyond a doubt, that the negro Sandy Campbell, now in custody, did not commit this robbery and murder, but that it was perpetrated by some unknown man, who has fled from the city. Our venerable and distinguished fellow townsman, Mr. Delamere, in whose employment this Campbell has been for many years, will vouch for his character, and states, furthermore, that Campbell was with him all last night, covering any hour at which this crime could have been committed."

"If Mr. Delamere will swear to that," said some one in the crowd, "the negro should not be lynched."

There were murmurs of dissent. The preparations had all been made. There would be great disappointment if the lynching did not occur.

"Let Mr. Delamere swear, if he wants to save the nigger," came again from the crowd.

"Certainly," assented Carteret. "Mr. Delamere can have no possible objection to taking the oath. Is there a notary public present, or a justice of the peace?"

A man stepped forward. "I am a justice of the peace," he announced.

"Very well, Mr. Smith," said Carteret, recognizing the speaker. "With your permission, I will formulate the oath, and Mr. Delamere may repeat it after me, if he will. I solemnly swear,"—

"I solemnly swear,"—

Mr. Delamere's voice might have come from the tomb, so hollow and unnatural did it sound.

"So help me God,"—

"So help me God,"—

"That the negro Sandy Campbell, now in jail on the charge of murder, robbery, and assault, was in my presence last night between the hours of eight and two o'clock."

Mr. Delamere repeated this statement in a firm voice; but to Ellis, who was in the secret, his words fell upon the ear like clods dropping upon the coffin in an open grave.

"I wish to add," said General Belmont, stepping forward, "that it is not our intention to interfere, by anything which may be done at this meeting, with the orderly process of the law, or to advise the prisoner's immediate release. The prisoner will remain in custody, Mr. Delamere, Major Carteret, and I guaranteeing that he will be proved entirely innocent at the preliminary hearing tomorrow morning."

Several of those present looked relieved; others were plainly disappointed; but when the meeting ended, the news went out that the lynching had been given up. Carteret immediately wrote and had struck off a handbill giving a brief statement of the proceedings, and sent out a dozen boys to distribute copies among the people in the streets. That no precaution might be omitted, a call was issued to the Wellington Grays, the crack independent military company of the city, who in an incredibly short time were on guard at the jail.

Thus a slight change in the point of view had demonstrated the entire ability of the leading citizens to maintain the dignified and orderly processes of the law whenever they saw fit to do so.

The night passed without disorder, beyond the somewhat rough handling of two or three careless negroes that came in the way of small parties of the disappointed who had sought alcoholic consolation.

At ten o'clock the next morning, a preliminary hearing of the charge against Campbell was had before a magistrate. Mr. Delamere, perceptibly older and more wizened than he had seemed the day before, and leaning heavily on the arm of a servant, repeated his statement of the evening before. Only one or two witnesses were called, among whom was Mr. Ellis, who swore positively that in his opinion the prisoner was not the man whom he had seen and at first supposed to be Campbell. The most sensational piece of testimony was that of Dr. Price, who had examined the body, and who swore that the wound in the head was not necessarily fatal, and might have been due to a fall,—that she had more than likely died of shock attendant upon the robbery, she being of advanced age and feeble health. There was no evidence, he said, of any personal violence.

Sandy was not even bound over to the grand jury, but was discharged upon the ground that there was not sufficient evidence upon which to hold him. Upon his release he received the congratulations of many present, some of whom would cheerfully have done him to death a few hours before. With the childish fickleness of a mob, they now experienced a satisfaction almost as great as, though less exciting than, that attendant upon taking life. We speak of the mysteries of inanimate nature. The workings of the human heart are the profoundest mystery of the universe. One moment they make us despair of our kind, and the next we see in them the reflection of the divine image. Sandy, having thus escaped from the Mr. Hyde of the mob, now received the benediction of its Dr. Jekyll. Being no cynical philosopher, and realizing how nearly the jaws of death had closed upon him, he was profoundly grateful for his escape, and felt not the slightest desire to investigate or criticise any man's motives.

With the testimony of Dr. Price, the worst feature of the affair came to an end. The murder eliminated or rendered doubtful, the crime became a mere vulgar robbery, the extent of which no one could estimate, since no living soul knew how much money Mrs. Ochiltree had had in the cedar chest. The absurdity of the remaining charge became more fully apparent in the light of the reaction from the excitement of the day before.

Nothing further was ever done about the case; but though the crime went unpunished, it carried evil in its train. As we have seen, the charge against Campbell had been made against the whole colored race. All over the United States the Associated Press had flashed the report of another dastardly outrage by a burly black brute,—all black brutes it seems are burly,—and of the impending lynching with its prospective horrors. This news, being highly sensational in its character, had been displayed in large black type on the front pages of the daily papers. The dispatch that followed, to the effect that the accused had been found innocent and the lynching frustrated, received slight attention, if any, in a fine-print paragraph on an inside page. The facts of the case never came out at all. The family honor of the Delameres was preserved, and the prestige of the white race in Wellington was not seriously impaired.

Upon leaving the preliminary hearing, old Mr. Delamere had requested General Bemmont to call at his house during the day upon professional business. This the general did in the course of the afternoon.

"Belmont," said Mr. Delamere, "I wish to make my will. I should have drawn it with my own hand; but you know my motives, and can testify to my soundness of mind and memory."

He thereupon dictated a will, by the terms of which he left to his servant, Sandy Campbell, three thousand dollars, as a mark of the testator's appreciation of services rendered and sufferings endured by Sandy on behalf of his master. After some minor dispositions, the whole remainder of the estate was devised to Dr. William Miller, in trust for the uses of his hospital and training-school for nurses, on condition that the institution be incorporated and placed under the management of competent trustees. Tom Delamere was not mentioned in the will.

"There, Belmont," he said, "that load is off my mind. Now, if you will call in some witnesses,—most of my people can write,—I shall feel entirely at ease."

The will was signed by Mr. Delamere, and witnessed by Jeff and Billy, two servants in the house, neither of whom received any information as to its contents, beyond the statement that they were witnessing their master's will.

"I wish to leave that with you for safe keeping, Belmont," said Mr. Delamere, after the witnesses had retired. "Lock it up in your safe until I die, which will not be very long, since I have no further desire to live."

An hour later Mr. Delamere suffered a third paralytic

stroke, from which he died two days afterwards, without having in the meantime recovered the power of speech.

The will was never produced. The servants stated, and General Belmont admitted, that Mr. Delamere had made a will a few days before his death; but since it was not discoverable, it seemed probable that the testator had destroyed it. This was all the more likely, the general was inclined to think, because the will had been of a most unusual character. What the contents of the will were, he of course did not state, it having been made under the seal of professional secrecy.

This suppression was justified by the usual race argument: Miller's hospital was already well established, and, like most negro institutions, could no doubt rely upon Northern philanthropy for any further support it might need. Mr. Delamere's property belonged of right to the white race, and by the higher law should remain in the possession of white people. Loyalty to one's race was a more sacred principle than deference to a weak old man's whims.

Having reached this conclusion, General Belmont's first impulse was to destroy the will; on second thoughts he locked it carefully away in his safe. He would hold it awhile. It might some time be advisable to talk the matter over with young Delamere, who was of a fickle disposition and might wish to change his legal adviser.

CHAPTER XXVIII

In Season and Out

WELLINGTON SOON RESUMED its wonted calm, and in a few weeks the intended lynching was only a memory. The robbery and assault, however, still remained a mystery to all but a chosen few. The affair had been dropped as absolutely as though it had never occurred. No colored man ever learned the reason of this sudden change of front, and Sandy Campbell's loyalty to his old employer's memory kept him silent. Tom Delamere did not offer to retain Sandy in his service, though he presented him with most of the old gentleman's wardrobe. It is only justice to Tom to state that up to this time he had not been informed of the contents of his grandfather's latest will. Major Carteret gave Sandy employment as butler, thus making a sort of vicarious atonement, on the part of the white race, of which the major felt himself in a way the embodiment, for the risk to which Sandy had been subjected.

Shortly after these events Sandy was restored to the bosom of the church, and, enfolded by its sheltering arms, was no longer tempted to stray from the path of rectitude, but became even a more rigid Methodist than before his recent troubles.

Tom Delamere did not call upon Clara again in the character of a lover. Of course they could not help meeting, from time to time, but he never dared presume upon their former relations. Indeed, the social atmosphere of Wellington remained so frigid toward Delamere that he left town, and did not return for several months.

Ellis was aware that Delamere had been thrown over, but a certain delicacy restrained him from following up immediately the advantage which the absence of his former rival gave him. It seemed to him, with the quixotry of a clean, pure mind, that Clara would pass through a period of mourning for her lost illusion, and that it would be indelicate, for the time being, to approach her with a lover's attentions. The work of the office had been unusually heavy of late. The major, deeply absorbed in politics, left the detail work of the paper to Ellis. Into the intimate counsels of the revolutionary committee Ellis had not been admitted, nor would he have desired to be. He knew, of course, in a general way, the results that it was sought to achieve; and while he did not see their necessity, he deferred to the views of older men, and was satisfied to remain in ignorance of anything which he might disapprove. Moreover, his own personal affairs occupied his mind to an extent that made politics or any other subject a matter of minor importance.

As for Dr. Miller, he never learned of Mr. Delamere's good intentions toward his institution, but regretted the old gentleman's death as the loss of a sincere friend and well-wisher of his race in their unequal struggle.

Despite the untiring zeal of Carteret and his associates, the campaign for the restriction of the suffrage, which was to form the basis of a permanent white supremacy, had seemed to languish for a while after the Ochiltree affair. The lull, however, was only temporary, and more apparent than real, for the forces adverse to the negro were merely gathering strength for a more vigorous assault. While little was said in Wellington, public sentiment all over the country became every day more favorable to the views of the conspirators. The nation was rushing forward with giant strides toward colossal wealth and world-dominion, before the exigencies of which mere abstract ethical theories must not be permitted to stand. The same argument that justified the conquest of an inferior nation could not be denied to those who sought the suppression of an inferior race. In the South, an obscure jealousy of the negro's progress, an obscure fear of the very equality so contemptuously denied, furnished a rich soil for successful agitation. Statistics of crime, ingeniously manipulated, were made to present a fearful showing against the negro. Vital statistics were made to prove that he had degenerated from an imaginary standard of physical excellence which had existed under the benign influence of slavery. Constant lynchings emphasized his impotence, and bred everywhere a growing contempt for his rights.

At the North, a new Pharaoh had risen, who knew not Israel,—a new generation, who knew little of the fierce passions which had played around the negro in a past epoch, and derived their opinions of him from the "coon song" and the police reports. Those of his old friends who survived were disappointed that he had not flown with clipped wings; that he had not in one generation of limited opportunity attained the level of the whites. The whole race question seemed to have reached a sort of *impasse*, a blind alley, of which no one could see the outlet. The negro had become a target at which any one might try a shot. Schoolboys gravely debated the question as to whether or not the negro should exercise the franchise. The pessimist gave him up in despair; while the optimist, smilingly confident that everything would come out all right in the end, also turned aside and went his buoyant way to more pleasing themes.

For a time there were white men in the state who opposed any reactionary step unless it were of general application. They were conscientious men, who had learned the ten commandments and wished to do right; but this class was a small minority, and their objections were soon silenced by the all-powerful race argument. Selfishness is the most constant of human motives. Patriotism, humanity, or the love of God may lead to sporadic outbursts which sweep away the heaped-up wrongs of centuries; but they languish at times, while the love of self works on ceaselessly, unwearyingly, burrowing always at the very roots of life, and heaping up fresh wrongs for other centuries to sweep away. The state was at the mercy of venal and self-seeking politicians, bent upon regaining their ascendency at any cost, stultifying their own minds by vague sophistries and high-sounding phrases, which deceived none but those who wished to be deceived, and these but imperfectly; and dulling the public conscience by a loud clamor in which the calm voice of truth was for the moment silenced. So the cause went on.

Carteret, as spokesman of the campaign, and sincerest of all its leaders, performed prodigies of labor. The Morning Chronicle proclaimed, in season and out, the doctrine of "White Supremacy." Leaving the paper in charge of Ellis, the major made a tour of the state, rousing the white people of the better class to an appreciation of the terrible danger which confronted them in the possibility that a few negroes might hold a few offices or dictate the terms upon which white men should fill them. Difficulties were explained away. The provisions of the Federal Constitution, it was maintained, must yield to the "higher law," and if the Constitution could neither be altered nor bent to this end, means must be found to circumvent it.

The device finally hit upon for disfranchising the colored people in this particular state was the notorious "grandfather clause." After providing various restrictions of the suffrage, based upon education, character, and property, which it was deemed would in effect disfranchise the colored race, an exception was made in favor of all citizens whose fathers or grandfathers had been entitled to vote prior to 1867. Since none but white men could vote prior to 1867, this exception obviously took in the poor and ignorant whites, while the same class of negroes were excluded.

It was ingenious, but it was not fair. In due time a constitutional convention was called, in which the above scheme was adopted and submitted to a vote of the people for ratification. The campaign was fought on the color line. Many white Republicans, deluded with the hope that by the elimination of the negro vote their party might receive accessions from the Democratic ranks, went over to the white party. By fraud in one place, by terrorism in another, and everywhere by the resistless moral force of the united whites, the negroes were reduced to the apathy of despair, their few white allies demoralized, and the amendment adopted by a large majority. The negroes were taught that this is a white man's country, and that the sooner they made up their minds to this fact, the better for all concerned. The white people would be good to them so long as they behaved themselves and kept their place. As theoretical equals,—practical equality being forever out of the question, either by nature or by law,—there could have been nothing but strife between them, in which the weaker party would invariably have suffered most.

Some colored men accepted the situation thus outlined, if not as desirable, at least as inevitable. Most of them, however, had little faith in this condescending friendliness which was to take the place of constitutional rights. They knew they had been treated unfairly; that their enemies had prevailed against them; that their whilom friends had stood passively by and seen them undone. Many of the most enterprising and progressive left the state, and those who remain still labor under a sense of wrong and outrage which renders them distinctly less valuable as citizens.

The great steal was made, but the thieves did not turn honest,—the scheme still showed the mark of the burglar's tools. Sins, like chickens, come home to roost. The South paid a fearful price for the wrong of negro slavery; in some form or other it will doubtless reap the fruits of this later iniquity.

Drastic as were these "reforms," the results of which we have anticipated somewhat, since the new Constitution was not to take effect immediately, they moved all too slowly for the little coterie of Wellington conspirators, whose ambitions and needs urged them to prompt action. Under the new Constitution it would be two full years before the "nigger amendment" became effective, and meanwhile the Wellington district would remain hopelessly Republican. The committee decided, about two months before the fall election, that an active local campaign must be carried on, with a view to discourage the negroes from attending the polls on election day.

The question came up for discussion one forenoon in a meeting at the office of the Morning Chronicle, at which all of the "Big Three" were present.

"Something must be done," declared McBane, "and that damn quick. Too many white people are saying that it will be better to wait until the amendment goes into effect. That would mean to leave the niggers in charge of this town for two years after the state has declared for white supremacy! I'm opposed to leaving it in their hands one hour,—them's my sentiments!"

This proved to be the general opinion, and the discussion turned to the subject of ways and means.

"What became of that editorial in the nigger paper?"

inquired the general in his blandest tones, cleverly directing a smoke ring toward the ceiling. "It lost some of its
point back there, when we came near lynching that nigger; but now that that has blown over, why wouldn't it
be a good thing to bring into play at the present junc-
ture? Let's read it over again."

Carteret extracted the paper from the pigeon-hole
where he had placed it some months before. The article
was read aloud with emphasis and discussed phrase by
phrase. Of its wording there could be little criticism,—it
was temperately and even cautiously phrased. As suggested by the general, the Ochiltree affair had proved
that it was not devoid of truth. Its great offensiveness lay
in its boldness: that a negro should publish in a newspaper what white people would scarcely acknowledge to
themselves in secret was much as though a Russian *mou-
jik* or a German peasant should rush into print to question the divine right of the Lord's Anointed. The article
was racial *lèse-majesté* in the most aggravated form. A
peg was needed upon which to hang a *coup d'état*, and
this editorial offered the requisite opportunity. It was
unanimously decided to republish the obnoxious article,
with comment adapted to fire the inflammable Southern
heart and rouse it against any further self-assertion of the
negroes in politics or elsewhere.

"The time is ripe!" exclaimed McBane. "In a month
we can have the niggers so scared that they won't dare
stick their heads out of doors on 'lection day."

"I wonder," observed the general thoughtfully, after
this conclusion had been reached, "if we couldn't have
Jerry fetch us some liquor?"

Jerry appeared in response to the usual summons. The
general gave him the money, and ordered three Calhoun
cocktails. When Jerry returned with the glasses on a tray,
the general observed him with pointed curiosity.

"What in h—ll is the matter with you, Jerry? Your
black face is splotched with brown and yellow patches,
and your hair shines as though you had fallen head-
foremost into a firkin of butter. What's the matter with
you?"

Jerry seemed much embarrassed by this inquiry.

"Nothin', suh, nothin'," he stammered. "It's—it's jes'

somethin' I be'n puttin' on my hair, suh, ter improve de quality, suh."

"Jerry," returned the general, bending a solemn look upon the porter, "you have been playing with edged tools, and your days are numbered. You have been reading the Afro-American Banner."

He shook open the paper, which he had retained in his hand, and read from one of the advertisements:—

" 'Kinky, curly hair made straight in two applications. Dark skins lightened two shades; mulattoes turned perfectly white.'

"This stuff is rank poison, Jerry," continued the general with a mock solemnity which did not impose upon Jerry, who nevertheless listened with an air of great alarm. He suspected that the general was making fun of him; but he also knew that the general would like to think that Jerry believed him in earnest; and to please the white folks was Jerry's consistent aim in life. "I can see the signs of decay in your face, and your hair will all fall out in a week or two at the latest,—mark my words!"

McBane had listened to this pleasantry with a sardonic sneer. It was a waste of valuable time. To Carteret it seemed in doubtful taste. These grotesque advertisements had their tragic side. They were proof that the negroes had read the handwriting on the wall. These pitiful attempts to change their physical characteristics were an acknowledgment, on their own part, that the negro was doomed, and that the white man was to inherit the earth and hold all other races under his heel. For, as the months had passed, Carteret's thoughts, centering more and more upon the negro, had led him farther and farther, until now he was firmly convinced that there was no permanent place for the negro in the United States, if indeed anywhere in the world, except under the ground. More pathetic even than Jerry's efforts to escape from the universal doom of his race was his ignorance that even if he could, by some strange alchemy, bleach his skin and straighten his hair, there would still remain, underneath it all, only the unbleached darky,—the ass in the lion's skin.

When the general had finished his facetious lecture, Jerry backed out of the room shamefacedly, though affecting a greater confusion than he really felt. Jerry had not reasoned so closely as Carteret, but he had realized that it was a distinct advantage to be white,—an advantage which white people had utilized to secure all the best things in the world; and he had entertained the vague hope that by changing his complexion he might share this prerogative. While he suspected the general's sincerity, he nevertheless felt a little apprehensive lest the general's prediction about the effects of the face-bleach and other preparations might prove true,—the general was a white gentleman and ought to know,—and decided to abandon their use.

This purpose was strengthened by his next interview with the major. When Carteret summoned him, an hour later, after the other gentlemen had taken their leave, Jerry had washed his head thoroughly and there remained no trace of the pomade. An attempt to darken the lighter spots in his cuticle by the application of printer's ink had not proved equally successful,—the retouching left the spots as much too dark as they had formerly been too light.

"Jerry," said Carteret sternly, "when I hired you to work for the Chronicle, you were black. The word 'negro' means 'black.' The best negro is a black negro, of the pure type, as it came from the hand of God. If you wish to get along well with the white people, the blacker you are the better,—white people do not like negroes who want to be white. A man should be content to remain as God made him and where God placed him. So no more of this nonsense. Are you going to vote at the next election?"

"What would you 'vise me ter do, suh?" asked Jerry cautiously.

"I do not advise you. You ought to have sense enough to see where your own interests lie. I put it to you whether you cannot trust yourself more safely in the hands of white gentlemen, who are your true friends, than in the hands of ignorant and purchasable negroes and unscrupulous white scoundrels?"

"Dere's no doubt about it, suh," assented Jerry, with a vehemence proportioned to his desire to get back into favor. "I ain' gwine ter have nothin' ter do wid de 'lection, suh! Ef I don' vote, I kin keep my job, can't I, suh?"

The major eyed Jerry with an air of supreme disgust. What could be expected of a race so utterly devoid of tact? It seemed as though this negro thought a white gentleman might want to bribe him to remain away from the polls; and the negro's willingness to accept the imaginary bribe demonstrated the venal nature of the colored, race,—its entire lack of moral principle!

"You will retain your place, Jerry," he said severely, "so long as you perform your duties to my satisfaction and behave yourself properly."

With this grandiloquent subterfuge Carteret turned to his next article on white supremacy. Jerry did not delude himself with any fine-spun sophistry. He knew perfectly well that he held his job upon the condition that he stayed away from the polls at the approaching election. Jerry was a fool—

> "The world of fools hath such a store,
> That he who would not see an ass,
> Must stay at home and shut his door
> And break his looking-glass."

But while no one may be entirely wise, there are degrees of folly, and Jerry was not all kinds of a fool.

CHAPTER XXIX

Mutterings of the Storm

EVENTS MOVED RAPIDLY during the next few days. The reproduction, in the Chronicle, of the article from the Afro-American Banner, with Carteret's inflammatory comment, took immediate effect. It touched the Southern white man in his most sensitive spot. To him such an article was an insult to white womanhood, and must be resented by some active steps,—mere words would be no answer at all. To meet words with words upon such a subject would be to acknowledge the equality of the negro and his right to discuss or criticise the conduct of the white people.

The colored people became alarmed at the murmurings of the whites, which seemed to presage a coming storm. A number of them sought to arm themselves, but ascertained, upon inquiring at the stores, that no white merchant would sell a negro firearms. Since all the dealers in this sort of merchandise were white men, the negroes had to be satisfied with oiling up the old army muskets which some of them possessed, and the few revolvers with which a small rowdy element generally managed to keep themselves supplied. Upon an effort being made to purchase firearms from a Northern city, the express company, controlled by local men, refused to accept the consignment. The white people, on the other hand, procured both arms and ammunition in large quantities, and the Wellington Grays drilled with great assiduity at their armory.

All this went on without any public disturbance of the town's tranquillity. A stranger would have seen nothing to excite his curiosity. The white people did their talking among themselves, and merely grew more distant in their manner toward the colored folks, who instinctively closed their ranks as the whites drew away. With each day that passed the feeling grew more tense. The editor of the Afro-American Banner, whose office had been quietly garrisoned for several nights by armed negroes, became frightened, and disappeared from the town between two suns.

The conspirators were jubilant at the complete success of their plans. It only remained for them to so direct this aroused public feeling that it might completely accomplish the desired end,—to change the political complexion of the city government and assure the ascendency of the whites until the amendment should go into effect. A revolution, and not a riot, was contemplated.

With this end in view, another meeting was called at Carteret's office.

"We are now ready," announced General Belmont, "for the final act of this drama. We must decide promptly, or events may run away from us."

"What do you suggest?" asked Carteret.

"Down in the American tropics," continued the general, "they have a way of doing things. I was in Nicaragua, ten years ago, when Paterno's revolution drove out Igorroto's government. It was as easy as falling off a log. Paterno had the arms and the best men. Igorroto was not looking for trouble, and the guns were at his breast before he knew it. We have the guns. The negroes are not expecting trouble, and are easy to manage compared with the fiery mixture that flourishes in the tropics."

"I should not advocate murder," returned Carteret. "We are animated by high and holy principles. We wish to right a wrong, to remedy an abuse, to save our state from anarchy and our race from humiliation. I don't object to frightening the negroes, but I am opposed to unnecessary bloodshed."

"I'm not quite so particular," struck in McBane. "They need to be taught a lesson, and a nigger more or less wouldn't be missed. There's too many of 'em now."

"Of course," continued Carteret, "if we should decide upon a certain mode of procedure, and the negroes should resist, a different reasoning might apply; but I will have no premeditated murder."

"In Central and South America," observed the general reflectively, "none are hurt except those who get in the way."

"There'll be no niggers hurt," said McBane contemptuously, "unless they strain themselves running. One white man can chase a hundred of 'em. I've managed five hundred at a time. I'll pay for burying all the niggers that are killed."

The conference resulted in a well-defined plan, to be put into operation the following day, by which the city government was to be wrested from the Republicans and their negro allies.

"And now," said General Belmont, "while we are cleansing the Augean stables, we may as well remove the cause as the effect. There are several negroes too many in this town, which will be much the better without them. There's that yellow lawyer, Watson. He's altogether too mouthy, and has too much business. Every nigger that gets into trouble sends for Watson, and white lawyers, with families to support and social positions to keep up, are deprived of their legitimate source of income."

"There's that damn nigger real estate agent," blurted out McBane. "Billy Kitchen used to get most of the nigger business, but this darky has almost driven him to the poorhouse. A white business man is entitled to a living in his own profession and his own home. That nigger don't belong here nohow. He came from the North a year or two ago, and is hand in glove with Barber, the nigger editor, which is enough of itself to damn him. *He'll* have to go!"

"How about the collector of the port?"

"We'd better not touch him. It would bring the government down upon us, which we want to avoid. We don't need to worry about the nigger preachers either. They want to stay here, where the loaves and the fishes are. We can make 'em write letters to the newspapers justifying our course, as a condition of their remaining."

"What about Billings?" asked McBane. Billings was the white Republican mayor. "Is that skunk to be allowed to stay in town?"

"No," returned the general, "every white Republican office-holder ought to be made to go. This town is only big enough for Democrats, and negroes who can be taught to keep their place."

"What about the colored doctor," queried McBane,

"with the hospital, and the diamond ring, and the carriage, and the other fallals?"

"I shouldn't interfere with Miller," replied the general decisively. "He's a very good sort of a negro, doesn't meddle with politics, nor tread on any one else's toes. His father was a good citizen, which counts in his favor. He's spending money in the community too, and contributes to its prosperity."

"That sort of nigger, though, sets a bad example," retorted McBane. "They make it all the harder to keep the rest of 'em down."

" 'One swallow does not make a summer,' " quoted the general. "When we get things arranged, there'll be no trouble. A stream cannot rise higher than its fountain, and a smart nigger without a constituency will no longer be an object of fear. I say, let the doctor alone."

"He'll have to keep mighty quiet, though," muttered McBane discontentedly. "I don't like smart niggers. I've had to shoot several of them in the course of my life."

"Personally, I dislike the man," interposed Carteret, "and if I consulted my own inclinations, would say expel him with the rest; but my grievance is a personal one, and to gratify it in that way would be a loss to the community. I wish to be strictly impartial in this matter, and to take no step which cannot be entirely justified by a wise regard for the public welfare."

"What's the use of all this hypocrisy, gentlemen?" sneered McBane. "Every last one of us has an axe to grind! The major may as well put an edge on his. We'll never get a better chance to have things our way. If this nigger doctor annoys the major, we'll run him out with the rest. This is a white man's country, and a white man's city, and no nigger has any business here when a white man wants him gone!"

Carteret frowned darkly at this brutal characterization of their motives. It robbed the enterprise of all its poetry, and put a solemn act of revolution upon the plane of a mere vulgar theft of power. Even the general winced.

"I would not consent," he said irritably, "to Miller's being disturbed."

McBane made no further objection.

There was a discreet knock at the door.

"Come in," said Carteret.

Jerry entered. "Mistuh Ellis wants ter speak ter you a minute, suh," he said.

Carteret excused himself and left the room.

"Jerry," said the general, "you lump of ebony, the sight of you reminds me! If your master doesn't want you for a minute, step across to Mr. Brown's and tell him to send me three cocktails."

"Yas, suh," responded Jerry, hesitating. The general had said nothing about paying.

"And tell him, Jerry, to charge them. I'm short on change to-day."

"Yas, suh; yas, suh," replied Jerry, as he backed out of the presence, adding, when he had reached the hall: "Dere ain' no change fer Jerry dis time, sho': I'll jes' make dat *fo'* cocktails, an' de gin'l won't never know de diffe'nce. I ain' gwine 'cross de road fer nothin', not ef I knows it."

Half an hour later, the conspirators dispersed. They had fixed the hour of the proposed revolution, the course to be pursued, the results to be obtained; but in stating their equation they had overlooked one factor,—God, or Fate, or whatever one may choose to call the Power that holds the destinies of man in the hollow of his hand.

CHAPTER XXX

The Missing Papers

MRS. CARTERET WAS very much disturbed. It was supposed that the shock of her aunt's death had affected her health, for since that event she had fallen into a nervous condition which gave the major grave concern. Much to the general surprise, Mrs. Ochiltree had left no will, and no property of any considerable value except her homestead, which descended to Mrs. Carteret as the natural heir. Whatever she may have had on hand in the way of ready money had undoubtedly been abstracted from the cedar chest by the midnight marauder, to whose visit her death was immediately due. Her niece's grief was held to mark a deep-seated affection for the grim old woman who had reared her.

Mrs. Carteret's present state of mind, of which her nervousness was a sufficiently accurate reflection, did in truth date from her aunt's death, and also in part from the time of the conversation which Mrs. Ochiltree, one afternoon, during and after the drive past Miller's new hospital. Mrs. Ochiltree had grown steadily more and more childish after that time, and her niece had never succeeded in making her pick up the thread of thought where it had been dropped. At any rate, Mrs. Ochiltree had made no further disclosure upon the subject.

An examination, not long after her aunt's death, of the papers found near the cedar chest on the morning after the murder had contributed to Mrs. Carteret's enlightenment, but had not promoted her peace of mind.

When Mrs. Carteret reached home, after her hurried exploration of the cedar chest, she thrust into a bureau drawer the envelope she had found. So fully was her mind occupied, for several days, with the funeral, and with the excitement attending the arrest of Sandy Campbell, that she deferred the examination of the contents of the envelope until near the end of the week.

One morning, while alone in her chamber, she drew the envelope from the drawer, and was holding it in her hand, hesitating as to whether or not she should open it, when the baby in the next room began to cry.

The child's cry seemed like a warning, and yielding to a vague uneasiness, she put the paper back.

"Phil," she said to her husband at luncheon, "Aunt Polly said some strange things to me one day before she died,—I don't know whether she was quite in her right mind or not; but suppose that my father had left a will by which it was provided that half his property should go to that woman and her child?"

"It would never have gone by such a will," replied the major easily. "Your Aunt Polly was in her dotage, and merely dreaming. Your father would never have been such a fool; but even if he had, no such will could have stood the test of the courts. It would clearly have been due to the improper influence of a designing woman."

"So that legally, as well as morally," said Mrs. Carteret, "the will would have been of no effect?"

"Not the slightest. A jury would soon have broken down the legal claim. As for any moral obligation, there would have been nothing moral about the affair. The only possible consideration for such a gift was an immoral one. I don't wish to speak harshly of your father, my dear, but his conduct was gravely reprehensible. The woman herself had no right or claim whatever; she would have been whipped and expelled from the town, if justice—blind, bleeding justice, then prostrate at the feet of slaves and aliens—could have had her way!"

"But the child"—

"The child was in the same category. Who was she, to have inherited the estate of your ancestors, of which, a few years before, she would herself have formed a part? The child of shame, it was hers to pay the penalty. But the discussion is all in the air, Olivia. Your father never did and never would have left such a will."

This conversation relieved Mrs. Carteret's uneasiness. Going to her room shortly afterwards, she took the envelope from her bureau drawer and drew out a bulky paper. The haunting fear that it might be such a will as her aunt had suggested was now removed; for such an instrument, in the light of what her husband had said confirming her own intuitions, would be of no valid effect. It might be just as well, she thought, to throw the paper in the fire without looking at it. She wished to think as well as might be of her father, and she felt that her respect for his memory would not be strengthened by the knowledge that he had meant to leave his estate away from her; for her aunt's words had been open to the construction that she was to have been left destitute. Curiosity strongly prompted her to read the paper. Perhaps the will contained no such provision as she had feared, and it might convey some request or direction which ought properly to be complied with.

She had been standing in front of the bureau while these thoughts passed through her mind, and now, dropping the envelope back into the drawer mechanically, she unfolded the document. It was written on legal paper, in her father's own hand.

Mrs. Carteret was not familiar with legal verbiage, and there were several expressions of which she did not perhaps appreciate the full effect; but a very hasty glance enabled her to ascertain the purport of the paper. It was a will, by which, in one item, her father devised to his daughter Janet, the child of the woman known as Julia Brown, the sum of ten thousand dollars, and a certain plantation or tract of land a short distance from the town of Wellington. The rest and residue of his estate, after deducting all legal charges and expenses, was bequeathed to his beloved daughter, Olivia Merkell.

Mrs. Carteret breathed a sigh of relief. Her father had not preferred another to her, but had left to his lawful daughter the bulk of his estate. She felt at the same time a growing indignation at the thought that that woman should so have wrought upon her father's weakness as to induce him to think of leaving so much valuable property to her bastard,—property which by right should go, and now would go, to her own son, to whom by every rule of law and decency it ought to descend.

A fire was burning in the next room, on account of the baby,—there had been a light frost the night before, and the air was somewhat chilly. For the moment the room was empty. Mrs. Carteret came out from her chamber and threw the offending paper into the fire, and watched it slowly burn. When it had been consumed, the carbon residue of one sheet still retained its form, and she could read the words on the charred portion. A sentence, which had escaped her eye in her rapid reading, stood out in ghostly black upon the gray background:—

"All the rest and residue of my estate I devise and bequeath to my daughter Olivia Merkell, the child of my beloved first wife."

Mrs. Carteret had not before observed the word "first." Instinctively she stretched toward the fire the poker which she held in her hand, and at its touch the shadowy remnant fell to pieces, and nothing but ashes remained upon the hearth.

Not until the next morning did she think again of the envelope which had contained the paper she had burned. Opening the drawer where it lay, the oblong blue envelope confronted her. The sight of it was distasteful. The indorsed side lay uppermost, and the words seemed like a mute reproach:—

"The Last Will and Testament of Samuel Merkell."

Snatching up the envelope, she glanced into it mechanically as she moved toward the next room, and perceived a thin folded paper which had heretofore escaped her notice. When opened, it proved to be a certificate of marriage, in due form, between Samuel Merkell and Julia Brown. It was dated from a county in South Carolina, about two years before her father's death.

For a moment Mrs. Carteret stood gazing blankly at this faded slip of paper. Her father *had* married this women!—at least he had gone through the form of marriage with her, for to him it had surely been no more than an empty formality. The marriage of white and colored persons was forbidden by law. Only recently she had read of a case where both the parties to such a crime, a colored man and a white woman, had been sentenced to long terms in the penitentiary. She even recalled the circumstances. The couple had been living together unlawfully,—they were very low people, whose private lives were beneath the public notice,—but influenced by a religious movement pervading the community, had sought, they said at the trial, to secure the blessing of God upon their union. The higher law, which imperiously demanded that the purity and prestige of the white race be preserved at any cost, had intervened at this point.

Mechanically she moved toward the fireplace, so dazed by this discovery as to be scarcely conscious of her own actions. She surely had not formed any definite intention of destroying this piece of paper when her fingers relaxed unconsciously and let go their hold upon it. The draught swept it toward the fireplace. Ere scarcely touching the flames it caught, blazed fiercely, and shot upward with the current of air. A moment later the record of poor Julia's marriage was scattered to the four winds of heaven, as her poor body had long since mingled with the dust of earth.

The letter remained unread. In her agitation at the discovery of the marriage certificate, Olivia had almost forgotten the existence of the letter. It was addressed to "John Delamere, Esq., as Executor of my Last Will and Testament," while the lower left-hand corner bore the direction: "To be delivered only after my death, with seal unbroken."

The seal was broken already; Mr. Delamere was dead; the letter could never be delivered. Mrs. Carteret unfolded it and read:—

MY DEAR DELAMERE,—I have taken the liberty of naming you as executor of my last will, because you are my friend, and the only man of my acquaintance whom I feel that I can trust to carry out my wishes, appreciate my motives, and preserve the silence I desire.

I have, first, a confession to make. Inclosed in this letter you will find a certificate of marriage between my child Janet's mother and myself. While I have never exactly repented of this marriage, I have never had the courage to acknowledge it openly. If I had not married Julia, I fear Polly Ochiltree would have married me by main force,—as she would marry you or any other gentleman unfortunate enough to fall in the way of this twice-widowed man-hunter. When my wife died, three years ago, her sister Polly offered to keep house for me and the child. I would sooner have had the devil in the house, and yet I trembled with alarm,—there seemed no way of escape,—it was so clearly and obviously the proper thing.

But she herself gave me my opportunity. I was on the point of consenting, when she demanded, as a condition of her coming, that I discharge Julia, my late wife's maid. She was laboring under a misapprehension in regard to the girl, but I grasped at the straw, and did everything to foster her delusion. I declared solemnly that nothing under heaven would induce me to part with Julia. The controversy resulted in my permitting Polly to take the chid, while I retained the maid.

Before Polly put this idea into my head, I had scarcely looked at Julia, but this outbreak turned my attention toward her. She was a handsome girl, and, as I soon found out, a good girl. My wife, who raised her, was a Christian woman, and had taught her modesty and virtue. She was free. The air was full of liberty, and equal rights, and all the abolition claptrap, and she made marriage a condition of her remaining longer in the house. In a moment of weakness I took her away to a place where we were not known, and married her. If she had left me, I should have fallen a victim to Polly Ochiltree,—to which any fate was preferable.

And then, old friend, my weakness kept to the fore. I was ashamed of this marriage, and my new wife saw it. Moreover, she loved me,—too well, indeed, to wish to make me unhappy. The ceremony had satisfied her conscience, had set her right, she said, with God; for the opinions of men she did not care, since I loved her,—she only wanted to compensate me, as best she could, for the great honor I had done my handmaiden,—for she had read her Bible, and I was the Abraham to her Hagar, compared with whom she considered herself at a great advantage. It was her own proposition that nothing be said of this marriage. If any shame should fall on her, it would fall lightly, for it would be undeserved. When the child came, she still kept silence. No one, she argued, could blame an innocent child for the accident of birth, and in the sight of God this child had every right to exist; while among her own people illegitimacy would involve but little stigma.

I need not say that I was easily persuaded to accept this sacrifice; but touched by her fidelity, I swore to provide handsomely for them both. This I have tried to do by the will of which I ask you to act as executor. Had I left the child more, it might serve as a ground for attacking the will; my acknowledgment of the tie of blood is sufficient to justify a reasonable bequest.

I have taken this course for the sake of my daughter Olivia, who is dear to me, and whom I would not wish to make ashamed; and in deference to public opinion, which it is not easy to defy. If, after my death, Julia should choose to make our secret known, I shall of course be beyond the reach of hard words; but loyalty to my memory will probably keep her silent. A strong man would long since have acknowledged her before the world and taken the consequences; but, alas! I am only myself, and the atmosphere I live in does not encourage moral heroism. I should like to be different, but it is God who hath made us, and not we ourselves!

Nevertheless, old friend, I will ask of you one favor. If in the future this child of Julia's and of mine should grow to womanhood; if she should prove to have her mother's gentleness and love of virtue; if, in the new era which is opening up for her mother's race, to which, unfortunately, she must belong, she should become, in time, an educated woman; and if the time should ever come when, by virtue of her education or the development of her people, it would be to her a source of shame or unhappiness that she was an illegitimate child,—if you are still alive, old friend, and have the means of knowing or divining this thing, go to her and tell her, for me, that she is my lawful child, and ask her to forgive her father's weakness.

When this letter comes to you, I shall have passed to—the Beyond; but I am confident that you will accept this trust, for which I thank you now, in advance, most heartily.

The letter was signed with her father's name, the same signature which had been attached to the will.

Having firmly convinced herself of the illegality of the papers, and of her own right to destroy them, Mrs. Carteret ought to have felt relieved that she had thus removed all traces of her dead father's folly. True, the other daughter remained,—she had seen her on the street only the day before. The sight of this person she had always found offensive, and now, she felt, in view of what she had just learned, it must be even more so. Never, while this woman lived in the town, would she be able to throw the veil of forgetfulness over this blot upon her father's memory.

As the day wore on, Mrs. Carteret grew still less at ease. To herself, marriage was a serious thing,—to a right-thinking woman the most serious concern of life. A marriage certificate, rightfully procured, was scarcely less solemn, so far as it went, than the Bible itself. Her own she cherished as the apple of her eye. It was the evidence of her wifehood, the seal of her child's legitimacy, her patent of nobility,—the token of her own and her child's claim to social place and consideration. She had burned this pretended marriage certificate because it meant nothing. Nevertheless, she could not ignore the knowledge of another such marriage, of which every one in the town knew,—a celebrated case, indeed, where a white man, of a family quite as prominent as her father's, had married a colored woman during the military occupation of the state just after the civil war. The legality of the marriage had never been questioned. It had been fully consummated by twenty years of subsequent cohabitation. No amount of social persecution had ever shaken the position of the husband. With an iron will he had stayed on in the town, a living protest against the established customs of the South, so rudely interrupted for a few short years; and, though his children were negroes, though he had never appeared in public with his wife, no one had ever questioned the validity of his marriage or the legitimacy of his offspring.

The marriage certificate which Mrs. Carteret had burned dated from the period of the military occupation. Hence Mrs. Carteret, who was a good woman, and would not have done a dishonest thing, felt decidedly uncomfortable. She had destroyed the marriage certificate, but its ghost still haunted her.

Major Carteret, having just eaten a good dinner, was in a very agreeable humor when, that same evening, his wife brought up again the subject of their previous discussion.

"Phil," she asked, "Aunt Polly told me that once, long before my father died, when she went to remonstrate with him for keeping that woman in the house, he threatened to marry Julia if Aunt Polly ever said another word to him about the matter. Suppose he *had* married her, and had *then* left a will,—would the marriage have made any difference, so far as the will was concerned?"

Major Carteret laughed. "Your Aunt Polly," he said, "was a remarkable woman, with a wonderful imagination, which seems to have grown more vivid as her memory and judgment weakened. Why should your father marry his negro housemaid? Mr. Merkell was never rated as a fool,—he had one of the clearest heads in Wellington. I saw him only a day or two before he died, and I could swear before any court in Christendom that he was of sound mind and memory to the last. These notions of your aunt were mere delusions. Your father was never capable of such a folly."

"Of course I am only supposing a case," returned Olivia. "Imagining such a case, just for the argument, would the marriage have been legal?"

"That would depend. If he had married her during the military occupation, or over in South Carolina, the marriage would have been legally valid, though morally and socially outrageous."

"And if he had died afterwards, leaving a will?"

"The will would have controlled the disposition of his estate, in all probability."

"Suppose he had left no will?"

"You are getting the matter down pretty fine, my dear! The woman would have taken one third of the real estate for life, and could have lived in the homestead until she died. She would also have had half the other property,— the money and goods and furniture, everything except the land,—and the negro child would have shared with you the balance of the estate. That, I believe, is according to the law of descent and distribution."

Mrs. Carteret lapsed into a troubled silence. Her father *had* married the woman. In her heart she had no doubt of the validity of the marriage, so far as the law was concerned; if one marriage of such a kind would stand, another contracted under similar conditions was equally as good. If the marriage had been valid, Julia's child had been legitimate. The will she had burned gave this sister of hers—she shuddered at the word—but a small part of the estate. Under the law, which intervened now that there was no will, the property should have been equally divided. If the woman had been white,—but the woman had *not* been white, and the same rule of moral conduct did not, *could* not, in the very nature of things, apply, as between white people! For, if this were not so, slavery had been, not merely an economic mistake, but a great crime against humanity. If it had been such a crime, as for a moment she dimly perceived it might have been, then through the long centuries there had been piled up a catalogue of wrong and outrage which, if the law of compensation be a law of nature, must some time, somewhere, in some way, be atoned for. She herself had not escaped the penalty, of which, she realized, this burden placed upon her conscience was but another installment.

If she should make known the facts she had learned, it would mean what?—a division of her father's estate, a recognition of the legality of her father's relations with Julia. Such a stain upon her father's memory would be infinitely worse than if he had not married her. To have lived with her without marriage was a social misdemeanor, at which society in the old days had winked, or at most had frowned. To have married her was to have committed the unpardonable social sin. Such a scandal Mrs. Carteret could not have endured. Should she seek to make restitution, it would necessarily involve the disclosure of at least some of the facts. Had she not destroyed the will, she might have compromised with her conscience by producing it and acting upon its terms, which had been so stated as not to disclose the marriage. This was now rendered impossible by her own impulsive act; she could not mention the will at all, without admitting that she had destroyed it.

Mrs. Carteret found herself in what might be called, vulgarly, a moral "pocket." She could, of course, remain silent. Mrs. Carteret was a good woman, according to her lights, with a cultivated conscience, to which she had always looked as her mentor and infallible guide.

Hence Mrs. Carteret, after this painful discovery, remained for a long time ill at ease,—so disturbed, indeed, that her mind reacted upon her nerves, which had never been strong; and her nervousness affected her strength, which had never been great, until Carteret, whose love for her had been deepened and strengthened by the advent of his son, became alarmed for her health, and spoke very seriously to Dr. Price concerning it.

CHAPTER XXXI

The Shadow of a Dream

MRS. CARTERET AWOKE, with a start, from a troubled dream. She had been sailing across a sunlit sea, in a beautiful boat, her child lying on a bright-colored cushion at her feet. Overhead the swelling sail served as an awning to keep off the sun's rays, which far ahead were reflected with dazzling brilliancy from the shores of a golden island. Her son, she dreamed, was a fairy prince, and yonder lay his kingdom, to which he was being borne, lying there at her feet, in this beautiful boat, across the sunlit sea.

Suddenly and without warning the sky was overcast. A squall struck the boat and tore away the sail. In the distance a huge billow—a great white wall of water—came sweeping toward their frail craft, threatening it with instant destruction. She clasped her child to her bosom, and a moment later found herself struggling in the sea, holding the child's head above the water. As she floated there, as though sustained by some unseen force, she saw in the distance a small boat approaching over the storm-tossed waves. Straight toward her it came, and she had reached out her hand to grasp its side, when the rower looked back, and she saw that it was her sister. The recognition had been mutual. With a sharp movement of one oar the boat glided by, leaving her clutching at the empty air.

She felt her strength begin to fail. Despairingly she signaled with her disengaged hand; but the rower, after one mute, reproachful glance, rowed on. Mrs. Carteret's strength grew less and less. The child became heavy as lead. Herself floating in the water, as though it were her native element, she could no longer support the child. Lower and lower it sank,—she was powerless to save it or to accompany it,—until, gasping wildly for breath, it threw up its little hands and sank, the cruel water gurgling over its head,—when she awoke with a start and a chill, and lay there trembling for several minutes before she heard little Dodie in his crib, breathing heavily.

She rose softly, went to the crib, and changed the child's position to an easier one. He breathed more freely, and she went back to bed, but not to sleep.

She had tried to put aside the distressing questions raised by the discovery of her father's will and the papers accompanying it. Why should she be burdened with such a responsibility, at this late day, when the touch of time had well-nigh healed these old sores? Surely, God had put his curse not alone upon the slave, but upon the stealer of men! With other good people she had thanked Him that slavery was no more, and that those who once had borne its burden upon their consciences could stand erect and feel that they themselves were free. The weed had been cut down, but its roots remained, deeply imbedded in the soil, to spring up and trouble a new generation. Upon her weak shoulders was placed the burden of her father's weakness, her father's folly. It was left to her to acknowledge or not this shameful marriage and her sister's rights in their father's estate.

Balancing one consideration against another, she had almost decided that she might ignore this tie. To herself, Olivia Merkell,—Olivia Carteret,—the stigma of base birth would have meant social ostracism, social ruin, the averted face, the finger of pity or of scorn. All the traditional weight of public disapproval would have fallen upon her as the unhappy fruit of an unblessed union. To this other woman it could have had no such significance,—it had been the lot of her race. To them, twenty-five years before, sexual sin had never been imputed as more than a fault. She had lost nothing by her supposed illegitimacy; she would gain nothing by the acknowledgment of her mother's marriage.

On the other hand, what would be the effect of this revelation upon Mrs. Carteret herself? To have it known that her father had married a negress would only be less dreadful than to have it appear that he had committed some terrible crime. It was a crime now, by the laws of every Southern State, for white and colored persons to intermarry. She shuddered before the possibility that at some time in the future some person, none too well informed, might learn that her father had married a colored woman, and might assume that she, Olivia Carteret, or her child, had sprung from this shocking *mésalliance*,—a fate to which she would willingly have preferred death. No, this marriage must never be made known; the secret should remain buried forever in her own heart!

But there still remained the question of her father's property and her father's will. This woman was her father's child,—of that there could be no doubt, it was written in her features no less than in her father's will. As his lawful child,—of which, alas! there could also be no question,—she was entitled by law to half his estate. Mrs. Carteret's problem had sunk from the realm of sentiment to that of material things, which, curiously enough, she found much more difficult. For, while the negro, by the traditions of her people, was barred from the world of sentiment, his rights of property were recognized. The question had become, with Mrs. Carteret, a question of *meum* and *tuum*. Had the girl Janet been poor, ignorant, or degraded, as might well have been her fate, Mrs. Carteret might have felt a vicarious remorse for her aunt's suppression of the papers; but fate had compensated Janet for the loss; she had been educated, she had married well; she had not suffered for lack of the money of which she had been defrauded, and did not need it now. She had a child, it is true, but this child's career would be so circumscribed by the accident of color that too much wealth would only be a source of unhappiness; to her own child, on the contrary, it would open every door of life.

It would be too lengthy a task to follow the mind and conscience of this much-tried lady in their intricate workings upon this difficult problem; for she had a mind as logical as any woman's, and a conscience which she wished to keep void of offense. She had to confront a situation involving the element of race, upon which the moral standards of her people were hopelessly confused. Mrs. Carteret reached the conclusion, ere daylight dawned, that she would be silent upon the subject of her father's second marriage. Neither party had wished it known,—neither Julia nor her father,—and she would respect her father's wishes. To act otherwise would be to defeat his will, to make known what he had carefully concealed, and to give Janet a claim of title to one half her father's estate, while he had only meant her to have the ten thousand dollars named in the will.

By the same reasoning, she must carry out her father's will in respect to this bequest. Here there was another difficulty. The mining investment into which they had entered shortly after the birth of little Dodie had tied up so much of her property that it would have been difficult to procure ten thousand dollars immediately; while a demand for half the property at once would mean bankruptcy and ruin. Moreover, upon what ground could she offer her sister any sum of money whatever? So sudden a change of heart, after so many years of silence, would raise the presumption of some right on the part of Janet in her father's estate. Suspicion once aroused, it might be possible to trace this hidden marriage, and establish it by legal proof. The marriage once verified, the claim for half the estate could not be denied. She could not plead her father's will to the contrary, for this would be to acknowledge the suppression of the will, in itself a criminal act.

There was, however, a way of escape. This hospital which had recently been opened was the personal property of her sister's husband. Some time in the future, when their investments matured, she would present to the hospital a sum of money equal to the amount her father had meant his colored daughter to have. Thus indirectly both her father's will and her own conscience would be satisfied.

Mrs. Carteret had reached this comfortable conclusion, and was falling asleep, when her attention was again drawn by her child's breathing. She took it in her own arms and soon fell asleep.

"By the way, Olivia," said the major, when leaving the house next morning for the office, "if you have any business down town to-day, transact it this forenoon. Under no circumstances must you or Clara or the baby leave the house after midday."

"Why, what's the matter, Phil?"

"Nothing to alarm you, except that there may be a little political demonstration which may render the streets unsafe. You are not to say anything about it where the servants might hear."

"Will there be any danger for you, Phil?" she demanded with alarm.

"Not the slightest, Olivia dear. No one will be harmed; but it is best for ladies and children to stay indoors."

Mrs. Carteret's nerves were still more or less unstrung from her mental struggles of the night, and the memory of her dream came to her like a dim foreboding of misfortune. As though in sympathy with its mother's feelings, the baby did not seem as well as usual. The new nurse was by no means an ideal nurse,—Mammy Jane understood the child much better. If there should be any trouble with the negroes, toward which her husband's remark seemed to point,—she knew the general political situation, though not informed in regard to her husband's plans,—she would like to have Mammy Jane near her, where the old nurse might be protected from danger or alarm.

With this end in view she dispatched the nurse, shortly after breakfast, to Mammy Jane's house in the negro settlement on the other side of the town, with a message asking the old woman to come immediately to Mrs. Carteret's. Unfortunately, Mammy Jane had gone to visit a sick woman in the country, and was not expected to return for several hours.

CHAPTER XXXII

The Storm Breaks

THE WELLINGTON RIOT began at three o'clock in the afternoon of a day as fair as was ever selected for a deed of darkness. The sky was clear, except for a few light clouds that floated, white and feathery, high in air, like distant islands in a sapphire sea. A salt-laden breeze from the ocean a few miles away lent a crisp sparkle to the air.

At three o'clock sharp the streets were filled, as if by magic, with armed white men. The negroes, going about, had noted, with uneasy curiosity, that the stores and places of business, many of which closed at noon, were unduly late in opening for the afternoon, though no one suspected the reason for the delay; but at three o'clock every passing colored man was ordered, by the first white man he met, to throw up his hands. If he complied, he was searched, more or less roughly, for firearms, and then warned to get off the street. When he met another group of white men the scene was repeated. The man thus summarily held up seldom encountered more than two groups before disappearing across lots to his own home or some convenient hiding-place. If he resisted any demand of those who halted him— But the records of the day are historical; they may be found in the newspapers of the following date, but they are more firmly engraved upon the hearts and memories of the people of Wellington. For many months there were negro families in the town whose children screamed with fear and ran to their mothers for protection at the mere sight of a white man.

Dr. Miller had received a call, about one o'clock, to attend a case at the house of a well-to-do colored farmer, who lived some three or four miles from the town, upon the very road, by the way, along which Miller had driven so furiously a few weeks before, in the few hours that intervened before Sandy Campbell would probably have been burned at the stake. The drive to his patient's home, the necessary inquiries, the filling of the prescription from his own medicine-case, which he carried along with him, the little friendly conversation about the weather and the crops, and, the farmer being an intelligent and thinking man, the inevitable subject of the future of their race,—these, added to the return journey, occupied at least two hours of Miller's time.

As he neared the town on his way back, he saw ahead of him half a dozen men and women approaching, with fear written in their faces, in every degree from apprehension to terror. Women were weeping and children crying, and all were going as fast as seemingly lay in their power, looking behind now and then as if pursued by some deadly enemy. At sight of Miller's buggy they made a dash for cover, disappearing, like a covey of frightened partridges, in the underbrush along the road.

Miller pulled up his horse and looked after them in startled wonder.

"What on earth can be the matter?" he muttered, struck with a vague feeling of alarm. A psychologist, seeking to trace the effects of slavery upon the human mind, might find in the South many a curious illustration of this curse, abiding long after the actual physical bondage had terminated. In the olden time the white South labored under the constant fear of negro insurrections. Knowing that they themselves, if in the negroes' place, would have risen in the effort to throw off the yoke, all their reiterated theories of negro subordination and inferiority could not remove that lurking fear, founded upon the obscure consciousness that the slaves ought to have risen. Conscience, it has been said, makes cowards of us all. There was never, on the continent of America, a successful slave revolt, nor one which lasted more than a few hours, or resulted in the loss of more than a few white lives; yet never was the planter quite free from the fear that there might be one.

On the other hand, the slave had before his eyes always the fear of the master. There were good men, according to their lights,—according to their training and environment,—among the Southern slaveholders, who treated their slaves kindly, as slaves, from principle, because they recognized the claims of humanity, even under the dark skin of a human chattel. There was many a one who protected or pampered his negroes, as the case might be, just as a man fondles his dog,—because they were his; they were a part of his estate, an integral part of the entity of property and person which made up the aristocrat; but with all this kindness, there was always present, in the consciousness of the lowest slave, the knowledge that he was in his master's power, and that he could make no effectual protest against the abuse of that authority. There was also the knowledge, among those who could think at all, that the best of masters was himself a slave to a system, which hampered his movements but scarcely less than those of his bondmen.

When, therefore, Miller saw these men and women scampering into the bushes, he divined, with this slumbering race consciousness which years of culture had not obliterated, that there was some race trouble on foot. His intuition did not long remain unsupported. A black head was cautiously protruded from the shrubbery, and a black voice—if such a description be allowable—addressed him:—

"Is dat you, Doctuh Miller?"

"Yes. Who are you, and what's the trouble?"

"What's de trouble, suh? Why, all hell's broke loose in town yonduh. De w'ite folks is riz 'gins' de niggers, an' say dey 're gwine ter kill eve'y nigger dey kin lay han's on."

Miller's heart leaped to his throat, as he thought of his wife and child. This story was preposterous; it could not be true, and yet there must be something in it. He tried to question his informant, but the man was so overcome with excitement and fear that Miller saw clearly that he must go farther for information. He had read in the Morning Chronicle, a few days before, the obnoxious editorial quoted from the Afro-American Banner, and had noted the comment upon it by the white editor. He had felt, as at the time of its first publication, that the editorial was ill-advised. It could do no good, and was calculated to arouse the animosity of those whose friendship, whose tolerance, at least, was necessary and almost indispensable to the colored people. They were living at the best, in a sort of armed neutrality with the whites; such a publication, however serviceable elsewhere, could have no other effect in Wellington than to endanger this truce and defeat the hope of a possible future friendship. The right of free speech entitled Barber to publish it; a larger measure of common-sense would have made him withhold it. Whether it was the republication of this article that had stirred up anew the sleeping dogs of race prejudice and whetted their thirst for blood, he could not yet tell; but at any rate, there was mischief on foot.

"Fer God's sake, doctuh, don' go no closeter ter dat town," pleaded his informant, "er you'll be killt sho'. Come on wid us, suh, an' tek keer er yo'se'f. We're gwine ter hide in de swamps till dis thing is over!"

"God, man!" exclaimed Miller, urging his horse forward, "my wife and child are in the town!"

Fortunately, he reflected, there were no patients confined in the hospital,—if there should be anything in this preposterous story. To one unfamiliar with Southern life, it might have seemed impossible that these good Christian people, who thronged the churches on Sunday, and wept over the sufferings of the lowly Nazarene, and sent missionaries to the heathen, could be hungering and thirsting for the blood of their fellow men; but Miller cherished no such delusion. He knew the history of his country; he had the threatened lynching of Sandy Campbell vividly in mind; and he was fully persuaded that to race prejudice, once roused, any horror was possible. That women or children would be molested of set purpose he did not believe, but that they might suffer by accident was more than likely.

As he neared the town, dashing forward at the top of his horse's speed, he heard his voice called in a loud and agitated tone, and, glancing around him, saw a familiar form standing by the roadside, gesticulating vehemently.

He drew up the horse with a suddenness that threw the faithful and obedient animal back upon its haunches. The colored lawyer, Watson, came up to the buggy. That he was laboring under great and unusual excitement was quite apparent from his pale face and frightened air.

"What's the matter, Watson?" demanded Miller, hoping now to obtain some reliable information.

"Matter!" exclaimed the other. "Everything's the mat-

ter! The white people are up in arms. They have disarmed the colored people, killing half a dozen in the
process, and wounding as many more. They have forced
the mayor and aldermen to resign, have formed a provisional city government à la française, and have ordered
me and half a dozen other fellows to leave town in forty-
eight hours, under pain of sudden death. As they seem
to mean it, I shall not stay so long. Fortunately, my wife
and children are away. I knew you were out here, however, and I thought I'd come out and wait for you, so
that we might talk the matter over. I don't imagine they
mean you any harm, personally, because you tread on
nobody's toes; but you're too valuable a man for the race
to lose, so I thought I'd give you warning. I shall want
to sell you my property, too, at a bargain. For I'm worth
too much to my family to dream of ever attempting to
live here again."

"Have you seen anything of my wife and child?" asked
Miller, intent upon the danger to which they might be
exposed.

"No; I didn't go to the house. I inquired at the drug-
store and found out where you had gone. You needn't
fear for them,—it is not a war on women and children."

"War of any kind is always hardest on the women and
children," returned Miller; "I must hurry on and see that
mine are safe."

"They'll not carry the war so far into Africa as that,"
returned Watson; "but I never saw anything like it. Yesterday I had a hundred white friends in the town, or
thought I had,—men who spoke pleasantly to me on the
street, and sometimes gave me their hands to shake. Not
one of them said to me to-day: 'Watson, stay at home
this afternoon.' I might have been killed, like any one of
half a dozen others who have bit the dust, for any word
that one of my 'friends' had said to warn me. When the
race cry is started in this neck of the woods, friendship,
religion, humanity, reason, all shrivel up like dry leaves
in a raging furnace."

The buggy, into which Watson had climbed, was meanwhile rapidly nearing the town.

"I think I'll leave you here, Miller," said Watson, as
they approached the outskirts, "and make my way home
by a roundabout path, as I should like to get there unmo-

lested. Home!—a beautiful word that, isn't it, for an ex-
iled wanderer? It might not be well, either, for us to be
seen together. If you put the hood of your buggy down,
and sit well back in the shadow, you may be able to
reach home without interruption; but avoid the main
streets. I'll see you again this evening, if we're both alive,
and I can reach you; for my time is short. A committee
are to call in the morning to escort me to the train. I am
to be dismissed from the community with public honors."

Watson was climbing down from the buggy, when a
small party of men were seen approaching, and big Josh
Green, followed by several other resolute-looking colored men, came up and addressed them.

"Dr. Miller," cried Green, "Mr. Watson,—we're lookin' fer a leader. De w'ite folks are killin' de niggers, an'
we ain' gwine ter stan' up an' be shot down like dogs.
We're gwine ter defen' ou' lives, an' we ain' gwine ter
run away f'm no place where we've got a right ter be;
an' woe be ter de w'ite man w'at lays han's on us! Dere's
two niggers in dis town ter eve'y w'ite man, an' ef we've
got ter be killt, we'll take some w'ite folks 'long wid us,
ez sho' ez dere's a God in heaven,—ez I s'pose dere is,
dough He mus' be 'sleep, er busy somewhar e'se ter-day.
Will you-all come an' lead us?"

"Gentlemen," said Watson, "what is the use? The negroes will not back you up. They haven't the arms, nor
the moral courage, nor the leadership."

"We'll git de arms, an' we'll git de courage, ef you'll
come an' lead us! We wants leaders,—dat's w'y we come
ter you!"

"What's the use?" returned Watson despairingly. "The
odds are too heavy. I've been ordered out of town; if I
stayed, I'd be shot on sight, unless I had a body-guard
around me."

"We'll be yo' body-guard!" shouted half a dozen
voices.

"And when my body-guard was shot, what then? I
have a wife and children. It is my duty to live for them.
If I died, I should get no glory and no reward, and my
family would be reduced to beggary,—to which they'll
soon be near enough as it is. This affair will blow over
in a day or two. The white people will be ashamed of
themselves to-morrow, and apprehensive of the conse-

quences for some time to come. Keep quiet, boys, and trust in God. You won't gain anything by resistance."

" 'God he'ps dem dat he'ps demselves,' " returned Josh stoutly. "Ef Mr. Watson won't lead us, will you, Dr. Miller?" said the spokesman, turning to the doctor.

For Miller it was an agonizing moment. He was no coward, morally or physically. Every manly instinct urged him to go forward and take up the cause of these leaderless people, and, if need be, to defend their lives and their rights with his own,—but to what end?

"Listen, men," he said. "We would only be throwing our lives away. Suppose we made a determined stand and won a temporary victory. By morning every train, every boat, every road leading into Wellington, would be crowded with white men,—as they probably will be any way,—with arms in their hands, curses on their lips, and vengeance in their hearts. In the minds of those who make and administer the laws, we have no standing in the court of conscience. They would kill us in the fight, or they would hang us afterwards,—one way or another, we should be doomed. I should like to lead you; I should like to arm every colored man in this town, and have them stand firmly in line, not for attack, but for defense; but if I attempted it, and they should stand by me, which is questionable,—for I have met them fleeing from the town,—my life would pay the forfeit. Alive, I may be of some use to you, and you are welcome to my life in that way,—I am giving it freely. Dead, I should be a mere lump of carrion. Who remembers even the names of those who have been done to death in the Southern States for the past twenty years?"

"I 'members de name er one of 'em," said Josh, "an' I 'members de name er de man dat killt 'im, an' I s'pec' his time is mighty nigh come."

"My advice is not heroic, but I think it is wise. In this riot we are placed as we should be in a war: we have no territory, no base of supplies, no organization, no outside sympathy,—we stand in the position of a race, in a case like this, without money and without friends. Our time will come,—the time when we can command respect for our rights; but it is not yet in sight. Give it up, boys, and wait. Good may come of this, after all."

Several of the men wavered, and looked irresolute.

"I reckon that's all so, doctuh," returned Josh, "an', de way you put it, I don' blame you ner Mr. Watson; but all dem reasons ain' got no weight wid me. I'm gwine in dat town, an' ef any w'ite man 'sturbs me, dere'll be trouble,—dere'll be double trouble,—I feels it in my bones!"

"Remember your old mother, Josh," said Miller.

"Yas, suh, I'll 'member her; dat's all I kin do now. I don' need ter wait fer her no mo', fer she died dis mo'nin'. I'd lack ter see her buried, suh, but I may not have de chance. Ef I gits killt, will you do me a favor?"

"Yes, Josh; what is it?"

"Ef I should git laid out in dis commotion dat's gwine on, will you collec' my wages f'm yo' brother, and see dat de ole 'oman is put away right?"

"Yes, of course."

"Wid a nice coffin, an' a nice fune'al, an' a head-bo'd an' a foot-bo'd?"

"Yes."

"All right, suh! Ef I don' live ter do it, I'll know it'll be 'tended ter right. Now we're gwine out ter de cotton compress, an' git a lot er colored men together, an' ef de w'ite folks 'sturbs me, I shouldn't be s'prise' ef dere'd be a mix-up;—an' ef dere is, me an *one* w'ite man 'll stan' befo' de jedgment th'one er God dis day; an' it won't be me w'at'll be 'feared er de jedgment. Come along, boys! Dese gentlemen may have somethin' ter live fer; but ez fer my pa't, I'd ruther be a dead nigger any day dan a live dog!"

CHAPTER XXXIII

Into the Lion's Jaws

THE PARTY UNDER Josh's leadership moved off down the road. Miller, while entirely convinced that he had acted wisely in declining to accompany them, was yet conscious of a distinct feeling of shame and envy that he, too, did not feel impelled to throw away his life in a hopeless struggle.

Watson left the buggy and disappeared by a path at the roadside. Miller drove rapidly forward. After entering the town, he passed several small parties of white men, but escaped scrutiny by sitting well back in his buggy, the presumption being that a well-dressed man with a good horse and buggy was white. Torn with anxiety, he reached home at about four o'clock. Driving the horse into the yard, he sprang down from the buggy and hastened to the house, which he found locked, front and rear.

A repeated rapping brought no response. At length he broke a window, and entered the house like a thief.

"Janet, Janet!" he called in alarm, "where are you? It is only I,—Will!"

There was no reply. He ran from room to room, only to find them all empty. Again he called his wife's name, and was about rushing from the house, when a muffled voice came faintly to his ear,—

"Is dat you, Doctuh Miller?"

"Yes. Who are you, and where are my wife and child?"

He was looking around in perplexity, when the door of a low closet under the kitchen sink was opened from within, and a woolly head was cautiously protruded.

"Are you *sho'* dat's you, doctuh?"

"Yes, Sally; where are"—

"An' not some w'ite man come ter bu'n down de house an' kill all de niggers?"

"No, Sally, it's me all right. Where is my wife? Where is my child?"

"Dey went over ter see Mis' Butler 'long 'bout two o'clock, befo' dis fuss broke out, suh. Oh, Lawdy, Lawdy, suh! Is all de cullud folks be'n killt 'cep'n' me an' you, suh? Fer de Lawd's sake, suh, you won' let 'em kill me, will you, suh? I'll wuk fer you fer nuthin', suh, all my bawn days, ef you'll save my life, suh!"

"Calm yourself, Sally. You'll be safe enough if you stay right here, I've no doubt. They'll not harm women,—of that I'm sure enough, although I haven't yet got the bearings of this deplorable affair. Stay here and look after the house. I must find my wife and child!"

The distance across the city to the home of the Mrs. Butler whom his wife had gone to visit was exactly one mile. Though Miller had a good horse in front of him, he was two hours in reaching his destination. Never will the picture of that ride fade from his memory. In his dreams he repeats it night after night, and sees the sights that wounded his eyes, and feels the thoughts—the haunting spirits of the thoughts—that tore his heart as he rode through hell to find those whom he was seeking.

For a short distance he saw nothing, and made rapid progress. As he turned the first corner, his horse shied at the dead body of a negro, lying huddled up in the collapse which marks sudden death. What Miller shuddered at was not so much the thought of death, to the sight of which his profession had accustomed him, as the suggestion of what it signified. He had taken with allowance the wild statement of the fleeing fugitives. Watson, too, had been greatly excited, and Josh Green's group were desperate men, as much liable to be misled by their courage as the others by their fears; but here was proof that murder had been done,—and his wife and children were in the town. Distant shouts, and the sound of firearms, increased his alarm. He struck his horse with the whip, and dashed on toward the heart of the city, which he must traverse in order to reach Janet and the child.

At the next corner lay the body of another man, with the red blood oozing from a ghastly wound in the forehead. The negroes seemed to have been killed, as the band plays in circus parades, at the street intersections, where the example would be most effective. Miller, with a wild leap of the heart, had barely passed this gruesome spectacle, when a sharp voice commanded him to halt, and emphasized the order by covering him with a revolver. Forgetting the prudence he had preached to others, he had raised his whip to strike the horse, when several hands seized the bridle.

"Come down, you damn fool," growled an authoritative voice. "Don't you see we're in earnest? Do you want to get killed?"

"Why should I come down?" asked Miller.

"Because we've ordered you to come down! This is the white people's day, and when they order, a nigger must obey. We're going to search you for weapons."

"Search away. You'll find nothing but a case of surgeon's tools, which I'm more than likely to need before this day is over, from all indications."

"No matter; we'll make sure of it! That's what we're here for. Come down, if you don't want to be pulled down!"

Miller stepped down from his buggy. His interlocutor, who made no effort at disguise, was a clerk in a dry-goods store where Miller bought most of his family and hospital supplies. He made no sign of recognition, however, and Miller claimed no acquaintance. This man, who had for several years emptied Miller's pockets in the course of more or less legitimate trade, now went through them, aided by another man, more rapidly than ever before, the searchers convincing themselves that Miller carried no deadly weapon upon his person. Meanwhile, a third ransacked the buggy with like result. Miller recognized several others of the party, who made not the slightest attempt at disguise, though no names were called by any one.

"Where are you going?" demanded the leader.

"I am looking for my wife and child," replied Miller.

"Well, run along, and keep them out of the streets when you find them; and keep your hands out of this affair, if you wish to live in this town, which from now on will be a white man's town, as you niggers will be pretty firmly convinced before night."

Miller drove on as swiftly as might be.

At the next corner he was stopped again. In the white man who held him up, Miller recognized a neighbor of his own. After a short detention and a perfunctory search, the white man remarked apologetically:—

"Sorry to have had to trouble you, doctuh, but them's the o'ders. It ain't men like you that we're after, but the vicious and criminal class of niggers."

Miller smiled bitterly as he urged his horse forward. He was quite well aware that the virtuous citizen who had stopped him had only a few weeks before finished a term in the penitentiary, to which he had been sentenced for stealing. Miller knew that he could have bought all the man owned for fifty dollars, and his soul for as much more.

A few rods farther on, he came near running over the body of a wounded man who lay groaning by the wayside. Every professional instinct urged him to stop and offer aid to the sufferer; but the uncertainty concerning his wife and child proved a stronger motive and urged him resistlessly forward. Here and there the ominous sound of firearms was audible. He might have thought this merely a part of the show, like the "powder play" of the Arabs, but for the bloody confirmation of its earnestness which had already assailed his vision. Somewhere in this seething caldron of unrestrained passions were his wife and child, and he must hurry on.

His progress was painfully slow. Three times he was stopped and searched. More than once his way was barred, and he was ordered to turn back, each such occasion requiring a detour which consumed many minutes. The man who last stopped him was a well-known Jewish merchant. A Jew—God of Moses!—had so far forgotten twenty centuries of history as to join in the persecution of another oppressed race! When almost reduced to despair by these innumerable delays, he perceived, coming toward him, Mr. Ellis, the sub-editor of the Morning Chronicle. Miller had just been stopped and questioned again, and Ellis came up as he was starting once more upon his endless ride.

"Dr. Miller," said Ellis kindly, "it is dangerous for you on the streets. Why tempt the danger?"

"I am looking for my wife and child," returned Miller

in desperation. "They are somewhere in this town,—I don't know where,—and I must find them."

Ellis had been horror-stricken by the tragedy of the afternoon, the wholly superfluous slaughter of a harmless people, whom a show of force would have been quite sufficient to overawe. Elaborate explanations were afterwards given for these murders, which were said, perhaps truthfully, not to have been premeditated, and many regrets were expressed. The young man had been surprised, quite as much as the negroes themselves, at the ferocity displayed. His own thoughts and feelings were attuned to anything but slaughter. Only that morning he had received a perfumed note, calling his attention to what the writer described as a very noble deed of his, and requesting him to call that evening and receive the writer's thanks. Had he known that Miss Pemberton, several weeks after their visit to the Sound, had driven out again to the hotel and made some inquiries among the servants, he might have understood better the meaning of this missive. When Miller spoke of his wife and child, some subtle thread of suggestion coupled the note with Miller's plight.

"I'll go with you, Dr. Miller," he said, "if you'll permit me. In my company you will not be disturbed."

He took a seat in Miller's buggy, after which it was not molested.

Neither of them spoke. Miller was sick at heart; he could have wept with grief, even had the welfare of his own dear ones not been involved in this regrettable affair. With prophetic instinct he foresaw the hatreds to which this day would give birth; the long years of constraint and distrust which would still further widen the breach between two peoples whom fate had thrown together in one community.

There was nothing for Ellis to say. In his heart he could not defend the deeds of this day. The petty annoyances which the whites had felt at the spectacle of a few negroes in office; the not unnatural resentment of a proud people at what had seemed to them a presumptuous freedom of speech and lack of deference on the part of their inferiors,—these things, which he knew were to be made the excuse for overturning the city government, he realized full well were no sort of justification for the wholesale murder or other horrors which might well ensue before the day was done. He could not approve the acts of his own people; neither could he, to a negro, condemn them. Hence he was silent.

"Thank you, Mr. Ellis," exclaimed Miller, when they had reached the house where he expected to find his wife. "This is the place where I was going. I am—under a great obligation to you."

"Not at all, Dr. Miller. I need not tell you how much I regret this deplorable affair."

Ellis went back down the street. Fastening his horse to the fence, Miller sprang forward to find his wife and child. They would certainly be there, for no colored woman would be foolhardy enough to venture on the streets after the riot had broken out.

As he drew nearer, he felt a sudden apprehension. The house seemed strangely silent and deserted. The doors were closed, and the venetian blinds shut tightly. Even a dog which had appeared slunk timidly back under the house, instead of barking vociferously according to the usual habit of his kind.

CHAPTER XXXIV

The Valley
of the Shadow

MILLER KNOCKED at the door. There was no response. He went round to the rear of the house. The dog had slunk behind the woodpile. Miller knocked again, at the back door, and, receiving no reply, called aloud.

"Mrs. Butler! It is I, Dr. Miller. Is my wife here?"

The slats of a near-by blind opened cautiously.

"Is it really you, Dr. Miller?"

"Yes, Mrs. Butler. I am looking for my wife and child,—are they here?"

"No, sir; she became alarmed about you, soon after the shooting commenced, and I could not keep her. She left for home half an hour ago. It is coming on dusk, and she and the child are so near white that she did not expect to be molested."

"Which way did she go?"

"She meant to go by the main street. She thought it would be less dangerous than the back streets. I tried to get her to stay here, but she was frantic about you, and nothing I could say would keep her. Is the riot almost over, Dr. Miller? Do you think they will murder us all, and burn down our houses?"

"God knows," replied Miller, with a groan. "But I must find her, if I lose my own life in the attempt."

Surely, he thought, Janet would be safe. The white people of Wellington were not savages; or at least their temporary reversion to savagery would not go as far as to include violence to delicate women and children. Then there flashed into his mind Josh Green's story of his "silly" mother, who for twenty years had walked the earth as a child, as the result of one night's terror, and his heart sank within him.

Miller realized that his buggy, by attracting attention, had been a hindrance rather than a help in his progress across the city. In order to follow his wife, he must practically retrace his steps over the very route he had come. Night was falling. It would be easier to cross the town on foot. In the dusk his own color, slight in the daytime, would not attract attention, and by dodging in the shadows he might avoid those who might wish to intercept him. But he must reach Janet and the boy at any risk. He had not been willing to throw his life away hopelessly, but he would cheerfully have sacrificed it for those whom he loved.

He had gone but a short distance, and had not yet reached the centre of mob activity, when he intercepted a band of negro laborers from the cotton compress, with big Josh Green at their head.

"Hello, doctuh!" cried Josh, "does you wan' ter jine us?"

"I'm looking for my wife and child, Josh. They're somewhere in this den of murderers. Have any of you seen them?"

No one had seen them.

"You men are running a great risk," said Miller. "You are rushing on to certain death."

"Well, suh, maybe we is; but we're gwine ter die fightin'. Dey say de w'ite folks is gwine ter bu'n all de cullud schools an' chu'ches, an' kill all de niggers dey kin ketch. Dey're gwine ter bu'n yo' new hospittle, ef somebody don' stop 'em."

"Josh—men—you are throwing your lives away. It is a fever; it will wear off to-morrow, or to-night. They'll not burn the schoolhouses, nor the hospital—they are not such fools, for they benefit the community; and they'll only kill the colored people who resist them. Every one of you with a gun or a pistol carries his death warrant in his own hand. I'd rather see the hospital burn than have one of you lose his life. Resistance only makes the matter worse,—the odds against you are too long."

"Things can't be any wuss, doctuh," replied one of the crowd sturdily. "A gun is mo' dange'ous ter de man in front of it dan ter de man behin' it. Dey're gwine ter kill us anyhow; an' we're tired,— we read de newspapers,— an' we're tired er bein' shot down like dogs, widout jedge er jury. We'd ruther die fightin' dan be stuck like pigs in a pen!"

"God help you!" said Miller. "As for me, I must find my wife and child."

"Good-by, doctuh," cried Josh, brandishing a huge knife. " 'Member 'bout de ole 'oman, ef you lives thoo dis. Don' fergit de headbo'd an' de footbo'd, an' a silver plate on de coffin, ef dere's money ernuff."

They went their way, and Miller hurried on. They might resist attack; he thought it extremely unlikely that they would begin it; but he knew perfectly well that the mere knowledge that some of the negroes contemplated resistance would only further inflame the infuriated whites. The colored men might win a momentary victory, though it was extremely doubtful; and they would as surely reap the harvest later on. The qualities which in a white man would win the applause of the world would in a negro be taken as the marks of savagery. So thoroughly diseased was public opinion in matters of race that the negro who died for the common rights of humanity might look for no need of admiration or glory. At such a time, in the white man's eyes, a negro's courage would be mere desperation; his love of liberty, a mere animal dislike of restraint. Every finer human instinct would be interpreted in terms of savagery. Or, if forced to admire, they would none the less repress. They would applaud his courage while they stretched his neck, or carried off the fragments of his mangled body as souvenirs, in much the same way that savages preserve the scalps or eat the hearts of their enemies.

But concern for the fate of Josh and his friends occupied only a secondary place in Miller's mind for the moment. His wife and child were somewhere ahead of him. He pushed on. He had covered about a quarter of a mile more, and far down the street could see the signs of greater animation, when he came upon the body of a woman lying upon the sidewalk. In the dusk he had almost stumbled over it, and his heart came up in his mouth. A second glance revealed that it could not be his wife. It was a fearful portent, however, of what her fate might be. The "war" had reached the women and children. Yielding to a professional instinct, he stooped, and saw that the prostrate form was that of old Aunt Jane

Letlow. She was not yet quite dead, and as Miller, with a tender touch, placed her head in a more comfortable position, her lips moved with a last lingering flicker of consciousness:—

"Comin', missis, comin'!"

Mammy Jane had gone to join the old mistress upon whose memorey her heart was fixed; and yet not all her reverence for her old mistress, nor all her deference to the whites, nor all their friendship for her, had been able to save her from this raging devil of race hatred which momentarily possessed the town.

Perceiving that he could do no good, Miller hastened onward, sick at heart. Whenever he saw a party of white men approaching,—these brave reformers never went singly,—he sought concealment in the shadow of a tree or the shrubbery in some yard until they had passed. He had covered about two thirds of the distance homeward, when his eyes fell upon a group beneath a lamp-post, at sight of which he turned pale with horror, and rushed forward with a terrible cry.

"Mine Enemy, O Mine Enemy!"

THE PROCEEDINGS OF the day—planned originally as a "demonstration," dignified subsequently as a "revolution," under any name the culmination of the conspiracy formed by Carteret and his colleagues—had by seven o'clock in the afternoon developed into a murderous riot. Crowds of white men and half-grown boys, drunk with whiskey or with license, raged through the streets, beating, chasing, or killing any negro so unfortunate as to fall into their hands. Why any particular negro was assailed, no one stopped to inquire; it was merely a white mob thirsting for black blood, with no more conscience or discrimination than would be exercised by a wolf in a sheepfold. It was race against race, the whites against the negroes; and it was a one-sided affair, for until Josh Green got together his body of armed men, no effective resistance had been made by any colored person, and the individuals who had been killed had so far left no marks upon the enemy by which they might be remembered.

"Kill the niggers!" rang out now and then through the dusk, and far down the street and along the intersecting thoroughfares distant voices took up the ominous refrain,—"Kill the niggers! Kill the damned niggers!"

Now, not a dark face had been seen on the street for half an hour, until the group of men headed by Josh made their appearance in the negro quarter. Armed with guns and axes, they presented quite a formidable appearance as they made their way toward the new hospital, near which stood a schoolhouse and a large church, both used by the colored people. They did not reach their destination without having met a number of white men, singly or in twos or threes; and the rumor spread with incredible swiftness that the negroes in turn were up in arms, determined to massacre all the whites and burn the town. Some of the whites became alarmed, and recognizing the power of the negroes, if armed and conscious of their strength, were impressed by the immediate necessity of overpowering and overawing them. Others, with appetites already whetted by slaughter, saw a chance, welcome rather than not, of shedding more black blood. Spontaneously the white mob flocked toward the hospital, where rumor had it that a large body of desperate negroes, breathing threats of blood and fire, had taken a determined stand.

It had been Josh's plan merely to remain quietly and peaceably in the neighborhood of the little group of public institutions, molesting no one, unless first attacked, and merely letting the white people see that they meant to protect their own; but so rapidly did the rumor spread, and so promptly did the white people act, that by the time Josh and his supporters had reached the top of the rising ground where the hospital stood, a crowd of white men much more numerous than their own party were following them at a short distance.

Josh, with the eye of a general, perceived that some of his party were becoming a little nervous, and decided that they would feel safer behind shelter.

"I reckon we better go inside de hospittle, boys," he exclaimed. "Den we'll be behind brick walls, an' dem other fellows'll be outside, an' ef dere's any fightin', we'll have de bes' show. We ain' gwine ter do no shootin' till we're pestered, an' dey'll be less likely ter pester us ef dey can't git at us widout runnin' some resk. Come along in! Be men! De gov'ner er de President is gwine ter sen' soldiers ter stop dese gwines-on, an' meantime we kin keep dem white devils f'm bu'nin' down our hospittles an' chu'ch-houses. W'en dey comes an' fin's out dat we jes' means ter pertect ou' prope'ty, dey'll go 'long 'bout deir own business. Er, ef dey wants a scrap, dey kin have it! Come erlong, boys!"

Jerry Letlow, who had kept out of sight during the day, had started out, after night had set in, to find Major Carteret. Jerry was very much afraid. The events of the day had filled him with terror. Whatever the limitations

of Jerry's mind or character may have been, Jerry had a
keen appreciation of the danger to the negroes when they
came in conflict with the whites, and he had no desire
to imperil his own skin. He valued his life for his own
sake, and not for any altruistic theory that it might be of
service to others. In other words, Jerry was something
of a coward. He had kept in hiding all day, but finding,
toward evening, that the riot did not abate, and fearing,
from the rumors which came to his ears, that all the
negroes would be exterminated, he had set out, somewhat desperately, to try to find his white patron and protector. He had been cautious to avoid meeting any white
men, and, anticipating no danger from those of his own
race, went toward the party which he saw approaching,
whose path would cross his own. When they were only
a few yards apart, Josh took a step forward and caught
Jerry by the arm.

"Come along, Jerry, we need you! Here's another
man, boys. Come on now, and fight fer yo' race!"

In vain Jerry protested. "I don' wan' ter fight," he
howled. "De w'ite folks ain' gwine ter pester me; dey're
my frien's. Tu'n me loose,—tu'n me loose, er we all
gwine ter git killed!"

The party paid no attention to Jerry's protestations.
Indeed, with the crowd of whites following behind, they
were simply considering the question of a position from
which they could most effectively defend themselves and
the building which they imagined to be threatened. If
Josh had released his grip of Jerry, that worthy could
easily have escaped from the crowd; but Josh maintained
his hold almost mechanically, and, in the confusion,
Jerry found himself swept with the rest into the hospital, the doors of which were promptly barricaded with
the heavier pieces of furniture, and the windows
manned by several men each, Josh, with the instinct of
a born commander, posting his forces so that they could
cover with their guns all the approaches to the building.
Jerry still continuing to make himself troublesome, Josh,
in a moment of impatience, gave him a terrific box on the
ear, which stretched him out upon the floor unconscious.

"Shet up," he said; "ef you can't stan' up like a man,
keep still, and don't interfere wid men w'at will fight!"

The hospital, when Josh and his men took possession,

had been found deserted. Fortunately there were no patients for that day, except one or two convalescents, and these, with the attendants, had joined the exodus of the colored people from the town.

A white man advanced from the crowd without toward the main entrance to the hospital. Big Josh, looking out from a window, grasped his gun more firmly, as his eyes fell upon the man who had murdered his father and darkened his mother's life. Mechanically he raised his rifle, but lowered it as the white man lifted up his hand as a sign that he wished to speak.

"You niggers," called Captain McBane loudly,—it was that worthy,—"you niggers are courtin' death, an' you won't have to court her but a minute er two mo' befo' she'll have you. If you surrender and give up your arms, you'll be dealt with leniently,—you may get off with the chain-gang or the penitentiary. If you resist, you'll be shot like dogs."

"Dat's no news, Mr. White Man," replied Josh, appearing boldly at the window. "We're use' ter bein' treated like dogs by men like you. If you w'ite people will go 'long an' ten' ter yo' own business an' let us alone, we'll ten' ter ou'n. You've got guns, an' we've got jest as much right ter carry 'em as you have. Lay down yo'n, an' we'll lay down ou'n,—we didn' take 'em up fust; but we ain' gwine ter let you bu'n down ou' chu'ches an' school'ouses, er dis hospittle, an' we ain' comin' out er dis house, where we ain' disturbin' nobody, fer you ter shoot us down er sen' us ter jail. You hear me!"

"All right," responded McBane. "You've had fair warning. Your blood be on your"—

His speech was interrupted by a shot from the crowd, which splintered the window-casing close to Josh's head. This was followed by half a dozen other shots, which were replied to, almost simultaneously, by a volley from within, by which one of the attacking party was killed and another wounded.

This roused the mob to frenzy.

"Vengeance! vengeance!" they yelled. "Kill the niggers!"

A negro had killed a white man,—the unpardonable sin, admitting neither excuse, justification, nor extenuation. From time immemorial it had been bred in the

Southern white consciousness, and in the negro consciousness also, for that matter, that the person of a white man was sacred from the touch of a negro, no matter what the provocation. A dozen colored men lay dead in the streets of Wellington, inoffensive people, slain in cold blood because they had been bold enough to question the authority of those who had assailed them, or frightened enough to flee when they had been ordered to stand still; but their lives counted nothing against that of a riotous white man, who had courted death by attacking a body of armed men.

The crowd, too, surrounding the hospital, had changed somewhat in character. The men who had acted as leaders in the early afternoon, having accomplished their purpose of overturning the local administration and establishing a provisional government of their own, had withdrawn from active participation in the rioting, deeming the negroes already sufficiently overawed to render unlikely any further trouble from that source. Several of the ringleaders had indeed begun to exert themselves to prevent further disorder, or any loss of property, the possibility of which had become apparent; but those who set in motion the forces of evil cannot always control them afterwards. The baser element of the white population, recruited from the wharves and the saloons, was now predominant.

Captain McBane was the only one of the revolutionary committee who had remained with the mob, not with any purpose to restore or preserve order, but because he found the company and the occasion entirely congenial. He had had no opportunity, at least no tenable excuse, to kill or maim a negro since the termination of his contract with the state for convicts, and this occasion had awakened a dormant appetite for these diversions. We are all puppets in the hands of Fate, and seldom see the strings that move us. McBane had lived a life of violence and cruelty. As a man sows, so shall he reap. In works of fiction, such men are sometimes converted. More often, in real life, they do not change their natures until they are converted into dust. One does well to distrust a tamed tiger.

On the outskirts of the crowd a few of the better class, or at least of the better clad, were looking on. The double volley described had already been fired, when the number of these was augmented by the arrival of Major Carteret and Mr. Ellis, who had just come from the Chronicle office, where the next day's paper had been in hasty preparation. They pushed their way towards the front of the crowd.

"This must be stopped, Ellis," said Carteret. "They are burning houses and killing women and children. Old Jane, good old Mammy Jane, who nursed my wife at her bosom, and has waited on her and my child within a few weeks, was killed only a few rods from my house, to which she was evidently fleeing for protection. It must have been by accident,—I cannot believe that any white man in town would be dastard enough to commit such a deed intentionally! I would have defended her with my own life! We must try to stop this thing!"

"Easier said than done," returned Ellis. "It is in the fever stage, and must burn itself out. We shall be lucky if it does not burn the town out. Suppose the negroes should also take a hand at the burning? We have advised the people to put the negroes down, and they are doing the job thoroughly."

"My God!" replied the other, with a gesture of impatience, as he continued to elbow his way through the crowd; "I meant to keep them in their places,—I did not intend wholesale murder and arson."

Carteret, having reached the front of the mob, made an effort to gain their attention.

"Gentlemen!" he cried in his loudest tones. His voice, unfortunately, was neither loud nor piercing.

"Kill the niggers!" clamored the mob.

"Gentlemen, I implore you"—

The crash of a dozen windows, broken by stones and pistol shots, drowned his voice.

"Gentlemen!" he shouted; "this is murder, it is madness; it is a disgrace to our city, to our state, to our civilization!"

"That's right!" replied several voices. The mob had recognized the speaker. "It *is* a disgrace, and we'll not put up with it a moment longer. Burn 'em out! Hurrah for Major Carteret, the champion of 'white supremacy'! Three cheers for the Morning Chronicle and 'no nigger domination'!"

"Hurrah, hurrah, hurrah!" yelled the crowd.

In vain the baffled orator gesticulated and shrieked in the effort to correct the misapprehension. Their oracle had spoken; not hearing what he said, they assumed it to mean encouragement and cooperation. Their present course was but the logical outcome of the crusade which the Morning Chronicle had preached, in season and out of season, for many months. When Carteret had spoken, and the crowd had cheered him, they felt that they had done all that courtesy required, and he was good-naturedly elbowed aside while they proceeded with the work in hand, which was now to drive out the negroes from the hospital and avenge the killing of their comrade.

Some brought hay, some kerosene, and others wood from a pile which had been thrown into a vacant lot near by. Several safe ways of approach to the building were discovered, and the combustibles placed and fired. The flames, soon gaining a foothold, leaped upward, catching here and there at the exposed woodwork, and licking the walls hungrily with long tongues of flame.

Meanwhile a desultory firing was kept up from the outside, which was replied to scatteringly from within the hospital. Those inside were either not good marksmen, or excitement had spoiled their aim. If a face appeared at a window, a dozen pistol shots from the crowd sought the spot immediately.

Higher and higher leaped the flames. Suddenly from one of the windows sprang a black figure, waving a white handkerchief. It was Jerry Letlow. Regaining consciousness after the effect of Josh's blow had subsided, Jerry had kept quiet and watched his opportunity. From a safe vantage-ground he had scanned the crowd without, in search of some white friend. When he saw Major Carteret moving disconsolately away after his futile effort to stem the torrent, Jerry made a dash for the window. He sprang forth, and, waving his handkerchief as a flag of truce, ran toward Major Carteret, shouting frantically:—

"Majah Carteret—O majah! It's me, suh, Jerry, suh! I didn' go in dere myse'f, suh,—I wuz drag' in dere! I wouldn' do nothin' 'g'inst de w'ite folks, suh,—no, 'ndeed, I wouldn', suh!"

Jerry's cries were drowned in a roar of rage and a

volley of shots from the mob. Carteret, who had turned away with Ellis, did not even hear his servant's voice. Jerry's poor flag of truce, his explanations, his reliance upon his white friends, all failed him in the moment of supreme need. In that hour, as in any hour when the depths of race hatred are stirred, a negro was no more than a brute beast, set upon by other brute beasts whose only instinct was to kill and destroy.

"Let us leave this inferno, Ellis," said Carteret, sick with anger and disgust. He had just become aware that a negro was being killed, though he did not know whom. "We can do nothing. The negroes have themselves to blame,—they tempted us beyond endurance. I counseled firmness, and firm measures were taken, and our purpose was accomplished. I am not responsible for these subsequent horrors,—I wash my hands of them. Let us go!"

The flames gained headway and gradually enveloped the burning building, until it became evident to those within as well as those without that the position of the defenders was no longer tenable. Would they die in the flames, or would they be driven out? The uncertainty soon came to an end.

The besieged had been willing to fight, so long as there seemed a hope of successfully defending themselves and their property; for their purpose was purely one of defense. When they saw the case was hopeless, inspired by Josh Green's reckless courage, they were still willing to sell their lives dearly. One or two of them had already been killed, and as many more disabled. The fate of Jerry Letlow had struck terror to the hearts of several others, who could scarcely hide their fear. After the building had been fired, Josh's exhortations were no longer able to keep them in the hospital. They preferred to fight and be killed in the open, rather than to be smothered like rats in a hole.

"Boys!" exclaimed Josh,—"men!—fer nobody but men would do w'at you have done,—the day has gone 'g'inst us. We kin see ou' finish; but fer my part, I ain' gwine ter leave dis worl' widout takin' a w'ite man 'long wid me, an' I sees my man right out yonder waitin',—I be'n waitin' fer him twenty years, but he won' have ter wait fer me mo' 'n 'bout twenty seconds. Eve'y one er you pick yo' man! We'll open de do', an' we'll give some w'ite men a chance ter be sorry dey ever started dis fuss!"

The door was thrown open suddenly, and through it rushed a dozen or more black figures, armed with knives, pistols, or clubbed muskets. Taken by sudden surprise, the white people stood motionless for a moment, but the approaching negroes had scarcely covered half the distance to which the heat of the flames had driven back the mob, before they were greeted with a volley that laid them all low but two. One of these, dazed by the fate of his companions, turned instinctively to flee, but had scarcely faced around before he fell, pierced in the back by a dozen bullets.

Josh Green, the tallest and biggest of them all, had not apparently been touched. Some of the crowd paused in involuntary admiration of this black giant, famed on the wharves for his strength, sweeping down upon them, a smile upon his face, his eyes lit up with a rapt expression which seemed to take him out of mortal ken. This impression was heightened by his apparent immunity from the shower of lead which less susceptible persons had continued to pour at him.

Armed with a huge bowie-knife, a relic of the civil war, which he had carried on his person for many years for a definite purpose, and which he had kept sharpened to a razor edge, he reached the line of the crowd. All but the bravest shrank back. Like a wedge he dashed through the mob, which parted instinctively before him, and all oblivious of the rain of lead which fell around him, reached the point where Captain McBane, the bravest man in the party, stood waiting to meet him. A pistol-flame flashed in his face, but he went on, and raising his powerful right arm, buried his knife to the hilt in the heart of his enemy. When the crowd dashed forward to wreak vengeance on his dead body, they found him with a smile still upon his face.

One of the two died as the fool dieth. Which was it, or was it both? "Vengeance is mine," saith the Lord, and it had not been left to Him. But they that do violence must expect to suffer violence. McBane's death was merciful, compared with the nameless horrors he had heaped upon the hundreds of helpless mortals who had fallen into his hands during his career as a contractor of convict labor.

Sobered by this culminating tragedy, the mob shortly afterwards dispersed. The flames soon completed their work, and this handsome structure, the fruit of old Adam Miller's industry, the monument of his son's philanthropy, a promise of good things for the future of the city, lay smouldering in ruins, a melancholy witness to the fact that our boasted civilization is but a thin veneer, which cracks and scales off at the first impact of primal passions.

CHAPTER XXXVI

Fiat Justitia

BY THE LIGHT of the burning building, which illuminated the street for several blocks, Major Carteret and Ellis made their way rapidly until they turned into the street where the major lived. Reaching the house, Carteret tried the door and found it locked. A vigorous ring at the bell brought no immediate response. Carteret had begun to pound impatiently upon the door, when it was cautiously opened by Miss Pemberton, who was pale, and trembled with excitement.

"Where is Olivia?" asked the major.

"She is upstairs, with Dodie and Mrs. Albright's hospital nurse. Dodie has the croup. Virgie ran away after the riot broke out. Sister Olivia had sent for Mammy Jane, but she did not come. Mrs. Albright let her white nurse come over."

"I'll go up at once," said the major anxiously. "Wait for me, Ellis,—I'll be down in a few minutes."

"Oh, Mr. Ellis," exclaimed Clara, coming toward him with both hands extended, "can nothing be done to stop this terrible affair?"

"I wish I could do something," he murmured fervently, taking both her trembling hands in his own broad palms, where they rested with a surrendering trustfulness which he has never since had occasion to doubt. "It has gone too far, already, and the end, I fear, is not yet; but it cannot grow much worse."

The editor hurried upstairs. Mrs. Carteret, wearing a worried and haggard look, met him at the threshold of the nursery.

"Dodie is ill," she said. "At three o'clock, when the trouble began, I was over at Mrs. Albright's,—I had left Virgie with the baby. When I came back, she and all the other servants had gone. They had heard that the white people were going to kill all the negroes, and fled to seek safety. I found Dodie lying in a draught, before an open window, gasping for breath. I ran back to Mrs. Albright's,—I had found her much better to-day,—and she let her nurse come over. The nurse says that Dodie is threatened with membranous croup."

"Have you sent for Dr. Price?"

"There was no one to send,—the servants were gone, and the nurse was afraid to venture out into the street. I telephoned for Dr. Price, and found that he was out of town; that he had gone up the river this morning to attend a patient, and would not be back until to-morrow. Mrs. Price thought that he had anticipated some kind of trouble in the town to-day, and had preferred to be where he could not be called upon to assume any responsibility."

"I suppose you tried Dr. Ashe?"

"I could not get him, nor any one else, after that first call. The telephone service is disorganized on account of the riot. We need medicine and ice. The drugstores are all closed on account of the riot, and for the same reason we couldn't get any ice."

Major Carteret stood beside the brass bedstead upon which his child was lying,—his only child, around whose curly head clustered all his hopes; upon whom all his life for the past year had been centred. He stooped over the bed, beside which the nurse had stationed herself. She was wiping the child's face, which was red and swollen and covered with moisture, the nostrils working rapidly, and the little patient vainly endeavoring at intervals to cough up the obstruction to his breathing.

"Is it serious?" he inquired anxiously. He had always thought of the croup as a childish ailment, that yielded readily to proper treatment; but the child's evident distress impressed him with sudden fear.

"Dangerous," replied the young woman laconically. "You came none too soon. If a doctor isn't got at once, the child will die,—and it must be a good doctor."

"Whom can I call?" he asked. "You know them all, I suppose. Dr. Price, our family physician, is out of town."

"Dr. Ashe has charge of his cases when he is away," replied the nurse. "If you can't find him, try Dr. Hooper.

The child is growing worse every minute. On your way back you'd better get some ice, if possible."

The major hastened downstairs.

"Don't wait for me, Ellis," he said. "I shall be needed here for a while. I'll get to the office as soon as possible. Make up the paper, and leave another stick out for me to the last minute, but fill it up in case I'm not on hand by twelve. We must get the paper out early in the morning."

Nothing but a matter of the most vital importance would have kept Major Carteret away from his office this night. Upon the presentation to the outer world of the story of this riot would depend the attitude of the great civilized public toward the events of the last ten hours. The Chronicle was the source from which the first word would be expected; it would give the people of Wellington their cue as to the position which they must take in regard to this distressful affair, which had so far transcended in ferocity the most extreme measures which the conspirators had anticipated. The burden of his own responsibility weighed heavily upon him, and could not be shaken off; but he must do first the duty nearest to him,—he must first attend to his child.

Carteret hastened from the house, and traversed rapidly the short distance to Dr. Ashe's office. Far down the street he could see the glow of the burning hospital, and he had scarcely left his own house when the fusillade of shots, fired when the colored men emerged from the burning building, was audible. Carteret would have hastened back to the scene of the riot, to see what was now going on, and to make another effort to stem the tide of bloodshed; but before the dread of losing his child, all other interests fell into the background. Not all the negroes in Wellington could weigh in the balance for one instant against the life of the feeble child now gasping for breath in the house behind him.

Reaching the house, a vigorous ring brought the doctor's wife to the door.

"Good-evening, Mrs. Ashe. Is the doctor at home?"

"No, Major Carteret. He was called to attend Mrs. Wells, who was taken suddenly ill, as a result of the trouble this afternoon. He will be there all night, no doubt."

"My child is very ill, and I must find some one."

"Try Dr. Yates. His house is only four doors away."

A ring at Dr. Yates's door brought out a young man.

"Is Dr. Yates in?"

"Yes, sir."

"Can I see him?"

"You might see him, sir, but that would be all. His horse was frightened by the shooting on the streets, and ran away and threw the doctor, and broke his right arm. I have just set it; he will not be able to attend any patients for several weeks. He is old and nervous, and the shock was great."

"Are you not a physician?" asked Carteret, looking at the young man keenly. He was a serious, gentlemanly looking young fellow, whose word might probably be trusted.

"Yes, I am Dr. Evans, Dr. Yates's assistant. I'm really little more than a student, but I'll do what I can."

"My only child is sick with the croup, and requires immediate attention."

"I ought to be able to handle a case of the croup," answered Dr. Evans, "at least in the first stages. I'll go with you, and stay by the child, and if the case is beyond me, I may keep it in check until another physician comes."

He stepped back into another room, and returning immediately with his hat, accompanied Carteret homeward. The riot had subsided; even the glow from the smouldering hospital was no longer visible. It seemed that the city, appalled at the tragedy, had suddenly awakened to a sense of its own crime. Here and there a dark face, emerging cautiously from some hiding-place, peered from behind fence or tree, but shrank hastily away at the sight of a white face. The negroes of Wellington, with the exception of Josh Green and his party, had not behaved bravely on this critical day in their history; but those who had fought were dead, to the last man; those who had sought safety in flight or concealment were alive to tell the tale.

"We pass right by Dr. Thompson's," said Dr. Evans. "If you haven't spoken to him, it might be well to call him for consultation, in case the child should be very bad."

"Go on ahead," said Carteret, "and I'll get him."

Evans hastened on, while Carteret sounded the old-fashioned knocker upon the doctor's door. A gray-haired negro servant, clad in a dress suit and wearing a white tie, came to the door.

"De doctuh, suh," he replied politely to Carteret's question, "has gone ter ampitate de ahm er a gent'eman who got one er his bones smashed wid a pistol bullet in de—fightin' dis atternoon, suh. He's jes' gone, suh, an' lef' wo'd dat he'd be gone a' hour er mo', suh."

Carteret hastened homeward. He could think of no other available physician. Perhaps no other would be needed, but if so, he could find out from Evans whom it was best to call.

When he reached the child's room, the young doctor was bending anxiously over the little frame. The little lips had become livid, the little nails, lying against the white sheet, were blue. The child's efforts to breathe were most distressing, and each gasp cut the father like a knife. Mrs. Carteret was weeping hysterically.

"How is he, doctor?" asked the major.

"He is very low," replied the young man. "Nothing short of tracheotomy—an operation to open the windpipe—will relieve him. Without it, in half or three quarters of an hour he will be unable to breathe. It is a delicate operation, a mistake in which would be as fatal as the disease. I have neither the knowledge nor the experience to attempt it, and your child's life is too valuable for a student to practice upon. Neither have I the instruments here."

"What shall we do?" demanded Carteret. "We have called all the best doctors, and none are available."

The young doctor's brow was wrinkled with thought. He knew a doctor who could perform the operation. He had heard, also, of a certain event at Carteret's house some months before, when an unwelcome physician had been excluded from a consultation,—but it was the last chance.

"There is but one other doctor in town who has performed the operation, so far as I know," he declared, "and that is Dr. Miller. If you can get him, he can save your child's life."

Carteret hesitated involuntarily. All the incidents, all

the arguments, of the occasion when he had refused to admit the colored doctor to his house, came up vividly before his memory. He had acted in accordance with his lifelong beliefs, and had carried his point; but the present situation was different,—this was a case of imperative necessity, and every other interest or consideration must give way before the imminence of his child's peril. That the doctor would refuse the call, he did not imagine: it would be too great an honor for a negro to decline,—unless some bitterness might have grown out of the proceedings of the afternoon. That this doctor was a man of some education he knew; and he had been told that he was a man of fine feeling,—for a negro,—and might easily have taken to heart the day's events. Nevertheless, he could hardly refuse a professional call,—professional ethics would require him to respond. Carteret had no reason to suppose that Miller had ever learned of what had occurred at the house during Dr. Burns's visit to Wellington. The major himself had never mentioned the controversy, and no doubt the other gentlemen had been equally silent.

"I'll go for him myself," said Dr. Evans, noting Carteret's hesitation and suspecting its cause. "I can do nothing here alone, for a little while, and I may be able to bring the doctor back with me. He likes a difficult operation."

It seemed an age ere the young doctor returned, though it was really only a few minutes. The nurse did what she could to relieve the child's sufferings, which grew visibly more and more acute. The mother, upon the other side of the bed, held one of the baby's hands in her own, and controlled her feelings as best she might. Carteret paced the floor anxiously, going every few seconds to the head of the stairs to listen for Evans's footsteps on the piazza without. At last the welcome sound was audible, and a few strides took him to the door.

"Dr. Miller is at home, sir," reported Evans, as he came in. "He says that he was called to your house once before, by a third person who claimed authority to act, and that he was refused admittance. He declares that he will not consider such a call unless it come from you personally."

"That is true, quite true," replied Carteret. "His position is a just one. I will go at once. Will—will—my child live until I can get Miller here?"

"He can live for half an hour without an operation. Beyond that I could give you little hope."

Seizing his hat, Carteret dashed out of the yard and ran rapidly to Miller's house; ordinarily a walk of six or seven minutes, Carteret covered it in three, and was almost out of breath when he rang the bell of Miller's front door.

The ring was answered by the doctor in person.

"Dr. Miller, I believe?" asked Carteret.

"Yes, sir."

"I am Major Carteret. My child is seriously ill, and you are the only available doctor who can perform the necessary operation."

"Ah! You have tried all the others,—and then you come to me!"

"Yes, I do not deny it," admitted the major, biting his lip. He had not counted on professional jealousy as an obstacle to be met. "But I *have* come to you, as a physician, to engage your professional services for my child,— my only child. I have confidence in your skill, or I should not have come to you. I request—nay, I implore you to lose no more time, but come with me at once! My child's life is hanging by a thread, and you can save it!"

"Ah!" replied the other, "as a father whose only child's life is in danger, you implore *me*, of all men in the world, to come and save it!"

There was a strained intensity in the doctor's low voice that struck Carteret, in spite of his own preoccupation. He thought he heard, too, from the adjoining room, the sound of some one sobbing softly. There was some mystery here which he could not fathom unaided.

Miller turned to the door behind him and threw it open. On the white cover of a low cot lay a childish form in the rigidity of death, and by it knelt, with her back to the door, a woman whose shoulders were shaken by the violence of her sobs. Absorbed in her grief, she did not turn, or give any sign that she had recognized the intrusion.

"There, Major Carteret!" exclaimed Miller, with the tragic eloquence of despair, "there lies a specimen of your handiwork! There lies *my* only child, laid low by a stray bullet in this riot which you and your paper have fomented; struck down as much by your hand as though you had held the weapon with which his life was taken!"

"My God!" exclaimed Carteret, struck with horror. "Is the child dead?"

"There he lies," continued the other, "an innocent child,—there he lies dead, his little life snuffed out like a candle, because you and a handful of your friends thought you must override the laws and run this town at any cost!—and there kneels his mother, overcome by grief. We are alone in the house. It is not safe to leave her unattended. My duty calls me here, by the side of my dead child and my suffering wife! I cannot go with you. There is a just God in heaven!—as you have sown, so may you reap!"

Carteret possessed a narrow, but a logical mind, and except when confused or blinded by his prejudices, had always tried to be a just man. In the agony of his own predicament,—in the horror of the situation at Miller's house,—for a moment the veil of race prejudice was rent in twain, and he saw things as they were, in their correct proportions and relations,—saw clearly and convincingly that he had no standing here, in the presence of death, in the home of this stricken family. Miller's refusal to go with him was pure, elemental justice; he could not blame the doctor for his stand. He was indeed conscious of a certain involuntary admiration for a man who held in his hands the power of life and death, and could use it, with strict justice, to avenge his own wrongs. In Dr. Miller's place he would have done the same thing. Miller had spoken the truth,—as he had sown, so must he reap! He could not expect, could not ask, this father to leave his own household at such a moment.

Pressing his lips together with grim courage, and bowing mechanically, as though to Fate rather than the physician, Carteret turned and left the house. At a rapid pace he soon reached home. There was yet a chance for his child: perhaps some one of the other doctors had come; perhaps, after all, the disease had taken a favorable turn,—Evans was but a young doctor, and might have been mistaken. Surely, with doctors all around him, his child would not be permitted to die for lack of medical attention! He found the mother, the doctor, and the nurse still grouped, as he had left them, around the suffering child.

"How is he now?" he asked, in a voice that sounded like a groan.

"No better," replied the doctor; "steadily growing worse. He can go on probably for twenty minutes longer without an operation."

"Where is the doctor?" demanded Mrs. Carteret, looking eagerly toward the door. "You should have brought him right upstairs. There's not a minute to spare! Phil, Phil, our child will die!"

Carteret's heart swelled almost to bursting with an intense pity. Even his own great sorrow became of secondary importance beside the grief which his wife must soon feel at the inevitable loss of her only child. And it was his fault! Would that he could risk his own life to spare her and to save the child!

Briefly, and as gently as might be, he stated the result of his errand. The doctor had refused to come, for a good reason. He could not ask him again.

Young Evans felt the logic of the situation, which Carteret had explained sufficiently. To the nurse it was even clearer. If she or any other woman had been in the doctor's place, she would have given the same answer.

Mrs. Carteret did not stop to reason. In such a crisis a mother's heart usurps the place of intellect. For her, at that moment, there were but two facts in all the world. Her child lay dying. There was within the town, and within reach, a man who could save him. With an agonized cry she rushed wildly from the room.

Carteret sought to follow her, but she flew down the long stairs like a wild thing. The least misstep might have precipitated her to the bottom; but ere Carteret, with a remonstrance on his lips, had scarcely reached the uppermost step, she had thrown open the front door and fled precipitately out into the night.

CHAPTER XXXVII

The Sisters

MILLER'S DOORBELL RANG loudly, insistently, as though demanding a response. Absorbed in his own grief, into which he had relapsed upon Carteret's departure, the sound was an unwelcome intrusion. Surely the man could not be coming back! If it were some one else— What else might happen to the doomed town concerned him not. His child was dead,—his distracted wife could not be left alone.

The doorbell rang clamorously, appealingly. Through the long hall and the closed door of the room where he sat, he could hear some one knocking, and a faint voice calling.

"Open, for God's sake, open!"

It was a woman's voice,—the voice of a woman in distress. Slowly Miller rose and went to the door, which he opened mechanically.

A lady stood there, so near the image of his own wife, whom he had just left, that for a moment he was well-nigh startled. A little older, perhaps, a little fairer of complexion, but with the same form, the same features, marked by the same wild grief. She wore a loose wrapper, which clothed her like the drapery of a statue. Her long dark hair, the counterpart of his wife's, had fallen down, and hung disheveled about her shoulders. There was blood upon her knuckles, where she had beaten with them upon the door.

"Dr. Miller," she panted, breathless from her flight and laying her hand upon his arm appealingly,—when he shrank from the contact she still held it there,—"Dr. Miller, you will come and save my child? You know what it is to lose a child! I am so sorry about your little boy! You will come to mine!"

"Your sorrow comes too late, madam," he said

harshly. "My child is dead. I charged your husband with his murder, and he could not deny it. Why should I save your husband's child?"

"Ah, Dr. Miller!" she cried, with his wife's voice,—she never knew how much, in that dark hour, she owed to that resemblance—"it is *my* child, and I have never injured you. It is my child, Dr. Miller, my only child. I brought it into the world at the risk of my own life! I have nursed it, I have watched over it, I have prayed for it,—and it now lies dying! Oh, Dr. Miller, dear Dr. Miller, if you have a heart, come and save my child!"

"Madam," he answered more gently, moved in spite of himself, "my heart is broken. My people lie dead upon the streets, at the hands of yours. The work of my life is in ashes,—and, yonder, stretched out in death, lies my own child! God! woman, you ask too much of human nature! Love, duty, sorrow, *justice*, call me here. I cannot go!"

She rose to her full height. "Then you are a murderer," she cried wildly. "His blood be on your head, and a mother's curse beside!"

The next moment, with a sudden revulsion of feeling, she had thrown herself at his feet,—at the feet of a negro, this proud white woman,—and was clasping his knees wildly.

"O God!" she prayed, in tones which quivered with anguish, "pardon my husband's sins, and my own, and move this man's hard heart, by the blood of thy Son, who died to save us all!"

It was the last appeal of poor humanity. When the pride of intellect and caste is broken; when we grovel in the dust of humiliation; when sickness and sorrow come, and the shadow of death falls upon us, and there is no hope elsewhere,—we turn to God, who sometimes swallows the insult, and answers the appeal.

Miller raised the lady to her feet. He had been deeply moved,—but he had been more deeply injured. This was his wife's sister,—ah, yes! but a sister who had scorned and slighted and ignored the existence of his wife for all her life. Only Miller, of all the world, could have guessed what this had meant to Janet, and he had merely divined it through the clairvoyant sympathy of love. This woman could have no claim upon him because of this unacknowledged relationship. Yet, after all, she *was* his wife's sister, his child's kinswoman. She was a fellow creature, too, and in distress.

"Rise, madam," he said, with a sudden inspiration, lifting her gently. "I will listen to you on one condition. My child lies dead in the adjoining room, his mother by his side. Go in there, and make your request of her. I will abide by her decision."

The two women stood confronting each other across the body of the dead child, mute witness of this first meeting between two children of the same father. Standing thus face to face, each under the stress of the deepest emotions, the resemblance between them was even more striking than it had seemed to Miller when he had admitted Mrs. Carteret to the house. But Death, the great leveler, striking upon the one hand and threatening upon the other, had wrought a marvelous transformation in the bearing of the two women. The sad-eyed Janet towered erect, with menacing aspect, like an avenging goddess. The other, whose pride had been her life, stood in the attitude of a trembling suppliant.

"*You* have come here," cried Janet, pointing with a tragic gesture to the dead child,—"*you*, to gloat over your husband's work. All my life you have hated and scorned and despised me. Your presence here insults me and my dead. What are you doing here?"

"Mrs. Miller," returned Mrs. Carteret tremulously, dazed for a moment by this outburst, and clasping her hands with an imploring gesture, "my child, my only child, is dying, and your husband alone can save his life. Ah, let me have my child," she moaned, heartrendingly. "It is my only one—my sweet child—my ewe lamb!"

"This was *my* only child!" replied the other mother; "and yours is no better to die than mine!"

"You are young," said Mrs. Carteret, "and may yet have many children,—this is my only hope! If you have a human heart, tell your husband to come with me. He leaves it to you; he will do as you command."

"Ah," cried Janet, "I have a human heart, and therefore I will not let him go. *My* child is dead—O God, my child, my child!"

She threw herself down by the bedside, sobbing hysterically. The other woman knelt beside her, and put her arm about her neck. For a moment Janet, absorbed in her grief, did not repulse her.

"Listen," pleaded Mrs. Carteret. "You will not let my baby die? You are my sister;—the child is your own near kin!"

"My child was nearer," returned Janet, rising again to her feet and shaking off the other woman's arm. "He was my son, and I have seen him die. I have been your sister for twenty-five years, and you have only now, for the first time, called me so!"

"Listen—sister," returned Mrs. Carteret. Was there no way to move this woman? Her child lay dying, if he were not dead already. She would tell everything, and leave the rest to God. If it would save her child, she would shrink at no sacrifice. Whether the truth would still further incense Janet, or move her to mercy, she could not tell; she would leave the issue to God.

"Listen, sister!" she said. "I have a confession to make. You *are* my lawful sister. My father was married to your mother. You are entitled to his name, and to half his estate."

Janet's eyes flashed with bitter scorn.

"And you have robbed me all these years, and now tell me that as a reason why I should forgive the murder of my child?"

"No, no!" cried the other wildly, fearing the worst. "I have known of it only a few weeks,—since my Aunt Polly's death. I had not meant to rob you,—I had meant to make restitution. Sister! for our father's sake, who did you no wrong, give me my child's life!"

Janet's eyes slowly filled with tears—bitter tears—burning tears. For a moment even her grief at her child's loss dropped to second place in her thoughts. This, then, was the recognition for which, all her life, she had longed in secret. It had come, after many days, and in larger measure than she had dreamed; but it had come, not with frank kindliness and sisterly love, but in a storm of blood and tears; not freely given, from an open heart, but extorted from a reluctant conscience by the agony of a mother's fears. Janet had obtained her heart's desire, and now that it was at her lips, found it but apples of Sodom, filled with dust and ashes!

"Listen!" she cried, dashing her tears aside. "I have but one word for you,—one last word,—and then I hope never to see your face again! My mother died of want, and I was brought up by the hand of charity. Now, when I have married a man who can supply my needs, you offer me back the money which you and your friends have robbed me of! You imagined that the shame of being a negro swallowed up every other ignominy,—and in your eyes I am a negro, though I am your sister, and you are white, and people have taken me for you on the streets,—and you, therefore, left me nameless all my life! Now, when an honest man has given me a name of which I can be proud, you offer me the one of which you robbed me, and of which I can make no use. For twenty-five years I, poor, despicable fool, would have kissed your feet for a word, a nod, a smile. Now, when this tardy recognition comes, for which I have waited so long, it is tainted with fraud and crime and blood, and I must pay for it with my child's life!"

"And I must forfeit that of mine, it seems, for withholding it so long," sobbed the other, as, tottering, she turned to go. "It is but just."

"Stay—do not go yet!" commanded Janet imperiously, her pride still keeping back her tears. "I have not done. I throw you back your father's name, your father's wealth, your sisterly recognition. I want none of them,—they are bought too dear! ah, God, they are bought too dear! But that you may know that a woman may be foully wronged, and yet may have a heart to feel, even for one who has injured her, you may have your child's life, if my husband can save it! Will," she said, throwing open the door into the next room, "go with her!"

"God will bless you for a noble woman!" exclaimed Mrs. Carteret. "You do not mean all the cruel things you have said,—ah, no! I will see you again, and make you take them back; I cannot thank you now! Oh, doctor, let us go! I pray God we may not be too late!"

Together they went out into the night. Mrs. Carteret tottered under the stress of her emotions, and would have fallen, had not Miller caught and sustained her with his arm until they reached the house, where he turned over her fainting form to Carteret at the door.

"Is the child still alive?" asked Miller.

"Yes, thank God," answered the father, "but nearly gone."

"Come on up, Dr. Miller," called Evans from the head of the stairs. "There's time enough, but none to spare."

The Sport
of the Gods

by

Paul Laurence Dunbar

CHAPTER I

The Hamiltons

FICTION HAS SAID so much in regret of the old days when there were plantations and overseers and masters and slaves, that it was good to come upon such a household as Berry Hamilton's, if for no other reason than that it afforded a relief from the monotony of tiresome iteration.

The little cottage in which he lived with his wife, Fannie, who was housekeeper to the Oakleys, and his son and daughter, Joe and Kit, sat back in the yard some hundred paces from the mansion of his employer. It was somewhat in the manner of the old cabin in the quarters, with which usage as well as tradition had made both master and servant familiar. But, unlike the cabin of the elder day, it was a neatly furnished, modern house, the home of a typical, good-living negro. For twenty years Berry Hamilton had been butler for Maurice Oakley. He was one of the many slaves who upon their accession to freedom had not left the South, but had wandered from place to place in their own beloved section, waiting, working, and struggling to rise with its rehabilitated fortunes.

The first faint signs of recovery were being seen when he came to Maurice Oakley as a servant. Through thick and thin he remained with him, and when the final upward tendency of his employer began his fortunes had increased in like manner. When, having married, Oakley bought the great house in which he now lived, he left the little servant's cottage in the yard, for, as he said laughingly, "There is no telling when Berry will be following my example and be taking a wife unto himself."

His joking prophecy came true very soon. Berry had long had a tenderness for Fannie, the housekeeper. As she retained her post under the new Mrs. Oakley, and as there was a cottage ready to his hand, it promised to be cheaper and more convenient all around to get married. Fannie was willing, and so the matter was settled.

Fannie had never regretted her choice, nor had Berry ever had cause to curse his utilitarian ideas. The stream of years had flowed pleasantly and peacefully with them. Their little sorrows had come, but their joys had been many.

As time went on, the little cottage grew in comfort. It was replenished with things handed down from "the house" from time to time and with others bought from the pair's earnings.

Berry had time for his lodge, and Fannie time to spare for her own house and garden. Flowers bloomed in the little plot in front and behind it; vegetables and greens testified to the housewife's industry.

Over the door of the little house a fine Virginia creeper bent and fell in graceful curves, and a cluster of insistent morning-glories clung in summer about its stalwart stock.

It was into this bower of peace and comfort that Joe and Kitty were born. They brought a new sunlight into the house and a new joy to the father's and mother's hearts. Their early lives were pleasant and carefully guarded. They got what schooling the town afforded, but both went to work early, Kitty helping her mother and Joe learning the trade of barber.

Kit was the delight of her mother's life. She was a pretty, cheery little thing, and could sing like a lark. Joe too was of a cheerful disposition, but from scraping the chins of aristocrats came to imbibe some of their ideas, and rather too early in life bid fair to be a dandy. But his father encouraged him, for, said he, "It's de p'opah thing fu' a man what waits on quality to have quality mannahs an' to waih quality clothes."

" 'Tain't no use to be a-humo'in' dat boy too much, Be'y," Fannie had replied, although she did fully as much "humo'in' " as her husband; "hit sho' do mek' him biggety, an' a biggety po' niggah is a 'bomination befo' de face of de Lawd; but I know 'tain't no use a-talkin' to you, fu' you plum boun' up in dat Joe."

Her own eyes would follow the boy lovingly and proudly even as she chided. She could not say very much, either, for Berry always had the reply that she was spoiling Kit out of all reason. The girl did have the prettiest clothes of any of her race in the town, and when she was to sing for the benefit of the A. M. E. church or for the benefit of her father's society, the Tribe of Benjamin, there was nothing too good for her to wear. In this too they were aided and abetted by Mrs. Oakley, who also took a lively interest in the girl.

So the two doting parents had their chats and their jokes at each other's expense and went bravely on, doing their duties and spoiling their children much as white fathers and mothers are wont to do.

What the less fortunate negroes of the community said of them and their offspring is really not worth while. Envy has a sharp tongue, and when has not the aristocrat been the target for the plebeian's sneers?

Joe and Kit were respectively eighteen and sixteen at the time when the preparations for Maurice Oakley's farewell dinner to his brother Francis were agitating the whole Hamilton household. All of them had a hand in the work: Joe had shaved the two men; Kit had helped Mrs. Oakley's maid; the mother had fretted herself weak over the shortcomings of a cook that had been in the family nearly as long as herself, while Berry was stern and dignified in anticipation of the glorious figure he was to make in serving.

When all was ready, peace again settled upon the Hamiltons. Mrs. Hamilton, in the whitest of white aprons, prepared to be on hand to annoy the cook still more; Kit was ready to station herself where she could view the finery; Joe had condescended to promise to be home in time to eat some of the good things, and Berry— Berry was gorgeous in his evening suit with the white waistcoat, as he directed the nimble waiters hither and thither.

CHAPTER II

A Farewell Dinner

MAURICE OAKLEY WAS not a man of sudden or violent enthusiasms. Conservatism was the quality that had been the foundation of his fortunes at a time when the disruption of the country had involved most of the men of his region in ruin.

Without giving any one ground to charge him with being lukewarm or renegade to his cause, he had yet so adroitly managed his affairs that when peace came he was able quickly to recover much of the ground lost during the war. With a rare genius for adapting himself to new conditions, he accepted the changed order of things with a passive resignation, but with a stern determination to make the most out of any good that might be in it.

It was a favourite remark of his that there must be some good in every system, and it was the duty of the citizen to find out that good and make it pay. He had done this. His house, his reputation, his satisfaction, were all evidences that he had succeeded.

A childless man, he bestowed upon his younger brother, Francis, the enthusiasm he would have given to a son. His wife shared with her husband this feeling for her brother-in-law, and with him played the rôle of parent, which had otherwise been denied her.

It was true that Francis Oakley was only a half-brother to Maurice, the son of a second and not too fortunate marriage, but there was no halving of the love which the elder man had given to him from childhood up.

At the first intimation that Francis had artistic ability, his brother had placed him under the best masters in America, and later, when the promise of his youth had begun to blossom, he sent him to Paris, although the expenditure just at that time demanded a sacrifice which might have been the ruin of Maurice's own career. Francis's promise had never come to entire fulfilment. He was always trembling on the verge of a great success without quite plunging into it. Despite the joy which his presence gave his brother and sister-in-law, most of his time was spent abroad, where he could find just the atmosphere that suited his delicate, artistic nature. After a visit of two months he was about returning to Paris for a stay of five years. At last he was going to apply himself steadily and try to be less the dilettante.

The company which Maurice Oakley brought together to say good-bye to his brother on this occasion was drawn from the best that this fine old Southern town afforded. There were colonels there at whose titles and the owners' rights to them no one could laugh; there were brilliant women there who had queened it in Richmond, Baltimore, Louisville, and New Orleans, and every Southern capital under the old régime, and there were younger ones there of wit and beauty who were just beginning to hold their court. For Francis was a great favourite both with men and women. He was a handsome man, tall, slender, and graceful. He had the face and brow of a poet, a pallid face framed in a mass of dark hair. There was a touch of weakness in his mouth, but this was shaded and half hidden by a full mustache that made much forgivable to beauty-loving eyes.

It was generally conceded that Mrs. Oakley was a hostess whose guests had no awkward half-hour before dinner. No praise could be higher than this, and tonight she had no need to exert herself to maintain this reputation. Her brother-in-law was the life of the assembly; he had wit and daring, and about him there was just that hint of charming danger that made him irresistible to women. The guests heard the dinner announced with surprise,— an unusual thing, except in this house.

Both Maurice Oakley and his wife looked fondly at the artist as he went in with Claire Lessing. He was talking animatedly to the girl, having changed the general trend of the conversation to a manner and tone directed more particularly to her. While she listened to him, her face glowed and her eyes shone with a light that every man could not bring into them.

As Maurice and his wife followed him with their gaze, the same thought was in their minds, and it had not just come to them, Why could not Francis marry Claire Lessing and settle in America, instead of going back ever and again to that life in the Latin Quarter? They did not believe that it was a bad life or a dissipated one, but from the little that they had seen of it when they were in Paris, it was at least a bit too free and unconventional for their traditions. There were, too, temptations which must assail any man of Francis's looks and talents. They had perfect faith in the strength of his manhood, of course; but could they have had their way, it would have been their will to hedge him about so that no breath of evil invitation could have come nigh to him.

But this younger brother, this half ward of theirs, was an unruly member. He talked and laughed, rode and walked, with Claire Lessing with the same free abandon, the same show of uninterested good comradeship, that he had used towards her when they were boy and girl together. There was not a shade more of warmth or self-consciousness in his manner towards her than there had been fifteen years before. In fact, there was less, for there had been a time, when he was six and Claire three, that Francis, with a boldness that the lover of maturer years tries vainly to attain, had announced to Claire that he was going to marry her. But he had never renewed this declaration when it came time that it would carry weight with it.

They made a fine picture as they sat together to-night. One seeing them could hardly help thinking on the instant that they were made for each other. Something in the woman's face, in her expression perhaps, supplied a palpable lack in the man. The strength of her mouth and chin helped the weakness of his. She was the sort of woman who, if ever he came to a great moral crisis in his life, would be able to save him if she were near. And yet he was going away from her, giving up the pearl that he had only to put out his hand to take.

Some of these thoughts were in the minds of the brother and sister now.

"Five years does seem a long while," Francis was saying, "but if a man accomplishes anything, after all, it seems only a short time to look back upon."

"All time is short to look back upon. It is the looking

forward to it that counts. It doesn't, though, with a man, I suppose. He's doing something all the while."

"Yes, a man is always doing something, even if only waiting; but waiting is such unheroic business."

"That is the part that usually falls to a woman's lot. I have no doubt that some dark-eyed mademoiselle is waiting for you now."

Francis laughed and flushed hotly. Claire noted the flush and wondered at it. Had she indeed hit upon the real point? Was that the reason that he was so anxious to get back to Paris? The thought struck a chill through her gaiety. She did not want to be suspicious, but what was the cause of that tell-tale flush? He was not a man easily disconcerted; then why so to-night? But her companion talked on with such innocent composure that she believed herself mistaken as to the reason for his momentary confusion.

Someone cried gayly across the table to her: "Oh, Miss Claire, you will not dare to talk with such little awe to our friend when he comes back with his ribbons and his medals. Why, we shall all have to bow to you, Frank!"

"You're wronging me, Esterton," said Francis. "No foreign decoration could ever be to me as much as the flower of approval from the fair women of my own State."

"Hear!" cried the ladies.

"Trust artists and poets to pay pretty compliments, and this wily friend of mine pays his at my expense."

"A good bit of generalship, that, Frank," an old military man broke in. "Esterton opened the breach and you at once galloped in. That's the highest art of war."

Claire was looking at her companion. Had he meant the approval of the women, or was it one woman that he cared for? Had the speech had a hidden meaning for her? She could never tell. She could not understand this man who had been so much to her for so long, and yet did not seem to know it; who was full of romance and fire and passion, and yet looked at her beauty with the eyes of a mere comrade. She sighed as she rose with the rest of the women to leave the table.

The men lingered over their cigars. The wine was old and the stories new. What more could they ask? There was a strong glow in Francis Oakley's face, and his laugh was frequent and ringing. Some discussion came up which sent him running up to his room for a bit of evidence. When he came down it was not to come directly to the dining-room. He paused in the hall and despatched a servant to bring his brother to him.

Maurice found him standing weakly against the railing of the stairs. Something in his air impressed his brother strangely.

"What is it, Francis?" he questioned, hurrying to him.

"I have just discovered a considerable loss," was the reply in a grieved voice.

"If it is no worse than loss, I am glad; but what is it?"

"Every cent of money that I had to secure my letter of credit is gone from my bureau."

"What? When did it disappear?"

"I went to my bureau to-night for something and found the money gone; then I remembered that when I opened it two days ago I must have left the key in the lock, as I found it to-night."

"It's a bad business, but don't let's talk of it now. Come, let's go back to our guests. Don't look so cut up about it, Frank, old man. It isn't as bad as it might be, and you mustn't show a gloomy face to-night."

The younger man pulled himself together, and re-entered the room with his brother. In a few minutes his gaiety had apparently returned.

When they rejoined the ladies, even their quick eyes could detect in his demeanour no trace of the annoying thing that had occurred. His face did not change until, with a wealth of fervent congratulations, he had bade the last guest good-bye.

Then he turned to his brother. "When Leslie is in bed, come into the library. I will wait for you there," he said, and walked sadly away.

"Poor, foolish Frank," mused his brother, "as if the loss could matter to him."

CHAPTER III

The Theft

FRANK WAS VERY PALE when his brother finally came to him at the appointed place. He sat limply in his chair, his eyes fixed upon the floor.

"Come, brace up now, Frank, and tell me about it."

At the sound of his brother's voice he started and looked up as though he had been dreaming.

"I don't know what you'll think of me, Maurice," he said; "I have never before been guilty of such criminal carelessness."

"Don't stop to accuse yourself. Our only hope in this matter lies in prompt action. Where was the money?"

"In the oak cabinet and lying in the bureau drawer. Such a thing as a theft seemed so foreign to this place that I was never very particular about the box. But I did not know until I went to it to-night that the last time I had opened it I had forgotten to take the key out. It all flashed over me in a second when I saw it shining there. Even then I didn't suspect anything. You don't know how I felt to open that cabinet and find all my money gone. It's awful."

"Don't worry. How much was there in all?"

"Nine hundred and eighty-six dollars, most of which, I am ashamed to say, I had accepted from you."

"You have no right to talk that way, Frank; you know I do not begrudge a cent you want. I have never felt that my father did quite right in leaving me the bulk of the fortune; but we won't discuss that now. What I want you to understand, though, is that the money is yours as well as mine, and you are always welcome to it."

The artist shook his head. "No, Maurice," he said, "I can accept no more from you. I have already used up all my own money and too much of yours in this hopeless fight. I don't suppose I was ever cut out for an artist, or

479

I'd have done something really notable in this time, and would not be a burden upon those who care for me. No, I'll give up going to Paris and find some work to do."

"Frank, Frank, be silent. This is nonsense. Give up your art? You shall not do it. You shall go to Paris as usual. Leslie and I have perfect faith in you. You shall not give up on account of this misfortune. What are the few paltry dollars to me or to you?"

"Nothing, nothing, I know. It isn't the money, it's the principle of the thing."

"Principle be hanged! You go back to Paris to-morrow, just as you had planned. I do not ask it, I command it."

The younger man looked up quickly.

"Pardon me, Frank, for using those words and at such a time. You know how near my heart your success lies, and to hear you talk of giving it all up makes me forget myself. Forgive me, but you'll go back, won't you?"

"You are too good, Maurice," said Frank impulsively, "and I will go back, and I'll try to redeem myself."

"There is no redeeming of yourself to do, my dear boy; all you have to do is to mature yourself. We'll have a detective down and see what we can do in this matter."

Frank gave a scarcely perceptible start. "I do so hate such things," he said; "and, anyway, what's the use? They'll never find out where the stuff went to."

"Oh, you need not be troubled in this matter. I know that such things must jar on your delicate nature. But I am a plain hard-headed business man, and I can attend to it without distaste."

"But I hate to shove everything unpleasant off on you. It's what I've been doing all my life."

"Never mind that. Now tell me, who was the last person you remember in your room?"

"Oh, Esterton was up there awhile before dinner. But he was not alone two minutes."

"Why, he would be out of the question anyway. Who else?"

"Hamilton was up yesterday."

"Alone?"

"Yes, for a while. His boy, Joe, shaved me, and Jack was up for a while brushing my clothes."

"Then it lies between Jack and Joe?"

Frank hesitated.

"Neither one was left alone, though."

"Then only Hamilton and Esterton have been alone for any time in your room since you left the key in your cabinet?"

"Those are the only ones of whom I know anything. What others went in during the day, of course, I know nothing about. It couldn't have been either Esterton or Hamilton."

"Not Esterton, no."

"And Hamilton is beyond suspicion."

"No servant is beyond suspicion."

"I would trust Hamilton anywhere," said Frank stoutly, "and with anything."

"That's noble of you, Frank, and I would have done the same, but we must remember that we are not in the old days now. The negroes are becoming less faithful and less contented, and more's the pity, and a deal more ambitious, although I have never had any unfaithfulness on the part of Hamilton to complain of before."

"Then do not condemn him now."

"I shall not condemn any one until I have proof positive of his guilt or such clear circumstantial evidence that my reason is satisfied."

"I do not believe that you will ever have that against old Hamilton."

"This spirit of trust does you credit, Frank, and I very much hope that you may be right. But as soon as a negro like Hamilton learns the value of money and begins to earn it, at the same time he begins to covet some easy and rapid way of securing it. The old negro knew nothing of the value of money. When he stole, he stole hams and bacon and chickens. These were his immediate necessities and the things he valued. The present laughs at this tendency without knowing the cause. The present negro resents the laugh, and he has learned to value other things than those which satisfy his belly."

Frank looked bored.

"But pardon me for boring you. I know you want to go to bed. Go and leave everything to me."

The young man reluctantly withdrew, and Maurice went to the telephone and rung up the police station.

As Maurice had said, he was a plain, hard-headed busi-

ness man, and it took very few words for him to put the
Chief of Police in possession of the principal facts of the
case. A detective was detailed to take charge of the case,
and was started immediately, so that he might be upon
the ground as soon after the commission of the crime as
possible.

When he came he insisted that if he was to do anything
he must question the robbed man and search his room
at once. Oakley protested, but the detective was ada-
mant. Even now the presence in the room of a man un-
initiated into the mysteries of criminal methods might be
destroying the last vestige of a really important clue. The
master of the house had no alternative save to yield.
Together they went to the artist's room. A light shone
out through the crack under the door.

"I am sorry to disturb you again, Frank, but may we
come in?"

"Who is with you?"

"The detective."

"I did not know he was to come to-night."

"The chief thought it better."

"All right in a moment."

There was a sound of moving around, and in a short
time the young fellow, partly undressed, opened the
door.

To the detective's questions he answered in substance
what he had told before. He also brought out the cabinet.
It was a strong oak box, uncarven, but bound at the
edges with brass. The key was still in the lock, where
Frank had left it on discovering his loss. They raised the
lid. The cabinet contained two compartments, one for
letters and a smaller one for jewels and trinkets.

"When you opened this cabinet, your money was
gone?"

"Yes."

"Were any of your papers touched?"

"No."

"How about your jewels?"

"I have but few and they were elsewhere."

The detective examined the room carefully, its approaches, and the hall-ways without. He paused knowingly at a window that overlooked the flat top of a porch.

"Do you ever leave this window open?"

"It is almost always so."

"Is this porch on the front of the house?"

"No, on the side."

"What else is out that way?"

Frank and Maurice looked at each other. The younger man hesitated and put his hand to his head. Maurice answered grimly, "My butler's cottage is on that side and a little way back."

"Uh huh! and your butler is, I believe, the Hamilton whom the young gentleman mentioned some time ago."

"Yes."

Frank's face was really very white now. The detective nodded again.

"I think I have a clue," he said simply. "I will be here again to-morrow morning."

"But I shall be gone," said Frank.

"You will hardly be needed, anyway."

The artist gave a sigh of relief. He hated to be involved in unpleasant things. He went as far as the outer door with his brother and the detective. As he bade the officer good-night and hurried up the hall, Frank put his hand to his head again with a convulsive gesture, as if struck by a sudden pain.

"Come, come, Frank, you must take a drink now and go to bed," said Oakley.

"I am completely unnerved."

"I know it, and I am no less shocked than you. But we've got to face it like men."

They passed into the dining-room, where Maurice poured out some brandy for his brother and himself. "Who would have thought it?" he asked, as he tossed his own down.

"Not I. I had hoped against hope up until the last that it would turn out to be a mistake."

"Nothing angers me so much as being deceived by the man I have helped and trusted. I should feel the sting of all this much less if the thief had come from the outside, broken in, and robbed me, but this, after all these years, is too low."

"Don't be hard on a man, Maurice; one never knows what prompts him to a deed. And this evidence is all circumstantial."

"It is plain enough for me. You are entirely too kindhearted, Frank. But I see that this thing has worn you out. You must not stand here talking. Go to bed, for you must be fresh for to-morrow morning's journey to New York."

Frank Oakley turned away towards his room. His face was haggard, and he staggered as he walked. His brother looked after him with a pitying and affectionate gaze.

"Poor fellow," he said, "he is so delicately constructed that he cannot stand such shocks as these"; and then he added: "To think of that black hound's treachery! I'll give him all that the law sets down for him."

He found Mrs. Oakley asleep when he reached the room, but he awakened her to tell her the story. She was horror-struck. It was hard to have to believe this awful thing of an old servant, but she agreed with him that Hamilton must be made an example of when the time came. Before that, however, he must not know that he was suspected.

They fell asleep, he with thoughts of anger and revenge, and she grieved and disappointed.

CHAPTER IV

From a Clear Sky

THE INMATES OF THE Oakley house had not been long in their beds before Hamilton was out of his and rousing his own little household.

"You, Joe," he called to his son, "git up f'om daih an' come right hyeah. You got to he'p me befo' you go to any shop dis mo'nin'. You, Kitty, stir yo' stumps, miss. I know yo' ma's a-dressin' now. Ef she ain't, I bet I'll be aftah huh in a minute, too. You all layin' 'roun', snoozin' w'en you all des' pint'ly know dis is de mo'nin' Mistah Frank go 'way f'om hyeah."

It was a cool Autumn morning, fresh and dew-washed. The sun was just rising, and a cool clear breeze was blowing across the land. The blue smoke from the "house," where the fire was already going, whirled fantastically over the roofs like a belated ghost. It was just the morning to doze in comfort, and so thought all of Berry's household except himself. Loud was the complaining as they threw themselves out of bed. They maintained that it was an altogether unearthly hour to get up. Even Mrs. Hamilton added her protest, until she suddenly remembered what morning it was, when she hurried into her clothes and set about getting the family's breakfast.

The good-humour of all of them returned when they were seated about their table with some of the good things of the night before set out, and the talk ran cheerily around.

"I do declaih," said Hamilton, "you all's as bad as dem white people was las' night. De way dey waded into dat food was a caution." He chuckled with delight at the recollection.

"I reckon dat's what dey come fu'. I wasn't payin' so much 'tention to what dey eat as to de way dem women

485

was dressed. Why, Mis' Jedge Hill was des' mo'n go'geous.''

"Oh, yes, ma, an' Miss Lessing wasn't no ways behin' her," put in Kitty.

Joe did not condescend to join in the conversation, but contented himself with devouring the good things and aping the manners of the young men whom he knew had been among last night's guests.

"Well, I got to be goin'," said Berry, rising. "There'll be early breakfas' at de 'house' dis mo'nin', so's Mistah Frank kin ketch de fus' train."

He went out cheerily to his work. No shadow of impending disaster depressed his spirits. No cloud obscured his sky. He was a simple, easy man, and he saw nothing in the manner of the people whom he served that morning at breakfast save a natural grief at parting from each other. He did not even take the trouble to inquire who the strange white man was who hung about the place.

When it came time for the young man to leave, with the privilege of an old servitor Berry went up to him to bid him good-bye. He held out his hand to him, and with a glance at his brother, Frank took it and shook it cordially. "Good-bye, Berry," he said. Maurice could hardly restrain his anger at the sight, but his wife was moved to tears at her brother-in-law's generosity.

The last sight they saw as the carriage rolled away towards the station was Berry standing upon the steps waving a hearty farewell and god-speed.

"How could you do it, Frank?" gasped his brother, as soon as they had driven well out of hearing.

"Hush, Maurice," said Mrs. Oakley gently; "I think it was very noble of him."

"Oh, I felt sorry for the poor fellow," was Frank's reply. "Promise me you won't be too hard on him, Maurice. Give him a little scare and let him go. He's possibly buried the money, anyhow."

"I shall deal with him as he deserves."

The young man sighed and was silent the rest of the way.

"Whether I fail or succeed, you will always think well of me, Maurice?" he said in parting; "and if I don't come up to your expectations, well—forgive me—that's all."

His brother wrung his hand. "You will always come up to my expectations, Frank," he said. "Won't he, Leslie?"

"He will always be our Frank, our good, generous-hearted, noble boy. God bless him!"

The young fellow bade them a hearty good-bye, and they, knowing what his feelings must be, spared him the prolonging of the strain. They waited in the carriage, and he waved to them as the train rolled out of the station.

"He seems to be sad at going," said Mrs. Oakley.

"Poor fellow, the affair of last night has broken him up considerably, but I'll make Berry pay for every pang of anxiety that my brother has suffered."

"Don't be revengeful, Maurice; you know what brother Frank asked of you."

"He is gone and will never know what happens, so I may be as revengeful as I wish."

The detective was waiting on the lawn when Maurice Oakley returned. They went immediately to the library, Oakley walking with the firm, hard tread of a man who is both exasperated and determined, and the officer gliding along with the cat-like step which is one of the attributes of his profession.

"Well?" was the impatient man's question as soon as the door closed upon them.

"I have some more information that may or may not be of importance."

"Out with it; maybe I can tell."

"First, let me ask if you had any reason to believe that your butler had any resources of his own, say to the amount of three or four hundred dollars?"

"Certainly not. I pay him thirty dollars a month, and his wife fifteen dollars, and with keeping up his lodges and the way he dresses that girl, he can't save very much."

"You know that he has money in the bank?"

"No."

"Well, he has. Over eight hundred dollars."

"What? Berry? It must be the pickings of years."

"And yesterday it was increased by five hundred more."

"The scoundrel!"

"How was your brother's money, in bills?"

"It was in large bills and gold, with some silver."

"Berry's money was almost all in bills of a small denomination and silver."

"A poor trick; it could easily have been changed."

"Not such a sum without exciting comment."

"He may have gone to several places."

"But he had only a day to do it in."

"Then some one must have been his accomplice."

"That remains to be proven."

"Nothing remains to be proven. Why, it's as clear as day that the money he has is the result of a long series of peculations, and that this last is the result of his first large theft."

"That must be made clear to the law."

"It shall be."

"I should advise, though, no open proceedings against this servant until further evidence to establish his guilt is found."

"If the evidence satisfies me, it must be sufficient to satisfy any ordinary jury. I demand his immediate arrest."

"As you will, sir. Will you have him called here and question him, or will you let me question him at once?"

"Yes."

Oakley struck the bell, and Berry himself answered it.

"You're just the man we want," said Oakley, shortly.

Berry looked astonished.

"Shall I question him," asked the officer, "or will you?"

"I will. Berry, you deposited five hundred dollars at the bank yesterday?"

"Well, suh, Mistah Oakley," was the grinning reply, "ef you ain't de beatenes' man to fin' out things I evah seen."

The employer half rose from his chair. His face was livid with anger. But at a sign from the detective he strove to calm himself.

"You had better let me talk to Berry, Mr. Oakley," said the officer.

Oakley nodded. Berry was looking distressed and excited. He seemed not to understand it at all.

"Berry," the officer pursued, "you admit having deposited five hundred dollars in the bank yesterday?"

"Sut'ny. Dey ain't no reason why I shouldn't admit it, 'ceptin' erroun' ermong dese jealous niggahs."

"Uh huh! well, now, where did you get this money?"

"Why, I wo'ked fu' it, o' co'se, whaih you s'pose I got it? 'Tain't drappin' off trees, I reckon, not roun' dis pa't of de country."

"You worked for it? You must have done a pretty big job to have got so much money all in a lump?"

"But I didn't git it in a lump. Why, man, I've been savin' dat money fu mo'n fo' yeahs."

"More than four years? Why didn't you put it in the bank as you got it?"

"Why, mos'ly it was too small, an' so I des' kep' it in a ol' sock. I tol' Fannie dat some day ef de bank didn't bus' wid all de res' I had, I'd put it in too. She was allus sayin' it was too much to have layin' 'roun' de house. But I des' tol' huh dat no robber wasn't goin' to bothah de po' niggah down in de ya'd wid de rich white man up at de house. But fin'lly I listened to huh an' sposited it yistiddy."

"You're a liar! you're a liar, you black thief!" Oakley broke in impetuously. "You have learned your lesson well, but you can't cheat me. I know where that money came from."

"Calm yourself, Mr. Oakley, calm yourself."

"I will not calm myself. Take him away. He shall not stand here and lie to me."

Berry had suddenly turned ashen.

"You say you know whaih dat money come f'om? Whaih?"

"You stole it, you thief, from my brother Frank's room."

"Stole it! My Gawd, Mistah Oakley, you believed a thing lak dat aftah all de yeahs I been wid you?"

"You've been stealing all along."

"Why, what shell I do?" said the servant helplessly. "I tell you, Mistah Oakley, ask Fannie. She'll know how long I been a-savin' dis money."

"I'll ask no one."

"I think it would be better to call his wife, Oakley."

"Well, call her, but let this matter be done with soon."

Fannie was summoned, and when the matter was explained to her, first gave evidences of giving way to grief, but when the detective began to question her, she calmed herself and answered directly just as her husband had.

"Well posted," sneered Oakley. "Arrest that man."

Berry had begun to look more hopeful during Fannie's recital, but now the ashen look came back into his face. At the word "arrest" his wife collapsed utterly, and sobbed on her husband's shoulder.

"Send the woman away."

"I won't go," cried Fannie stoutly; "I'll stay right hyeah by my husband. You sha'n't drive me away f'om him."

Berry turned to his employer. "You b'lieve dat I stole f'om dis house aftah all de yeahs I've been in it, aftah de caih I took of yo' money an' yo' valybles, aftah de way I've put you to bed f'om many a dinnah, an' you woke up to fin' all yo' money safe? Now, can you b'lieve dis?"

His voice broke, and he ended with a cry.

"Yes, I believe it, you thief, yes. Take him away."

Berry's eyes were bloodshot as he replied, "Den, damn you! damn you! ef dat's all dese yeahs counted fu', I wish I had a-stoled it."

Oakley made a step forward, and his man did likewise, but the officer stepped between them.

"Take that damned hound away, or, by God! I'll do him violence!"

The two men stood fiercely facing each other, then the handcuffs were snapped on the servant's wrist.

"No, no," shrieked Fannie, "you mustn't, you mustn't. Oh, my Gawd! he ain't no thief. I'll go to Mis' Oakley. She nevah will believe it." She sped from the room.

The commotion had called a crowd of curious servants into the hall. Fannie hardly saw them as she dashed among them, crying for her mistress. In a moment she returned, dragging Mrs. Oakley by the hand.

"Tell 'em, oh, tell 'em, Miss Leslie, dat you don't believe it. Don't let 'em 'rest Berry."

"Why, Fannie, I can't do anything. It all seems perfectly plain, and Mr. Oakley knows better than any of us, you know."

Fannie, her last hope gone, flung herself on the floor, crying, "O Gawd! O Gawd! he's gone fu' sho'!"

Her husband bent over her, the tears dropping from his eyes. "Nevah min', Fannie," he said, "nevah min'. Hit's boun' to come out all right."

She raised her head, and seizing his manacled hands pressed them to her breast, wailing in a low monotone, "Gone! gone!"

They disengaged her hands, and led Berry away.

"Take her out," said Oakley sternly to the servants; and they lifted her up and carried her away in a sort of dumb stupor that was half a swoon.

They took her to her little cottage, and laid her down until she could come to herself and the full horror of her situation burst upon her.

CHAPTER V

The Justice of Men

THE ARREST OF Berry Hamilton on the charge preferred by his employer was the cause of unusual commotion in the town. Both the accuser and the accused were well known to the citizens, white and black,—Maurice Oakley as a solid man of business, and Berry as an honest, sensible negro, and the pink of good servants. The evening papers had a full story of the crime, which closed by saying that the prisoner had amassed a considerable sum of money, it was very likely from a long series of smaller peculations.

It seems a strange irony upon the force of right living, that this man, who had never been arrested before, who had never even been suspected of wrong-doing, should find so few who even at the first telling doubted the story of his guilt. Many people began to remember things that had looked particularly suspicious in his dealings. Some others said, "I didn't think it of him." There were only a few who dared to say, "I don't believe it of him."

The first act of his lodge, "The Tribe of Benjamin," whose treasurer he was, was to have his accounts audited, when they should have been visiting him with comfort, and they seemed personally grieved when his books were found to be straight. The A. M. E. church, of which he had been an honest and active member, hastened to disavow sympathy with him, and to purge itself of contamination by turning him out. His friends were afraid to visit him and were silent when his enemies gloated. On every side one might have asked, Where is charity? and gone away empty.

In the black people of the town the strong influence of slavery was still operative, and with one accord they turned away from one of their own kind upon whom had been set the ban of the white people's displeasure. If they had sympathy, they dared not show it. Their own interests, the safety of their own positions and firesides, demanded that they stand aloof from the criminal. Not then, not now, nor has it ever been true, although it has been claimed, that negroes either harbour or sympathise with the criminal of their kind. They did not dare to do it before the sixties. They do not dare to do it now. They have brought down as a heritage from the days of their bondage both fear and disloyalty. So Berry was unbefriended while the storm raged around him. The cell where they had placed him was kind to him, and he could not hear the envious and sneering comments that went on about him. This was kind, for the tongues of his enemies were not.

"Tell me, tell me," said one, "you needn't tell me dat a bird kin fly so high dat he don' have to come down some time. An' w'en he do light, honey, my Lawd, how he flop!"

"Mistah Rich Niggah," said another. "He wanted to dress his wife an' chillen lak white folks, did he? Well, he foun' out, he foun' out. By de time de jedge git thoo wid him he won't be hol'in' his haid so high."

"W'y, dat gal o' his'n," broke in old Isaac Brown indignantly, "w'y, she wouldn' speak to my gal, Minty, when she met huh on de street. I reckon she come down off'n huh high hoss now."

The fact of the matter was that Minty Brown was no better than she should have been, and did not deserve to be spoken to. But none of this was taken into account either by the speaker or the hearers. The man was down, it was time to strike.

The women too joined their shrill voices to the general cry, and were loud in their abuse of the Hamiltons and in disparagement of their high-toned airs.

"I knowed it, I knowed it," mumbled one old crone, rolling her bleared and jealous eyes with glee. "W'enevah you see niggahs gittin' so high dat dey own folks ain' good enough fu' 'em, look out."

"W'y, la, Aunt Chloe, I knowed it too. Dem people got so owdacious proud dat dey wouldn't walk up to de collection table no mo' at chu'ch, but allus set an' waited twell de basket was passed erroun'."

"Hit's de livin' trufe, an' I's been seein' it all 'long. I

ain't said nuffin', but I knowed what 'uz gwine to happen. Ol' Chloe ain't lived all dese yeahs fu' nuffin', an' ef she got de gif' o' secon' sight, 'tain't fu' huh to say."

The women suddenly became interested in this half assertion, and the old hag, seeing that she had made the desired impression, lapsed into silence.

The whites were not neglecting to review and comment on the case also. It had been long since so great a bit of wrong-doing in a negro had given them cause for speculation and recrimination.

"I tell you," said old Horace Talbot, who was noted for his kindliness towards people of colour, "I tell you, I pity that darky more than I blame him. Now, here's my theory." They were in the bar of the Continental Hotel, and the old gentleman sipped his liquor as he talked. "It's just like this: The North thought they were doing a great thing when they come down here and freed all the slaves. They thought they were doing a great thing, and I'm not saying a word against them. I give them the credit for having the courage of their convictions. But I maintain that they were all wrong, now, in turning these people loose upon the country the way they did, without knowledge of what the first principle of liberty was. The natural result is that these people are irresponsible. They are unacquainted with the ways of our higher civilisation, and it'll take them a long time to learn. You know Rome wasn't built in a day. I know Berry, and I've known him for a long while, and a politer, likelier darky than him you would have to go far to find. And I haven't the least doubt in the world that he took that money absolutely without a thought of wrong, sir, absolutely. He saw it. He took it, and to his mental process, that was the end of it. To him there was no injury inflicted on any one, there was no crime committed. His elemental reasoning was simply this; This man has more money than I have; here is some of his surplus,—I'll just take it. Why, gentlemen, I maintain that that man took that money with the same innocence of purpose with which one of our servants a few years ago would have appropriated a stray ham."

"I disagree with you entirely, Mr. Talbot," broke in Mr. Beachfield Davis, who was a mighty hunter.— "Make mine the same, Jerry, only add a little syrup.—I disagree with you. It's simply total depravity, that's all. All niggers are alike, and there's no use trying to do anything with them. Look at that man, Dodson, of mine. I had one of the finest young hounds in the State. You know that white pup of mine, Mr. Talbot, that I bought from Hiram Gaskins? Mighty fine breed. Well, I was spendin' all my time and patience trainin' that dog in the daytime. At night I put him in that nigger's care to feed and bed. Well, do you know, I came home the other night and found that black rascal gone? I went out to see if the dog was properly bedded, and by Jove, the dog was gone too. Then I got suspicious. When a nigger and a dog go out together at night, one draws certain conclusions. I thought I had heard bayin' way out towards the edge of the town. So I stayed outside and watched. In about an hour here came Dodson with a possum hung over his shoulder and my dog trottin' at his heels. He'd been possum huntin' with my hound—with the finest hound in the State, sir. Now, I appeal to you all, gentlemen, if that ain't total depravity, what is total depravity?"

"Not total depravity, Beachfield, I maintain, but the very irresponsibility of which I have spoken. Why, gentlemen, I foresee the day when these people themselves shall come to us Southerners of their own accord and ask to be re-enslaved until such time as they shall be fit for freedom." Old Horace was nothing if not logical.

"Well, do you think there's any doubt of the darky's guilt?" asked Colonel Saunders hesitatingly. He was the only man who had ever thought of such a possibility. They turned on him as if he had been some strange, unnatural animal.

"Any doubt!" cried Old Horace.

"Any doubt!" exclaimed Mr. Davis.

"Any doubt" almost shrieked the rest. "Why, there can be no doubt. Why, Colonel, what are you thinking of? Tell us who has got the money if he hasn't? Tell us where on earth the nigger got the money he's been putting in the bank? Doubt? Why, there isn't the least doubt about it."

"Certainly, certainly," said the Colonel, "but I thought, of course, he might have saved it. There are several of those people, you know, who do a little business and have bank accounts."

"Yes, but they are in some sort of business. This man makes only thirty dollars a month. Don't you see?"

The Colonel saw, or said he did. And he did not answer what he might have answered, that Berry had no rent and no board to pay. His clothes came from his master, and Kitty and Fannie looked to their mistress for the larger number of their supplies. He did not call to their minds that Fannie herself made fifteen dollars a month, and that for two years Joe had been supporting himself. These things did not come up, and as far as the opinion of the gentlemen assembled in the Continental bar went, Berry was already proven guilty.

As for the prisoner himself, after the first day when he had pleaded "Not guilty" and been bound over to the Grand Jury, he had fallen into a sort of dazed calm that was like the stupor produced by a drug. He took little heed of what went on around him. The shock had been too sudden for him, and it was as if his reason had been for the time unseated. That it was not permanently overthrown was evidenced by his waking to the most acute pain and grief whenever Fannie came to him. Then he would toss and moan and give vent to his sorrow in passionate complaints.

"I didn't tech his money, Fannie, you know I didn't. I wo'ked fu' every cent of dat money, an' I saved it myself. Oh, I'll nevah be able to git a job ag'in. Me in de lock-up—me, aftah all dese yeahs!"

Beyond this, apparently, his mind could not go. That his detention was anything more than temporary never seemed to enter his mind. That he would be convicted and sentenced was as far from possibility as the skies from the earth. If he saw visions of a long sojourn in prison, it was only as a nightmare half consciously experienced and which with the struggle must give way before the waking.

Fannie was utterly hopeless. She had laid down whatever pride had been hers and gone to plead with Maurice Oakley for her husband's freedom, and she had seen his hard, set face. She had gone upon her knees before his wife to cite Berry's long fidelity.

"Oh, Mis' Oakley," she cried, "ef he did steal de

money, we've got enough saved to mek it good. Let him go! let him go!"

"Then you admit that he did steal?" Mrs. Oakley had taken her up sharply.

"Oh, I didn't say dat; I didn't mean dat."

"That will do, Fannie. I understand perfectly. You should have confessed that long ago."

"But I ain't confessin'! I ain't! He didn't——"

"You may go."

The stricken woman reeled out of her mistress's presence, and Mrs. Oakley told her husband that night, with tears in her eyes, how disappointed she was with Fannie,—that the woman had known it all along, and had only just confessed. It was just one more link in the chain that was surely and not too slowly forging itself about Berry Hamilton.

Of all the family Joe was the only one who burned with a fierce indignation. He knew that his father was innocent, and his very helplessness made a fever in his soul. Dandy as he was, he was loyal, and when he saw his mother's tears and his sister's shame, something rose within him that had it been given play might have made a man of him, but, being crushed, died and rotted, and in the compost it made all the evil of his nature flourished. The looks and gibes of his fellow-employees at the barber-shop forced him to leave his work there. Kit, bowed with shame and grief, dared not appear upon the streets, where the girls who had envied her now hooted at her. So the little family was shut in upon itself away from fellowship and sympathy.

Joe went seldom to see his father. He was not heartless; but the citadel of his long desired and much vaunted manhood trembled before the sight of his father's abject misery. The lines came round his lips, and lines too must have come round his heart. Poor fellow, he was too young for this forcing process, and in the hothouse of pain he only grew an acrid, unripe cynic.

At the sitting of the Grand Jury Berry was indicted. His trial followed soon, and the town turned out to see it. Some came to laugh and scoff, but these, his enemies, were silenced by the spectacle of his grief. In vain the lawyer whom he had secured showed that the evidence against him proved nothing. In vain he produced proof

of the slow accumulation of what the man had. In vain
he pleaded the man's former good name. The judge and
the jury saw otherwise. Berry was convicted. He was
given ten years at hard labour.

He hardly looked as if he could live out one as he
heard his sentence. But Nature was kind and relieved
him of the strain. With a cry as if his heart were bursting,
he started up and fell forward on his face unconscious.
Some one, a bit more brutal than the rest, said, "It's
five dollars' fine every time a nigger faints," but no one
laughed. There was something too portentous, too tragic
in the degradation of this man.

Maurice Oakley sat in the court-room, grim and relent-
less. As soon as the trial was over, he sent for Fannie,
who still kept the cottage in the yard.

"You must go," he said. "You can't stay here any
longer. I want none of your breed about me."

And Fannie bowed her head and went away from him
in silence.

All the night long the women of the Hamilton household lay in bed and wept, clinging to each other in their
grief. But Joe did not go to sleep. Against all their en-
treaties, he stayed up. He put out the light and sat staring
into the gloom with hard, burning eyes.

CHAPTER VI

Outcasts

WHAT PARTICULARLY IRRITATED Maurice Oakley was that Berry should to the very last keep up his claim of innocence. He reiterated it to the very moment that the train which was bearing him away pulled out of the station. There had seldom been seen such an example of criminal hardihood, and Oakley was hardened thereby to greater severity in dealing with the convict's wife. He began to urge her more strongly to move, and she, dispirited and humiliated by what had come to her, looked vainly about for the way to satisfy his demands. With her natural protector gone, she felt more weak and helpless than she had thought it possible to feel. It was hard enough to face the world. But to have to ask something of it was almost more than she could bear.

With the conviction of her husband the last five hundred dollars had been confiscated as belonging to the stolen money, but their former deposit remained untouched. With this she had the means at her disposal to tide over their present days of misfortune. It was not money she lacked, but confidence. Some inkling of the world's attitude towards her, guiltless though she was, reached her and made her afraid.

Her desperation, however, would not let her give way to fear, so she set forth to look for another house. Joe and Kit saw her go as if she were starting on an expedition into a strange country. In all their lives they had known no home save the little cottage in Oakley's yard. Here they had toddled as babies and played as children and been happy and care-free. There had been times when they had complained and wanted a home off by themselves, like others whom they knew. They had not failed, either, to draw unpleasant comparisons between their mode of life and the old plantation quarters system. But now all this was forgotten, and there were only grief and anxiety that they must leave the place and in such a way.

Fannie went out with little hope in her heart, and a short while after she was gone Joe decided to follow her and make an attempt to get work.

"I'll go an' see what I kin do, anyway, Kit. 'Tain't much use, I reckon, trying to get into a bahbah shop where they shave white folks, because all the white folks are down on us. I'll try one of the coloured shops."

This was something of a condescension for Berry Hamilton's son. He had never yet shaved a black chin or put shears to what he termed "naps," and he was proud of it. He thought, though, that after the training he had received from the superior "Tonsorial Parlours" where he had been employed, he had but to ask for a place and he would be gladly accepted.

It is strange how all the foolish little vaunting things that a man says in days of prosperity wax a giant crop around him in the days of his adversity. Berry Hamilton's son found this out almost as soon as he had applied at the first of the coloured shops for work.

"Oh, no, suh," said the proprietor, "I don't think we got anything fu' you to do; you're a white man's bahbah. We don't shave nothin' but niggahs hyeah, an' we shave 'em in de light o' day an' on de groun' flo'."

"W'y, I hyeah you say dat you couldn't git a paih of sheahs thoo a niggah's naps. You ain't been practisin' lately, has you?" came from the back of the shop, where a grinning negro was scraping a fellow's face.

"Oh, yes, you're done with burr-heads, are you? But burr-heads are good enough fu' you now."

"I think," the proprietor resumed, "that I hyeahed you say you wasn't fond o' grape pickin'. Well, Josy, my son, I wouldn't begin it now, 'specially as anothah kin' o' pickin' seems to run in yo' fambly."

Joe Hamilton never knew how he got out of that shop. He only knew that he found himself upon the street outside the door, tears of anger and shame in his eyes, and the laughs and taunts of his tormentors still ringing in his ears.

It was cruel, of course it was cruel. It was brutal. But

only he knew how just it had been. In his moments of pride he had said all those things, half in fun and half in earnest, and he began to wonder how he could have been so many kinds of a fool for so long without realising it.

He had not the heart to seek another shop, for he knew that what would be known at one would be equally well known at all the rest. The hardest thing that he had to bear was the knowledge that he had shut himself out of all the chances that he now desired. He remembered with a pang the words of an old negro to whom he had once been impudent, "Nevah min', boy, nevah min', you's bo'n, but you ain't daid!"

It was too true. He had not known then what would come. He had never dreamed that anything so terrible could overtake him. Even in his straits, however, desperation gave him a certain pluck. He would try for something else for which his own tongue had not disqualified him. With Joe, to think was to do. He went on to the Continental Hotel, where there were almost always boys wanted to "run the bells." The clerk looked him over critically. He was a bright, spruce-looking young fellow, and the man liked his looks.

"Well, I guess we can take you on," he said. "What's your name?"

"Joe," was the laconic answer. He was afraid to say more.

"Well, Joe, you go over there and sit where you see those fellows in uniform, and wait until I call the head bellman."

Young Hamilton went over and sat down on a bench which ran along the hotel corridor and where the bellman were wont to stay during the day awaiting their calls. A few of the blue-coated Mercuries were there. Upon Joe's advent they began to look askance at him and to talk among themselves. He felt his face burning as he thought of what they must be saying. Then he saw the head bellman talking to the clerk and looking in his direction. He saw him shake his head and walk away. He could have cursed him. The clerk called to him.

"I didn't know," he said,—"I didn't know that you were Berry Hamilton's boy. Now, I've got nothing against you myself. I don't hold you responsible for what your father did, but I don't believe our boys would work with you. I can't take you on."

Joe turned away to meet the grinning or contemptuous glances of the bellmen on the seat. It would have been good to be able to hurl something among them. But he was helpless.

He hastened out of the hotel, feeling that every eye was upon him, every finger pointing at him, every tongue whispering, "There goes Joe Hamilton, whose father went to the penitentiary the other day."

What should he do? He could try no more. He was proscribed, and the letters of his ban were writ large throughout the town, where all who ran might read. For a while he wandered aimlessly about and then turned dejectedly homeward. His mother had not yet come.

"Did you get a job?" was Kit's first question.

"No," he answered bitterly, "no one wants me now."

"No one wants you? Why, Joe—they—they don't think hard of us, do they?"

"I don't know what they think of ma and you, but they think hard of me, all right."

"Oh, don't you worry; it'll be all right when it blows over."

"Yes, when it all blows over; but when'll that be?"

"Oh, after a while, when we can show 'em we're all right."

Some of the girl's cheery hopefulness had come back to her in the presence of her brother's dejection, as a woman always forgets her own sorrow when some one she loves is grieving. But she could not communicate any of her feeling to Joe, who had been and seen and felt, and now sat darkly waiting his mother's return. Some presentiment seemed to tell him that, armed as she was with money to pay for what she wanted and asking for nothing without price, she would yet have no better tale to tell than he.

None of these forebodings visited the mind of Kit, and as soon as her mother appeared on the threshold she ran to her, crying, "Oh, where are we going to live, ma?"

Fannie looked at her for a moment, and then answered with a burst of tears, "Gawd knows, child, Gawd knows."

The girl stepped back astonished. "Why, why!" and

then with a rush of tenderness she threw her arms about her mother's neck. "Oh, you're tired to death," she said; "that's what's the matter with you. Never mind about the house now. I've got some tea made for you, and you just take a cup."

Fannie sat down and tried to drink her tea, but she could not. It stuck in her throat, and the tears rolled down her face and fell into the shaking cup. Joe looked on silently. He had been out and he understood.

"I'll go out to-morrow and do some looking around for a house while you stay at home an' rest, ma."

Her mother looked up, the maternal instinct for the protection of her daughter at once aroused. "Oh, no, not you, Kitty," she said.

Then for the first time Joe spoke: "You'd just as well tell Kitty now, ma, for she's got to come across it anyhow."

"What you know about it? Whaih you been to?"

"I've been out huntin' work. I've been to Jones's bah-bah shop an' to the Continental Hotel." His light-brown face turned brick red with anger and shame at the memory of it. "I don't think I'll try any more."

Kitty was gazing with wide and saddening eyes at her mother.

"Were they mean to you too, ma?" she asked breathlessly.

"Mean? Oh Kitty! Kitty! you don't know what it was like. It nigh killed me. Thaih was plenty of houses an' owned by people I've knowed fu' yeahs, but not one of 'em wanted to rent to me. Some of 'em made excuses 'bout one thing er t'other, but de res' come right straight out an' said dat we'd give a neighbourhood a bad name ef we moved into it. I've almos' tramped my laigs off. I've tried every decent place I could think of, but nobody wants us."

The girl was standing with her hands clenched nervously before her. It was almost more than she could understand.

"Why, we ain't done anything," she said. "Even if they don't know any better than to believe that pa was guilty, they know we ain't done anything."

"I'd like to cut the heart out of a few of 'em," said Joe in his throat.

"It ain't goin' to do no good to look at it that a-way, Joe," his mother replied. "I know hit's ha'd, but we got to do de bes' we kin."

"What are we goin' to do?" cried the boy fiercely. "They won't let us work. They won't let us live any-whaih. Do they want us to live on the levee an' steal, like some of 'em do?"

"What are we goin' to do?" echoed Kitty helplessly. "I'd go out ef I thought I could find anythin' to work at."

"Don't you go anywhaih, child. It 'ud only be worse. De niggah men dat ust to be bowin' an' scrapin' to me an' tekin' off dey hats to me laughed in my face. I met Minty—an' she slurred me right in de street. Dey'd do worse fu' you."

In the midst of the conversation a knock came at the door. It was a messenger from the "House," as they still called Oakley's home, and he wanted them to be out of the cottage by the next afternoon, as the new servants were coming and would want the rooms.

The message was so curt, so hard and decisive, that Fannie was startled out of her grief into immediate action.

"Well, we got to go," she said, rising wearily.

"But where are we goin'?" wailed Kitty in affright. "There's no place to go to. We haven't got a house. Where'll we go?"

"Out o' town someplace as fur away from this damned hole as we kin git." The boy spoke recklessly in his anger. He had never sworn before his mother before.

She looked at him in horror. "Joe, Joe," she said, "you're mekin' it wuss. You're mekin' it ha'dah fu' me to baih when you talk dat a-way. What you mean? Whaih you think Gawd is?"

Joe remained sullenly silent. His mother's faith was too stalwart for his comprehension. There was nothing like it in his own soul to interpret it.

"We'll git de secon'-han' dealah to tek ouah things to-morrer, an' then we'll go away some place, up No'th maybe."

"Let's go to New York," said Joe.

"New Yo'k?"

They had heard of New York as a place vague and far

away, a city that, like Heaven, to them had existed by faith alone. All the days of their lives they had heard of it, and it seemed to them the centre of all the glory, all the wealth, and all the freedom of the world. New York. It had an alluring sound. Who would know them there? Who would look down upon them?

"It's a mighty long ways off fu' me to be sta'tin' at dis time o' life."

"We want to go a long ways off."

"I wonder what pa would think of it if he was here," put in Kitty.

"I guess he'd think we was doin' the best we could."

"Well, den, Joe," said his mother, her voice trembling with emotion at the daring step they were about to take, "you set down an' write a lettah to yo' pa, an' tell him what we goin' to do, an' to-morrer—to-morrer—we'll sta't."

Something akin to joy came into the boy's heart as he sat down to write the letter. They had taunted him, had they? They had scoffed at him. But he was going where they might never go, and some day he would come back holding his head high and pay them sneer for sneer and jibe for jibe.

The same night the commission was given to the furniture dealer who would take charge of their things and sell them when and for what he could.

From his window the next morning Maurice Oakley watched the wagon emptying the house. Then he saw Fannie come out and walk about her little garden, followed by her children. He saw her as she wiped her eyes and led the way to the side gate.

"Well, they're gone," he said to his wife. "I wonder where they're going to live?"

"Oh, some of their people will take them in," replied Mrs. Oakley languidly.

Despite the fact that his mother carried with her the rest of the money drawn from the bank, Joe had suddenly stepped into the place of the man of the family. He attended to all the details of their getting away with a promptness that made it seem untrue that he had never been more than thirty miles from his native town. He was eager and excited. As the train drew out of the station, he did not look back upon the place which he hated, but Fannie and her daughter let their eyes linger upon it until the last house, the last chimney, and the last spire faded from their sight, and their tears fell and mingled as they were whirled away toward the unknown.

CHAPTER VII

In New York

TO THE PROVINCIAL coming to New York for the first
time, ignorant and unknown, the city presents a notable
mingling of the qualities of cheeriness and gloom. If he
have any eye at all for the beautiful, he cannot help
experiencing a thrill as he crosses the ferry over the river
filled with plying craft and catches the first sight of the
spires and buildings of New York. If he have the right
stuff in him, a something will take possession of him that
will grip him again every time he returns to the scene
and will make him long and hunger for the place when
he is away from it. Later, the lights in the busy streets
will bewilder and entice him. He will feel shy and helpless amid the hurrying crowds. A new emotion will take
his heart as the people hasten by him,—a feeling of loneliness, almost of grief, that with all of these souls about
him he knows not one and not one of them cares for
him. After a while he will find a place and give a sigh
of relief as he settles away from the city's sights behind
his cosey blinds. It is better here, and the city is cruel
and cold and unfeeling. This he will feel, perhaps, for
the first half-hour, and then he will be out in it all again.
He will be glad to strike elbows with the bustling mob
and be happy at their indifference to him, so that he may
look at them and study them. After it is all over, after
he has passed through the first pangs of strangeness and
homesickness, yes, even after he has got beyond the
stranger's enthusiasm for the metropolis, the real fever
of love for the place will begin to take hold upon him.
The subtle, insidious wine of New York will begin to
intoxicate him. Then, if he be wise, he will go away, any
place,—yes, he will even go over to Jersey. But if he be
a fool, he will stay and stay on until the town becomes
all in all to him; until the very streets are his chums and

certain buildings and corners his best friends. Then he is hopeless, and to live elsewhere would be death. The Bowery will be his romance, Broadway his lyric, and the Park his pastoral, the river and the glory of it all his epic, and he will look down pityingly on all the rest of humanity.

It was the afternoon of a clear October day that the Hamiltons reached New York. Fannie had some misgivings about crossing the ferry, but once on the boat these gave way to speculations as to what they should find on the other side. With the eagerness of youth to take in new impressions, Joe and Kitty were more concerned with what they saw about them than with what their future would hold, though they might well have stopped to ask some such questions. In all the great city they knew absolutely no one, and had no idea which way to go to find a stopping-place.

They looked about them for some coloured face, and finally saw one among the porters who were handling the baggage. To Joe's inquiry he gave them an address, and also proffered his advice as to the best way to reach the place. He was exceedingly polite, and he looked hard at Kitty. They found the house to which they had been directed, and were a good deal surprised at its apparent grandeur. It was a four-storied brick dwelling on Twenty-seventh Street. As they looked from the outside, they were afraid that the price of staying in such a place would be too much for their pockets. Inside, the sight of the hard, gaudily upholstered instalment-plan furniture did not disillusion them, and they continued to fear that they could never stop at this fine place. But they found Mrs. Jones, the proprietress, both gracious and willing to come to terms with them.

As Mrs. Hamilton—she began to be Mrs. Hamilton now, to the exclusion of Fannie—would have described Mrs. Jones, she was a "big yellow woman." She had a broad good-natured face and a tendency to run to bust.

"Yes," she said, "I think I could arrange to take you. I could let you have two rooms, and you could use my kitchen until you decided whether you wanted to take a flat or not. I has the whole house myself, and I keeps roomers. But latah on I could fix things so's you could have the whole third floor ef you wanted to. Most o' my gent'men 's railroad gent'men, they is. I guess it must 'a' been Mr. Thomas that sent you up here."

"He was a little bright man down at de deepo."

"Yes, that's him. That's Mr. Thomas. He's always lookin' out to send some one here, because he's been here three years hisself an' he kin recommend my house."

It was a relief to the Hamiltons to find Mrs. Jones so gracious and home-like. So the matter was settled, and they took up their abode with her and sent for their baggage.

With the first pause in the rush that they had experienced since starting away from home, Mrs. Hamilton began to have time for reflection, and their condition seemed to her much better as it was. Of course, it was hard to be away from home and among strangers, but the arrangement had this advantage,—that no one knew them or could taunt them with their past trouble. She was not sure that she was going to like New York. It had a great name and was really a great place, but the very bigness of it frightened her and made her feel alone, for she knew that there could not be so many people together without a deal of wickedness. She did not argue the complement of this, that the amount of good would also be increased, but this was because to her evil was the very present factor in her life.

Joe and Kit were differently affected by what they saw about them. The boy was wild with enthusiasm and with a desire to be a part of all that the metropolis meant. In the evening he saw the young fellows passing by dressed in their spruce clothes, and he wondered with a sort of envy where they could be going. Back home there had been no place much worth going to, except church and one or two people's houses. But these young fellows seemed to show by their manners that they were neither going to church nor a family visiting. In the moment that he recognised this, a revelation came to him,—the knowledge that his horizon had been very narrow, and he felt angry that it was so. Why should those fellows be different from him? Why should they walk the streets so knowingly, so independently, when he knew not whither to turn his steps? Well, he was in New York, and now he would learn. Some day some greenhorn from the

South should stand at a window and look out envying him, as he passed, red-cravated, patent-leathered, intent on some goal. Was it not better, after all, that circumstances had forced them thither? Had it not been so, they might all have stayed home and stagnated. Well, thought he, it's an ill wind that blows nobody good, and somehow, with a guilty under-thought, he forgot to feel the natural pity for his father, toiling guiltless in the prison of his native State.

Whom the Gods wish to destroy they first make mad. The first sign of the demoralisation of the provincial who comes to New York is his pride at his insensibility to certain impressions which used to influence him at home. First, he begins to scoff, and there is no truth in his views nor depth in his laugh. But by and by, from mere pretending, it becomes real. He grows callous. After that he goes to the devil very cheerfully.

No such radical emotions, however, troubled Kit's mind. She too stood at the windows and looked down into the street. There was a sort of complacent calm in the manner in which she viewed the girls' hats and dresses. Many of them were really pretty, she told herself, but for the most part they were not better than what she had had down home. There was a sound quality in the girl's make-up that helped her to see through the glamour of mere place and recognise worth for itself. Or it may have been the critical faculty, which is prominent in most women, that kept her from thinking a five-cent cheese-cloth any better in New York than it was at home. She had a certain self-respect which made her value herself and her own traditions higher than her brother did his.

When later in the evening the porter who had been kind to them came in and was introduced as Mr. William Thomas, young as she was, she took his open admiration for her with more coolness than Joe exhibited when Thomas offered to show him something of the town some day or night.

Mr. Thomas was a loquacious little man with a confident air born of an intense admiration of himself. He was the idol of a number of servant-girls' hearts, and altogether a decidedly dashing back-area-way Don Juan.

"I tell you, Miss Kitty," he burst forth, a few minutes

after being introduced, "they ain't no use talkin', N' Yawk'll give you a shakin' up 'at you won't soon forget. It's the only town on the face of the earth. You kin bet your life they ain't no flies on N' Yawk. We git the best shows here, we git the best concerts—say now, what's the use o' my callin' it all out?—we simply git the best of everything."

"Great place," said Joe wisely, in what he thought was going to be quite a man-of-the-world manner. But he burned with shame the next minute because his voice sounded so weak and youthful. Then too the oracle only said "Yes" to him, and went on expatiating to Kitty on the glories of the metropolis.

"D'jever see the statue o' Liberty? Great thing, the statue o' Liberty. I'll take you 'round some day. An' Cooney Island—oh, my, now that's the place; and talk about fun! That's the place for me."

"La, Thomas," Mrs. Jones put in, "how you do run on! Why, the strangers'll think they'll be talked to death before they have time to breathe."

"Oh, I guess the folks understan' me. I'm one o' them kin' o' men' at believe in whooping things up right from the beginning. I'm never strange with anybody. I'm a N' Yawker, I tell you, from the word go. I say, Mis' Jones, let's have some beer, an' we'll have some music purty soon. There's a fellah in the house 'at plays 'Rag-time' out o' sight."

Mr. Thomas took the pail and went to the corner. As he left the room, Mrs. Jones slapped her knee and laughed until her bust shook like jelly.

"Mr. Thomas is a case, sho'," she said; "but he likes you all, an' I'm mighty glad of it, fu' he's mighty curious about the house when he don't like the roomers."

Joe felt distinctly flattered, for he found their new acquaintance charming. His mother was still a little doubtful, and Kitty was sure she found the young man "fresh."

He came in pretty soon with his beer, and a half-dozen crabs in a bag.

"Thought I'd bring home something to chew. I always like to eat something with my beer."

Mrs. Jones brought in the glasses, and the young man filled one and turned to Kitty.

"No, thanks," she said with a surprised look.

"What, don't you drink beer? Oh, come now, you'll get out o' that."

"Kitty don't drink no beer," broke in her mother with mild resentment. "I drinks it sometimes, but she don't. I reckon maybe de chillen better go to bed."

Joe felt as if the "chillen" had ruined all his hopes, but Kitty rose.

The ingratiating "N' Yawker" was aghast.

"Oh, let 'em stay," said Mrs. Jones heartily; "a little beer ain't goin' to hurt 'em. Why, sakes, I know my father gave me beer from the time I could drink it, and I knows I ain't none the worse fu' it."

"They'll git out o' that, all right, if they live in N' Yawk," said Mr. Thomas, as he poured out a glass and handed it to Joe. "You neither?"

"Oh, I drink it," said the boy with an air, but not looking at his mother.

"Joe," she cried to him, "you must ricollect you ain't at home. What 'ud yo' pa think?" Then she stopped suddenly, and Joe gulped his beer and Kitty went to the piano to relieve her embarrassment.

"Yes, that's it, Miss Kitty, sing us something," said the irrepressible Thomas, "an' after while we'll have that fellah down that plays 'Rag-time.' He's out o' sight, I tell you."

With the pretty shyness of girlhood, Kitty sang one or two little songs in the simple manner she knew. Her voice was full and rich. It delighted Mr. Thomas.

"I say, that's singin' now, I tell you," he cried. "You ought to have some o' the new songs. D' jever hear 'Baby, you got to leave'? I tell you, that's a hot one. I'll bring you some of 'em. Why, you could git a job on the stage easy with that voice o' yourn. I got a frien' in one o' the comp'nies an' I'll speak to him about you."

"You ought to git Mr. Thomas to take you to the th'atre some night. He goes lots."

"Why, yes, what's the matter with to-morrer night? There's a good coon show in town. Out o' sight. Let's all go."

"I ain't nevah been to nothin' lak dat, an' I don't know," said Mrs. Hamilton.

"Aw, come, I'll git the tickets an' we'll all go. Great singin', you know. Whatd' you say?"

The mother hesitated, and Joe filled the breach.

"We'd all like to go," he said. "Ma, we'll go if you ain't too tired."

"Tired? Pshaw, you'll furgit all about your tiredness when Smithkins gits on the stage. Y' ought to hear him sing, 'I bin huntin' fu' wo'k'! You'd die laughing."

Mrs. Hamilton made no further demur, and the matter was closed.

Awhile later the "Rag-time" man came down and gave them a sample of what they were to hear the next night. Mr. Thomas and Mrs. Jones two-stepped, and they sent a boy after some more beer. Joe found it a very jolly evening, but Kit's and the mother's hearts were heavy as they went up to bed.

"Say," said Mr. Thomas when they had gone, "that little girl's a peach, you bet; a little green, I guess, but she'll ripen in the sun."

CHAPTER VIII

An Evening Out

FANNIE HAMILTON, tired as she was, sat long into the night with her little family discussing New York,—its advantages and disadvantages, its beauty and its ugliness, its morality and immorality. She had somewhat receded from her first position, that it was better being here in the great strange city than being at home where the very streets shamed them. She had not liked the way that their fellow lodger looked at Kitty. It was bold, to say the least. She was not pleased, either, with their new acquaintance's familiarity. And yet, he had said no more than some stranger, if there could be such a stranger, would have said down home. There was a difference, however, which she recognised. Thomas was not the provincial who puts every one on a par with himself, nor was he the metropolitan who complacently patronises the whole world. He was trained out of the one and not up to the other. The intermediate only succeeded in being offensive. Mrs. Jones' assurance as to her guest's fine qualities did not do all that might have been expected to reassure Mrs. Hamilton in the face of the difficulties of the gentleman's manner.

She could not, however, lay her finger on any particular point that would give her the reason for rejecting his friendly advances. She got ready the next evening to go to the theatre with the rest. Mr. Thomas at once possessed himself of Kitty and walked on ahead, leaving Joe to accompany his mother and Mrs. Jones,—an arrangement, by the way, not altogether to that young gentleman's taste. A good many men bowed to Thomas in the street, and they turned to look enviously after him. At the door of the theatre they had to run the gantlet of a dozen pairs of eyes. Here, too, the party's guide seemed to be well known, for some one said, before they passed

514

out of hearing, "I wonder who that little light girl is that Thomas is with tonight? He's a hot one for you."

Mrs. Hamilton had been in a theatre but once before in her life, and Joe and Kit but a few times oftener. On those occasions they had sat far up in the peanut gallery in the place reserved for people of colour. This was not a pleasant, cleanly, nor beautiful locality, and by contrast with it, even the garishness of the cheap New York theatre seemed fine and glorious.

They had good seats in the first balcony, and here their guide had shown his managerial ability again, for he had found it impossible, or said so, to get all the seats together, so that he and the girl were in the row in front and to one side of where the rest sat. Kitty did not like the arrangement, and innocently suggested that her brother take her seat while she went back to her mother. But her escort overruled her objections easily, and laughed at her so frankly that from very shame she could not urge them again, and they were soon forgotten in her wonder at the mystery and glamour that envelops the home of the drama. There was something weird to her in the alternate spaces of light and shade. Without any feeling of its ugliness, she looked at the curtain as at a door that should presently open between her and a house of wonders. She looked at it with the fascination that one always experiences for what either brings near or withholds the unknown.

As for Joe, he was not bothered by the mystery or the glamour of things. But he had suddenly raised himself in his own estimation. He had gazed steadily at a girl across the aisle until she had smiled in response. Of course, he went hot and cold by turns, and the sweat broke out on his brow, but instantly he began to swell. He had made a decided advance in knowledge, and he swelled with the consciousness that already he was coming to be a man of the world. He looked with a new feeling at the swaggering, sporty young negroes. His attitude towards them was not one of humble self-depreciation any more. Since last night he had grown, and felt that he might, that he would, be like them, and it put a sort of chuckling glee into his heart.

One might find it in him to feel sorry for this small-souled, warped being, for he was so evidently the jest of

Fate, if it were not that he was so blissfully, so conceitedly, unconscious of his own nastiness. Down home he had shaved the wild young bucks of the town, and while doing it drunk in eagerly their unguarded narrations of their gay exploits. So he had started out with false ideals as to what was fine and manly. He was afflicted by a sort of moral and mental astigmatism that made him see everything wrong. As he sat there tonight, he gave to all he saw a wrong value and upon it based his ignorant desires.

When the men of the orchestra filed in and began tuning their instruments, it was the signal for an influx of loiterers from the door. There were a large number of coloured people in the audience, and because members of their own race were giving the performance, they seemed to take a proprietary interest in it all. They discussed its merits and demerits as they walked down the aisle in much the same tone that the owners would have used had they been wondering whether the entertainment was going to please the people or not.

Finally the music struck up one of the numerous negro marches. It was accompanied by the rhythmic patting of feet from all parts of the house. Then the curtain went up on a scene of beauty. It purported to be a grove to which a party of picnickers, the ladies and gentlemen of the chorus, had come for a holiday, and they were telling the audience all about it in crescendos. With the exception of one, who looked like a faded kid glove, the men discarded the grease paint, but the women under their make-ups ranged from pure white, pale yellow, and sickly greens to brick reds and slate grays. They were dressed in costumes that were not primarily intended for picnic going. But they could sing, and they did sing, with their voices, their bodies, their souls. They threw themselves into it because they enjoyed and felt what they were doing, and they gave almost a semblance of dignity to the tawdry music and inane words.

Kitty was enchanted. The airily dressed women seemed to her like creatures from fairy-land. It is strange how the glare of the footlights succeeds in deceiving so many people who are able to see through other delusions. The cheap dresses on the street had not fooled Kitty for an instant, but take the same cheese-cloth, put a little water starch into it, and put it on the stage, and she could see only chiffon.

She turned around and nodded delightedly at her brother, but he did not see her. He was lost, transfixed. His soul was floating on a sea of sense. He had eyes and ears and thoughts only for the stage. His nerves tingled and his hands twitched. Only to know one of those radiant creatures, to have her speak to him, smile at him! If ever a man was intoxicated, Joe was. Mrs. Hamilton was divided between shame at the clothes of some of the women and delight with the music. Her companion was busy pointing out who this and that actress was, and giving jelly-like appreciation to the doings on the stage.

Mr. Thomas was the only cool one in the party. He was quietly taking stock of his young companion,—of her innocence and charm. She was a pretty girl, little and dainty, but well developed for her age. Her hair was very black and wavy, and some strain of the South's chivalric blood, which is so curiously mingled with the African in the veins of most coloured people, had tinged her skin to an olive hue.

"Are you enjoying yourself?" he leaned over and whispered to her. His voice was very confidential and his lips near her ear, but she did not notice.

"Oh, yes," she answered, "this is grand. How I'd like to be an actress and be up there!"

"Maybe you will some day."

"Oh, no, I'm not smart enough."

"We'll see," he said wisely; "I know a thing or two."

Between the first and second acts a number of Thomas's friends strolled up to where he sat and began talking, and again Kitty's embarrassment took possession of her as they were introduced one by one. They treated her with a half-courteous familiarity that made her blush. Her mother was not pleased with the many acquaintances that her daughter was making, and would have interfered had not Mrs. Jones assured her that the men clustered about their host's seat were some of the "best people in town." Joe looked at them hungrily, but the man in front with his sister did not think it necessary to include the brother or the rest of the party in his miscellaneous introductions.

One brief bit of conversation which the mother over-heard especially troubled her.

"Not going out for a minute or two?" asked one of the men, as he was turning away from Thomas.

"No, I don't think I'll go out to-night. You can have my share."

The fellow gave a horse laugh and replied, "Well, you're doing a great piece of work, Miss Hamilton, whenever you can keep old Bill from goin' out an' lushin' between acts. Say, you got a good thing; push it along."

The girl's mother half rose, but she resumed her seat, for the man was going away. Her mind was not quiet again, however, until the people were all in their seats and the curtain had gone up on the second act. At first she was surprised at the enthusiasm over just such dancing as she could see any day from the loafers on the street corners down home, and then, like a good, sensible, humble woman, she came around to the idea that it was she who had always been wrong in putting too low a value on really worthy things. So she laughed and applauded with the rest, all the while trying to quiet something that was tugging at her away down in her heart.

When the performance was over she forced her way to Kitty's side, where she remained in spite of all Thomas's palpable efforts to get her away. Finally he proposed that they all go to supper at one of the coloured cafés.

"You'll see a lot o' the show people," he said.

"No, I reckon we'd bettah go home," said Mrs. Hamilton decidedly. "De chillen ain't ust to stayin' up all hours o' nights, an' I ain't anxious fu' 'em to git ust to it."

She was conscious of a growing dislike for this man who treated her daughter with such a proprietary air. Joe winced again at "de chillen."

Thomas bit his lip, and mentally said things that are unfit for publication. Aloud he said, "Mebbe Miss Kitty'ud like to go an' have a little lunch."

"Oh, no, thank you," said the girl; "I've had a nice time and I don't care for a thing to eat."

Joe told himself that Kitty was the biggest fool that it had ever been his lot to meet, and the disappointed suitor satisfied himself with the reflection that the girl was green yet, but would get bravely over that.

He attempted to hold her hand as they parted at the

parlour door, but she drew her fingers out of his clasp and said, "Good-night; thank you," as if he had been one of her mother's old friends.

Joe lingered a little longer.

"Say, that was out o' sight," he said.

"Think so?" asked the other carelessly.

"I'd like to get out with you some time to see the town," the boy went on eagerly.

"All right, we'll go some time. So long."

"So long."

Some time. Was it true? Would he really take him out and let him meet stage people? Joe went to bed with his head in a whirl. He slept little that night for thinking of his heart's desire.

CHAPTER IX

His Heart's Desire

WHATEVER ELSE HIS VISIT to the theatre may have done for Joe, it inspired him with a desire to go to work and earn money of his own, to be independent both of parental help and control, and so be able to spend as he pleased. With this end in view he set out to hunt for work. It was a pleasant contrast to his last similar quest, and he felt it with joy. He was treated everywhere he went with courtesy, even when no situation was forthcoming. Finally he came upon a man who was willing to try him for an afternoon. From the moment the boy rightly considered himself engaged, for he was master of his trade. He began his work with heart elate. Now he had within his grasp the possibility of being all that he wanted to be. Now Thomas might take him out at any time and not be ashamed of him.

With Thomas, the fact that Joe was working put the boy in an entirely new light. He decided that now he might be worth cultivating. For a week or two he had ignored him, and, proceeding upon the principle that if you give corn to the old hen she will cluck to her chicks, had treated Mrs. Hamilton with marked deference and kindness. This had been without success, as both the girl and her mother held themselves politely aloof from him. He began to see that his hope of winning Kitty's affections lay, not in courting the older woman but in making a friend of the boy. So on a certain Saturday night when the Banner Club was to give one of its smokers, he asked Joe to go with him. Joe was glad to, and they set out together. Arrived, Thomas left his companion for a few moments while he attended, as he said, to a little business. What he really did was to seek out the proprietor of the club and some of its hangers on.

"I say," he said, "I've got a friend with me to-night.

He's got some dough on him. He's fresh and young and easy."

"Whew!" exclaimed the proprietor.

"Yes, he's a good thing, but push it along kin' o' light at first; he might get skittish."

"Thomas, let me fall on your bosom and weep," said a young man who, on account of his usual expression of innocent gloom, was called Sadness. "This is what I've been looking for for a month. My hat was getting decidedly shabby. Do you think he would stand for a touch on the first night of our acquaintance?"

"Don't you dare? Do you want to frighten him off? Make him believe that you've got coin to burn and that it's an honour to be with you."

"But, you know, he may expect a glimpse of the gold."

"A smart man don't need to show nothin'. All he's got to do is to act."

"Oh, I'll act; we'll all act."

"Be slow to take a drink from him."

"Thomas, my boy, you're an angel. I recognise that more and more every day, but bid me do anything else but that. That I refuse: it's against nature"; and Sadness looked more mournful than ever.

"Trust old Sadness to do his part," said the portly proprietor; and Thomas went back to the lamb.

"Nothin' doin' so early," he said; "let's go an' have a drink."

They went, and Thomas ordered.

"No, no, this is on me," cried Joe, trembling with joy.

"Pshaw, your money's counterfeit," said his companion with fine generosity. "This is on me, I say. Jack, what'll you have yourself?"

As they stood at the bar, the men began strolling up one by one. Each in his turn was introduced to Joe. They were very polite. They treated him with a pale, dignified, high-minded respect that menaced his pocket-book and possessions. The proprietor, Mr. Turner, asked him why he had never been in before. He really seemed much hurt about it, and on being told that Joe had only been in the city for a couple of weeks expressed emphatic surprise, even disbelief, and assured the rest that any one would have taken Mr. Hamilton for an old New Yorker.

Sadness was introduced last. He bowed to Joe's "Happy to know you, Mr. Williams."

"Better known as Sadness," he said, with an expression of deep gloom. "A distant relative of mine once had a great grief. I have never recovered from it."

Joe was not quite sure how to take this; but the others laughed and he joined them, and then, to cover his own embarrassment, he did what he thought the only correct and manly thing to do,—he ordered a drink.

"I don't know as I ought to," said Sadness.

"Oh, come on," his companions called out, "don't be stiff with a stranger. Make him feel at home."

"Mr. Hamilton will believe me when I say that I have no intention of being stiff, but duty is duty. I've got to go down town to pay a bill, and if I get too much aboard, it wouldn't be safe walking around with money on me."

"Aw, shut up, Sadness," said Thomas. "My friend Mr. Hamilton 'll feel hurt if you don't drink with him."

"I cert'n'y will," was Joe's opportune remark, and he was pleased to see that it caused the reluctant one to yield.

They took a drink. There was quite a line of them. Joe asked the bartender what he would have. The men warmed towards him. They took several more drinks with him and he was happy. Sadness put his arm about his shoulder and told him, with tears in his eyes, that he looked like a cousin of his that had died.

"Aw, shut up, Sadness!" said some one else. "Be respectable."

Sadness turned his mournful eyes upon the speaker. "I won't," he replied. "Being respectable is very nice as a diversion, but it's tedious if done steadily." Joe did not quite take this, so he ordered another drink.

A group of young fellows came in and passed up the stairs. "Shearing another lamb?" said one of them significantly.

"Well, with that gang it will be well done."

Thomas and Joe left the crowd after a while, and went to the upper floor, where, in a long, brilliantly lighted room, tables were set out for drinking-parties. At one end of the room was a piano, and a man sat at it listlessly strumming some popular air. The proprietor joined them pretty soon, and steered them to a table opposite the door.

"Just sit down here, Mr. Hamilton," he said, "and you can see everybody that comes in. We have lots of nice people here on smoker nights, especially after the shows are out and the girls come in."

Joe's heart gave a great leap, and then settled as cold as lead. Of course, those girls wouldn't speak to him. But his hopes rose as the proprietor went on talking to him and to no one else. Mr. Turner always made a man feel as if he were of some consequence in the world, and men a good deal older than Joe had been fooled by his manner. He talked to one in a soft, ingratiating way, giving his whole attention apparently. He tapped one confidentially on the shoulder, as who should say, "My dear boy, I have but two friends in the world, and you are both of them."

Joe, charmed and pleased, kept his head well. There is a great deal in heredity, and his father had not been Maurice Oakley's butler for so many years for nothing.

The Banner Club was an institution for the lower education of negro youth. It drew its pupils from every class of people and from every part of the country. It was composed of all sorts and conditions of men, educated and uneducated, dishonest and less so, of the good, the bad, and the—unexposed. Parasites came there to find victims, politicians for votes, reporters for news, and artists of all kinds for colour and inspiration. It was the place of assembly for a number of really bright men, who after days of hard and often unrewarded work came there and drunk themselves drunk in each other's company, and when they were drunk talked of the eternal verities.

The Banner was only one of a kind. It stood to the stranger and the man and woman without connections for the whole social life. It was a substitute—poor, it must be confessed—to many youths for the home life which is so lacking among certain classes in New York.

Here the rounders congregated, or came and spent the hours until it was time to go forth to bout or assignation. Here too came sometimes the curious who wanted to see something of the other side of life. Among these, white visitors were not infrequent,—those who were young enough to be fascinated by the bizarre, and those who were old enough to know that it was all in the game. Mr. Skaggs, of the New York *Universe*, was one of the former class and a constant visitor,—he and a "lady friend" called "Maudie," who had a penchant for dancing to "Rag-time" melodies as only the "puffessor" of such a club can play them. Of course, the place was a social cesspool, generating a poisonous miasma and reeking with the stench of decayed and rotten moralities. There is no defence to be made for it. But what do you expect when false idealism and fevered ambition come face to face with catering cupidity?

It was into this atmosphere that Thomas had introduced the boy Joe, and he sat there now by his side, firing his mind by pointing out the different celebrities who came in and telling highly flavoured stories of their lives or doings. Joe heard things that had never come within the range of his mind before.

"Aw, there's Skaggsy an' Maudie—Maudie's his girl, y' know, an' he's a reporter on the N' Yawk *Universe*. Fine fellow, Skaggsy."

Maudie—a portly, voluptuous-looking brunette—left her escort and went directly to the space by the piano. Here she was soon dancing with one of the coloured girls who had come in.

Skaggs started to sit down alone at a table, but Thomas called him, "Come over here, Skaggsy."

In the moment that it took the young man to reach them, Joe wondered if he would ever reach that state when he could call that white man Skaggsy and the girl Maudie. The new-comer set all of that at ease.

"I want you to know my friend, Mr. Hamilton, Mr. Skaggs."

"Why, how d' ye do, Hamilton? I'm glad to meet you. Now, look a here; don't you let old Thomas here string you about me bein' any old 'Mr.!' Skaggs. I'm Skaggsy to all of my friends. I hope to count you among 'em."

It was such a supreme moment that Joe could not find words to answer, so he called for another drink.

"Not a bit of it," said Skaggsy, "not a bit of it. When I meet my friends I always reserve to myself the right of ordering the first drink. Waiter, this is on me. What'll you have, gentlemen?"

They got their drinks, and then Skaggsy leaned over confidentially and began talking.

"I tell you, Hamilton, there ain't an ounce of prejudice in my body. Do you believe it?"

Joe said that he did. Indeed Skaggsy struck one as being aggressively unprejudiced.

He went on: "You see, a lot o' fellows say to me, 'What do you want to go down to that nigger club for?' That's what they call it,—'nigger club.' But I say to 'em, 'Gentlemen, at that nigger club, as you choose to call it, I get more inspiration than I could get at any of the greater clubs in New York.' I've often been invited to join some of the swell clubs here, but I never do it. By Jove! I'd rather come down here and fellowship right in with you fellows. I like coloured people, anyway. It's natural. You see, my father had a big plantation and owned lots of slaves,—no offence, of course, but it was the custom of that time,—and I've played with little darkies ever since I could remember."

It was the same old story that the white who associates with negroes from volition usually tells to explain his taste.

The truth about the young reporter was that he was born and reared on a Vermont farm, where his early life was passed in fighting for his very subsistence. But this never troubled Skaggsy. He was a monumental liar, and the saving quality about him was that he calmly believed his own lies while he was telling them, so no one was hurt, for the deceiver was as much a victim as the deceived. The boys who knew him best used to say that when Skaggs got started on one of his debauches of lying, the Recording Angel always put on an extra clerical force.

"Now look at Maudie," he went on; "would you believe it that she was of a fine, rich family, and that the coloured girl she's dancing with now used to be her servant? She's just like me about that. Absolutely no prejudice."

Joe was wide-eyed with wonder and admiration, and he couldn't understand the amused expression on Thomas's face, nor why he surreptitiously kicked him under the table.

Finally the reporter went his way, and Joe's sponsor

explained to him that he was not to take in what Skaggsy said, and that there hadn't been a word of truth in it. He ended with, "Everybody knows Maudie, and that coloured girl is Mamie Lacey, and never worked for anybody in her life. Skaggsy's a good fellah, all right, but he's the biggest liar in N' Yawk."

The boy was distinctly shocked. He wasn't sure but Thomas was jealous of the attention the white man had shown him and wished to belittle it. Anyway, he did not thank him for destroying his romance.

About eleven o'clock, when the people began to drop in from the plays, the master of ceremonies opened proceedings by saying that "The free concert would now begin, and he hoped that all present, ladies included, would act like gentlemen, and not forget the waiter. Mr. Meriweather will now favour us with the latest coon song, entitled 'Come back to yo' Baby, Honey.'"

There was a patter of applause, and a young negro came forward, and in a strident, music-hall voice, sung or rather recited with many gestures the ditty. He couldn't have been much older than Joe, but already his face was hard with dissipation and foul knowledge. He gave the song with all the rank suggestiveness that could be put into it. Joe looked upon him as a hero. He was followed by a little, brown-skinned fellow with an immature Vandyke beard and a lisp. He sung his own composition and was funny; how much funnier than he himself knew or intended, may not even be hinted at. Then, while an instrumentalist, who seemed to have a grudge against the piano, was hammering out the opening bars of a march, Joe's attention was attracted by a woman entering the room, and from that moment he heard no more of the concert. Even when the master of ceremonies announced with an air that, by special request, he himself would sing "Answer,"—the request was his own,—he did not draw the attention of the boy away from the yellow-skinned divinity who sat at a near table, drinking whiskey straight.

She was a small girl, with fluffy dark hair and good features. A tiny foot peeped out from beneath her rattling silk skirts. She was a good-looking young woman and daintily made, though her face was no longer youthful, and one might have wished that with her complexion she had not run to silk waists in magenta.

Joe, however, saw no fault in her. She was altogether lovely to him, and his delight was the more poignant as he recognised in her one of the girls he had seen on the stage a couple of weeks ago. That being true, nothing could keep her from being glorious in his eyes,—not even the grease-paint which adhered in unneat patches to her face, nor her taste for whiskey in its unreformed state. He gazed at her in ecstasy until Thomas, turning to see what had attracted him, said with a laugh, "Oh, it's Hattie Sterling. Want to meet her?"

Again the young fellow was dumb. Just then Hattie also noticed his intent look, and nodded and beckoned to Thomas.

"Come on," he said, rising.

"Oh, she didn't ask for me," cried Joe, tremulous and eager.

His companion went away laughing.

"Who's your young friend?" asked Hattie.

"A fellah from the South."

"Bring him over here."

Joe could hardly believe in his own good luck, and his head, which was getting a bit weak, was near collapsing when his divinity asked him what he'd have? He began to protest, until she told the waiter with an air of authority to make it a little " 'skey." Then she asked him for a cigarette, and began talking to him in a pleasant, soothing way between puffs.

When the drinks came, she said to Thomas, "Now, old man, you've been awfully nice, but when you get your little drink, you run away like a good little boy. You're superfluous."

Thomas answered, "Well, I like that," but obediently gulped his whiskey and withdrew, while Joe laughed until the master of ceremonies stood up and looked sternly at him.

The concert had long been over and the room was less crowded when Thomas sauntered back to the pair.

"Well, good-night," he said. "Guess you can find your way home, Mr. Hamilton"; and he gave Joe a long wink.

"Goo'-night," said Joe, woozily, "I be a' ri'. Goo'-night."

"Make it another 'skey," was Hattie's farewell remark.

It was late the next morning when Joe got home. He had a headache and a sense of triumph that not even his illness and his mother's reproof could subdue.

He had promised Hattie to come often to the club.

CHAPTER X

A Visitor from Home

MRS. HAMILTON BEGAN to question very seriously whether she had done the best thing in coming to New York as she saw her son staying away more and more and growing always farther away from her and his sister. Had she known how and where he spent his evenings, she would have had even greater cause to question the wisdom of their trip. She knew that although he worked he never had any money for the house, and she foresaw the time when the little they had would no longer suffice for Kitty and her. Realising this, she herself set out to find something to do.

It was a hard matter, for wherever she went seeking employment, it was always for her and her daughter, for the more she saw of Mrs. Jones, the less she thought it well to leave the girl under her influence. Mrs. Hamilton was not a keen woman, but she had a mother's intuitions, and she saw a subtle change in her daughter. At first the girl grew wistful and then impatient and rebellious. She complained that Joe was away from them so much enjoying himself, while she had to be housed up like a prisoner. She had receded from her dignified position, and twice of an evening had gone out for a car-ride with Thomas; but as that gentleman never included the mother in his invitation, she decided that her daughter should go no more, and she begged Joe to take his sister out sometimes instead. He demurred at first, for he now numbered among his city acquirements a fine contempt for his woman relatives. Finally, however, he consented, and took Kit once to the theatre and once for a ride. Each time he left her in the care of Thomas as soon as they were out of the house, while he went to find or to wait for his dear Hattie. But his mother did not know all this, and Kit did not tell her. The quick poison of the unreal life about her had already begun to affect her character. She had grown secretive and sly. The innocent longing which in a burst of enthusiasm she had expressed that first night at the theatre was growing into a real ambition with her, and she dropped the simple old songs she knew to practise the detestable coon ditties which the stage demanded.

She showed no particular pleasure when her mother found the sort of place they wanted, but went to work with her in sullen silence. Mrs. Hamilton could not understand it all, and many a night she wept and prayed over the change in this child of her heart. There were times when she felt that there was nothing left to work or fight for. The letters from Berry in prison became fewer and fewer. He was sinking into the dull, dead routine of his life. Her own letters to him fell off. It was hard getting the children to write. They did not want to be bothered, and she could not write for herself. So in the weeks and months that followed she drifted farther away from her children and husband and all the traditions of her life.

After Joe's first night at the Banner Club he had kept his promise to Hattie Sterling and had gone often to meet her. She had taught him much, because it was to her advantage to do so. His greenness had dropped from him like a garment, but no amount of sophistication could make him deem the woman less perfect. He knew that she was much older than he, but he only took this fact as an additional sign of his prowess in having won her. He was proud of himself when he went behind the scenes at the theatre or waited for her at the stage door and bore her off under the admiring eyes of a crowd of gapers. And Hattie? She liked him in a half-contemptuous, half-amused way. He was a good-looking boy and made money enough, as she expressed it, to show her a good time, so she was willing to overlook his weakness and his callow vanity.

"Look here," she said to him one day, "I guess you'll have to be moving. There's a young lady been inquiring for you to-day, and I won't stand for that."

He looked at her, startled for a moment, until he saw the laughter in her eyes. Then he caught her and kissed her. "What're you givin' me?" he said.

"It's a straight tip, that's what."

"Who is it?"

"It's a girl named Minty Brown from your home."

His face turned brick-red with fear and shame. "Minty Brown!" he stammered.

Had that girl told all and undone him? But Hattie was going on about her work and evidently knew nothing.

"Oh, you needn't pretend you don't know her," she went on banteringly. "She says you were great friends down South, so I've invited her to supper. She wants to see you."

"To supper!" he thought. Was she mocking him? Was she restraining her scorn of him only to make his humiliation the greater after a while? He looked at her, but there was no suspicion of malice in her face, and he took hope.

"Well, I'd like to see old Minty," he said. "It's been many a long day since I've seen her."

All that afternoon, after going to the barber-shop, Joe was driven by a tempest of conflicting emotions. If Minty Brown had not told his story, why not? Would she yet tell, and if she did, what would happen? He tortured himself by questioning if Hattie would cast him off. At the very thought his hand trembled, and the man in the chair asked him if he hadn't been drinking.

When he met Minty in the evening, however, the first glance at her reassured him. Her face was wreathed in smiles as she came forward and held out her hand.

"Well, well, Joe Hamilton," she exclaimed, "if I ain't right-down glad to see you! How are you?"

"I'm middlin', Minty. How's yourself?" He was so happy that he couldn't let go her hand.

"An' jes' look at the boy! Ef he ain't got the impidence to be waihin' a mustache too. You must 'a' been lettin' the cats lick yo' upper lip. Didn't expect to see me in New York, did you?"

"No, indeed. What you doin' here?"

"Oh, I got a gent'man friend what's a porter, an' his run's been changed so that he comes hyeah, an' he told me, if I wanted to come he'd bring me thoo fur a visit, so, you see, hyeah I am. I allus was mighty anxious to see this hyeah town. But tell me, how's Kit an' yo' ma?"

"They're both right well." He had forgotten them and their scorn of Minty.

"Whaih do you live? I'm comin' roun' to see 'em."

He hesitated for a moment. He knew how his mother, if not Kit, would receive her, and yet he dared not anger this woman, who had his fate in the hollow of her hand.

She saw his hesitation and spoke up. "Oh, that's all right. Let by-gones be by-gones. You know I ain't the kin' o' person that holds a grudge ag'in anybody."

"That's right, Minty, that's right," he said, and gave her his mother's address. Then he hastened home to prepare the way for Minty's coming. Joe had no doubt but that his mother would see the matter quite as he saw it, and be willing to temporise with Minty; but he had reckoned without his host. Mrs. Hamilton might make certain concessions to strangers on the score of expediency, but she absolutely refused to yield one iota of her dignity to one whom she had known so long as an inferior.

"But don't you see what she can do for us, ma? She knows people that I know, and she can ruin me with them."

"I ain't never bowed my haid to Minty Brown an' I ain't a-goin' to do it now," was his mother's only reply.

"Oh, ma," Kitty put in, "you don't want to get talked about up here, do you?"

"We'd jes' as well be talked about fu' somep'n we didn' do as fu' somep'n we did do, an' it wouldn' be long befo' we'd come to dat if we made frien's wid dat Brown gal. I ain't a-goin' to do it. I'm ashamed o' you, Kitty, fu' wantin' me to."

The girl began to cry, while her brother walked the floor angrily.

"You'll see what'll happen," he cried; "you'll see."

Fannie looked at her son, and she seemed to see him more clearly than she had ever seen him before,—his foppery, his meanness, his cowardice.

"Well," she answered with a sigh, "it can't be no wuss den what's already happened."

"You'll see, you'll see," the boy reiterated.

Minty Brown allowed no wind of thought to cool the fire of her determination. She left Hattie Sterling's soon after Joe, and he was still walking the floor and uttering dire forebodings when she rang the bell below and asked for the Hamiltons.

Mrs. Jones ushered her into her fearfully upholstered parlour, and then puffed up stairs to tell her lodgers that there was a friend there from the South who wanted to see them.

"Tell huh," said Mrs. Hamilton, "dat dey ain't no one hyeah wants to see huh."

"No, no," Kitty broke in.

"Heish," said her mother; "I'm goin' to boss you a little while yit."

"Why, I don't understan' you, Mis' Hamilton," puffed Mrs. Jones. "She's a nice-lookin' lady, an' she said she knowed you at home."

"All you got to do is to tell dat ooman jes' what I say."

Minty Brown downstairs had heard the little colloquy, and, perceiving that something was amiss, had come to the stairs to listen. Now her voice, striving hard to be condescending and sweet, but growing harsh with anger, floated up from below:

"Oh, nevah min', lady, I ain't anxious to see 'em. I jest called out o' pity, but I reckon dey 'shamed to see me 'cause de ol' man's in penitentiary an' dey was run out o' town."

Mrs. Jones gasped, and then turned and went hastily downstairs.

Kit burst out crying afresh, and Joe walked the floor muttering beneath his breath, while the mother sat grimly watching the outcome. Finally they heard Mrs. Jones' step once more on the stairs. She came in without knocking, and her manner was distinctly unpleasant.

"Mis' Hamilton," she said, "I've had a talk with the lady downstairs, an' she's tol' me everything. I'd be glad if you'd let me have my rooms as soon as possible."

"So you goin' to put me out on de wo'd of a stranger?"

"I'm kin' o' sorry, but everybody in the house heard what Mis' Brown said, an' it'll soon be all over town, an' that 'ud ruin the reputation of my house."

"I reckon all dat kin be 'splained."

"Yes, but I don't know that anybody kin 'splain your daughter allus being with Mr. Thomas, who ain't even divo'ced from his wife." She flashed a vindictive glance at the girl, who turned deadly pale and dropped her head in her hands.

"You daih to say dat, Mis' Jones, you dat fust inter-duced my gal to dat man and got huh to go out wid him? I reckon you'd bettah go now."

And Mrs. Jones looked at Fannie's face and obeyed.

As soon as the woman's back was turned, Joe burst out, "There, there! see what you've done with your damned foolishness."

Fannie turned on him like a tigress. "Don't you cuss hyeah befo' me; I ain't nevah brung you up to it, an' I won't stan' it. Go to dem whaih you larned it, an whaih de wo'ds soun' sweet." The boy started to speak, but she checked him. "Don't you daih to cuss ag'in or befo' Gawd dey'll be somep'n fu' one o' dis fambly to be rottin' in jail fu'!"

The boy was cowed by his mother's manner. He was gathering his few belongings in a bundle.

"I ain't goin' to cuss," he said sullenly, "I'm goin' out o' your way."

"Oh, go on," she said, "go on. It's been a long time sence you been my son. You on yo' way to hell, an' you is been fu' lo dese many days."

Joe got out of the house as soon as possible. He did not speak to Kit nor look at his mother. He felt like a cur, because he knew deep down in his heart that he had only been waiting for some excuse to take this step.

As he slammed the door behind him, his mother flung herself down by Kit's side and mingled her tears with her daughter's. But Kit did not raise her head.

"Dey ain't nothin' lef' but you now, Kit"; but the girl did not speak, she only shook with hard sobs.

Then her mother raised her head and almost screamed, "My Gawd, not you, Kit!" The girl rose, and then dropped unconscious in her mother's arms.

Joe took his clothes to a lodging-house that he knew of, and then went to the club to drink himself up to the point of going to see Hattie after the show.

CHAPTER XI

Broken Hopes

WHAT JOE HAMILTON lacked more than anything else in the world was some one to kick him. Many a man who might have lived decently and become a fairly respectable citizen has gone to the dogs for the want of some one to administer a good resounding kick at the right time. It is corrective and clarifying.

Joe needed especially its clarifying property, for though he knew himself a cur, he went away from his mother's house feeling himself somehow aggrieved, and the feeling grew upon him the more he thought of it. His mother had ruined his chance in life, and he could never hold up his head again. Yes, he had heard that several of the fellows at the club had shady reputations, but surely to be the son of a thief or a supposed thief was not like being the criminal himself.

At the Banner he took a seat by himself, and, ordering a cocktail, sat glowering at the few other lonely members who had happened to drop in. There were not many of them, and the contagion of unsociability had taken possession of the house. The people sat scattered around at different tables, perfectly unmindful of the bartender, who cursed them under his breath for not "getting together."

Joe's mind was filled with bitter thoughts. How long had he been away from home? he asked himself. Nearly a year. Nearly a year passed in New York, and he had come to be what he so much desired,—a part of its fast life,—and now in a moment an old woman's stubbornness had destroyed all that he had builded.

What would Thomas say when he heard it? What would the other fellows think? And Hattie? It was plain that she would never notice him again. He had no doubt but that the malice of Minty Brown would prompt her

535

to seek out all of his friends and make the story known. Why had he not tried to placate her by disavowing sympathy with his mother? He would have had no compunction about doing so, but he had thought of it too late. He sat brooding over his trouble until the bartender called with respectful sarcasm to ask if he wanted to lease the glass he had.

He gave back a silly laugh, gulped the rest of the liquor down, and was ordering another when Sadness came in. He came up directly to Joe and sat down beside him. "Mr. Hamilton says 'Make it two, Jack,'" he said with easy familiarity. "Well, what's the matter, old man? You're looking glum."

"I feel glum."

"The divine Hattie hasn't been cutting any capers, has she? The dear old girl hasn't been getting hysterical at her age? Let us hope not."

Joe glared at him. Why in the devil should this fellow be so sadly gay when he was weighted down with sorrow and shame and disgust?

"Come, come now, Hamilton, if you're sore because I invited myself to take a drink with you, I'll withdraw the order. I know the heroic thing to say is that I'll pay for the drinks myself, but I can't screw my courage up to the point of doing so unnatural a thing."

Young Hamilton hastened to protest. "Oh, I know you fellows now well enough to know how many drinks to pay for. It ain't that."

"Well, then, out with it. What is it? Haven't been up to anything, have you?"

The desire came to Joe to tell this man the whole truth, just what was the matter, and so to relieve his heart. On the impulse he did. If he had expected much from Sadness he was disappointed, for not a muscle of the man's face changed during the entire recital.

When it was over, he looked at his companion critically through a wreath of smoke. Then he said: "For a fellow who has had for a full year the advantage of the education of the New York clubs, you are strangely young. Let me see, you are nineteen or twenty now—yes. Well, that perhaps accounts for it. It's a pity you weren't born older. It's a pity most men aren't. They wouldn't have to take so much time and lose so many good things learning. Now, Mr. Hamilton, let me tell you, and you will pardon me for it, that you are a fool. Your case isn't half as bad as that of nine-tenths of the fellows that hang around here. Now, for instance, my father was hung."

Joe started and gave a gasp of horror.

"Oh yes, but it was done with a very good rope and by the best citizens of Texas, so it seems that I really ought to be very grateful to them for the distinction they conferred upon my family, but I am not. I am ungratefully sad. A man must be very high or very low to take the sensible view of life that keeps him from being sad. I must confess that I have aspired to the depths without ever being fully able to reach them.

"Now look around a bit. See that little girl over there? That's Viola. Two years ago she wrenched up an iron stool from the floor of a lunch-room, and killed another woman with it. She's nineteen,—just about your age, by the way. Well, she had friends with a certain amount of pull. She got out of it, and no one thinks the worse of Viola. You see, Hamilton, in this life we are all suffering from fever, and no one edges away from the other because he finds him a little warm. It's dangerous when you're not used to it; but once you go through the parching process, you become inoculated against further contagion. Now, there's Barney over there, as decent a fellow as I know; but he has been indicted twice for pocket-picking. A half-dozen fellows whom you meet here every night have killed their man. Others have done worse things for which you respect them less. Poor Wallace, who is just coming in, and who looks like a jaunty rag-picker, came here about six months ago with about two thousand dollars, the proceeds from the sale of a house his father had left him. He'll sleep in one of the club chairs to-night, and not from choice. He spent his two thousand learning. But, after all, it was a good investment. It was like buying an annuity. He begins to know already how to live on others as they have lived on him. The plucked bird's beak is sharpened for other's feathers. From now on Wallace will live, eat, drink, and sleep at the expense of others, and will forget to mourn his lost money. He will go on this way until, broken and useless, the poorhouse or the potter's field gets him. Oh, it's a fine, rich life, my lad. I know you'll like it. I said you would the first time I saw you. It has plenty of stir in it, and a man never gets lonesome. Only the rich are lonesome. It's only the independent who depend upon others."

Sadness laughed a peculiar laugh, and there was a look in his terribly bright eyes that made Joe creep. If he could only have understood all that the man was saying to him, he might even yet have turned back. But he didn't. He ordered another drink. The only effect that the talk of Sadness had upon him was to make him feel wonderfully "in it." It gave him a false bravery, and he mentally told himself that now he would not be afraid to face Hattie.

He put out his hand to Sadness with a knowing look. "Thanks, Sadness," he said, "you've helped me lots."

Sadness brushed the proffered hand away and sprung up. "You lie," he cried, "I haven't; I was only fool enough to try"; and he turned hastily away from the table.

Joe looked surprised at first, and then laughed at his friend's retreating form. "Poor old fellow," he said, "drunk again. Must have had something before he came in."

There was not a lie in all that Sadness had said either as to their crime or their condition. He belonged to a peculiar class,—one that grows larger and larger each year in New York and which has imitators in every large city in this country. It is a set which lives, like the leech, upon the blood of others,—that draws its life from the veins of foolish men and immoral women, that prides itself upon its well-dressed idleness and has no shame in its voluntary pauperism. Each member of the class knows every other, his methods and his limitations, and their loyalty one to another makes of them a great hulking, fashionably uniformed fraternity of indolence. Some play the races a few months of the year; others, quite as intermittently, gamble at "shoestring" politics, and waver from party to party as time or their interests seem to dictate. But mostly they are like the lilies of the field.

It was into this set that Sadness had sarcastically invited Joe, and Joe felt honoured. He found that all of his former feelings had been silly and quite out of place; that all he had learned in his earlier years was false. It was very plain to him now that to want a good reputation was the sign of unpardonable immaturity, and that dishonour was the only real thing worth while. It made him feel better.

He was just rising bravely to swagger out to the theatre when Minty Brown came in with one of the club-men he knew. He bowed and smiled, but she appeared not to notice him at first, and when she did she nudged her companion and laughed.

Suddenly his little courage began to ooze out, and he knew what she must be saying to the fellow at her side, for he looked over at him and grinned. Where now was the philosophy of Sadness? Evidently Minty had not been brought under its educating influences, and thought about the whole matter in the old, ignorant way. He began to think of it too. Somehow old teachings and old traditions have an annoying way of coming back upon us in the critical moments of life, although one has long ago recognised how much truer and better some newer ways of thinking are. But Joe would not allow Minty to shatter his dreams by bringing up these old notions. She must be instructed.

He rose and went over to her table.

"Why, Minty," he said, offering his hand, "you ain't mad at me, are you?"

"Go on away f'om hyeah," she said angrily; "I don't want none o' thievin' Berry Hamilton's fambly to speak to me."

"Why, you were all right this evening."

"Yes, but jest out o' pity, an' you was nice 'cause you was afraid I'd tell on you. Go on now."

"Go on now," said Minty's young man; and he looked menacing.

Joe, what little self-respect he had gone, slunk out of the room and needed several whiskeys in a neighbouring saloon to give him courage to go to the theatre and wait for Hattie, who was playing in vaudeville houses pending the opening of her company.

The closing act was just over when he reached the stage door. He was there but a short time, when Hattie tripped out and took his arm. Her face was bright and smiling, and there was no suggestion of disgust in the dancing eyes she turned up to him. Evidently she had not heard, but the thought gave him no particular pleasure, as it left him in suspense as to how she would act when she should hear.

"Let's go somewhere and get some supper," she said; "I'm as hungry as I can be. What are you looking so cut up about?"

"Oh, I ain't feelin' so very good."

"I hope you ain't lettin' that long-tongued Brown woman bother your head, are you?"

His heart seemed to stand still. She did know, then.

"Do you know all about it?"

"Why, of course I do. You might know she'd come to me first with her story."

"And you still keep on speaking to me?"

"Now look here, Joe, if you've been drinking, I'll forgive you; if you ain't, you go on and leave me. Say, what do you take me for? Do you think I'd throw down a friend because somebody else talked about him? Well, you don't know Hat Sterling. When Minty told me that story, she was back in my dressing-room, and I sent her out o' there a-flying, and with a tongue-lashing that she won't forget for a month o' Sundays."

"I reckon that was the reason she jumped on me so hard at the club." He chuckled. He had taken heart again. All that Sadness had said was true, after all, and people thought no less of him. His joy was unbounded.

"So she jumped on you hard, did she? The cat!"

"Oh, she didn't say a thing to me."

"Well, Joe, it's just like this. I ain't an angel, you know that, but I do try to be square, and whenever I find a friend of mine down on his luck, in his pocketbook or his feelings, why, I give him my flipper. Why, old chap, I believe I like you better for the stiff upper lip you've been keeping under all this."

"Why, Hattie," he broke out, unable any longer to control himself, "you're—you're—"

"Oh, I'm just plain Hat Sterling, who won't throw down her friends. Now come on and get something to eat. If that thing is at the club, we'll go there and show her just how much her talk amounted to. She thinks she's the whole game, but I can spot her and then show her that she ain't one, two, three."

When they reached the Banner, they found Minty still

there. She tried on the two the same tactics that she had employed so successfully upon Joe alone. She nudged her companion and tittered. But she had another person to deal with. Hattie Sterling stared at her coldly and indifferently, and passed on by her to a seat. Joe proceeded to order supper and other things in the nonchalant way that the woman had enjoined upon him. Minty began to feel distinctly uncomfortable, but it was her business not to be beaten. She laughed outright. Hattie did not seem to hear her. She was beckoning Sadness to her side. He came and sat down.

"Now look here," she said, "you can't have any supper because you haven't reached the stage of magnificent hunger to make a meal palatable to you. You've got so used to being nearly starved that a meal don't taste good to you under any other circumstances. You're in on the drinks, though. Your thirst is always available.—Jack," she called down the long room to the bartender, "make it three.—Lean over here, I want to talk to you. See that woman over there by the wall? No, not that one,—the big light woman with Griggs. Well, she's come here with a story trying to throw Joe down, and I want you to help me do her."

"Oh, that's the one that upset our young friend, is it?" said Sadness, turning his mournful eyes upon Minty.

"That's her. So you know about it, do you?"

"Yes, and I'll help do her. She mustn't touch one of the fraternity, you know." He kept his eyes fixed upon the outsider until she squirmed. She could not at all understand this serious conversation directed at her. She wondered if she had gone too far and if they contemplated putting her out. It made her uneasy.

Now, this same Miss Sterling had the faculty of attracting a good deal of attention when she wished to. She brought it into play to-night, and in ten minutes, aided by Sadness, she had a crowd of jolly people about her table. When, as she would have expressed it, "everything was going fat," she suddenly paused and, turning her eyes full upon Minty, said in a voice loud enough for all to hear,—

"Say, boys, you've heard that story about Joe, haven't you?"

They had.

"Well, that's the one that told it; she's come here to try to throw him and me down. Is she going to do it?"

"Well, I guess not!" was the rousing reply, and every face turned towards the now frightened Minty. She rose hastily and, getting her skirts together, fled from the room, followed more leisurely by the crestfallen Griggs. Hattie's laugh and "Thank you, fellows," followed her out.

Matters were less easy for Joe's mother and sister than they were for him. A week or more after this, Kitty found him and told him that Minty's story had reached their employers and that they were out of work.

"You see, Joe," she said sadly, "we've took a flat since we moved from Mis' Jones', and we had to furnish it. We've got one lodger, a race-horse man, an' he's mighty nice to ma an' me, but that ain't enough. Now we've got to do something."

Joe was so smitten with sorrow that he gave her a dollar and promised to speak about the matter to a friend of his.

He did speak about it to Hattie.

"You've told me once or twice that your sister could sing. Bring her down here to me, and if she can do anything, I'll get her a place on the stage," was Hattie's answer.

When Kitty heard it she was radiant, but her mother only shook her head and said, "De las' hope, de las' hope."

CHAPTER XII

"All the World's a Stage"

KITTY PROVED HERSELF Joe's sister by falling desperately in love with Hattie Sterling the first time they met. The actress was very gracious to her, and called her "child" in a pretty, patronising way, and patted her on the cheek.

"It's a shame that Joe hasn't brought you around before. We've been good friends for quite some time."

"He told me you an' him was right good friends."

Already Joe took on a new importance in his sister's eyes. He must be quite a man, she thought, to be the friend of such a person as Miss Sterling.

"So you think you want to go on the stage, do you?"

"Yes, 'm, I thought it might be right nice for me if I could."

"Joe, go out and get some beer for us, and then I'll hear your sister sing."

Miss Sterling talked as if she were a manager and had only to snap her fingers to be obeyed. When Joe came back with the beer, Kitty drank a glass. She did not like it, but she would not offend her hostess. After this she sang, and Miss Sterling applauded her generously, although the young girl's nervousness kept her from doing her best. The encouragement helped her, and she did better as she became more at home.

"Why, child, you've got a good voice. And, Joe, you've been keeping her shut up all this time. You ought to be ashamed of yourself."

The young man had little to say. He had brought Kitty almost under a protest, because he had no confidence in her ability and thought that his "girl" would disillusion her. It did not please him now to find his sister so fully under the limelight and himself "up stage."

Kitty was quite in a flutter of delight; not so much with

the idea of working as with the glamour of the work she might be allowed to do.

"I tell you, now," Hattie Sterling pursued, throwing a brightly stockinged foot upon a chair, "your voice is too good for the chorus. Gi' me a cigarette, Joe. Have one, Kitty?—I'm goin' to call you Kitty. It's nice and home-like, and then we've got to be great chums, you know."

Kitty, unwilling to refuse anything from the sorceress, took her cigarette and lighted it, but a few puffs set her off coughing.

"Tut, tut, Kitty, child, don't do it if you ain't used to it. You'll learn soon enough."

Joe wanted to kick his sister for having tried so delicate an art and failed, for he had not yet lost all of his awe of Hattie.

"Now, what I was going to say," the lady resumed after several contemplative puffs, "is that you'll have to begin in the chorus any way and work your way up. It wouldn't take long for you, with your looks and voice, to put one of the 'up and ups' out o' the business. Only hope it won't be me. I've had people I've helped try to do it often enough."

She gave a laugh that had just a touch of bitterness in it, for she began to recognise that although she had been on the stage only a short time, she was no longer the all-conquering Hattie Sterling, in the first freshness of her youth.

"Oh, I wouldn't want to push anybody out," Kit expostulated.

"Oh, never mind, you'll soon get bravely over that feeling, and even if you didn't it wouldn't matter much. The thing has to happen. Somebody's got to go down. We don't last long in this life: it soon wears us out, and when we're worn out and sung out, danced out and played out, the manager has no further use for us; so he reduces us to the ranks or kicks us out entirely."

Joe here thought it time for him to put in a word. "Get out, Hat," he said contemptuously; "you're good for a dozen years yet."

She didn't deign to notice him, save so far as a sniff goes.

"Don't you let what I say scare you, though, Kitty. You've got a good chance, and maybe you'll have more sense than I've got, and at least save money—while you're in it. But let's get off that. It makes me sick. All you've got to do is to come to the opera-house to-morrow and I'll introduce you to the manager. He's a fool, but I think we can make him do something for you."

"Oh, thank you, I'll be around to-morrow, sure."

"Better come about ten o'clock. There's a rehearsal to-morrow, and you'll find him there. Of course, he'll be pretty rough, he always is at rehearsals, but he'll take to you if he thinks there's anything in you and he can get it out."

Kitty felt herself dismissed and rose to go. Joe did not rise.

"I'll see you later, Kit," he said; "I ain't goin' just yet. Say," he added, when his sister was gone, "you're a hot one. What do you want to give her all that con for? She'll never get in."

"Joe," said Hattie, "don't you get awful tired of being a jackass? Sometimes I want to kiss you, and sometimes I feel as if I had to kick you. I'll compromise with you now by letting you bring me some more beer. This got all stale while your sister was here. I saw she didn't like it, and so I wouldn't drink any more for fear she'd try to keep up with me."

"Kit is a good deal of a jay yet," Joe remarked wisely.

"Oh, yes, this world is full of jays. Lots of 'em have seen enough to make 'em wise, but they're still jays, and don't know it. That's the worst of it. They go around thinking they're it, when they ain't even in the game. Go on and get the beer."

And Joe went, feeling vaguely that he had been sat upon.

Kit flew home with joyous heart to tell her mother of her good prospects. She burst into the room, crying, "Oh, ma, ma, Miss Hattie thinks I'll do to go on the stage. Ain't it grand?"

She did not meet with the expected warmth of response from her mother.

"I do' know as it'll be so gran'. F'om what I see of dem stage people dey don't seem to 'mount to much. De way dem gals shows demse'ves is right down bad to me. Is you goin' to dress lak dem we seen dat night?"

Kit hung her head.

"I guess I'll have to."

"Well, ef you have to, I'd ruther see you daid any day. Oh, Kit, my little gal, don't do it, don't do it. Don't you go down lak yo' brothah Joe. Joe's gone."

"Why, ma, you don't understand. Joe's somebody now. You ought to 've heard how Miss Hattie talked about him. She said he's been her friend for a long while."

"Her frien', yes, an' his own inimy. You needn' pattern aftah dat gal, Kit. She ruint Joe, an' she's aftah you now."

"But nowadays everybody thinks stage people respectable up here."

"Maybe I'm ol'-fashioned, but I can't believe in any ooman's ladyship when she shows herse'f lak dem gals does. Oh, Kit, don't do it. Ain't you seen enough? Don't you know enough already to stay away f'om dese hyeah people? Dey don't want nothin' but to pull you down an' den laugh at you w'en you's dragged in de dust."

"You mustn't feel that away, ma. I'm doin' it to help you."

"I do' want no sich help. I'd ruther starve."

Kit did not reply, but there was no yielding in her manner.

"Kit," her mother went on, "dey's somep'n I ain't nevah tol' you dat I'm goin' to tell you now. Mistah Gibson ust to come to Mis' Jones's lots to see me befo' we moved hyeah, an' he's been talkin' 'bout a good many things to me." She hesitated. "He say dat I ain't noways ma'ied to my po' husban', dat a pen'tentiary sentence is de same as a divo'ce, an' if Be'y should live to git out, we'd have to ma'y ag'in. I wouldn't min' dat, Kit, but he say dat at Be'y's age dey ain't much chanst of his livin' to git out, an' hyeah I'll live all dis time alone, an' den have no one to tek keer o' me w'en I git ol'. He wants me to ma'y him, Kit. Kit, I love yo' fathah; he's my only one. But Joe, he's gone, an' ef yo go, befo' Gawd I'll tell Tawm Gibson yes."

The mother looked up to see just what effect her plea would have on her daughter. She hoped that what she said would have the desired result. But the girl turned around from fixing her neck-ribbon before the glass, her face radiant. "Why, it'll be splendid. He's such a nice man, an' race-horse men 'most always have money. Why don't you marry him, ma? Then I'd feel that you was safe an' settled, an' that you wouldn't be lonesome when the show was out of town."

"You want me to ma'y him an' desert yo' po' pa?"

"I guess what he says is right, ma. I don't reckon we'll ever see pa again an' you got to do something. You got to live for yourself now."

Her mother dropped her head in her hands. "All right," she said, "I'll do it; I'll ma'y him. I might as well go de way both my chillen's gone. Po' Be'y, po' Be'y. Ef you evah do come out, Gawd he'p you to baih what you'll fin'." And Mrs. Hamilton rose and tottered from the room, as if the old age she anticipated had already come upon her.

Kit stood looking after her, fear and grief in her eyes. "Poor ma," she said, "an' poor pa. But I know, an' I know it's for the best."

On the next morning she was up early and practising hard for her interview with the managing star of "Martin's Blackbirds."

When she arrived at the theatre, Hattie Sterling met her with frank friendliness.

"I'm glad you came early, Kitty," she remarked, "for maybe you can get a chance to talk with Martin before he begins rehearsal and gets all worked up. He'll be a little less like a bear then. But even if you don't see him before then, wait, and don't get scared if he tries to bluff you. His bark is a good deal worse than his bite."

When Mr. Martin came in that morning, he had other ideas than that of seeing applicants for places. His show must begin in two weeks, and it was advertised to be larger and better than ever before, when really nothing at all had been done for it. The promise of this advertisement must be fulfilled. Mr. Martin was late, and was out of humour with every one else on account of it. He came in hurried, fierce, and important.

"Mornin', Mr. Smith, mornin', Mrs. Jones. Ha, ladies and gentlemen, all here?"

He shot every word out of his mouth as if the after-taste of it were unpleasant to him. He walked among the chorus like an angry king among his vassals, and his glance was a flash of insolent fire. From his head to his feet he was the very epitome of self-sufficient, brutal conceit.

Kitty trembled as she noted the hush that fell on the people at his entrance. She felt like rushing out of the room. She could never face this terrible man. She trembled more as she found his eyes fixed upon her.

"Who's that?" he asked, disregarding her, as if she had been a stick or a stone.

"Well, don't snap her head off. It's a girl friend of mine that wants a place," said Hattie. She was the only one who would brave Martin.

"Humph. Let her wait. I ain't got no time to hear any one now. Get yourselves in line, you all who are on to that first chorus, while I'm getting into my sweat-shirt."

He disappeared behind a screen, whence he emerged arrayed, or only half arrayed, in a thick absorbing shirt and a thin pair of woollen trousers. Then the work began. The man was indefatigable. He was like the spirit of energy. He was in every place about the stage at once, leading the chorus, showing them steps, twisting some awkward girl into shape, shouting, gesticulating, abusing the pianist.

"Now, now," he would shout, "the left foot on that beat. Bah, bah, stop! You walk like a lot of tin soldiers. Are your joints rusty? Do you want oil? Look here, Taylor, if I didn't know you, I'd take you for a truck. Pick up your feet, open your mouths, and move, move, move! Oh!" and he would drop his head in despair. "And to think that I've got to do something with these things in two weeks—two weeks!" Then he would turn to them again with a sudden reaccession of eagerness. "Now, at it again, at it again! Hold that note, hold it! Now whirl, and on the left foot. Stop that music, stop it! Miss Coster, you'll learn that step in about a thousand years, and I've got nine hundred and ninety-nine years and fifty weeks less time than that to spare. Come here and try that step with me. Don't be afraid to move. Step like a chicken on a hot griddle!" And some blushing girl would come forward and go through the step alone before all the rest.

Kitty contemplated the scene with a mind equally divided between fear and anger. What should she do if he should so speak to her? Like the others, no doubt, smile sheepishly and obey him. But she did not like to believe

it. She felt that the independence which she had known
from babyhood would assert itself, and that she would
talk back to him, even as Hattie Sterling did. She felt
scared and discouraged, but every now and then her
friend smiled encouragingly upon her across the ranks of
moving singers.

Finally, however, her thoughts were broken in upon
by hearing Mr. Martin cry: "Oh, quit, quit, and go rest
yourselves, you ancient pieces of hickory, and let me
forget you for a minute before I go crazy. Where's that
new girl now?"

Kitty rose and went toward him, trembling so that she
could hardly walk.

"What can you do?"

"I can sing," very faintly.

"Well, if that's the voice you're going to sing in, there
won't be many that'll know whether it's good or bad.
Well, let's hear something. Do you know any of these?"

And he ran over the titles of several songs. She knew
some of them, and he selected one. "Try this. Here,
Tom, play it for her."

It was an ordeal for the girl to go through. She had
never sung before at anything more formidable than a
church concert, where only her immediate acquaintances
and townspeople were present. Now to sing before all
these strange people, themselves singers, made her feel
faint and awkward. But the courage of desperation came
to her, and she struck into the song. At the first her
voice wavered and threatened to fail her. It must not.
She choked back her fright and forced the music from
her lips.

When she was done, she was startled to hear Martin
burst into a raucous laugh. Such humiliation! She had
failed, and instead of telling her, he was bringing her to
shame before the whole company. The tears came into
her eyes, and she was about giving way when she caught
a reassuring nod and smile from Hattie Sterling, and
seized on this as a last hope.

"Haw, haw, haw!" laughed Martin, "haw, haw, haw!
The little one was scared, see? She was scared, d' you
understand? But did you see the grit she went at it with?
Just took the bit in her teeth and got away. Haw, haw,
haw! Now, that's what I like. If all you girls had that

spirit, we could do something in two weeks. Try another one, girl."

Kitty's heart had suddenly grown light. She sang the second one better because something within her was singing.

"Good!" said Martin, but he immediately returned to his cold manner. "You watch these girls close and see what they do, and to-morrow be prepared to go into line and move as well as sing."

He immediately turned his attention from her to the chorus, but no slight that he could inflict upon her now could take away the sweet truth that she was engaged and to-morrow would begin work. She wished she could go over and embrace Hattie Sterling. She thought kindly of Joe, and promised herself to give him a present out of her first month's earnings.

On the first night of the show pretty little Kitty Hamilton was pointed out as a girl who wouldn't be in the chorus long. The mother, who was soon to be Mrs. Gibson, sat in the balcony, a grieved, pained look on her face. Joe was in a front row with some of the rest of the gang. He took many drinks between the acts, because he was proud.

Mr. Thomas was there. He also was proud, and after the performance he waited for Kitty at the stage door and went forward to meet her as she came out. The look she gave him stopped him, and he let her pass without a word.

"Who'd 'a' thought," he mused, "that the kid had that much nerve? Well, if they don't want to find out things, what do they come to N' Yawk for? It ain't nobody's old Sunday-school picnic. Guess I got out easy, anyhow."

Hattie Sterling took Joe home in a hansom.

"Say," she said, "if you come this way for me again, it's all over, see? Your little sister's a comer, and I've got to hustle to keep up with her."

Joe growled and fell asleep in his chair. One must needs have a strong head or a strong will when one is the brother of a celebrity and would celebrate the distinguished one's success.

CHAPTER XIII

The Oakleys

A YEAR AFTER the arrest of Berry Hamilton, and at a time when New York had shown to the eyes of his family so many strange new sights, there were few changes to be noted in the condition of affairs at the Oakley place. Maurice Oakley was perhaps a shade more distrustful of his servants, and consequently more testy with them. Mrs. Oakley was the same acquiescent woman, with unbounded faith in her husband's wisdom and judgment. With complacent minds both went their ways, drank their wine, and said their prayers, and wished that brother Frank's five years were past. They had letters from him now and then, never very cheerful in tone, but always breathing the deepest love and gratitude to them.

His brother found deep cause for congratulation in the tone of these epistles.

"Frank is getting down to work," he would cry exultantly. "He is past the first buoyant enthusiasm of youth. Ah, Leslie, when a man begins to be serious, then he begins to be something." And her only answer would be, "I wonder, Maurice, if Claire Lessing will wait for him?"

The two had frequent questions to answer as to Frank's doing and prospects, and they had always bright things to say of him, even when his letters gave them no such warrant. Their love for him made them read large between the lines, and all they read was good.

Between Maurice and his brother no word of the guilty servant ever passed. They each avoided it as an unpleasant subject. Frank had never asked and his brother had never proffered aught of the outcome of the case.

Mrs. Oakley had once suggested it. "Brother ought to know," she said, "that Berry is being properly punished."

"By no means," replied her husband. "You know that

it would only hurt him. He shall never know if I have to tell him."

"You are right, Maurice, you are always right. We must shield Frank from the pain it would cause him. Poor fellow! he is so sensitive."

Their hearts were still steadfastly fixed upon the union of this younger brother with Claire Lessing. She had lately come into a fortune, and there was nothing now to prevent it. They would have written Frank to urge it, but they both believed that to try to woo him away from his art was but to make him more wayward. That any woman could have power enough to take him away from this jealous mistress they very much doubted. But they could hope, and hope made them eager to open every letter that bore the French postmark. Always it might contain news that he was coming home, or that he had made a great success, or, better, some inquiry after Claire. A long time they had waited, but found no such tidings in the letters from Paris.

At last, as Maurice Oakley sat in his library one day, the servant brought him a letter more bulky in weight and appearance than any he had yet received. His eyes glistened with pleasure as he read the postmark. "A letter from Frank," he said joyfully, "and an important one, I'll wager."

He smiled as he weighed it in his hand and caressed it. Mrs. Oakley was out shopping, and as he knew how deep her interest was, he hesitated to break the seal before she returned. He curbed his natural desire and laid the heavy envelope down on the desk. But he could not deny himself the pleasure of speculating as to its contents.

It was such a large, interesting-looking package. What might it not contain? It simply reeked of possibilities. Had any one banteringly told Maurice Oakley that he had such a deep vein of sentiment, he would have denied it with scorn and laughter. But here he found himself sitting with the letter in his hand and weaving stories as to its contents.

First, now, it might be a notice that Frank had received the badge of the Legion of Honour. No, no, that was too big, and he laughed aloud at his own folly, wondering the next minute, with half shame, why he laughed, for did he, after all, believe anything was too big for that brother of his? Well, let him begin, anyway, away down. Let him say, for instance, that the letter told of the completion and sale of a great picture. Frank had sold small ones. He would be glad of this, for his brother had written him several times of things that were a-doing, but not yet of anything that was done. Or, better yet, let the letter say that some picture, long finished, but of which the artist's pride and anxiety had forbidden him to speak, had made a glowing success, the success it deserved. This sounded well, and seemed not at all beyond the bounds of possibility. It was an alluring vision. He saw the picture already. It was a scene from life, true in detail to the point of very minuteness, and yet with something spiritual in it that lifted it above the mere copy of the commonplace. At the Salon it would be hung on the line, and people would stand before it admiring its workmanship and asking who the artist was. He drew on his memory of old reading. In his mind's eye he saw Frank, unconscious of his own power or too modest to admit it, stand unknown among the crowds around his picture waiting for and dreading their criticisms. He saw the light leap to his eyes as he heard their words of praise. He saw the straightening of his narrow shoulders when he was forced to admit that he was the painter of the work. Then the windows of Paris were filled with his portraits. The papers were full of his praise, and brave men and fair women met together to do him homage. Fair women, yes, and Frank would look upon them all and see reflected in them but a tithe of the glory of one woman, and that woman Claire Lessing. He roused himself and laughed again as he tapped the magic envelope.

"My fancies go on and conquer the world for my brother," he muttered. "He will follow their flight one day and do it himself."

The letter drew his eyes back to it. It seemed to invite him, to beg him even. "No, I will not do it; I will wait until Leslie comes. She will be as glad to hear the good news as I am."

His dreams were taking the shape of reality in his mind, and he was believing all that he wanted to believe.

He turned to look at a picture painted by Frank which

hung over the mantel. He dwelt lovingly upon it, seeing in it the touch of a genius.

"Surely," he said, "this new picture cannot be greater than that, though it shall hang where kings can see it and this only graces the library of my poor house. It has the feeling of a woman's soul with the strength of a man's heart. When Frank and Claire marry, I shall give it back to them. It is too great a treasure for a clod like me. Heigho, why will women be so long a-shopping?"

He glanced again at the letter, and his hand went out involuntarily towards it. He fondled it, smiling.

"Ah, Lady Leslie, I've a mind to open it to punish you for staying so long."

He essayed to be playful, but he knew that he was trying to make a compromise with himself because his eagerness grew stronger than his gallantry. He laid the letter down and picked it up again. He studied the postmark over and over. He got up and walked to the window and back again, and then began fumbling in his pockets for his knife. No, he did not want it; yes, he did. He would just cut the envelope and make believe he had read it to pique his wife; but he would not read it. Yes, that was it. He found the knife and slit the paper. His fingers trembled as he touched the sheets that protruded. Why would not Leslie come? Did she not know that he was waiting for her? She ought to have known that there was a letter from Paris to-day, for it had been a month since they had had one.

There was a sound of footsteps without. He sprang up, crying, "I've been waiting so long for you!" A servant opened the door to bring him a message. Oakley dismissed him angrily. What did he want to go down to the Continental for to drink and talk politics to a lot of muddle-pated fools when he had a brother in Paris who was an artist and a letter from him lay unread in his hand? His patience and his temper were going. Leslie was careless and unfeeling. She ought to come; he was tired of waiting.

A carriage rolled up the driveway and he dropped the letter guiltily, as if it were not his own. He would only say that he had grown tired of waiting and started to read it. But it was only Mrs. Davis's footman leaving a note for Leslie about some charity.

He went back to the letter. Well, it was his. Leslie had forfeited her right to see it as soon as he. It might be mean, but it was not dishonest. No, he would not read it now, but he would take it and show her that he had exercised his self-control in spite of her shortcomings. He laid it on the desk once more. It leered at him. He might just open the sheets enough to see the lines that began it, and read no further. Yes, he would do that. Leslie could not feel hurt at such a little thing.

The first line had only "Dear Brother." "Dear Brother"! Why not the second? That could not hold much more. The second line held him, and the third, and the fourth, and as he read on, unmindful now of what Leslie might think or feel, his face turned from the ruddy glow of pleasant anxiety to the pallor of grief and terror. He was not half-way through it when Mrs. Oakley's voice in the hall announced her coming. He did not hear her. He sat staring at the page before him, his lips apart and his eyes staring. Then, with a cry that echoed through the house, crumpling the sheets in his hand, he fell forward fainting to the floor, just as his wife rushed into the room.

"What is it?" she cried. "Maurice! Maurice!"

He lay on the floor staring up at the ceiling, the letter clutched in his hands. She ran to him and lifted up his head, but he gave no sign of life. Already the servants were crowding to the door. She bade one of them to hasten for a doctor, others to bring water and brandy, and the rest to be gone. As soon as she was alone, she loosed the crumpled sheets from his hand, for she felt that this must have been the cause of her husband's strange attack. Without a thought of wrong, for they had no secrets from each other, she glanced at the opening lines. Then she forgot the unconscious man at her feet and read the letter through to the end.

The letter was in Frank's neat hand, a little shaken, perhaps, by nervousness.

"DEAR BROTHER," it ran, "I know you will grieve at receiving this, and I wish that I might bear your grief for you, but I cannot, though I have as heavy a burden as this can bring to you. Mine would have been lighter to-day, perhaps, had you been more straightforward with me. I am not blaming you, however, for I know that my hypocrisy made you believe me possessed of a really soft heart, and you thought to spare me. Until yesterday, when in a letter from Esterton he casually mentioned the matter, I did not know that Berry was in prison, else this letter would have been written sooner. I have been wanting to write it for so long, and yet have been too great a coward to do so.

"I know that you will be disappointed in me, and just what that disappointment will cost you I know; but you must hear the truth. I shall never see your face again, or I should not dare to tell it even now. You will remember that I begged you to be easy on your servant. You thought it was only my kindness of heart. It was not; I had a deeper reason. I knew where the money had gone and dared not tell. Berry is as innocent as yourself—and I—well, it is a story, and let me tell it to you.

"You have had so much confidence in me, and I hate to tell you that it was all misplaced. I have no doubt that I should not be doing it now but that I have drunken absinthe enough to give me the emotional point of view, which I shall regret to-morrow. I do not mean that I am drunk. I can think clearly and write clearly, but my emotions are extremely active.

"Do you remember Claire's saying at the table that night of the farewell dinner that some dark-eyed mademoiselle was waiting for me? She did not know how truly she spoke, though I fancy she saw how I flushed when she said it: for I was already in love—madly so.

"I need not describe her. I need say nothing about her, for I know that nothing I say can ever persuade you to forgive her for taking me from you. This has gone on since I first came here, and I dared not tell you, for I saw whither your eyes had turned. I loved this girl, and she both inspired and hindered my work. Perhaps I would have been successful had I not met her, perhaps not.

"I love her too well to marry her and make of our devotion a stale, prosy thing of duty and compulsion. When a man does not marry a woman, he must keep her better than he would a wife. It costs. All that you gave me went to make her happy.

"Then, when I was about leaving you, the catastrophe came. I wanted much to carry back to her. I gambled to make more. I would surprise her. Luck was against me. Night after night I lost. Then, just before the dinner, I woke from my frenzy to find all that I had was gone. I would have asked you for more, and you would have given it; but that strange, ridiculous something which we misname Southern honour, that honour which strains at a gnat and swallows a camel, withheld me, and I preferred to do worse. So I lied to you. The money from my cabinet was not stolen save by myself. I am a liar and a thief, but your eyes shall never tell me so.

"Tell the truth and have Berry released. I can stand it. Write me but one letter to tell me of this. Do not plead with me, do not forgive me, do not seek to find me, for from this time I shall be as one who has perished from the earth; I shall be no more.

> "Your brother,
>
> "FRANK."

By the time the servants came they found Mrs. Oakley as white as her lord. But with firm hands and compressed lips she ministered to his needs pending the doctor's arrival. She bathed his face and temples, chafed his hands, and forced the brandy between his lips. Finally he stirred and his hands gripped.

"The letter!" he gasped.

"Yes, dear, I have it; I have it."

"Give it to me," he cried. She handed it to him. He seized it and thrust it into his breast.

"Did—did—you read it?"

"Yes, I did not know——"

"Oh, my God, I did not intend that you should see it. I wanted the secret for my own. I wanted to carry it to my grave with me. Oh, Frank, Frank, Frank!"

"Never mind, Maurice. It is as if you alone knew it."

"It is not, I say, it is not!"

He turned upon his face and began to weep passionately, not like a man, but like a child whose last toy has been broken.

"Oh, my God," he moaned, "my brother, my brother!"

" 'Sh, dearie, think—it's—it's—Frank."

"That's it, that's it—that's what I can't forget. It's Frank,—Frank, my brother."

Suddenly he sat up and his eyes stared straight into hers.

"Leslie, no one must ever know what is in this letter," he said calmly.

"No one shall, Maurice; come, let us burn it."

"'Burn it? No, no," he cried, clutching at his breast. "It must not be burned. What! burn my brother's secret? No, no, I must carry it with me,—carry it with me to the grave."

"But, Maurice——"

"I must carry it with me."

She saw that he was overwrought, and so did not argue with him.

When the doctor came, he found Maurice Oakley in bed, but better. The medical man diagnosed the case and decided that he had received some severe shock. He feared too for his heart, for the patient constantly held his hands pressed against his bosom. In vain the doctor pleaded; he would not take them down, and when the wife added her word, the physician gave up, and after prescribing, left, much puzzled in mind.

"It's a strange case," he said; "there's something more than the nervous shock that makes him clutch his chest like that, and yet I have never noticed signs of heart trouble in Oakley. Oh, well, business worry will produce anything in anybody."

It was soon common talk about the town about Maurice Oakley's attack. In the seclusion of his chamber he was saying to his wife:

"Ah, Leslie, you and I will keep the secret. No one shall ever know."

"Yes, dear, but—but—what of Berry?"

"What of Berry?" he cried, starting up excitedly. "What is Berry to Frank? What is that nigger to my brother? What are his sufferings to the honour of my family and name?"

"Never mind, Maurice, never mind, you are right."

"It must never be known, I say, if Berry has to rot in jail."

So they wrote a lie to Frank, and buried the secret in their breasts, and Oakley wore its visible form upon his heart.

CHAPTER XIV

Frankenstein

FIVE YEARS IS but a short time in the life of a man, and yet many things may happen therein. For instance, the whole way of a family's life may be changed. Good natures may be made into bad ones and out of a soul of faith grow a spirit of unbelief. The independence of respectability may harden into the insolence of defiance, and the sensitive cheek of modesty into the brazen face of shamelessness. It may be true that the habits of years are hard to change, but this is not true of the first sixteen or seventeen years of a young person's life, else Kitty Hamilton and Joe could not so easily have become what they were. It had taken barely five years to accomplish an entire metamorphosis of their characters. In Joe's case even a shorter time was needed. He was so ready to go down that it needed but a gentle push to start him, and once started, there was nothing within him to hold him back from the depths. For his will was as flabby as his conscience, and his pride, which stands to some men for conscience, had no definite aim or direction.

Hattie Sterling had given him both his greatest impulse for evil and for good. She had at first given him his gentle push, but when she saw that his collapse would lose her a faithful and useful slave she had sought to check his course. Her threat of the severance of their relations had held him up for a little time, and she began to believe that he was safe again. He went back to the work he had neglected, drank moderately, and acted in most things as a sound, sensible being. Then, all of a sudden, he went down again, and went down badly. She kept her promise and threw him over. Then he became a hanger-on at the clubs, a genteel loafer. He used to say in his sober moments that at last he was one of the boys that Sadness had spoken of. He did not work, and yet he lived and ate and was proud of his degradation. But he soon tired of being separated from Hattie, and straightened up again. After some demur she received him upon his former footing. It was only for a few months. He fell again. For almost four years this had happened intermittently. Finally he took a turn for the better that endured so long that Hattie Sterling again gave him her faith. Then the woman made her mistake. She warmed to him. She showed him that she was proud of him. He went forth at once to celebrate his victory. He did not return to her for three days. Then he was battered, unkempt, and thick of speech.

She looked at him in silent contempt for a while as he sat nursing his aching head.

"Well, you're a beauty," she said finally with cutting scorn. "You ought to be put under a glass case and placed on exhibition."

He groaned and his head sunk lower. A drunken man is always disarmed.

His helplessness, instead of inspiring her with pity, inflamed her with an unfeeling anger that burst forth in a volume of taunts.

"You're the thing I've given up all my chances for—you, a miserable, drunken jay, without a jay's decency. No one had ever looked at you until I picked you up and you've been strutting around ever since, showing off because I was kind to you, and now this is the way you pay me back. Drunk half the time and half drunk the rest. Well, you know what I told you the last time you got 'loaded'? I mean it too. You're not the only star in sight, see?"

She laughed meanly and began to sing, "You'll have to find another baby now."

For the first time he looked up, and his eyes were full of tears—tears both of grief and intoxication. There was an expression of a whipped dog on his face.

"Do'—Ha'ie, do'—" he pleaded, stretching out his hands to her.

Her eyes blazed back at him, but she sang on insolently, tauntingly.

The very inanity of the man disgusted her, and on a sudden impulse she sprang up and struck him full in the face with the flat of her hand. He was too weak to resist the blow, and, tumbling from the chair, fell limply to the floor, where he lay at her feet, alternately weeping aloud and quivering with drunken, hiccoughing sobs.

"Get up!" she cried; "get up and get out o' here. You sha'n't lay around my house."

He had already begun to fall into a drunken sleep, but she shook him, got him to his feet, and pushed him outside the door. "Now, go, you drunken dog, and never put your foot inside this house again."

He stood outside, swaying dizzily upon his feet and looking back with dazed eyes at the door, then he muttered: "Pu' me out, wi' you? Pu' me out, damn you! Well, I ki' you. See 'f I don't"; and he half walked, half fell down the street.

Sadness and Skaggsy were together at the club that night. Five years had not changed the latter as to wealth or position or inclination, and he was still a frequent visitor at the Banner. He always came in alone now, for Maudie had gone the way of all the half-world, and reached depths to which Mr. Skaggs's job prevented him from following her. However, he mourned truly for his lost companion, and to-night he was in a particularly pensive mood.

Some one was playing rag-time on the piano, and the dancers were wheeling in time to the music. Skaggsy looked at them regretfully as he sipped his liquor. It made him think of Maudie. He sighed and turned away.

"I tell you, Sadness," he said impulsively, "dancing is the poetry of motion."

"Yes," replied Sadness, "and dancing in rag-time is the dialect poetry."

The reporter did not like this. It savoured of flippancy, and he was about entering upon a discussion to prove that Sadness had no soul, when Joe, with bloodshot eyes and dishevelled clothes, staggered in and reeled towards them.

"Drunk again," said Sadness. "Really, it's a waste of time for Joe to sober up. Hullo there!" as the young man brought up against him; "take a seat." He put him in a chair at the table. "Been lushin' a bit, eh?"

"Gi' me some'n' drink."

"Oh, a hair of the dog. Some men shave their dogs clean, and then have hydrophobia. Here, Jack!"

They drank, and then, as if the whiskey had done him good, Joe sat up in his chair.

"Ha'ie's throwed me down."

"Lucky dog! You might have known it would have happened sooner or later. Better sooner than never."

Skaggs smoked in silence and looked at Joe.

"I'm goin' to kill her."

"I wouldn't if I were you. Take old Sadness's advice and thank your stars that you're rid of her."

"I'm goin' to kill her." He paused and looked at them drowsily. Then, bracing himself up again, he broke out suddenly, "Say, d' ever tell y' 'bout the ol' man? He never stole that money. Know he di' n'."

He threatened to fall asleep now, but the reporter was all alert. He scented a story.

"By Jove!" he exclaimed, "did you hear that? Bet the chap stole it himself and's letting the old man suffer for it. Great story, ain't it? Come, come, wake up here. Three more, Jack. What about your father?"

"Father? Who's father. Oh, do' bother me. What?"

"Here, here, tell us about your father and the money. If he didn't steal it, who did?"

"Who did? Tha' 's it, who did? Ol' man di' n' steal it, know he di' n'."

"Oh, let him alone, Skaggsy, he don't know what he's saying."

"Yes, he does, a drunken man tells the truth."

"In some cases," said Sadness.

"Oh, let me alone, man. I've been trying for years to get a big sensation for my paper, and if this story is one, I'm a made man."

The drink seemed to revive the young man again, and by bits Skaggs was able to pick out of him the story of his father's arrest and conviction. At its close he relapsed into stupidity, murmuring, "She throwed me down."

"Well," sneered Sadness, "you see drunken men tell the truth, and you don't seem to get much guilt out of our young friend. You're disappointed, aren't you?"

"I confess I am disappointed, but I've got an idea, just the same."

"Oh, you have? Well, don't handle it carelessly; it might go off." And Sadness rose. The reporter sat thinking for a time and then followed him, leaving Joe in a drunken sleep at the table. There he lay for more than two hours. When he finally awoke, he started up as if some determination had come to him in his sleep. A part of the helplessness of his intoxication had gone, but his first act was to call for more whiskey. This he gulped down, and followed with another and another. For a while he stood still, brooding silently, his red eyes blinking at the light. Then he turned abruptly and left the club.

It was very late when he reached Hattie's door, but he opened it with his latch-key, as he had been used to do. He stopped to help himself to a glass of brandy, as he had so often done before. Then he went directly to her room. She was a light sleeper, and his step awakened her.

"Who is it?" she cried in affright.

"It's me." His voice was steadier now, but grim.

"What do you want? Didn't I tell you never to come here again? Get out or I'll have you taken out."

She sprang up in bed, glaring angrily at him.

His hands twitched nervously, as if her will were conquering him and he were uneasy, but he held her eye with his own.

"You put me out to-night," he said.

"Yes, and I'm going to do it again. You're drunk."

She started to rise, but he took a step towards her and she paused. He looked as she had never seen him look before. His face was ashen and his eyes like fire and blood. She quailed beneath the look. He took another step towards her.

"You put me out to-night," he repeated, "like a dog."

His step was steady and his tone was clear, menacingly clear. She shrank back from him, back to the wall. Still his hands twitched and his eye held her. Still he crept slowly towards her, his lips working and his hands moving convulsively.

"Joe, Joe!" she said hoarsely, "what's the matter? Oh, don't look at me like that."

The gown had fallen away from her breast and showed the convulsive fluttering of her heart.

He broke into a laugh, a dry, murderous laugh, and his hands sought each other while the fingers twitched over one another like coiling serpents.

"You put me out—you—you, and you made me what I am." The realisation of what he was, of his foulness and degradation, seemed just to have come to him fully. "You made me what I am, and then you sent me away. You let me come back, and now you put me out."

She gazed at him fascinated. She tried to scream and she could not. This was not Joe. This was not the boy that she had turned and twisted about her little finger. This was a terrible, terrible man or a monster.

He moved a step nearer her. His eyes fell to her throat. For an instant she lost their steady glare and then she found her voice. The scream was checked as it began. His fingers had closed over her throat just where the gown had left it temptingly bare. They gave it the caress of death. She struggled. They held her. Her eyes prayed to his. But his were the fire of hell. She fell back upon her pillow in silence. He had not uttered a word. He held her. Finally he flung her from him like a rag, and sank into a chair. And there the officers found him when Hattie Sterling's disappearance had become a strange thing.

CHAPTER XV

"Dear, Damned, Delightful Town"

WHEN JOE WAS TAKEN, there was no spirit or feeling left in him. He moved mechanically, as if without sense or volition. The first impression he gave was that of a man over-acting insanity. But this was soon removed by the very indifference with which he met everything concerned with his crime. From the very first he made no effort to exonerate or to vindicate himself. He talked little and only in a dry, stupefied way. He was as one whose soul is dead, and perhaps it was; for all the little soul of him had been wrapped up in the body of this one woman, and the stroke that took her life had killed him too.

The men who examined him were irritated beyond measure. There was nothing for them to exercise their ingenuity upon. He left them nothing to search for. Their most damning question he answered with an apathy that showed absolutely no interest in the matter. It was as if some one whom he did not care about had committed a crime and he had been called to testify. The only thing which he noticed or seemed to have any affection for was a little pet dog which had been hers and which they sometimes allowed to be with him after the life sentence had been passed upon him and when he was awaiting removal. He would sit for hours with the little animal in his lap, caressing it dumbly. There was a mute sorrow in the eyes of both man and dog, and they seemed to take comfort in each other's presence. There was no need of any sign between them. They had both loved her, had they not? So they understood.

Sadness saw him and came back to the Banner, torn and unnerved by the sight. "I saw him," he said with a shudder, "and it'll take more whiskey than Jack can give me in a year to wash the memory of him out of me. Why, man, it shocked me all through. It's a pity they didn't send him to the chair. It couldn't have done him much harm and would have been a real mercy."

And so Sadness and all the club, with a muttered "Poor devil!" dismissed him. He was gone. Why should they worry? Only one more who had got into the whirl-pool, enjoyed the sensation for a moment, and then swept dizzily down. There were, indeed, some who for an earnest hour sermonised about it and said, "Here is another example of the pernicious influence of the city on untrained negroes. Oh, is there no way to keep these people from rushing away from the small villages and country districts of the South up to the cities, where they cannot battle with the terrible force of a strange and unusual environment? Is there no way to prove to them that woollen-shirted, brown-jeaned simplicity is infinitely better than broad-clothed degradation?" They wanted to preach to these people that good agriculture is better than bad art,—that it was better and nobler for them to sing to God across the Southern fields than to dance for rowdies in the Northern halls. They wanted to dare to say that the South has its faults—no one condones them—and its disadvantages, but that even what they suffered from these was better than what awaited them in the great alleys of New York. Down there, the bodies were restrained, and they chafed; but here the soul would fester, and they would be content.

This was but for an hour, for even while they ex-claimed they knew that there was no way, and that the stream of young negro life would continue to flow up from the South, dashing itself against the hard necessities of the city and breaking like waves against a rock,—that, until the gods grew tired of their cruel sport, there must still be sacrifices to false ideals and unreal ambitions.

There was one heart, though, that neither dismissed Joe with gratuitous pity nor sermonised about him. The mother heart had only room for grief and pain. Already it had borne its share. It had known sorrow for a lost husband, tears at the neglect and brutality of a new com-panion, shame for a daughter's sake, and it had seemed already filled to overflowing. And yet the fates had put in this one other burden until it seemed it must burst with the weight of it.

To Fannie Hamilton's mind now all her boy's short-comings became as naught. He was not her wayward, erring, criminal son. She only remembered that he was her son, and wept for him as such. She forgot his curses, while her memory went back to the sweetness of his baby prattle and the soft words of his tenderer youth. Until the last she clung to him, holding him guiltless, and to her thought they took to prison, not Joe Hamilton, a convicted criminal, but Joey, Joey, her boy, her first-born,—a martyr.

The pretty Miss Kitty Hamilton was less deeply impressed. The arrest and subsequent conviction of her brother was quite a blow. She felt the shame of it keenly, and some of the grief. To her, coming as it did just at a time when the company was being strengthened and she more importantly featured than ever, it was decidedly inopportune, for no one could help connecting her name with the affair.

For a long time she and her brother had scarcely been upon speaking terms. During Joe's frequent lapses from industry he had been prone to "touch" his sister for the wherewithal to supply his various wants. When, finally, she grew tired and refused to be "touched," he rebuked her for withholding that which, save for his help, she would never have been able to make. This went on until they were almost entirely estranged. He was wont to say that "now his sister was up in the world, she had got the big head," and she to retort that her brother "wanted to use her for a 'soft thing.'"

From the time that she went on the stage she had begun to live her own life, a life in which the chief aim was the possession of good clothes and the ability to attract the attention which she had learned to crave. The greatest sign of interest she showed in her brother's affair was, at first, to offer her mother money to secure a lawyer. But when Joe confessed all, she consoled herself with the reflection that perhaps it was for the best, and kept her money in her pocket with a sense of satisfaction. She was getting to be so very much more Joe's sister. She did not go to see her brother. She was afraid it might make her nervous while she was in the city, and she went on the road with her company before he was taken away.

Miss Kitty Hamilton had to be very careful about her nerves and her health. She had had experiences, and her voice was not as good as it used to be, and her beauty had to be aided by cosmetics. So she went away from New York, and only read of all that happened when some one called her attention to it in the papers.

Berry Hamilton in his Southern prison knew nothing of all this, for no letters had passed between him and his family for more than two years. The very cruelty of destiny defeated itself in this and was kind.

CHAPTER XVI

Skaggs's Theory

THERE WAS, PERHAPS, more depth to Mr. Skaggs than most people gave him credit for having. However it may be, when he got an idea into his head, whether it were insane or otherwise, he had a decidedly tenacious way of holding to it. Sadness had been disposed to laugh at him when he announced that Joe's drunken story of his father's troubles had given him an idea. But it was, nevertheless, true, and that idea had stayed with him clear through the exciting events that followed on that fatal night. He thought and dreamed of it until he had made a working theory. Then one day, with a boldness that he seldom assumed when in the sacred Presence, he walked into the office and laid his plans before the editor. They talked together for some time, and the editor seemed hard to convince.

"It would be a big thing for the paper," he said, "if it only panned out; but it is such a rattle-brained, harum-scarum thing. No one under the sun would have thought of it but you, Skaggs."

"Oh, it's bound to pan out. I see the thing as clear as day. There's no getting around it."

"Yes, it looks plausible, but so does all fiction. You're taking a chance. You're losing time. If it fails——"

"But if it succeeds?"

"Well, go and bring back a story. If you don't, look out. It's against my better judgment anyway. Remember I told you that."

Skaggs shot out of the office, and within an hour and a half had boarded a fast train for the South.

It is almost a question whether Skaggs had a theory or whether he had told himself a pretty story and, as usual, believed it. The editor was right. No one else would have thought of the wild thing that was in the reporter's mind.

The detective had not thought of it five years before, nor had Maurice Oakley and his friends had an inkling, and here was one of the New York *Universe*'s young men going miles to prove his idea about something that did not at all concern him.

When Skaggs reached the town which had been the home of the Hamiltons, he went at once to the Continental Hotel. He had as yet formulated no plan of immediate action and with a fool's or a genius' belief in his destiny he sat down to await the turn of events. His first move would be to get acquainted with some of his neighbours. This was no difficult matter, as the bar of the Continental was still the gathering-place of some of the city's choice spirits of the old régime. Thither he went, and his convivial cheerfulness soon placed him on terms of equality with many of his kind.

He insinuated that he was looking around for business prospects. This proved his open-sesame. Five years had not changed the Continental frequenters much, and Skaggs's intention immediately brought Beachfield Davis down upon him with the remark, "If a man wants to go into business, business for a gentleman, suh, Gad, there's no finer or better paying business in the world than breeding blooded dogs—that is, if you get a man of experience to go in with you."

"Dogs, dogs," drivelled old Horace Talbot, "Beachfield's always talking about dogs. I remember the night we were all discussing that Hamilton nigger's arrest, Beachfield said it was a sign of total depravity because his man hunted 'possums with his hound." The old man laughed inanely. The hotel whiskey was getting on his nerves.

The reporter opened his eyes and his ears. He had stumbled upon something, at any rate.

"What was it about some nigger's arrest, sir?" he asked respectfully.

"Oh, it wasn't anything much. Only an old and trusted servant robbed his master, and my theory——"

"But you will remember, Mr. Talbot," broke in Davis, "that I proved your theory to be wrong and cited a conclusive instance."

"Yes, a 'possum-hunting dog."

"I am really anxious to hear about the robbery,

though. It seems such an unusual thing for a negro to steal a great amount."

"Just so, and that was part of my theory. Now——"

"It's an old story and a long one, Mr. Skaggs, and one of merely local repute," interjected Colonel Saunders. "I don't think it could possibly interest you, who are familiar with the records of the really great crimes that take place in a city such as New York."

"Those things do interest me very much, though. I am something of a psychologist, and I often find the smallest and most insignificant-appearing details pregnant with suggestion. Won't you let me hear the story, Colonel?"

"Why, yes, though there's little in it save that I am one of the few men who have come to believe that the negro, Berry Hamilton, is not the guilty party."

"Nonsense! nonsense!" said Talbot; "of course Berry was guilty, but, as I said before, I don't blame him. The negroes——"

"Total depravity," said Davis. "Now look at my dog——"

"If you will retire with me to the further table I will give you whatever of the facts I can call to mind."

As unobtrusively as they could, they drew apart from the others and seated themselves at a more secluded table, leaving Talbot and Davis wrangling, as of old, over their theories. When the glasses were filled and the pipes going, the Colonel began his story, interlarding it frequently with comments of his own.

"Now, in the first place, Mr. Skaggs," he said when the tale was done, "I am lawyer enough to see for myself how weak the evidence was upon which the negro was convicted, and later events have done much to confirm me in the opinion that he was innocent."

"Later events?"

"Yes." The Colonel leaned across the table and his voice fell to a whisper. "Four years ago a great change took place in Maurice Oakley. It happened in the space of a day, and no one knows the cause of it. From a social, companionable man, he became a recluse, shunning visitors and dreading society. From an openhearted, unsuspicious neighbour, he became secretive and distrustful of his own friends. From an active business man, he has become a retired brooder. He sees no one if he can help it. He writes no letters and receives none, not even from his brother, it is said. And all of this came about in the space of twenty-four hours."

"But what was the beginning of it?"

"No one knows, save that one day he had some sort of nervous attack. By the time the doctor was called he was better, but he kept clutching his hand over his heart. Naturally, the physician wanted to examine him there, but the very suggestion of it seemed to throw him into a frenzy; and his wife too begged the doctor, an old friend of the family, to desist. Maurice Oakley had been as sound as a dollar, and no one of the family had had any tendency to heart affection."

"It is strange."

"Strange it is, but I have my theory."

"His actions are like those of a man guarding a secret."

"Sh! His negro laundress says that there is an inside pocket in his undershirts."

"An inside pocket?"

"Yes."

"And for what?" Skaggs was trembling with eagerness. The Colonel dropped his voice lower.

"We can only speculate," he said; "but, as I have said, I have my theory. Oakley was a just man, and in punishing his old servant for the supposed robbery it is plain that he acted from principle. But he is also a proud man and would hate to confess that he had been in the wrong. So I believed that the cause of his first shock was the finding of the money that he supposed gone. Unwilling to admit this error, he lets the misapprehension go on, and it is the money which he carries in his secret pocket, with a morbid fear of its discovery, that has made him dismiss his servants, leave his business, and refuse to see his friends."

"A very natural conclusion, Colonel, and I must say that I believe you. It is strange that others have not seen as you have seen and brought the matter to light."

"Well, you see, Mr. Skaggs, none are so dull as the people who think they think. I can safely say that there is not another man in this town who has lighted upon the real solution of this matter, though it has been openly talked of for so long. But as for bringing it to light, no one would think of doing that. It would be sure to hurt Oakley's feelings, and he is of one of our best families."

"Ah, yes, perfectly right."

Skaggs had got all that he wanted; much more, in fact, than he had expected. The Colonel held him for a while yet to enlarge upon the views that he had expressed.

When the reporter finally left him, it was with a cheery "Good-night, Colonel. If I were a criminal, I should be afraid of that analytical mind of yours!"

He went upstairs chuckling. "The old fool!" he cried as he flung himself into a chair. "I've got it! I've got it! Maurice Oakley must see me, and then what?" He sat down to think out what he should do to-morrow. Again, with his fine disregard of ways and means, he determined to trust to luck, and as he expressed it, "brace old Oakley."

Accordingly he went about nine o'clock the next morning to Oakley's house. A gray-haired, sad-eyed woman inquired his errand.

"I want to see Mr. Oakley," he said.

"You cannot see him. Mr. Oakley is not well and does not see visitors."

"But I must see him, madam; I am here upon business of importance."

"You can tell me just as well as him. I am his wife and transact all of his business."

"I can tell no one but the master of the house himself."

"You cannot see him. It is against his orders."

"Very well," replied Skaggs, descending one step; "it is his loss, not mine. I have tried to do my duty and failed. Simply tell him that I came from Paris."

"Paris?" cried a querulous voice behind the woman's back. "Leslie, why do you keep the gentleman at the door? Let him come in at once."

Mrs. Oakley stepped from the door and Skaggs went in. Had he seen Oakley before he would have been shocked at the change in his appearance; but as it was, the nervous, white-haired man who stood shiftily before him told him nothing of an eating secret long carried. The man's face was gray and haggard, and deep lines were cut under his staring, fish-like eyes. His hair tumbled in white masses over his pallid forehead, and his lips twitched as he talked.

"You're from Paris, sir, from Paris?" he said. "Come in, come in."

His motions were nervous and erratic. Skaggs followed him into the library, and the wife disappeared in another direction.

It would have been hard to recognise in the Oakley of the present the man of a few years before. The strong frame had gone away to bone, and nothing of his old power sat on either brow or chin. He was as a man who trembled on the brink of insanity. His guilty secret had been too much for him, and Skaggs's own fingers twitched as he saw his host's hands seek the breast of his jacket every other moment.

"It is there the secret is hidden," he said to himself, "and whatever it is, I must have it. But how—how? I can't knock the man down and rob him in his own house." But Oakley himself proceeded to give him his first cue.

"You—you—perhaps have a message from my brother—my brother who is in Paris. I have not heard from him for some time."

Skaggs's mind worked quickly. He remembered the Colonel's story. Evidently the brother had something to do with the secret. "Now or never," he thought. So he said boldly, "Yes, I have a message from your brother."

The man sprung up, clutching again at his breast. "You have? you have? Give it to me. After four years he sends me a message! Give it to me!"

The reporter looked steadily at the man. He knew that he was in his power, that his very eagerness would prove traitor to his discretion.

"Your brother bade me to say to you that you have a terrible secret, that you bear it in your breast—there—there. I am his messenger. He bids you to give it to me."

Oakley had shrunken back as if he had been struck.

"No, no!" he gasped, "no, no! I have no secret."

The reporter moved nearer him. The old man shrunk against the wall, his lips working convulsively and his hand tearing at his breast as Skaggs drew nearer. He attempted to shriek, but his voice was husky and broke off in a gasping whisper.

"Give it to me, as your brother commands."

"No, no, no! It is not his secret; it is mine. I must

carry it here always, do you hear? I must carry it till I die. Go away! Go away!"

Skaggs seized him. Oakley struggled weakly, but he had no strength. The reporter's hand sought the secret pocket. He felt a paper beneath his fingers. Oakley gasped hoarsely as he drew it forth. Then raising his voice gave one agonised cry, and sank to the floor frothing at the mouth. At the cry rapid footsteps were heard in the hallway, and Mrs. Oakley threw open the door.

"What is the matter?" she cried.

"My message has somewhat upset your husband," was the cool answer.

"But his breast is open. Your hand has been in his bosom. You have taken something from him. Give it to me, or I shall call for help."

Skaggs had not reckoned on this, but his wits came to the rescue.

"You dare not call for help," he said, "or the world will know!"

She wrung her hands helplessly, crying, "Oh, give it to me, give it to me. We've never done you any harm."

"But you've harmed some one else; that is enough."

He moved towards the door, but she sprang in front of him with the fierceness of a tigress protecting her young. She attacked him with teeth and nails. She was pallid with fury, and it was all he could do to protect himself and yet not injure her. Finally, when her anger had taken her strength, he succeeded in getting out. He flew down the hall-way and out of the front door, the woman's screams following him. He did not pause to read the precious letter until he was safe in his room at the Continental Hotel. Then he sprang to his feet, crying, "Thank God! thank God! I was right, and the *Universe* shall have a sensation. The brother is the thief, and Berry Hamilton is an innocent man. Hurrah! Now, who is it that has come on a wild-goose chase? Who is it that ought to handle his idea carefully? Heigho, Saunders my man, the drinks'll be on you, and old Skaggsy will have done some good in the world."

CHAPTER XVII

A Yellow Journal

MR. SKAGGS HAD no qualms of conscience about the manner in which he had come by the damaging evidence against Maurice Oakley. It was enough for him that he had it. A corporation, he argued, had no soul, and therefore no conscience. How much less, then, should so small a part of a great corporation as himself be expected to have them?

He had his story. It was vivid, interesting, dramatic. It meant the favour of his editor, a big thing for the *Universe*, and a fatter lining for his own pocket. He sat down to put his discovery on paper before he attempted anything else, although the impulse to celebrate was very strong within him.

He told his story well, with an eye to every one of its salient points. He sent an alleged picture of Berry Hamilton as he had appeared at the time of his arrest. He sent a picture of the Oakley home and of the cottage where the servant and his family had been so happy. There was a strong pen-picture of the man, Oakley, grown haggard and morose from carrying his guilty secret, of his confusion when confronted with the supposed knowledge of it. The old Southern city was described, and the opinions of its residents in regard to the case given. It was there— clear, interesting, and strong. One could see it all as if every phase of it were being enacted before one's eyes. Skaggs surpassed himself.

When the editor first got hold of it he said "Huh!" over the opening lines,—a few short sentences that instantly pricked the attention awake. He read on with increasing interest. "This is good stuff," he said at the last page. "Here's a chance for the *Universe* to look into the methods of Southern court proceedings. Here's a chance for a spread."

The *Universe* had always claimed to be the friend of all poor and oppressed humanity, and every once in a while it did something to substantiate its claim, whereupon it stood off and said to the public, "Look you what we have done, and behold how great we are, the friend of the people!" The *Universe* was yellow. It was very so. But it had power and keenness and energy. It never lost an opportunity to crow, and if one was not forthcoming, it made one. In this way it managed to do a considerable amount of good, and its yellowness became forgivable, even commendable. In Skaggs's story the editor saw an opportunity for one of its periodical philanthropies. He seized upon it. With headlines that took half a page, and with cuts authentic and otherwise, the tale was told, and the people of New York were greeted next morning with the announcement of—

"A Burning Shame!
A Poor and Innocent Negro made to Suffer
For a Rich Man's Crime!
Great Exposé by the 'Universe'!
A 'Universe' Reporter to the Rescue!
The Whole Thing to be Aired that the
People May Know!"

Then Skaggs received a telegram that made him leap for joy. He was to do it. He was to go to the capital of the State. He was to beard the Governor in his den, and he, with the force of a great paper behind him, was to demand for the people the release of an innocent man. Then there would be another write-up and much glory for him and more shekels. In an hour after he had received his telegram he was on his way to the Southern capital.

Meanwhile in the house of Maurice Oakley there were sad times. From the moment that the master of the house had fallen to the floor in impotent fear and madness there had been no peace within his doors. At first his wife had tried to control him alone, and had humoured the wild babblings with which he woke from his swoon. But these changed to shrieks and cries and curses, and she was forced to throw open the doors so long closed and call in help. The neighbours and her old friends went to her assistance, and what the reporter's story had not done, the ravings of the man accomplished; for, with a show of matchless cunning, he continually clutched at his breast, laughed, and babbled his secret openly. Even then they would have smothered it in silence, for the honour of one of their best families; but too many ears had heard, and then came the yellow journal bearing all the news in emblazoned headlines.

Colonel Saunders was distinctly hurt to think that his confidence had been imposed on, and that he had been instrumental in bringing shame upon a Southern name.

"To think, suh," he said generally to the usual assembly of choice spirits,—"to think of that man's being a reporter, such, a common, ordinary reporter, and that I sat and talked to him as if he were a gentleman!"

"You're not to be blamed, Colonel," said old Horace Talbot. "You've done no more than any other gentleman would have done. The trouble is that the average Northerner has no sense of honour, suh, no sense of honour. If this particular man had had, he would have kept still, and everything would have gone on smooth and quiet. Instead of that, a distinguished family is brought to shame, and for what? To give a nigger a few more years of freedom when, likely as not, he don't want it; and Berry Hamilton's life in prison has proved nearer the ideal reached by slavery than anything he has found since emancipation. Why, suhs, I fancy I see him leaving his prison with tears of regret in his eyes."

Old Horace was inanely eloquent for an hour over his pet theory. But there were some in the town who thought differently about the matter, and it was their opinions and murmurings that backed up Skaggs and made it easier for him when at the capital he came into contact with the official red tape.

He was told that there were certain forms of procedure, and certain times for certain things, but he hammered persistently away, the murmurings behind him grew louder, while from his sanctum the editor of the *Universe* thundered away against oppression and high-handed tyranny. Other papers took it up and asked why this man should be despoiled of his liberty any longer? And when it was replied that the man had been convicted, and that the wheels of justice could not be stopped or turned back by the letter of a romantic artist or the ravings of a madman, there was a mighty outcry against the farce of justice that had been played out in this man's case.

The trial was reviewed; the evidence again brought up and examined. The dignity of the State was threatened. At this time the State did the one thing necessary to save its tottering reputation. It would not surrender, but it capitulated, and Berry Hamilton was pardoned.

Berry heard the news with surprise and a half-bitter joy. He had long ago lost hope that justice would ever be done to him. He marvelled at the word that was brought to him now, and he could not understand the strange cordiality of the young white man who met him at the warden's office. Five years of prison life had made a different man of him. He no longer looked to receive kindness from his fellows, and he blinked at it as he blinked at the unwonted brightness of the sun. The lines about his mouth where the smiles used to gather had changed and grown stern with the hopelessness of years. His lips drooped pathetically, and hard treatment had given his eyes a lowering look. His hair, that had hardly shown a white streak, was as white as Maurice Oakley's own. His erstwhile quick wits were dulled and imbruted. He had lived like an ox, working without inspiration or reward, and he came forth like an ox from his stall. All the higher part of him he had left behind, dropping it off day after day through the wearisome years. He had put behind him the Berry Hamilton that laughed and joked and sang and believed, for even his faith had become only a numbed fancy.

"This is a very happy occasion, Mr. Hamilton," said Skaggs, shaking his hand heartily.

Berry did not answer. What had this slim, glib young man to do with him? What had any white man to do with him after what he had suffered at their hands?

"You know you are to go New York with me?"

"To New Yawk? What fu'?"

Skaggs did not tell him that, now that the *Universe* had done its work, it demanded the right to crow to its heart's satisfaction. He said only, "You want to see your wife, of course?"

Berry had forgotten Fannie, and for the first time his heart thrilled within him at the thought of seeing her again.

"I ain't hyeahed f'om my people fu' a long time. I didn't know what had become of 'em. How's Kit an' Joe?"

"They're all right," was the reply. Skaggs couldn't tell him, in this the first hour of his freedom. Let him have time to drink the sweetness of that all in. There would be time afterwards to taste all of the bitterness.

Once in New York, he found that people wished to see him, some fools, some philanthropists, and a great many reporters. He had to be photographed—all this before he could seek those whom he longed to see. They printed his picture as he was before he went to prison and as he was now, a sort of before-and-after-taking comment, and in the morning that it all appeared, when the *Universe* spread itself to tell the public what it had done and how it had done it, they gave him his wife's address.

It would be better, they thought, for her to tell him herself all that happened. No one of them was brave enough to stand to look in his eyes when he asked for his son and daughter, and they shifted their responsibility by pretending to themselves that they were doing it for his own good: that the blow would fall more gently upon him coming from her who had been his wife. Berry took the address and inquired his way timidly, hesitatingly, but with a swelling heart, to the door of the flat where Fannie lived.

CHAPTER XVIII

What Berry Found

HAD NOT BERRY's years of prison life made him forget what little he knew of reading, he might have read the name Gibson on the door-plate where they told him to ring for his wife. But he knew nothing of what awaited him as he confidently pulled the bell. Fannie herself came to the door. The news the papers held had not escaped her, but she had suffered in silence, hoping that Berry might be spared the pain of finding her. Now he stood before her, and she knew him at a glance, in spite of his haggard countenance.

"Fannie," he said, holding out his arms to her, and all of the pain and pathos of long yearning was in his voice, "don't you know me?"

She shrank away from him, back in the hall-way.

"Yes, yes, Be'y, I knows you. Come in."

She led him through the passage-way and into her room, he following with a sudden sinking at his heart. This was not the reception he had expected from Fannie.

When they were within the room he turned and held out his arms to her again, but she did not notice them. "Why, is you 'shamed o' me?" he asked brokenly.

" 'Shamed? No! Oh, Be'y," and she sank into a chair and began rocking to and fro in her helpless grief.

"What's de mattah, Fannie? Ain't you glad to see me?"

"Yes, yes, but you don't know nothin', do you? Dey lef' me to tell you?"

"Lef' you to tell me? What's de mattah? Is Joe or Kit daid? Tell me."

"No, not daid. Kit dances on de stage fu' a livin', an', Be'y, she ain't de gal she ust to be. Joe—Joe—Joe—he's in pen'tentiary fu' killin' a ooman."

Berry started forward with a cry, "My Gawd! my Gawd! my little gal! my boy!"

"Dat ain't all," she went on dully, as if reciting a rote lesson; "I ain't yo' wife no mo'. I's ma'ied ag'in. Oh Be'y, Be'y, don't look at me lak dat. I couldn't he'p it. Kit an' Joe lef' me, an' dey said de pen'tentiary divo'ced you an' me, an' dat you'd nevah come out nohow. Don't look at me lak dat, Be'y."

"You ain't my wife no mo'? Hit's a lie, a damn lie! You is my wife. I's a innocent man. No pen'tentiary kin tek you erway f'om me. Hit's enough what dey've done to my chillen." He rushed forward and seized her by the arm. "Dey sha'n't do no mo', by Gawd! dey sha'n't, I say!" His voice had risen to a fierce roar, like that of a hurt beast, and he shook her by the arm as he spoke.

"Oh, don't, Be'y, don't, you hu't me. I couldn't he'p it."

He glared at her for a moment, and then the real force of the situation came full upon him, and he bowed his head in his hands and wept like a child. The great sobs came up and stuck in his throat.

She crept up to him fearfully and laid her hand on his head.

"Don't cry, Be'y," she said; "I done wrong, but I loves you yit."

He seized her in his arms and held her tightly until he could control himself. Then he asked weakly, "Well, what am I goin' to do?"

"I do' know, Be'y, 'ceptin' dat you'll have to leave me."

"I won't! I'll never leave you again," he replied doggedly.

"But, Be'y, you mus'. You'll only mek it ha'der on me, an' Gibson'll beat me ag'in."

"Ag'in!"

She hung her head: "Yes."

He gripped himself hard.

"Why cain't you come on off wid me, Fannie? You was mine fus'."

"I couldn't. He would fin' me anywhaih I went to."

"Let him fin' you. You'll be wid me, an' we'll settle it, him an' me."

"I want to, but oh, I can't, I can't," she wailed.

"Please go now, Be'y, befo' he gits home. He's mad anyhow, 'cause you're out."

Berry looked at her hard, and then said in a dry voice, "An' so I got to go an' leave you to him?"

"Yes, you mus'; I'm his'n now."

He turned to the door, murmuring, "My wife gone, Kit a nobody, an' Joe, little Joe, a murderer, an' then I—I—ust to pray to Gawd an' call him 'Ouah Fathah.' " He laughed hoarsely. It sounded like nothing Fannie had ever heard before.

"Don't, Be'y, don't say dat. Maybe we don't un'erstan'."

Her faith still hung by a slender thread, but his had given way in that moment.

"No, we don't un'erstan'," he laughed as he went out of the door. "We don't un'erstan'."

He staggered down the steps, blinded by his emotions, and set his face towards the little lodging that he had taken temporarily. There seemed nothing left in life for him to do. Yet he knew that he must work to live, although the effort seemed hardly worth while. He remembered now that the *Universe* had offered him the under janitorship in its building. He would go and take it, and some day, perhaps— He was not quite sure what the "perhaps" meant. But as his mind grew clearer he came to know, for a sullen, fierce anger was smouldering in his heart against the man who through lies had stolen his wife from him. It was anger that came slowly, but gained in fierceness as it grew.

Yes, that was it, he would kill Gibson. It was no worse than his present state. Then it would be father and son murderers. They would hang him or send him back to prison. Neither would be hard now. He laughed to himself.

And this was what they had let him out of prison for? To find out all this. Why had they not left him there to die in ignorance? What had he to do with all these people who gave him sympathy? What did he want of their sympathy? Could they give him back one tithe of what he had lost? Could they restore to him his wife or his son or his daughter, his quiet happiness or his simple faith?

He went to work for the *Universe*, but night after night, armed, he patrolled the sidewalk in front of Fannie's house. He did not know Gibson, but he wanted to see them together. Then he would strike. His vigils kept him from his bed, but he went to the next morning's work with no weariness. The hope of revenge sustained him, and he took a savage joy in the thought that he should be the dispenser of justice to at least one of those who had wounded him.

Finally he grew impatient and determined to wait no longer, but to seek his enemy in his own house. He approached the place cautiously and went up the steps. His hand touched the bell-pull. He staggered back.

"Oh, my Gawd!" he said.

There was crape on Fannie's bell. His head went round and he held to the door for support. Then he turned the knob and the door opened. He went noiselessly in. At the door of Fannie's room he halted, sick with fear. He knocked, a step sounded within, and his wife's face looked out upon him. He could have screamed aloud with relief.

"It ain't you!" he whispered huskily.

"No, it's him. He was killed in a fight at the race-track. Some o' his frinds are settin' up. Come in."

He went in, a wild, strange feeling surging at his heart. She showed him into the death-chamber.

As he stood and looked down upon the face of his enemy, still, cold, and terrible in death, the recognition of how near he had come to crime swept over him, and all his dead faith sprang into new life in a glorious resurrection. He stood with clasped hands, and no word passed his lips. But his heart was crying, "Thank God! thank God! this man's blood is not on my hands."

The gamblers who were sitting up with the dead wondered who the old fool was who looked at their silent comrade and then raised his eyes as if in prayer.

When Gibson was laid away, there were no formalities between Berry and his wife; they simply went back to each other. New York held nothing for them now but sad memories. Kit was on the road, and the father could not bear to see his son; so they turned their faces southward, back to the only place they could call home. Surely the people could not be cruel to them now, and even if they were, they felt that after what they had endured no wound had power to give them pain.

Leslie Oakley heard of their coming, and with her own hands re-opened and refurnished the little cottage in the yard for them. There the white-haired woman begged them to spend the rest of their days and be in peace and comfort. It was the only amend she could make. As much to satisfy her as to settle themselves, they took the cottage, and many a night thereafter they sat together with clasped hands listening to the shrieks of the madman across the yard and thinking of what he had brought to them and to himself.

It was not a happy life, but it was all that was left to them, and they took it up without complaint, for they knew they were powerless against some Will infinitely stronger than their own.

BIBLIOGRAPHY

Andrews, William L. *The Literary Career of Charles W. Chesnutt*. Baton Rouge: Louisiana State University Press, 1980.

Baker, Houston A. *Blues, Ideology, and Afro-American Literature*. Chicago: University of Chicago Press, 1984.

Bell, Bernard. *The Afro-American Novel and Its Tradition*. Amherst: University of Massachusetts Press, 1987.

Bone, Robert A. *The Negro Novel in America*. 2d ed. New Haven: Yale University Press, 1965.

Bruce, Dickson D. *Black American Writing from the Nadir: The Evolution of a Literary Tradition 1877–1915*. Baton Rouge: Louisiana State University Press, 1989.

Carby, Hazel. *Reconstructing Womanhood: The Emergence of the Afro-American Woman Novelist*. New York: Oxford University Press, 1987.

Elder, Arlene A. *The "Hindered Hand": Cultural Implications of Early African-American Fiction*. Westport, CT: Greenwood Press, 1978.

Gayle, Addison. *Oak and Ivy: A Biography of Paul Laurence Dunbar*. Garden City, NY: Doubleday, 1971.

Gloster, Hugh M. *Negro Voices in American Fiction*. Chapel Hill: University of North Carolina Press, 1948.

Harper, Frances Ellen Watkins. *A Brighter Coming Day: A Frances Ellen Watkins Harper Reader*. Ed. Frances Smith Foster. New York: Feminist Press, 1990.

Jackson, Blyden. *A History of Afro-American Literature. Vol. 1. The Long Beginning, 1746–1895*. Baton Rouge: Louisiana State University Press, 1989.

Loggins, Vernon. *The Negro Author in America: His Development to 1900*. New York: Columbia University Press, 1931.

Redding, J. Saunders. *To Make a Poet Black*. Chapel Hill: University of North Carolina Press, 1939.

Ø

Recommended Reading from SIGNET